*The supreme
novelist of the
Nineteenth Century*

Lev Tolstoy, born a member of the
Russian nobility, became one of its
sharpest critics. His novels,
WAR AND PEACE,
ANNA KARENINA,
RESURRECTION, and
his later moralistic writings put
him squarely in the camp of
social reform that swept across Europe
in the nineteenth century. Despite
Tolstoy's bitter attacks on the
Russian social system, his prestige
was so enormous that even the Czar
did not dare to challenge him.
In his lifetime, Tolstoy became the
center of a group of disciples that
extended as far as the shores of
America. His literary and philosophical
genius exerts its influence on
each successive generation.

ANNA KARENINA

Lev Tolstoy

Translated by
Morris S. Gurin
and
Jacob Gurin

WASHINGTON SQUARE PRESS, INC. • NEW YORK

ANNA KARENINA

A *Washington Square Press* edition

1st printing........................March, 1966

Anna Karenina was first published serially in Russian in *Russki Vestnik*, St. Petersburg, 1876–1877.

Published by

L

Washington Square Press, Inc., 630 Fifth Avenue, New York, N.Y.

WASHINGTON SQUARE PRESS editions are distributed in the U.S. by Affiliated Publishers, a division of Pocket Books, Inc., 630 Fifth Avenue, New York 20, N.Y. and in Canada by Pocket Books of Canada, Ltd., Richmond Hill, Ontario.

Contents

▶ *A BRIEF CHRONOLOGY OF*
  MAIN EVENTS IN THE LIFE
  OF LEV NIKOLAYEVICH TOLSTOY

1828   Tolstoy born on August 28th at the family seat, Yasnaya Poliana.

1830   Mother dies when he is only eighteen months old.

1837   The whole family moves temporarily to Moscow. Father dies when Tolstoy is nine.

1841   The remainder of the family moves to Kazan, where the children come under the guardianship of P. I. Yushkov, wife of the governor of Kazan.

1844   Enters Kazan University with the intention of majoring in Oriental languages.

1845   Transfers to law school. Studies badly. Occupies spare time reading Rousseau, Sterne, Voltaire.

1847   Inherits the estate of Yasnaya Poliana. Leaves university without graduating.

1849   Goes to St. Petersburg with intention of joining University law school there. Abandons his attempt almost immediately.

1852   Publishes his first major work, *Childhood,* anonymously in the St. Petersburg literary magazine *The Contemporary.* The work is an immediate success.

1852–54 Writes a series of Caucasian tales including *The Raid* and *The Woodcutting.* Also writes *Boyhood* and begins *The Cossacks.*

1854   Signs up in the artillery. Is made an ensign, serving at first with the Army of the Danube and later in the Crimea. Reads Plato, Hume, Karamzin, Pushkin, Lermontov and Dickens.

1854–55 Takes part in the Crimean War, particularly the siege of Sevastopol. Writes *Sevastopol in December, 1854, Sevastopol in May, 1855* and *Sevastopol in August, 1855,* all three of which are published in *The Contemporary* and make Tolstoy something of a literary celebrity.

1856   Resigns from the army with the rank of lieutenant.
         Goes to St. Petersburg and becomes the darling of
         the literary salons. Writes *Youth, Notes of a Billiard
         Marker, Two Hussars* and *A Landlord's Morning.*
         Returns to Yasnaya Poliana and makes plans to free
         his serfs. The plans are not realized, however.

1857   Makes his first journey abroad. Visits France,
         Switzerland, Italy and Germany. Writes short stories
         Lucerne and *Albert.* Reads Balzac, Goethe, Dumas
         fils, Proudhon and the Gospels.

1859   Establishes his first school for peasant children with
         himself as teacher. Devotes himself wholeheartedly
         to popular education.

1860   Goes abroad to study Western European methods of
         education. Visits Germany, Switzerland and France
         in company with his favorite brother, Nikolai. In
         France Nikolai dies of tuberculosis. Tolstoy deeply
         shocked by this death.

1861   Visits Italy and England to study their schools. Hears
         Dickens speak in London. Visits Proudhon in Brus-
         sels. Revisits Germany.

1862   Founds a monthly pedagogical journal entitled
         Yasnaya Poliana. Expands his school for peasants.
         Quarrels with Turgenev and challenges him to a
         duel. The duel does not take place, however. Writes
         Polikushka, finishes *The Cossacks.* In September
         marries Sofia Andreyevna Behrs.

1863   Begins to write *War and Peace.*

1867   *War and Peace* begins to appear in separate volumes.

1869   *War and Peace* completed. Tolstoy reads Schopen-
         hauer, plans to translate him into Russian.

1871   Returns to problems of peasant education and to his
         school.

1872   Writes an *ABC Book* for children, containing para-
         bles, folk tales and snippets of scientific information.

1873   Begins to write *Anna Karenina.*

1875   *Anna Karenina* begins to be serialized in *The Rus-
         sian Messenger.*

1877   *Anna Karenina* completed. Onset of spiritual crisis.

1879   Begins to write *My Confession,* first systematization
         of his developing religious beliefs.

1880   Writes *An Examination of Dogmatic Theology.*

1881   *My Confession* completed. Begins to write *A Union and Translation of the Four Gospels.*

1883   Writes *What I Believe.* Begins *The Death of Ivan Ilyich.* Meets V. G. Chertkov.

1884   Together with Chertkov and another disciple, P. Biryukov, founds the publishing house The Intermediary.

1885   Writes *What Then Must We Do?*

1886   Writes *On Life, How Much Land Does a Man Need?* and *The Power of Darkness.*

1887   Begins *The Kreutzer Sonata.* Hears the story for *Resurrection* from A. F. Koni.

1889   Completes *The Kreutzer Sonata.* Begins *Resurrection.*

1890   Begins *The Kingdom of God Is Within You.*

1891   *The Kreutzer Sonata* published. Completes *The Fruits of Enlightenment.* Begins *The Devil* and *Father Sergius.* Renounces copyright on all works written since 1881.

1891–93 Works to alleviate suffering caused by famine.

1893   Completes *The Kingdom of God Is Within You.*

1894–95 Writes *Master and Man.* Becomes acquainted with the Dukhobors.

1896   Begins *Hadji Murad, The Teaching of Christ* and *What Is Art?*

1897   Completes *What Is Art?* Chertkov and Biryukov exiled.

1898   The Dukhobors sail for Canada.

1899   Completes *Resurrection.*

1900   Writes *The Living Corpse.*

1901   Excommunicated by the Russian Orthodox Church.

1903   Writes *On Shakespeare and the Drama.*

1904   Completes *Hadji Murad.*

1904–5 Compiles *The Circle of Reading,* an anthology of wise sayings.

1910   Leaves home for an unknown destination, dies November 7th at the way station of Astapovo.

EXPLANATORY NOTES

SINCE Russian names often puzzle English-speaking readers unfamiliar with the language, a few remarks on their forms and usage seem to be pertinent.

Surnames of women take the feminine ending -*a* added to the masculine form with the final consonant: Mr. Karenin—Mrs. (Miss) Karenina; or the masculine ending -*i* (-*y*) is replaced by the feminine -*aia*: Mr. Dostoevsky—Mrs. (Miss) Dostoevskaya. Surnames ending in -*ch* and -*o* do not change. This gender inflection of surnames is usually not rendered in modern translations, the masculine form being used for both.

First names alone in an address to an adult can be used only by relatives and very close friends. Their use by mere acquaintances indicates that the owner of the name holds a socially inferior position (Matvei, the valet).

Each first name has its traditional nickname or a nickname may be devised by the speaker; e.g., Dolinka, or Dashenka from Daria; Kitty, from Ekaterina; Varia or Varenka from Varvara, etc. Nicknames are first applied to children but often are retained as the child grows up. Again this is the privilege of relatives and close friends only. All first names and their nicknames can take a variety of endings that show the attitude of the speaker to the person addressed. Verochka, from Vera; Kolenka, Nikolasha, from Nikolai, are indicative of tenderness and affection. Varka, Sashka, Vaska are disparaging forms showing the speaker's anger or displeasure with the person addressed or are indicative of the inferior social position of the person thus spoken to. Modern translations, as a rule, avoid rendering these diminutive or disparaging forms unless a character is called in this manner throughout the whole work.

Patronymics are formed by adding -*ovich* or -*ievich* (for a male), -*ovna* or -*ievna* to the father's first name and are used in combination with the first name of the person addressed. This is the *only* way in Russian of addressing an adult with whom one is on not too familiar terms. The use of surname and title in the Western manner is considered too stiff and is used on formal occasions only. The prince's full name is Aleksandr Dmitrievich Shcherbatsky, that is, Aleksandr, the son of Dmitri, with the family name of Shcherbatsky. His daughter is

named Ekaterina Aleksandr*ovna* (daughter of Aleksandr).
After marriage the woman changes her surname but never her
patronymic. It is habitual for peasants to address each other
by their patronymics only. In rural dialects as well as in quick
speech the ending *-ovich* often gets shortened to *-ich*.

The name-and-patronymic form of address is such an intrinsic feature of Russian life and so indicative of the social
standing of the person and his or her relationship with others
that it can be neither omitted nor "simplified" in a translation.

A Reference List of Personal Names
Found in *ANNA KARENINA*

AGÁFIA MIKHÁILOVNA	Levin's housekeeper
ALEKSÁNDR DMÍTRIE-VICH SHCHERBÂTSKY	Prince; Kitty's father
ALEKSÁNDR VRÓNSKY	Aleksei Vronsky's brother
ALEKSÉI ALEKSÁNDRO-VICH KARÉNIN	Anna's husband
ALEKSÉI KIRÍLLOVICH VRÓNSKY	Count; Anna's lover
ALYÓSHA	Aleksei Kirillovich Vronsky
ANNA ARKÁDIEVNA KARÉNINA	
ANNA PÁVLOVNA	Petrov's wife
ÁNNUSHKA	Anna Karenina's maid
ÁNNY	Anna Karenina's daughter
BETSY TVERSKÓY	Princess; Anna Karenina's friend
CHÍRIKOV	Friend of Levin
DÀRIA ALEKSÁN-DROVNA OBLÓNSKY	Princess; wife of Stepan Oblon-sky; daughter of Prince and Princess Shcherbatsky; sister of Kitty and Natalie
DÁSHENKA	Daria Aleksandrovna
DMÍTRI or MÍTIA	Levin's son
DÓLINKA	Daria Aleksandrovna
DÓLLENKA	Daria Aleksandrovna
DÓLLY	Daria Aleksandrovna
EGÓRUSHKA KORSÚNSKY	Member of the social set
EKATERÍNA ALEKSÁNDROVNA	Kitty
ERMÍLIN PROKHÓR	Peasant
FILÍPP	Levin's coachman
FIÓDOR	Karenin's coachman
FIÓDOR	Peasant employed by Levin
GOLENÍSHCHEV	Friend of Vronsky

GRINÉVICH	Friend of Oblonsky
GRÍSHA	Son of Oblonsky
HANNAH	Anna Karenina's protegée
IGNÁT	Levin's coachman
KAMERÓVSKY	Officer
KAPITÓNYCH	Karenin's doorman
KARÉNINA, ANNA ARKÁDIEVNA	
KARÉNIN, ALEKSÉI ALEKSÁNDROVICH	Anna's husband
KATAVÁSOV	Professor; Levin's friend
KÁTENKA	Kitty
KATERÍNA ALEKSÁNDROVNA	Kitty
KITTY	Young Princess Shcherbatsky; later Levin's wife
KONSTANTÍN DMÍTRIEVICH LÉVIN	
KORNÉI	Karenin's servant
KORSÚNSKY, EGÓRUSHKA	Member of the social set
KORSÚNSKY, LÝDIE	Egorushka Korsunsky's wife
KÓSTIA	Konstantin Levin
KÓZNYSHEV, SERGÉI IVÁNOVICH	Levin's half-brother
KRÍTSKY	Nikolai Levin's friend
KUZMÁ	Levin's servant
LÉVIN, KONSTANTÍN DMÍTRIEVICH	Usually referred to as Levin
LÉVIN, NIKOLÁI	Konstantin Levin's brother; Koznyshev's half-brother
LÍZA MERKÁLOV	Member of high society
LIZAVÉTA PETRÓVNA	Midwife
LVÓV, NATALIE	Sister of Kitty and Dolly
LVÓV	Natalie's husband
LYDIA IVÁNOVNA	Countess; friend of Karenin
MAKHÓTIN	Officer
MÁRIA ANDRÉYEVNA	Nikolai Levin's mistress
MÁRIA VLÁSIEVNA	Midwife
MÁSHA	Countess Nordston

MÁSHA	Maria Andreyevna
MÁSHA	Dolly's daughter
MATRIÓNA FILIMÓNOVNA	Nurse in the Oblonsky household
MATVÉI	Oblonsky's valet
MIÁKHKY	Princess
MIKHÁILA	Levin's office clerk
MIKHÁILA	Karenin's coachman
MIKHÁILOV	Painter
MÍTIA	Levin's son
NATÁLIA ALEKSÁNDROVNA	Natalie Lvov
NATALÍE LVOV	Sister of Kitty and Dolly
NEVEDÓVSKY	Nobleman
NIKÍTIN	Friend of Oblonsky
NIKOLÁI DMÍTRIEVICH LÉVIN	Levin's brother
NIKOLÁI IVÁNOVICH SVIÁZHSKY	Friend of Levin
NIKOLÁI SHCHERBÁTSKY	Kitty's cousin
NIKÓLENKA	Nikolai Levin
NÓRDSTON	Countess; Kitty's friend
OBLÓNSKY, STEPÁN ARKÁDIEVICH	Prince; Dolly's husband; Anna's brother
OBLÓNSKY, VARVÁRA	Princess; Anna's aunt
PARMÉNICH	Peasant
PESTSÓV	Friend of Oblonsky
PETRÍTSKY	Friend of Vronsky
PETRÓV	Painter
PIÓTR DMÍTRIEVICH	Kitty's doctor
PIÓTR	Karenina's servant
RTÍSHCHEV, MÁRIA EVGÉNIEVNA	Friend of Princess Shcherbatsky
SAPPHO STOLZ	Member of the high society
SHCHERBÁTSKY, ALEKSÁNDR DMÍTRIEVICH	Prince; father of Natalie, Dolly and Kitty
SERGÉI IVÁNOVICH KÓZNYSHEV	Levin's half-brother
SERYÓZHA	Anna's son

INTRODUCTION

LEV NIKOLAYEVICH TOLSTOY was born on August 28, 1828, on the family estate Yasnaya Poliana, about 120 miles from Moscow. He came from a long line of aristocrats. His mother, born Princess Volkonsky, was a direct descendant of Rurik, a ninth-century prince and the founder of Russia. His father's family could be traced back to 1353, when a German mercenary named Indris arrived in Southern Russia. Indris was accompanied by three thousand soldiers, and offered his services to the local prince. Indris' grandson migrated to Moscow and entered the service of the Grand Duke of Muscovy, who gave him the name Tolstoy. One of his descendants distinguished himself in the reign of Peter the Great, and when Catherine I ascended the throne she granted him the hereditary title of count. Thus began the long line of Counts Tolstoy.

When Lev Tolstoy was a year and a half old, his mother died. In his reminiscences he mentions that there remained no portrait of her, and that he could not visualize her as a physical being. He could imagine only her spiritual nature, and from everything he heard about her, she appeared to have been a kind and gifted person.

Of his father, Nikolai Ilitch Tolstoy, he had a clear recollection. Tolstoy mentions that his father, as a youth of seventeen, entered military service and took part in the campaigns of 1813 and 1814 against Napoleon. But he soon lost interest in military life, retired and moved to Kazan to live with his parents. Nikolai's father died soon afterward, leaving more debts than means to pay them. At that time he married Princess Volkonsky and moved to Yasnaya Poliana,* his wife's ancestral estate. Nine years later, in 1831 his wife died.

Nikolai Tolstoy, a kindhearted man, never subjected his peasants to corporal punishment, although that was the common practice. His time was taken up with management of the estate, endless litigations resulting from his father's debts, and hunting. He was an avid reader and possessed a well-stocked library of French classics, history, and natural science.

After the death of Tolstoy's mother, a distant relative, Tatiana Aleksandrovna Ergolsky, took upon herself the care of

---

* Also frequently spelled Polyana.

the family. Next to his father and the memory of his mother, she exerted the greatest influence upon Tolstoy.

In 1836, the family moved to Moscow in order to provide a better education for the older boys. There, in 1837, Tolstoy's father suddenly died. The loss made a strong impression upon Tolstoy, confronting the nine-year old for the first time with the problem of life and death. For a long time he could not believe that his father was really dead. An aunt, who lived in Kazan, became the children's guardian, and in 1841 the entire family moved to Kazan.

Even as an adolescent, Tolstoy showed the introspection that characterized his adult life. "My favorite and most frequent subjects for reflection were unusual for my age and condition," he wrote in _Childhood, Adolescence and Youth._ "Once the thought occurred to me that happiness does not depend on the conditions in which we find ourselves, but on our attitude toward them."

During these years, his friendship with his brother Dmitri had a great influence upon Tolstoy. Dmitri was a serious-minded youth, devoutly religious, gentle, but given to outbursts of anger. He did not mingle with his contemporaries, paid little attention to his appearance, and avoided the usual aristocratic pleasures. "My friendship with Dmitri," wrote Tolstoy, "revealed to me a new view of life and its purpose. . . . This view consisted of the conviction that man's purpose is moral perfection."

The family spent five years in Kazan. Every summer they moved to Yasnaya Poliana and in the fall returned to Kazan. In 1844, Tolstoy passed the entrance tests at the Faculty of Oriental Languages of Kazan University. But his time was taken up with attending balls, masquerades, and the theater; as a result, he failed in his examinations. He transferred to the Faculty of Law, became interested in his studies, but then neglected them and again failed. He left the University and returned to Yasnaya Poliana.

He had lost faith in the religion in which he had been raised. "When I was sixteen years old," he wrote, "I gave up praying and stopped going to chuch voluntarily. I no longer believed in what I had been told in childhood, but I believed in something. But what I believed in, I could not say. I believed in God, or rather did not deny His existence, but what kind of God, I could not say. Nor did I reject Christ and His teachings, but what His teachings were, I could not say."

At that time, Russia was engaged in a war with the mountaineers of the Caucasus. In April 1851, Tolstoy's older brother Nikolai, who was serving in the army in the Caucasus, came home on furlough, and when he returned to the Caucasus, Tolstoy accompanied him. Nature in the majestic Caucasus, and the courage of the Cossacks and simplicity of life in their villages impressed Tolstoy deeply. His short novel, *The Cossacks* is partly autobiographical, for Olenin, the hero of the story, is a young aristocrat who had been disappointed in the life of civilized society.

During that period Tolstoy completed his story, "Childhood," and sent the manuscript to the magazine *Sovremennik*. Nekrasov, the editor, replied with the famous letter in which Tolstoy's genius was recognized for the first time. The story was also a success with the magazine's readers.

In the meantime Tolstoy continued his life as a soldier. He took part in several skirmishes with the mountaineers and was nearly taken prisoner. In 1854, he was made an officer and given leave to go home. But Russia was then involved in the Crimean War, and Tolstoy soon received orders to join the Army of the Danube, where he arrived in March of 1854.

The army suffered defeat, and Tolstoy left for the Crimea. In November he arrived in Sevastopol during the siege, one of the great episodes in the military history of Russia. Stirred by the courage and humility of the Russian sailors and soldiers, Tolstoy wrote the Sevastopol stories, which made him famous. When Sevastopol surrendered, Tolstoy was sent to Petersburg as a courier.

In Petersburg he joined the literary circle of the *Sovremennik*. A new life opened to him. But Tolstoy did not fully agree with the members of his circle, and he often clashed with them, particularly with Turgenev—who, nevertheless, admired Tolstoy's literary genius. In May 1856, Tolstoy left Petersburg for Moscow and by the end of that year had retired from military service.

He gave himself up to worldly pleasures. His letters, however, show that he also searched for true love and an ideal family life. He courted a young lady, Valeria Arseniev. They appeared to be engaged, but after six months Tolstoy wrote her that their marriage would bring them only suffering, and they parted. He went abroad to Paris, where he visited Versailles, the Louvre, the opera, theaters, cabarets and other places of pleasure.

In August 1857, Tolstoy returned from abroad. During the next few years he traveled frequently from Yasnaya Poliana to Moscow and Petersburg. He enjoyed the pleasures of social life, but the feeling of dissatisfaction with himself never left him. Still seeking the meaning of life and death, he wrote "Three Deaths" during this period.

In 1860, Tolstoy made his second trip abroad, to attend to his sick brother, Nikolai, and to study the general state of education in Europe. In February 1861, while Tolstoy was abroad, the Russian serfs were emancipated by an Imperial Manifesto. A new era began in Russia; liberals were inspired by a zeal for public service.

Returning to Yasnaya Poliana, Tolstoy was appointed public arbitrator for his district, responsible for settling conflicts that arose among the newly freed serfs and the landowners. Still concerned with the problems and questions of education, he not only wrote on the subject but founded a school for peasant children. But Tolstoy was not satisfied; he wrote of that period, in his *Confession,* that "I would have come to the same state of despair to which I had come fifteen years earlier, if another aspect of life had not remained, one which I had not yet experienced but which promised me salvation—family life."

Tolstoy was a close friend and frequent visitor of the family of a Dr. Behrs. There were three daughters in the family, and it was expected that Tolstoy would propose to the eldest. Instead, he declared his love to the youngest daughter, Sofia Andreyevna. He did it by writing a row of letters on a card table with a piece of chalk; they were the initial letters of the words he meant to say. Sofia made out the sentence and answered him in the same manner. Tolstoy later made use of this device in *Anna Karenina* when Levin and Kitty declare their love for each other. On September 23, 1862, Tolstoy and Sofia Andreyevna were married in the Court Church in the Kremlin. After the wedding they left for Yasnaya Poliana. The bride was eighteen and Tolstoy was thirty-four.

Sofia was beautiful and intelligent, and she loved and admired her husband. Their marriage lasted forty-eight years. Sofia was Tolstoy's close friend and collaborator; she created a serene and calm atmosphere in which he wrote his two masterpieces; she copied his works in her own hand; and she bore him thirteen children. Her love for Tolstoy never lessened, and survived the crises of their later years. But along with love and devotion she had a strong feeling of possessiveness. She wanted to have her husband for herself, and later for herself and her family.

Soon after his marriage, Tolstoy began to work on *War and Peace*. He eagerly studied the historical documents of the era described in the novel and spoke to many eyewitnesses of events. He visited Borodino and made and attached to the novel a plan of the battlefield. The novel was completed in the fall of 1869. During the following few years, Tolstoy again devoted himself to his educational activities, teaching his own and the peasants' children. Then in March 1873, he began *Anna Karenina*, his second masterpiece.

These were years of a profound internal evolution which culminated in the great crisis of Tolstoy's life, the choice between moral philosophy and art. Tolstoy had always sought a purpose in life; he was obsessed with the need to find the meaning of life and death; he was always aroused by the injustice, cruelty, idleness, and depravity of the society in which he lived. Within his soul there had always been a struggle between the artist and the moralist, and in 1880, the moralist prevailed. In the meantime, his wife wrote in her diary of the hardships she had to endure and of the change in her husband, which frightened her.

In his search for the meaning of life, Tolstoy often was in a state of despair. He sought an answer to his questions in science, in philosophy, and in the lives of people of his circle; but he found no satisfaction in any of these. "A change has taken place within me," he wrote, "one which has long been in preparation and for which the foundations have long been within me. The life of our circle, of the rich and the learned, not only filled me with aversion, but lost all its meaning. All our actions, judgments, science, art, all this I saw in a new light. I understood that all this was nothing but diversion, that no meaning could be found in it. But I understood the true meaning of the life of the toiling people, of all those who create life. I understood that this was life itself, that the meaning of this life was true, and I accepted it." He gained peace of mind. He accepted the teachings of Christ but rejected the church, which had distorted those teachings. Later, in 1901, the church excommunicated him.

The family now spent winters in Moscow. But Tolstoy, instead of receiving and visiting friends and attending the theater and balls, devoted himself to manual labor. He often dressed in a sheepskin coat and marched with the lumber-jacks to the woods at the outskirts of Moscow to chop trees. He became more and more isolated from his family, and only the birth of another child, Aleksandra, in 1884, prevented him from leaving the family and turning into a vagabond. Aleksandra eventually became her father's devoted disciple and aide. She later migrated to the United States and wrote a biography of her father.

In 1883, in an article entitled "My Religion," Tolstoy had expressed a basic principle of Tolstoyism: "Do not resist evil with violence." Toward 1885, Tolstoy completely changed his way of life. He now dressed like a peasant and cleaned his own room, learned to mend shoes, to mow, to lay bricks. He transferred all his goods to his wife's name. His aim was to give up all his possessions, to abandon the life of luxury, to live with the peasants as they lived.

In June 1889, he completed *The Kreutzer Sonata*. It was suppressed by the censor, but later was published through the intervention of Emperor Aleksander III, who admired Tolstoy's genius. The same year Tolstoy worked on *Resurrection*, his third major novel.

His fame had now become world-wide. Anything he wrote was translated into many languages, and visitors from all lands came to Yasnaya Poliana. But the differences between Tolstoy and his wife were growing deeper. In September 1891, he gave up all rights to his works published after 1881; rights to works published before that date were retained by the family.

During this period there appeared in the Tolstoy house-hold a new individual, V. G. Chertkov, Tolstoy's most devoted disciple and a propagandist for his ideas. He and Sofia Andreyevna became the opposing poles in the struggle for Tolstoy's soul. Their struggle embittered the final years of Tolstoy's life. Sofia Andreyevna feared that her husband had written a secret will and diary. She tried frantically to obtain these papers, and on the night of October 28, 1910, she entered his room in search of them. Believing that he was asleep, she searched the drawers of his desk. This was the last time he saw her. Early the following morning he sat down at his desk and wrote a farewell letter to her. Then he left Yasnaya Poliana in the company of a faithful disciple, Dr. Douchan Makovitsky. They traveled by train to a monastery, Optyna Pustyn, which Tolstoy had previously visited several times, and then to the Chamardino Convent to visit his sister. He stayed there until November 12th. While journeying from the convent he fell sick, and, accompanied by Makovitsky and his daughter Aleksandra, who had joined him by that time, he left the train at Astapovo, a small railroad station. He had developed pneumonia, and was placed in the stationmaster's room. He died there on November 20, 1910.

A few days earlier, Chertkov and Sofia Andreyevna had arrived. But while her husband was on his deathbed, Sofia Andreyevna was not allowed to see him. Three days before his death, Tolstoy asked his daughter Tatiana about her mother, but she did not dare to tell him that she was there. At five o'clock in the morning of November 20, when Tolstoy was in a coma, an hour before his death, Sofia Andreyevna was finally admitted to him.

Tolstoy's wife died in 1919, at the age of seventy-five.

Tolstoy began work on *Anna Karenina* on March 18, 1873, and in May of that year he informed his friend Strakhov that a rough draft had been completed. He sold the rights to Katkov, the publisher of *Russki Vestnik*, a monthly periodical. The novel appeared serially in 1875, 1876, and 1877, in the January, February, March, and April issues of each year. With the death of Anna in the seventh part of the novel, the book seemed to come to an end, but Tolstoy added an eighth part, without Anna. It is devoted partly to a discussion of the political problems of that day, partly to telling the story of Vronsky and the secondary characters of the novel after Anna's death, and mainly to Levin and his inner struggle. Katkov, who disagreed with Tolstoy's views on the Slav problem as expressed by Levin in this part of the novel, refused to publish it in his magazine, and the section appeared as a separate book.

Anna Karenina is unique in the literature of the nineteenth century. It deals with such contrasting topics as the story of an all-absorbing passion and the downfall of a family, the story of a happy love, the political and economic problems of the day, and problems of philosophy, religion, art, science, and agriculture. A wide panorama of Russian life of the period is depicted. Guards, officers and peasants, princes and servants, landowners and laborers, aristocratic ladies and their attendants, old men and children crowd the pages of the book.

Hunts, a magnificent ball, races, haymaking, the sufferings of childbirth, the agony of death, a fashionable wedding, and a frightful act of suicide are some of the unforgettable scenes of joy and excitement or sorrow and compassion. And the composition of the novel is not based on an intricate plot, but runs along two lines, which cross each other only in the beginning and then much later on in the novel. The two lines are the story of the tragic love of Anna and Vronsky, and the story of the idyllic love of Kitty and Levin.

Two main ideas are developed as the novel proceeds along its two story lines. One, as demonstrated by the life of Anna, is expressed in the epigraph, taken from the Epistle of St. Paul to the Romans (12:19). It speaks of the moral law that must not be transgressed. Violation of this law leads to destruction—which judgment is not pronounced by man but by God. Tolstoy contracts this negative idea with a positive one—that man must not live for himself alone; he must live for his soul and serve God.

A considerable portion of the novel is autobiographical. In the person of Levin, Tolstoy represented much of himself. Many of Levin's thoughts are Tolstoy's own, and many episodes in the story of Levin and Kitty are taken from the lives of Tolstoy and his wife.

Nevertheless, Tolstoy's style is that of a keen but detached observer. With few exceptions, he refrains from expressing his own opinions. Examples of such exceptions are found in the first paragraph of the novel, and in the first paragraph of Chapter 23, Part Seven. In general, however, the scenes of the novel are described by the author with complete impartiality. Thus, after reading the scene (Chapter 1, Part Five) in which Levin confesses to the priest that he doubts everything, even the existence of God, and the priest criticizes his views and chides him in a fatherly manner, the reader would find it difficult to decide with whom Tolstoy sympathized. On the basis of the largely autobiographical treatment of Levin, the reader would be inclined to think that Tolstoy shared Levin's beliefs. Actually, as seen from a letter to a friend, he agreed wholeheartedly with the priest.

The influence of Pushkin, whom Tolstoy admired deeply, can be seen in the style and structure of the novel. As in Pushkin's works, Tolstoy's heroes are individuals endowed with traits common to all humanity; they are not sociological or psychological types, as in most of the Russian literature of

the nineteenth century, beginning with Gogol. The years
during which Tolstoy wrote *Anna Karenina* mark a dividing
line in his life. The novel was written under the influence of
this changing state, and the eighth part, which describes
Levin's inner contradictions and his search for the meaning
of life, mirrors Tolstoy's own experience of that period.

The literature on Tolstoy and his works is voluminous. A
list of some of these works is appended to this preface.

Since Russian proper names usually create difficulty for
the reader who is unfamiliar with the Russian language, all
names in this book, with the exception of Anna Karenina,
have been rendered in the masculine form to avoid confusion.
For example, both Prince and Princess Shcherbatsky are given
the same form of their surname, rather than referring to the
Princess' as Shcherbatskaya. A reference list of most of the
proper names mentioned in the novel is furnished, marked to
indicate the syllables stressed in pronunciation.

—Morris S. Gurin

Silver Spring, Maryland
October, 1964

Vengeance is mine;
I will repay.

> Romans, 12:19

PART ONE

1

ALL HAPPY FAMILIES resemble one another; every unhappy family is unhappy in its own way.

The Oblonsky household was in a state of complete confusion. The wife had learned of her husband's affair with the French governess who had formerly lived with them, and she declared that she could not remain in the same house with him. Such had been the situation for the past three days, and it caused suffering to husband and wife, the other members of the family and the rest of the household. All the members of the family and the household felt that there was no reason to stay together, that people who met accidentally in some inn would be closer to each other than they were. The wife had not emerged from her rooms; the husband was away for the third successive day; the bewildered children ran all over the house; the English governess had an argument with the housekeeper and sent a note to her friend asking that another position be found for her; the family cook had left the previous day at dinnertime; the servants' cook and the coachman had asked to be released.

On the third day after the quarrel, Prince Stepan Arkadievich Oblonsky—Stiva, as he was called by his friends—woke at eight o'clock in the morning, his usual hour. He was not in his wife's bedroom but in his study, on the morocco divan. He turned his portly, well-groomed body on the springs of the divan as if to slip back into a deep sleep, tightly grasping the pillow and pressing his cheek firmly against it. Suddenly he started, sat up on the divan, and opened his eyes.

Let's see, how was it? he thought, recalling his dream. Yes, how was it? Ah! Alabin was giving a dinner in Darmstadt; no, it was not Darmstadt, but something American.

1

Well, there was Darmstadt in America. Yes, Alabin was giving a dinner on tables made of glass, and the tables sang *Il mio tesoro*, yet not *Il mio tesoro* but something nicer; and there were small decanters, which also were women, he recalled.

Stepan Arkadievich's eyes glistened with joy, and still smiling, he was lost in thought. Yes, it was very good, very good. There were many other delights there, but even when awake you can't express them in words or describe them in your thoughts. He noticed a band of light that broke through the side of the window drape. He cheerfully swung over the side of the divan. With his feet he searched for and found his slippers, finished in golden morocco and embroidered by his wife (last year's birthday present), and following his unbroken, nine-year-old habit he reached, without rising, for the place where his robe usually hung. And here he suddenly recalled how it had happened and why he had slept not in his wife's bedroom but in his study. The smile vanished from his face, and he frowned.

"Ah, ah, ah! Ah!" he muttered, recalling all that had happened. His imagination brought back all the details of his quarrel with his wife, the hopelessness of his situation, and what was most painful, the sense of his own guilt.

Well, she'll never forgive me, and she can't forgive me. And, what's most terrible, it's all my fault, my fault; but I'm not really guilty. This is the real drama of the situation, he thought. "Ah, ah, ah!" he repeated in despair, recollecting the most painful impressions of the quarrel.

Most unpleasant was the first moment, when, returning home from the theater, gay and happy, holding in his hand an enormous pear, a present for his wife, he did not find her in the drawing room. To his surprise, he did not find her in the sitting room either. At last he saw her in her bedroom, with that unfortunate note in her hand, the note that had revealed everything.

Dolly, who was always occupied, always bustling about, and who, in his opinion, was not very bright, was sitting motionless with the note in her hand. She stared at him with an expression of horror, despair, and anger.

"What is this?" she asked, pointing to the note.

As is often the case, in his recollection Stepan Arkadievich was tormented not so much by the event itself as by the answer he had given his wife. What happened to him at that timber in his wife's estate. The timber had to be sold, but it was out of the question to sell it now, before peace had been made with his wife. It was most embarrassing to find this pecuniary consideration involved in the matter of reconciliation with his wife. He felt offended at the thought that he might be influenced by this circumstance, and that he might seek reconciliation with his wife for the sake of selling the timber.

When he was through with the letters, Stepan Arkadievich reached for the office papers, quickly looked over two of them, made some notes with his large pencil and, putting them aside, turned to the coffee. While drinking it, he opened the morning newspaper, which was still damp, and began to read. Stepan Arkadievich subscribed to and read a newspaper that though liberal, never leaned to radical opinions but to those that were accepted by the majority. Though he was not greatly interested in art, or science, or politics, he faithfully took the views on these subjects that were accepted by the majority and by his newspaper, and he changed them only when the majority changed them. Actually, he did not change them; they changed unnoticeably within him.

Stepan Arkadievich never really selected either his views or his opinions—these views and opinions came to him themselves—just as he never selected the shapes of his hat or his coat but accepted the ones that were in style. And it was as necessary for him to possess some opinions as to possess a hat. This was required both by the society he belonged to and by the urge for mental activity that usually comes to a man in his mature years. If there was any reason for accepting the liberal point of view in preference to the conservative, which was shared by most members of his circle, it was not that he considered the liberal point of view more reasonable than the conservative but that it was more suited to his way of life. The liberal party insisted that everything in Russia was bad, and indeed, Stepan Arkadievich was deeply in debt and had very little money. The liberal party held that marriage was an outmoded institution and had to be reformed. Indeed, Stepan Arkadievich's family life afforded him little pleasure, forcing him to lie and to pretend, which was so against his nature. The liberal party declared, or rather implied, that religion was but a bridle to hold in check the barbarian portion of the population. Indeed, Stepan Arkadievich could not stand through even a short church service without developing pains in his legs, and could not understand the reason for all these terrible, high-sounding words about the world beyond when, in this world, life could be so pleasant. At the same time Stepan Arkadievich, who enjoyed a witty joke, found pleasure in confusing a meek person by asserting that if one wishes to boast of his ancestry, he must not stop with Rurik and renounce his first forefather, the ape. Thus it had become Stepan Arkadievich's custom to pass judgment from the liberal point of view, and he liked his newspaper just as he liked his after-dinner cigar, for the slight fog which it created in his head. He read an editorial that pointed out that there was no reason for lamenting that radicalism was going to swallow up all the conservative elements, or any reason for the government to take measures to destroy the revolutionary hydra. On the contrary, "It is our opinion that danger lies not in the imagined revolutionary hydra, but in the persistent nature of tradition, which impedes progress," and so on. He read another article, on finance, which mentioned Bentham and Mill and took a dig at the ministry. With his usual perspicacity, he caught the meaning of every dig. He knew who had made it, against whom it was directed, and the reason that provoked it. As always, this gave him pleasure. But today this pleasure was marred by the recollection of Matriona Filimonovna's advice and by the unhappiness that reigned in the house. He read about the rumors that Count Beist had left for Wiesbaden, about a remedy for gray hair, about a light carriage offered for sale, he read an advertisement put in by a young person. But these bits of information no longer provided him the quiet, ironical pleasure they had in the past.

After he was through with the newspaper, a second cup of coffee and a piece of buttered bread, he got up, brushed the crumbs from his vest, straightened, and smiled happily, but not because he felt any special pleasure in his heart. The happy smile was evoked by his good digestion.

But this happy smile reminded him of all that had happened, and he became thoughtful.

He heard the voices of two of his children behind the door, and recognized the voice of Grisha, the younger boy, and Tania, the older girl. They dropped something that they had been carrying.

"I told you, passengers aren't allowed on the roof!" cried the girl in English. "Pick them up!"

Everything is topsy-turvy, thought Stepan Arkadievich. Look at the children running around all on their own. He went up to the door and called them. They left the box, which was supposed to represent a train, and entered the room.

The girl, her father's darling, unhesitantly ran up to him, embraced him with loud laughter, and hung on his neck, enjoying, as always, the familiar scent of the perfume from his side whiskers. As he bent toward her, she kissed his face, which turned red from stooping but shone with tenderness. She released him and would have run away, but her father stopped her.

"How is Mama?" he asked, stroking his daughter's smooth tender neck. "And how are you?" he smilingly replied to the boy's greeting.

He knew well that he loved his son less than his daughter, but he always tried to treat them impartially. The boy, however, sensed this and did not respond to his father's cool smile.

"Mama? She is up," replied the girl.

Stepan Arkadievich sighed. She had another sleepless night, he thought.

"Is she cheerful?"

The girl knew that father and mother had quarreled, that mother could not be cheerful, that father surely knew about it, and that he was not sincere when he asked about it in such a casual way. She was ashamed of her father and blushed. Noticing this, he also blushed.

"I don't know," she said. "She told us to have no classes today, but to take a walk with Miss Hull and visit Grandma."

"Well, go, my Tanchurochka. No, wait," he said, stopping her and caressing her delicate little hand.

He reached for the box of candy he had left on the mantelpiece the day before and handed her two of the kinds she liked most, one chocolate and the other cream-filled.

"Is this for Grisha?" she asked, pointing at the chocolate candy.

"Yes, yes," he replied, and once again gently patting her little shoulder, he kissed her hair and her neck and let her go.

"The coach is ready," said Matvei. "A woman petitioner is here," he added.

"How long has she been here?" asked Stepan Arkadievich.

"About half an hour."

"How many times have I ordered you to report to me about these visitors without delay?"

"But I had to let you have your coffee," said Matvei in the gruff but friendly way that could arouse no anger.

"Well, hurry and ask her to come in," said Oblonsky, frowning in annoyance.

The petitioner, the widow of a junior captain named Kalinin, explained her request, which was difficult to understand and impossible to grant. But Stepan Arkadievich, in his customary way, put her at ease, listened to her attentively without interrupting, gave her detailed advice, pointed out to whom and how to apply, and as a further help, he quickly and easily wrote a note to a person who might assist her. He wrote in a large, well-spaced, handsome and legible hand. After dismissing the captain's widow, Stepan Arkadievich picked up his hat, then stopped to make sure that he had not forgotten anything. As it turned out, he had not forgotten anything except what he wished to forget: the quarrel with his wife.

Ah, yes! He lowered his head, and his handsome face saddened. Shall I go to see her or not? he asked himself.

His inner voice told him that there was no purpose in going to see her. It would produce nothing but falsehood; it was impossible to improve and repair their relations, because it was impossible to turn her anew into an attractive and desirable woman or to turn him into an old man incapable of loving. Nothing but falsehood and deception would come of it, and falsehood and deception were alien to his nature.

At some point, however, it will have to be done. Things cannot remain as they are, he told himself, trying to summon all his courage. He straightened, reached for a cigarette, which, after a couple of puffs, he threw into the mother-of-pearl ash tray. He briskly passed by the somber drawing room, and opened the door that led to his wife's bedroom.

4

DARIA ALEKSANDROVNA stood in the disordered room in front of a chiffonier from which she was taking something. She was dressed in a light jacket. The braids of her hair, now thinning but once so thick and beautiful, were coiled on the back of her head. Her face was thin and worn, and this accentuated her large frightened eyes. On hearing her husband's steps, she stopped and glanced at the door, vainly trying to assume a severe and contemptuous expression. She was afraid of him and she feared the coming interview. Just now, for the tenth time, she was trying to do something that she had been attempting for the past three days: to select the children's and her own belongings to take with them to her mother's. But she could not bring herself to do it, and even now she repeated to herself, as she had before, that this state of affairs could continue no longer. She must do something; she must punish him, put him to shame, take revenge at least for a small part of that suffering which he had caused her. She still repeated that she was going to leave him, but she felt that this was impossible. It was impossible because she could not cease regarding him as her husband and she could not stop loving him. Moreover, she felt that if here, in her house, it was hard for her to care properly for her five children, they would fare much worse where they were going. Even here, within these past three days, the youngest of the children had fallen sick from being fed a badly cooked bouillon, and the others had gone almost without dinner the previous day. She knew that she could not leave, but in her self-delusion she kept on sorting the belongings they would need, pretending that she would leave.

At the sight of her husband she put her hand into the drawer of the chiffonier, as if trying to find something, and glanced at him only when he came very close to her. But her face, which she wished to keep severe and determined, showed only embarrassment and suffering.

"Dolly!" he said in a soft, timid voice. He pulled his head into his shoulders and tried to appear pitiful and submissive, but instead he exuded an air of health and vigor.

Her glance swept him from top to toe; his entire body exuded health and vigor. Yes, he's happy and contented, she thought. But I? This repugnant goodness that everybody loves and praises him for so much! I hate this goodness of his, she thought. Her mouth contracted; a muscle trembled in the right cheek of her pale, nervous face.

"What do you want?" she asked rapidly in a low voice, not her own.

"Dolly!" he repeated in a trembling voice, "Anna is coming today."

"What's that to me? I cannot see her," she cried.

"But you must, Dolly!"

"Go away, go away!" she cried without looking at him, as if forced to cry out by physical pain.

Stepan Arkadievich could rest undisturbed when thinking about his wife, could assume that everything would *come out right in the end*, as Matvei had put it, and could calmly read his paper and drink his coffee. But when he saw this suffering, tortured face, when he heard the sound of her voice, a voice of despair and submission to fate, his breath stopped short, he felt a lump in his throat, and tears glistened in his eyes.

"My God, what have I done! Dolly! For God's sake! Please . . ." and choked by sobs, he could not continue.

She slammed the chiffonier shut and looked at him.

"Dolly, what can I say? Only one thing: forgive me, forgive me. After all, cannot nine years of our life compensate for a few moments only, a few moments?"

She lowered her eyes and listened, waiting for his words, as if begging him to prove that she was wrong.

"Moments of infatuation," he muttered, and was going to continue, but at these words her lips again tightened, again a muscle twitched in her right cheek as if from physical pain.

"Go away, get out of here!" she cried in a voice still shriller. "Don't talk to me about your infatuation and about your loathsome adventures."

She wanted to leave, but she tottered and gripped the back of a chair for support. Her face was distorted, her lips quivered, and tears filled her eyes.

"Dolly!" he said, sobbing. "For God's sake, think of the children. They are not at fault. I'm guilty; punish me! Tell me how to atone for my guilt. I'll do whatever I can; I am ready for anything. I'm guilty, and there are no words to describe my guilt. Please, Dolly, forgive me!"

She sat down. He listened to her heavy, labored breathing, and his pity for her was boundless. She tried a few times to say something, but could not. He waited.

"You think about the children only because you like to play with them, but I think about them because I know that they are lost now," she said. This evidently was one of those sentences that she had repeated to herself these past three days.

She addressed him now in the familiar "thou." He looked

at her gratefully and attempted to take her hand, but she shrank from him in disgust.

"I always think about the children, and therefore would do anything to save them; but I don't know myself whether it would be better to take them away from their father or to leave them with a dissolute father. Yes, a dissolute father. . . . But tell me, after this . . . after what's happened, is it possible for us to live together? Is it possible? Tell me, is it possible?" she kept on repeating, raising her voice. "After my husband, the father of my children, has had a love affair with his children's governess . . . ?"

"But what's to be done? What's to be done?" he asked in a pitiful voice, without knowing what he was saying, and letting his head droop lower and lower.

"You are vile. I loathe you!" she cried out, growing more and more excited. "Your tears are nothing but water. You've never loved me; you possess neither a heart nor any noble feelings. You are loathsome and vile, a stranger to me. Yes, a total stranger!" In pain and anger she shouted the word "stranger," a word which filled her with horror.

He looked at her, and the anger in her face astonished and frightened him. He could not understand that his pity only exasperated her. She saw in him only pity, not love. No, he thought, she hates me. She will not forgive me.

"It's terrible! Terrible!" he said.

At this moment, in the next room a child cried out, probably as the result of a fall. Daria Aleksandrovna listened, and her face quickly grew tender. For a few seconds she could not decide what to do, then she suddenly got up and moved to the door.

But she surely loves my child, he thought, as he watched the change in her face caused by the child's cry. *My* child. Then how can she hate me?

"Dolly, one more word!" he said, following her.

"If you follow me, I will call the servants and the children. I will let everyone know that you are a scoundrel. I am leaving today, and you may remain here with your paramour," She left, slamming the door.

Stepan Arkadievich sighed, wiped his face, and softly stepped out of the room. Matvei says that everything will come out right in the end, but how? I don't see how it's possible. Ah, how terrible! And how common was her shouting, he said to himself, recalling her words "scoundrel" and "paramour." Could the maids have heard it? How terribly, terribly common! Stepan Arkadievich remained standing for a few seconds, wiped his eyes, sighed, straightened, and left the room.

It was Friday, and in the dining room the old German watchmaker was winding the clock. Stepan Arkadievich smiled as he recalled his joke about this punctual, bald-headed watchmaker: the German was wound up for life to wind clocks. Stepan Arkadievich loved a witty joke. Perhaps everything will *come out right in the end!* Well put: It will *come out right.* I must repeat that to somebody.

"Matvei," he called. "Get Maria and she'll help you arrange the sitting room for Anna Arkadievna."

"Very well."

Stepan Arkadievich put on his fur coat and went out on the porch.

"Will you have dinner at home?" asked Matvei.

"I'm not sure. Here's your expense money," he said, taking ten rubles out of his wallet. "Is it enough?"

"It will have to do, whether it is enough or not," said Matvei, shutting the door of the coach and stepping back to the porch.

In the meantime, Daria Aleksandrovna calmed the child. By the sound of the coach she knew that he had left, and she returned to her bedroom. This was her only retreat from the domestic worries that absorbed her as soon as she emerged from it. Even during the short time she had been in the nursery, the English governess and Matriona Filimonovna had managed to present her with a few urgent problems to which she alone could give the answer: How to dress the children for their walk? Should they be given milk? Should a new cook be hired?

"Oh, leave me alone, leave me alone," she had said, returning to her bedroom and sitting in the same place where she had had the argument with her husband. She wrung her emaciated hands, her rings slipping down on her bony fingers, and tried to recollect all the words of the argument. He left! But what is he going to do about *her?* she thought. Is it possible that he still sees her? Why didn't I ask him? No, no, a reconciliation is out of the question. Even if we remain in the same house, we will remain as strangers. Strangers forever! she repeated again, giving a particular meaning to this word that so frightened her. How much I loved him. My God, how much I loved him! How much I loved him! And now, don't I still love him? Don't I love him more than before? But what a terrible thing, especially—she began, but could not finish her thought, for Matriona Filimonovna appeared at the door.

"Please have someone fetch my brother," the nurse said, "and he will prepare dinner. Otherwise, the children will remain without food until six o'clock again."

"All right, I'll be there right away and see to it. By the way, have you sent for fresh milk?"

Daria Aleksandrovna engrossed herself in the routine of the day, and in it she drowned all her troubles for a while.

5

IN SCHOOL Stepan Arkadievich had been a good student, thanks to his abilities, but he was lazy and mischievous and therefore had graduated among the last in the class. Though he lived a life of pleasure, held a low rank, and was still comparatively young, he occupied a respectable and well-paid position as the head of one of the Moscow council chambers. He had obtained this position through the husband of his sister Anna, Aleksei Aleksandrovich Karenin, who held one of the most important positions in the ministry to which the Moscow council chamber belonged. But if Karenin had not appointed his brother-in-law to this position, then Stiva Oblonsky would have obtained through any of hundreds of other persons—brothers, sisters, cousins, aunts, and uncles—this position or a similar one, at a yearly salary of about six thousand rubles, which he needed, for his personal affairs were in a bad state in spite of his wife's wealth.

Half of Moscow and Petersburg were Stepan Arkadievich's kinsmen and friends. He had been born into that group of people who were or had become the powerful ones in the world. One-third of the men in high offices, the old-timers, were his father's friends and had known him since his childhood. Another third addressed him as "thou," and the last third were close acquaintances. Therefore those who dealt out earthly blessings, such as positions, leases, concessions, and the like, were all his friends and would not neglect him. Oblonsky did not have to exert any effort in order to obtain a well-paying position; all he had to do was to refuse no offer, to envy no one, to argue with no one, and to take no offense at anyone. He followed all these rules without effort, thanks to his good nature. He would laugh at the idea that he might be refused a position at a salary that he needed, particularly since his demands were never exorbitant. All he asked for were the privileges given to others of his age; he fulfilled his duties in no worse fashion than any of them.

All who knew Stepan Arkadievich admired him, and not just for his good and happy nature and unquestioned honesty. His handsome serene looks, shining eyes, black eyebrows and hair, and healthy complexion aroused an almost physical sensation of friendliness and cheer in anyone who met him. "Ah! Stiva! Oblonsky! Here he is!" were the usual happy greetings with which he was met. And if occasionally after a conversation with him nothing particularly cheerful occurred, he was nevertheless greeted with the same cheer the next day, and the day after.

In the three years since he had become the head of one of the Moscow council chambers, Stepan Arkadievich had gained not only the affection but also the respect of his associates, subordinates, and superiors and of anyone else who dealt with him. The main qualities of Stepan Arkadievich that brought him this general respect were: first, his unusual tolerance for others, based on an awareness of his own shortcomings; second, his truly democratic sentiments, which he had not derived from reading his newspaper but which were in his blood and which made him treat all people alike, regardless of their status and calling; third, and most important, his absolute indifference toward his job, an attitude that saved him both from undue enthusiasm and from possible blunders.

Arriving at his place of work, Stepan Arkadievich went into his small study, carrying his briefcase and followed by the respectful doorkeeper. He put on his uniform and entered the chamber. The clerks and other employees rose and cheerfully and respectfully greeted him. As usual, he hurriedly walked up to his seat, shook hands, and sat down. After a few joking remarks appropriate to the occasion, he turned to his work. No one but Stepan Arkadievich could so neatly set the limits to freedom, familiarity and formality, that were so essential to make the work enjoyable. His secretary came up with the papers respectfully and cheerfully, the way everyone acted in Stepan Arkadievich's presence, and spoke a few words in the familiar and free manner that had been introduced by Stepan Arkadievich.

"At last we have received the information we needed from the Penza government office. Here, if you please."

"It has come at last!" repeated Stepan Arkadievich, putting his fingers on the paper. "Well, gentlemen . . ." and the office day began.

If they could only have seen, he thought, lowering his head with an air of great importance and listening to the report, what a guilty boy their chief was only half an hour ago. He smiled with his eyes during the reading. Until two o'clock this work had to go on without interruption, and at two o'clock there was a break and lunch.

It was not yet two o'clock when the large glass doors of the chamber opened, and someone walked in. All the council members, grateful for the interruption, turned toward the door, looking from under a portrait and behind the statuette of Justice. But immediately the doorkeeper put out the intruder and closed the glass door behind him.

When the report had been read, Stepan Arkadievich rose, stretched, and following the new free ways, reached for a cigarette here in the office, and left for his study. His two friends, the veteran Nikitin and Grinevich, a Gentleman of the Bedchamber, accompanied him.

"We'll have time enough to complete the case after lunch," said Stepan Arkadievich.

"We'll have plenty of time!" said Nikitin.

"He certainly is some knave, that Fomin!" remarked Grinevich concerning one of the persons involved in the case which they had been deciding.

Stepan Arkadievich frowned at Grinevich's remark, indicating how improper it was to form premature conclusions, but did not say anything.

"Who was the man that came in?" he asked the doorkeeper.

"Your excellency, someone tried to get in without permission while I was busy. He asked for you. I told him that as soon as the council members came outside, then. . . ."

"Where is he?"

"I believe he's in the entrance hall. He's been here all this time. There he is," said the doorkeeper, pointing to a well-built, broad-shouldered and curly bearded man who, with his fur cap on his head, was briskly and easily running up the worn steps of the stone staircase. One of the officials, a thin man, who was going down with his briefcase in his hand, stopped, looked disapprovingly at the feet of the running man, then turned his questioning glance to Oblonsky.

Stepan Arkadievich stood at the top of the staircase. His face, smiling gently above the embroidered collar of his uniform, grew still brighter when he recognized the man who was running up to him.

"Well, well! Levin, at last!" he exclaimed with a friendly jocular smile, as he looked at Levin coming up to him. "How could you bring yourself to look for me in this den?" said Stepan Arkadievich. Not content with just a handshake, he kissed his friend. "When did you arrive?"

"A little while ago, and I'm very anxious to speak to you," replied Levin. He looked about him shyly and with a mixture of anger and annoyance.

"Well, let's go to my study," said Stepan Arkadievich, who was aware of his friend's touchy and resentful shyness. Seizing his hand, he drew him behind himself as if leading him through a dangerous place.

Stepan Arkadievich used the familiar "thou" with almost all his acquaintances: sexagenarians, youngsters of twenty, actors, ministers of state, merchants, adjutants-general. Thus many of these people whom he addressed familiarly could be found on both ends of the social ladder, and they would have been greatly astonished had they known that through Oblonsky they had something in common. He "thoued" everyone with whom he drank champagne, and he drank champagne with everyone. Occasionally, in the presence of his subordinates, he would come across a "disreputable" friend, as he jokingly called some of those whom he addressed familiarly. Then, with his usual tact, he found a way to ease the unfavorable impression which the meeting might have made upon the subordinates. Levin was not one of the "disreputable" ones, but Oblonsky, tactful as usual, felt that Levin might suspect him of unwillingness to show their friendship to his subordinates. He therefore was in a hurry to take him to his study.

Levin was almost of the same age as Oblonsky, and they addressed each other as "thou" not just because they had shared champagne. Levin was a companion and friend of early youth. In spite of the difference in their characters and their tastes, they liked each other as two friends whose friendship was formed in early youth. In spite of this, as often happens between those who have chosen different careers, each within his own heart had little respect for his friend's occupation, although reason told him he should approve. Each believed that the life he led was the only real life and that the one his friend led was only a mirage. On seeing Levin, Oblonsky could not restrain a slight, jesting smile. It was not the first time that he had met Levin as he arrived in Moscow from the country, where he was engaged in something, although Stepan Arkadievich could never fully grasp what it actually was, nor did he have any interest in it. Whenever Levin arrived in Moscow he was upset, rushed, somewhat embarrassed, and ashamed of his embarrassment. He usually brought with him completely new and unexpected attitudes. Stepan Arkadievich laughed at them, but he was liked by them. Likewise, in his heart, Levin had little regard either for the city life that his friend led or for his position, which he considered worthless and ridiculous. Yet there was a difference between them. Oblonsky, doing everything that everybody else did, laughed with self-confidence and good humor, whereas Levin's laughter lacked self-confidence and sometimes sounded bitter.

"We've been waiting for you for a long time," said Stepan Arkadievich, entering the study and releasing Levin's hand, as if to indicate that here he was out of danger. "I'm very, very glad to see you," he continued. "Well, how are you? When did you arrive?"

Levin remained silent, looking at Oblonsky's two friends, unknown to him, and particularly at the hands of the elegant Grinevich, with their long white fingers and long, yellow, curving nails, and the large shiny buttons on his shirt. Evidently these hands had so captured his attention, he could not think of anything else. Oblonsky immediately noticed this and smiled.

"Oh, yes! May I present to you my friends," he said, "Filipp Ivanovich Nikitin, Mikhail Stanislavich Grinevich," and, pointing to Levin, "meet an active member of the zemstvo,* a modern man, a gymnast who lifts one hundred and eighty pounds with one hand, a cattle breeder and a hunter, my friend Konstantin Dmitrievich Levin, the brother of Sergei Ivanovich Koznyshev."

"I am glad to meet you," said the old man.

"I have the honor of knowing your brother Sergei Ivano-

---

* An elected district council in Russia, created in 1864.

vich," said Grinevich, holding out his thin hand with its long nails.

Levin frowned, shook hands coldly, and immediately turned to Oblonsky. Though he held his half-brother, a writer famous throughout Russia, in great esteem, he could not bear to be known not as Konstantin Levin but as the brother of the famous Koznyshev.

"But I'm no longer active in the zemstvo. I've quarrelled with all of them, and no longer attend the meetings," he said, addressing Oblonsky.

"So soon?" smiled Oblonsky. "But how? And why?"

"It's a long story. Some day I'll tell you about it," said Levin, but he began his story at once. "To make it short, I have become convinced that no zemstvo activity does or can amount to anything," he started with an injured air. "On the one hand, to them it is a toy. They play at parliament, and I'm neither young enough nor old enough to amuse myself with toys. On the other hand," he said haltingly, "it's a way for the county coterie to make a ruble. Formerly they had the trusteeship offices and the courts; now it's the zemstvo. The salary they receive, though not a bribe, is not really earned," he argued heatedly, as if one of his listeners had challenged his opinion.

"Oho! I see this is a new phase. You are a conservative now," said Stepan Arkadievich. "Well, we'll speak about it later."

"Yes, later. But I have to see you," said Levin, staring with aversion at Grinevich's hands.

Stepan Arkadievich smiled faintly.

"Didn't you say that you would never again wear a European suit?" he asked, looking at Levin's new suit, obviously the creation of a French tailor. "Yes, I see. A new phase."

Levin blushed suddenly, not the way adults blush, lightly, unaware of it, but the way boys blush who realize how ridiculous their shyness is. Ashamed, they blush still more, and are almost reduced to tears. It was so embarrassing to see this intelligent, manly face reduced to such a childish state that Oblonsky averted his gaze.

"Where shall we meet? I'm very, very anxious to speak to you," said Levin.

Oblonsky seemed to be lost in thought.

"Listen, let's go to Gurin's for lunch, and we can talk there. I'm free until three o'clock."

"No," said Levin after a moment. "I have another call to make."

"All right, then let's dine together."

"Dine? But really, I have nothing special to tell you, just a word or two, a question, and then we can talk."

"Then let me hear that word or two now, and we'll have our conversation at dinner."

"Here are those two words," said Levin, "although it does not matter." His face suddenly turned angry, as a result of his attempt to overcome his shyness. "How are the Shcherbatskys? As usual?" he asked.

Stepan Arkadievich, who had known for a long time that Levin was in love with Kitty, his sister-in-law, smiled faintly, though his eyes sparkled with merriment. "A matter of two words, you said. But I cannot answer in just two words, because. . . . Excuse me for a minute."

The secretary entered, showing a respect tinged with familiarity. Like all secretaries, he was modestly conscious of his superiority over his chief in understanding the problems of his office. He came up to Oblonsky with some papers, and, while pretending to ask his advice, began to clear up a difficult point. Stepan Arkadievich interrupted the secretary and gently put his hand on his sleeve.

"No, please do as I asked," he said, smiling to ease the effect of his remark. He briefly explained how he understood the case, pushed aside the papers, and said, "Please do it this way, Zakhar Nikitich."

The abashed secretary left. During Oblonsky's conversation with the secretary, Levin had completely recovered from his embarrassment. He stood behind a chair, leaning on it with both hands, smiling ironically.

"I don't understand. I don't understand," he said.

"What don't you understand?" Oblonsky asked, smiling gaily and reaching for a cigarette. He waited for some sort of odd explanation from Levin.

"I don't understand what you do here," said Levin, with a shrug of his shoulders. "How can you take it seriously?"

"Why do you ask?"

"Because you actually do nothing."

"That's what you think. We are overburdened with work."

"Paper work. Well, you have a knack for it," added Levin.

"You really mean that I lack something."

"Perhaps you do," said Levin. "Nevertheless, I delight in

your high status and feel proud that my friend is such a great man. But you haven't answered my question," he added, trying his best to look Oblonsky straight in the eye.

"Well, never mind. Wait a bit and you too will come to this. It's all very well for you to talk this way, with your three-thousand dessiatines of land in Karazin County, your strong muscles, and the bloom of a twelve-year-old in your cheeks. But you, too, will become one of us. Now about your question: nothing has changed, but it's a pity that you haven't been there for such a long time."

"Why?" asked Levin in alarm.

"No special reason," replied Oblonsky. "We will talk about it later. But what's the real purpose of your visit?"

"Well, about this, too, we will speak later," said Levin, again blushing to the roots of his hair.

"Well, I know," said Stepan Arkadievich. "You see, I would invite you to my house, but my wife is not quite well. But listen, if you want to see them, you'll most probably find them in the Zoological Park between four and five o'clock. Kitty skates there. Go there, I'll come over, and we'll dine somewhere."

"Excellent; I'll see you later."

"Remember, now. I know you well, and you may forget about it or suddenly leave for the country," said Stepan Arkadievich, laughing.

"No, I'll be there."

Levin left the room, and only at the door did he recall that he had not taken leave of Oblonsky's friends.

"He must be a very energetic gentleman," said Grinevich when Levin left.

"Yes, my good friend," said Stepan Arkadievich, shaking his head. "A fortunate man! Three thousand dessiatines in Karazin County, everything to look forward to, and such vigor! Unlike our fate."

"Why are you complaining, Stepan Arkadievich?"

"It is bad, very bad," said Stepan Arkadievich with a heavy sigh.

6

WHEN OBLONSKY asked Levin what the real purpose of his visit was, Levin blushed and then got angry with himself for having blushed. He could not answer, "I have come to propose to your sister-in-law," although this was the only purpose of his visit.

The families Levin and Shcherbatsky descended from old Moscow nobility, and the relations between them were always close and friendly. This bond grew still stronger during Levin's college years. He had studied for the examinations and entered the university together with young Prince Shcherbatsky, the brother of Kitty and Dolly. During that period Levin often visited the home of the Shcherbatskys and fell in love with the home of the Shcherbatskys. It may seem strange, but Konstantin Levin actually fell in love with the home and the family, particularly with the female half of the family Shcherbatsky. Levin did not remember his own mother, and his only sister was older than he. Therefore, in the home of the Shcherbatskys he met for the first time a family descended from old nobility, an educated and honorable family, a kind he had never known because of the early death of his father and mother. All members of this family, particularly the female half, seemed to him enveloped in some mysterious poetic veil. Not only did he not see any flaws in them, but he believed that under the poetic veil that covered them there resided the most sublime sentiments and every possible perfection. Why should these three young ladies speak French one day and English the next? Why should they, at set hours, take turns in playing the piano, the sound of which could be heard in their brother's room upstairs, where the students studied their lessons? What was the purpose of that constant stream of teachers of French literature, music, drawing, and dancing? Why, at set hours, should the three ladies, accompanied by Mlle. Linon, ride in the carriage along Tverskoy Boulevard, all dressed in fur-lined satin coats, Dolly in a long one, Natalie in a half-length coat, and Kitty in a very short one, which exposed to full view her shapely legs tightly encased in red stockings? Why should they take a walk along Tverskoy Boulevard, followed by a servant with a gold ornament in his hat? All of these, and many other events in their mysterious world, he did not understand, but he knew that everything in that world was beautiful, and he was particularly enamored of the mystery surrounding these happenings.

In his college days he nearly fell in love with the older sister, Dolly, but she was soon married to Oblonsky. Then he began to fall in love with the next sister. He had a feeling that he must fall in love with one of the sisters, and could not decide which one. But Natalie married the diplomat Lvov as soon as she was introduced to society. Kitty was still a child when Levin graduated from the university. The young Shcherbatsky had joined the Navy and drowned in the Baltic Sea, and Levin's visits to the Shcherbatsky family became much less frequent in spite of his friendship with Oblonsky. In the early winter of the same year, Levin arrived in Moscow after staying for a whole year in the country. When he visited the Shcherbatskys, he knew which of the three sisters fortune had selected as his true love.

He was of good stock, rich rather than poor, thirty-two years old, and it was most natural that he should propose to Princess Shcherbatsky. In all probability he would be accepted as a good match for her. But Levin was in love, and he therefore believed that Kitty was so perfect in every respect, a creature standing so high above all earthly things, that it was utterly improbable that either she or the others might accept him, such a common earthly creature, as worthy of her. After a dazed two months in Moscow, seeing Kitty almost daily at social affairs, which he began to frequent in order to meet her, Levin suddenly decided that nothing would come of it, and he left for the country.

His conviction that nothing would come of it was based on the fact that Kitty's relatives considered him an unsuitable and unworthy match for the charming Kitty, and that Kitty herself could not love him. In the opinion of her family, Levin had no definite occupation and held no position recognized by society, whereas some of his friends at the age of thirty-two were colonels or aides-de-camp, others were professors, bank directors, railway presidents, or heads of council chambers like Oblonsky. He, however (he knew very well how he must appear to others), was just a landowner, busy with cow breeding, snipe hunting, and with his farm buildings. In other words, he was a fellow of no talents, who had accomplished little, and who, according to society's standards, was a misfit.

The charming, mysterious Kitty surely could never love such a homely man as he thought himself to be, and what was more important, such an ordinary, undistinguished man. Moreover, he found his having formerly treated Kitty as a child (in view of his friendship with her brother) an additional obstacle to his love for her. He assumed that a homely, good man, such as he thought himself, could be loved only as a friend; that to be loved the way he himself loved Kitty, one must be a handsome, and, what was most important, an extraordinary man.

He had heard that women often loved homely, simple men, but he did not believe it, for he knew very well that he himself could love only beautiful, mysterious, and extraordinary women.

But, after he had spent two lonely months in the country, he convinced himself that this love was unlike the loves of his early youth; that this feeling gave him not a moment's peace; that he could not go on without finding an answer to the question of whether or not she would become his wife; that his despair had been born of his imagination; that he had no proof that he would be refused if he proposed. Then he went to Moscow with the firm resolve to propose and marry, if accepted. Or . . . he could not even think of what would happen if he were refused.

7

ON ARRIVING in Moscow on an early train, Levin stopped at the house of his older half-brother Koznyshev. He changed his clothes and went to see him in his study. He intended to explain to him the purpose of his visit immediately and to seek his advice, but his brother was not alone. He had with him a famous professor of philosophy, who had come from Kharkov for the sole purpose of straightening out a misunderstanding between them concerning a very important philosophical problem. The professor had been carrying on a heated attack against the materialists. Sergei Koznyshev had followed this controversy closely, and after he had read the professor's latest article, he had written him a letter in which he explained his objections to the professor's theory. He reproached him for yielding to the materialists on too many points. The professor arrived without delay to settle their differences. The problem under discussion, in vogue at that time, was whether there is any boundary that divides man's psychological functions from his physiological, and if there is, where is it?

Sergei Ivanovich met his brother with his usual cool yet kindly smile, introduced him to the professor, and resumed the conversation.

The professor, a short, yellowed, bespectacled man with a narrow forehead, interrupted the conversation for a moment to greet Levin, then renewed his speech, paying no further attention to him. Levin sat down, waiting for the professor to leave, but soon became interested in the subject of conversation.

Levin had come across the magazine articles they were discussing, and had read them. While at the university he had studied natural science, and these articles had aroused his interest as an explanation of the foundation on which the study of nature was based. But he had never before connected these scientific conclusions concerning the animal origin of man, reflexes, biology, and sociology with another problem which lately had come to his mind with increasing frequency, namely, what did life and death mean to him?

As he listened to the conversation between his brother and the professor, he noticed that they had established a connection between scientific and spiritual problems, that at times they almost touched on these problems. But every time they approached a problem that he considered important, they hurriedly retreated and became deeply involved anew in the subjects of subdivisions, mental reservations, quotations, allusions, and references to authoritative sources. He could scarcely understand what they were talking about.

"I cannot agree," said Sergei Ivanovich, his words clear and distinct as usual, and his diction refined. "In no way can I agree with Keiss and accept the fact that my entire conception of the outside world is produced by impressions. The basic conception of *being* I have not acquired through sensation, for there exists no special organ for this purpose."

"Yes, but Wurst, and Knaust, and Pripasov would reply to you that your conception of being is brought about by the sum total of sensations, that this conception of being is the result of sensations. Wurst even goes so far as to assert that without sensation, there can be no conception of being."

"I would say just the opposite," began Sergei Ivanovich.

Once more it appeared to Levin that now so close to the main problem, they had retreated once more, and he decided to ask the professor a question.

"Does this mean that if my senses are destroyed, if my body dies, my existence comes to an end?" he asked.

Annoyed and, as it seemed, intellectually pained by this interruption, the professor glanced at the strange inquirer who looked more like a barge hauler than a philosopher. He then shifted his eyes to Sergei Ivanovich, as if to ask: What can one say? But Sergei Ivanovich's manner of speaking differed considerably from that of the professor, whose speech was laborious and ideas biased. He had left in his mind enough room both to reply to the professor and to understand how simple and natural was the questioner's point of view. He smiled and said, "We have no right yet to seek the solution to this problem."

"We have no facts," confirmed the professor, and he continued with his argument. "No," he said, "I am only pointing out that if, as Pripasov plainly says, sensation is based on impression, then we must make a clear distinction between these two conceptions."

Levin was no longer listening and waited for the professor to leave.

8

WHEN THE professor had left, Sergei Ivanovich turned to his brother.

"I'm very glad that you came. You will stay? How are the affairs of the estate?"

Levin knew that his older brother was little interested in the affairs of the estate, and that he inquired about them only to please him. So he told him only about the sale of wheat and about his finances.

Levin thought of telling his brother about his intention to marry, and of asking his advice. He had even firmly decided to do so, but when he saw his brother, listened to his conversation with the professor and noticed the somewhat condescending way his brother inquired about their affairs (their mother's estate had remained undivided, and Levin supervised both parts of it), Levin felt that somehow he would not be able to start a conversation with his brother about his decision to get married. He felt that his brother would not receive the news in a way that would please him.

"Well, how is the zemstvo?" asked Sergei Ivanovich, who was greatly interested in the zemstvo and considered it very important.

"Truly, I don't know. . . ."

"Why not? Are you no longer a member of the board?"

"No, I'm no longer a member. I've resigned." replied Levin. "And I no longer attend the meetings."

"It's a pity," said Sergei Ivanovich, frowning.

In his defense, Levin went into an explanation of what went on at the county meetings.

"It's always like this," interrupted Sergei Ivanovich. "We, the Russians, always act this way. Perhaps it's a good trait of ours, this ability to see our failures. But we overdo it; we seek our consolation in an irony which comes easily to our tongues. I am sure that were the privileges of the zemstvo institutions given to some other European nation, such as the Germans or the English, they would use them as foundations for liberty, whereas all we do is to treat them as a laughing matter."

"But what's to be done?" said Levin apologetically. "It was my last attempt. I have tried with all my heart, but I failed; I am unfit for this work."

"You are not unfit," said Sergei Ivanovich. "You just have the wrong attitude toward it."

"Perhaps," dejectedly answered Levin.

"You know, our brother Nikolai is here again."

Nikolai was the older brother of Konstantin Levin and the half-brother of Sergei Ivanovich. He was a lost man, having squandered most of his fortune, consorted with the strangest and lowest sort of people, and quarreled with his brothers.

"What are you saying?" cried Levin in dismay. "How do you know?"

"Prokofi saw him in the street."

"Here, in Moscow? Do you know where he is?" Levin rose from his chair, as if prepared to search for him immediately.

"I'm sorry I told you," said Sergei Ivanovich, and he shook his head at his younger brother's agitation. "I found out where he lives, and sent him the promissory note that he had given to Trubin, which I paid. Here's his answer."

Sergei Ivanovich reached for the note from under a paperweight and handed it to Levin.

Levin read the note, which was written in an odd but familiar hand. "I respectfully beg you to leave me alone. This is the only demand I make of my loving brothers. Nikolai Levin."

After Levin had read it, he remained standing before Sergei Ivanovich without raising his head, the note in his hand.

In his heart his desire to forget for the moment his unfortunate brother struggled against his belief that it would be wrong to do so.

"Apparently he wants to insult me," continued Sergei Ivanovich, "but he will fail, for I wish to help him with all my heart. Yet I know I cannot do so."

"Yes, yes," repeated Levin. "I understand and appreciate your feelings toward him, but I'll go to see him."

"Go if you wish, but I wouldn't advise you to do so," said Sergei Ivanovich. "I'm not concerned about myself, and I don't believe that he can provoke you against me. But for your own sake I wouldn't advise you to go. It's hopeless. However, do as you like."

"Perhaps it's hopeless, but I feel, and particularly at this moment—but that's another matter—I feel that I can't remain still."

"Well, this I do not understand," said Sergei Ivanovich. "I do know, however," he added, "that I have learned a lesson in humility. Ever since Nikolai became what he is today I've developed a different and more tolerant view of what is commonly called depravity. You know what he did. . . ."

"Ah, it's terrible," said Levin.

Sergei Ivanovich's servant gave Levin his brother's address, and he was going to leave at once, then decided to postpone his visit until evening. First, to gain peace of mind, he had to settle the matter that had brought him to Moscow. From his brother's, Levin went to Oblonsky's office, inquired about the Shcherbatsky family, then left for the place where he was told he might meet Kitty.

9

AT FOUR O'CLOCK Levin, his heart pounding, alighted from a carriage at the Zoological Park, and walked along a path to the hill and the skating pond, certain that he would meet her there, for he had seen the Shcherbatskys' coach at the entrance.

It was a clear, frosty day. The approach to the skating pond was crowded with long rows of coaches, sleighs, carriages and gendarmes. The gentry, resplendent in their hats in the bright sunshine, thronged near the entrance and along the swept paths between the Russian-style pavilions decorated with carved birds. In the garden, spreading old birches, all their branches weighted with snow, seemed to be bedecked in new festive robes.

He walked along a path to the skating pond, talking to himself: I must keep calm. What's the matter with you? What ails you? Quiet, you fool, he said, addressing his heart. But the more he tried to compose himself, the more labored his breathing became. An acquaintance passed by and greeted him, but Levin did not even notice who it was. He came up to the hill, where the air was filled with the clanking of the chains on the sleds as they were pulled up and came down again, the clash of the colliding toboggans, and the sound of happy voices. He took a few more steps. The skating pond lay open before him, and he immediately recognized her in the crowd of skaters.

The joy and fear that filled his heart told him that she was here. She stood on the opposite side of the pond, talking to a lady. Neither her dress nor her manner was distinctive in any way, yet Levin recognized her in this crowd as easily as he would a rose in a field of nettles. She cast a radiance all about her, her smile enveloping all in its brilliance. Could I really go onto the ice? Could I approach her? he thought. The place where she was standing seemed to him unapproachable and sacred, and for a moment he felt such a dread that he thought of turning back. He had to force himself to realize that all sorts of people were near her, and that he himself might by chance have come there to skate. He went down, refraining from looking at her directly, as one refrains from looking at the sun. But just as one can see the sun without looking at it, he could see her.

On this day of the week and at this hour, there gathered on the ice a group of people who belonged to the same circle and were all acquainted with each other. Here were the virtuoso skaters who flaunted their skill; the learners, who held on to chairs, moving timidly and awkwardly; the boys; and the old men, who skated for the sake of health. All of them, thought Levin, were fortune's favorites, because they were here, near her. All the skaters seemed to pass her or to catch up with her with ease. They even spoke to her, or enjoyed themselves without any regard for her, taking advantage of the perfect ice and the beautiful weather.

Nikolai Shcherbatsky, Kitty's cousin, in a short jacket and tight pants, sat on a bench, wearing his skates. On seeing Levin, he cried:

"Here is Russia's greatest skater! When did you arrive? The ice is perfect. Hurry and put on your skates."

"But I have no skates," replied Levin, surprised at this ease and unconcern displayed in her presence. Though he did not look at her directly, he never lost sight of her. He felt that the sun was approaching him. She was in the corner of the pond. Her slender feet, in their high shoes, were set at an angle, and she skated toward him somewhat fearfully. A boy, dressed in the Russian style, tried to pass her, desperately swinging his arms and bending toward the ground. She skated hesitantly. She had withdrawn her hands from her little muff, which hung on a cord, and now held them out for protection. She looked at Levin and recognized him, smiling both at him and at her own fears. When she reached the end of the turn, her firm slender legs had brought her directly to Shcherbatsky. She held on to him with her hand and, smiling, she nodded to Levin. She was more beautiful than he had imagined.

In his mind he could picture her very distinctly, particularly her charming little blond head, which displayed the serenity and goodness of a child and was held so effortlessly by her shapely, girlish shoulders. The childlike expression of her face, combined with the beauty of her slender figure, created that extraordinary charm which he remembered so well. But most surprisingly impressive were the look in her eyes, gentle, calm, and sincere, and especially her smile, which always transported Levin into that enchanted state in which he felt tenderly moved, the way he had been, he recollected, only rarely in the early years of his childhood.

"How long have you been here?" she said, giving him her hand. "Thank you," she added, as he picked up the handkerchief which had fallen from her muff.

"I? Not long, I came yesterday, no . . . today," replied Levin, who, in his excitement, failed at first to understand her question. "I wanted to come to see you," he said, and, recalling why he had looked for her, he blushed with embarrassment, "I didn't know that you loved skating, and that you were such an excellent skater."

She looked at him attentively, as if trying to understand the cause of his embarrassment.

"Your praise is most welcome. Your fame as a champion skater is still alive here," she said, and with her small black-gloved hand she brushed off the hoarfrost which covered her muff.

"Yes, some time ago I was an avid skater. I was anxious to reach perfection."

"It seems that you do everything avidly," she said with a smile. "I'm anxious to see you skate. Put on your skates, and let's skate together."

To skate together! Is it possible? thought Levin, looking at her.

"I'll put them on right away," he said, and he left to get the skates.

"It's been a long time since you were here, sir," said the attendant, holding Levin's foot and fastening the skate on his heel. "Since you, there have been no great skaters among the gentlemen. Is this all right?" he asked, adjusting the strap.

"Very good, very good. But please hurry," replied Levin, scarcely able to hold back the happy smile which spread over his features. Yes! he thought, this is life, this is happiness. "*Together*," she said. "*Let's skate together!*" Shall I tell her now? But just because I'm happy now, happy at least in my hopes, I'm afraid to tell her . . . But later? I must! I must, I must! Now brace up!

Levin stood up, took off his coat, sped over the rough ice near the pavilion, and reached the smooth area. He glided along without any effort as though able to increase and decrease his speed and change his direction by will alone. He came over to her shyly, but again her smile reassured him.

She gave him her hand, and they went off together, increasing their speed. The faster they moved, the more tightly she pressed his arm.

"I would learn more quickly if you were my teacher. Somehow I have confidence in you," she said.

"I, too, have confidence in myself, when you lean on me," he said, but immediately was frightened by his words, and blushed. Indeed, as soon as he said these words, all tenderness disappeared from her face, as the sun behind the clouds. Levin noticed the familiar play of her facial features, which betrayed mental exertion. A wrinkle marred her smooth forehead.

"Is something troubling you? But then I have no right to ask," he said quickly.

"Why not? No, nothing is troubling me," she answered coldly, and immediately added:

"Have you seen Mlle. Linon?"

"Not yet."

"Go to her. She is so fond of you."

What can it be? thought Levin. I have upset her! Oh! God, help me! He rushed over to the bench on which was seated the old Frenchwoman with her gray curls. Smiling and showing her false teeth, she greeted him as an old friend.

"Yes, we keep growing up," she said, pointing with her eyes at Kitty, "and getting old. The tiny bear has grown up," continued the Frenchwoman with a laugh, and she reminded him of his joke about the three young ladies whom he had called "the Three Bears," as in the English fairy tale. "Do you remember how you used to tell it?"

He did not remember it at all, but for about ten years she had laughed at this joke and enjoyed it.

"Well, go ahead and skate. Our Kitty skates well now, doesn't she?"

When Levin came up to Kitty, her face had lost its coldness. Her eyes were sincere and gentle, but in this gentleness Levin noticed a strange, deliberately calm quality. He felt sad. They discussed the old governess and her peculiarities, and she inquired about his life.

"Aren't you bored in the country during the winter?" she asked.

"No, I don't get bored. I keep very busy," he said, and felt that she was overwhelming him with that calm tone, from which he would be powerless to escape, as had happened earlier that winter.

"How long will you stay?"

"I don't know," he replied, without thinking of what he was saying. The thought had occurred to him that he might again succumb to this mood of hers, one of calm friendship, that he might again leave for the country without resolving anything, and he decided to resist.

"Why don't you know?"

"I don't know. It depends on you," he said, and was seized with dismay at his words.

She either did not hear his words or did not want to. She thrust her foot out twice as though about to trip, and hurriedly skated away from him. She skated up to Mlle. Linon, said something to her and made for the pavilion, where the ladies took off their skates.

My God, what have I done! My Lord, help me, enlighten me, thought Levin, praying and at the same time feeling the need for strenuous activity. He began to race on his skates, describing inside and outside turns.

At this moment one of the young men, the best among the new skaters, came out of the coffee house with a cigarette in his mouth and skates on his feet. He dashed to the staircase and clattered down the steps. On reaching the last step, he sped forward, without changing in the least the easy position of his arms, and glided over the ice.

Well, that's a new trick! said Levin to himself, and immediately rushed upstairs to perform this new trick.

"Don't get killed! You have to know how to do it," Nikolai Shcherbatsky warned him.

On the top landing of the staircase, Levin sprinted at top speed and then rushed down the steps, swinging his arms for balance in this unfamiliar kind of motion. On the last step he tripped, but, scarcely touching the ice with his hands, he straightened with a violent motion and glided on, laughing.

How good and dear he is, Kitty thought as she came out from the pavilion with Mlle. Linon. She looked at him with a soft, tender smile, as at a dear brother. Am I really guilty? Have I done anything wrong? They call it coquetry. I know that I love another, but it is such a pleasure to be with him; he is so good. But why did he say that? she thought.

Seeing that Kitty and her mother, who had met at the staircase, were leaving, Levin, his face red from the exertion, stopped and for a moment was lost in thought. He took off his skates and caught up with both mother and daughter at the entrance to the park.

"I am very glad to see you," said the princess. "We receive on Thursdays, as usual."

"Then may I come today?"

"We will be happy to see you," replied the princess coldly. This coldness upset Kitty, and she could not restrain her desire to atone for it. She turned to him and said with a smile:

"Goodbye."

At this moment, Stepan Arkadievich, his hat askew, his face and eyes shining, entered the park with the air of a happy victor. But when he came up to his mother-in-law, his face grew sad and guilty as he answered her inquiries about Dolly's health. When he finished the subdued, cheerless conversation with his mother-in-law, he straightened and took Levin's arm.

"Well, are we going?" he asked. "I've been thinking about you all this time and am very, very glad that you have come," he said, looking into his eyes meaningfully.

"Let's go, let's go," Levin answered happily. He still heard the sound of that voice that had told him "goodbye," and still saw the smile that had accompanied it.

"To the England or the Hermitage?"

"It doesn't matter."

"Well, to the England then," said Stepan Arkadievich. He preferred the England, for he owed more there than at the Hermitage and considered it wrong to stay away from it. "Is your carriage here? Splendid, for I've dismissed my coach."

The friends remained silent during the ride. Levin reflected upon the meaning of the change of expression on Kitty's face. At one moment he felt sure that there was hope, and at the next he fell into despair and saw clearly that his hope was absurd. Yet all the while he knew that now he was a completely different man, in no way resembling what he had been before he had seen her smile and heard her "goodbye."

On the way to the hotel, Stepan Arkadievich decided on what they would have for dinner.

"You like turbot, don't you?" he asked Levin as they arrived at the hotel.

"What?" asked Levin, repeating the question, "turbot? Yes, I am *terribly* fond of turbot."

10

When Levin entered the hotel with Oblonsky, he could not help noticing a certain strange air, a kind of restrained glow in the face and in the manner of Stepan Arkadievich. Oblonsky took off his coat and, with his hat cocked, passed into the dining room, giving his order to the Tartar waiters who, in swallow-tailed coats and with napkins on their arms, clustered about him. Bowing right and left to the many acquaintances who greeted him here amiably, as they did everywhere, he walked up to the buffet, had a vodka and some fish, and said a few words to the Frenchwoman who, painted and bedecked with ribbons, laces, and curls, was behind the counter. His words pleased her, and she responded with hearty laughter. Levin, however, would not drink, just because this Frenchwoman appeared so vulgar, and, it seemed, was all false hair, *poudre de riz*, and *vinaigre de toilette*. He hurried away from her as from something unclean. His soul was filled with memories of Kitty, and his smiling eyes shone with triumph and happiness.

"Here, Your Excellency, if you please, nobody will disturb Your Excellency here," said one of the waiters to Oblonsky. He was particularly tenacious, a fair-skinned old Tartar with the tails of his coat spread apart over his wide back.

"Please, Your Excellency," he addressed Levin, looking after the guest as well, as a sign of respect for Stepan Arkadievich.

He quickly spread a fresh tablecloth over the one that covered the round table under the bronze sconce, moved up the velvet-covered chairs, and remained standing with a napkin and a bill of fare in his hands, waiting for Stepan Arkadievich's order.

"Would you like, Your Excellency, to dine in a private room? It will be vacant in a few minutes. Prince Golitzin and a lady. We have received some fresh oysters."

"Ah, oysters!" Stepan Arkadievich thought for a moment. "Shouldn't we change our order, Levin?" he said, resting his finger on the card. His face showed how serious this matter was to him. "Are the oysters good? You had better be sure."

"Flensburg oysters, Your Excellency. We have none from Ostend."

"They may be from Flensburg, but are they fresh?"

"They arrived yesterday."

"Well, shall we start with oysters and then change the whole order? What do you think?"

"It makes no difference to me. I would prefer cabbage soup and kasha, but they do not serve such things here."

"Kasha *à la russe*?" asked the Tartar, bending over Levin as nurse over a child.

"No, truly, whatever you choose will suit me. The skating made me hungry. And please don't think," he added, noticing the expression of annoyance on Oblonsky's face, "that I do not approve of your order. I'll enjoy the meal."

"Of course! You may say what you want but this is one of life's pleasures," said Stepan Arkadievich. "Well, my good fellow, bring in some oysters, two, or no, it won't be enough, three dozen; vegetable soup. . . ."

"*Printanière*," quickly repeated the Tartar, but Stepan Arkadievich evidently refused to give him the pleasure of ordering the dishes by their French names.

"I said vegetable soup. Then turbot in a thick sauce, and . . . roast beef. But make sure that it's good. Then some capons and dessert."

The Tartar, recalling Stepan Arkadievich's habit of never calling the dishes by their French names, did not repeat each item as he ordered, but it gave him much pleasure to reread the whole order from the bill of fare "*Soup printanière, turbot sauce Beaumarchais, poulard à l'estragon, macédoine de fruits,*" he said, and quickly, as if worked by springs, he deposited the card in its cover, picked up another one, a wine list, and presented it to Stepan Arkadievich.

"What shall we drink?"

"I? Whatever you like, but not much—champagne," said Levin.

"What! Start with champagne? All right, let's try it. Do you like the White Seal brand?"

"*Cachet blanc,*" was the Tartar's quick response.

"Well, bring us this wine with the oysters, and then we'll see."

"Very well, sir. Any wine with your dinner?"

"Bring us some *Nuits*. No, a classic Chablis would be better."

"Very well, sir. Some of *your* special cheese?"

"All right, Parmesan. But perhaps you prefer some other kind?"

"No, it makes no difference to me," replied Levin, scarcely able to restrain a smile.

The Tartar, the tails of his coat flapping, hurried away, and within five minutes came flying back, carrying a tray of oysters on the half-shell and holding a bottle of wine between his fingers.

Stepan Arkadievich crumpled the starched napkin, tucked it into his vest, made himself comfortable, and started at the oysters.

"Not bad," he said. Using a small silver fork, he scraped the quivering oysters from their mother-of-pearl shells and swallowed them one after the other. "Not bad," he repeated, setting his moist, shining eyes now on Levin and now on the Tartar.

Levin, too, ate the oysters, though he would have preferred white bread and cheese. He watched Oblonsky with pleasure. Even the Tartar, after he had uncorked the bottle and poured the sparkling wine into the slender, gilt-edged goblets, stole glances at Stepan Arkadievich with a smile of undisguised admiration, all the while adjusting his white tie.

"Don't you care for oysters?" asked Stepan Arkadievich, emptying his goblet. "Or do you have something on your mind?"

He would have liked to see Levin cheerful. Levin was not so unhappy as he was embarrassed. Conscious of what was going on in his heart, he felt ill at ease and frightened in this tavern with its private rooms, where men dined with their ladies, amidst this hustle and bustle, amidst all these bronze, mirrors, gaslight, and Tartars. All this was so offensive to him he feared it would soil what now filled his soul.

"I do have something on my mind, and, in addition, all this embarrasses me," he said. "You can't imagine how alien all this is to me, a man from the country. Those fingernails of the gentleman whom I met in your office. . . ."

"Yes, I noticed how preoccupied you were with poor Grinevich's fingernails," said Stepan Arkadievich, smiling.

"It's beyond me," replied Levin. "Try to put yourself in my place. Judge from the point of view of a man from the country. We in the country try to keep our hands ready for work. Accordingly, we cut our fingernails and sometimes we roll up our sleeves. But here they deliberately let their nails grow as long as possible and wear cufflinks as large as small saucers, which, of course, prevents their hands from doing any work."

Stepan Arkadievich smiled broadly.

"It proves that there's no need for him to do manual work. He uses his mind."

"Perhaps. But it seems strange to me, just as it seems strange that whereas we in the country try to eat quickly so as to be ready to get back to our work, you and I are dragging this meal out as long as possible, and that is why we are eating oysters—"

"Of course," replied Stepan Arkadievich quickly. "But this is the real aim of civilization: to turn everything into a source of pleasure."

"Well, if this is the aim, then I would prefer to be a savage."

"You are a savage anyway. All you Levins are savages."

Levin sighed. He thought of his brother Nikolai and frowned in a pang of conscience. But now Oblonsky mentioned a matter that completely absorbed him.

"Well, are you going to see our Shcherbatskys this evening?" he asked with a meaningful glint in his eye, as he pushed aside the coarse, empty shells and reached for the cheese.

"Yes, I certainly am," replied Levin, "though it seemed to me that the princess was not very anxious to have me."

"How can you say that? Nonsense! It's her way. . . . Well, my friend, the soup! It's her way, the *grande dame*," said Stepan Arkadievich. "I'll be there too, but first I must go to Countess Banin's for choir rehearsal. Well, aren't you a savage? Otherwise, how can we account for your sudden disappearance from Moscow last year? The Shcherbatskys kept asking me about you, as if I should know. But I know only one thing: you behave in a manner all your own."

"Yes," Levin said slowly, in a troubled voice. "You are right. I'm a savage—not because I left then, but because I have come back. Now I'm back. . . ."

"Oh, what a fortunate man you are!" cried Stepan Arkadievich, looking into Levin's eyes.

"Why?"

" 'I can tell a spirited horse by its breed, an enamored young man by his eyes,' " recited Stepan Arkadievich. "Your future lies before you."

"And with you, is everything in the past?"

"No, not in the past. But yours is the future, and mine is the present, a present with its ups and downs."

"What's the matter?"

"Well, it's bad, but I'm not going to talk about myself and, besides, it's so hard to explain everything," said Stepan Arkadievich. "Now what's the real purpose of your visit to Moscow? . . . Waiter!" he called to the Tartar.

"Then you've guessed?" replied Levin. A light shone deep in his eyes, which he kept fixed on Stepan Arkadievich.

"I have, but I'm reluctant to broach the subject. By this alone you can judge whether my guess is right or wrong," said Stepan Arkadievich, looking at Levin with a subtle smile.

"What are you trying to say?" asked Levin in a trembling voice, feeling all his facial muscles quiver, "What is your opinion?"

Stepan Arkadievich slowly drank his glass of Chablis, his eyes fixed on Levin.

"I could wish for nothing better than this," said Stepan Arkadievich. "It's the best thing that could happen."

"But aren't you mistaken? Do you know what we're talking about?" said Levin quickly, his eyes looking eagerly at his companion. "Do you think it's possible?"

"I think it's possible. Why shouldn't it be?"

"No, do you really think it's possible? Tell me just what you think. But if I'm refused? And I'm almost sure. . . ."

"What makes you think so?" said Stepan Arkadievich, smiling at his friend's excitement.

"That's the way it seems to me sometimes. Really, it would be terrible both for myself and for her."

"Well, there is nothing terrible in such a matter for the girl, whatever the outcome. To be proposed to makes any girl proud."

"Yes, any girl, but not her."

Stepan Arkadievich smiled. He knew very well this feeling of Levin's: for Levin, all the girls in the world were divided into two groups. One consisted of all the girls in the world except her, and these girls possessed all the human frailties; they were most ordinary. The other group consisted of her alone, possessed no weaknesses at all, and stood high above ordinary mortals.

"Wait, have some of this sauce," he said, restraining Levin, who was pushing aside the sauce.

Levin obediently put some sauce on his plate, but did not give Stepan Arkadievich a chance to eat.

"No, listen to me," he said. "I want you to understand that, for me, this is a matter of life and death. I have never spoken about it to anyone. To no one else can I speak about it as to you. True, our tastes, our views, everything in us is completely different. But I know that you love me and understand me, and therefore I love you deeply. But for God's sake, be completely sincere with me."

"I'm telling you what I think," said Stepan Arkadievich, smiling. "But I'll tell you something else. My wife, a most exceptional woman. . . ." Stepan Arkadievich sighed, recalling the state of his relationship with his wife. Then, after a moment's silence, he continued. "She has the gift of foresight. She reads men's hearts; but in addition to that she foresees everything, particularly in matrimonial matters. For instance, she predicted that Miss Shakhovsky would marry Brenteln. Nobody wanted to believe her, but it turned out her way. She's on your side."

"What do you mean?"

"I mean she not only loves you, but she says that Kitty will surely be your wife."

At these words Levin's face suddenly brightened with a smile, the kind that is close to tender tears.

"Is that what she says?" exclaimed Levin. "I have always said that your wife is a wonderful person. But enough, let's not talk about it any longer," he said, rising from his seat.

"Very well, but sit down."

But Levin could not remain seated. He strode twice up and down the tiny room with resolute steps, blinked to hide his tears, and only then resumed his seat at the table.

"I wish you would understand," he said, "that this is not love. I have been in love, but this is not the same. This is not my own feeling, but some external force that has taken possession of me. I left for one reason alone. I decided that this could never be, since, as you know, such happiness can never be in this world. But I have struggled with myself over this and I see that there's no life without it. I must come to a decision. . . ."

"Then why did you leave?"

"Ah, wait! Oh, how many thoughts are going through my mind! How many questions must be answered! Listen: you cannot imagine what your words have done for me. I'm so happy that it's almost wicked. I've forgotten everything else. Today I found out that my brother Nikolai . . . he is here, you know, and I even forgot about him. It seems to me that he, too, is happy. Perhaps it is madness. But one thing is terrible . . . you are married and know the feeling . . . it is terrible that we, the older people, with our past . . . a past not of love, but of sin . . . suddenly are drawn close to a pure, innocent creature. It's shameful, and therefore one cannot but feel unworthy."

"Well, your sins are few."

"Nevertheless," said Levin, "nevertheless, 'looking back at my life with disgust, I shudder, curse, and lament bitterly.' It's true!"

"What can you do? Life is like that," said Stepan Arkadievich.

"There's one consolation. In that prayer, one I've always been fond of, we ask for forgiveness not for our merits but through mercy. So may she also forgive me."

11

LEVIN EMPTIED his goblet, and they fell into silence.

"I must tell you something else. Do you know Vronsky?" Stepan Arkadievich asked Levin.

"No, I don't. Why do you ask?"

"Bring us another," said Stepan Arkadievich to the Tartar, who was filling the goblets and hovering about just when he was not needed.

"Why should I know Vronsky?"

"The reason you must know Vronsky is that he is one of your rivals."

"Who is this Vronsky?" asked Levin, and his face, which a moment ago had so pleased Oblonsky with its expression of childish rapture, suddenly turned angry and unpleasant.

"Vronsky is one of the sons of Count Kirill Ivanovich Vronsky and one of the best representatives of Petersburg's gilded youth. I met him in Tver when I was in service there, and he came on a recruiting mission. Exceedingly rich, handsome, best connections, aide-de-camp, and at the same time a very decent and good fellow. He's more than just a decent fellow! As I have found out here, he's well educated and very intelligent. He's a man who will go far."

Levin frowned and kept silent.

"Well, he showed up here soon after you left and, as I understand, he's head over heels in love with Kitty. And you know, her mother. . . ."

"Pardon me, but I don't understand," said Levin with a scowl. At once his thoughts turned to his brother Nikolai. He loathed himself for having forgotten him.

"Wait, wait," said Stepan Arkadievich, smiling and touching his hand. "I've told you what I know, and repeat that in this fine and delicate matter, as far as I can tell, the odds are in your favor."

Levin leaned back in his chair, his face pale.

"But I would advise you to settle the matter as soon as possible," continued Oblonsky, refilling Levin's goblet.

"No, thanks, I can't drink any more," said Levin, pushing aside the goblet. "I'll get drunk. . . . But how are you getting along?" he continued, evidently wishing to change the subject.

"One more word. I advise you by all means to settle the matter soon. I would not advise you to talk about it today," said Stepan Arkadievich. "Go there tomorrow morning, propose to her in the traditional way, and may God bless you!"

"You've intended all this time to come to my place to hunt. Well, come in the spring," said Levin.

With all his heart he regretted now that he had started this conversation with Stepan Arkadievich. This *very special* feeling had been polluted by talk of rivalry with some Petersburg officer, and by the conjectures and advice of Stepan Arkadievich.

Stepan Arkadievich smiled. He knew what was going on in Levin's heart. "I'll come some time," he said. "Yes, my friend, women—they are the pivot on which everything turns. I, too, am in trouble, in great trouble, and it's all because of women. Tell me frankly," he continued, taking a cigar, and holding the goblet in his other hand, "give me your advice."

"About what?"

"Here is the problem. Suppose you are married, you love your wife, and you become infatuated with another woman. . . ."

"Excuse me, but I absolutely do not understand that . . . as I do not understand how, after such a dinner as this, I could go directly to a bakery and steal a loaf of bread."

Stepan Arkadievich's eyes shone more brightly than usual. "Why not? Sometimes a loaf of bread smells so good that you cannot resist it.

> *"Himmlisch ist's, wenn ich bezwungen*
> *Meine irdishe Begier;*
> *Aber noch wenn's nicht gelungen*
> *Hatt' ich auch recht hübsch Plaisir!"*

Stepan Arkadievich recited these verses with a subtle smile. Nor could Levin refrain from smiling.

"Now, all joking aside," continued Oblonsky. "Don't you see, here is a woman, a kind, meek, loving creature, poor and lonely, who has sacrificed everything. Now, the deed done, shall I desert her? Suppose we must part, to preserve our family life, but shouldn't I pity her, help her, soften the blow?"

"Well, you must excuse me. You know that for me women are divided into two kinds . . . no . . . actually there are women and there are. . . . I have never seen any charming fallen creatures and never will. I loathe such women as that painted Frenchwoman behind the counter with her curls, and all fallen women are the same."

"And the woman of the Gospel?"

"Oh, stop! Christ would never have said those words had he known how much they would be abused. They're the only words in all the Gospels that people remember. . . . But I'm not saying what I think, only what I feel. I loathe fallen women. You're afraid of spiders, and I'm afraid of these vermin. Most surely you have not studied spiders and their ways; the same is true of me."

"It's all right for you to talk this way. You remind me of one of Dickens' characters who with his left hand cast over his right shoulder all his difficult problems. By denying a fact you don't explain it. But what's to be done? Tell me, what's to be done? Your wife is aging, but you remain full of life. It doesn't take long before all your love for her is gone, no matter how much you respect her. Now suddenly a new love turns up, and you are lost, lost!" Stepan Arkadievich said with dejection and despair.

Levin smiled ironically.

"Yes, you're lost," continued Oblonsky. "But what's to be done?"

"Don't steal bread."

Stepan Arkadievich laughed outright.

"What a moralizer! But look—here are two women. One insists only on her rights. Your love for her is her right, but you cannot give it to her. The other sacrifices everything for your sake and demands nothing in return. What can you do? How should you act? It's a terrible drama."

"If you want to know my sincere view in this matter, I must tell you that I don't find anything dramatic in it. Here's why. In my opinion, love . . . both kinds of love, which, as you remember, Plato discusses in his *Symposium*, are men's touchstone. Some accept only one kind, and others the other. Those who accept only the non-Platonic love vainly talk about dramatic conflicts. This kind of love leads to no drama. 'I thank you for the pleasure. My compliments!' and there's the whole drama. As for Platonic love, it can create no drama, because such love is serene and pure, because. . . ."

At this moment Levin recalled his own sins and the inner struggle he had lived through, and he added suddenly:

"On the other hand, perhaps you are right. It's very possible . . . but I don't know, I really don't know."

"You see," said Stepan Arkadievich, "you're an idealist, which is both your strength and your weakness. Yours is an idealistic character; you expect life to be made up of phenomena that correspond with your ideals, and this doesn't happen. For example, you scoff at government or public service, because you demand that acts always fit the ideal, but this doesn't happen. You also expect each man's activities to be purposeful, and love and family life to be the same, but this doesn't happen. All the diversity, all the charm, all the beauty of life is made up of light and shadow."

Levin sighed and made no reply. His thoughts turned inward, and he no longer heard Oblonsky.

Then both felt that, though they were friends, though they had just dined and wined together, something that should have drawn them still closer, each one thought only of his own problems now, with no concern for the other's. It was not the first time that Oblonsky had had the experience after dinner of two friends drawing apart instead of coming closer, and he knew what to do about it.

"Check, please," he called and went into the next room, where he met one of his acquaintances, an adjutant. They talked about a certain actress and the man who kept her. In this conversation Oblonsky found immediate repose and relief from his exchange with Levin, who always overtaxed his mind and soul.

When the Tartar returned with a bill for twenty-six rubles and change, not counting the tip, Levin, who as a man from the country ordinarily would have been horrified by his share of fourteen rubles, this time paid no attention to it. He paid his share and left for home to dress and then to go to the Shcherbatskys', where his fate would be decided.

12

PRINCESS KITTY SHCHERBATSKY was eighteen years old. This was the first winter since her debut. Her social success had been greater than that of her two sisters, greater even than her mother had expected. Almost all the young men who danced at the Moscow balls were in love with Kitty. Moreover, during this same first winter there had appeared two serious contenders for her hand: Levin, and immediately after his departure, Count Vronsky.

Levin's arrival in early winter, his frequent visits, and his undisguised love for Kitty, brought about the first serious discussions between her parents concerning Kitty's future. This resulted in a disagreement between the prince and the princess. The prince favored Levin and said that he could not wish for a better husband for Kitty. But the princess, with a woman's habit of ignoring the problem, maintained that Kitty was too young, that Levin had in no way shown that his intentions were serious, that Kitty had no affection for him, and so on. Yet she had never mentioned her main objection, namely, that she was waiting for a better match for her daughter, that she had no liking for Levin, and that she did not understand him. But when Levin suddenly left, the princess was happy, and she triumphantly told her husband, "You see, I was right!" And when Vronsky appeared, she was still happier, firmly convinced that Kitty's must be not merely a good match but a brilliant one.

In the mother's opinion, no comparison could be made between Levin and Vronsky. She disliked in Levin his strange, rude notions, his awkwardness in society, which, in her opinion, was brought about by his pride, his life in the country, the life of an uncivilized person, as she understood it, which had to do with cattle and moujiks. In addition, she was highly displeased that he, in love with her daughter, had visited them regularly for a month and a half, but had seemed hesitant and watchful, as if undecided whether to condescend to propose. He did not understand that, visiting the home of a marriageable young lady, he was expected to declare his intentions. But he left suddenly, without having declared them. Fortunately, she thought, he is so unattractive that Kitty could never fall in love with him.

In Vronsky she found the answer to all her requirements. He was very rich and intelligent, a person of quality, embarked on a brilliant career as an officer and courtier; and he was a charming person. One could wish for none better.

At the balls, Vronsky openly courted Kitty and danced with her. He visited her house, and all this showed without any doubt that his intentions were serious. In spite of this, all that winter her mother had been upset and very worried.

The princess herself had married thirty years earlier, in a match arranged by her aunt. The groom, of whom everything was known beforehand, arrived, saw the bride, and was seen himself. The matchmaking aunt inquired about the impressions they had made on each other and reported them; the impressions were good. Then on an appointed day he proposed, and the parents, who had expected it, accepted him. Everything had been so easy and simple; at least, so it seemed to the princess. But now, in arranging the marriages of her daughters, she had learned what a complicated affair it was, though it looked so easy and simple. How many were the fears she had lived through, how many problems she had pondered, how much money had been spent, how numerous the clashes with her husband, before the two older daughters, Daria and Natalia, were married off! Now, with the youngest one, the same fears, the same doubts, but still sharper arguments with her husband. The old prince, like all fathers, was particularly sensitive in everything which concerned the honor and purity of his daughters. He was unreasonably jealous regarding his daughters, especially Kitty, who was his darling, and quite often he went into tantrums, accusing his wife of damaging the reputation of their daughter. The princess had become used to this at the time of their older daughters' marriages, but now, she felt, the prince had more reason to be so sensitive. She noticed that many changes had been accepted recently in society, and that the duties of a mother had become more difficult. She noticed that young people of Kitty's age formed some new associations, attended some schools unknown to her, mingled freely with the opposite sex, and rode on the streets on their own. Many of them had given up curtsying, and, most important, they all were convinced that it was their concern to choose a husband, and not their parents'. "Nowadays nobody marries off a girl the way they used to," was the opinion of all these young girls, and even of older people. But how they married them off these days, the princess could not find out from anyone. The French custom, to let the parents decide the fate of their children, had been condemned and rejected. The English custom, to give full freedom to the girl, was not accepted either, and, in Russian society, was inadmissible. The Russian custom of matchmaking was considered offensive, and everyone laughed at it, including the princess herself. Yet how to marry off and how to get married, no one seemed to know. Everyone with whom the princess happened to discuss the subject invariably remarked: "Truly, it's time to give up these old ways. It's the young people who get married, not the parents. You must therefore let the young people arrange their own affairs as well as they can." Such views well suited those who had no daughters of their own, but the old princess knew that, given freedom, a young lady might fall in love, and fall in love with a man who had no intention of getting married, or with one who was not fit to be her husband. And no matter how much one tried to convince the princess that nowadays young people must arrange their own lives, she could no more accept this than she could accept the idea that a loaded pistol could ever become a fit toy for five-year-old children. Therefore the princess worried about Kitty more than she had about her older daughters.

She was apprehensive lest Vronsky limit himself only to courting her daughter. She saw that her daughter was already in love with him, but she knew that Vronsky was an honest man who would do nothing wrong, and this allayed her fears. At the same time, she realized how easy the modern ways of life made it for a girl to lose her head, and in what little regard a man usually held these matters. The week before, Kitty had told her mother about the conversation she had had with Vronsky while dancing with him. The princess felt somewhat relieved at Kitty's words, but still not completely reassured. Vronsky told Kitty that he and his brother were so accustomed to strict obedience to their mother that they would never undertake anything important without seeking her advice. "And now I am waiting for my mother's arrival from Petersburg as for a happy event," he said.

Kitty told her mother about this, without reading anything of particular importance into his words. But her mother understood them differently. She knew that the old lady had been expected any day; she knew that the old lady would gladly approve her son's choice. It seemed strange to her that he, out of respect for his mother, had not proposed. Nevertheless, she was so eager to arrange the match and, especially, to allay her worries, that she believed all this. Though she was deeply affected by the misfortunes of her older daughter Dolly, who intended to leave her husband, she had become completely engrossed in her worries about the approaching fateful decisions concerning the future of her youngest daughter. With Levin's arrival that day, her worries increased. She was afraid that her daughter, who it seemed, some time ago had felt some affection toward Levin, might be moved by undue faithfulness, refuse Vronsky, and that, in general, Levin's arrival might complicate and delay what was so close to fulfillment.

"When did he arrive?" asked the princess when they returned home. She was referring to Levin.

"Today, *Maman*."

"I wish to say just one thing . . ." began the princess, and by the serious and animated expression on her mother's face, Kitty guessed what she was about to say.

"Mama," she said, flaring up and quickly turning toward her, "please don't say anything about this, please don't. I understand perfectly."

Although she agreed with her mother's wishes, she found her motives offensive.

"I just want to say that, having raised the hopes of one. . . ."

"Mama, darling, for heaven's sake, don't say any more. It's frightening to speak about it."

"All right!" said her mother, seeing tears in her daughter's eyes. "Yet one thing, my darling. You promised not to keep any secrets from me. You won't, will you?"

"I never will, never," replied Kitty, blushing and looking squarely at her mother. "But now I have nothing to tell you. Even if I wanted to . . . I don't know what to say and how . . . I don't know. . . ."

With such eyes she can tell no lies, thought her mother, smiling at her excitement and happiness. The princess smiled, for she knew how tremendously important to the poor girl all this was that was now going on in her heart.

13

FROM AFTER dinner until the early evening, Kitty felt the way a youth feels before battle. Her heart pounded and she could not concentrate on anything. She felt that this evening, when the two men would meet for the first time, must decide her fate. In her mind she saw them constantly, either apart or together. When she thought of the past, she dwelled with pleasure and tenderness on the memories of her association with Levin. Memories of childhood and memories of Levin's friendship with her late brother added a singular poetical charm to her association with Levin. His love for her, of which she was sure, flattered her and filled her with joy. It was so easy to think about Levin. But her thoughts about Vronsky were always mingled with some embarrassment, though he always was most courteous and fully relaxed. She sensed some falsehood, not in him, for he was sincere and kind, but in herself, whereas with Levin she was completely at ease. But as soon as her thoughts turned to her future, with Vronsky it appeared brilliant and happy, with Levin confused.

She went upstairs to dress for the evening. Looking in the mirror, she was happy to see that this was one of her good days, and that she was in full control of herself, something so urgently needed to face what was coming. She had a feeling of outward calmness, and her movements were graceful and relaxed.

At half past seven, as soon as she came down into the drawing room, the servant announced: "Konstantin Dmitrievich Levin." The princess was still in her room, and the prince had not yet come in. The time has come, thought Kitty, and all her blood rushed to her heart. She was startled at the sight of her pale face in the mirror.

She was now sure that he had purposely arrived early in order to find her alone and to propose to her. And only now, for the first time, did she see this matter in an entirely different, new light. Only now did she understand that the forthcoming decision concerned not her alone, as if she had only to decide which of the two would bring her happiness and which of them she loved. She saw that at this very moment she must offend a man she loved, and offend him cruelly . . . and why? Because he, gentle soul, loved her, was truly in love with her. But it could not be helped; it had to be done.

My God, do I really have to tell him myself? she thought. And what will I tell him? Will I really tell him that I do not love him? It would be untrue. Then what will I tell him? That I love another? No, I cannot. I'll leave, I'll go away.

She was already near the door when she heard his steps. No, it would be dishonest. But what do I have to fear? I didn't do anything wrong. What will be, will be. I'll tell him the truth. I'm always at ease with him. Here he is, she said to herself as she saw him, so strong and gentle, looking at her with his shining eyes. She looked directly at him, as if begging for mercy, and gave him her hand.

"I believe I've come at the wrong time. I'm too early," he said, looking about the empty drawing room. When he saw that everything was happening the way he wished, that nothing prevented his declaring himself, his face darkened.

"Oh, no," said Kitty. She sat down at the table.

"I really wanted to find you alone," he said, without sitting down and without looking at her lest he lose his courage.

"Mother will be right in. Yesterday she was very tired. Yesterday. . . ."

She spoke without knowing what her lips were saying and without lowering her tender, imploring gaze.

He looked at her. She blushed and fell silent.

"I told you that I didn't know how long I would stay in Moscow. . . . It depends on you."

She bent her head lower and lower, and did not know what answer she would give to the forthcoming question.

"It depends on you," he repeated. "I wanted to say . . . I wanted to say . . . I have come for the purpose that . . . to be my wife!" he said, without knowing what he was saying but only that now the terrifying words had been said. He stopped and looked at her.

She was breathing heavily, avoiding his eyes. She was enraptured. Her soul was filled with happiness. She never had expected that this declaration of love would move her so profoundly. But all this lasted only for a moment. Her thoughts turned to Vronsky. She looked at Levin with her clear, frank eyes and, seeing his despairing face, hurriedly replied:

"It cannot be . . . forgive me."

How close to him she was only a moment ago, how important in his life, and now so alien and distant!

"It could not be otherwise," he said without looking at her. He bowed and started to leave.

14

AT THIS VERY moment the princess came in. An expression of fear appeared on her face as she found them alone and saw how disturbed they were. Levin bowed to her and said nothing. Kitty kept silent, her eyes lowered. Thank God— she refused him, the princess thought, and her face lit up with the same smile with which she usually received her Thursday visitors. She sat down and asked Levin about his life in the country. Levin resumed his seat and waited for the other guests to arrive so he could leave without being noticed.

Within five minutes, Kitty's friend, Countess Nordston, entered. She had married the count last year.

She was a thin, yellowed, sickly, nervous woman with black shining eyes. She loved Kitty and wished her to marry according to her own ideal of happiness—such are always the wishes of married women for their unmarried friends—and her choice was Vronsky. She had never liked Levin, whom she had often seen earlier that winter, and at these meetings her favorite sport had been to ridicule him.

"I love it when he looks down at me from the height of his majesty, or when he abruptly cuts off his clever conversation with me, a stupid woman. He stoops toward me, and this amuses me. I'm glad that he cannot stand me," she went on about him.

She was right. Levin, indeed, could not stand her. He despised everything that she was proud of and that she prized so highly in herself: her nervousness and her refined contempt and disregard for everything that was common and coarse.

The relationship between Countess Nordston and Levin was of a kind that is not uncommon in high society: two people, though outwardly remaining on friendly terms, feel such mutual contempt that they cannot take each other seriously and cannot even insult each other.

Countess Nordston immediately attacked Levin. "Ah! Konstantin Dmitrievich! You are here again in our depraved Babylon," she said, giving him her tiny yellowed hand and recalling his words of last winter, when he had referred to Moscow as Babylon. "Well, has Babylon reformed or have you turned wicked?" she added, casting ironical looks at Kitty.

"I am flattered, Countess, that you still remember my words," replied Levin, who by this time had succeeded in composing himself, and at once assumed his usual jestingly hostile attitude toward Countess Nordston. "I believe they made a deep impression on you."

"Of course! I take it all down. Well, Kitty, have you gone skating again?"

She began a conversation with Kitty. Though it would have been ungracious on Levin's part to leave now, he would have preferred to do so rather than to remain there all evening watching Kitty, who only rarely looked at him and avoided his glances. He was about to rise when the princess, noticing his silence, turned to him:

"How long are you going to stay in Moscow? I understand that you're active in the zemstvo and cannot remain long."

"No, Princess, I am no longer in the zemstvo," he said. "I have come for just a few days."

There's something strange about him, thought Countess Nordston, looking at his stern, serious face. "He's reluctant to be drawn into one of his long discussions. But I'll bait him. I'm very anxious to show Kitty how ridiculous he is, and I intend to do so.

"Konstantin Dmitrievich," she said to him, "please explain to me what this means—you, of course, know about it—in our Kaluga village all our moujiks and their women have squandered all they had on liquor and now do not pay us anything. What does it mean? You always praise the moujiks so highly!"

At this moment another lady entered the room, and Levin rose.

"Forgive me, Countess, I really don't know anything about it and have nothing to say," he said, and turned toward the officer who came in following the lady.

This must be Vronsky, thought Levin, and to confirm this he looked at Kitty. She already had caught sight of Vronsky and then had turned to cast a glance at Levin. From the involuntary sparkle in her eyes, Levin understood that she loved this man, understood it as well as if she had told him in her own words. But what kind of man was he?

Now, come what may, Levin had to remain. He had to find out with what sort of a man Kitty had fallen in love.

In every contest there are those who, on meeting their fortunate rivals, are ready to disregard any good qualities in them and see only their bad ones. On the other hand, there are those who are anxious to find in their fortunate rivals those good qualities through which they have triumphed, and with a gnawing pain in their hearts they seek in them only what is good. Levin was such a person. And he had no difficulty in finding the good and attractive in Vronsky. They were immediately evident. Vronsky was of medium height, well built, dark-haired, with handsome, good-natured, very calm and strong features. Everything about him was simple yet elegant, from his closely cropped black hair and clean-shaven chin to the expanse of his brand-new uniform. After stepping aside at the door for the lady, Vronsky came up to the princess and then to Kitty.

As he approached her, his handsome eyes shone with particular tenderness. With a slight, happy, and modestly triumphant smile (so it seemed to Levin), he respectfully and gently bent over her, and extended his hand, which was not large, but wide.

After he had greeted the other guests and exchanged a few words with them, he sat down without looking even once at Levin, whose eyes remained fixed upon him.

"I would like you to know each other," said the princess, pointing to Levin. "Konstantin Dmitrievich Levin. Count Aleksei Kirillovich Vronsky."

Vronsky rose, and with a friendly look at Levin, shook his hand.

"I believe that some time this winter I had a dinner appointment with you," he said, smiling his frank and sincere smile, "but you suddenly left for the country."

"Konstantin Dmitrievich despises and detests the city and us, its inhabitants," said Countess Nordston.

"It seems that my words impress you so deeply that you cannot forget them," said Levin, and he blushed as he remembered that he had said these words before.

Vronsky glanced at Levin and Countess Nordston and smiled.

"Do you stay in the country all through the year?" he asked. "It must be boring there in the winter."

"It isn't boring if you're busy, and it isn't boring to be with oneself," curtly answered Levin.

"I love the country," said Vronsky, noticing Levin's tone but pretending not to.

"But I hope, Count, that you would never agree to spend your entire life in the country," said Countess Nordston.

"I don't know. I never tried it for any length of time. I had a strange experience once," he continued. "I have never been so lonesome for the country, the Russian village, with its moujiks and their bast sandals, as in Nice, when I spent the winter there with my mother. Nice, as you know, is a very boring place, and Naples and Sorrento are fine for only a short while. And these are the very places where you so vividly remember Russia, particularly the Russian village. They are like. . . ."

He spoke, addressing both Kitty and Levin and turning his calm, friendly look from one to the other. Evidently he was saying what came first to his mind.

Noticing that Countess Nordston was waiting to say something, he stopped without finishing his sentence, and attentively listened to her.

The conversation did not stop for a moment. The princess always held in reserve two topics, in the event that conversation might flag. One was classical compared with scientific education, the other was the problem of compulsory military service. But at present she was in no need of these two old reliable devices, and the countess had no opportunity to tease Levin.

Levin wanted to take part in the general conversation but could not. He kept reminding himself, Now I must go, but he remained, as though he were waiting for something.

The conversation turned to spirits and moving tables, and Countess Nordston, who believed in spiritism, began telling about the seances she had witnessed.

"Ah, Countess, please take me, please take me to them. I've never witnessed anything supernatural, though I seek it everywhere," said Vronsky with a smile.

"Very well. Next Saturday," replied Countess Nordston. "And you, Konstantin Dmitrievich, do you believe in it?" she asked Levin.

"Why do you ask me? You know what I'll say."

"But I want to hear your opinion."

"Here's my opinion," replied Levin. "These moving tables just prove that the so-called educated classes are in no way superior to the moujiks. They believe in the evil eye, sorcery, and charms, while we. . . ."

"So you don't believe in it?"

"I cannot believe, Countess."

"Even if I have seen it with my own eyes?"

"Peasant women also say that they have seen brownies with their own eyes."

"Then you think that I am telling an untruth?" she said, and laughed heartily.

"No, Masha, Konstantin Dmitrievich just says that he can't believe in such things," said Kitty, blushing for Levin. He noticed it and, his annoyance growing, was ready with his reply when Vronsky, smiling unaffectedly and cheerfully, came to the rescue of the conversation, which was on the verge of turning unpleasant.

"Then you don't admit the possibility at all?" he asked. "Why not? We admit the existence of electricity without knowing its nature; why, then, can't we admit the existence of a new force, still unknown, which . . ."

"When electricity was discovered," Levin interrupted quickly, "only a phenomenon was revealed, but its source and effects remained unknown. It took centuries to learn how to use it. The spiritists, on the other hand, begin by telling us that they have found messages on tables and that spirits have visited them. Then only do they tell us that all this has been produced by an unknown force."

Vronsky listened to Levin attentively, as he always did, evidently interested in what he had to say.

"Yes, the spiritists say, 'We don't know yet what kind of force this is, but it exists, and here are the conditions under which it operates. Let the scientists discover the nature of this force.' No, I don't see why this can't be a new force, if it. . . ."

"Because," Levin interrupted again, "in the case of electricity, every time you rub amber on wool, a certain effect is produced, whereas here the effect does not always take place. Therefore it's not a natural phenomenon."

Vronsky apparently sensed that, for a drawing-room conversation, the discussion was becoming too serious. He therefore did not add to it and, to change the subject, turned to the ladies with a smile.

"Let us try now, Countess—" he began, but Levin was eager to prove his point.

"I believe," he continued, "that this attempt of the spiritists to explain their miracles by the existence of some new force has been most unsuccessful. Evidently they are speaking of a spiritual force, but at the same time they try to subject it to physical experimentation."

Everybody was waiting for him to stop, and he felt it.

"I believe that you would make an excellent medium," said Countess Nordston. "There is something ecstatic about you."

Levin opened his mouth, was about to say something but then blushed and said nothing.

"Let's test the tables, please," said Vronsky. "Princess, with your permission?"

Vronsky rose to search for a table.

Kitty got up to help and, as she passed Levin, she met his look. She pitied him with all her heart, the more so because she was the cause of his unhappiness. If I may be forgiven, her look pleaded, please forgive me; I am so happy. But his look replied, I hate everyone, I hate you and myself, and he reached for his hat. But he was not yet fated to leave. As the guests at the table made ready to take their places and Levin prepared to leave, the old prince entered, and, after greeting the ladies, he turned to Levin.

"Ah!" he exclaimed cheerfully, "how long have you been here? I didn't know that you were here. I'm very happy to see you."

The old prince addressed Levin either as "thou" or "you." He embraced Levin now and, while conversing with him, took no notice of Vronsky, who rose and waited patiently for the prince to recognize him.

Kitty felt that after what had happened, her father's friendliness was oppressing Levin. She also noticed that her father had at last replied coldly to Vronsky's greeting, and that Vronsky, friendly but puzzled, looked at him, vainly trying to understand how anyone could feel any unfriendliness toward him. She blushed.

"Prince, let Konstantin Dmitrievich come over to us," said Countess Nordston. "We want to perform an experiment."

"What experiment? Moving tables? Well, excuse me, ladies and gentleman, a child's game would be more entertaining," said the prince, looking at Vronsky and suspecting that it was his idea. "There's at least some sense in a child's game."

Surprised, Vronsky turned his steady gaze toward the prince, but then, with a faint smile, he quickly engaged Countess Nordston in a conversation concerning the next week's grand ball.

"You'll be there, I hope?" he asked Kitty.

As soon as the old prince had turned away from him, Levin left, unnoticed. His last impression of the evening was of Kitty's happy, smiling face, as she answered Vronsky's question about the ball.

15

AFTER THE GUESTS had left, Kitty told her mother about her conversation with Levin, and, in spite of the pity she felt for him, she was happy that she had been *proposed to*. She didn't doubt that she had done the right thing, but she was a long time in falling asleep after retiring. One impression stubbornly persisted. It was Levin's face, with his kind eyes looking gloomy and dejected under his frowning brows as he stood there, listening to her father and glancing at her and at Vronsky. She felt so sorry for him that tears came to her eyes. But immediately her thoughts turned to the man of her choice. She vividly recollected those manly, firm features, that noble composure, and that kindness toward everyone, which was radiated by his entire being. She was loved by him whom she loved; her soul was filled with joy, and with a happy smile she lay her head on the pillow. It's a pity, she said to herself, but what can I do? I'm not at fault. But an inner voice contradicted her. She could not tell whether she regretted having encouraged Levin or having refused him, and these doubts marred her happiness. Lord, have mercy, Lord, have mercy! she kept repeating until she fell asleep.

In the meantime, downstairs in the prince's small study, a frequently recurring scene was taking place, the cause of which was a beloved daughter.

"Well, do you know what this means?" shouted the prince, waving his arms and wrapping his squirrel-fur robe tightly about him. "It means that you have no pride, no dignity, that you are disgracing, and ruining our daughter with this idiotic, despicable matchmaking."

"Please, for heaven's sake, Prince, what have I done?" said the princess, nearly in tears.

She had been very happy and pleased with the conversation with her daughter and, as usual, had come to say good night to the prince. Although she had no intention of telling him that Levin had proposed and that Kitty had refused, she hinted to her husband that, regarding Vronsky, everything seemed to be settled, and that all that was needed was the arrival of his mother. On hearing this, the prince suddenly exploded and began to shout, using strong language.

"What have you done? First, you lead the young man on; all Moscow will gossip about it, and for good reason. If you arrange a gathering, then invite everybody, and not only these selected prospective bridegrooms. Invite all those *pups*," (as the prince referred to the young men of Moscow) "hire a piano player, and let them dance, not the way you did it today, with your prospective bridegrooms. It was disgusting to watch you turn the little girl's head. Levin is a thousand times the better man. As for this little Petersburg dandy, they are all machine made, they are all alike and all trash. Even if he were a prince of the blood, my daughter would have no need of him!"

"But what have I done?"

"I'll tell you," the prince exclaimed angrily.

"I know that if I listen to you," interrupted the princess, "our daughter will never get married. If that's the case, it would be better to leave for the country."

"It would be better to go."

"But wait. Am I asking any special favors of them? Not at all. Here's a young man, and a very good one, who falls in love, and she, it seems . . ."

"Yes, that's what you think. But what if she's really in love with him, while he thinks as much of getting married as I? Ah, I wish I didn't have to witness it. 'Ah, spiritism! Ah, Nice! Ah, the ball!' " and the prince, imitating his wife, curtsied with each word. "But if we cause Katinka's unhappiness, if she really gets it into her head that. . . ."

"But what makes you think this will happen?"

"I don't think so, I know so. This is something men see more clearly than women. Here's a man whose intentions are serious—Levin; and here's a bird, a dandy, interested only in a good time."

"Well, once your mind is made up . . ."

"You'll see that I was right, but it will be too late, as it was with Dashenka."

"Well, let's not talk about it," interrupted the princess, remembering poor Dolly.

"All right then, good night!"

They crossed each other, kissed, and parted, still feeling that neither's opinion had been changed.

At first, the princess was quite sure that this evening had decided Kitty's fate, that nobody could doubt that Vronsky's intentions were serious; but her husband's words had upset her. When she returned to her room, she was frightened by the uncertainties of the future and, like Kitty, she repeated in her heart: Lord, have mercy. Lord, have mercy.

16

VRONSKY HAD NEVER known family life. In her youth his mother had been a brilliant woman of fashion who, while she was married and particularly later, had had many love affairs, which were well known in society. He scarcely remembered his father, and had been brought up in the School of Pages.

After he was graduated as a very young, dashing officer, he immediately slipped into the rut of the wealthy Petersburg military. Though he occasionally visited high society, all his love interests lay outside it.

In Moscow, where he arrived after a life of luxury and dissipation in Petersburg, he tasted for the first time the delight of close association with a sweet, innocent young lady of fashion, who loved him. It never occurred to him that there was anything wrong in his relations with Kitty. At the balls he danced mostly with her. He visited her home. He spoke with her about the trifling matters usually discussed in high society, but, in his view, these trifling matters took on a singular meaning. Though he never told her anything which he could not say in the presence of others, he felt that her dependence on him grew stronger, and the more he felt it the more pleased he was and the more tender were his feelings toward her. He did not realize that his conduct toward Kitty could be described only as leading a young lady on without any intention of marrying her, and that this was an insidious deception commonly indulged in by young men of the smart set such as he. It seemed to him that he was the first who had discovered this pastime, and this discovery delighted him.

If he could have heard her parents' conversation that evening, if he could have seen the matter from the family's point of view, if he had been told that Kitty would be unhappy if he did not marry her, he would have been surprised and would not have believed it. He could not believe that anything that brought such great pleasure to him and, what was more important, to her, could be wrong. Still less could he believe that he should marry her.

He never believed that he would marry. Not only did he dislike married life, but, in accordance with the general opinion of the bachelor set to which he belonged, he always saw something alien, hostile, and worst of all, ridiculous in every family, and particularly in a husband. Though Vronsky could not surmise the topic of the elder Shcherbatskys' conversation, as he left the Shcherbatskys' that evening, he felt that the mysterious spiritual bond that existed between him and Kitty had grown so strong that he ought to do something about it. But he was unable to decide what he could or should do.

As always Vronsky left the home of the Shcherbatskys with a pleasant feeling of cleanliness and freshness, partly because he had not smoked there for the whole evening. A new feeling was added to this as he was returning from their home now. He felt how tenderly moved he was by her love for him. It is most delightful, he thought, that nothing was said either by myself or by her, that we understood each other in an unspoken conversation of looks and intonations, and that today, more clearly than ever, she told me that she loves me. And with what charm, what simplicity, what trust she said it! I feel that I am better, purer! I feel that I have a heart, and that there is much good in me. Those sweet eyes full of love! When she said: *"and very much. . . ."*

Well, then what? Then nothing—so be it! It's good for me, good for her. And he began to think about how to conclude the evening.

He turned over in his mind the places he could go. The club? A game of cards, a glass of champagne with Ignatov? No, I won't go there. *Château des Fleurs.* I'll find Oblonsky there, songs, cancan. No, I'm tired of it. I love to visit the Shcherbatskys just because it makes a better man of me. I'll go home.

He went straight to his suite at the Dusseau, had his supper, undressed, and as soon as his head touched the pillow, fell into his usual deep sleep.

17

ON THE NEXT DAY, at eleven o'clock in the morning, Vronsky left for the Petersburg railroad station to meet his mother. The first person he met at the steps of the large staircase was Oblonsky, who had come to meet his sister, who was arriving on the same train.

"Ah! Your Excellency!" cried Oblonsky. "Whom have you come to meet?"

"My mother," replied Vronsky, smiling as everybody smiled on meeting Oblonsky. They shook hands and walked up the stairs together. "She's arriving from Petersburg today."

"I waited for you until two o'clock. Where did you go from the Shcherbatskys?"

"Home," replied Vronsky. "I must confess that I had such a pleasant evening with the Shcherbatskys that I had no desire to go anywhere else."

" 'I know a spirited horse by its breed, an enamored youth by his eyes,' " recited Stepan Arkadievich, the way he had to Levin.

Vronsky smiled, making no attempt to contradict him, but immediately changed the subject.

"And whom have you come to meet?" he asked.

"A pretty lady," said Oblonsky.

"Well, well!"

"*Honi soit qui mal y pense!* My sister Anna."

"Ah, Karenina!" said Vronsky.

"You probably have met her."

"I think I have. Perhaps not . . . I really don't remember," absently replied Vronsky. In his mind he vaguely connected the name Karenina with something prim and dull.

"But you've surely met Aleksei Aleksandrovich, my famous brother-in-law. The whole world knows him."

"I know him by reputation and sight only. I know that he's clever, learned and somewhat righteous. . . . But, you know, that's not in my line," said Vronsky.

"Yes, he's an outstanding person, somewhat on the conservative side, but a nice man," remarked Stepan Arkadievich. "A nice man."

"Well, good for him," said Vronsky with a smile. "Ah, there you are," he said, turning to his mother's tall old servant, who was standing at the door. "Come on in."

Of late, Vronsky not only shared the general admiration for Oblonsky, but also felt personally bound to him, for in his imagination he connected him with Kitty.

"Well, shall we give a supper for the diva on Sunday?" he said, smiling and taking his friend's arm.

"By all means. I'll collect subscriptions. By the way, did you meet my friend Levin yesterday?" asked Stepan Arkadievich.

"Oh, yes. But he left rather early."

"He's a good fellow," continued Oblonsky. "Don't you think so?"

"I don't know," replied Vronsky. "Why is there always something brusque about all Moscovites, present company excepted, of course," he jestingly added. "Something brusque. They always have a chip on their shoulder. They are angry, as if always anxious to press their point home. . . ."

"Yes, it's true, yes . . ." said Stepan Arkadievich, smiling gaily.

"Well, how soon?" Vronsky asked the attendant.

"The train has left and is on the way," replied the attendant.

Everything was being readied for the arrival of the train. The porters bustled about; the gendarmes and the attendants took their places; the visitors crowded together. Their breath steaming, the workmen, dressed in sheepskin coats and soft felt boots, made their way across the rails of the curving road. From far off could be heard the whistle of the locomotive and the heavy rumble of the train.

"No," said Stepan Arkadievich, who was eager to tell Vronsky about Levin's intentions concerning Kitty, "no, you were wrong about my friend Levin. He's a very nervous man and may often seem disagreeable. But, on the other hand, sometimes he's very gentle. His nature is honest and sincere; he has a heart of gold. But yesterday there was a particular reason," Stepan Arkadievich added with a meaningful smile, completely forgetting the sincere feeling of sympathy he had had last night toward his friend. He had the same feeling now, but this time it was toward Vronsky. "He had a good reason to be either especially happy or especially unhappy."

Vronsky stopped and asked bluntly, "What do you mean? Did he propose to your *belle-soeur* last night?"

"Perhaps," said Stepan Arkadievich. "I believe he did. Yes, he did, if he left early and in a bad mood . . . He has been in love with her for a long time, and I feel sorry for him."

"Well, well! . . . I believe she can make a better match," said Vronsky, and, squaring his shoulders, he resumed walking. "On the other hand, I don't know him," he added. "Yes, it must be hard to bear. That's why most of us prefer to deal with the Klaras. With them, a lack of success proves only that you were short of money; but here your dignity is at stake. Here comes the train."

And indeed, the train's whistle now sounded closer. Within a few minutes the platform began to quake. The locomotive rolled by, puffing steam against the oppressive weight of the frosty air, the lever of the middle wheel moving slowly and rhythmically; the engineer, bundled up and covered with hoarfrost, waved his greeting; the baggage car with a whining dog in it followed the tender, causing the platform to shake more slowly and severely; finally the passenger cars drew up, shuddering as they came to a stop.

The dashing conductor, blowing his whistle while the train was still moving, jumped down, and following him, the impatient passengers emerged one by one: an officer of the Guards, erect and stern-looking; a fidgety tradesman, holding his satchel and smiling cheerfully; a moujik with a bag on his shoulder.

Vronsky stood next to Oblonsky, watching the cars with their emerging passengers, having completely forgotten about his mother. The news he just had heard about Kitty filled him with excitement and joy. He unconsciously thrust his chest forward and his eyes gleamed. He rejoiced in his triumph.

"The countess is in this compartment," the sprightly conductor said, coming up to Vronsky.

The conductor's words roused him, turning his thoughts to his mother and their forthcoming meeting. In his heart he did not respect his mother and, without realizing it, did not love her, though, according to the standards of his set and by his upbringing, he could not think of any other relationship with his mother than one of deep deference and respect. The less he loved and respected her in his heart, the greater were his outward signs of deference and respect.

18

VRONSKY FOLLOWED the conductor into the car, and, at the entrance to the compartment, he stopped to give way to a lady who was emerging. Because of his long experience as a gentleman in society, by a single look at the lady he knew that she was a member of the upper class. He apologized and, as he was about to enter the car, he felt a compulsion to look at her once more, not because of her beauty or the elegance and modest grace of her person but because there was something unusually gentle and tender in the expression of her lovely face as she passed by. As he looked at her, she also turned her head. Her shining gray eyes appeared dark under her thick lashes. She looked at him with friendly interest, as if she recognized him, then she turned toward the passing crowd, as though searching for someone. In this brief glance, Vronsky noticed a restrained vivacity, which played on her features and flitted between her shining eyes and the faint smile curving her rosy lips. In spite of herself, the radiance of her look and her smile seemed to express what overflowed her being so forcefully. She deliberately turned off the glow in her eyes, but, against her will, it showed now in her faint smile.

Vronsky entered the car. His mother, a dried-up old woman with black eyes and small curls, squinted as she looked at her son, her thin lips smiling faintly. She rose from her narrow seat, handed her bag to the maid, gave her son her thin hand, and lifting his head from her hand, she kissed his face.

"Did you receive my telegram? Are you well? Thank God!"

"Did you have a good trip?" asked her son, sitting down next to her and involuntarily listening to a woman's voice behind the door. He knew that it was the voice of the same lady he had met at the entrance.

"I still do not agree with you," he heard the lady saying.

"That's what you people in Petersburg think."

"Not we in Petersburg, but just we, the women," she answered.

"Well, let me kiss your hand."

"Goodbye, Ivan Petrovich. Please see if my brother is here and send him to me," she said at the door, and re-entered the compartment.

"Well, have you found your brother?" asked Countess Vronsky, turning to the lady.

Vronsky remembered now that this was Karenina.

"Your brother is here," he said, rising. "Forgive me, I did not recognize you. We knew each other for such a short time," said Vronsky, bowing, "that you probably don't remember me."

"Oh, no! I recognize you, for it seems that all the way here your mother and I spoke only of you," she said, finally permitting a smile to express the animation which begged to be shown on her face. "But my brother is still not here."

"Then go and fetch him, Alyosha," said the old countess.

Vronsky went to the platform and shouted, "Oblonsky! Here!"

But Karenina did not wait for her brother to come. When she caught sight of him, she walked out of the car with light, firm steps. And as soon as her brother reached her, she placed her left hand on his neck, drew him to herself, and kissed him heartily. All this she did with a grace and sureness that amazed Vronsky. He watched her fixedly and smiled without knowing why. Then he remembered that his mother was waiting for him, and he returned to the car.

"Isn't she charming?" asked the countess, referring to Karenina. "Her husband placed her next to me, to my great pleasure. We chatted all the way. But you, they say—*vous filez le parfait amour. Tant mieux, mon cher, tant mieux.*"

"I don't know what you mean, *Maman*," her son replied coldly. "Let's go, *Maman*."

Karenina re-entered the car to say goodbye to the countess.

"Well, Countess, you've found your son, and I my brother," she said gaily. "I've already told you all my stories; I have no others to tell."

"No," said the countess, taking her hand, "I wouldn't be bored by you, even if we went around the world together. You are one of those sweet women with whom it's pleasant either to talk or to remain silent. And, please, don't worry about your son; it's impossible to avoid partings."

Karenina remained standing, erect and motionless, her eyes smiling.

"Anna Arkadievna," explained the countess to her son, "has a little boy, eight years old, I believe. She has never parted with him, and now she worries about having left him."

"Yes, the countess and I chattered all the way, I about my son, and she about hers," said Karenina, and again a smile lit up her face, a kind smile directed at him.

"I am sure you grew tired of it," he said, quick to seize the flirtatious hint she had thrown him. But apparently the tone of the conversation no longer pleased her, and she turned to the old countess.

"I am very grateful to you. I didn't notice how the day passed yesterday. Goodbye, Countess."

"Goodbye, my dear friend," answered the countess. "Let me kiss your pretty face. I must tell you openly, as befits an old woman, that I have fallen in love with you."

Karenina sincerely believed these words and was glad to hear them, however stilted they might sound. She blushed, bent slightly, offered her face to the countess' lips, straightened, and, with the same smile flitting between her eyes and her lips, she gave her hand to Vronsky. He shook the little hand she extended to him, surprised and pleased at the heartiness of her response, so firm and unhesitating. She left with a brisk step, which carried her rather ample figure with surprising ease.

"Very charming," said the old lady.

Her son thought the same. He followed her with his eyes as far as her graceful figure could be seen, and a smile remained on his face. Through the window he saw her come up to her brother, take his arm, and enter into a lively conversation on subjects that apparently were in no way concerned with himself, and this annoyed him.

"Well, *Maman,* are you really in good health?" he repeated, turning to his mother.

"I am fine. Alexandre was very sweet. And Marie has become very pretty; she is charming."

She began again to tell him about the matters that interested her most: about her grandson's christening, for which she had made this trip to Petersburg, and the singular kindness the Czar had shown toward her older son.

"Here's Lavrenti," said Vronsky, looking at the window. "Let's go, now, please."

The old butler, who had accompanied the countess on the trip, came into the car to announce that everything was ready. The countess rose, ready to leave.

"Let's go now. There are only a few people about," said Vronsky.

The maid took a bag and the lap dog; the butler and the porter carried the other bags. Vronsky took his mother's arm. As they were emerging from the car, several men with frightened faces rushed past them, among them the stationmaster in his brightly colored cap. Evidently something terrible had happened. The crowd ran to the rear of the train.

"What has happened?" "Where?" "He threw himself under!" "He was crushed!" could be heard in the crowd.

Stepan Arkadievich, arm-in-arm with his sister, their faces frightened, returned and stopped at the entrance to the car to avoid the crowd.

The ladies re-entered the car, and Vronsky and Stepan Arkadievich followed the crowd to find out the details of the accident.

Whether because he was drunk, or because he was too heavily bundled up against the frost, a watchman had not heard the train backing up and had been crushed.

Even before Vronsky and Oblonsky came back, the ladies learned the details from the butler.

Both Oblonsky and Vronsky saw the maimed body. Apparently Oblonsky was deeply moved. His face was distorted, and he seemed to be on the verge of tears.

"Oh, what a terrible thing! Oh, Anna, if you could see it! Oh, what a terrible thing!" he kept repeating.

Vronsky remained silent, his handsome face serious but perfectly calm.

"Oh, if you could see it, Countess," said Stepan Arkadievich. "And his wife was there. . . . It was terrible to look at her. . . . She threw herself on the body. They say he was the sole support of a large family. It's terrible!"

"Couldn't we do something for her?" asked Karenina in a whisper choked with emotion.

Vronsky glanced at her and immediately left the car.

"I'll be right back, *Maman*," he said, turning toward her from the door.

When he returned a few minutes later, Stepan Arkadievich and the countess had begun to talk about a new singer, and the countess cast impatient glances at the door, waiting for her son.

"Now let's go," said Vronsky, as he came into the car.

They left together, Vronsky with his mother, and Oblonsky and his sister following behind. At the exit the stationmaster caught up with Vronsky.

"You handed two hundred rubles to my assistant. Will you be good enough to tell me whom it's for?"

"For the widow," said Vronsky with a shrug. "Why do you ask?"

"You gave money?" cried Oblonsky from behind, and pressing his sister's arm, he added: "How kind! How kind! He's a fine man, isn't he? My compliments, Countess."

His sister and he stopped, looking for her maid. By the time they came out of the station Vronsky's coach had departed. The emerging crowd was still talking about the accident.

"A terrible death," said one man, passing by. "They say he was cut in two."

"On the contrary, I think it was a very easy, quick death," remarked another.

"Why don't they do something about it?" said a third.

Karenina took her seat in the coach, and Stepan Arkadievich was surprised to see that her lips were trembling and that she could scarcely restrain her tears.

"What's the matter, Anna?" he asked, after they had gone a few hundred yards.

"It's a bad omen."

"Nonsense," said Stepan Arkadievich. "The only thing that counts is that you are here. . . . You can't imagine how much I count on you."

"Have you known Vronsky for a long time?" she asked.

"Yes. You know, we hope that he'll marry Kitty."

"Oh?" Anna said softly. "Well, now let's talk about you," she said, with a toss of her head, as if, by a purely physical action, she were trying to rid herself of what was unwanted and disturbing. "Let's talk about your problems. I received your letters and here I am."

"Yes, I'm pinning all my hopes on you," said Stepan Arkadievich.

"Well, tell me everything."

And Stepan Arkadievich began his story.

When they reached his house, Oblonsky helped his sister to alight, sighed, shook her hand, and then left for the council chamber.

19

WHEN ANNA ENTERED the house, Dolly was in the small drawing room with her blond, chubby son, who already resembled his father, listening to him recite his French lesson. The boy read, twisting and tugging on a button that was precariously attached to his small jacket. Several times his mother restrained him, but each time his plump little hand took hold of the button again. Finally his mother tore the button off and put it in her pocket.

"Stop fussing with your hands, Grisha," she said. She resumed her knitting, an old pastime, which she always returned to when feeling depressed. She knitted nervously now, counting the stitches, which she threw over with her fingers. Though she had let her husband know yesterday that she did not care whether his sister arrived or not, she had prepared everything for her arrival and waited for her impatiently.

Dolly was crushed by her misfortune; she was overwhelmed by it. But she remembered that Anna, her sister-in-law, was the wife of one of the most important persons in Petersburg and herself a Petersburg *grande-dame*. So she did not, as she had told her husband she would, forget that her sister-in-law was arriving. After all, thought Dolly, Anna is in no way at fault; all I know about her is the very best, and she always treats me kindly and amiably. In truth, as she remembered the impression which the Karenins had made upon her in Petersburg, she did not like their home. There was something basically false in their family life. But why shouldn't I receive her? she thought. I only hope she doesn't plan on consoling me. All this consolation, advice, Christian forgiveness—I've thought of them a thousand times, and they are of no use.

Dolly had spent all these days alone with the children. She did not like to talk about her misfortune, but, with the misfortune weighing on her heart, she could not talk about anything else. She knew that somehow she would tell Anna everything. Sometimes she was glad at the thought of doing so, but then she became vexed at the prospect of talking about her humiliation to her, his sister, and to hear from her those stilted words of advice and consolation.

As often happens, though she was watching the clock and expected her guest momentarily, she missed the moment of her arrival and did not hear the bell ring.

On hearing the rustle of a dress and the sound of light steps right at the door, she turned around, and the expression on her worn face was not of joy, but of surprise. She rose and embraced her sister-in-law.

"My, you have already arrived?" she said, kissing her.

"Dolly, I'm so glad to see you!"

"And I'm glad, too," said Dolly, smiling weakly. She watched the expression on Anna's face, trying to guess whether she knew what had happened. Probably she knows, she thought, noting the consoling expression. "Well, let's go. I'll show you to your room," she said, trying to postpone the forthcoming conversation as long as possible.

"Is that Grisha? My goodness, how he's grown!" said Anna, kissing him, and, keeping her eyes on Dolly, she stopped and blushed. "No, let's stay here."

She took off her kerchief and hat, which caught on a lock of black, wavy hair. Tossing her head, she freed it.

"You're the picture of health and happiness," said Dolly, almost envious.

"I? . . . Yes," said Anna. "Good heavens, Tania! She is the same age as my Seryozha," she added, turning to the girl, who came running in. She lifted her in her arms and kissed her. "A lovely child. Show me all of them."

She named them all, remembering not only their names, but their ages to the year and the month, their habits, and their sicknesses. Dolly could not help being grateful for this.

"Well, let's go and see them. I'm sorry that Vasia is asleep."

After the visit to the children they sat down together in the drawing room to have coffee. Anna reached for the tray and then pushed it aside.

"Dolly," she said, "he told me."

Dolly looked coldly at Anna. She waited now for those words of pretended sympathy, but Anna did not say anything of the kind.

"Dolly, my dear," she said, "I am not going either to defend him or to console you. That would be wrong. But, my dear, I pity you, I pity you with all my heart."

Tears suddenly appeared underneath her thick eyelashes,

filling her shining eyes. She moved closer to her sister-in-law and took her hand in her own strong little one. Dolly did not move away, but her face did not lose its cold expression. She said:

"Nobody can console me. All is lost after what has happened. All is lost!"

As soon as she said this, her face softened. Anna took Dolly's dry thin hand, kissed it and said:

"But, Dolly, what's to be done? What's to be done? What is the best thing to do in this terrible situation? This is what we have to consider now."

"Everything is over, and nothing can be done," said Dolly. "But you must understand. The worst is that I cannot leave him. I must consider the children. But I cannot live with him; it is torture for me to be with him."

"Dolly, my darling, he told me. But I'd like to hear about it from you. Tell me everything."

Dolly looked at her questioningly.

She read sincere sympathy and love in Anna's face.

"All right," she said suddenly, "but I'll start from the beginning. You know how I married. Brought up by *Maman*, I was not only innocent, but also naïve. I didn't know anything. I heard that husbands tell their wives about their past, but Stiva . . ." she corrected herself, "Stepan Arkadievich never told me anything. You won't believe it, but until now I thought that I was the only woman he had ever known. I have lived this way for eight years, and not only have I not suspected him of unfaithfulness, but I considered such a thing impossible. And now, just imagine, after thinking this way, to learn suddenly of all this horror, all this vileness! Try to understand, I felt so sure of my happiness and of his, and suddenly . . ." continued Dolly, restraining her sobs, "and then to see this letter . . . a letter from him to his mistress, to my governess. No, it's too terrible!" She hurriedly reached for her handkerchief and covered her face. After a short silence, she continued. "It's one thing to be temporarily infatuated, but it's something else to deceive me deliberately and cunningly . . . and with whom? To continue to be my husband and have this affair with her . . . it's terrible! You couldn't possibly understand. . . ."

"Oh, no, I understand! I understand, my dear Dolly, I understand," repeated Anna, pressing Dolly's hand.

"And do you think that he understands how terrible my

situation is?" continued Dolly. "Not at all! He's happy and contented."

"Oh, no!" Anna interrupted quickly. "He's miserable; he is crushed by remorse."

"Is he capable of remorse?" interrupted Dolly, watching her sister-in-law's face carefully.

"Yes. I know him. He appeared so pitiful. Both of us know him. He's kind, but proud; and now he's so deeply humiliated. But what has really moved me"—here Anna guessed what could affect Dolly most—"two things torment him: he is ashamed to face his children, and he knows that he, who loves you—yes, yes, who loves you more than anything else in the world," she hastily interrupted Dolly, who was about to contradict her, "he knows that he has caused you such suffering, such anguish. He keeps saying, 'No no, she won't forgive me.'"

While listening to her words, Dolly looked past her sister-in-law thoughtfully.

"Yes, I realize that he's in a terrible situation. It's worse to be guilty than innocent," she said, "if he feels that he's the cause of all this misfortune. But how can I forgive him? How can I again become his wife after this? It will be torture for me to live with him simply because I cherish my past love for him. . . ."

And sobs interrupted her words.

It seemed that every time her anger abated, she deliberately returned to the one subject so painful to her.

"She's young, she's pretty," Dolly continued, "but isn't it true that I have been robbed of my beauty, my youth? And by whom? By him and the children. I devoted myself to serving him and, in this service, gave up everything. But now, of course, he finds more pleasure with this fresh, vulgar creature. They probably discussed me, or, what is still worse, they were silent on the subject. Do you understand?" and again her eyes lit up with hatred. "And after all this he can still speak to me. . . . Well, can I trust him? Never. No, everything is over, everything in which I have found consolation, reward for my toil and suffering. . . . Would you believe it? I've just gone over Grisha's lesson. It used to be a joy; now it's torture. Why do I try, why do I struggle? Why should I work with the children? It's terrible, but suddenly my heart has completely changed, and instead of love and kindness, I feel only hatred for him, yes, hatred. . . . I would kill him and—"

"My darling Dolly, I understand, but don't torture yourself. You feel so deeply insulted and are so aroused that you don't see things as they really are."

Dolly calmed down, and for a few moments they were silent.

"What's to be done, Anna? Help me. I've thought it all over, but I find no way out."

Anna did not know what to say, but her heart sincerely responded to every word, to every expression of her sister-in-law's face.

"Let me tell you one thing," began Anna. "I'm his sister; I know his nature, his ability to forget everything, everything —" she made a gesture at her forehead—"his tendency to lose his head, and to repent deeply afterward. Now he cannot believe, he cannot understand how he could have done what he did."

"He understands now, and he understood it then," interrupted Dolly. "But I . . . you are forgetting about me . . . does this make it any easier for me?"

"Wait. I confess that when he spoke to me, I didn't yet understand all the horror of your situation. I thought only of him and of the crisis in your family life. I pitied him, but now, after talking to you, I, as a woman, see the other side. I see how you suffer, and I cannot tell you how I pity you! Dolly, my darling, I fully understand how deeply you suffer, but one thing I don't know. . . . I don't know how much love for him there is in your heart, and whether there is still enough of it to forgive him. Only you know this. If there is enough, then forgive him."

"No," began Dolly, but Anna interrupted her, again kissing her hand.

"I know society better than you," she said. "I know how people like Stiva look at such matters. You say that he discussed you with *her*. He didn't. They may be unfaithful, but to every one of them, home and wife are sacred. Somehow they despise these women, and they don't let them interfere with their family life. They draw some impassable line between their families and these people. I don't understand it, but it is so."

"Yes, but he kissed her . . ."

"Wait, Dolly, my darling. I remember Stiva when he fell in love with you. I remember that time well. He used to come to me and cry, telling me what a sublime being you were to him, and I know that the longer he has lived with you the loftier you have risen in his eyes. We used to laugh at him, as he added to his every word: 'Dolly is a wonderful woman.' You always were and have remained his idol, and this temporary infatuation has not touched his soul. . . ."

"But if this infatuation is repeated?"

"It cannot be, as I see it. . . ."

"Would you forgive?"

"I don't know, I can't judge. . . . No, I think I can," added Anna as an afterthought, turning over in her mind the whole situation and weighing it carefully, "Yes, I can, I can. I would forgive him. I would not remain unchanged, yet I would forgive him as though this had not happened, had never happened."

"Of course," Dolly interrupted quickly, as if expressing a thought which had occurred to her many times, "this is the only way to forgive. You must forgive completely, completely. Now come, let me show you to your room." She rose, and while they were walking, she embraced Anna. "My dear, how glad I am that you've come. I feel better now, so much better."

20

ANNA SPENT the entire day at the Oblonskys and would see no one, though some of her acquaintances, already informed of her arrival, called on her the very same day. Anna spent the entire morning with Dolly and the children. She just sent a note to her brother, asking him by all means to come home for dinner. "Come, God is merciful," she wrote.

Oblonsky dined at home. Everybody took part in the conversation, and his wife talked to him, using the "thou," which she had not done earlier. Husband and wife still remained estranged, but now there was no more talk of parting, and Stepan Arkadievich felt that an explanation and reconciliation were possible.

Right after dinner Kitty arrived. She knew Anna Arkadievna, but only slightly, and she now came to her sister's with some misgivings about the reception that this Petersburg society lady, so highly regarded by everyone, would accord her. But Anna Arkadievna liked her, which Kitty noticed at once. Evidently Anna admired her beauty and youth, and Kitty, without noticing it, not only fell under her spell, but fell in love with her, the way young girls are prone to fall in love with married and older women. Anna did not look like a lady of fashion or like the mother of an eight-year-old boy. By the grace of her movements, her freshness, and the constant vivacity of her features, which showed now in her smile and now in her look, she could have been taken for a twenty-year-old girl, were it not for the serious, sometimes sad expression of her eyes, which impressed Kitty and attracted her. Kitty felt that Anna was completely frank and hid nothing, but that within her there existed some other, loftier world of complex and poetical interests, one that Kitty could not reach.

After dinner Dolly left for her room. Anna quickly rose and came over to her brother, who was smoking a cigar.

"Stiva," she said to him with a gay wink, making the sign of the cross over him and indicating the door with her eyes, "go, and may God be with you."

He understood, put down the cigar, and disappeared behind the door.

When Stepan Arkadievich left, she resumed her seat on the divan, with the children around her. Either because the children knew that their mother loved this aunt, or because they themselves delighted in her singular charm, the older two and then the younger ones, as always happens with children, had clung to their new aunt since before dinner, and refused to be parted from her. They made a kind of game of it, trying to see who could sit closest to their aunt, to touch her, to hold her small hand, to kiss her, to toy with her ring, or just to touch the flounce of her dress.

"Come, let us sit as before," said Anna Arkadievna, taking her seat.

And again Grisha pushed his head under her arm, rested it against her dress, and lit up with pride and happiness.

"When will they hold the ball?" she asked Kitty.

"Next week. A magnificent ball, one of those balls that are always great fun."

"And are there any that are not always great fun?" asked Anna with tender irony.

"It may seem strange, but there are. You always enjoy yourself at the Bobrishchevs', and at the Nikitins', but it's always boring at the Mezhkovs'. Haven't you noticed it?"

"No, my dear, I no longer find balls enjoyable," said Anna, and in her eyes Kitty caught a glimpse of that world that was closed to her. "It's just that I find some less tiresome and boring . . ."

"How could *you* be bored at a ball?"

"Why shouldn't *I* be bored at a ball?" asked Anna.

Kitty felt that Anna knew what answer would follow. "Because no one can compare with you."

Anna could still blush. She did so and said: "First of all, it's not so; secondly, if it were so, what good would it do me?"

"Are you going to this ball?" asked Kitty.

"I think I'll have to. Here, take this," she said to Tania, who was pulling at a ring that slipped easily off Anna's white, tapering finger.

"I'll be very glad if you go. I would like so much to see you at the ball."

"If I have to go, I'll at least be happy to know that it gives you pleasure. . . . Grisha, please don't pull. My hair is already rumpled," she said, rearranging an unruly lock that Grisha had been playing with.

"I can just see you at the ball in a lilac dress."

"Why lilac?" asked Anna Arkadievna with a smile. "Well, children, you must go. Can't you hear? Miss Hull is calling you to tea," she said, freeing herself from the children and sending them off to the dining room.

"I know why you are inviting me to the ball. You expect much of this ball, and you want everybody to be present and to take part in it."

"How did you know? It's true."

"Oh! What a good age is yours!" continued Anna. "I remember so well that azure haze, like in the Swiss mountains. It's a haze that veils everything at that blessed age, when childhood is just about to end. And the road leading through this immense, happy, and gay circle grows narrower and narrower; and though this appears light and beautiful, you start it both with joy and fear. Who hasn't gone through this?"

Kitty smiled and remained silent. But how could she have gone through it? she thought. How I'd like to know the whole story of her life, thought Kitty, remembering the unromantic appearance of Aleksei Aleksandrovich, Anna's husband.

"I know. Stiva told me, and best wishes are in order. I like him very much," continued Anna. "I met him at the railroad station."

"Oh, was he there?" asked Kitty, blushing. "What did Stiva tell you?"

"Stiva blurted out everything. And I was very glad. I traveled with Vronsky's mother yesterday, and she kept talking about him all the way. He's her darling. I know how partial mothers are, but . . ."

"What did his mother tell you?"

"Oh, many things. I know that he's her darling, but you can see that he's a noble knight. . . . For instance, she told me that he planned to give his entire estate to his brother, and while still a child he had performed an extraordinary deed by saving a drowning woman. In a word, a hero," said Anna, smiling and recollecting the two hundred rubles he had donated at the railroad station.

But she did not tell her about the two hundred rubles. For some reason she did not like to think about it. She felt that there was something about it that concerned her, something that should not have been.

"She begged me to visit her," continued Anna. "I'll be glad to see the old lady, I'm going to visit her tomorrow. And now, thank God, Stiva has been in Dolly's room for quite a while," added Anna, changing the subject. She rose as if something had displeased her, or so it seemed to Kitty.

"No, I'm first! No, I!" the children shouted. They had finished their tea and were rushing in to see Aunt Anna.

"All together!" said Anna, smiling. She ran up to meet them, embraced them, and tumbled into one pile the whole group of swarming children, who shrieked with delight.

21

AT TEA TIME for the adults, Dolly emerged from her room, but Stepan Arkadievich did not. Apparently he had left his wife's room by a back door.

"I'm afraid that you may feel cold upstairs," remarked Dolly, turning to Anna. "I'd like to transfer you downstairs— We'd be closer then."

"Please don't worry about me," replied Anna, looking intently at Dolly's face in an attempt to find out whether they had made up or not.

"You'll have more light down here," said her sister-in-law.

"I told you that I sleep like a top, always and anywhere."

"What's all this about?" asked Stepan Arkadievich, coming out of the study and addressing his wife.

From his tone both Kitty and Anna knew immediately that they had made up.

"I would like to transfer Anna downstairs, but first we have to change the curtains. Nobody else knows how to do it, and I'll have to do it myself," replied Dolly, turning to him.

Heaven only knows whether they made up completely, thought Anna on hearing the cold, calm tone of Dolly's voice.

"Oh, stop, Dolly! You make everything difficult," said her husband. "I'll do it, if you wish. . . ."

Yes, they probably have made up, thought Anna.

"I know how you'll do it," replied Dolly. "You'll give impossible instructions to Matvei, then you'll leave, and he'll confuse everything." As she said this her usual ironical smile curved Dolly's lips.

Complete, complete reconciliation, thought Anna. Complete, thank God. Happy that she had been the cause of it, she came over to Dolly and kissed her.

"That's not so. Why do you have such a low opinion of Matvei and myself?" asked Stepan Arkadievich, addressing his wife with a faint smile.

As usual, during the whole of the evening Dolly retained her ironical attitude toward her husband, and Stepan Arkadievich felt gay and contented, but was careful to show that, though forgiven, he had not forgotten his guilt.

At half-past nine, the exceptionally enjoyable and pleasant family evening conversation at the Oblonsky's table was interrupted by an event that, although most ordinary, for some reason appeared strange to everyone. As they were talking about a mutual Petersburg friend, Anna suddenly rose.

"Her picture is in my album," she said. "And by the way, I will show you my Seryozha," she added with a mother's proud smile.

It was almost ten o'clock, the time when she usually said good night to her son and very often put him to bed herself before leaving for a ball. She now felt very sad to be so far away from him. No matter what they spoke about, her thoughts now and again turned to her curly-haired Seryozha. She wanted to look at his picture and to talk about him. Under a convenient pretext she rose and, with her light, resolute step, she went for the album. The stairs to her room started from the landing of the large inside entrance staircase.

As she was leaving the drawing room, the bell rang in the entrance hall.

"Who could that be?" said Dolly.

"It's too early for someone to be calling for me, but too late for a visitor," remarked Kitty.

"Probably some papers from the office," Stepan Arkadievich added. As Anna passed near the staircase, a servant ran up to announce the visitor. The visitor himself was standing near the lamp. Looking down, Anna immediately recognized Vronsky, and a strange feeling both of pleasure and fear suddenly stirred in her heart. He stood there without taking off his coat, and took something out of his pocket. When she reached the middle of the staircase, he lifted his eyes, saw her, and he seemed somewhat embarrassed and startled. She inclined her head slightly and went on. Then she heard Stepan Arkadievich's loud voice inviting him to come in, and the soft, gentle, and calm voice of Vronsky declining the invitation.

When Anna returned with the album, Vronsky had gone, and Stepan Arkadievich told her that he had come in connection with a dinner they were to give the next day for a visiting celebrity.

"He absolutely refused to come in. He acted strangely," added Stepan Arkadievich.

Kitty blushed. She thought that she alone knew why he had come and why he would not stay. He was in our house, she thought, didn't find me there, and decided that I was here. He wouldn't come in because he thought it was late, and because Anna is here.

All of them exchanged looks without saying anything and turned to Anna's album.

There was nothing unusual or strange about a person stopping at a friend's house at half-past-nine to inquire about a forthcoming dinner without staying, yet it seemed strange to everyone. It seemed most strange and most wrong to Anna.

22

THE BALL HAD just begun when Kitty and her mother ascended the large staircase, which was flooded with light and adorned with flowers and powdered servants in red jackets. From the staircase they could hear a rhythmic rustle emanating from the rooms as from a beehive. While they were arranging their hair and their dresses in front of a mirror on the landing, amidst potted trees, they heard the precise and clear sounds of the violins of the orchestra in the main ballroom playing the first waltz. An old gentleman in civilian clothes arranged his thinning locks at another mirror and emitted a scent of perfume. Finding himself in their way at the staircase, he stepped aside with obvious admiration for Kitty, whom he had not met. A beardless youth in a low-cut vest—one of those society youngsters whom old Prince Shcherbatsky called *"pups"*—bowed to them, ran past them, straightening his white tie as he went, returned, and invited Kitty to dance a quadrille. The first quadrille had been promised to Vronsky, so she promised the youth the second one. An officer, buttoning his glove, stood sidewise at the door, stroking his mustache and looking with admiration at Kitty, with her rosy charm.

Her toilette, coiffure, and preparations for the ball had taken much planning and effort. Nevertheless, as she now entered the ballroom, dressed in an elaborate tulle dress with its rose slip, she felt completely at ease, as if all these rosettes and laces, all these details of her toilette, had been prepared and attended to by her and by her maids without the slightest effort. It was as if she had been born in this tulle and lace, with this high coiffure, topped with a rose and two leaves.

When, at the entrance to the ballroom, the old princess tried to straighten a twisted ribbon on Kitty's belt, Kitty stepped away gently. She felt that everything about her should by itself be beautiful and graceful, and that nothing more remained to be adjusted.

This was one of Kitty's happy days. The dress was nowhere too tight; no part of the lace bertha had slipped; the rosettes did not crumple and were holding in place; the rose slippers, with their high, curved heels did not press, they caressed her little feet. The thick blond rolls clung to her little head like her own hair. All three buttons fastened without tearing her long glove, which encased her hand without altering its shape. The black velvet ribbon of her medallion entwined her neck with singular daintiness. It was charming, this velvet ribbon, and at home, looking in the mirror at her neck, Kitty felt what this velvet ribbon signified. Whatever her doubts about the rest of her costume, the velvet ribbon was charming. Here at the ball, Kitty smiled once more as she looked at it in the mirror. In her bare shoulders and arms Kitty felt as cool as marble, a feeling she particularly loved. Her eyes shone, and her rosy lips could not help smiling, for she knew how attractive she was. No sooner had she entered the ballroom and approached a group of ladies in colorful tulles, ribbons, and laces waiting to be invited to dance (Kitty would never stay long with such a group), she was invited to a waltz. Her partner was none other than a gentleman most famous among the dancing set, a well-known dance leader, master of ceremonies, the married, handsome, elegant Egorushka Korsunsky. He had just left Countess Banin, with whom he had danced the first waltz. Looking over his domain, which now consisted of only a few dancing couples, he noticed Kitty entering the room and ran up to her with the peculiar trot that is typical of dance leaders. He bowed, and without even waiting for her assent, he raised his arm to encircle her slender waist. She turned around to hand her fan to someone. Her hostess took it, smiling.

"It's so good that you have arrived in time," he said, putting his arm around her waist. "What a strange habit it is to come late!"

Bending her left arm, she rested her hand on his shoulder, and her tiny feet in their rose slippers, quickly, lightly, and rhythmically glided along the slippery parquet floor in time to the music.

"It's so restful to dance with you," he told her, during the first slow steps of the waltz. "What unusual lightness and precision!" he told her, as he told almost all of his dancing partners.

She smiled at his compliment and, looking over her shoulder, she continued to glance about the room. She was no novice at attending these balls, to whom all the faces blended into one enchanting impression. Nor was she one of those girls who frequent balls too often and to whom all these faces have become too familiar and tiresome. She was equally far from both these extremes. She was animated, and at the same time in control of her feelings, so that she could observe all that was going on around her. She saw the elite gathering in the left corner of the hall. The beautiful Lydie,

Korsunsky's wife, her gown décolleté in the extreme, was there. The hostess was there. There shone the bald head of Krivin, who never failed to cling to the elite. The young people looked in that direction, not daring to approach. There Kitty noticed Stiva, and then she saw the beautiful figure and head of Anna, in a black velvet dress. And *he* was there. Kitty had not seen him since the evening she had refused Levin. With her keen eye Kitty recognized him at once, and even noticed that he looked at her.

"Well, another waltz, if you aren't tired?" asked Korsunsky, puffing slightly.

"No, thank you."

"Where would you like to go?"

"I believe Karenina is here . . . take me to her."

"I would be happy to."

And Korsunsky, waltzing and slowing down his steps, led her directly to the group in the left corner of the ballroom, constantly repeating, "*Pardon, mesdames, pardon, pardon, mesdames.*" He made his way through this sea of laces, tulles, and ribbons, without so much as disturbing a ruffle, and then spun his partner about with an abrupt motion, which revealed her slender feet in openwork stockings and blew her train high in the air, landing it on Krivin's knees. Korsunsky bowed, straightened, and offered his arm to take her to Anna Karenina. Kitty, her face flushed, took her train off Krivin's knees, and, slightly dizzy, looked around for Anna. Anna's dress was not lilac, as Kitty had so eagerly desired, but black velvet with a low décolletage that bared her full shoulders and breast of chiseled, seasoned ivory and her round arms with their tiny wrists. The entire dress was trimmed with Venetian guipure. She had a small cluster of pansies in her black hair, which was all her own, and a similar one on the black ribbon of her belt amidst white lace. Her coiffure was simple. Its beauty lay in the display of short, unruly ringlets of her waving hair against her neck and temples. A string of pearls hung around her firm, chiseled neck.

Kitty saw Anna every day, was in love with her, and in her imagination always visualized her in lilac. But now, seeing her in black, she felt how little she knew of her charm. She looked surprisingly new to her now. Now she understood that Anna should not wear lilac, that Anna always stood out from her attire, that her attire was never noticed, and that this was the real source of her charm. And this black dress, with its magnificent lace, was not visible on her. It formed but a frame, and she alone was seen, simple, natural, elegant, yet gay and vivacious.

She stood there, erect as always, and when Kitty came up, she was talking to her host, her head tilted slightly toward him.

"No, I won't cast a stone," she answered to some question of his, "though I don't understand," she continued, shrugging her shoulders. And immediately, with a tender protective smile, she turned to Kitty. With a woman's quick glance she examined Kitty's dress. With a scarcely noticeable nod, well understood by Kitty, she signaled approval of her dress and general appearance. "You seem to dance even when you come into the room," she added.

"She's one of my most faithful assistants," said Korsunsky, bowing to Anna Arkadievna, whom he had not seen yet that evening. "The young princess makes the ball gay and magnificent. Anna Arkadievna, a waltz?" he asked, bowing.

"Have you met?" asked the host.

"Is there anybody whom I have not met? My wife and I are like white wolves. Everybody knows us," answered Korsunsky. "A waltz, Anna Arkadievna?"

"I don't dance when I can avoid it," she said.

"But you can't avoid it today," replied Korsunsky.

At this moment Vronsky came up.

"Well, if we can't avoid it today, then let's dance," she said, without noticing Vronsky's bow, and quickly raised her hand to Korsunsky's shoulder.

Why is she displeased with him? thought Kitty, as she noticed that Anna deliberately did not respond to Vronsky's bow. Vronsky came up to Kitty. He reminded her of the first quadrille and expressed regret that all this time he had not had the pleasure of seeing her. Kitty looked with admiration at Anna as she danced, and listened to him. She expected him to invite her to waltz, but he did not, and she glanced at him with surprise. He blushed and quickly invited her, but as soon as he put his arm around her slender waist and took the first step, the music suddenly stopped. Kitty looked at his face, which was so near to her, and, for many long years afterward, the love with which she had looked at him then and to which he had not responded filled her heart with tormenting shame.

"Pardon, pardon! Waltz, waltz!" shouted Korsunsky from the other side of the ballroom, and seizing the first available young lady, he began to waltz with her.

23

VRONSKY AND KITTY waltzed around the room several times. After the waltz Kitty went up to her mother, and she had scarcely exchanged a few words with Nordston, when Vronsky came to take her to the first quadrille. They did not speak about anything in particular during the quadrille. The conversation varied, touching now on the Korsunskys, husband and wife, whom he jokingly described as nice forty-year-old children, and now on the future of the public theater. Only once did the conversation sting her to the quick: it was when he asked her about Levin, inquiring whether he was here and adding that he liked him very much. But Kitty did not expect very much of the quadrille. She waited for the mazurka with a sinking heart. She believed that during the mazurka everything would be decided. The fact that he did not invite her to the mazurka during the quadrille did not trouble her. She was certain that she would dance the mazurka with him, as she had at previous balls, and she refused five invitations to the mazurka, saying that it was taken. The whole ball, until the last quadrille, seemed to Kitty an enchanting dream of gay colors, sounds and movements. She missed a dance only when she felt too tired and begged to be excused. But as she danced the last quadrille with one of the dull young men whom she could not refuse, she happened to be facing Vronsky and Anna. She had not been with Anna since those days just after her arrival, and here she suddenly saw her again, this time in a completely new and unexpected light. She saw in her the animation brought about by success, something she knew so well in herself. She saw that Anna was intoxicated by the admiration she had aroused. She knew this feeling, knew its symptoms, and saw them in Anna. She saw the shimmering sparkle in her eyes, the happy and lively smile that unconsciously curved her lips, and the distinct grace, ease, and exactness of her movements.

Who? she asked herself. Everybody or just one? The young man she was dancing with lost the thread of their conversation and vainly tried to recapture it. She gave him no aid in his suffering, and, outwardly obeying the gay, loud, imperious shouts of Korsunsky, who threw everyone now into a *grand rond*, now into a *chaîne*, she watched, and her heart sank deeper and deeper.

No, she thought, it's not the crowd's admiration that intoxicates her, it's the admiration of one man. And who is this man? Can it be he?

Every time he spoke to Anna, her eyes lit up gaily, and a happy smile curved her rosy lips. It seemed that she was forcing herself to conceal these signs of happiness, but they appeared on her face nevertheless. But what about him? Kitty glanced at him and was horrified. She saw in him what Anna's face mirrored so clearly. Where was his usual calm and confident bearing, his calm and unconcerned expression? No, every time he turned to her now, he bent his head slightly, as if ready to fall on his knees, and his look expressed nothing but submission and awe. "All I want," the look seemed to repeat, "is to wrong no one and to save myself. But I don't know how." The expression on his face was one which she had never seen before.

They were speaking about their mutual friends, and in general it was a most ordinary conversation, but it seemed to Kitty that her fate depended on every word they said. And it was strange indeed that though they spoke about Ivan Ivanovich and his funny French, and about Miss Eletsky, who could have made a better match, they, like Kitty, read the same importance into these words. For Kitty this ball, the entire world, everything, had become enveloped in a mist. Only the strict training she had received upheld her now and made her do everything which was required of her, made her dance, reply to questions, speak, even smile. But as they began to rearrange the chairs to make ready for the mazurka, and some couples emerged from the smaller rooms, Kitty was seized with despair and horror. She had refused five invitations, and she had no partner for the mazurka. There was no reason to hope that anybody would invite her now, for she was so popular that everyone would think she had already been invited. She should have told her mother that she was not well and left for home, but she lacked the courage to do it. She felt crushed.

She went into the far corner of a small drawing room and sank into an armchair. The ethereal skirt of her dress rose like a cloud around her slender waist. One of her thin, bare, delicate, maidenly arms, dangling helplessly, sank into the rose folds of her dress. In the other hand she held a fan, and fluttering it, she cooled her burning face. She looked like a butterfly which had just come to rest on a blade of grass, but was ready to take to the air and to spread its rainbow-colored wings. But her heart was oppressed with horror and despair.

Perhaps I'm mistaken; perhaps it isn't really so, she thought. And again she recalled all that she had seen.

"Kitty, what's the matter?" asked Countess Nordston, who approached her noiselessly across the carpet. "I don't understand this."

Kitty's lower lip quivered. She rose quickly.

"Kitty, aren't you going to dance the mazurka?"

"No, no," said Kitty, her voice trembling and choked with tears.

"I heard him invite her to the mazurka," said Nordston, knowing that Kitty would understand who "he" and "she" were. "But she said, 'Aren't you going to dance with Princess Shcherbatsky?'"

"Oh, I don't care!" replied Kitty.

No one but she understood her situation. No one else knew that yesterday she had refused a man whom she perhaps loved, refusing she had put her trust in another.

Countess Nordston found Korsunsky, with whom she was supposed to dance the mazurka, and asked him to invite Kitty.

Kitty was in the first pair of dancers, and to her good fortune, there was no need to speak, for Korsunsky was completely occupied with his duties. Vronsky and Anna were sitting almost directly across from her. She saw them there with her keen eyes, and also saw them up close when the dancing pairs came face to face. And the more she saw them, the more convinced she became that her misfortune was complete. She saw that they felt themselves to be all alone in this crowded ballroom. And on Vronsky's face, always so firm and self-assured, she saw now, to her amazement, an expression of embarrassment and submission, as of a clever dog caught at some mischief.

Anna smiled, and this smile infected him. She grew thoughtful, and he grew serious. Some supernatural force drew Kitty's eyes to Anna's face. She was lovely in her simple black dress, lovely were her full arms with their bracelets, lovely her firm neck with its strings of pearls, lovely the waving hair of her disarrayed coiffure, lovely the graceful, light movements of her small feet and hands, lovely her beautiful, animated face, but there was something terrible and cruel in all this loveliness.

Kitty admired her still more than before, and her suffering grew deeper and deeper. Kitty felt crushed, and her face showed it. When Vronsky looked at her, as their paths crossed during the mazurka, he scarcely recognized her, she had changed so much.

"A magnificent ball!" he said to her just to say something.

"Yes," she answered.

In the middle of the mazurka, while performing some complicated figure recently invented by Korsunsky, Anna came out into the center of the circle, followed by two partners, and asked Kitty and another lady to join her. Kitty came over to her, with fear in her eyes. Anna looked at her with partly closed eyes and smiled, pressing her hand. But when she noticed that Kitty's face displayed only despair and surprise in response to her smile, she turned away from her and began a gay conversation with another lady.

Yes, there is something strange about her. Something devilish and charming, said Kitty to herself.

Anna had no intention of staying for supper, but her host insisted.

"Now, Anna Arkadievna!" Korsunsky broke in, enfolding her bare arm with his sleeved one, "I have a wonderful idea for a cotillion! *Un bijou!*"

And he slowly moved on, trying to draw her back. The host smiled approvingly.

"No, I won't stay," replied Anna, smiling. But in spite of this smile, by the resolute way in which Anna replied to them, both Korsunsky and the host understood that she would not remain.

"No. As it is I have danced more at just one of your Moscow balls than I did all this winter in Petersburg," said Anna, looking at Vronsky who was standing near her. "I must rest before my journey."

"Are you definitely leaving tomorrow?" asked Vronsky.

"Yes, I believe so," replied Anna, as if surprised at his daring question, but the uncontrollable, shimmering sparkle of her eyes and smile seared him as she said this.

Anna Arkadievna left without staying for supper.

24

YES, THERE IS something unpleasant, something repulsive about me, thought Levin, as he left the Shcherbatskys and walked to his brother's. I'm of no use to other people. They call it pride. But I have no pride about me. If I were proud, I wouldn't have put myself in such a situation. And he thought of Vronsky, happy, kind, clever, and calm, who most surely had never been in such a terrible situation as the one in which he found himself this evening. Yes, he thought, she could be expected to select him. That's how it should be, and I have no complaint against anyone or anything. It's my own fault. What right did I have to think that she would want to join her life with mine? Who am I? And what am I? A worthless man, of no use to anybody and unfit for anything. He thought of his brother Nikolai and was glad to be able to think of him. Isn't he right, he thought, when he says that everything in this world is evil and distasteful? And I doubt whether we judge or have judged our brother Nikolai fairly. Of course, from the point of view of Prokofi, who saw him dressed in a tattered coat and drunk, he's a despicable man, but I know him differently. I know his heart and know that he and I are alike. And, instead of going to see him, I went to dinner, and to this place.

Levin went up to the lamp post, read his brother's address, which he had in his wallet, and hailed a cab. Throughout the long ride to his brother's, Levin vividly recalled all the events in his brother's life that were known to him. He recollected that during his college years and for a year after graduation, though ridiculed by his friends, he had lived the life of a monk, strictly observing all religious rites, offices, and fasts, and avoiding all kinds of pleasure, particularly women. And then, as if something had suddenly burst within him, he joined the company of the most revolting persons and sank into a life of unrestrained dissipation. Then he recalled the story of the boy Nikolai had taken from the village to bring up, and had beaten so badly in a fit of anger that a suit was brought against him for injuries. He also recalled the story of the sharper to whom Nikolai had lost all his money and had given a promissory note, and against whom Nikolai himself had brought a complaint that he had been cheated (this was the money that

Sergei Ivanovich had paid). Then he recalled the night his brother had spent in jail for disorderly conduct. He recalled the shameful lawsuit that Nikolai entered against his brother Sergei Ivanovich, claiming that Sergei Ivanovich had not paid him his part of their mother's estate. And the last case, when he had left to serve in a western province and was brought to trial there for beating a foreman. All this was terribly repulsive, but to Levin it was less revolting than to those who did not know Nikolai Levin, did not know the story of his life, and did not know his heart.

Levin remembered that during the period when Nikolai had devoted himself to piety, observed fasts, associated with monks, attended church services, and looked to religion as a means of restraining his passionate nature, nobody supported him. On the contrary, everyone, including himself, had laughed at him. They teased him, calling him Noah and a monk. And when he broke down no one helped him, and everyone turned from him in horror and digust.

Levin felt that, despite the infamy of his life, Nikolai, within his heart, at the very bottom of his heart, was no more immoral than those who despised him. It was not his fault that he was born with an intractable nature and a troubled mind. But he always wanted to be good. I will tell him everything, Levin thought. I will make him tell me everything, and I will prove to him that I love him and understand him, Levin decided in his heart as, at about eleven o'clock, he arrived at the hotel where his brother lived.

"Upstairs. Rooms twelve and thirteen," replied the doorman to Levin's inquiry.

"Is he at home?"

"Most probably he is."

A thick cloud of cheap, weak tobacco smoke curled in the band of light which emerged through the half-open door of room twelve. Levin heard an unfamiliar voice, but he immediately knew that his brother was there by the sound of his cough.

When he came up to the door, the unfamiliar voice said:

"It all depends on how reasonably and competently this affair will be conducted."

Konstantin Levin looked inside and noticed the speaker, a young man in a Russian-style coat, with an immense shock of hair. A young, slightly pockmarked woman in a woolen dress, collarless and cuffless, sat on a divan. His brother was nowhere to be seen. Konstantin's heart ached at the thought that his brother lived amidst such strangers. No one heard him come in, and Konstantin, taking off his rubbers, listened to the words of the stranger. They were talking about some enterprise.

"Well, may the devil take them, those privileged classes," said his brother after a fit of coughing. "Masha! Bring us some supper and the wine, if there is any left. If not, send for some."

The woman rose, came out from behind the partition, and saw Konstantin.

"A gentleman is here, Nikolai Dmitrievich," she said.

"What does he want?" Nikolai Levin said in an angry voice.

"It's me," replied Konstantin Levin, as he stepped into the light.

"Who is 'me'?" Nikolai repeated in a still angrier voice.

One could hear him quickly getting up and tripping, and then he appeared in the doorway. Though he knew his brother so well, Levin was struck by his wild and sickly appearance, by his immense, haggard, stooping figure, and by his large, frightened eyes.

He looked even more haggard than three years ago, when Konstantin Levin had seen him last. He was dressed in a short coat. His hands and his wide frame appeared still larger. His hair had thinned, but the same straight mustache hung over his lips, the same eyes looked strangely and naïvely at the visitor.

"Ah, Kostia!" he said quickly, recognizing his brother, and his eyes lit up with pleasure. But at the same moment he glanced at the young man, and, with a movement so familiar to Konstantin, he jerked his head and neck, as if his collar were too tight. His worn face assumed an entirely different expression now, wild, suffering and cruel.

"I wrote to you and to Sergei Ivanovich that I don't know you and don't wish to know you. What is it that you want?"

He was completely different from that man whom Konstantin had seen in his imagination. Everything in his nature that was most oppressive and evil, everything that made it so hard to associate with him, Konstantin Levin had forgotten when he thought of him. He recollected all this now, as he saw his face and particularly the jerking movement of his head.

"I don't want anything of you," he meekly answered. "I've just come to see you."

His brother's meekness evidently softened Nikolai. His lips twitched.

"Oh, is that so!" he said. "Well, come in, sit down. Would you like some supper? Masha, bring some supper for three. No, wait. You know who he is?" he said turning to his brother and pointing to the stranger. "This is Mr. Kritsky, my friend, whom I knew in Kiev, an extraordinary person. Of course, the police are after him, for he is no scoundrel."

And, following his habit, he glanced at everyone in the room. Seeing that the woman, who stood at the door, was ready to leave, he cried, "Wait, I said." And, again glancing at everyone, he began talking in the awkward, halting manner that was so familiar to Konstantin. He told his brother Kritsky's story: how he had been expelled from the university for forming a needy students' aid society; how he had organized a school for the poor; how he had become a teacher in a village school and was expelled from it, too; how he had been brought to trial on some charges.

An awkward silence followed. To break it, Konstantin Levin turned to Kritsky.

"Are you a graduate of Kiev University?" he asked him.

"Yes, Kiev," Kritsky said with a sullen scowl.

"And this woman," interrupted Nikolai Levin, pointed to her, "my life's companion, Maria Nikolayevna. I took her from a house," he said, jerking his head. "But I love and respect her and I expect everyone who wishes to know me," he added raising his voice and frowning, "to love and respect her. She is just like a wife to me, just like a wife. Now you know with whom you are dealing. But if you think it will degrade you, there's the door."

And again his questioning eyes scanned the faces around him.

"I cannot understand why it should degrade me."

"Then, Masha, order our supper. Supper for three, vodka, and wine. No, wait. . . . No, don't. . . . Go!"

25

"You see," continued Nikolai Levin, wrinkling his brow in concentration and twitching. Evidently he found it difficult to decide what he was going to say or do. "You see . . ." he said, pointing at some iron bars, tied together in the corner of the room. "You see that? It's the beginning of a new undertaking that we're organizing. It's an industrial cooperative. . . ."

Konstantin barely listened to him. He looked at his sickly, tubercular face, his pity for him growing deeper and deeper, and he could not force himself to listen to his brother's description of the cooperative. He knew that his brother was pinning all his hopes for saving himself from self-contempt on this cooperative. Nikolai Levin continued:

"You know that capital oppresses the worker. Our workers, the moujiks, bear the full load of toil, and no matter how much they toil, they cannot extricate themselves from their position as beasts of burden. All the gains derived from their low income, all the profits, which could improve their state and afford them leisure and education, are taken away by the capitalists. And our society is so organized that the more the moujiks work, the more profit accrues to the merchants and to the landowners, while they themselves will forever remain beasts of burden. This order must be changed," he concluded, with a questioning look at his brother.

"Yes, of course," said Konstantin, watching a flush appear on his brother's face under his protuding cheekbones.

"We are, therefore, organizing a metal-working cooperative, where all the work and profits, and, what is most important, the implements of production, will be owned in common."

"Where will you have this cooperative?" asked Konstantin Levin."

"In the village Vozdrema, in Kazan province."

"Why in a village? I believe that there is already enough to do in the villages. Why have a metal-working cooperative in a village?"

"Because the peasants are still slaves, as they have been all along, and therefore you and Sergei Ivanovich find no pleasure in seeing them freed from this slavery," said Nikolai Levin, angered by Konstantin's objection.

Konstantin Levin sighed, looking about the gloomy and dirty room. Evidently this sigh further angered Nikolai.

"I know your and Sergei Ivanovich's artistocratic views; I know that he uses all his ingenuity to justify the existing evil."

"Well now, why do you say this about Sergei Ivanovich?" asked Levin, smiling.

"About Sergei Ivanovich? Here's why!" suddenly shouted Nikolai Levin on hearing Sergei Ivanovich's name. "Here's why. . . . But what's the use of talking? Yet, one question. . . . Why have you come here? You despise this. Very well then, go on your way," he cried, rising from his chair. "Go, go!"

"I don't despise this at all," said Konstantin Levin shyly. "I'm not even arguing with you."

At that moment Maria Nikolayevna came back. Nikolai Levin glanced at her angrily. She quickly came over and whispered something to him.

"I'm not well. I've become irritable," said Nikolai Levin, calming down and breathing heavily, "and here you come, talking to me about Sergei Ivanovich and his article. It's such nonsense, such lies, such self-deception. How can a man write about justice, if he knows nothing about it? Have you read his article?" he asked, turning to Kritsky. He resumed his seat at the table and pushed aside a pile of half-filled cigarettes to make room.

"I haven't read it," replied Kritsky gloomily. Evidently he had no desire to enter the conversation.

"Why?" asked Nikolai Levin, turning on Kritsky with irritation.

"Because I don't want to waste my time on such a thing."

"But let me ask you, how do you know that you're going to waste your time on it? Many will find it impossible to understand this article; it's above them. But it's different with me. I understand his ideas thoroughly and therefore see their weakness."

Everyone grew silent. Kritsky slowly rose and reached for his hat.

"Won't you stay for supper? Well, goodbye. Come tomorrow with the metal worker."

As soon as Kritsky had left, Nikolai Levin smiled and winked.

"He isn't any good either," he said, "I see it. . . ."

But at that moment Kritsky called him from the entrance hall.

"What does he want now?" he asked and went into the hall to see him. When he remained alone with Maria Nikolayevna, Levin asked her:

"How long have you been with my brother?"

"This is the second year. His health is very bad. He drinks too much," she said.

"What do you mean?"

"He drinks vodka, and it isn't good for him."

"Does he drink a lot?" whispered Levin.

"Yes," she said, looking fearfully at the door, and Nikolai walked in.

"What have you been talking about?" he asked, frowning and shifting his frightened eyes from one to the other.

"About nothing," replied Konstantin in embarrassment.

"Well, if you don't want to tell me, don't. But there's nothing for you to talk to her about. She's a wench, and you're a gentleman," he said, jerking his head.

"Well now, you've listened and passed judgment and pity me for my delusions," he continued, raising his voice.

"Nikolai Dmitrievich, Nikolai Dmitrievich," again whispered Maria Nikolayevna, approaching him.

"All right, all right! . . . What about supper? Here it is," he said, noticing the waiter with the tray. "Here, put it here," he said angrily, and at once reached for the vodka, filled a glass, and drank it greedily. "A drink?" he asked Konstantin, his spirits quickly rising. "Well, enough about Sergei Ivanovich. All in all, I'm glad to see you. We're not strangers, after all. Well, have a drink. Tell me, what are you doing?" he continued, greedily chewing a piece of bread and filling another glass. "How are you getting along?"

"I live by myself in the country, as always, and manage the estate," replied Konstantin. It frightened him to see how greedily his brother drank and ate, but he tried to hide his feelings.

"Why haven't you married?"

"I've had no opportunity," Konstantin replied, blushing.

"Why? As for me, of course, all is over. I've ruined my life. I've said, and say it now, that if I'd been given my portion when I needed it, my life would have been entirely different."

Konstantin Dmitrievich quickly changed the subject.

"You know, your Vaniushka is employed by me as a clerk in Pokrovskoe," he said.

Nikolai jerked his head and was lost in thought.

"Please tell me what is going on in Pokrovskoe. Is the house still there, the birch trees, our classroom? And Filipp, the gardener, is he still alive? How well I remember the arbor and the divan. See to it that nothing is changed in the house, get married soon, and recapture the past. I'll come to visit you, if you have a good wife."

"Why don't you come now?" asked Levin. "How nicely we could arrange everything!"

"I'd come if I were sure I wouldn't see Sergei Ivanovich there."

"You wouldn't. We live our own lives."

"Yet, whatever you say, you must choose between me and him," he said, looking timidly at his brother. This timidity moved Konstantin.

"If you would like to know my sincere opinion on this matter, I take no part in this quarrel between you and Sergei Ivanovich. Both of you are at fault. But you are guilty in your deeds, and he in his thoughts."

"Aha! So you do understand, after all?" cried Nikolai happily.

"But I, if you want to know, set more store by friendship with you, because. . . ."

"Why? Why?"

Konstantin could not tell him that he valued his friendship more highly because Nikolai was so unhappy and was in need of a friend. But Nikolai understood that Konstantin wanted to say this very thing and he frowned and reached again for the vodka.

"Enough, Nikolai Dmitrievich," said Maria Nikolayevna, reaching for the decanter with her plump, bare arm.

"Leave me alone. Don't bother me! I'll beat you!" he shouted.

Maria Nikolayevna smiled her kind, timid smile, which communicated itself to Nikolai, and removed the vodka.

"You think that she doesn't understand anything?" said Nikolai. "She understands everything better than we. There's something good and kind about her, don't you think?"

"Have you been in Moscow before?" asked Levin, just to say something to her.

"Don't speak to her with the formal 'you'! She's afraid of it. Only the justice of the peace, who tried her for her attempt to flee from the brothel, ever said that to her. My God, how senseless everything is in this world!" he suddenly cried out. "These new institutions, these justices of the peace, zemstvos. What a horror!"

And he began to tell him about his encounters with these new institutions.

Konstantin Levin listened to him, and although he himself often spoke about the purposelessness of all these public institutions, he found it unpleasant to hear these opinions shared by his brother and coming from his lips.

"We'll understand all this in the next world," he said jestingly.

"In the next world? Oh, I dislike that world. I dislike it," he said, staring at his brother with his wild, frightened eyes. "And though it seems that it would be so good to get away from all this confusion and abomination, my own and that of others, I fear death; I fear death terribly." He shuddered. "Well, have a drink. Would you like some champagne? Or let's go somewhere. Let's go to the gypsies. You know, I have developed a great liking for the gypsies and for Russian songs."

His tongue became thick, and he began to skip from one subject to another. With Masha's help, Konstantin persuaded him to stay home, and they put him to bed, dead drunk.

Masha promised Konstantin to write to him when in need of help, and to persuade Nikolai Levin to go to stay with his brother.

26

IN THE MORNING, Konstantin Levin left Moscow, arriving home toward evening. On the way he spoke to his fellow travelers in the car on politics, about the new railroads, and, as in Moscow, he was overcome by his intellectual confusion, by his dissatisfaction with himself, by an undefinable shame. But when he alighted at his station and saw his one-eyed coachman, Ignat, with the collar of his coat raised; when, in the dim light from the station windows, he found his sleigh with its rug wraps, his horses with their tails tied up, their harness with its rings and tassels; and when the coachman Ignat, even before they started on their way, had managed to tell him all the village news, that the contractor had come and that Pava had calved, he felt that the confusion was slowly lifting and that the shame and dissatisfaction with himself were passing. This he began to feel at the first sight of Ignat and the horses. After he had put on the sheepskin coat which they had brought him, sat down in the sleigh, and wrapped himself, they left. As he thought of his forthcoming work and looked at the trace horse, a former Don riding horse, overstrained but spirited, he began to see what had happened to him in quite a different light. He felt that he was himself and did not wish to be anyone else. He only wanted to be better than he had been before. First, he decided that from this day on he would entertain no hope for the singular happiness that marriage would have brought him, and therefore he would no longer be so neglectful of the present. Secondly, he would never again allow himself to be carried away by vile passion, the memory of which had tormented him so much when he intended to propose. Then, recalling his brother Nikolai, he resolved that never again would he let himself forget about him, that he would keep informed about him in order to be ready to give him help when he needed it. This, he felt, would be soon. Then, his brother's discussion of communism, which at that time he had taken so lightly, now caused him to ponder. The idea of changing economic conditions he considered absurd, but he always felt the injustice of his affluence when compared with the poverty of the people, and he resolved that though he had always worked hard and had seldom indulged in luxury, from now on, in order to be free from all sense of guilt, he would work still harder and indulge still less in luxury. And all this seemed to him so easy to achieve that all the way home he was lost in the most pleasant dreams. With an invigorating feeling of hope for a new and better life, he arrived home about nine o'clock in the evening.

Light shone through the windows of Agafia Mikhailovna's room onto the snow piled on the front landing. The old nurse, who now performed the duties of housekeeper, was not asleep yet. She awakened Kuzma, and he ran out on the porch, sleepy and barefoot. The pointer bitch Laska almost tripped Kuzma and ran after him, yelping. She rubbed against Levin's knees and, rearing, wanted to but dared not put her front paws against his chest.

"You have returned so soon, little father," said Agafia Mikhailovna.

"I was homesick, Agafia Mikhailovna. It's good to be a guest, but home is better," he answered, and went to his study.

The candle that had been brought in slowly lit up the study. It brought out all the familiar details: the stag's antlers, the shelves of books, the mirror, the tile stove with its vent that had long needed repair, his father's divan, the large table, the open book on the table, the chipped ash tray, the notebook in his handwriting. When he saw all this, he was seized for a moment with doubt whether he would be able to achieve that change in his life he had dreamt of on his way home. All these mementoes of his life seemed to have taken hold of him and said, "You won't escape us. You won't change, but you will stay the same as you have been, with your doubts, your constant dissatisfaction with yourself, your vain attempts to improve, your failures, and your constant expectation of happiness which hasn't been given to you and won't be."

This is what these inanimate objects said to him, but another voice, the voice of his heart, told him that one must not give in to the past, and that one is the master of his own fate. Obeying this voice, he went over to the corner of the room, reached for the heavy dumbbells he kept there, and began to exercise in an attempt to restore his vigor. At the sound of squeaking steps behind the door, he quickly put down the dumbbells.

The steward came in and reported that everything, thank God, was in good order, but he added that the buckwheat had burnt slightly in the new drier. This news upset Levin. The new drier had been built and partly designed by him. The steward had always been opposed to this drier, and now, secretly triumphant, he was giving him the news about the burnt buckwheat. But Levin was firmly convinced that if the buckwheat had burnt, it was only through lack of proper attention, which he had asked for so many times. He was annoyed and reprimanded the steward. But one important and happy event had occurred. Pava, his best and most expensive cow, one he had bought at an exhibition, had calved.

"Kuzma, give me my sheepskin coat. And you," he told the steward, "tell them to fetch a lantern. I'm going to take a look."

The cattle shed where the better cows were kept was right behind the house. They passed through the yard, near the snowdrift at the lilac bush, and came up to the cattle shed. They opened the door, which had frozen shut. A smell of warm manure filled the air, and the cows, surprised at the sudden light of the lantern, stirred in the fresh straw. He caught a glimpse of the smooth, broad, black-mottled back of the Dutch Belted cow. Berkut, the bull, rested with the ring through his lip, and was about to rise, but changed his mind and just puffed twice as they passed him. The red beauty Pava, enormous as a hippopotamus, stood with her back to them, screening the calf from the visitor and sniffing at it.

Levin went into the stall, looked over Pava, and raised the mottled red calf to its long, shaky legs. The worried Pava mooed, but calmed down as soon as Levin set the calf next to her. After a deep breath, she began licking her with her rough tongue. The hungry calf pushed her muzzle between her mother's legs and wagged her little tail.

"Bring the light over here, Fiodor," said Levin, examining the calf. "Just like her mother! Though the coloring is her father's. She's fine. She has a long frame and deep flanks. She's fine, Vasily Fiodorovich, isn't she?" he asked the steward. Because of his joy over the calf, he no longer bore any grudge against him on account of the buckwheat.

"How could she be otherwise? Semyon the contractor came the day after you left. We must settle the price with him, Konstantin Dmitrievich," said the steward. "I have already reported to you about the machine."

And starting with this one problem, Levin became engrossed in all the details of his work, complex and important. From the cattle shed he went straight to his office, and after a talk with the steward and Semyon the contractor, he returned home and went directly upstairs into the drawing room.

27

THE HOUSE was large and ancient, and though Levin lived alone, he heated and occupied the whole house. He knew it was foolish to do it, that it was even wrong and against his new resolutions, but for Levin this house was an entire world. This was a world in which Levin's father and mother had lived and died. They had lived a life that Levin considered the model of perfection and that he dreamt of recapturing with his own wife and family.

Levin faintly remembered his mother. Her memory was sacred to him and he imagined that, in his wife, that beautiful and sacred ideal of womanhood, which his mother had been, would be resurrected.

Not only was he unable to think of love for a woman without marriage, but in his imagination he first saw his future family and only then the woman who would give him this family. Therefore his idea of marriage was different from the ideas of most of his acquaintances, for whom marriage was one of many other events in life. For Levin it was the chief event, on which all happiness depended. And now he had to give it up!

When he entered the small drawing room where he always

had his tea, he ensconced himself in his armchair with a book. Agafia Mikhailovna brought him tea, and with her usual, "I will sit down, little father," sat in a chair at the window. Strange as it may seem, he now felt that he had not abandoned his dreams and that he could not live without them. It will happen he thought, with her or with another, but it will happen. He read the book, thought about what he was reading, stopped, and listened to Agafia Mikhailovna, who chattered ceaselessly. At the same time, different pictures of his future family life and his work were passing, disconnected, through his mind. Deep in his heart was growing a feeling of order, harmony and balance.

He listened as Agafia Mikhailovna told him about Prokhor, who had forsaken his God: instead of buying a horse with the money Levin had given him as a present, he was on a continuous drinking spree, and he had mercilessly beaten his wife. Levin listened, read the book, and reviewed the whole course of the thoughts that were aroused by his reading. It was Tindall's book on heat. He recalled his criticism of Tindall for his feeling of self-satisfaction, brought on by his skill in experimentation, and for his failure to view things philosophically. Suddenly a happy thought flashed through his mind: In two years I will have two Dutch Belted cows in my herd. Pava herself may still be alive then, twelve young daughters sired by Berkut, and then to have these three cows exhibited . . . how wonderful! He turned back to the book.

Well, electricity and heat, he thought, are one and the same. But in the equation that would solve this problem, can we substitute one quantity for the other? No. What then? The bond between the different natural forces can be known even by instinct. . . . It's a particular pleasure to think that Pava's calf will grow into a red mottled cow, and the whole herd, to which these three will be added . . . splendid! To come out with my wife and guests to see the herd. . . . My wife will say: "Kostia and I nursed this calf!" "How can you be interested in such things?" a guest will ask. "Everything that interests him interests me." But who will she be? and he remembered all that had happened in Moscow. . . . And what can be done? It's not my fault. But now everything will be different. It's nonsensical to say that life will not allow it, that the past will not allow it. You must strive to live better, much better. . . . He raised his head and was lost in thought. Old Laska was not yet fully over her happiness at Levin's arrival; she ran out into the yard to bark, returned bringing with her the aroma of the outdoors, and wagging her tail, she came over to him, shoved her head under his arm, and whimpered plaintively, asking to be patted.

"She all but speaks," said Agafia Mikhailovna. "A dog . . . yet she understands that the master has arrived and that he is troubled."

"Why should I be troubled?"

"Don't I see, little father? It's time indeed for me to know the masters' ways. I have grown up with them from childhood. But it doesn't matter, little father, as long as you have good health and a clear conscience."

Levin stared at her, surprised that she should read his thoughts.

"Well, shall I bring you some more tea?" she asked, and taking his cup, she left the room.

Laska was still shoving her head under his arm. He patted her. She curled up right at his feet, putting her head on her outstretched hind paws, and to prove that now all was well and safe, she opened her mouth slightly, smacked her lips, and adjusting her sticky lips against her old teeth, fell silent in a blissful calm. Levin closely watched these last movements of hers.

That's how it is for me, too! he said to himself. That's how it is for me, too! Yes, all is well.

28

EARLY IN THE MORNING after the ball, Anna Arkadievna sent a telegram to her husband informing him that she was leaving Moscow that same day.

"No, I must go, I must," she said to her sister-in-law, announcing the change in her plans, and she said it in a tone that implied that she had recalled how urgently she was needed at home. "Yes, I must go today."

Stepan Arkadievich was not coming for dinner, but promised to be at home at seven o'clock to see his sister off.

Kitty did not come either. She sent a note saying that she had a headache. Dolly and Anna dined with the children and the English governess. Today the children did not play with their aunt, did not show their love for her, and did not care in the least that she was leaving. This change was partly due to the fickleness of children and partly to their sensitiveness. They felt that today Anna was no longer the one with whom they had fallen in love, and no longer cared for them. All that morning Anna had been busy getting ready to leave. She wrote a few notes to her Moscow friends, recorded her expenditures, and packed. In general it seemed to Dolly that something was troubling Anna, that she was in that preoccupied mood, so familiar to her, that one falls into, not without reason, and that most often masks dissatisfaction with oneself. After dinner Anna went into her room to dress, and Dolly followed her.

"You're acting so strangely today!" said Dolly.

"I am? Do you think so? I'm not acting strangely; I'm bad. This happens to me. I feel like crying. It's foolish but it passes," Anna said quickly, lowering her flushed face to the little bag, into which she was putting her nightcap and her batiste handkerchiefs. Her eyes, continuously tear-filled, shone with a strange brightness. "Just as I didn't want to leave Petersburg, I don't want to leave now."

"You have come and done such a good deed," said Dolly, watching her attentively.

Anna looked at her with eyes moist with tears.

"Don't say that, Dolly. I haven't done and couldn't have done anything. I often wonder why everybody's agreed to spoil me. What have I done—and what could I have done? It's the great love in your heart that made you forgive."

"Yet God knows what would have happened without you! How happy you are, Anna! Everything in your heart is so good and serene!"

"But every heart has its skeletons, as the English say."

"But your heart surely has no skeletons. Everything about you is so serene."

"It has!" suddenly said Anna, and it was surprising to see, right after her tears, such an arch, ironical smile curving her lips.

"Then they must be funny, your skeletons, not gloomy," Dolly said, smiling.

"No, they're gloomy. Do you know why I'm leaving today and not tomorrow? There's something that depresses me and I want to make a full confession to you," added Anna, sitting up straight in her chair with an air of resolution and looking squarely at Dolly.

To her great surprise, Dolly saw Anna blushing to the tips of her ears and to the roots of her hair, which curled in black ringlets around her neck.

"Well," continued Anna, "do you know why Kitty didn't come for dinner? She is jealous of me. I have ruined. . . . It was because of me that, instead of joy, that ball brought her suffering. But, I assure you, I was not guilty, or perhaps only a little guilty," she said, slowly stretching the words *a little* in a thin voice.

"You sounded so much like Stiva when you said that," said Dolly with a laugh.

Anna felt hurt. "Oh, no! Oh, no! I'm not Stiva," she said, frowning. "I'm telling you this because I will not permit myself, even for a moment, to lose faith with myself."

But as soon as she spoke these words, she knew that they were not true. Not only had she lost faith with herself, but she was perturbed by thoughts of Vronsky, and she was leaving earlier than she had intended only in order to avoid seeing him.

"Yes, Stiva told me that you danced the mazurka with him, and that he. . . ."

"You can't imagine how ridiculously everything turned out. I just wanted to be a matchmaker, but something very different happened. Perhaps I, against my will. . . ."

She blushed and stopped.

"Oh, they sense such things immediately," said Dolly.

"But it would break my heart to think that there might have been anything serious on his part," Anna interrupted. "And I'm sure that everything will be forgotten and that Kitty won't hate me any more."

"To tell you the truth, Anna, my heart is not fully set on this match for Kitty. And if he could fall in love with you at first sight, it would be better for them to part now."

"My God, how foolish it was!" said Anna, and again she flushed deeply with pleasure on hearing the words that expressed her secret thoughts. "And so I'm leaving, after making an enemy of Kitty, whom I've grown so fond of. How charming she is! Will you set things right, Dolly? Please."

Dolly could scarcely restrain a smile. She loved Anna, but she was pleased to see that she had her weaknesses.

"An enemy? That's impossible."

"How much I would like all of you to love me as I love

you, and how much I love you now!" she said with tears in her eyes. "Oh, how foolish I am today!"

She ran her handkerchief over her face and began dressing. Stepan Arkadievich, his face flushed with happiness, and smelling of wine and cigars, arrived late, just before Anna left.

Anna's sentiments communicated themselves to Dolly, and when she embraced her sister-in-law for the last time, she whispered:

"Remember, Anna, that I will never forget what you've done for me. And remember that I've always loved you and shall love you as my dearest friend!"

"I don't deserve it," said Anna, kissing her and suppressing her tears.

"You have always understood me. Goodbye, my dear!"

29

WELL, IT'S ALL OVER, thank God, was Anna Arkadievna's first thought as, for the last time, she said goodbye to her brother, who had blocked the entrance to the railroad car until the third bell rang. She took her seat next to Annushka and looked around in the dim light of the sleeping car. Thank God, tomorrow I'll see Seryozha and Aleksei Aleksandrovich, and life will again be familiar and secure. In the same preoccupied mood she had been in all day, Anna now enjoyed attending to all the requisites for a comfortable trip. With her skillful small hands she opened and then closed the red bag, reached for the small pillow, put it on her lap, wrapped her legs neatly, and made herself comfortable. A sick lady was preparing for the night. Two other ladies addressed Anna, and a stout old lady wrapped her legs and made some remarks about the heating. Anna replied with a few words, but she was not interested in their conversation. She asked Annushka to get a small lantern, attached it to the arm of the chair, and reached for a paper knife and an English novel from her small bag. At first she could not concentrate on reading. She was distracted by the general bustle and by the passengers pacing up and down. Then, when the train started, she could not help listening to the sounds it made. The snow beat against the window on the left side and clung to the glass. The conductor, bundled up against the cold, passed by, one side of him covered with snow. The passengers talked about the snowstorm raging outside. All this distracted Anna. Then the scene kept repeating itself. The same shaking and rattling of the train, the same snow beating at the window, the same extremes of steaming heat and blasts of cold air, the same faces flitting by in the semidarkness, the same voices. Anna resumed her reading and now could concentrate on it. Annushka dozed. On her large hands, with which she held the small red bag in her lap, she wore a pair of gloves, one of which was torn. Anna could concentrate on her reading now, but she found no pleasure in following the story of other people's lives—she was too eager to live her own life. When she read how the heroine of the novel nursed the sick man, she wanted to be able to tiptoe noiselessly about the sick room. When she read about a member of parliament delivering a speech, she wanted to hear herself delivering that speech. And when she read about Lady Mary riding to the hounds, annoying her sister-in-law, and surprising everyone by her courage, she wanted to do the same. With nothing else to occupy her, she forced herself to read, her little hands toying with the smooth paper knife.

The hero of the novel was now reaching the height of English good fortune, a baronetcy and an estate, and Anna wished to follow him to that estate, but she suddenly felt that he should be ashamed, and that she was ashamed for the same reason. But why should he be ashamed? And what am I ashamed of? she asked herself, surprised and offended. She put aside the book, threw herself back in the chair, gripping the smooth paper knife with both hands. There was nothing to be ashamed of. She remembered all that had happened in Moscow; the memories were good and pleasant. She recalled the ball, recalled Vronsky and his enamored, shy face, recalled their relationship. There was nothing to be ashamed of. But at the same time, with this recollection, the feeling of shame grew stronger, as though at the very moment when she thought of Vronsky, an inner voice told her, You are warm, very warm, burning. But what of it? she said firmly, stirring in her chair—What does it mean? Am I afraid to face it? Why should I? And between this boyish officer and myself is there or can there be anything other than a casual acquaintance? She smiled contemptuously and turned back to the book, but now she could not understand a word she read. She pressed the paper knife against the windowpane, placed its smooth cold surface against her cheek, and almost laughed aloud with a joyful feeling that suddenly and for no reason seized her. She felt that her nerves were drawn tighter and tighter, as violin strings are drawn on their pegs. She felt that her eyes were opening wider and wider, that her fingers and toes were twitching nervously, that something within her made her breathing labored, and she was startled by the unusual clarity of all these sounds and shapes in the quivering semidarkness. She was continually seized by fits of doubt, and was not sure whether the train was moving forward or backward, or was standing still. Was that Annushka sitting near her or a stranger? What is lying on the arm of the seat, her fur coat or some animal? She thought. And who am I? Am I myself or someone else? It was frightening to succumb to this confusion. But something drew her into it, and she could succumb at will or resist. She sat up to clear her mind, threw aside the wrap, and took off her cape. She recovered for a moment and understood that the tall, gaunt moujik who had entered, dressed in a long nankeen coat with one of its buttons missing, was the stove tender, that he looked at the thermometer, and that he let in a blast of wind and snow as he opened the door. But again everything grew confused. This long-waisted moujik began to gnaw at something on the wall; the old lady stretched her legs the entire length of the car and filled it with a black cloud. Then there was a terrible screeching and hammering, as if someone were being torn apart. A red light blinded her and everything disappeared behind a wall. Anna felt that she had fallen, as though into an abyss. But all this was not frightening, but funny. A man, bundled up and covered with snow, shouted something into her ear. She rose and came to her senses. She realized that they were nearing a station, and that the man was the conductor. She asked Annushka to hand her her cape and the shawl. She put them on and turned to the door.

"Are you going outside?" asked Annushka.

"Yes, I need a breath of air. It's too hot in here."

She opened the door. She was met by a blast of wind and snow that contended with her for the door. She enjoyed the struggle, then opened the door and went outside. As though it had been waiting for her, the wind whistled joyously, trying to seize her and carry her away. She caught on to the cold railing and, holding her skirt, alighted on the platform and took a turn around the car. The wind was bitter between the cars, but it was calm on the platform, which was screened by the cars. She was delighted to draw deep breaths of the snowy, frosty air. Standing near the car, she looked around the platform and the illuminated station.

30

THE TERRIBLE STORM raged on. It whistled between the wheels of the cars and along the posts at the corner of the platform. The snow had drifted against one side of the cars, the posts, the people, against everything that could be seen, and still kept drifting. For a moment the storm abated, but then renewed with such violent blasts that nothing, it seemed, could resist it. All this time people scurried about, chattering with animation. Their steps squeaked on the boards of the platform, and they ceaselessly opened and closed the large doors. The bent shadow of a man glided by her feet, and she heard the sounds of a hammer rapping on iron. "Send a telegram!" an angry voice was heard shouting through the stormy darkness. "Here, please! Number twenty-eight!" shouted other voices, and shapes, bundled up and covered with snow, scurried by. Two gentlemen with lit cigarettes in their mouths passed near her. She breathed deeply once more to have her fill of fresh air, and as she took her hand from her muff to grasp the railing and enter the car, a man in a military coat, standing close to her, screened the flickering light of the street lamp. She turned around and at once recognized Vronsky's face. He saluted her, bowed, and asked her whether she needed anything, and whether he could be of any help to her. She looked at him for quite a while without saying anything, and though he stood in the shadow, she saw, or it seemed to her that she saw, the expression of his face and eyes. It was the same expression of respectful admiration that had impressed her so deeply the day before. Many a time during the past few days, and even only a little while ago, she had said to herself that Vronsky was just one of hundreds of other young men, all alike, whom she met everywhere, and of whom she would not even permit herself to think. But now, the moment she saw him, a feeling of joyous pride possessed her. She did not have to ask him why he was there. She knew, as well as if he himself had told her, that he was there to be where she was.

"I didn't know that you were on the train. Why are you making this trip?" she asked, dropping her hand, which she had raised to grasp the rail. And unrestrained joy and admiration shone on her face.

"Why am I making this trip?" he repeated, looking at her squarely. "You know. I'm on this train to be with you," he said. "I can't help it."

At this moment the wind seemed to have burst all bounds. It blew the snow off the roofs of the cars and it flapped a loosened iron sheet. From up ahead could be heard the plaintive, gloomy, and throaty whistle of the locomotive. All the fury of the snowstorm now seemed to her still more beautiful. He had said exactly what her heart desired but what her mind feared. She did not say anything, and on her face he saw the struggle taking place.

"Forgive me, if what I've said displeased you," he said gently.

He spoke courteously and respectfully, but with such firmness and such forcefulness that for a long time she could not answer him.

"What you say is wrong, and I ask you, if you are a good man, to forget what you have said, as I will forget it," she said at last.

"I will not and can never forget even one word of yours, one movement of yours."

"Please, enough!" she cried, vainly trying to assume a severe expression on her face as he stared at her eagerly. And taking hold of the cold railing, she ascended the stairs and hurriedly went into the vestibule of the car. But in this small vestibule she stopped, recollecting all that had happened. Without remembering either his or her own words, she felt instinctively that this momentary conversation had brought them terribly close to each other. It frightened her and made her happy. She remained standing for a few moments, then entered the car and took her seat. The state of tension that had tormented her earlier not only returned, but grew stronger, and she feared that at any moment something within her would snap. She did not sleep at all that night. But there was nothing unpleasant or depressing in this state of tension or the reveries that crowded her mind. On the contrary, there was something joyful, exciting, glowing in it. Toward morning Anna dozed in her chair, and when she woke it was already daylight and the train was approaching Petersburg. At once she became engrossed in thoughts of her home, her husband, her son, and everyday cares.

As soon as the train arrived at Petersburg, she came out of the car, and the first face that attracted her attention was her husband's. Oh, my God! Where did he get those ears, she thought, looking at his forbidding, distinguished figure and with particular surprise at the cartilage of his ears, which supported the brim of his round hat. When he caught sight of her, he came over to meet her, curving his lips into his customary mocking smile and looking at her squarely with his large, tired eyes. When she met his direct, weary look, an unpleasant feeling made her heart sink, as if she had expected him to look different. She was particularly surprised at the dissatisfaction with herself she felt as she met him. It was an old, familiar feeling, close to hypocrisy, which she had always felt in her relationship with her husband. But whereas formerly she had not understood this feeling, she was conscious of it now, painfully and clearly.

"As you see, your tender husband, as tender as he was in the second year of our marriage, has been burning with desire to see you," he said in his slow, thin voice and in the manner in which he almost always addressed her, a manner that showed how he ridiculed those who would actually speak this way.

"Is Seryozha well?" she asked.

"Is this the only reward for my ardor?" he asked. "He is well, he is well. . . ."

31

ALL THAT NIGHT Vronsky did not even try to fall asleep. He sat in his chair, either staring straight ahead or looking at the people entering and leaving. If he had previously impressed or annoyed those who did not know him by his air of unshakable calm, he now seemed prouder and even more self-assured. He regarded people as mere objects. This air of haughtiness aroused hatred against him in a young, nervous court clerk who sat opposite him. The young man asked him for a match, spoke to him, even jostled him, to show him that he was not an object but a man, yet Vronsky looked at him the way he looked at the lantern. The young man's face became contorted, and he felt that he was losing his self-control through this denial of his humanity.

Vronsky saw nothing and no one. He felt like a king: not because he believed that he had made an impression on Anna —he did not believe this yet—but because the impression she made on him made him proud and happy.

He did not know what this would lead to and did not even think of it. He felt that all the forces of his nature, formerly scattered and loose, had now concentrated, and their terrible power was directed to one blissful purpose, and this made him happy. He only knew that he had told her the truth, that his path lay with hers, that all the happiness of his life, his only purpose in living, was to see and to hear her. When he had come out of the car at Bologovo to have a drink of seltzer water and saw Anna, the first words that he involuntarily uttered mirrored his thoughts. He was happy that he had told her, that now she knew it and thought about it. He did not sleep the entire night. On returning to the car, he kept recalling all the circumstances in which he had seen her, all her words, and his imagination, painting pictures of what might be, made his heart sink.

When he came out of the car at Petersburg after a sleepless night, he felt refreshed and invigorated, as after a cold bath. He stopped at his car, waiting for her to come out. I will see her once more, he said to himself, smiling without realizing it. I will again see her face, her walk. She may say something, turn her head, look at me, and perhaps smile. But before he could see her, he saw her husband, whom the stationmaster respectfully conducted through the crowd. Ah, yes! Her husband! Only now, for the first time, did Vronsky realize that there existed a bond between her and her husband. He knew that she had a husband, but he had not believed in his existence, and was convinced only now, when he saw him, with his head, shoulders, his legs in black trousers, and particularly when he saw this husband taking her arm with a calm feeling of possession.

On seeing Aleksei Aleksandrovich, with his ruddy Petersburg face, his austere self-confidence, his round hat, and his slightly stooped back, he believed in his existence and had an unpleasant feeling, like a man who, suffering from thirst, reaches a spring only to find that a dog, sheep, or pig has drunk there and muddied the water. Vronsky was particularly offended by Aleksei Aleksandrovich's gait and the way he moved his back and stubby legs. He admitted only his own incontestable right to love her. But she had remained unchanged. The sight of her affected him, enlivened him physically, aroused him and filled his heart with happiness. His German servant hastily came over to him from a second-class car. He ordered him to take care of his luggage and walked up to her. He watched husband and wife greet each other, and with the perspicacity of a man in love he noticed the slight embarrassment with which she spoke to her husband. No, he decided, she does not and cannot love him.

He was happy to notice that while he was still approaching Anna Arkadievna from behind, she knew that he was there, turned around, recognized him, and turned back to her husband.

"Did you have a comfortable night?" he asked, bowing both to her and her husband, and leaving it to Aleksei Aleksandrovich either to acknowledge his bow and recognize him or not.

"Thank you, very comfortable," she replied.

Her face looked tired, and it did not show the vivacity which usually appeared either in her smile or in her eyes, but as she looked at him, her eyes brightened, and though this lasted only a moment, it made him happy. She looked at her husband to see whether he knew Vronsky. Aleksei Aleksandrovich looked at Vronsky with displeasure, absent-mindedly trying to recall who he was. Vronsky's calmness and self-confidence struck against the forbidding self-confidence of Aleksei Aleksandrovich like a scythe against a rock.

"This is Count Vronsky," said Anna.

"Ah! We've met, it seems to me," Aleksei Aleksandrovich said indifferently, extending his hand. "You traveled there with the mother and back with the son," he added, speaking with precision, as if each of his words was supposed to delight his listener's heart. "You are probably returning from leave?" he asked and, without waiting for an answer, he addressed his wife in his usual jesting tone, "Well, I suppose that many tears were shed when you left Moscow."

By turning to his wife, he indicated to Vronsky that he wished to remain alone with her. Facing him again, he tipped his hat, but Vronsky turned to Anna Arkadievna.

"I hope to have the honor of visiting you," he said.

Aleksei Aleksandrovich glanced at Vronsky with his tired eyes.

"We will be happy to see you," he said coldly. "We receive

on Mondays." Then, ignoring Vronsky, he addressed his wife. "I am glad that I had a free half hour to meet you and to show you my tenderness," he continued in the same bantering tone.

"By stressing your tenderness you make it hard for me to appreciate it fully," she answered in the same mocking tone, unconsciously listening to Vronsky's footsteps as he walked behind them. But what do I care? she thought, and she asked her husband how Seryozha had spent the time without her.

"Oh, very well! Mariette says that he was a very good boy and . . . I regret to tell you . . . he hasn't missed you, not like your husband. And thank you again, my dear, for the gift of an extra day. Our dear Samovar will be delighted." (He called the famous Countess Lydia Ivanovna "the Samovar" because everything always fired her with zeal and excitement.) "She inquired about you. By the way, with your permission I would advise you to visit her today. Her heart bleeds for everyone. In addition to her other cares, she's concerned about the reconciliation of the Oblonskys."

Countess Lydia Ivanovna was her husband's friend and the center of one of the circles of Petersburg society, with which, through her husband, Anna was most closely connected.

"But I wrote her."

"And yet she wants to know all the details. Go to her, my dear, if you're not tired. And now, Kondrati will bring up the coach for you, and I'll go to the committee. My dinners will no longer be lonely," continued Aleksei Aleksandrovich, this time without his mocking tone. "You have no idea how accustomed I have become . . ."

He clung to her hand, and with a special kind of smile he helped her to the coach.

32

THE FIRST PERSON Anna met at home was her son. He dashed down the stairs to meet her, disregarding the admonition of the governess, and with unrestrained delight cried, "Mama, Mama!" On reaching her, he clung to her, his arms around her neck.

"I told you it was Mama!" he cried to the governess. "I knew!"

And, just as her husband had, her son stirred in her a feeling akin to disappointment. She had imagined him to be better than he actually was. She had to stoop to reality to delight in him as he really was. And even so, he was charming, with his blond curls, blue eyes, and his plump, well-shaped legs in their tight stockings. His closeness and tenderness gave Anna a sensation of almost physical delight and of moral composure, as she met his frank, trusting, and loving look, and listened to his naïve questions. Anna reached for the presents Dolly's children had sent him, and told her son about the nice girl Tania, who lived in Moscow, could read, and even taught other children to read.

"Well, am I not as good as she is?" asked Seryozha.

"To me you're the best in the whole world."

"I know," said Seryozha, smiling.

Anna had not yet finished her coffee when they announced the arrival of Countess Lydia Ivanovna. Countess Lydia Ivanovna was a tall, stout woman with a sickly, yellowish complexion and beautiful, black, melancholy eyes. Anna loved her, but it seemed that today, for the first time, she saw her with all her shortcomings.

"Well, my friend, did you bring them the olive branch?" asked Countess Lydia Ivanovna, as soon as she entered the room.

"Yes, everything is settled, but it wasn't as serious as we had thought," replied Anna. "My belle-soeur is, in general, a very determined lady."

But Countess Lydia Ivanovna, who was interested in everything that did not concern her, also had the habit of paying no attention even to what interested her. She interrupted Anna:

"Yes, there's much evil and sorrow in this world, and I'm so tired today."

"What's the matter?" asked Anna, trying to restrain her smile.

"I'm getting tired of vainly taking up the cudgel in defense of the truth, and often feel completely worn out. Take the case of the Little Sisters." (This was a philanthropic, religious-patriotic society.) "All would be well but for these gentlemen, with whom it is impossible to accomplish anything," added Countess Lydia Ivanovna, with mock submission to her fate. "They caught hold of the idea, but have distorted it, and now indulge in petty and worthless talk. Only two or three persons, your husband among them, understand the importance of this case, whereas all the others belittle it. Yesterday Pravdin wrote to me. . . ."

Pravdin was a famous pan-Slavist who lived abroad. Countess Lydia Ivanovna recited the contents of his letter.

The countess then told her about some of her other troubles, about the intrigues against the unification of the churches, and then left in a hurry, for that day she still had to attend a meeting of a society and a session of the Slav committee.

All this was going on before. Why didn't I notice it then? Anna asked herself. Is it because she was overwrought today? But, truly, all this is ridiculous. Virtue is her purpose; she is a Christian, but she's always angry. Everybody is her enemy, and all are enemies of her Christianity and virtue.

After Lydia Ivanovna had left, a friend arrived, a director's wife, who brought her up to date on all the news of the town. At three o'clock her friend left and promised to be back for dinner. Aleksei Aleksandrovich was in his office at the ministry. Remaining alone, Anna spent the rest of the time before dinner in her son's company at his meal (he ate separately), in arranging her things, and in reading and replying to the numerous notes and letters that had accumulated on her desk.

She no longer had that feeling of unfounded shame that had perturbed her during the trip. In the familiar surroundings of her life, she again felt confident and beyond reproach.

With surprise she recalled the state she had been in yesterday. What was it about? she asked herself. Nothing. Vronsky said something foolish, something that could easily be quashed, and I replied as I should have. There's no need to tell it to my husband, and it mustn't be told. Talking about it would only lend importance to something that doesn't warrant it. She recalled that once, in Petersburg, a young man, a subordinate of her husband's, had all but declared his love for her. She told Aleksei Aleksandrovich about it, and his reply was that this might have happened to any lady of her station, that he had full confidence in her judgment, and that he would never permit jealousy to humiliate her or himself. Then there's no reason to discuss it—yes, thank God, there's nothing to discuss, she said to herself.

33

ALEKSEI ALEKSANDROVICH returned from the ministry at four o'clock, but, as often happened, he had no time to stop in to see her. He went into his study to receive the petitioners who were waiting for him, and to sign some papers his office manager had sent him. At dinnertime the invited guests arrived (the Karenins always had several people for dinner): an old lady cousin of Aleksei Aleksandrovich's, a director of a department and his wife, and a young man who had been recommended to Aleksei Aleksandrovich in the ministry. Anna came into the drawing room to entertain them. Exactly at five o'clock, as the bronze Peter the First clock sounded the fifth stroke, Aleksei Aleksandrovich emerged from his study. He had to make a formal call after dinner, and therefore was wearing a white tie and a swallow-tailed coat with two decorations. Every minute of Aleksei Aleksandrovich's life was occupied and accounted for. He was most punctual, and this enabled him to perform all his numerous daily duties. "Without haste and without rest" was his motto. He entered the room, greeted the guests, and hurriedly sat down, smiling at his wife.

"Yes, my loneliness has come to an end. You would scarcely believed how awkward" (he stressed the word *awkward*) "it is to dine alone."

At dinner he spoke to his wife about the news from Moscow, and with his mocking smile he inquired about Stepan Arkadievich, but general conversation touched mainly upon government and social affairs. After dinner he spent about half an hour with the guests, and, smiling again, he shook his wife's hand and left for the council meeting. That day Anna neither went to see Princess Betsy Tverskoy, who, informed of her arrival, had invited her for the evening, nor to the theater, where she had a box for the evening. She went nowhere, primarily because the dress she had expected was not ready. And other things annoyed her as, after the guests had left, she busied herself with her wardrobe. She had a talent for dressing both well and inexpensively, and before she left for Moscow, she had given her seamstress three dresses to be altered. The alterations should have made them completely unrecognizable, and the seamstress should have brought them three days earlier. But, as it turned out, two dresses were not ready, and the third had not been altered the way Anna had expected. The seamstress came to clear up the matter, insisting that hers was the right way, and Anna became so upset that later she was ashamed of herself. To calm herself completely, she went into her son's room and spent the whole evening with him, put him to bed herself, crossed him and covered him with his blanket. She was glad that she had not gone anywhere and that she had had such a pleasant evening. She felt relaxed and calm, and now saw clearly that everything that had seemed to her of such great importance during the trip constituted a most ordinary and insignificant incident of life in society, and that she had nothing to be ashamed of either in her own eyes or the eyes of others. She sat down at the fireplace with an English novel to wait for her husband. At exactly half-past nine she heard him ring the bell, and he entered the room.

"At last you are here!" she said, extending her hand to him.

He kissed her hand and sat next to her.

"I see that your trip was successful," he said.

"Yes, very successful," she replied, and began to tell him all about it from the beginning: about traveling with Countess Vronsky, about her arrival in Moscow, and about the accident at the railroad station. Then she told him how sorry she had felt first for her brother, and then for Dolly.

"I don't believe that such a man should be forgiven, though he is your brother," Aleksei Aleksandrovich said sternly.

Anna smiled. She understood that he said this to show clearly that even considerations of kinship would not stop him from expressing his sincere opinions. She knew this trait of her husband's and admired it.

"I'm glad that everything has ended well, and that you're back," he continued. "Well, what do they say there about my new proposal, which was passed by the council?"

Anna knew nothing about this new proposal, and she felt ashamed that she could have so easily overlooked a matter that was of such great importance to him.

"Here, on the contrary, it raised quite a stir," he said, with a self-satisfied smile.

She saw that Aleksei Aleksandrovich wanted to share with her the pleasure which this matter had brought him, and she assisted his explanation with her questions. With the same self-satisfied smile, he described the ovations that were given him on account of this new proposal.

"I am very, very glad. It proves that at last we're beginning to judge this matter from a reasonable and positive point of view."

After his second glass of tea with cream and bread, Aleksei Aleksandrovich rose to leave for his study.

"But you didn't go anywhere this evening. You must have been bored," he said.

"Oh, no!" she said, rising after him and accompanying him to his study through the dining room. "What are you reading now?" she asked.

"I am reading *Poésie des enfers* by Duc de Lille," he answered. "A very remarkable book."

Anna smiled, as one always smiles at the weaknesses of loved ones. Holding his arm, she accompanied him to the doors of his study. She knew this habit of his, which had now become a compulsion, to read every evening. She knew that though he was always engrossed in his official business, he considered it his duty to follow all the great events in the intellectual world. She also knew that his interests lay in books on politics, philosophy, and theology; that he was completely incapable of enjoying works of art, and that in spite of this, or rather because of it, Aleksei Aleksandrovich never missed any book in this field that attracted general attention; he considered it his duty to read it. She knew that in matters of politics, philosophy, and theology, Aleksei Aleksandrovich was a skeptic or a seeker; but in art and poetry, and particularly in music, of which he knew absolutely nothing, his opinions were well defined and firm. He loved to speak of Shakespeare, Raphael, Beethoven, of the new schools of poetry and music, all of them defined by him very clearly and consistently.

"Well, God be with you!" she said at the door of his study. Inside, a shaded candle and a decanter of water had been readied for him next to his chair. "I'll write a few letters to Moscow." He took her hand and kissed it again.

After all, he's a good man, honest, kind, and remarkable in his own sphere, said Anna Arkadievna to herself when she had returned to her room, as though defending him against someone who was criticizing him and who said that he could not be loved. But why do his ears protrude so strangely? Is it because he had his hair cut?

Exactly at twelve o'clock, while Anna was still at her desk, finishing a letter to Dolly, she heard his measured tread in his slippers, and Aleksei Aleksandrovich, washed and combed, with a book under his arm, came over to her.

"It's time, it's time," he said with a peculiar smile, and went to the bedroom.

And what right did he have to look at him that way? thought Anna, recalling Vronsky's look at Aleksei Aleksandrovich.

She undressed and went into the bedroom. Not only had her face lost that vivacity that in Moscow had shone so brightly from her eyes and smile, but on the contrary, the glow seemed now to have disappeared completely or to have hidden somewhere deep within her.

34

WHEN VRONSKY had departed from Petersburg, he left his large apartment on Morskaya Street in charge of his favorite friend, Petritsky.

Petritsky was a young lieutenant, not a very high-ranking nobleman and not only not rich but deep in debt, always drunk toward evening and often confined to the guardhouse for ridiculous and unsavory escapades; but he was beloved by his friends and superiors. When, around twelve o'clock, Vronsky arrived at his house from the railroad station, he saw a familiar hired coach near the entrance. Even while he rang, he heard from behind the door the boisterous laughter of men, the jabber of a young woman, and a shout from Petritsky: "If it's one of those rascals, don't let him in." Vronsky told his orderly not to announce him and tiptoed into the first room. Baroness Shilton, Petritsky's friend, all aglitter in her lilac satin dress, her rosy little face, and her blond hair, chirped like a canary and filled the whole room with her Parisian chatter. She sat at the round table making coffee. Seated around her were Petritsky in a coat, and Captain Kamerovsky, evidently just off duty, in full uniform.

"Bravo! Vronsky!" shouted Petritsky, jumping up, his chair scraping the floor. "Here is the master of the house himself!

Baroness, give him a cup of coffee from the new coffee pot. What a surprise! I hope you approve of the new ornament in your study," he said, pointing at the baroness. "You've met, I hope."

"Of course!" said Vronsky, smiling gaily and shaking the baroness' little hand. "Of course! We are old friends!"

"You've just come from a trip," said the baroness. "I had better go. Oh, I'll go at once, if I'm in the way."

"Wherever you are, you are most welcome, Baroness," said Vronsky. "How are you, Kamerovsky?" he added coldly, shaking hands with Kamerovsky.

"You never learned to say such fine words," said the baroness, turning to Petritsky.

"Is that so? Well, after dinner I'll match him."

"But after dinner doesn't count. Well, I'll pour you some coffee. Go, wash and change," said the baroness, resuming her seat and carefully opening the new coffee pot. "Pierre, hand me some more coffee," she said, turning to Petritsky. She called him Pierre, deriving it from his surname Petritsky, without any attempt to hide their relationship. "I'll add some to the pot."

"You'll ruin it."

"No, I won't. Well, how is your wife?" suddenly asked the baroness, interrupting Vronsky's conversation with his friend. "We have married you off here. Have you brought your wife with you?"

"No, baroness. I was born a gypsy and I'll die a gypsy."

"So much the better, so much the better. Give me your hand."

The baroness would not let Vronsky go and began telling him of her latest plans and asking his advice, all the time interspersing her conversation with jesting remarks.

"He still refuses to give me a divorce. Well, what can I do?" (*He* was her husband.) "I have decided to bring suit against him. What would you advise? Kamerovsky, watch the coffee. . . . He has left. You see how busy I am? I want to bring suit against him, because I need my property. You know the foolish things they say about me, that I'm unfaithful to him," she said contemptuously, "and that's why he wants to take my property away from me."

Vronsky listened with pleasure to the gay chatter of this pretty woman, nodded encouragingly, gave her half-serious advice, and in general quickly assumed his usual manner in dealing with women of this kind. To him the members of the Petersburg world belonged to two distinct groups. One was the lower group, to which belonged the common, stupid, and, what is more, the ridiculous types, who believed that a husband should live with only one wife, the one he had married, that a girl should be chaste, a woman modest, a man manly, self-disciplined and steadfast, that children must be educated, one's living earned, debts paid, and other such nonsense. This was the old-fashioned, ridiculous group. But there was another group of real people, to which all of his circle belonged, where it was important only to be elegant, handsome, generous, brave, and gay, and where one could yield to any passion without blushing and laugh at everything else.

Still under the impression of the completely different world he had found in Moscow, Vronsky at first felt utterly confused, but this lasted only for a moment, and, as if putting on his old slippers, he re-entered his former gay and pleasant world.

In spite of everything, there was no coffee. It spattered everyone as it overflowed, but by causing roars of laughter and by soiling the expensive rug and the baroness' dress, it served its purpose.

"Well, now I must say goodbye, or you'll never wash and my conscience will be burdened by the worst crime a well-bred man may commit, that of being unclean. Would you advise me to put a knife to his throat?"

"By all means, and see that your little hand touches his lips. He will kiss your little hand, and everything will end well."

"Well, I'll see you at the French theater tonight," she said, and, her dress rustling, she disappeared.

Kamerovsky also rose, and Vronsky, without waiting for him to leave, shook hands with him and went into his dressing room. While he washed, Petritsky described in a few words his present state, which had changed so drastically since Vronsky's departure. He was absolutely penniless. His father would not give him any money and refused to pay his debts. The tailor wanted to sue him, and someone else threatened to do the same. The commander of the regiment had declared that unless these excesses were halted, he would have to resign. He was sick and tired of the baroness, particularly because she always insisted on giving him money. And there was a charming creature here, he would show her to Vronsky, a marvel, in the classic Oriental style, "in the genre of Rebecca's servant, you know." He had quarrelled with Berkoshev yesterday and intended to send his seconds, but, of course, nothing would come of it. But in general everything was fine and most pleasant. Petritsky did not let his friend inquire too deeply into the details of his situation, and began telling him all the interesting news. Listening to Petritsky's familiar stories in this familiar setting, in the apartment that he had occupied for the past three years, Vronsky experienced the pleasant sensation of returning to the customary, carefree way of life in Petersburg.

"It's impossible!" he cried, releasing the pedal of the washstand at which he was washing his healthy, ruddy neck. "It's impossible!" he cried, on hearing that Lora had dropped Fertinhof and gone over to Mileiev. "Is he still as stupid and contented? Well, what about Buzulukov?"

"Ah! Listen to what happened to Buzulukov. What a story!" cried Petritsky. "You know how crazy he is about balls, and how he doesn't miss a single court ball. He went to the grand ball wearing his new helmet. Have you seen these new helmets? Very comfortable, much lighter. Well, there he stood. . . . But listen to me."

"I'm listening," replied Vronsky, drying himself with a rough towel.

"The grand duchess passed by with some ambassador, and to his bad luck, their conversation touched on the new helmets. The grand duchess wanted to show the ambassador the new helmet. . . . They saw our friend standing there." (Petritsky mimicked him standing there in his helmet.) "The grand duchess asked him to hand her his helmet, but he refused. What happened? They winked at him, they nodded at him, they frowned at him. 'Let us have the helmet,' they said. He still refused, standing there as if frozen. You can easily imagine. . . . But he . . . what's his name . . . tried to grab the helmet, but he still held on to it. At last he snatched it and handed it to the grand duchess. 'Here is the new-style helmet,' says the grand duchess. She turned the helmet over, and, just imagine. Plop! Out fell a pear, candy, two pounds of candy, to which our friend had helped himself."

Vronsky burst into laughter. And for a long time after, as they discussed different subjects, when he recalled the story of the new helmet, he laughed heartily, showing his strong, even teeth.

After hearing all the news, Vronsky put on his uniform with

who had seen life, was endowed with good health, and was not a fool, he did not believe in medicine, and in his heart he was vexed by this comedy, the more so because probably he alone knew the real cause of Kitty's illness. Some cackler! he thought, borrowing this name from the hunters' vocabulary and applying it to the renowned doctor as he listened to his prattle about the symptoms of his daughter's illness. The doctor, on the other hand, could scarcely conceal his contempt for this old gent and had to exert himself to stoop to his low intellectual level. He understood that there was no use in talking to this old man, and that the mother was the head of the family. It was before her that he intended to cast his pearls. At that moment the old princess and the family doctor came into the room. The prince stepped aside. He did not want to show them how ridiculous this comedy appeared to him. The princess was puzzled and did not know what to do. She felt guilty before Kitty.

"Well, Doctor, our fate is in your hands," said the princess. "Tell me everything." She was going to add, Is there any hope? but her lips trembled and she could not utter this question. "Well, doctor?"

"One minute, Princess. I will just exchange a few words with my colleague, and then I will have the honor to report my findings to you."

"Should I leave you?"

"As you wish."

The princess sighed and walked out.

When the doctors remained alone, the family doctor timidly began to expound his opinion. He considered that this was the beginning of a tubercular infection, but . . . and so on. The renowned doctor listened to him, and in the middle of the speech looked at his massive gold watch.

"Yes," he said, "but. . . ."

The family doctor respectfully fell silent in the middle of his speech.

"You know that we cannot ascertain the beginning of a tubercular infection. There is nothing definite about it before the lung tissue is damaged. Yet we may suspect it. And there are symptoms of it: impaired nutrition, nervous excitation, and so on. The problem is this: when a tubercular infection is suspected, what must be done to sustain nutrition?"

"But as you know, some other causes, moral or emotional,

always underlie such cases," the family doctor dared to interject with a subtle smile.

"Yes, of course," replied the renowned doctor, again looking at his watch. "Pardon me. Is the bridge over Yausa repaired, or do we still have to make a detour?" he asked. "Ah, it is repaired. Then I may be there within twenty minutes. Just as you were saying, the problem is this: how to sustain nutrition and ease nervous tension. One is related to the other, and we must treat both simultaneously."

"How about a trip abroad?" asked the family doctor.

"I am opposed to such trips. And here is why, if you please: if a tubercular infection has set in, something we cannot ascertain, then a trip abroad will not help. A remedy is needed, one that will sustain nutrition and will do no harm."

And the renowned doctor expounded his method of treatment with Soden waters. The main reason for prescribing them, it seemed, was that they were harmless.

The family doctor listened to him attentively and respectfully.

"Yet I would mention some advantages of a trip abroad, such as a change from surroundings that are connected with unpleasant memories, and a new daily routine. Moreover, the mother is anxious to go," he said.

"Ah! In that case, well, let them go. But those German charlatans may do harm. . . . They must follow. . . . Well, let them go."

He looked at his watch again.

"Oh, it's time," he said, and went to the door.

The renowned doctor declared to the princess that he must again see the patient (decorum demanded it).

"What! Another examination!" exclaimed the horrified mother.

"Oh, no. Just a few details, Princess."

"As you wish."

The princess, followed by the doctor, entered the drawing room. Kitty stood in the middle of the room. She was thin, her eyes gleamed strangely, and her face was flushed with the shame she had endured. When the doctor entered she flared up, and her eyes filled with tears. All her illness and its treatment seemed to her so foolish, even laughable. The treatment seemed to her as ridiculous as an attempt to put together fragments of a broken vase. Her heart was broken. What use were the treatments, the pills and the powders? But she could not hurt her mother, especially since her mother believed that it was all her fault.

"Will you kindly sit down, Princess," said the renowned doctor to Kitty.

Smiling, he sat down facing her, took her pulse, and resumed his tedious questioning. She answered him, then suddenly grew angry and rose.

"Forgive me, Doctor, but, truly, all this is of no use. You have already asked me the same questions three times."

The renowned doctor was not offended.

"Nervous tension," he told the princess, when Kitty left. "But I am through anyway. . . ."

And, addressing the princess as a person of exceptional understanding, the doctor expounded to her the scientific aspects of Kitty's case and concluded with instructions on how to take the waters, something completely useless. Asked whether they should make the trip abroad, the doctor fell into deep thought, as if trying to solve a complicated problem. At last he announced his decision: they should make the trip, but they should be wary of those charlatans, and they should .pply to him for any advice.

Everybody felt relieved when the doctor left. The mother felt cheerful as she came back to her daughter, and Kitty also made believe that she had cheered up. Lately, she had to pretend often, almost always.

"Truly, *Maman*, I am well. But if you want to, let's go," she said. Trying to prove that she was interested in the forthcoming trip, she began discussing all the necessary preparations for it.

2

IMMEDIATELY AFTER the doctor's departure, Dolly arrived. She knew there was going to be a medical consultation that day, and though she had only recently left the confinement bed (she had given birth to a daughter at the end of the winter) and though she had troubles and cares of her own, she left an infant and a sick girl at home in order to come and inquire about Kitty's fate, which was to be decided that day.

"Well, what news is there?" she asked, entering the drawing room without taking off her hat. "You all look so cheerful. All is well, I hope!"

They tried to tell her what the doctor had said, but it seemed that although the doctor had spoken flowingly and at length, no one really could tell what he had said. The most interesting news was that it had been decided that they should go abroad.

Dolly sighed unwittingly. Her sister, who was her best friend, was going to leave. Hers was an unhappy life. Her relationship with Stepan Arkadievich after the reconciliation had become humiliating. The repair made by Anna proved short-lived, and family peace had broken down again, and on the same grounds. Although she had no definite grounds for suspecting him of infidelity, Stepan Arkadievich was almost never at home, there was almost never enough money in the house, and Dolly was constantly tormented by suspicion. Now, however, she tried to rid herself of it, remembering the tortures of jealousy she had suffered. That first fit of jealousy, once experienced, could not be repeated. Even the discovery of his infidelity could not affect her now as it had the first time. Such a discovery would now only disrupt her family life, and she yielded to self-deception, despising him and, most of all, herself for her weakness. Moreover, she was always beset by worries about her large family: either she had trouble with the infant's feeding, or the nurse left her, or, as now, one of the children fell sick.

"Well, how is your family?" asked her mother.

"Ah, *Maman*, we too have our troubles. Lily is sick, and I'm afraid it's scarlet fever. I've purposely come to find out what has happened, because if it is scarlet fever, God forbid, I shall be confined to the house."

After the doctor had left, the old prince also came out from his study, offered Dolly his cheek, exchanged a few words with her, and turning to his wife, said:

"What have you decided? Are you going? And what are you going to do about me?"

"I believe that it's best for you to remain here, Aleksandr."

"As you wish."

"*Maman*, why shouldn't Father come with us?" asked Kitty. "He would be happier, and we would, too."

The old man rose and stroked Kitty's hair. She raised her face and looked at him, forcing a smile. She always believed that he understood her better than anyone else in the family, though he spoke little about her. The youngest child, she was her father's pet, and it seemed to her that his love for her gave him special understanding. When she saw the look in his kind, blue eyes, which were fixed on her, it seemed to her that he saw through her and perceived all the wickedness within her. Blushing, she leaned toward him, hoping to be kissed. But he just tugged gently at her hair and said:

"These stupid chignons! You want to touch your own daughter, and instead you stroke some dead peasant woman's hair. Well, Dolinka," he said, turning to his older daughter, "what is your hero up to?"

"Nothing, Papa," replied Dolly, understanding that he was referring to her husband. "He's always going somewhere; I almost never see him," she could not help adding with a sarcastic smile.

"He still hasn't gone to the country to sell the timber?"

"He's still getting ready to do it."

"Is that so!" said the prince. "Well, shall I get ready, too? As you wish," he said, turning to his wife, and sat down. "Now, then, Katya," he added, again turning to his youngest daughter, "some day you must wake up and say to yourself, 'I am really all well and happy, and will take a walk again with Papa early on this frosty morning.' Well?"

Everything her father said seemed so simple, but at these words Kitty grew utterly confused, as if caught in some shameful act. Yes, she thought, he knows everything, understands everything, and he's telling me that though ashamed, one should overcome the shame. She could not gather the courage to reply to him. She tried to say something, but suddenly burst into tears and ran out of the room.

"See what your jokes lead to!" cried the princess, berating her husband. "You always! . . ." and she launched into a reproachful tirade.

For quite a while the prince kept silent and listened to the princess' reproaches, the gloom on his face deepening.

"She's so pitiful, the poor thing, so pitiful. And you don't know how painful it is to her to be reminded of the reason. Ah, how wrong you can be about people!" said the princess, and by the change in her tone both Dolly and the prince knew that she was now talking about Vronsky. "I'm surprised that there are no laws against such loathsome, ignoble people."

"Oh, I wish I didn't have to listen to this," the prince said gloomily. He rose from his chair and was going to leave, but stopped at the door. "There are laws, Mother, and since you have brought me to it, I'll tell you whose fault all this is: yours, and yours alone. There are and there always have been laws against such fellows. Yes, if things were as they should be, I myself, old man that I am, would challenge this dandy. And now go ahead and cure her. Call in all these charlatans."

The prince, it seemed, had more to say, but as soon as the princess heard the tone of his voice, she immediately shrank and repented her words, as she always did in her serious discussions with her husband.

"Alexandre, Alexandre," she whispered, fidgeting and finally bursting into tears.

At the sight of her tears, the prince grew silent. He came over to her.

"Well, that's enough, that's enough! I know how hard it is on you, too. What can we do? It's not such a great misfortune. God is merciful . . . thank you . . ." he said, without knowing what he was saying, in reply to the princess' tearful kiss which he felt on his hand. Then he left the room.

Dolly's maternal and family experience had immediately told her that this was a matter for women to decide. She had known it ever since Kitty had left the room in tears, and now she was ready to do her part. She took off her hat and figuratively rolled up her sleeves, ready for action. During her mother's attack upon her father, she attempted to restrain her within the limits permitted a respectful daughter. At her father's outburst she kept silent. She was embarrassed for her mother and felt tenderly toward her father for the good nature to which he had immediately reverted. But when her father had left, she was ready to do what was most important: to see Kitty and to calm her.

"I've wanted to tell you something for a long time, *Maman*. Do you know that Levin was going to propose to Kitty when he was here last? He told Stiva."

"What of it? I don't understand. . . ."

"Perhaps Kitty refused him. . . . Did she say anything to you about it?"

"No, she didn't tell me anything about one or the other; she's too proud. But I know that this was the cause. . . ."

"Yes, just imagine. She refused Levin, and I know that she wouldn't have refused him but for the other one, and then that other one so cruelly deceived her."

The princess dreaded to think how much she had wronged her daughter, and she grew angry.

"Oh, nothing makes sense! Now they all want to live their own lives, they don't tell their mothers anything, and then. . . ."

"*Maman,* I'm going to see her."

"Go. I won't stop you," said her mother.

3

As SHE ENTERED Kitty's small room, pretty and rose-colored, with its small *vieux-saxe* dolls, as pretty, rosy, and gay as Kitty herself had been only two months ago, Dolly remembered how the two of them had fitted out this room last year with such love and pleasure. Her heart sank when she saw Kitty sitting in a low chair next to the door, her eyes motionless, staring at the corner of the rug. Kitty looked up at her sister, and the cold, somewhat stern expression on her face did not change.

"I'm leaving soon. I'll be confined to my house, and you won't be able to see me," said Daria Aleksandrovna, sitting down near her. "I do so want to talk to you."

"About what?" Kitty asked quickly, raising her head in alarm.

"Is there anything to talk about but your sorrow?"

"I have no sorrow."

"Come now, Kitty. Do you really think that I don't know? I know everything. And believe me, it's all so insignificant. . . . We've all gone through it."

Kitty kept silent and looked stern.

"He's not worth your suffering," continued Daria Aleksandrovna, getting to the heart of the matter.

"Is it because he slighted me?" said Kitty in a trembling voice. "Don't talk about it! Please don't talk about it!"

"But who told you that? No one said so. I'm sure that he was in love with you and still is, but—"

"Oh, I'm sick and tired of these condolences," cried Kitty, suddenly flaring up. She turned in her chair, her face flushed. She twisted a belt she was holding in her fingers, squeezing the buckle first in one hand, then in the other. Dolly knew this habit of her sister's, to pass objects from hand to hand when in a state of excitement. She knew that at such moments

Kitty was prone to be carried away by her anger and to say many uncalled for and unpleasant words. Dolly wanted to calm her, but it was too late.

"What are you suggesting?" Kitty asked quickly. "That I was in love with a man who did not want me, and that I'm now dying of love for him? Can these be the words of my sister who thinks that . . . that . . . she sympathizes with me? I don't want this sympathy and this sham."

"Kitty, you're unjust."

"Why are you torturing me?"

"On the contrary. . . . I see that you're suffering. . . ."

But in her excitement Kitty would not listen to her.

"I have nothing to break my heart over and nothing to be consoled for. I feel too proud to permit myself to love a man who doesn't love me."

"But I never said you did. . . . One more thing. Tell me the truth," said Daria Aleksandrovna, taking her hand. "Did Levin propose to you?"

At the sound of Levin's name, Kitty seemed to lose all self-control. She jumped up from the chair, threw the buckle on the floor, and, gesturing rapidly, said:

"But what has Levin to do with it? I can't understand why you like to torture me. I've told you and tell you again that I am proud and never, *never* will do as you do. You go back to a man who was unfaithful to you and who has fallen in love with another woman. I cannot, cannot understand this. You can do it, but not I."

With these words she looked at her sister. Dolly was silent and bowed her head sadly. Kitty was about to leave, but instead sat down at the door, lowered her head, and buried her face in her handkerchief.

The silence lasted for about two minutes. Dolly thought about herself. The humiliation she constantly felt was particularly painful now, when she was reminded of it by her sister. She had not expected such cruelty from her sister, and she was angry with her. But at that moment she heard the rustle of a dress and the burst of muffled sobs, and two hands entwined her neck from below. Kitty was kneeling in front of her.

"Dolinka, I'm so unhappy," she said in a guilty whisper, and buried her lovely face, moist with tears, in Daria Aleksandrovna's skirt.

It seemed that tears were the lubricant without which the

machinery of mutual communication between the two sisters could not properly function. After the tears had been shed, the sisters spoke no longer about those matters which bothered them. But even while speaking about irrelevant matters, they knew that they understood each other. Kitty knew that her poor sister was deeply hurt by her harsh words about her husband's infidelity and her profound humiliation, but she knew that Dolly had forgiven her. Dolly, on the other hand, now knew everything she had wanted to know. She was convinced that she had guessed right and that Levin had proposed to Kitty, that she had refused him, that Vronsky had deceived her, and that she was now prepared to love Levin and hate Vronsky, and that all this was the cause of Kitty's sorrow, her unconsolable sorrow. Kitty did not say a word about all this; she spoke only about her emotional state.

"I have no sorrow," she said, calming down, "I would like you to understand how abhorrent, repugnant, and mean, everything, most of all myself, seems to me now. You can't imagine how vile my present thoughts are."

"But what kind of vile thoughts could you have?" Dolly asked with a smile.

"The vilest and meanest. I can't explain it to you. It's neither depression nor boredom, but something much worse. It's as if everything that was good within me has disappeared, and only my vileness remains. How can I make it clear to you?" she continued, seeing how puzzled her sister looked. "Papa was just talking to me . . . it seems that he thinks only about one thing: that I must get married. Mother takes me to the balls, and it seems that she takes me there with one purpose only, to marry me off as soon as possible and get rid of me. I know it isn't true, but I can't rid myself of these thoughts. The so-called bridegrooms I cannot stand. I have a feeling that they just appraise me. Formerly it was sheer delight to go somewhere dressed in an evening gown, and I admired myself, but now I'm ashamed and embarrassed. Well, what can I do? The doctor . . . well. . . ."

Kitty stopped in confusion. She wanted to add that ever since that change had taken place in her, she could not bear the presence of Stepan Arkadievich, and that when she saw him she could not help thinking what seemed to her the vilest and the meanest thoughts.

"Yes, everything appears to me in the vilest and meanest

guise," she continued. "This is the nature of my illness.
Perhaps it will pass. . . ."

"But try not to think about it. . . ."

"I can't. I feel at ease only with the children, only at your
house."

"It's a pity that you won't be able to come to see me."

"No, I'll come. I had scarlet fever, and I'll talk *Maman*
into it."

Kitty had her way, moved to her sister's, and took care of
the children during the whole course of the scarlet fever,
which they had contracted as had been expected. Under the
care of both sisters, all six children recovered fully, but Kitty's
health did not improve. During Lent the Shcherbatskys went
abroad.

4

THERE WAS ACTUALLY only one group in Petersburg high
society: everyone knew everyone else and visited each other.
But this large group had its subdivisions. Anna Arkadievna
Karenina's friends and acquaintances belonged to three different circles. The first was her husband's official circle, which
comprised his colleagues and subordinates, who, in their
social relationships, were either bound or separated in the
most diverse and whimsical way. Anna could now scarcely
recollect the feeling of almost reverent respect she had
formerly held these people in. She knew all of them, now, as
well as people come to know each other in a small town. She
knew their habits and weaknesses, knew where the shoe
pinched one foot or another. She knew their relationships to
each other and to the center of the circle. She knew who was
dependent on whom and to what degree, and who agreed or
disagreed with whom and on what points. But this was a
circle of officials, of men whose interests she never shared,
and she avoided this circle in spite of Countess Lydia
Ivanovna's admonitions.

Another circle, with which Anna Arkadievna was closely
connected, was one that helped Aleksei Aleksandrovich in
his career. The center of this circle was Countess Lydia
Ivanovna. This group comprised old, ugly, virtuous, and de-
vout women, and learned, clever, ambitious men. One of the

clever members of this circle called it "the conscience of Petersburg society." Aleksei Aleksandrovich valued this circle highly, and Anna, who could get along so well with everyone, found friends even in this circle during the early period of her life in Petersburg. But now, after her return from Moscow, she found this circle unbearable. It seemed to her that they were all hypocrites, including herself, and she became so bored and ill at ease in this group that she visited Lydia Ivanovna as rarely as possible.

The third and last circle with which she was connected was the true elite. Theirs was a world of balls, dinners, and glittering toilettes. The elite clung to the court so that it might not descend to the level of the lower circle. Its members fancied that they despised those of the lower circle, but actually the tastes of both were not similar but identical. Anna was connected with this circle through the wife of her cousin, Princess Betsy Tverskoy, who had a yearly income of a hundred and twenty thousand rubles. Betsy took a particular liking to Anna from her first appearance in society, looked after her, and drew her into her own circle, deriding Lydia Ivanovna's circle.

"When I get old and ugly, I'll become like them," Betsy would say, "but for you, young and pretty as you are, it's too early to enter that old people's home."

At first, Anna avoided Princess Tverskoy's circle as much as she could because it involved her in expense above her means, and the first circle had more appeal to her. But after the trip to Moscow, her attitude changed. She avoided her pious friends and frequented this elite group. Here she often met Vronsky, and at these meetings she felt the thrill of joy. Most often she met Vronsky at Betsy's, who was born a Vronsky and was his cousin. Vronsky went everywhere he could meet Anna and, when he could, he spoke to her of his love. She never invited it, but whenever she met him, the same vivacity kindled in her heart as on that day in the railroad car when she saw him for the first time. She herself felt that at the sight of him, joy shone in her eyes and curved her lips into a smile, and she could not conceal the signs of this joy.

He permitted himself to seek her company, and in the beginning Anna believed sincerely that this annoyed her. But soon after her return from Moscow, when she came to a party where she had expected him but did not find him, she felt sad. This plainly proved to her that she was deceiving herself, that not only was she not displeased that he sought her company but it was now the chief interest in her life.

A celebrated singer was giving her second concert, and all of the elite turned out. From his seat in the first row, Vronsky noticed his cousin, and without waiting for the intermission, he went up to her box.

"Why didn't you come for dinner? I admire this clairvoyance of the enamored," she said, and added, smiling, so that only he could hear her words: "*She was not there.* But come after the performance."

Vronsky looked at her questioningly. She lowered her head. He thanked her with a smile and sat near her.

"How well I remember your sarcastic comments," continued Princess Betsy, who took particular pleasure in following the course of this love affair. "Where are they now? You are trapped, my friend!"

"But I could wish for nothing better than to be trapped," answered Vronsky with his quiet, good-natured smile. "And to tell the truth, my complaint is that I'm not fully trapped yet. I'm beginning to lose hope."

"But what hope could you have?" said Betsy, feeling offended for her friend. "*Entendons nous.*" But the sparkle in her eyes showed that she understood as well as he what hope he could have.

"None," replied Vronsky, smiling and showing his even teeth. "Excuse me," he added, and taking the binoculars from her hand, he scanned the opposite tier of boxes over her bare shoulder. "I'm afraid I'm becoming ridiculous."

He knew very well that he was in no danger of appearing ridiculous, either in the eyes of Betsy or of the other members of their group. He knew very well that in the eyes of these people, the role of an unfortunate lover of a girl or of an unmarried woman in general might seem ridiculous. But the role of a man who pursued a married woman, and who had set as the firm purpose of his life to entice her into adultery, could never look ridiculous; there was something beautiful and majestic about it. Therefore, with a proud and gay smile playing under his mustache, he lowered the binoculars and looked at his cousin.

"Why didn't you come for dinner?" she asked, looking at him with admiration.

"I must tell you the story. I was busy, but you know with what? You'd never, never guess. I tried to make peace between a husband and a man who had insulted his wife. I really did."

"Well, did you succeed?"

"Almost."

"You must tell me the whole story," she said, rising. "Come back during the intermission."

"I can't. I'm going to the French theater."

"After Nielson?" asked Betsy with horror, although she actually would not have known the difference between Nielson and a chorus girl.

"What can I do? I must meet someone there in connection with this peacemaking affair."

" 'Blessed are the peacemakers, for they shall be saved,' " said Betsy, repeating words that, it seemed to her she had heard from someone. "Well, sit down and tell me all about it."

And she resumed her seat.

5

"It is somewhat risqué, but so charming that I am terribly anxious to tell it," said Vronsky, looking at her with his smiling eyes. "I'll not mention any names."

"But I'll guess them, which is still better."

"Now listen. Two cheerful young men are riding—"

"Officers of your regiment, of course?"

"I'm not saying that they were officers, just two young men who have had their lunch—"

"In other words, tipsy."

"Perhaps. They are going to have dinner with a friend, and they are in the happiest frame of mind. They see a pretty lady passing in a cab. She turns around and beckons and smiles at them, at least so it seems to them. They follow her, of course, galloping with all their might. To their surprise, the beauty stops at the entrance of the same house to which they are headed. The beauty runs up to the top floor. All they see is her rosy lips under the short veil, and her pretty little feet."

"You're telling it with such feeling that it seems to me that you were one of those two!"

"And what did you tell me a minute ago? Well, our young men enter their friend's apartment. He's giving a farewell dinner, and here, of course, they have a few drinks, perhaps a few too many, as always happens at farewell dinners. And at the dinner they ask who lives on the top floor. Nobody knows, and when they ask the servant whether any *mademoiselles* live upstairs, he answers that there are many of them here. After dinner our young men enter their host's study and write a letter to the mysterious lady. It is a passionate letter, a declaration of love, and they themselves go upstairs to deliver the letter and to explain what the letter might not make perfectly clear."

"Why are you telling me such awful things? Go on!"

"They ring the bell. A maid comes out, they give her the letter and assure the maid that they are so deeply enamored that they are going to die right now, here at the door. The maid is puzzled and argues with them. Suddenly a gentleman with sausage-shaped whiskers emerges, red as a lobster, declares that nobody but he and his wife live in this apartment, and throws them out."

"And how do you know that this gentleman, as you say, had sausage-shaped whiskers?"

"But listen. Today I went to make peace."

"Well, what happened?"

"We're coming to the point of the story. It turns out that this is a happy couple, a titular councilor and his spouse. The titular councilor registers a complaint. I become peacemaker, and what a peacemaker! I assure you that Talleyrand couldn't compare with me."

"And why was it so difficult?"

"You just listen. . . . We apologize deeply. 'We are heartbroken; we ask forgiveness for this unfortunate misunderstanding.' The titular councilor with his sausage-shaped whiskers begins to melt, but wants to express his own feelings, and as soon as he begins expressing them, grows excited and abusive, and again I must use all my diplomatic gifts. 'I admit that they acted badly, but please take into consideration their youth and inexperience. Moreover, the young men had just lunched. You understand. They repent with all their hearts, and ask you to forgive them for what they have done.' The titular councilor softens again. 'I agree with you, Count. I am ready to forgive, but you understand, my wife, an honorable lady, is subjected to abuse, harassment, and insolence from some rascals, some. . . .' And, you understand, that young scoundrel is right there and I have to make peace between them. Again I resort to my diplomatic gifts, and again, as the case nears its conclusion, the titular councilor blows up, reddens, his whiskers bristle, and again I'm a model of subtle diplomacy."

"Oh, I must tell you this story," said Betsy with a laugh to a lady who was just entering the box. "He's so amusing."

"Well, *bonne chance*," she added, extending to Vronsky the one finger of her hand not occupied in holding her fan. With a shrug of her shoulders, she lowered the bodice of her dress in order to be uncovered as much as possible when she moved up to the railing and appeared under the gaslight and in full view of the public.

Vronsky went to the French theater, where he had to see his regimental commander, who never missed an evening in the French theater. He wanted to talk to him about his peacemaking mission, which had occupied and amused him for the past three days. Petritsky, whom he loved, and young Prince Kedrov, a fine fellow and good comrade who had recently joined their regiment, were implicated in this affair. But, what was more important, it involved the honor of the regiment.

Both men belonged to Vronsky's squadron. The official, Titular Councilor Venden, had come to see the regimental commander and had registered a complaint against the officers who had insulted his wife. His young wife, explained Venden (he had been married for half a year), was in church with her mother when she suddenly felt ill—something which happens to ladies in a certain condition—and, no longer able to stand, left for home in the first better-grade cab that came by. Then, pursued by the officers and taking fright, she ran up the staircase, and this worsened her condition. When Venden came home from his office, he heard the bell and some voices, came into the entrance hall, saw drunken officers with a letter, and threw them out. He insisted on strict punishment.

"You must admit," said the regimental commander to Vronsky, when he had come to his house at the commander's invitation, "that Petritsky is becoming impossible. Not a week passes without some scandal. This official will not leave the matter as it stands; he will appeal to higher echelons."

Vronsky saw how improper all this looked, knew that in this case a duel was out of the question, and that all efforts had to be made to mollify this titular councilor and hush up the whole affair. The regimental commander summoned Vronsky precisely because he knew what an honorable and clever man he was and, what was most important, how highly he prized the honor of the regiment, After a short consultation they decided that Petritsky and Kedrov, together with Vronsky, would visit the titular councilor and apologize to him. But both the regimental commander and Vronsky understood that Vronsky's name and the emblems of an aide-de-camp on his uniform would be of great help in appeasing the titular councilor. And indeed, these two factors did prove effective to some degree, but the final conclusion of peace was not certain yet, as Vronsky had explained.

When Vronsky arrived at the French theater, he went into a corner of the lobby with the regimental commander and there reported his mixed success. After deliberation, the regimental commander decided to leave the matter as it stood, but for his own amusement he inquired of Vronsky about the details of the interview. For a long time he could not restrain his laughter as he listened to Vronsky relate how the mollified titular councilor would suddenly become furious when he recalled the details of the affair, and how Vronsky, taking advantage of the shaky truce he had at last established, retreated, pushing Petritsky ahead of him.

"A nasty affair, but not without humor. It is unthinkable to have Kedrov fight this gentleman! So he was furious?" he asked again, laughing. "And what do you say about Claire? She is marvelous today!" he said, referring to the new French actress. "She has a fresh appeal no matter how often you see her. Leave it to the French."

6

PRINCESS BETSY left the theater without waiting for the last act. She scarcely had time to enter her dressing room, powder her long pale face and remove the excess, fix her hair, and order tea to be served in the large drawing room, when one coach after another began rolling up at her vast house on Bolshaya Morskaya. The guests emerged onto the wide porch, and the corpulent doorman, who in the mornings read a newspaper behind the glass door to impress the passers-by, noise-lessly opened the enormous door to let the guests in.

Almost at the same time as the hostess opened her door, her hair rearranged and face refreshed, the guests came in through the other one. They entered the large drawing room with its somber walls, thick rugs, and brilliantly lighted table. The white tablecloth, the silver samovar, and the transparent por-celain of the tea service sparkled in the bright light of the candles.

The hostess sat down at the samovar and took off her gloves. The servants inconspicuously moved up chairs, and the guests took their seats and separated into two groups: one was near the hostess at the samovar, the other at the opposite side of the drawing room, around an ambassador's wife, a beautiful wom-an in black velvet and with black, sharply outlined eyebrows. In both groups the conversation wavered as if seeking the right topic, as it usually does in the first few minutes of a soirée; the banter was interrupted by greetings, exclamations, and offers of tea.

"She's an excellent actress. You can see that she has studied Kaulbach thoroughly," said a diplomat in the group around the ambassador's wife. "Did you notice the way she fell? . . ."

"Oh, please, let's not talk about Nielson! You can't say any-thing new about her," said a stout, red-faced, fair-haired lady, who had no eyebrows, wore no chignon, and was dressed in an old silk dress. This was Princess Miakhky, known for the blunt-ness and rudeness of her speech, and nicknamed *Enfant Ter-rible.* Princess Miakhky sat between the two groups, listened to both of them, and took part in the conversation of both alternately. "I've heard this same reference to Kaulbach tonight from three different men, as though they had all agreed to repeat it. And I don't know why they are so taken with it."

This remark interrupted the conversation, and a new topic had to be introduced.

"Tell me something amusing but not malicious," said the ambassador's wife, skilled at the type of elegant conversation that the English call "small talk." She had addressed the dip-lomat, who, like the rest of the group, did not know how to begin.

"I believe that would be quite difficult: they say only malice is amusing," he began with a smile. "But I will try. Mention a subject. It all depends on the subject. If the subject is given, it is easy to develop. I often think that the famous conversationalists of the last century would find it hard to speak cleverly today. We are tired of all this clever talk."

"That was said a long time ago," interrupted the ambassador's wife, laughing.

The conversation had begun on a pleasant note, perhaps too pleasant, for it stopped for this very reason. The group had to resort to that time-tested, never-failing device—gossip.

"Don't you think Tushkevich has something of Louis XV about him?" he asked, indicating with his eyes a handsome, fair-haired young man who was standing at the table.

"Oh, yes! He is the same style as this drawing room, that's why he comes here often."

The conversation continued, for it was made up of hints at a matter which could not be mentioned in this drawing room, namely, the relationship between Tushkevich and the lady of of the house.

In the meantime, the conversation at the samovar also wavered for some time between three unavoidable topics: the latest society news, the theater, and gossip about friends. Finally it settled on the last, on gossip.

"Have you heard that Maltishchev—not the daughter, but the mother—has ordered for herself a suit of *diable rose*?"

"You don't say! How charming!"

"I'm surprised—she is so clever; she's far from a fool—that she doesn't see how ridiculous she is."

Everybody had something to add to this condemnation and ridicule of the unfortunate Madame Maltishchev, and the conversation crackled as gaily as a blazing bonfire.

Princess Betsy's husband, a good-natured, corpulent man, an ardent collector of engravings, hearing that his wife had visitors, came into the drawing room before leaving for his club. Noiselessly walking on the soft rug, he came over to Princess Miakhky.

"How did you like Nielson?" he asked.

"Oh, why did you steal up so softly? You frightened me," she answered. "Please do not talk to me about opera; you understand nothing about music. I would rather stoop to your level and talk about your majolica and engravings. Well, what treasures have you brought recently at the flea market?"

"Would you like me to show it to you? But you know nothing about such things."

"Show it to me. I have learned something from those bankers

. . . what's their name . . . they have some beautiful engravings. They showed them to me."

"Don't tell me that you've been to the Schützburgs'?" asked her hostess, who was at the samovar.

"I have, *ma chère*. They invited my husband and me to dinner, and I was told that the sauce served at that dinner cost a thousand rubles," said Princess Miakhky in a loud voice, aware that everyone was listening to her. "But it was a terrible sauce, something green. Then I had to invite them. I prepared a sauce that cost me eighty-five kopecks, and everyone was happy. These thousand-ruble sauces are not for me."

"She's unique!" said the hostess.

"Remarkable!" said someone else.

The effect produced by Princess Miakhky's words was always the same. She spoke on simple, common-sense subjects, although, as in the present case, not always to the point, and in this lay the secret of the effect that her words always had. In the society she lived in these words had the same effect as the wittiest of jokes. Princess Miakhky could not understand why they had such an effect, but she knew that they did, and she made use of it.

Since everyone had listened to Princess Miakhky tell her story, and the conversation around the ambassador's wife had stopped, the hostess tried to unite the two circles. Turning to the ambassador's wife, she said:

"Are you sure you don't want any tea? Come over to us."

"No, we're fine here," answered the ambassador's wife with a smile, and she resumed the conversation they had begun.

It was a pleasant conversation. They passed judgment on the Karenins, husband and wife.

"Anna's changed a great deal since her trip to Moscow. There's something strange about her," said her friend.

"The main change is that she brought the shadow of Aleksei Vronsky with her," said the ambassador's wife.

"But what of it? Grimm wrote a tale about a man who had no shadow, whose shadow had been taken from him. It was his punishment for something he'd done. I never could understand what kind of punishment that would be. But it must be very unpleasant for a woman to have no shadow."

"True enough, but women followed by a shadow always come to a bad end," said Anna's friend.

"Bite your tongue," suddenly exclaimed Princess Miakhky

on hearing these words. "Karenina is a fine woman. I don't like her husband, but I like her very much."

"Why don't you like her husband? He's such a remarkable person," said the ambassador's wife. "My husband says there are few such statesmen in Europe."

"My husband says the same, but I don't believe him," said Princess Miakhky. "But for our husbands' talk, we would see things as they really are, and Aleksei Aleksandrovich, in my opinion, is just plain stupid. I say this in a whisper. . . . Isn't it true that everything becomes clear? Earlier, when they would have had me believe that he was clever, I kept searching for what was so clever about him; I found nothing and decided that I must be stupid. But as soon as I told myself, in a whisper, 'he is stupid,' everything became clear, don't you see?"

"How nasty you are today!"

"Not at all. I have no choice. One of us is stupid. And, you know, nobody wants to admit it about himself."

" 'No one is satisfied with his circumstances, but everyone is satisfied with his wisdom,' " said the diplomat, reciting a French verse.

"How true," said Princess Miakhky quickly turning to him. "But I won't let you have Anna. She's so dear and sweet. Is it her fault that everyone's in love with her, and that everyone follows her like a shadow?"

"But I have no intention of criticizing her," said Anna's friend apologetically.

"If nobody follows us like shadows, it doesn't prove that we've the right to judge others."

And after duly berating Anna's friend, Princess Miakhky rose and, together with the ambassador's wife, joined the group at the table, where the conversation centered on the King of Prussia.

"Whom have you been maligning?" asked Betsy.

"The Karenins. The princess gave her opinion of Aleksei Aleksandrovich," answered the ambassador's wife, smiling and taking a seat at the table.

"It's a pity we didn't hear it," said the hostess, glancing at the entrance door. "Here you are at last!" she said, turning with a smile to Vronsky, who was entering the room.

Vronsky not only knew everyone here, but saw them every day, and therefore he entered the room with the calm air of one who enters a room and sees there the people he has just left.

"Where am I coming from?" he said in reply to a question

from the ambassador's wife. "What can I do? I must confess—
from the Bouffe. I must have been there a hundred times, but
always with renewed pleasure. It's wonderful! I'm ashamed to
say it, but I fall asleep at the opera, whereas at the Bouffe I
remain to the very end of the last act, and enjoy it thoroughly.
Today. . . ."

He mentioned a French actress and was going to tell them
something about her, but the ambassador's wife interrupted
him in mock fright:

"Please don't talk about such horrible things!"

"Well then, I won't, especially since everyone knows about
them."

"And everybody would go there if it were as socially accepted as the opera," interjected Princess Miakhky.

7

THE SOUND OF STEPS was heard at the entrance door, and Princess Betsy, who knew that this was Karenina coming, glanced
at Vronsky. He looked at the door, and a new and strange expression appeared on his face. He fixed a happy, shy look on
the new arrival and rose slowly. Anna entered the drawing
room. Erect, as always, she walked with a quick, firm, light
step, different from the step of other ladies of fashion, and,
without changing the direction of her eyes, she took the few
steps that separated her from her hostess, shook hands with
her, smiled, and with that smile glanced at Vronsky. Vronsky
bowed deeply and offered her a chair.

She replied to his greetings only with a slight nod of her
head, blushed and frowned. Immediately thereafter, having
nodded quickly to her friends and shaken the hands extended
to her, she addressed the hostess:

"I was at Countess Lydia's and wanted to come earlier, but
was delayed there. Sir John was there. A very interesting
person."

"Oh, is he the missionary?"

"Yes. He told us very interesting stories about life in India."

The conversation, interrupted by her arrival, again flickered
like the fitful flame of a dying lamp.

"Sir John—oh yes, Sir John. I've seen him. He's a good
speaker; Madame Vlasyev is completely enchanted with him."

"Is it true that the youngest of the Vlasyev girls is going to marry Topov?"

"Yes, they say it's all settled."

"I'm surprised at the parents. I believe it's a marriage of love."

"Of love? What an antediluvian idea! Who speaks of love nowadays?" asked the ambassador's wife.

"What can you do? These foolish old-fashioned ideas are still alive," said Vronsky.

"So much the worse for those who follow them. The only happy marriages are arranged marriages."

"Still, how often does the happiness of such married people crumble into dust as soon as they taste the passion that they hadn't known before!" said Vronsky.

"But we consider that an arranged marriage is effective only after both parties have tasted life. It's like scarlet fever. Everyone catches it eventually."

"Then we have to learn how to inoculate against love, as we do against smallpox."

"When I was young, I was in love with a sexton," said Princess Miakhky. "But I can scarcely believe that it was of any help to me."

"No, joking aside. I believe that in order to know love you must first make a mistake, and then correct it," said Princess Betsy.

"Even after marriage?" the ambassador's wife asked jokingly.

" ' It's never too late to repent,' " said the diplomat, quoting an English saying.

"That's it exactly," interjected Betsy. "You must make a mistake and then correct it. What's your opinion?" she asked, turning to Anna, who had kept silent, listening to this conversation with a scarcely noticeable but persistent smile on her lips.

"I think," said Anna, toying with the glove she had taken off, "I think that there are as many minds as there are heads, and as many kinds of love as there are hearts."

Vronsky had been looking at Anna, awaiting her words with a sinking heart. He sighed on hearing them, as if he had escaped from danger.

Suddenly Anna turned to him and said:

"I've received a letter from Moscow. They write that Kitty Shcherbatsky is very ill."

"Is that so?" Vronsky said with a frown.

"Aren't you interested?" said Anna, looking at him sternly.

"I certainly am, very much so. May I know exactly what they write?" he asked.

Anna rose and went over to Betsy.

"May I have a cup of tea?" she said, stopping at her chair. While Princess Betsy poured the tea, Vronsky went over to Anna.

"What do they write?" he asked.

"I often think that men don't understand what is dishonorable, though they often speak about it," said Anna, without answering his question. "I've wanted to tell you about it for a long time," she added, and after taking a few steps, she sat down in the corner at a table with albums on it.

"I don't quite understand the meaning of your words," he said, handing her the cup.

She glanced at the divan near her, and he immediately sat down.

"Yes, I've wanted to tell you," she said without looking at him, "that you acted badly, very, very badly."

"Don't I know that I acted badly? But whose fault was it that I acted that way?"

"Why are you saying that to me?" she asked, looking at him sternly.

"You know why," he answered, boldly and happily, meeting her look and keeping his eyes fixed on her.

It was not he who became embarrassed, but she.

"It only proves that you have no heart," she said. Her glance told him that she knew that he had a heart, and this was the very reason she feared him.

"What you have just been talking about was a mistake, not love."

"You must remember that I have forbidden you to mention that word, that awful word," said Anna with a start. But at once she realized that with these words, *"I have forbidden you,"* she showed that she assumed certain rights over him and thus had encouraged him to talk of love. "I've wanted to tell you for a long time," she continued, looking steadily into his eyes, her face flushed and burning. "I deliberately came here today, knowing that I would see you. I came to tell you that this must end. I never had reason to blush before anyone, but somehow you make me feel guilty."

He looked at her and was struck by a new, spiritual beauty in her face.

"What do you want me to do?" he asked, simply and gravely.

"I want you to go to Moscow and ask Kitty's forgiveness," she said.

"You don't want that," he answered.

He saw that she was saying what she forced herself to say, not what she wished to say.

"If you love me, as you say," she whispered, "then do what will bring me peace."

His face brightened.

"You are my entire life, as you know, but I know no peace and cannot give it to you. All of myself, my love . . . this I can give you. I cannot think about you and myself as being apart. To me, you and I are one. . . . And the future holds no possibility of peace either for you or for myself. I see the possibility of despair and misery . . . but I also see the possibility of happiness, great happiness. . . . Don't you think it is possible?" he added, using just his lips, but she heard him.

She exerted all the powers of her mind to say what she should, but instead she bestowed on him her look, full of love, and said nothing.

There you are! he thought in rapture. Just when I had given in to despair and when my cause seemed hopeless, lo and behold! She loves me, she confesses it!

"Then for my sake, never say these words to me again and let us remain good friends," she said. These were her words, but her look communicated something quite different.

"We won't be friends, you know that. But it is within your power to make us either the happiest or the unhappiest of people."

She wanted to say something, but he interrupted her.

"I ask for one thing alone. I ask for the right to hope and suffer, as I do now. But if even this may not be, tell me to disappear, and I shall disappear. You won't see me, if you find my presence burdensome."

"I don't wish to drive you away."

"Just leave everything unchanged. Leave it as it is," he said in a trembling voice. "Here is your husband."

Indeed, at this moment Aleksei Aleksandrovich entered the drawing room, his gait slow and awkward.

He glanced at his wife and Vronsky, walked over to the hostess, and, taking a cup of tea, he sat down and began to talk in his unhurried, always audible voice, his tone, as usual, jesting and bantering.

"Your Rambouillet is well attended," he said, viewing the company, "and favored by the graces and the muses."

But Princess Betsy could not stand this tone of his, sneering, as she called it, and skilled hostess that she was, she immediately engaged him in a serious conversation about compulsory military service. This subject at once engrossed Aleksei Aleksandrovich, and he went into a stubborn defense of the new law, which Princess Betsy attacked.

Vronsky and Anna were still at the small table.

"This is becoming improper," whispered one of the ladies, her look indicating Vronsky, Karenina, and her husband.

"What did I tell you?" replied Anna's friend.

And not only these ladies but almost everyone in the drawing room, even Princess Miakhky and Betsy herself, glanced frequently at the couple, as if inconvenienced by their keeping to themselves. Only Aleksei Aleksandrovich did not look even once in their direction and was not distracted from his interest in the conversation he had started.

Princess Betsy noticed this general embarrassment. She had one of the guests take her place to listen to Aleksei Aleksandrovich, and she went over to Anna.

"I always marvel at the clarity and precision of your husband's words," she said. "The most abstruse conceptions become clear to me when he expounds on them."

"Oh, yes," said Anna. She smiled, sparkling with happiness, and understood not a word of what Betsy had said to her. She walked over to the large table and involved herself in the general conversation.

About half an hour later, Aleksei Aleksandrovich came over to his wife and offered to take her home. Without looking at him, she replied that she was going to stay for supper. Aleksei Aleksandrovich excused himself and left.

In the driveway, the old stout Tartar, Karenina's coachman, dressed in a shiny leather coat, could scarcely restrain the gray trace horse, which was chilled and restless. The servant opened the door of the coach and waited. The doorman held open the outer entrance door. With her nimble little hands Anna Arkadievna tried to loosen the lace of her sleeve, caught in the hook of her fur coat, and, her head inclined, she listened with rapture to the words of Vronsky, who was escorting her.

"You haven't said anything, but I'm not demanding anything," he said. "Yet you know that it's not friendship that I need. There's only one happiness life can bring me, and that is expressed by the word you dislike so much . . . yes, love. . . ."

"Love . . ." she repeated slowly within herself, and suddenly, the lace at last loosened, she added:

"The reason I dislike that word is that it means so much to me, much more than you can understand." She looked into his eyes. "Good night!"

She extended her hand to him, passed the doorman with her brisk, springy step, and disappeared into the coach.

Her look and the touch of her hand set him afire. He kissed his palm at the spot where she had touched it and went home, happy in the knowledge that he had come closer to the achievement of his goal this evening than at any time during the past two months.

8

When he saw Anna and Vronsky sitting together at a separate table engrossed in a lively conversation, Aleksei Aleksandrovich found it neither strange nor improper. But he noticed that to the other guests it seemed strange and improper, and therefore it seemed improper to him, too. He decided that he should speak to his wife about it.

When he returned home, Aleksei Aleksandrovich went into his study, as was his custom, sat down in the armchair, opened a book on popes at the place marked by a paper knife, and read until one o'clock, as he usually did. At rare intervals he rubbed his high forehead with his hand and tossed his head, as if trying to rid himself of something. At the usual hour he rose and made ready for the night. Anna Arkadievna had not yet returned. He went upstairs with the book under his arm. But this evening his thoughts were taken up not by the affairs of his office, as they usually were, but by his wife and the unpleasantness in which she was involved. Contrary to his custom, he did not go to bed, but, clasping his hands behind his back, began to walk up and down the rooms, He felt that he could not go to sleep before thinking over the situation that had just developed.

When Aleksei Aleksandrovich had decided that he must speak to his wife, it seemed to him an easy and simple decision, but now, as he began to ponder this newly arisen situation, it seemed to him complicated and difficult.

Aleksei Aleksandrovich was not a jealous man. Jealousy, in his opinion, was an insult to one's wife, and one should trust his wife. He did not ask himself why he should trust Anna, or, in other words, why he should be so confident that his young wife would always love him. But he felt no distrust of her; therefore he had the confidence in her that he assured himself he should have. But now, though he still firmly believed that jealousy was a shameful feeling and that one should be trustful, he felt that he had come face to face with something illogical and nonsensical, and he did not know what to do about it. Aleksei Aleksandrovich came face to face with life, with the possibility that his wife might love not him but someone else, and this seemed to him preposterous and incomprehensible, for this was life itself. All his years Aleksei Aleksandrovich had lived and worked in official circles, which dealt only with life's reflections. And every time he came up against life itself, he shunned it. He now felt like a man who confidently walks on a bridge over a chasm and suddenly comes upon a part of the bridge that has been pulled down, the chasm yawning below. This chasm was life itself; the bridge was the artifical life that Aleksei Aleksandrovich had led. For the first time he thought it possible that his wife might fall in love with someone else, and the thought terrified him.

He did not undress, but with measured tread paced up and down the resounding parquet floor of the dining room, which was lit by a single lamp. He continued onto the carpet of the dark drawing room, where the only light was the reflection from the large, recently painted portrait of himself that hung over the divan; and went through to Anna's sitting room, where two candles shone on the portraits of her relatives and friends and on the desk, with its beautiful knickknacks so familiar to him. In her sitting room he approached the door of the bedroom and then turned back.

In each section of his walk he paused from time to time, mostly on the parquet floor of the lighted dining room, saying to himself, Yes, I must come to a decision, I must put an end to this, must explain my view on this matter and my decision.

Then he turned back. But what must I explain? What decision? he asked himself in the drawing room, finding no answer. But actually, he asked himself before turning into the sitting room, what has happened? Nothing. She had a long conversation with him. What of it? Aren't there many to whom a lady of fashion may talk? And then to be jealous is to humiliate both myself and her, he said to himself, entering her sitting room, but this reasoning, which used to carry so much weight with him, carried none now and was meaningless.

At the door to the bedroom he turned back, and as soon as he re-entered the dark drawing room, a voice told him he was wrong, and that since others had noticed it, it was important. In the dining room he again said to himself, I must come to a decision, must put an end to this, must express my view. . . . And again in the dining room, before turning, he asked himself what decision he must make. He asked himself what had happened, replied, Nothing, and recalled that jealousy was a feeling that was an insult to his wife. But when he returned to the drawing room he felt convinced that something really had happened. His thoughts as well as his body had made a full circle, without turning up anything new. He realized this, rubbed his forehead, and sat down in her sitting room.

Here, at the sight of her desk, an unfinished note and a malachite blotting pad on it, his thoughts suddenly took a new turn. He began to think about her, about her feelings and her thoughts. For the first time he clearly envisaged her personal life, her thoughts, her desires. And the thought that she had— and should have—her own personal life frightened him; he hastened to rid himself of it. This was the chasm into which it was so terrifying to look. To put himself into another person's place, to know that person's feelings and thoughts, was an emotional act alien to Aleksei Aleksandrovich. He considered such an emotional act harmful and dangerous daydreaming.

And what's most annoying, he thought, is that right now, when my case is reaching its completion (he was thinking about the project on which he had been working) and when I need complete peace of mind and full control of my mental powers, I'm weighted down by this senseless trouble. But what's to be done? I'm not one of those who endure their troubles and anxieties and can't summon the courage to face up to them.

"I must think this over, make a decision, and dismiss it from my mind," he said aloud.

Her own feelings, everything that has been going on and may be going on within her heart—that's not my concern; it's the concern of her conscience and lies within the domain of religion, he said to himself, relieved at finding a legalistic point of view from which to judge this new situation.

And so, said Aleksei Aleksandrovich to himself, all her feelings are the concern of her conscience, and do not concern me. My duties are well defined. As the head of the family, my duty is to guide her, and therefore I am partly responsible. I must point out to her the dangers which I see; I must warn her, even resort to my authority. I must speak out.

And in his mind, Aleksei Aleksandrovich clearly decided what he was going to tell his wife. Pondering on what he was going to say, he regretted that here, in his privacy, he had to waste his time and mental powers on these domestic problems. Nevertheless, he outlined in his mind, clearly and in detail, the speech he would make, as formal and logical as an official report. I must say and say clearly the following: first, I must explain the importance of public opinion and the proprieties; second, I must explain the religious nature of marriage; third, if necessary, I must remind her of the misfortune that might befall our son; fourth, I must remind her of her own possible unhappiness. Aleksei Aleksandrovich laced his fingers, palms down, and, pulling on his hands, cracked his knuckles.

This gesture, this bad habit of joining his hands and cracking his knuckles, always calmed him and set everything in order, something he needed now so badly. He heard the sound of the coach rolling up to the entrance porch. Aleksei Aleksandrovich stopped in the middle of the room.

The sound of a woman's footsteps could be heard on the stairs. Aleksei Aleksandrovich, ready for his speech, stood stretching his crossed fingers, and waiting to hear some of the knuckles crack. One did.

The sound of her light steps on the staircase told him that she was approaching, and though he was pleased with the speech he had prepared, the forthcoming confrontation terrified him. . . .

9

HER HEAD LOWERED, Anna walked in, playing with the tassels of her hood. Her eyes gleamed brightly, but it was not a joyful gleam; it was more like the terrifying glare of a fire in the darkness of night. On noticing her husband, Anna raised her head, and as though awakening from a dream, she smiled at him.

"Aren't you in bed yet? How strange!" she said. She threw off her hood, and without stopping, went to her dressing room. "It's late, Aleksei Aleksandrovich," she said from behind the door.

"Anna, I wish to talk to you."

"To me?" said Anna, surprised. She came from behind the door and looked at him. "What about?" she asked, sitting down. "Well, let's talk, if we have to. But I'd rather go to sleep."

Anna said whatever came to her mind, and was herself surprised to hear how easily she could lie. How simple and natural were her words, and how credible her desire to go to sleep! She felt as though she were encased in an impenetrable armor of lies. She felt that some unseen power helped and supported her.

"Anna, I must warn you," he said.

"Warn me?" she said. "Against what?"

Her look was so unaffected and so cheerful that only those who knew her as her husband did could suspect that there was anything unnatural either in the sound or the meaning of her words. But he knew her too well. He knew that if he happened to go to bed five minutes later than usual, she would notice it and inquire about the cause. He knew that she had always been quick to share with him her happiness, joys, and troubles. Therefore he found it very significant that she refused to notice his present state and did not want to say anything about herself. He saw that the recesses of her heart, formerly always open to him, were closed now. Moreover, by the tone of her voice he understood that this did not embarrass her. It was as though she had bluntly told him: Yes, it's closed, and that's the way it should be and will be. He had the feeling of a man who returns home and finds his house locked. But perhaps the key may yet be found, thought Aleksei Aleksandrovich.

"I want to warn you," he said in a soft voice, "that through your thoughtlessness and imprudence you may become a subject of public gossip. This evening your unduly animated conversation with Count Vronsky" (he pronounced this name firmly, calmly, and deliberately) "attracted general attention."

As he spoke, he looked into her laughing eyes. He was frightened, now, by their impenetrability. Even as he spoke, he knew that his words were useless and idle.

"That's just like you," she answered, as if completely at a loss to understand him, and of all his words deliberately grasping only the last ones. "Either you're annoyed when I'm bored, or you're annoyed when I'm gay. I wasn't bored. Is that what offends you?"

Aleksei Aleksandrovich started, and laced his fingers so as to crack his knuckles.

"Please stop doing that. I don't like it," she said.

"Anna, I'm surprised at you," said Aleksei Aleksandrovich softly, forcing himself to control his hands.

"What's really the matter?" she asked, with genuine and merry surprise. "What do you want of me?"

Aleksei Aleksandrovich fell silent, rubbing his hand across his forehead and eyes. He felt that instead of warning his wife against committing a social blunder, as he had intended to do, he had involuntarily involved himself in a matter of her conscience, and had figuratively come up against a stone wall.

"Here's what I must tell you," he continued, coldly and calmly. "Please listen to me. As you know, in my opinion jealousy is an offensive and humiliating feeling, and I will never permit myself to be governed by this feeling. But there are certain rules of propriety that one may not violate with impunity. This evening, judging by the impression that you made upon the guests, all of them, though not I, noticed that you acted and behaved in a manner which left much to be desired."

"I positively do not understand you," said Anna, shrugging her shoulders. He doesn't care, she thought. His only worry is that the guests noticed. "You're not well, Aleksei Aleksandrovich," she added. She rose and was about to leave, but he made a gesture as though he wished to stop her.

His face was unpleasant and gloomy, in a way that Anna had never seen before. She stopped, tilted her head to the back and to one side, and with her nimble fingers began to remove her hairpins.

"Well, I'm listening. Go on!" she said, calmly and derisively. "I'm even anxious to hear you, for I would like to know what this is about."

As she spoke, she wondered at her natural, self-assured tone and her choice of words.

"I've no right to go into the details of your feelings and, in general, I consider it useless and even harmful," began Aleksei Aleksandrovich. "When we search our hearts, we often find there something that might otherwise have remained undiscovered. Your feelings are the concern of your own conscience, but it is my duty to you, to myself, and to God to remind you of your duties. Our lives are bound together, and bound not by man but by God. Only a crime can break that bond, and such a crime is severely punished."

"I don't understand a word. And, my God, just tonight, when I'm so sleepy," she said. She quickly ran her fingers through her hair, looking for more hairpins.

"Anna, for God's sake, don't talk like this," he said gently. "Perhaps I'm mistaken, but believe me, what I'm saying is as much for my own sake as for yours. I'm your husband and I love you."

For a moment her face fell, and the derisive gleam left her eyes, but the words "I love you" provoked her anew. He loves me? she thought. Is he able to love? If he had never heard of love, he'd never use the word. He doesn't know what love is.

"Truly, Aleksei Aleksandrovich, I don't understand you," she said. "Tell me clearly what you mean. . . ."

"Please let me finish. I love you, but I'm not talking about myself. Our son and you are the important ones in this matter. It's quite possible, I repeat, that my words seem to you useless and out of place. Perhaps I say them because I am mistaken. If that is so, please forgive me. But if you yourself feel that there exists any basis at all for my thoughts, I beg you to think it over and, if possible, to open your heart to me. . . ."

Aleksei Aleksandrovich did not notice that his words were quite different from those he had prepared.

"I've nothing to say. And . . ." she said, and she could hardly restrain a sudden smile, "really, it's time to go to sleep."

Aleksei Aleksandrovich sighed and, without saying anything else, went into the bedroom.

When she came into the room, he was already in bed. His lips were tightly closed, and he did not look in her direction. Anna lay down in her bed and expected that any minute he would speak to her. She both feared his speaking and wished it. But he kept silent. She remained motionless for a long time, and then soon forgot about him. She thought of another, saw him, and felt this thought move her heart and fill it with wicked joy. Then suddenly she could hear a calm, even, nasal whistle. At first it seemed that Aleksei Aleksandrovich was startled by his own whistling and stopped it. He took two deep breaths, and then the whistle resounded with new, undisturbed regularity.

"It's late, very late," she whispered, smiling. For a long time she lay motionless with open eyes, and it seemed to her that she herself saw their glitter in the darkness.

10

From that evening on, a new life began for Aleksei Aleksandrovich and for his wife. Nothing in particular happened. As always, Anna continued her social activities, was a particularly frequent guest of Princess Betsy, and met Vronsky everywhere. Aleksei Aleksandrovich saw this, but could do nothing about it. To resist all his attempts to draw her into explanations, she surrounded herself with an impenetrable wall of gay bewilderment. Outwardly, everything remained as it had been, but their inner relationship had completely changed. Aleksei Aleksandrovich, so effective in dealing with affairs of state, felt helpless here. Like a bull, he submissively bent his head and waited for the blow from the hammer that he felt poised over him. Every time he thought of it, he felt that he ought to try once more, that there still was some hope of saving her, of bringing her back to her senses, by kindness, tenderness, and persuasion; and every day he intended to talk to her. But every time he began to talk to her, he felt that the spirit of evil and deceit that had possessed her possessed him too, and his words and tone were entirely different from what he intended. As he spoke to her, he unconsciously used a tone that mocked those who would speak thus. And in this tone one could not say what had to be said to her.

11

What had been for almost a whole year Vronsky's only desire, to the exclusion of all other former desires; what had been

Anna's impossible, terrifying, and therefore all the more enchanting dream of happiness—that desire was fulfilled. Pale, his jaw trembling, he stood before her, begging her to calm herself, not knowing himself how or why.

"Anna! Anna!" he said, his voice trembling. "Anna, for God's sake! . . ."

But the louder he spoke, the lower she hung her head, once so proud and gay, but now disgraced. Crumpling, she sank from the divan she had been sitting on, toward the floor, toward his feet, and would have fallen onto the rug, but for his support.

"Oh God, forgive me!" she said, sobbing, and pressing his hand to her heart.

She felt so wicked and guilty that nothing remained for her but to humble herself and ask forgiveness. She had no one in her life now but him, and therefore it was to him that she directed all her prayers for forgiveness. Looking at him, she felt physically humiliated and could not say anything else. And he felt as a murderer must feel when he looks at the body he has deprived of life. The body whose life he had taken was their love, the first stage of their love. It was horrifying and revolting to recall that for which they had to pay such a terrible, shameful price. The shame of her spiritual nakedness oppressed her and communicated itself to him. But in spite of the murderer's horror at the sight of his victim's body, the body must be cut up, must be hidden, and the murderer must reap the rewards of his crime.

And like the murderer who, impassioned by his anger, assails the body, drags it away and cuts it up, so he covered her face and shoulders with kisses. She held his hand and did not move. Yes, she thought, these are the kisses we paid for with our disgrace. And this hand, the only hand that will forever be mine, is the hand of my accomplice. She raised the hand and kissed it. He kneeled to look at her, but she hid her face in silence. At last, she forced herself to rise and pushed him aside. Her face was as beautiful as ever, and therefore all the more pitiful.

"Everything is finished," she said. "You are all that I have left. Never forget it."

"I cannot forget what is my entire life. For a moment of this happiness. . . ."

"What happiness?" she said, with horror and disgust, and against his will, this feeling of horror was imparted to him.

"For God's sake, not one word more, not a single word." She rose quickly and stepped away from him. "Not a single word," she repeated, and as they parted, he was astonished to see on her face an expression of bleak despair. She knew that at this moment she could not express in words the feeling of shame, joy, and fright with which she was entering a new life. She did not want to speak of it, to debase this feeling with inadequate words. But even later, the next day and the day after, she lacked not only the words to express all the complexity of her feelings, but also the appropriate thoughts with which to reflect on all that was within her heart.

She told herself, No, I can't think about it now; I'll do it later, when I am calmer. But this peace of mind never arrived. Every time she happened to think of what she had done, what the future held for her, and what she must do, she became frightened and tried to rid herself of these thoughts.

Later, she said to herself, later, when I feel calmer.

But in her dreams, when she had no control over her thoughts, her situation appeared in all its ugly nakedness. One dream visited her almost nightly. She dreamt that both men were her husbands, and that both of them showered their caresses on her. Aleksei Aleksandrovich was crying, kissing her hands and saying, "How good it is now!" And Aleksei Vronsky was there. He, too, was her husband. She was surprised that formerly this had seemed to her impossible, but now she laughingly explained to them that it was very simple, and both of them now were happy and contented. But this dream oppressed her like a nightmare, and she awakened terrified.

12

FOR A WHILE after his return from Moscow, Levin would start and blush whenever he recalled the disgrace of the refusal, and he would say to himself, I started and blushed the same way and considered myself lost forever when I failed in college physics and had to repeat the year. I likewise considered myself lost when I mismanaged my sister's affairs, which had been entrusted to me. And now—the years have passed, and it seems strange that such things could have worried me. The same will happen with this misfortune. Time will pass, and it will no longer trouble me.

But three months passed, he was still troubled by it, and the recollection remained as painful as it had been in the early days. He could find no peace, for though he had dreamt of family life so long, and felt so completely prepared for it, he was still single and was now farther than ever from marriage. Like everyone else around him, he felt acutely that it was not good for a man of his age to remain single. He recalled that, before leaving for Moscow, he had told Nikolai, his cowherd, a simple-minded moujik with whom he liked to talk, "Well, Nikolai, I want to get married," to which Nikolai hurriedly replied, as if talking of a matter which admits no doubt, "It's about time, Konstantin Dmitrievich." But now marriage seemed farther away than ever. The place was taken, and in his imagination he found it utterly impossible to substitute another girl. Moreover, he was painfully ashamed at the recollection of the refusal and the part he had played in it. No matter how many times he reassured himself that it was not his fault, this recollection made him shrink and blush, as did other similarly humiliating recollections. Like anyone else, in his past he had done some things that, he admitted, were wrong, and that should have weighed on his conscience. But he suffered far less from the recollection of these wrong acts than from the insignificant yet humiliating ones. Those wounds never healed. The refusal, and the pitiful state in which he must have appeared to others that evening, were now part of such recollections. Yet time and work did their part. These painful memories were increasingly overshadowed by the routine but important events of life in the country. With each passing week he thought of Kitty less frequently. He waited with impatience for news that she had married or was about to marry, in the hope that such news would bring him complete relief, as a toothache is relieved by the extraction of the diseased tooth.

In the meantime spring had arrived, beautiful and kindly, not one of those deceptive springs, vainly awaited, but one of those rare springs in which plants, animals, and men rejoice alike. This beautiful spring raised Levin's spirits still higher and strengthened his resolve to renounce completely his former ways in order to organize a stable, independent, solitary life for himself. Though many of the plans he had when he returned to the country had not been executed, he strictly observed his main resolution, that of leading a pure life. He no longer felt the shame that had always tortured him after a fall from grace, and he could look anyone straight in the eye. Back in February he had received a letter from Maria Nikolayevna. She wrote that his brother's health was failing, but that he refused to see a doctor. On receipt of this letter, Levin made a trip to Moscow to see his brother. He persuaded him to consult a doctor and to go abroad. Without making him angry, he prevailed upon his brother to borrow the money he needed for the trip from himself. The entire matter gave him much satisfaction. In addition to the management of the estate, which demanded his attention, particularly in the springtime, and in addition to his reading, Levin had that winter begun to write a book on agriculture. The main thesis of the book was that in agriculture the nature of the farm worker must be considered as a fundamental element, like the climate or the soil, and that therefore all laws of agriculture should be based not on the study of the soil and the climate only, but on the study of the soil, climate, and the obvious and unchangeable nature of the farm worker. Therefore, in spite of his seclusion, or because of it, he had a very full life, and only rarely did he yearn to share the thoughts that crowded his mind with anyone other than Agafia Mikhailovna, with whom he very often discussed physics, economics, and particularly philosophy. Philosophy was Agafia Mikhailovna's favorite subject.

Spring was slow in unfolding. During the last weeks of Lent the days were clear and frosty. In the daytime the snow melted in the sun, and at night the mercury dropped to seven degrees. The hard sheet of ice served as a road for the carts. It was a white Easter. Suddenly, on the second day of Easter week, a warm wind blew, the clouds gathered, and there followed a violent downpour of warm rain, which lasted for three days and three nights. On Thursday the wind calmed, a thick gray fog moved in, as if trying to hide the mysterious seasonal changes. The fog was heavy with water, the ice cracked and stirred, the foaming, muddy streams picked up speed, and one evening the following week the fog lifted, the clouds parted, the weather cleared, and real spring arrived. In the morning the bright rising sun quickly freed the waters from their glaze of ice, and everywhere the warm air quivered, filled with the tepid exhalations of the reviving earth. The old grass, and the sprouting blades of the new, turned green; the buds swelled on the white hazel tree, the currant bush, and the sticky birch tree; and around the willow, strewn with golden pollen, a newly emerged bee hummed, trying its wings. The invisible larks broke into song high above the velvety green meadows and the stubbled field, still ice-glazed. The pewit cried above the lowlands filled with remnants of rain-water, and above the swamps. The cranes and geese, cackling their vernal cry, winged by high in the sky. The thin-haired cows, with only a few patches of their skin not shed, lowed in the pastures. Bandy-legged lambs frisked around their bleating, fleece-shedding mothers. Barefoot boys skipped along, leaving their footprints in the drying paths. The pond resounded with the gay voices of peasant women washing their linen, and in the yards could be heard the sound of the peasant's axes as they repaired their plows and harrows. Spring had really come.

13

LEVIN PUT ON his high boots and, for the first time this season, a cloth coat instead of his fur coat and went about the farm. He passed through streams of water glaring in the bright sun-light, and stepped on thin ice and into heavy mire.

Spring is the season of plans and intentions. Levin came out into the yard, and like a tree in springtime, which does not yet know how its swollen buds will sprout and in what direction its young shoots and branches will grow, he did not fully know which of his favorite undertakings he would now begin. But he did feel full of the very best of plans and intentions. First of all, he visited the cattle shed. The cows were out in the yard. Shiny in their new growth of smooth hair, they basked in the sun, lowed, and begged to be taken to the field. After admiring the cows, so familiar to him even in the smallest detail, Levin ordered them driven to the field and the calves let into the yard. The shepherd ran up happily to drive the cows to the field. The dairymaids, gathering their skirts, splashed in the mire with their white feet, which the sun had not yet tanned. With switches in their hands, they herded into the yard the lowing calves, which were trans-ported by vernal happiness.

He admired this year's exceedingly large increase, the young calves as large as the moujiks' cows, and Pava's off-spring, three months old, as large as a year-old cow. Levin ordered the trough to be brought to them and some hay put behind the racks. But it turned out that the racks, which had been built in the fall and had not been used in the yard during the winter, were broken. He sent for the carpenter, who was supposed to work that day at the threshing machine. Instead, the carpenter was fixing the harrows, which should have been fixed by Shrovetide. Levin found this exceedingly annoying. He was annoyed by the constant carelessness against which he had been fighting with all his might for so many years. He found that the racks, not in use during the winter, had been transferred to the workhorses' stable and had been damaged there, for they were not sturdy enough, having been built for the calves. Moreover, all this indicated that the harrows and other agricultural implements had not yet been fixed. They should have been inspected and repaired during the winter, and for this purpose he had hired three carpenters. But the harrows were being repaired only now, when it was time to begin the harrowing. Levin sent for the steward, then abruptly left to look for him himself. The steward, aglow like everything else that day and dressed in a short sheepskin coat trimmed with lambskin, came from the threshing floor, crumpling a piece of straw in his hands.

"Why isn't the carpenter at the threshing machine?"

"I was going to report to you about it yesterday. The harrows have to be fixed. It's time for plowing."

"Why wasn't it done during the winter?"

"But what do you need the carpenter for?"

"Where are the calves' racks?"

"I told them to put them where they belong. What can you do with these people?" said the steward, waving his hands.

"Not with these people, but with this steward," said Levin angrily. "What do I pay you for?" he cried. But realizing that nothing would be accomplished this way, he stopped in the middle of his speech and just sighed. "Well, is it time for sowing?" he asked after a silence.

"We can start beyond Turkin tomorrow or the day after."

"And how about the clover?"

"I sent Vasili and Mishka out to sow. I hope they get there; it's a mire."

"How many dessiatines are you going to plant?"

"Six."

"Why not the entire lot?" cried Levin. The fact that they

were going to plant only six dessiatines in clover instead of all twenty annoyed Levin further. The best time for planting clover, according to theory and his own experience, was in early spring, immediately after the snow. But Levin could never get this done.

"We don't have enough men. What can you do with them? Three men didn't report for work, and Semion. . . ."

"You should have taken them off work on the straw."

"I did just that."

"So where are they all?"

"Five of them are preparing the compote." (This is what he called compost.) "Four are busy with the oats. I hope it's not touched, Konstantin Dmitrievich."

Levin knew very well that these words, "I hope it's not touched," meant that the English oats, intended for seeding, were already spoiled, and that they had again disobeyed his orders.

"But I spoke to you about the pipes at Lent," he cried.

"Don't worry. Everything will be done in time."

Angered, Levin waved his hands and went to the granary to inspect the oats and then turned back to the stable. The oats had not spoiled yet. But the workmen were using shovels, whereas the oats could have been poured directly into the lower granary. Levin ordered this done, and thus gained two extra men for clover planting. Levin's annoyance with the steward disappeared. It was hard to be angry with anyone on such a beautiful day.

"Ignat!" he called to his coachman, who, his sleeves rolled up, was washing the carriage at the well. "Saddle a horse."

"Which one would you like?"

"Kolpik, perhaps."

"Very well."

While they saddled the horse, Levin called the steward again, who was nearby. He wanted to make up his differences with him, and started a conversation about the forthcoming spring work and his projects.

Moving of manure had to start earlier, so that they might be through with it before the early meadow mowing. They had to keep plowing all of the distant field to keep it fallow and free from vegetation. All the mowing had to be done by hired workers, and the mowing fields were not to be leased on a share basis.

The steward listened attentively and, evidently, tried his

best to approve of his master's plans. But he still had that hopeless and unenthusiastic look that Levin knew so well and found so irritating. The look said, "All this is fine, but everything is in God's hands."

Nothing vexed Levin more than this attitude. But this was the usual attitude of all the stewards he had employed. They all had the same attitude toward his plans, and therefore he no longer grew angry but was chagrined, and even resolved more firmly to fight this elemental force that always resisted him. He called it "what God wills," for lack of a better name.

"If we manage to do it, Konstantin Dmitrievich," said the steward.

"Why shouldn't we?"

"We absolutely must hire about fifteen more men. But they don't show up. A few were here today and asked seventy rubles for the summer."

Levin fell silent. That force again resisted him. He knew that no matter how much they tried, they could not hire more than forty, more likely thirty-seven or thirty-eight men, at the right pay. Only forty applied, no more. But he decided to do his best.

"Send to Sury and to Chefirovka if they don't come. You have to look everywhere."

"I'll do it," Vasili Fedorovich said dispiritedly. "And now the horses are failing."

"We'll buy some more. But I know," he added, laughing, "that you're good at doing less and doing it worse, but this year I'll not let you have it your way. I'll do everything myself."

"Even now, it seems, you don't get enough sleep. But we like to have the master around. . . ."

"So they're planting clover beyond Berezovy Dol. I'll go take a look," he said, mounting the small bay, Kolpik, which the coachman had brought up.

"You'll not make it through the creek, Konstantin Dmitrievich," cried the coachman.

"Then I'll go through the wood."

The good, eager horse ambled over the puddles, snorting and asking for freer rein. Levin rode over the mire in the yard, through the gates, and out into the field.

Levin felt even more cheerful in the field than in the cattle shed or in the granary. Swaying in rhythm with the amble of his good horse, inhaling the warm but fresh smell of snow and air, and passing through the wood over formless patches of spongy, sunken snow that still remained here and there, he rejoiced at the sight of each of his trees, with their swollen buds and the reviving lichens on their bark. When he came out of the wood, an immense velvety, smooth green carpet of winter crops opened before his eyes, with no bare spots, with no stretches of water. Only in the hollows did there remain a few patches of snow, blackened and thawing. He was not annoyed when he saw a peasant's horse and its colt that had trampled his crops (he simply asked a peasant he met to drive them away). Nor was he annoyed by the foolish reply made to his question by the moujik Ipat, whom he met on the way. When asked, "Well, Ipat, will it soon be time to sow?" Ipat answered, "First you must plow, Konstantin Dmitrievich."

The farther Levin went the happier he felt. He thought of all the work he was going to do, and each project exceeded the previous one in importance: planting willow trees along the southern edge of the fields as a snow-break; fertilizing six fields with manure and keeping three in reserve for grass sowing; building a cow shed in the far end of the field; digging a pond; and erecting movable fences so that the cattle might fertilize the fields. Then not one dessiatine of land would be wasted; there would be three hundred in wheat, a hundred in potatoes, and a hundred and fifty in clover.

Lost in such dreams and carefully leading the horse along the border paths to avoid trampling the winter crop, he came to the place where the workers were planting clover. They had placed the cart of seed, not in the open place between the fields, but on the plowed land itself, and the winter wheat had been crushed by the cart's wheels and uprooted by the horse. The two workers were sitting on the boundary path; they had evidently been sharing their pipe. In the cart the soil, which was mixed with the seeds, remained unkneaded, lumped in hard, frozen clods. On seeing the master, Vasili walked over to the cart, and Mishka began planting. All this was wrong, but Levin very seldom scolded his workers. When Vasili came over, Levin ordered him to take the horse off the plowed field.

"It's all right, sir, it will right itself."

"Don't argue, please," said Levin, "and do as you are told."

"Yes sir," said Vasili, and he reached for the horse's head. "The sowing, Konstantin Dmitrievich," he said ingratiatingly, "is first class. But it's very hard to walk; fifty pounds of soil stick to each leg."

"Why hasn't the soil been sifted?"

"But we're kneading it," replied Vasili, taking some of the seed and working the earth between his palms.

It was not Vasili's fault that he had been given unsifted soil, but still it annoyed Levin.

He possessed a sure remedy, one that he had tried more than once, for overcoming his annoyance and for rectifying what seemed wrong to him. He used this remedy now. He watched Mishka as he walked along with huge clods of earth sticking to his legs. Levin dismounted, took Vasili's sowing basket, and started to sow.

"Where did you stop?"

Vasili pointed with his foot to the mark. Levin went on and, as well as he could, sowed the seeds, which were mixed with the soil. It was as difficult to walk as in a morass, and after covering half a dessiatine he was sweating profusely. He stopped and returned the sowing basket to Vasili.

"Well, master, in the summer don't blame me for this section," said Vasili.

"Why?" asked Levin cheerfully, feeling his remedy having its effect.

"You'll see in the summer. The difference will show. Now look at what I sowed last year. How well I did it! Konstantin Dmitrievich, I'm trying my best for you, as I would for my own father. I myself don't like to do things badly and advise others not to do so. What's good for the master is good for us. As I look there," said Vasili, pointing to the field, "my heart rejoices."

"And it's a fine spring, Vasili."

"Yes, such a spring the old folks don't remember. Back at home, an old man sowed three measures of wheat; he says you could take it for rye."

"When did you start sowing wheat?"

"You yourself taught us to do it two years ago. You kindly gave us two measures. Part of it we sold; the rest we sowed."

"Look, knead the clods well," said Levin, walking up to his horse, "and watch Mishka. And if the crop is good, you'll get fifty kopecks for each dessiatine."

"Many thanks. Even without this we're much obliged to you."

Levin mounted his horse and left for the field with last

year's clover, then for another which had been plowed for spring wheat.

The clover sprouted richly on the stubblefield. It rose firmly and showed its verdure among the broken stalks of last year's wheat. The horse sank up to its fetlocks and made a smacking noise as it withdrew its feet from the partly thawed ground. It was completely impossible to ride on the plowed field. The horse still could make it where the ice remained, but in the furrows, where the ground had thawed, it sank above its fetlocks. The plowland looked excellent; it would be ready for harrowing and sowing in two days. Everything was fine; everything looked cheering. Levin turned back across the stream in the hope that the water had subsided. He crossed it, as he had expected, and surprised two ducks. Most probably there are woodcocks here, too, he thought, and when he turned toward his house, he met the forester, who confirmed the fact that there were woodcocks about.

Levin rode home at a trot in order to have time for dinner and to prepare his gun for the evening.

14

APPROACHING THE HOUSE in the happiest frame of mind, Levin heard the sound of a bell coming from the direction of the main entrance to the house.

Probably some visitor has come by train, he thought. It is just time for the Moscow train. . . . Who could it be? Perhaps my brother Nikolai? I remember that he said, "Perhaps I'll go to the spas, or possibly I'll go to see you."

At first, for a moment, he was upset and displeased; the presence of his brother Nikolai would disturb his present happy, springlike mood. But he was ashamed of this feeling and now he felt that his heart had opened and that with tender joy and true sincerity he wanted and expected the visitor to be his brother. He spurred his horse, and as he emerged from behind the acacia bush, he saw the railroad station troika drive up to the house. There was a fur-coated gentleman in it, but he was not his brother. Ah, perhaps someone with whom I may have a pleasant conversation, he thought.

"Ah!" cried Levin happily, raising both arms. "What a welcome guest! How wonderful to see you!" he shouted, recognizing Stepan Arkadievich. I'll surely find out, he thought, whether she's married or is going to marry.

And on this beautiful spring day, he felt that thinking of her caused him no pain.

"Well, you didn't expect me?" asked Stepan Arkadievich, climbing out of the sleigh, lumps of mud on the bridge of his nose, on his cheek and eyebrows, and beaming with health and good cheer. "First of all, I wanted to see you," he said, embracing and kissing his friend. "Secondly, I want to do some hunting; and thirdly, I want to sell the timber in Ergushovo."

"Splendid! And what a beautiful spring. Why did you come in the sleigh?"

"It would have been worse in the carriage, Konstantin Dmitrievich," replied the coachman, who knew him.

"Well, I'm very, very happy to see you," said Levin, smiling sincerely with his joyful, boyish smile.

Levin showed his visitor to the guestroom, where they brought Stepan Arkadievich's luggage: his bag, a gun in its covered case, and a cigar case. He left him to wash up and change, while he himself went to the office to give orders for the plowing and clover planting. Agafia Mikhailovna, who always worried about the honor of the house, met him in the entrance hall and asked him about dinner.

"Do as you please, but hurry," he told her, and went to see the steward.

When he returned, Stepan Arkadievich—washed, combed, and beaming—came out of his room, and they went upstairs together.

"How glad I am that at last I've found my way to you! Now I'll learn about the mysteries you perform here. But I truly envy you! What a home! How pleasant everything is here! And how light, how cheerful!" said Stepan Arkadievich, forgetting that it was not always springtime, and that the days were not always so bright. "And your nurse is a darling. Of course, a pretty chambermaid with her little apron would be preferable; but the old woman fits in well with your strict, monkish style."

Stepan Arkadievich gave him all the interesting news. Of special interest to Levin was the fact that his brother Sergei Ivanovich planned to visit him that summer.

Stepan Arkadievich did not say a word about Kitty and the Shcherbatskys in general; he just gave him regards from his wife. Levin was grateful to him for his tact and was very happy with his guest. As always, during this long period of solitude he had accumulated a host of thoughts and feelings he could not share with those around him, and now he unburdened himself to Stepan Arkadievich. He spoke about the poetic joy of spring, about his plans and failures in the management of the estate, his thoughts and opinions about the books he was reading, and particularly the subject of his own book, which, though he had not noticed it himself, was based on his criticism of all former works on agriculture, Stepan Arkadievich, always kind, always quick to understand, was particularly kind to him this time. Levin was flattered as he noticed the esteem and, it seemed, the tenderness with which his friend now treated him.

Though Agafia Mikhailovna and the cook had done their utmost to prepare an exceptionally good dinner, the two starving comrades went after the *zakuska*, gorged themselves with bread and butter, smoked fish and pickled mushrooms; then Levin ordered the soup served without the patties the cook had planned to impress the guest with. But Stepan Arkadievich, though used to other dinners, greatly enjoyed everything: the herb-brandy, the bread, butter, and particularly the smoked fish, the mushrooms, nettle soup, chicken in white sauce, and white Crimean wine; everything was tasty and wonderful.

"Excellent, excellent," he said, lighting a thick cigarette after the roast. "I feel as if I've landed upon a calm shore after riding a noisy and jolting steamboat. So you say that we should study the worker as an important element in agriculture. You know that I'm ignorant in these matters, but it seems to me that your theory and its application will have an influence on the worker, too."

"Wait a minute. I'm not talking about political economy; I'm talking about agricultural science. It should follow the methods of natural science, should observe existing facts, and the worker with his economic, ethnographic—"

But at this moment Agafia Mikhailovna came in with some preserves.

"Well, Agafia Mikhailovna," said Stepan Arkadievich, kissing the tips of his plum fingers, "what delicious smoked fish you prepared, what herb-brandy! And now, isn't it time to go, Kostia?" he added.

Levin looked through the window at the sun setting behind the bare treetops. "It's time, it's time," he said. "Kuzma, get the carriage ready," and he ran downstairs.

Stepan Arkadievich went downstairs, carefully took the canvas cover off the varnished case, opened it, and began to assemble his expensive gun, a late model. Kuzma, who smelled a good tip coming, did not leave Stepan Arkadievich, but helped him to put on his stockings and boots, which Stepan Arkadievich willingly let him do.

"Kostia, order your people to receive the merchant Riabinin if he comes, and to ask him to wait for me. I invited him to come to see me this evening."

"Is it to Riabinin that you're selling the timber?"

"Yes, do you know him?"

"Of course. I had some business with him 'definitely and positively.'"

Stepan Arkadievich laughed. "Definitely and positively" were the favorite words of the merchant. "Yes, his speech is very funny." He added, "She understands where her master is going!" patting Laska, who was under Levin's feet, whining and licking first his hand, then his boots, and then his gun.

When they came out, the carriage was waiting for them at the porch.

"I ordered it, although it's not far. Perhaps you'd rather walk?"

"No, let's ride," said Stepan Arkadievich, coming up to the carriage. He sat down, wrapped his legs with the tiger-skin cover, and lit a cigar. "How strange that you don't smoke! Smoking a cigar is not only a pleasure, it is the crowning pleasure. This is the life! Wonderful! This is the way I'd like to live."

"What keeps you from doing so?" asked Levin, smiling.

"Yes, you're a happy man. You have everything that you love. You love horses, and you have them; you love dogs, and you have them too; you have your hunting, your estate."

"Perhaps I'm pleased with what I have and don't worry about what I don't have," said Levin, thinking of Kitty.

Stepan Arkadievich understood, glanced at him, but said nothing.

Levin was grateful to Oblonsky, who, with his usual tact, when he saw that Levin feared talking about the Shcherbatskys, refrained from mentioning their name. But now Levin was anxious to allay his tormenting doubts, and yet lacked the courage to broach the subject.

"And how are your affairs?" asked Levin, realizing how wrong it was on his part to think only of himself.

Stepan Arkadievich's eyes sparkled gaily.

"But you don't admit that you may hanker for sweets even after your stomach is full; you consider it a crime. I, on the other hand, don't accept life without love," he replied, making his own interpretation of Levin's question. "What can I do? I was born that way. And in the long run this brings you so much pleasure, while it causes so little harm to others. . . ."

"Well, is anything else new?" asked Levin.

"Yes, my friend. You know the women of that type, like Ossian's—the ones you see in your dreams. . . . But there are such women in real life too . . . such women are frightening. A woman, my friend, is the sort of subject that study it as much as you will, it remains quite new."

"Then it's better not to study it."

"No. A mathematician once said that pleasure comes from the search for the truth rather than its discovery."

Levin listened to him in silence, and no matter how he tried, he could not penetrate into his friend's mind, could not understand his feelings, nor could he comprehend the delights brought about by the study of such women.

15

THE HUNT WAS to take place not far from the stream, in a sparse aspen grove. When they arrived, Levin alighted and took Oblonsky to one corner of a mossy, swampy field, from which the snow had already melted. He himself returned to a double-trunked birch tree on the other side of the field, leaned his gun against the fork of the lower branches, took off his coat, rearranged his belt, and made sure that nothing encumbered him.

Old gray Laska, who had followed him closely, sat down cautiously, facing him, and pricked her ears. The sun was setting behind the dense woods; in the light of the sunset the birch trees, scattered among the aspens, stood out clearly, their branches hanging down, their swollen buds ready to burst.

From the thick woods, where snow still lay on the ground, there came the faint sound of water flowing in winding runnels. Small birds chirped, and now and then flew from tree to tree.

In the intervals of complete silence there could be heard the rustle of last year's leaves, stirred by the thawing snow and the growing grass.

How wonderful! You can hear and see the grass growing! said Levin to himself, noticing a slate-colored, wet aspen leaf stirring near a blade of young grass. He stood there, listened, and looked down; now at the wet, mossy ground; now at Laska, her ears pricked; now at the expanse of bare treetops, spread before him under the hill; and now at the darkening sky, streaked with white clouds. A hawk, slowly flapping its wings, flew high over the far side of the woods; another winged in the same direction, then disappeared. The bustle and chirp of the birds in the woods grew louder. Not far away, an owl hooted. Laska trembled, took a few cautious steps and listened, bending her head sideways. A cuckoo called from beyond the stream; it cuckooed twice in its usual way, then issued a few hurried, hoarse, confused sounds.

"Listen, the cuckoo!" said Stepan Arkadievich, coming out from behind the bush.

"Yes, I hear it," said Levin, resenting his own voice for breaking the silence of the woods. "It won't be long now."

Stepan Arkadievich again hid himself behind the bush, and all that Levin could see was the bright flame of a match, then the red glow of a cigarette and the thin bluish smoke.

Click, click, he heard as Stepan Arkadievich cocked his gun.

"What's making that sound?" asked Oblonsky, calling Levin's attention to a drawn-out whine, like the thin neighing of a frisking colt.

"Don't you know? It's a male hare. But enough talking. Listen, here they come!" Levin almost shouted as he cocked his gun.

The sound of a thin whistle came from afar, and after an interval of two seconds, as hunters have learned to expect, another whistle, then a third, and after that a guttural cry.

Levin looked to the right and left, and then, in the murky blue sky right in front of him, above the faintly distinguishable young shoots of the aspen crowns, he saw a flying bird. It was flying directly at him; the sounds of its cry, which resembled rhythmic scraping on a tightly drawn fabric, came nearer and now could be heard right above his head. He could easily make out the bird's long beak and neck, and at the moment when Levin aimed, a flash came from behind the bush where Oblonsky was standing. The bird plummeted downward and then shot straight up. There was another flash, followed by a thud; the bird flapped its wings, as if trying to remain aloft, stopped for a moment, and then tumbled heavily onto the swampy ground.

"Is it a miss?" cried Stepan Arkadievich. Because of the smoke, he could not see what had happened.

"There it is," said Levin, pointing to Laska, who, pricking one ear and waving the raised tip of her fluffy tail, walked slowly, as if wishing to prolong the pleasure, and as though with a smile, brought the dead bird up to her master. "Well, I'm glad you didn't miss," said Levin, now envious that it was not he who had killed the woodcock.

"I missed my shot with the right barrel," replied Stepan Arkadievich, reloading his gun. "Shh . . . there's another."

And, indeed, they heard two shrill whistles, one right after the other. Two woodcocks, racing playfully, whistling but emitting no cries, flew directly over the heads of the hunters. Four shots sounded, and, like swallows, the woodcocks turned abruptly and disappeared.

It had been a magnificent hunt. Stepan Arkadievich killed two more birds, and Levin got two, of which one was not retrieved. It was getting dark. Low in the western sky, Venus, clear and silvery, shone gently through the young birch trees, and high over the eastern horizon, somber Arcturus shimmered in its red light. Above his head, Levin caught sight of and then lost the stars of the Great Bear. The woodcocks flew no more, and Levin decided to wait a little longer until Venus, which he saw below the branch of the birch tree, would rise above it, and when all the stars of the Great Bear would shine clearly. Venus rose above the branch, the chariot of the Great Bear and its shaft stood out clearly in the dark blue sky, but still he waited.

"Isn't it time to go?" asked Stepan Arkadievich.

By now the woods were silent, and not a bird stirred.

"Let's stay a little longer," said Levin.

"As you wish."

They were now standing about fifteen steps apart.

"Stiva," suddenly asked Levin, "why don't you tell me whether your sister-in-law is married or is about to marry?"

Levin now felt so secure and calm that no answer, he believed, could upset him. But he was totally unprepared for the answer that Stepan Arkadievich gave him.

"She wasn't and isn't thinking of marrying, but she's very sick, and the doctors sent her abroad. They even fear for her life."

"What are you saying!" cried Levin. "Very sick? What's the matter with her? Is she. . . ."

During this conversation, Laska pricked up her ears, looked at the sky and then, with reproach, at them.

A fine time for talking! she thought. *One is coming. Here it is. They'll miss it. . . .*

But at this moment a shrill whistle struck their ears; they both seized their guns, and there were two flashes followed by the sound of two simultaneous hits. High above, the woodcock instantly folded its wings and fell into the woods, bending the young shoots.

"Splendid! This belongs to both of us," exclaimed Levin, and he ran into the woods with Laska to look for the woodcock. *What was that unpleasant news?* he thought, trying to recall. *Oh, yes, Kitty is sick. . . . I'm sorry, but what can I do?*

"Ah, you found it! A smart dog," he said, taking the warm bird from Laska's mouth and putting it in his game bag, which was almost full now. "I found it, Stiva!" he cried.

16

ON THEIR WAY home, Levin inquired about all the details of Kitty's illness and about the Shcherbatskys' plans, and though he was ashamed to admit it, the news pleased him. He was pleased because there still remained some hope, and was still more pleased because she suffered, she who had caused him so much suffering. But when Stepan Arkadievich began to explain the causes of Kitty's illness and mentioned Vronsky's name, Levin interrupted him.

"I have no right to know the family's secrets and, to tell you the truth, they don't interest me."

Stepan Arkadievich smiled faintly, noticing the instantaneous change in Levin's face, so familiar to him; it made him look as gloomy now as he was cheerful a moment ago.

"Have you come to a final settlement with Riabinin about the timber?" asked Levin.

"Yes, I have. The price is very good: thirty-eight thousand. Eight thousand down, and the rest within six years. It took me a long time to settle it. Nobody offered me more!"

"It means that you gave the timber away for nothing," said Levin gloomily.

"What do you mean, for nothing?" asked Stepan Arkadievich good-naturedly; he knew that now everything would look bad to Levin.

"Because the timber is worth at least five hundred rubles a dessiatine," replied Levin.

"Oh, these country squires!" said Stepan Arkadievich jestingly. "This tone of contempt for your city cousins! Yet when it comes to business, we always do better. Believe me, I considered everything; and sold the timber so profitably that I'm afraid he might back out. You have to remember that this timber can't be used for construction, only for fuel," he said, hoping that with this remark he would fully convince Levin how unjust his doubts were. "And he'll pay two hundred rubles a dessiatine, though it'll only yield two hundred and ten board feet."

Levin smiled derisively. I recognize this kind of behavior, he thought, and he's not alone in this. He's like all city folk. They visit the country perhaps twice in ten years, pick up a few country words, use them appropriately or not, and feel sure that they know everything. "Timber for construction," "yield," "board feet"—he uses terms he doesn't understand at all.

"I don't try to teach you how to run council-chamber affairs, and if I ever need such information, I'll ask you," he said, "but you're so sure that you know everything about the timber business. It isn't easy. Did you count the trees?"

"How could I count the trees?" asked Stepan Arkadievich, smiling and still eager to see his friend change his mood. "Though a great mind could count the grains of sand and the rays of the planets. . . ."

"Well, Riabinin's great mind can. And no merchant would buy timber without counting the trees, unless he's getting it free, as in your case. I know your woods; I hunt there every year and know that it's worth fully five hundred rubles cash, and he pays you two hundred, and in installments. It means that you made him a present of thirty thousand rubles."

"Well, let's not make too much of it," said Stepan Arkadievich piteously. "Then why did no one offer me more?"

"Because he's in collusion with the other merchants; he bribed them. I've had business with them; I know them well. They aren't merchants, they are forestallers. They are not interested in any deal bringing ten or fifteen per cent. They expect a profit of twenty kopecks on every ruble."

"Oh, it isn't so! You're in a bad mood."

"Not at all," replied Levin gloomily, as they reached the house.

A carriage was already waiting at the entrance. It was tightly covered with leather and iron; its well-fed horse was tightly harnessed in wide collar-straps. Riabinin's steward, who also served him as a coachman, tightly belted and ruddy-complexioned, was sitting in the carriage. Riabinin himself was inside the house, and met the friends in the entrance hall. Riabinin was a tall, lean, middle-aged man, with a mustache, a clean-shaven, jutting chin, and misty, bulging eyes. He was dressed in a long blue coat, with buttons in the back below the belt, and in tall boots, wrinkled at the ankles but smooth on the calves, with large galoshes over the boots. He mopped his face with a handkerchief and adjusted his coat, which already sat quite well on him. He smiled, greeted the arrivals, and extended his hand to Stepan Arkadievich as though about to seize something.

"So here you are," said Stepan Arkadievich, giving him his hand. "Splendid!"

"I have not dared to disobey Your Excellency's orders, though the road is very bad. I positively walked all the way, but have come in time. My compliments, Konstantin Dmitrievich," he said, turning to Levin and trying to seize his hand. But Levin frowned, pretended that he did not notice his hand and was busy removing the woodcocks from the bag.

"So you have been pleased to amuse yourselves with hunting. And what kind of bird is this?" Riabinin added comtemptuously, looking at the woodcocks. "Tasty, perhaps." He shook his head disapprovingly, as if in grave doubt concerning the worth of the entire enterprise.

"Would you like to go into the study?" Levin asked Stepan

Arkadievich, in French and with a sullen frown. "Go into the study; discuss your business there."

"Of course, anywhere you please," said Riabinin with disdainful dignity, as if to show that while some might find it difficult to deal with all kinds of people, he would never and under no circumstances have such difficulties.

On entering the study, Riabinin looked around, as was his custom, apparently seeking an icon; but finding none, he did not cross himself. He viewed the closets and shelves of books with the same mistrust with which he had viewed the woodcocks, smiled disdainfully and shook his head in disapproval, fully convinced that all this had no worth.

"Well, have you brought the money?" asked Oblonsky. "Sit down."

"We mustn't let the question of money worry us. But I have come to see you and to talk things over."

"What's there to talk about? But sit down."

"This I will do," said Riabinin, sitting down and leaning on the back of the chair with the greatest discomfort. "You have to come down, prince. Justice demands it. And the money is ready definitely, to the last kopeck. We must not let the question of money worry us."

Levin, who had just put his gun into the closet and was ready to leave, stopped at the door on hearing the merchant say these words.

"You know full well that you got the timber for nothing," he said. "He came to see me too late, or I'd have set the price."

Riabinin rose, smiled, and keeping silent, looked upward at Levin.

"Konstantin Dmitrievich is very stingy," he said with a smile, addressing Stepan Arkadievich. "You definitely cannot buy anything from him. I tried to buy his wheat; I offered a good price."

"Why should I give you mine for nothing? I don't find it accidentally, nor do I steal it."

"God forbid! In our times it is positively impossible to steal. Nowadays we definitely have open law courts to take care of this; everything is now done in a noble way, not at all by stealing. Ours were honorable dealings. He asks too much for his timber; I will hardly make anything on it. I am asking him to come down at least a little."

"Is your deal set or not? If it is, there's no use in bargaining, and if it isn't," said Levin, "I'll buy the timber."

The smile suddenly vanished from Riabinin's face, which took on a hawklike, rapacious, hard expression. With his bony fingers he quickly opened his coat, displaying his shirt, which he wore outside his trousers, the brass buttons of his vest and his watch chain, and he quickly brought out his old, thick wallet.

"The timber is mine, if you please," he said, quickly crossed himself, and extended his hand. "Here is the money, and the timber is mine. This is how Riabinin does business, he doesn't pinch pennies," he said, frowning and waving his wallet.

"In your place I'd be in no hurry," said Levin.

"But wait," said Oblonsky, surprised, "I gave him my word."

Levin walked out of the room, slamming the door. Riabinin looked after him, smiling and shaking his head.

"Ah, youth, youth. It is definitely pure childishness. Believe me, I am buying it just, so to say, for glory only. Let them know that Riabinin, and no one else, has bought Oblonsky's timber. But God only knows whether I will make anything on it. Believe me. And now, please, let us draw up the contract."

An hour later the merchant carefully buttoned his coat, wrapped his overcoat about him, and, with the contract in his pocket, sat down in his carriage, which was tightly mounted with iron, and left for his home.

"Oh, those gentlemen!" he said to his steward. "What a bunch!"

"Sure enough," answered the steward, handing him the reins, and buttoning the leather apron. "And how about your little deal, Mikhail Ignatich?"

"Well, well. . . ."

17

STEPAN ARKADIEVICH, his pockets bulging with the three months' advance payment made by the merchant, went upstairs. The sale of the timber was concluded, the money was in his pocket, and the hunt had been magnificent. Stepan Arkadievich was now in the happiest frame of mind, and therefore was particularly anxious to see his friend change his mood. He wished to see the day conclude, at suppertime, as happily as it had begun.

Indeed, Levin was in a bad humor, and though he tried to be kind and hospitable to his dear guest, he could not take hold of himself. The heady news that Kitty had not married gradually began to have its effect on him.

Kitty had not married and had fallen ill out of love for the man who had rejected her. It was though the offense had been committed against him. Vronsky had rejected her and she had rejected Levin. Accordingly, Vronsky had the right to despise Levin and therefore was his enemy. But this was not the way Levin saw it. He had a vague feeling that somehow he had been insulted, but he vented his resentment not against the cause of his annoyance, but against everything that came his way. This stupid timber deal, this trick played on Oblonsky, in his house, annoyed him.

"Well, are you through?" he said to Stepan Arkadievich as he came upstairs. "Would you like some supper?"

"I won't refuse. What a wonderful appetite I have in the country! Why didn't you offer Riabinin something to eat?"

"The devil with him."

"The way you treat him!" said Oblonsky. "You didn't even offer him your hand. Why shouldn't you offer him your hand?"

"Because I don't offer my hand to a lackey, and a lackey is a hundred times worthier than he."

"What a reactionary you are! And what about the equality of classes?" said Oblonsky.

"Let him practice it who likes it, but to me it seems disgusting."

"I see you are a convinced reactionary!"

"I assure you that I've never given the matter any thought. I am Konstantin Levin, and that's all!"

"And a Konstantin Levin who's in a bad mood," said Stepan Arkadievich with a smile.

"Yes, in a bad mood, and do you know why? I'm sorry to tell you, but it's on account of your stupid deal. . . ."

Stepan Arkadievich grimaced good-naturedly, like someone who has been offended and disturbed without reason.

"Well, don't worry about it," he said. "Isn't it usually true that when a man has sold something, he's told, 'This was worth much more.' But while he's selling it, nobody offers more. . . . No, I see that you have a great dislike for this unfortunate Riabinin."

"Perhaps I have. And do you know why? You'll again say that I'm a reactionary or you may use some other terrible word. But I'm annoyed and offended when I watch this continuous impoverishment of the class of noblemen to which I belong and to which I am proud to belong in spite of the fusion of classes. And were this impoverishment brought about by a life of luxury, I'd accept it; to live in luxury is a nobleman's privilege, and only the nobleman knows how to do it. But now moujiks buy the lands around us, and this offends me. The master doesn't do anything; the moujik works hard and displaces the idle man. That's how it should be. I'm glad for the moujik. But it hurts me to watch this impoverishment, which is caused by, I really don't know just what to call it, naïveté. Take the landlady, residing in Nice, who sold her magnificent estate at half price to her Polish leaseholder. Or when land is leased to a merchant at a ruble an acre, when it is really worth ten rubles. And you made this rogue a gift of thirty-thousand rubles for no reason."

"What else could I have done? Count the trees?"

"Of course. You didn't count them, but Riabinin did. Riabinin's children will be provided with a living and education, and yours probably won't."

"You'll have to forgive me, but there's something petty in keeping all these accounts. We have our occupation, and they have theirs, and making profit is what they are after. Well, that's that and it's all over. Ah, here's my favorite—fried eggs. And Agafia Mikhailovna, will you give me some of that wonderful herb-brandy?"

Stepan Arkadievich sat down at the table, joked with her and assured her that he had not had such a dinner and supper for a long time.

"At least you praise it," said Agafia Mikhailovna, "but to Konstantin Dmitrievich it makes no difference what you give him, even if it's just a crust of bread; he has his meal and leaves."

No matter how much Levin tried to take hold of himself, he still remained gloomy and silent. He had to ask one more question of Stepan Arkadievich, but he could not resolve to do it, could not decide on how to phrase it, nor could he find the right time for it. Stepan Arkadievich had by this time gone downstairs, undressed, washed again, put on a ruffled night shirt, and lain down. Levin lingered in Oblonsky's room, spoke about trifles, but could not gather the courage to ask him his question.

"What wonderful soap they make now!" he said, unwrapping and examining a bar of fragrant soap that Agafia Mikhailovna had prepared for the guest, but Oblonsky had not used. "Isn't it a work of art?"

"Yes, they have now improved everything," said Stepan Arkadievich, yawning blissfully and heartily. "Take, for instance, the theaters and amusement places . . . ah—ah—ah!" he yawned. "Electric light all over, ah—ah!"

"Yes, electric light," said Levin. "Yes. And where's Vronsky now?" he asked, suddenly putting aside the soap.

"Vronsky?" said Stepan Arkadievich, stifling a yawn. "He's in Petersburg. He left soon after you did, and since then hasn't once returned to Moscow. And, Kostia, I must tell you the truth," he continued, leaning his elbow on the table. He rested his rosy handsome face on his hand, his sentimental, kind and sleepy eyes shining like stars. "It's all your fault. You were afraid of your rival. And, as I told you then, I don't know which of the two of you had the better chance. Why didn't you follow through? I told you then. . . ." He yawned with his jaws only, without opening his mouth.

Does he or doesn't he know that I proposed? thought Levin, looking at him. Yes, there's something shrewd and diplomatic in his face. He felt that he was blushing, and in silence he looked squarely at Stepan Arkadievich.

"She was carried away by appearances, and that's all that happened to her," continued Oblonsky. "You know, his aristocratic nature and his brilliant career impressed not her but her mother."

Levin frowned. The burning pain caused by the refusal began anew; the old wound in his heart opened. But he was at home, and at home the very walls help.

"Wait a minute, wait a minute," he said, interrupting Oblonsky. "You speak about his aristocratic nature. May I ask what is this aristocratic nature of Vronsky's or of anybody else that made them reject me? You consider that Vronsky is an aristocrat, and I am not. A man whose father made his way in life through knavery, whose mother had God knows how many affairs. . . . No, you must forgive me, but I consider that *I* am an aristocrat, as are people like me, who can proudly point to three or four honorable generations preceding them, all highly educated—as to natural intellectual gifts, that's a different question—who never curried favor with anyone, never needed anybody's help. That's the way my father and grandfather lived, and I know many others like them. You consider it humiliating to count the trees in the woods, and you make Riabinin a gift of thirty thousand rubles, but you'll get a lease or some other awards, whereas I'll get nothing, therefore I prize what was left to me by my ancestors and what I've acquired by my work. . . . We're the aristocrats, not those who can live only by handouts from the people in power and whose price is but twenty kopecks."

"But whom are you attacking? I agree with you," said Stepan Arkadievich, sincerely and cheerfully, though he felt that Levin was including him among those whose price was twenty kopecks. He sincerely liked to see Levin so animated. "Whom do you have in mind? Though much of what you've said about Vronsky isn't true, this isn't what I want to tell you. I'm telling you bluntly that in your place I would now go to Moscow—"

"Well, I don't know whether you know it or not, and it makes no difference. I want to tell you that I proposed and was refused, and that the thought of Katerina Aleksandrovna now brings me only pain and shame."

"Why? What nonsense!"

"Let's not talk about it. I ask your forgiveness for being so ill-humored," said Levin. Now, having unburdened himself, he felt much as he had in the morning. "You're not angry with me, Stiva? Please, don't be angry," he said, smiling and taking his hand.

"No, I'm not angry at all, far from it. I'm glad that we now understand each other. You know, sometimes a hunt in the early morning can be fine. Shall we go? I won't sleep anyway, and right from the hunt we can go to the station."

"Splendid."

18

THOUGH VRONSKY'S inner life was all taken up with his passion, his external life rolled on, without change and without restraint, along his former, familiar pattern, shaped by his social and regimental interests and connections. Vronsky's regiment played an important part in his life, both because he loved his regiment, and even more because he was loved by his regiment. And in the regiment they not only loved Vronsky, they respected him and were proud of him. They were proud that he, a man immensely rich, with excellent education and abilities, one to whom the road to every kind of success, advancement, and magnificence lay open, that such a man rejected all this and held his regiment and comrades nearer to his heart than any other interest in his life. Vronsky was aware of his fellow officers' opinion, and he not only loved the life he led but also considered it his duty to sustain this generally accepted opinion.

It goes without saying that he spoke to none of his fellow officers of his love. He said not a word about it even at the wildest drinking parties (he was never so drunk as to lose his self-control), and he cut short any of his thoughtless friends who tried to hint at his love affair. In spite of the fact that his love was known all over the city—everyone guessed, more or less accurately, the nature of his relationship with Karenina— most of the young men envied him especially for the great difficulties in which his love involved him. These were caused by the high social standing of Karenina, which made the love affair so conspicuous.

Most of the young women, who envied Anna and who for a long time had been tired of hearing Anna called *"the right-eous one,"* were glad that their conjectures had proved true; they were only waiting for the change in public opinion so that they might assault her with all the weight of their scorn. They had already prepared clods of mud with which to spatter her when the time came. Most of the older people and those of high standing were displeased with this forthcoming public scandal.

Vronsky's mother, on hearing of his love affair, was pleased at first, both because she believed that there was nothing like a fashionable love affair to add the final touch of refinement to a brilliant young man, and because Karenina, whom she liked so much and who spoke to her so much about her son, nevertheless well fitted Countess Vronsky's general opinion of all beautiful and honorable women. But she had recently discovered that her son had refused a position of great importance to his career just to remain with the regiment and thus be able to see Karenina. She had also learned that some highly placed people were displeased with this, so she changed her opinion. And the information she had received about this love affair also displeased her. It was not one of those brilliant, graceful, fashionable affairs of which she would approve; she was told that it was an all-absorbing passion, like Werther's, which might lead her son to some foolish acts. She had not seen him since his sudden departure from Moscow and, through her older son, demanded that he come to see her.

The older brother was also displeased. He did not care what kind of love affair his younger brother had, great or little, passionate or passionless, wicked or not (he himself, the father of several children, kept a dancing girl, so he was liberal in his opinions), but he knew that this was an affair that displeased those who must be kept pleased, and therefore he did not approve of his brother's behavior.

In addition to his regiment and the social circle, Vronsky had another interest: horses, of which he was a passionate admirer.

Officers' steeplechase races were announced for that year. Vronsky entered, bought a full-blooded English mare, and in spite of his love, and though he tried to restrain himself, became passionately interested in the forthcoming races.

These two passions were not in each other's way. On the contrary, he needed some occupation and an all-absorbing diversion, unconnected with his love, to refresh him and bring him respite from his violent emotions.

19

ON THE DAY of the races at Krasnoye Selo, Vronsky arrived earlier than usual at the regimental mess to have his steak. He did not have to watch his diet too closely, for he was at the required weight, just around one-hundred and sixty pounds; but he still had to avoid putting on weight, and therefore he stayed away from starches and sweets. He sat, his coat unbuttoned over his white vest, leaning on the table with both arms while waiting for the steak, and looked into a book, a French novel open on his plate. He looked into the book only to avoid conversation with officers who were entering and leaving, for he was lost in thought.

He thought of Anna, who had promised to see him that day after the races. He had not seen her for three days; her husband had returned from abroad, and Vronsky did not know now whether she could come today or not, nor did he know how to find out about it. The last time he had seen her had been at his cousin Betsy's country house. But he visited Karenina's country home as little as possible. He now planned a visit there and was wondering how to arrange it.

Of course, he thought; I'll tell her that Betsy sent me to inquire whether she was coming to the races. Of course I'll go there, he decided in his own mind, raising his face from the book. His face shone with vivid happiness in the anticipation of seeing her.

"Send somebody to my house to ready my troika," he told the waiter, who served him the steak on a hot silver plate; and Vronsky reached for the plate and began to eat.

From the billiard room next door came the sounds of crashing balls, conversation, and laughter. Two officers emerged from the room: one of them, young, with a weak, thin face, had only recently graduated from the Corps of Pages and joined their regiment; the other was an older, plump officer, with a bracelet on his wrist and with small, puffy eyes.

Vronsky glanced at them, frowned, pretended not to notice, and looking sideways at his book, began to eat and read simultaneously.

"So you are building yourself up for your work?" said the plump officer, sitting down next to him.

"As you see," said Vronsky, without looking at him. He frowned and wiped his mouth.

"Aren't you afraid you'll put on weight?" he asked, offering a chair to the young officer.

"What?" said Vronsky angrily, his face expressing utter displeasure and showing his even teeth.

"Aren't you afraid you'll put on weight?"

"Waiter, some sherry!" said Vronsky without answering, and placing the book on the other side of him, he continued to read.

The plump officer took the wine list and turned to the younger officer.

"You choose the drinks," he said, handing him the list and looking at him.

"Rhenish, perhaps," said the young officer, glancing shyly at Vronsky and trying to tug at his scrubby mustache with his fingers.

Seeing that Vronsky was paying no attention to them, the young officer rose.

"Let's go to the billiard room," he said.

The plump officer rose obediently, and they went toward the billiard room.

At that moment the tall, well-built Captain Yashvin entered the room, and giving a disdainful upward nod to the two officers, he went over to Vronsky.

"Ah! Here he is!" he said, with a strong slap of his large hand on Vronsky's shoulder strap. Vronsky looked up angrily, but immediately his face brightened and showed its usual calm and self-assured kindness.

"Good for you, Alyosha," said the captain in his loud baritone voice. "Eat now and have only one small glass of wine."

"But I'm not hungry."

"The inseparable ones," added Yashvin, looking derisively at the two officers who at that moment were leaving the room. He sat down near Vronsky. The chair was too low for him, and he had to bend his thighs and shinbones into a sharp angle in his tight trousers. "Why didn't you come to the Krasnensky Theater last night? Numerova wasn't bad at all. Where were you?"

"I was delayed at the Tverskoys'," replied Vronsky.

"Ah!" came Yashvin's reply.

Yashvin, a gambler and a rake, a man devoid of any principles but immoral ones, was Vronsky's closest friend in the regiment. Vronsky loved him for his unusual physical strength, which he displayed mostly by drinking without end and spending sleepless nights without feeling any ill effect. He loved him for the steadfastness he showed both in his relations to his superiors and to his fellow officers—who repaid him with fearful respect—and at the gambling table, where the stakes were in the tens of thousands of rubles, and where, in spite of the amount of wine he happened to consume, he always remained so shrewd and self-confident that in the English club he was considered the foremost gambler. Vronsky particularly loved and respected him because he felt that Yashvin loved him not for his name and wealth but for his own sake. He was the only person to whom Vronsky could speak about his love. He felt that only Yashvin, in spite of his seeming disdain for all emotions, could understand the strong passion that now filled his life. Moreover, he was sure that Yashvin did not relish the current malicious gossip but properly understood his feelings, in the proper way, that is to say, that he believed that love was not a trifle, not a pastime, but something more serious, more important.

Vronsky did not talk to him about his love, but he knew that Yashvin knew all about it and understood it properly, and it pleased him to read this in his eyes.

"Ah, yes!" Yashvin said, thinking of Vronsky's visit to the Tverskoys'. And his black eyes twinkling, he pulled on the end of his left mustache, as if to chew on its tip, a bad habit of his.

"And how did you do yesterday? Did you win?" asked Vronsky.

"Eight thousand. But I'm not sure of three; most probably he won't pay."

"Then you can afford to lose, betting on me," said Vronsky, laughing. Yashvin had bet heavily on Vronsky.

"I won't lose. You just have to watch out for Makhotin."

And their conversation turned to the forthcoming race, which now occupied all of Vronsky's thought.

"Let's go. I'm through," said Vronsky. He rose and walked to the door. Yashvin also rose, straightening his huge legs and long back.

"It's too early for dinner, but there's time for a drink. I'll follow you in a minute. Wine!" he shouted in his powerful voice, which made windows shake, a voice that was famous on the parade ground. "No, never mind," he added quickly, shouting again. "If you're going home, I'll go with you."

They walked out together.

20

VRONSKY STAYED IN a spacious and clean Finnish cottage, divided by a partition into two parts. Petritsky also shared these quarters with him during the summer exercises. Petritsky was asleep when Vronsky and Yashvin came into the house.

"Get up. You've slept enough," said Yashvin, walking behind the partition and shaking Petritsky, who was asleep, his hair ruffled and his nose stuck into the pillow.

Petritsky rose to his knees with a start and looked about him.

"Your brother was here," he told Vronsky. "He woke me up, may the devil take him, and said he'd be back." With that he threw himself on the pillow and pulled up the blanket. "Stop, Yashvin," he said angrily to Yashvin, who tried to pull his blanket off. "Stop." He turned around and opened his eyes. "You'd better tell me what I should drink. I have such an awful taste in my mouth that. . . ."

"Vodka is best of all," said Yashvin in his deep voice. "Tereshchenko! Vodka and pickles for your master," he shouted, evidently enjoying the sound of his own voice.

"Vodka, you think? Eh?" asked Petritsky, grimacing and rubbing his eyes. "Will you have a drink? Let's all have a drink. Vronsky, will you have a drink?" said Petritsky, getting up and wrapping himself to the armpits in a tiger-skin blanket. He came into the doorway of the partition, raised his hands, and sang in French, " 'There was a king in Thu-u-le.' Vronsky, will you have a drink?"

"Go away," said Vronsky, who was putting on his coat with the assistance of his valet.

"Where to now?" Yashvin asked him. "Your troika is here," he added, seeing the carriage coming up to the house.

"To the stables, and then I have to see Briansky, too, about the horses," answered Vronsky.

Vronsky really had promised Briansky, who lived ten versts from Peterhof, that he would bring the money he owed him for the horses. He was anxious to keep the appointment. But his friends understood immediately that this was not the only place he was going.

Petritsky kept on singing, winked, and pursed his lips, as if to say, "We know who *that* Briansky is."

"See that you're not late," said Yashvin, changing the topic of the conversation. "How's my roan? Serving you well?" he asked, looking out the window and referring to the thill horse he had sold to Vronsky.

"Wait!" shouted Petritsky to Vronsky, who was now leaving. "Your brother left a letter and a note. Wait, where are they?"

Vronsky stopped.

"Well, where are they?"

"Where are they? That's the question!" said Petritsky solemnly, moving his index finger from his nose into the air.

"Don't be a fool. Tell we where they are," said Vronsky, smiling.

"I made no fire in the fireplace. They must be somewhere here."

"Enough of your lies! Where's the letter?"

"Upon my word, I forgot. Perhaps it was only a dream. Wait, wait, why should you get angry? If you'd had four bottles, as each of us had yesterday, you wouldn't know where you were either. Wait, give me a minute to remember!"

Petritsky went behind the partition and lay down on his bed.

"Wait a minute! I was lying here, and he was standing there. Yes, yes, yes. . . . Here it is," and Petritsky pulled out the letter from under the mattress where he had hidden it.

Vronsky took the letter and his brother's note. It was what he had expected, a letter from his mother, reproaching him for not coming to see her, and a note from his brother, stating that he had to talk to him. Vronsky knew that it all concerned the same matter. "What business is it of theirs?" he thought, and, crumpling the letters, he shoved them between the buttons of his coat, intending to read them more carefully during the ride. In the entrance hall he met two officers, one from his regiment and the other from a different one.

Vronsky's apartment was always a hangout for officers.

"Where to?"

"On business to Peterhof."

"Has the horse arrived from Tsarskoye?"

"Yes, but I haven't seen it yet."

"They say Makhotin's Gladiator limps!"

"Nonsense! But how will you race in this mud?" the other asked.

"Here are my saviors!" cried Petritsky when he caught sight of the newcomers. His orderly was standing before him, holding a tray with vodka and pickled cucumber. "Yashvin tells me I must take a drink to refresh myself."

"You certainly caused us a lot of trouble yesterday," said one of the newcomers. "We couldn't sleep at all the whole night."

"But listen to how it ended," said Petritsky. "Volkov climbs onto the roof and says that he feels sad. I say, 'Give us some music, a funeral march!' And there he fell asleep, to the strains of the funeral march."

"Have a drink, a drink of vodka by all means, then some seltzer water and plenty of lemon," said Yashvin, standing over Petritsky like a mother who makes her child take medicine. "And then a little champagne, about one bottle."

"That makes sense. Wait, Vronsky, let's have a drink."

"No. Goodbye, gentlemen, no drinks for me today."

"Why not? Afraid to get too heavy? Well, we'll have a drink without you. Bring us some seltzer water and a lemon."

"Vronsky!" someone called as he was already leaving the entrance hall.

"What is it?"

"You'd better get a haircut; your hair is too heavy, particularly on the bald spot."

Vronsky, in fact, was balding prematurely. He laughed gaily, showing his even teeth, and, covering the bald spot with his cap, he left and seated himself in the coach.

"To the stable!" he said. He was about to reach for the letters, meaning to read them, but he changed his mind; he did not want to be distracted before he had examined the horse. Later, he thought.

21

THE TEMPORARY STABLE, a wooden structure, had been erected right next to the race track, and on the previous day his horse was to have been brought there, but he had not seen her yet. During the last few days he had not exercised her himself, but had entrusted the trainer to do it, and now he was completely ignorant of the horse's condition. As soon as he alighted from the carriage, his groom, referred to as "boy," recognized the carriage from afar and called the trainer. The lean Englishman, dressed in high boots and a short jacket, with his beard a tuft of hair under his chin, came out to meet him, walking with the awkward gait of a jockey, swaying, with his elbows out.

"How's Frou-Frou?" Vronsky asked, in English.

"All right, sir," said the Englishman, his voice issuing from somewhere in his throat. "It's better not to go in," he added, tipping his hat. "I've put on a muzzle, and the horse is disturbed. It's better not to go in; it will upset the horse."

"No, I'll go in. I want to see her."

"Let's go then," replied the Englishman, still without opening his mouth. He frowned and, swinging his elbows, walked ahead with his disjointed gait.

They went to the small yard adjoining the stable. The boy on duty, dressed in a white jacket, trim and sprightly, with a broom in his hand, met the arrivals and followed them. There were five horses in the stalls of the stable, and Vronsky knew that that day his chief rival, Makhotin's chestnut Gladiator, which was over sixteen hands, was to be brought here. Vronsky had not yet seen Gladiator and was more eager to see him than his own horse. But Vronsky knew that, according to the rules of the sport, it was not only forbidden to see him, it was improper to inquire about him. As they walked along the corridor, the boy opened the door to the second stall on the left, and Vronsky saw a tall chestnut horse with white legs. He knew that this was Gladiator, and with the feeling of a man who turns away from an open letter that was not addressed to him, he turned away and went to Frou-Frou's stall.

"That's the horse which belongs to Makh . . . Makh . . . I can never pronounce his name," said the Englishman over his shoulder, pointing with his dirty thumb at Gladiator's stall.

"Makhotin? He's my most dangerous rival," said Vronsky.

"If you'd ride him," said the Englishman, "I'd bet on you."

"Frou-Frou is more spirited, but this one is stronger," said Vronsky, pleased with this praise of his riding skill.

"In the steeplechase, all that counts is riding skill and pluck," said the Englishman.

Not only did Vronsky feel that he possessed enough pluck, but, what was more important, he was fully convinced that no one in the world possessed more than he.

"Are you sure that she needs no more exercise?"

"She doesn't," replied the Englishman. "Please don't talk so loud. The horse is disturbed," he added, indicating the closed stall with his head. They stood before it now, and from within came the sound of straw rustling under the horse's feet.

He opened the door, and Vronsky entered the stall, dimly lit by one small window. A dark, muzzled bay stood there, shifting her feet on the fresh straw. In the semidarkness of the stall, Vronsky again took in at a glance all the features of his beloved horse. Frou-Frou was of middle stature, and her form was not without defects. Her bones were narrow, and though her breastbone protruded, her chest was narrow. Her back sloped downward, and her front legs, and even more so her hind ones, were noticeably turned inward. The muscles of her hind and front legs were not very large, but she was unusually large in the saddle girth, which, thanks to the training she had undergone and the leanness of her belly, was now particularly striking. The bones of her legs below the knee seemed no thicker than a finger when viewed from the front, but unusually broad when viewed from the side. All her body except her ribs seemed compressed from the sides and elongated. But her most outstanding characteristic, one that caused all her defects to be forgotten, was her *blood;* and it was that blood that, according to the English saying, *would tell.* Her muscles, sharply outlined under a network of veins, spread under her mobile, thin, and smooth-as-satin skin, looking as strong as her bones. Her lean head, with its shining, gay, protruding eyes, widened toward the nose, her nostrils flaring, the membrane between them rich with blood. All her body, and particularly her head, clearly expressed vigor combined with gentleness. She was one of those animals that, it would seem, do not speak only because the structure of their mouths does not permit them to do so.

It seemed, at least to Vronsky, that she understood all that he felt now as he looked at her.

As soon as Vronsky came in, she breathed sharply, and turning her protruding eye sideways so that the white of it filled with blood, she looked at the visitors from the farther side of the stall, shaking her muzzle and shifting her springy legs.

"You see how upset she is," said the Englishman.

"Oh, you darling! Oh!" said Vronsky, coming over to her. But the nearer he came to her, the more excited she grew. Only when he came over to her head did she calm down suddenly, the muscles quivering under her thin, delicate skin. Vronsky stroked her sturdy neck, straightened a lock of her mane, which fell on the other side of her withers, and moved his face toward her extended nostrils, thin as a bat's wing. She took in a noisy breath and then exhaled it through her straining nostrils, started, dropped her pointed ear, and extended her black, firm lip to Vronsky, as if intending to catch his sleeve. But that reminded her of the muzzle; she shook it and again began to shift her small chiseled legs.

"Calm down, dear, calm down!" he said, stroking her back, and happy to know that the horse was in absolutely perfect shape, he left the stall.

The horse's excitement communicated itself to Vronsky; he felt that the blood was rushing to his heart and, like the horse, he wanted to move and to bite; he was both frightened and happy.

"Well, I rely on you," he told the Englishman. "Be on the spot at exactly six-thirty."

"Everything is just fine," said the Englishman. "And where are you going now, Milord?" he asked, suddenly using the word "Milord," which he almost never used.

Vronsky, surprised, raised his head and looked at the Englishman, not at his eyes but at his forehead, as he was capable of doing. He was surprised at the boldness of the question. But he understood that the Englishman, in asking the question, saw in him not his employer, but a jockey, and answered:

"I have to see Briansky; I'll be back at home within an hour."

How many times today have I been asked that same question? he asked himself, and blushed, something he seldom did. The Englishman looked at him attentively. And, as if he knew where Vronsky was going, he added:

"It's most important to be calm before the race. Don't get into a bad humor and don't let anything disturb you."

"All right," Vronsky said, smiling. Jumping up into his carriage, he told his coachman to take him to Peterhof.

They had traveled only a short distance when the cloud, which since that morning had threatened to bring rain, drew near, and with it came a downpour.

Too bad! thought Vronsky, raising the top of his carriage. It was muddy enough; now it'll be a quagmire. Secluded in his closed carriage, he reached for his mother's letter and his brother's note and read them.

Yes, it was all the same. Everyone, including his mother and his brother, considered it his duty to interfere with the affairs of his heart. This interference aroused his enmity, a feeling he seldom experienced. What business is it of theirs? he thought. Why does everyone consider it his duty to worry about me? Why are they annoying me? Because this is something they can't understand. If this were the usual vulgar liaison of people of fashion, they would leave me alone. But they feel that this is something different. It isn't a pastime; this woman is dearer to me than my own life. They can't understand this, that's why it annoys them. Whatever our fate holds for us, we ourselves have shaped it, and we don't complain about it, he thought, with this word "we" joining Anna and himself together. No, they have to teach us how to live. They have no idea what happiness is; they don't know that without this love there's no happiness for us, no unhappiness, no life, he thought.

He was angry at all of them for interfering in his affairs precisely because, within his heart, he felt that they, all of them, were right. He felt that the love that bound him to Anna was not a temporary infatuation that, like all other love affairs in the fashionable world, would pass, leaving in the lives of the partners nothing but pleasant or unpleasant memories. He felt all the poignancy of his situation and hers, all the strain in trying to hide their love, to lie and deceive, being so exposed in the social world. He felt the effort of trying to lie, to deceive, to beguile, and to think constantly of others, when the passion that bound them was so strong that both of them remained oblivious of anything but their love.

He recalled vividly all the frequently recurring instances when he had to resort to lies and deception, so contrary to his nature; he recalled with singular vividness that he often saw her ashamed for being forced to resort to lies and deception. And since the beginning of his affair with Anna, he had often experienced a strange feeling. He felt that he loathed something; whether it was Aleksei Aleksandrovich, or himself, or all the social set, he did not quite know. But he always tried to rid himself of this feeling. Collecting himself, he continued along this line of thought.

Yes, he thought, she was unhappy before, but she had her pride and serenity; now she no longer has her serenity and dignity, though their absence doesn't show. Yes, this situation must come to an end, he decided.

And for the first time, the thought came clearly to his mind that this deception had to come to an end, and the sooner the better. We'll leave everything behind he said to himself, she and I; we'll secrete ourselves, alone with our love.

22

THE DOWNPOUR did not last long. The thill horse trotted at full speed, pulling the side horses, which were now given free rein and galloped over the muddy ground. When Vronsky neared his destination, the sun reappeared, the roofs of the villas and the old linden trees in the gardens on both sides of the main street sparkled with wet brilliance, the tree branches dripped gaily and water ran down the roofs. He no longer worried that the rain would mar the race track but felt happy that, thanks to the rain, he would surely find her at home, and probably alone, for he knew that Aleksei Aleksandrovich, who had recently returned from the spas, had not yet arrived from Petersburg,

Hoping to find her alone, Vronsky alighted before crossing the bridge, as he always did to arouse less attention and walked on foot. He did not enter through the front entrance but through the yard.

"Has the master arrived?" he asked the gardener.

"No, but the mistress is at home. Would you rather go through the front entrance? Somebody will open the door for you," said the gardener.

"No, I'll enter through the garden."

He was sure to find her alone and wanted to surprise her, for he had not promised to come that day, and most probably she did not think that he would come before the races. He walked along, holding his saber and carefully stepping on the gravel of the path, flanked by flowers, that led toward the terrace facing the garden. All the thoughts he had had on the way here, regarding their situation and its difficulties, were now forgotten. He thought about one thing only, that he was going to see her now, not in his imagination, but in person, all of her, the way she actually was. Coming up the sloping steps of the terrace, and placing his weight so as to make the least noise, he suddenly remembered what he always tended to forget, and which was the most tormenting part, of his relationship with her: her son, with his questioning and, it seemed to him, hostile eyes.

More often than anything else, this boy was the obstacle to their relations. In his presence Vronsky and Anna would not permit themselves to say anything that they would not repeat in the presence of other people; they did not even permit themselves to drop any hints the boy would not understand. They had never agreed between themselves to act this way; the rule came by itself. They would have considered it an insult to themselves to deceive this child. In his presence they spoke like old friends. Yet, in spite of these precautions, Vronsky often saw the attentive and puzzled look the boy fixed on him, and noticed his strange shyness. The boy's relationship with him was uneven: sometimes tender, at other times cold and shy. It seemed that the boy felt that there existed some important relationship between this man and his mother, the meaning of which he could not understand.

And, in fact, the boy felt that he could not understand this relationship and tried to make clear to himself what feeling he should have toward this man; but he was unable to do it. With a child's sensitiveness to other people's reactions, he clearly saw that his father, the governess, the nurse, all of them not only disliked Vronsky but regarded him with fear and repugnance, though they did not say anything about him; but he saw that his mother considered him her best friend.

What does this mean? thought the child: Who is he? Should I love him? If I don't understand him, it is probably my fault, or else I'm a stupid or a bad boy. And this resulted in that seeking, questioning, partly unfriendly expression of his, the shyness and changeability that so embarrassed Vronsky. The boy's presence always stirred in him that unreasonable feeling of disgust which he had lately experienced. The presence of this child stirred in Vronsky and Anna a feeling like that of a navigator who, watching his compass, sees that the direction he is rapidly moving in is at considerable variance with the prescribed course, yet he is powerless to stop; each minute takes him farther from his prescribed course, but to confess that he must retreat would be a confession that he is lost.

This child, with his naïve view of life, was the compass that showed them the degree of their deviation from what they knew but did not want to know.

This time Seryozha was not at home, and Anna was alone. She sat on the terrace, waiting for her son, who had gone for a walk and been caught in the rain. She had sent a manservant and a girl to look for him. She sat there, in the corner of the terrace behind the flowers, in a white dress with a good deal of embroidery, and did not hear him coming. She inclined her head, with its black curls, and pressed her forehead against the cold watering can that stood on the balustrade and which she held with her beautiful hands, the rings on her fingers so familiar to him. The beauty of her whole person, of her head, her neck, her hands, always came to him as a revelation. He stopped and looked at her, enraptured. But as he was going to take a step to approach her, she felt his approach, set aside the watering can, and turned her flushed face toward him.

"What is it? Aren't you well?" he asked in French, coming up to her. He wanted to run up to her, but recalling that some-one else might be there, he glanced at the door leading to the terrace, and blushed, as he always did when he had to be fearful and watchful.

"No, I am well," she said, rising and squeezing his outstretched hand. "I didn't expect you."

"My God, how cold your hands are!" he said.

"You frightened me," she replied. "I'm alone and am waiting for Seryozha, who went for a walk; they'll soon bring him here."

And though she tried to look calm, her lips trembled.

"Please forgive me. I'm here because I couldn't spend a day without seeing you," he continued in French, which he always used, thus avoiding both the Russian "you," unbearably cold in their relationship, and the dangerous Russian "thou."

"You have nothing to apologize for. I'm so glad."

"But you're not well, or perhaps worried," he continued, bending over her without letting her hand go. "What have you been thinking about?"

"About the same thing," she said, smiling.

She was telling him the truth. At any moment, if asked what she was thinking about, she could truthfully answer: about one thing only, about her happiness and unhappiness. And at this moment, when he surprised her, she was thinking why it was that a matter that other people, Betsy for example, treated so lightly (she knew about her secret affair with Tushkevich), was the cause of torment for her. For some reason, this thought particularly tormented her today. She asked him about the race. He answered, and seeing that she was troubled, he tried to distract her and in the simplest terms began to explain all the preparations for the race.

Shall I tell him or shall I not? she thought, looking at his calm tender eyes. He's so happy, so busy with his race, that he won't understand how all-important this event is for us.

"But you haven't told me what you were thinking of when I came in," he said, interrupting his account. "Please tell me."

She did not answer, and inclining her head slightly, gave him a questioning look from underneath her long eyelashes, her eyes sparkling. Her hand, which was playing with a leaf, trembled. He saw it, and his face expressed that submissiveness, that slavish devotion, which always moved her.

"I see that something has happened. Can I be calm even for a moment, knowing that I don't share your worry? Please tell me, for God's sake!" he begged her.

But I can't forgive him if he fails to understand the full

importance. Perhaps it would be better not to say anything. Why test him? she thought, still looking at him the same way, but feeling that the hand that held the leaf trembled more and more.

"For God's sake!" he repeated, taking her hand.

"Should I tell you?"

"Yes, yes, yes. . . ."

"I am pregnant," she said, slowly and softly.

The leaf in her hand trembled even more violently. She did not lower her eyes, but watched how he would take it. He paled, wanted to say something, but held back. He let her hand go and lowered his head. Yes, he understands the full importance of this event, she thought, and she gratefully pressed his hand.

But she was mistaken, thinking that he had understood the importance of this news in the same way as she, as a woman, had understood it. At this news he felt ten-fold the strange, ill-defined disgust he had experienced repeatedly. At the same time he understood that the crisis he wished for had arrived, that it was no longer possible to keep their secret from her husband, that the present unnatural situation had to come to an end in some manner. Moreover, her agitation was now directly imparted to him. He looked at her with his tender, submissive look, kissed her hand, rose, and in silence paced up and down the terrace.

"Yes," he said, walking up to her resolutely. "Neither you nor I have considered our relationship a pastime, and now our fate is sealed. We must bring an end," he said, looking around, "to this state of deception in which we live."

"Bring it to an end? How, Aleksei?" she asked softly. She was calm now, and her face shone with a tender smile.

"Leave your husband and join our lives together."

"They are joined even now," she answered, in a hardly audible voice.

"Yes, but to join them completely, completely."

"But how, Aleksei? Show me how we can do it," she said, her melancholy humor now directed at the hoplessness of their situation. "Is there really a way out of such a situation? Am I not my husband's wife?"

"There is a way out of every situation. We have to make a decision," he said. "Any situation would be better than that in which you find yourself. I see how much suffering everything causes you: society, your son, your husband."

"Ah, not my husband," she said with a frank smile. "I don't know anything about him; I don't think about him, he doesn't exist. . . ."

"You don't really mean that. I know you. You suffer on account of him, too."

"And he doesn't even know it," she said, and suddenly a bright blush covered her face. Her cheeks, forehead and neck reddened, and tears of shame filled her eyes. "Let's not talk about him."

23

VRONSKY HAD several times attempted, though not with such determination as now, to lead her into a discussion of her situation, but each time she had responded to his attempts with superficial and trifling remarks, as she did now. It seemed that there was something in this subject that she could not or would not see clearly; that as soon as she started to talk about it, she, the real Anna, withdrew somewhere within herself, and another woman appeared, strange and unknown, whom he did not love but feared, and who resisted him. But today he made up his mind to clear up the whole matter.

"Whether he knows or not," said Vronsky in his usual firm and calm manner, "whether he knows or not doesn't concern me at all. We cannot . . . you cannot live any longer under these circumstances, particularly now."

"What's to be done, then?" she asked in the same lightly mocking tone. She, who had so feared that he would take the news of her pregnancy too lightly, was annoyed that he was using it as the compelling reason for taking decisive action.

"He must be told all, and you must leave him."

"Very well, suppose I do it," she said. "Do you know what it will lead to? I'll tell you everything in advance," and a wicked fire kindled in her eyes, so tender a moment ago. " 'Well, you love another man and you have a *criminal* liaison with him.' " (She was mimicking her husband, and, like Aleksei Aleksandrovich, she underscored the word criminal.) " 'I have warned you of its results in every respect, religious, civilian and familial. You have not heeded my advice. Now I cannot expose to disgrace my name' "—she was going to add "and my son," but decided that she could not jest this way about her son—" 'to disgrace my name,' or something else of this kind," she added. "In a word, he'll state, clearly and exactly, in the manner of a high official, that he cannot release me; that he will take all necessary measures to suppress the scandal. And he'll do all these things calmly and precisely. That's what will happen. This is not a man but a machine, and an evil machine when it gets angry," she added, recalling Aleksei Aleksandrovich in every detail, his way of speaking, his nature, holding against him all the wrongs she could find in him but allowing nothing for the horrible crime against him she herself was guilty of.

"But Anna," said Vronsky in a persuasive, soft voice, trying to calm her, "we still must tell him, to see how he'll react, and then make our plans accordingly."

"What then? Will we elope?"

"Why not? I don't see how this can possibly continue. I'm not talking about myself. I see how much you suffer."

"Yes, to elope, and then I become your mistress?" she said bitterly.

"Anna," he said, with a tender reproach.

"Yes," she continued, "to become your mistress and to ruin everything. . . ."

She again wanted to say "for my son" but she could not pronounce the words.

Vronsky could not understand how she, with her strong and honest nature, could endure this state of deceit and have no desire to free herself from it. He did not realize that the main cause of this was her *son*, whom she could not bring herself to mention. When she thought of her son, and of the feelings he would have toward a mother who had forsaken his father, she felt so horrified at what she had done that, as a woman, she did not use reason, but only tried to soothe herself with false words and arguments in order to leave everything unchanged and to avoid the terrifying problem of her son's future.

"Please, I beg of you," she said suddenly, in an entirely different, sincere, and tender tone, taking his hand. "Never bring up the subject again."

"But, Anna. . . ."

"Never. Leave everything to me. I know all the vileness and baseness of my situation, but to find a way out of it is not as easy as you think. Leave everything to me and do as I say. Never speak to me about it. Do you promise? . . . No, promise me. . . ."

"I promise you everything, but I can't remain calm, particularly after what you've told me. I can't remain calm if you're not calm. . . ."

"I?" she repeated. "Yes, sometimes I suffer deeply, but it will pass, if you never mention it again. It only torments me when you mention it."

"I don't understand," he said.

"I know," she interrupted, "how hard it is for you, who are so honest, to lie, and I sympathize with you. I often think that for my sake you've ruined your life."

"I was just thinking the same thing," he said. "How could you sacrifice everything for my sake? I can't forgive myself when I see that you are unhappy."

"I unhappy?" she asked, coming nearer to him and looking at him, her smile enraptured and loving. "I? I am the hungry man who was given food. Perhaps he is cold, his clothes tattered; he feels ashamed, but he is not unhappy. I unhappy? No, here's my happiness!"

She heard the voice of her son, who had returned, and with a quick glance around the terrace, she rose abruptly. Her eyes lit up with a familiar flame. She hastily raised her beautiful hands, covered with rings, took his head, gave him a long look, and, her lips parted and smiling, she brought her face close to his, hurriedly kissed his mouth and both eyes, then pushed him aside. She wanted to go, but he restrained her.

"When?" he whispered, looking at her in rapture.

"Tonight at one o'clock," she whispered. She sighed heavily, and left with her light, quick step to meet her son.

Seryozha and his nurse had been caught in the rain in the large garden and had waited in the bower until it passed.

"Well, goodbye," she told Vronsky. "It will soon be time to go to the races. Betsy promised to take me there."

Vronsky looked at his watch and left hurriedly.

24

WHEN VRONSKY looked at his watch on the Karenins' terrace, he was so disturbed and preoccupied that, though he saw the hands of the dial, the time didn't register in his mind. He went to the road and, carefully stepping through the mud, headed toward his carriage. He was so completely taken up with his feelings toward Anna that he never thought about the hour and it did not occur to him that he might not have enough time to go to see Briansky. As often happens, all he remembered was the sequence of the things he had decided to do. He came over to the coachman, who was dozing on his box in the deepening shadows of a leafy linden tree, admired the shifting pillars of midges which hovered over the well-fed horses, and after awakening the coachman, he jumped into the carriage and ordered him to take him to Briansky's. Only after they had gone about seven miles, and he had looked at his watch again, did he realize that it was half-past five, and that he was late.

Several races were scheduled for that day: the convoy race, the two-verst officer's race, the four-verst race, and the one in which Vronsky was to take part. If he went to Briansky's, he had enough time to make his race but he would arrive at the races after all the court had already assembled. This would be unthinkable. But he had promised Briansky that he would be there that day, so he decided to go, ordering the coachman to have no pity on the troika.

He arrived at Briansky's, spent only five minutes with him, and raced back. The speed of the ride calmed him. All that was troublesome in his relationship with Anna, all that their discussion had left unanswered, all of that ceased to worry him. With delight and excitement he now thought of the race, for which he would surely be on time; and now and again the anticipation of the happiness that evening's rendezvous would provide shone brightly in his imagination.

His preoccupation with the forthcoming race grew as he plunged deeper and deeper into the atmosphere of the races, overtaking carriages journeying from the country villas and from Petersburg to the race track.

No one was at his apartment; everyone was at the races, and his servant was waiting for him at the gate. While he changed, the servant informed him that the second round of races had started, that many gentlemen had come to ask for him, and that the boy from the stable had come twice.

After he had unhurriedly changed (he never hurried and never lost his self-control), Vronsky ordered his driver to take him to the stables. When he reached the stables, he could see a sea of carriages, pedestrians and soldiers standing around the race track, and people crowding the pavilions. Evidently the second group of races were running, because as he entered the stable, he heard the bell. As he came nearer, he saw

Makhotin's white-legged chestnut, Gladiator, being led to the track, covered by an orange cloth trimmed with blue. The horse's bluish ears were pulled back against his head and appeared unusually large.

"Where's Cord?" he asked the stableboy.

"In the stable, saddling."

Frou-Frou, already saddled, stood in the open stall. They were ready to lead her out.

"I'm not late, am I?"

"It's all right! It's all right! Everything is fine, everything is fine," said the Englishman. "Don't get excited."

And again Vronsky glanced at the beautiful shape of his beloved horse, whose whole body quivered, and with difficulty tore himself away from this beautiful sight and left the stable. He rode over to the pavilions, choosing a time when he would attract the least attention. The two-verst race had just ended, and all eyes were riveted upon a Horse Guards man followed by a hussar of the Life Guards, who with all their remaining strength spurred on their horses as they approached the finish line. From outside and inside the large circle, everyone crowded toward the finish line, and a group of Horse Guards officers and soldiers shouted loudly, expressing their joy in anticipation of victory of their comrade and officer. Unnoticed, Vronsky slipped into the middle of the crowd just at the sound of the bell announcing the end of the race. The tall, mud-spattered Horse Guard, who had come in first, lowered himself into the saddle and slowly gave rein to his gray, heavily breathing stallion, darkened by sweat.

Straining his legs, the stallion slowed the motion of his heavy body. The Horse Guard looked around and made an effort to smile, like a man awakened from a heavy sleep. A crowd of friends and strangers surrounded him.

Vronsky deliberately shunned the elite high-society crowd, which moved about in front of the pavilions freely and unhurriedly, engaging in conversation. He found out that Karenina was there, and Betsy, and his sister-in-law, but he did not go over to them to avoid distraction. He was repeatedly stopped by acquaintances who related to him all the details of the previous races and inquired why he was late.

When those who had participated in the race were called to the pavilion to receive their prizes, and everyone moved in that direction, Vronsky's older brother Aleksandr, a colonel wearing shoulder knots, came over to him. He was of medium height and as stocky as Aleksei, but more handsome and rosy, with a red nose and an open, drunken face.

"Did you receive my note?" he asked. "One can never get you."

Aleksandr Vronsky, though a famous rake and unrestrained drunkard, was a true courtier. And now, speaking to his brother on a matter which was very unpleasant to him, and knowing that many eyes might be fixed on them, he assumed a gay air, as if they were exchanging some trifling remarks.

"I received it, and I must confess that I don't understand what *you* are worried about."

"I'm worried because I've just been reminded that you weren't here, and that on Monday they had seen you in Peterhof."

"There are some matters which should be discussed only by those whom they concern, and the matter that worries you is one of them. . . ."

"But then those people aren't in the service, aren't—"

"Please don't interfere in my affairs, that's all." Aleksei Vronsky's frowning face paled, and his protruding jaw trembled, something which very seldom happened to him. A very kindhearted man, he seldom grew angry, but when he did, his chin trembled, and he was dangerous, as Alexandr Vronsky well knew. Alexandr Vronsky smiled gaily.

"I just wanted to deliver our mother's letter. Write to her and don't get upset before your race. *Bonne chance,*" he added and smiling, left him.

And now a friendly greeting stopped Vronsky. "You don't know your friends any longer! How are you, *mon cher?*" said Stepan Arkadievich, and even here, in this brilliant Petersburg set, no less than in Moscow, he shone with his rosy face and sleek, well-groomed side whiskers. "I arrived yesterday and I'm happy to be present at your triumph. Where shall we meet?"

"Come to the mess tomorrow," said Vronsky, and he pressed his arm, apologized, and left for the track, where they were already leading out the horses for the great steeplechase.

The sweating horses, tired by the races, were being walked by the grooms and then led to their stalls. New ones appeared one after another, mostly English horses, ready for the forthcoming race, fresh, wearing their hoods, their bellies drawn, and resembling strange, huge birds. Vronsky's beauty, Frou-Frou, was led by on his right. She was lean, and she walked as though on springs, her pasterns resilient and quite long. Not far from her, they were taking the cloth off lop-eared Gladiator. Vronsky's attention was drawn involuntarily by the large, beautiful, regular features of the stallion, and his marvelous back and unusually short pasterns right above his hoofs. He wanted to go over to the horse, but another acquaintance stopped him.

"Ah, there's Karenin!" said the friend with whom he was talking. "He's looking for his wife. She's inside the pavilion. Haven't you seen her?"

"No, I haven't," replied Vronsky and, without even looking toward the pavilion, where, he had been told, Karenina was, he went over to his horse,

Vronsky had intended to give instructions concerning his saddle, but he hardly had time to look at it when the riders were called to draw their numbers and take their places. Seventeen officers, their faces serious and severe, many pale, crowded the pavilion and took their numbers. Vronsky drew number seven. The command to mount was sounded.

Feeling that he and the other riders were the cynosure upon which all the eyes were fixed, Vronsky, now in that state of tension in which he usually kept his movements calm and deliberate, walked over to his horse. On this festive day of the races, Cord had put on his formal dress: a black buttoned-up coat, a stiffly starched collar which reached his cheeks, a round black hat, and jackboots. As always, he was calm, looked important, and, standing in front of the mare, himself held her by both reins. Frou-Frou kept trembling as if in a fever. Her eye, full of fire, peered sideways at Vronsky as he came up to her. Vronsky put his finger under the saddle band. Her eye glowed still more brightly, and she showed her teeth and pulled her ear back. The Englishman puckered his lips and ventured a condescending smile at the attempt to check his way of saddling.

"Mount her and you won't worry so much."

For the last time, Vronsky glanced at his rivals. He knew that during the race he would not see them. Two of them were already riding up to the starting point. Galtsin, a dangerous rival and a friend of Vronsky's, was busy with his bay stallion, which would not let him mount. A little hussar of the Life Guards, in tight riding pants, galloped by, bent like a cat over the horse's croup, in attempt to imitate the English. Prince Kuzovlev sat pale on his full-blooded Grabovsky mare, his

Englishman holding the bridle. Vronsky and all his comrades knew Kuzovlev, his "unsteady" nerves, and his unusual egoism. They knew that he was afraid of everything and dreaded riding a race horse. But now, just because it was dangerous, because riders often broke their necks and because at every obstacle there was a doctor on duty as well as a nurse, and an ambulance with a red cross painted on it, just because of all of this, he decided to race. Their eyes met and Vronsky winked at him, kindly and approvingly. However, he had not yet caught sight of his chief rival, Makhotin, on Gladiator.

"Take your time," Cord said to Vronsky, "and remember one thing: don't hold her back at the jumps and don't push her. Let her choose her own way."

"All right, all right," said Vronsky, taking the reins.

"If possible, take the lead, but don't give up until the last minute, even if you are last."

The horse had not yet moved when Vronsky, with a strong and facile motion, put his foot in the indented steel stirrup and sat his solid body firmly on the squeaking leather of the saddle. With his right foot he took the other stirrup, and in his customary way lined up the two reins between his fingers. Cord let go. As if undecided about which foot to put forward, Frou-Frou, pulling the reins with her long neck, stepped forward as though on springs, rocking her rider on her supple back. Cord followed them, hurrying to keep up. The excited horse pulled the reins now to one side, now to the other, trying to deceive her rider, and in vain Vronsky tried to calm her by his voice and by his hand.

They were now nearing the dammed stream, heading toward the starting point. Many of the riders were ahead of him, others behind him, when Vronsky suddenly heard behind him the sound of a horse galloping through the mud, and Makhotin passed him on his white-legged, lop-eared Gladiator. Makhotin smiled, displaying his long teeth, but Vronsky looked at him angrily. He had never liked him, but now he considered him his most dangerous rival, and he was annoyed that he had galloped by, disturbing his horse. Frou-Frou raised her left leg, took two or three steps at a gallop, but, angered by the taut reins, changed to an uneven trot, jolting her rider. Cord also frowned and almost had to run to keep up with Vronsky.

25

IN ALL, there were seventeen officers in the race. The track was a four-verst ellipse facing the pavilion. The ellipse contained nine jumps: a stream; a large, solid barrier nearly five feet high built right in front of the pavilion; a dry ditch; a ditch filled with water; a slope; an Irish embankment (one of the most difficult obstacles) comprising an embankment with dry branches protruding from it, beyond which, invisible to the horse, was another ditch, so that the horse had to clear both obstacles or perish; there followed two more ditches with water and one dry, and then came the end of the race track, in front of the pavilion. But the race began not on the ellipse, but at some distance outside it. The first obstacle was here, the dammed stream about seven feet wide, which the riders could jump over or ford, as they pleased.

Three times the horses formed up at the starting line, but each time one of the horses did not hold, and they had to start all over again. The skilled starter, Colonel Sestrin, was just about to lose his patience when at last, after the fourth try, he gave the command, "Go!" and the riders started.

All eyes, all binoculars had been fixed on the multicolored group of horsemen while they were trying to take their places in line.

"They've started! They're off!" was heard now on all sides, after the silent waiting.

Groups of people and single pedestrians now ran from place to place to get a better view. From the very first moment, the crowded group of horsemen spread out and, as they approached the stream, they could be seen following one another in groups of two or three. It seemed to the viewers that all of the riders had started simultaneously, but they had not, and these momentary differences were of great importance to them.

The disturbed and overwrought Frou-Frou had lost the first moment, and a few horses started earlier than she. But even before reaching the stream, Vronsky, who with all his might tried to control his horse, which strained the reins, easily passed three riders. Now ahead of him were only Makhotin's chestnut Gladiator, his back rocking rhythmically directly in front of Vronsky, and, leading all of them, the beautiful Diana, carrying the half-dead Kuzovlev.

For the first few minutes, Vronsky could not quite control either himself or his horse. Until he reached the first obstacle, the stream, he could not direct his horse's movements.

Gladiator and Diana were nearing the obstacle together and reached it almost at the same moment. As one, they rose above the stream and landed on the other side. Effortlessly, as if flying, Frou-Frou rose into the air, following them, but at this moment Vronsky, suspended in the air, saw, almost under the feet of his horse, Kuzovlev wresting with Diana on the other side of the stream (Kuzovlev had given her free rein after the jump, and the horse had leaped forward, throwing him over her head). These details Vronsky learned later, but now he only saw that Frou-Frou's legs might land directly upon the head and legs of Diana. But, like a falling cat, she twisted her legs and back while still in the air, bypassed the horse and rushed onward.

Oh, you darling! thought Vronsky.

Beyond the stream Vronsky gained full control over the horse and began to restrain her, intending to clear the large barrier after Makhotin and only during the next open stretch to try to pass him.

The large barrier was right in front of the Czar's pavilion. The Czar, the whole court, and crowds of people were watching him and, one length in front of him, Makhotin, as they neared the devil (as the solid barrier was called). Vronsky felt these looks directed at him from all sides, but did not see anything except the ears and neck of his horse, the ground racing past him, and the croup and white legs of Gladiator, pounding rhythmically and rapidly at a fixed distance from him. Gladiator rose into the air noiselessly, flicked his short tail, and disappeared from Vronsky's view.

"Bravo!" a lone voice shouted.

At that same moment, the boards of the barrier flashed in front of Vronsky's eyes. Without the slightest change in her motion, the horse rose underneath him, the boards vanished, and only a thump was heard behind him. Aroused by Gladiator running in front of her, the horse rose far before the fence and hit it with a hind hoof. But her gait did not change, and Vronsky, a clod of dirt hitting his face, knew that he was still no closer to Gladiator. Again he saw in front of him his croup, his short tail, and the same fast-moving, white legs, which, at any rate, were not gaining.

At the very moment when Vronsky thought that it was the right time to pass Makhotin, Frou-Frou herself, aware of his intention and not requiring any urging, increased her speed, and began to close in toward Makhotin on the more advantageous side, the side close to the rope. But Makhotin held close to the rope. As soon as Vronsky decided that he could pass Makhotin on the other side, Frou-Frou also changed her direction and began to pull up on that side. Frou-Frou's shoulder, already darkening with perspiration, caught up with Gladiator's croup. They galloped side by side for a short distance. But before reaching the jump which was coming up, Vronsky, in order to avoid losing ground, began working the reins, and as they reached the slope, he quickly passed Makhotin. He had a glimpse of his face, bespattered with mud. It even seemed to him that he smiled. Vronsky had passed Makhotin, but he felt him hard on his heels, and heard right behind his back the ceaseless, even gallop and the short, yet vigorous breathing of Gladiator's nostrils.

The next two jumps, the ditch and the barrier, he cleared easily, but the sound of Gladiator's gallop and snorting grew nearer. He gave freer rein to the horse and was happy to feel that she easily picked up speed, and that Gladiator's hoofs now sounded again from the former distance.

Vronsky was leading the race. That was what he had wished, what Cord had advised him to do, and he was now sure of victory. His agitation, his happiness and his tenderness toward Frou-Frou grew greater. He wished to look back, but dared not; he tried to keep calm and to keep the horse reined to maintain in her a reserve of strength equal to that which he felt Gladiator still possessed. There still remained one jump, the most difficult. If he cleared this one before the others, he would come in first. They were nearing the Irish embankment. Both he and Frou-Frou caught sight of this embankment from afar, and both horse and rider were seized with a momentary qualm. The horse's ears, it seemed to him, betrayed some hesitancy, and he raised his riding stick, but felt immediately that his doubt was ill-founded: the horse knew what had to be done. She added speed, and, just as he had expected, she rose evenly, pushing herself off the ground and abandoning herself to the force of inertia which transported her far beyond the ditch. Effortlessly, starting with the same leg on which she had landed, preserving the same speed, she resumed the race.

"Bravo, Vronsky!" shouted a group standing near the jump. He knew that they were his friends and members of his regiment; Yashvin's voice was unmistakable, although he could not see him.

"Oh, my darling!" he said, thinking of Frou-Frou and listening to the sounds behind him. He made it, he thought, hearing Gladiator's stride behind him. There remained only the last ditch, filled with water, a yard-and-a-half wide. Vronsky didn't even look at it and, aiming to be far ahead, began working the reins in a circular motion, lifting and lowering the horse's head in rhythm with the gallop. He felt that the horse was using her last reserves. Not only were her neck and shoulders wet but drops of sweat appeared on her withers, her head, and her pointed ears; her breathing was short and labored. But he knew that this reserve was greater than was needed for the remaining five hundred or so yards. Only because he felt himself closer to the ground and by the singular suppleness of her movements, did he know that she had greatly increased her speed. She flew over the ditch without seeming to notice it. She flew over it like a bird. But at the same moment, to his horror, Vronsky felt that he had not followed the horse's movement properly, and without knowing why he did it, he made a wrong, unforgivable move, letting himself down in the saddle. Suddenly his situation changed, and he knew that something terrible had happened. He could not yet realize what it was, but right in front of him flashed the white legs of the chestnut stallion, and Makhotin rushed past him in a headlong gallop. One of Vronsky's feet was touching the ground, and his horse was falling toward that foot. He hardly had time to get it out of the way, when she fell on one side, wheezing heavily, and, stretching her thin, perspiring neck in a vain effort to rise, she fluttered on the ground at his feet like a wounded bird. The awkward movement which Vronsky had made had broken her spine. But he did not know this until much later. Now he could only see Makhotin rapidly drawing ahead while he, tottering, stood there alone on the muddy ground that was no longer rushing by. In front of him lay Frou-Frou; she was breathing heavily, and, turning her head toward him, she looked at him with her beautiful eyes. Still unaware of what had happened,

Vronsky pulled on the reins. She struggled like a small fish, flapping the saddle, and freed her front legs; unable to lift her back, she again struggled helplessly and fell over on her side. His pale face distorted with terror, his jaw trembling, Vronsky kicked her belly with his heel and again pulled on the reins. But she did not move, pressed her nose to the ground, and just looked at her master with a meaningful look.

"Aaah!" muttered Vronsky, clutching his head. "What have I done! I've lost the race! It's my fault. It's shameful, unforgivable! And this unfortunate, dear, shattered horse! Aaah! What have I done!"

A crowd, including the doctor and his assistant, and his fellow officers, ran up to him. To his sorrow, he felt that he was safe and unharmed. The horse had suffered a broken spine, and it was decided that she must be shot. Vronsky could not answer any questions, and could speak to no one. He turned away and, without picking up his cap, which had fallen off, he left the race track, unaware of where he was going. He felt crushed. For the first time in his life he had suffered a great misfortune, an irreparable misfortune of which he alone was the cause.

Yashvin, holding Vronsky's cap, caught up with him, saw him to his house, and within half an hour Vronsky had recovered. But this race remained with him for a long time as a most oppressing and tormenting memory.

26

OUTWARDLY, THE RELATIONSHIP between Aleksei Aleksandrovich and his wife remained unchanged, the only difference being that now he kept even busier than before. As in former years, with the arrival of spring, he went abroad to restore his health, which was always affected by the winter's labors. As usual, he returned in July and at once resumed his customary work with increased energy. As always, his wife moved to the country, while he remained in Petersburg.

Since the discussion they had had after the evening at Princess Tverskoy's, he never spoke to Anna about his suspicions and jealousy, and his usual mocking tone was most suitable for his present relationship with his wife. He behaved somewhat more coldly to her. It seemed that he was rather displeased with that first discussion that evening, in which she had declined to take part. There was a trace of annoyance in his relationship with her, but nothing else. You refused to give an explanation, he seemed to say, addressing her in his thoughts. So much the worse for you. Now it is you who will ask me for an explanation, and it will be I who will decline. So much the worse for you, he said to himself, like a man who, vainly trying to put out a fire, grows annoyed with his own efforts and says, It serves you right! Now you will burn down!

Clever and shrewd in his official duties, he did not fully understand the abnormality of such a relationship with his wife. He did not understand because he was too frightened to face his present situation, and within his heart he closed, locked, and sealed that compartment which contained his feelings toward his family, that is, toward his wife and son. He had always been a thoughtful father, but since the end of the winter he had grown particularly cold toward his son and treated him with the same ridicule as his wife. "Oh! Young man!" was his way of addressing him.

Aleksei Aleksandrovich said and thought that he had never been so occupied with his official duties as this year. But he did not realize that much of this year's business he had created himself, that this was one way to keep locked the compartment containing his feelings toward his wife and family and his thoughts about them, which grew more terrible the longer they were confined there. If anyone had had the right to ask Aleksei Aleksandrovich what he thought of his wife's behavior, the mild and quiet Aleksei Aleksandrovich would not have replied, but would have become very angry with the questioner. And just for this reason there was something haughty and stern in the expression on Aleksei Aleksandrovich's face when he was asked about his wife. Aleksei Aleksandrovich did not want to think about his wife's behavior and feelings, and, in fact, did not think of them at all.

Aleksei Aleksandrovich's permanent country residence was in Peterhof, where Countess Lydia Ivanovna also usually spent her summers. She lived not far from Anna, and they saw each other often. This year, Countess Lydia Ivanovna refused to go to Peterhof, paid not even one visit to Anna Arkadievna, and hinted to Aleksei Aleksandrovich that Anna's close association with Betsy and Vronsky was embarrassing.

Aleksei Aleksandrovich cut her off with the remark that his wife was above any suspicion, but since then he had avoided Countess Lydia Ivanovna. He did not want to see, and he did not see, that many members of the social set already looked askance at his wife; he did not want to understand, and he did not understand, why his wife had been so persistent in her desire to move to Tsarskoye, where Betsy lived, and which was not far from Vronsky's regimental camp. He did not permit himself to think of it, and so he did not. Nevertheless, though he never said it to himself and though he was unable not only to prove it but even to surmise it, deep within his heart he felt without doubt that he was a husband whose wife was deceiving him, and this made him profoundly unhappy.

How many times during eight years of happy married life, seeing how other wives were unfaithful and husbands deceived, had Aleksei Aleksandrovich said to himself, How can they allow it? Why don't they put an end to this ugly situation? But now, when misfortune had befallen him, he not only refused to think of how to put an end to the situation, he did not even want to recognize its existence, and he did not want to admit it just because it was so horrible, so unnatural.

Since his return from abroad, Aleksei Aleksandrovich had been at the country house twice. Once he stayed for dinner, and the other time he spent the evening with the guests, but not once did he stay overnight, contrary to his custom of former years.

The day of the races was a very busy one for Aleksei Aleksandrovich. In the morning he prepared a schedule for his entire day and decided that right after an early dinner he would go to the country to take his wife to the races, where all the court would be present, and where his presence was required. He would visit his wife because he had decided to see her once a week for the sake of propriety. Moreover, this was the fifteenth of the month, when, according to an established rule, he gave her expense money.

With his usual mental control, after he had thought about his wife as much as was needed, he did not allow himself to think any more about her.

It was a busy morning for Aleksei Aleksandrovich. The previous evening Lydia Ivanovna had sent him a brochure of a famous traveler in China, who was at that time in Petersburg, and a letter asking him to receive the traveler, a man who, for various reasons, was very interesting and important. Aleksei Aleksandrovich had not had time to finish the brochure the previous evening and did it that morning. Then he became busy with petitioners, reports, visitors, appointments, releases, matters of rewards, pensions, salaries, correspondence, all routine matters, as Aleksei Aleksandrovich called them, which always took up so much time. Then a personal matter, the doctor's visit, and the visit of his private secretary. The secretary did not take up much of his time. He just handed Aleksei Aleksandrovich the money he needed and made a short business report. The report was not very favorable, for, as it happened, because of the Karenins' busy social calendar their expenses were large, and the account showed a deficit. But the doctor, a famous Petersburg resident on friendly terms with Aleksei Aleksandrovich, took up much time. Aleksei Aleksandrovich had not expected him today; he was surprised at his arrival, the more so because the doctor carefully inquired about his health, examined his chest, tapped him and palpated him. Aleksei Aleksandrovich did not know that his friend Lydia Ivanovna, noticing that this year Aleksei Aleksandrovich's health had declined, had asked the doctor to go to examine him. "Do it for my sake," said Countess Lydia Ivanovna when she asked him to examine him.

"I'll do it for Russia, Countess," answered the doctor.

"He's an invaluable man," said Countess Lydia Ivanovna.

The doctor was quite dissatisfied with the state of Aleksei Aleksandrovich's health. He found that his liver was considerably enlarged, that his digestion was impaired, and that the water cure had had no effect. He advised him to be as active physically as he could and to avoid mental exertion as much as possible, and he particularly warned him against worrying which, of course, Aleksei Aleksandrovich could no more stop doing than he could stop breathing. He departed, leaving Aleksei Aleksandrovich with the unpleasant feeling that something was wrong with him and that it was not remediable.

After leaving Aleksei Aleksandrovich, the doctor came out on the porch and met Sliudin, Aleksei Aleksandrovich's manager, whom he knew well. They had been university classmates and, though they seldom met, they respected each other and were good friends. Therefore to no one but Sliudin would the doctor express his sincere opinion about Aleksei Aleksandrovich's condition.

"I'm so glad that you saw him," said Sliudin. "He's not well, and it seems to me. . . . What do you say?"

"Here's my opinion," said the doctor, motioning over Sliudin's head to his coachman to bring up the carriage. "Here's my opinion," said the doctor again, drawing his kid glove over one finger with his white hand. "If you try to break a string which has not been stretched, it will prove very difficult. But stretch it as taut as possible and it will snap at the touch of the finger. His assiduity, his utter devotion to his work, have put an unbearable strain on him, and he is subjected to an outside pressure, a heavy pressure," concluded the doctor, meaningfully raising his eyebrows.

"Are you going to the races?" he added, as he descended to his carriage, which the coachman had brought up. "Yes, of course, it takes much time," said the doctor in reply to Sliudin's words, which he could not make out.

After the doctor, who had taken up so much of his time, came the famous traveler, and Aleksei Aleksandrovich, availing himself of the facts he had learned from the brochure and his general information on the subject, impressed the traveler both by the depth of his knowledge and the breadth of his enlightened views.

Simultaneously with the appearance of the traveler was announced the arrival of a provincial marshal of nobility, who had arrived in Petersburg and whom Aleksei Aleksandrovich had to interview. After his departure there were some routine matters to go over with his office manager, and then he had to see a highly placed person on a serious and important matter. Aleksei Aleksandrovich did not return until five o'clock; then he had dinner with the office manager, and invited him to accompany him to the country and to the races.

Without realizing it, Aleksei Aleksandrovich was looking for any excuse to have a third person present at his meetings with his wife.

27

ANNA WAS UPSTAIRS, standing before the mirror, and with Annushka's help was attaching the last bow to her dress when she heard the sound of wheels on the gravel in the driveway.

It's too early for Betsy, she thought, and looking through

the window, she saw the coach, a black hat emerging from it, and the familiar ears of Aleksei Aleksandrovich. Just at the wrong time. Will he really spend the night? she thought, and everything to which this could lead appeared to her so horrible and so frightening that, without a moment's thought, she came out to meet them, her face sparkling with cheer. The familiar spirit of deceit and lies possessed her, and at once she abandoned herself to this spirit and began to talk, not knowing herself what she was going to say.

"How nice!" she said, giving her hand to her husband and greeting their family friend Sliudin with a smile. "You will stay overnight, I hope?" were the first words that the spirit of deceit made her say. "We'll go to the races together. But it's a pity; I promised Betsy I'd wait for her. She's coming to pick me up."

Aleksei Aleksandrovich frowned at the mention of Betsy's name.

"Oh, I wouldn't think of separating inseparable friends," he said in his usual jesting manner. Mikhail Vasilievich and I will go together. The doctors want me to walk. I'll take a walk on the way and make believe that I am at the spa."

"There's no hurry," said Anna. "Would you like tea?" She rang the bell.

"Serve tea and tell Seryozha that Aleksei Aleksandrovich has arrived. Well, how is your health? Mikhail Vasilievich, you've never been here. Look how nice it is on the balcony," she said, turning first to one and then to the other.

Her words were simple and natural, but she spoke too much and too quickly. She felt it herself, the more so because she noticed the inquisitive and watchful look which Mikhail Vasilievich cast in her direction.

Mikhail Vasilievich immediately went out onto the balcony. She sat down next to her husband.

"You don't look quite well," she said.

"Yes," he said, "the doctor came to see me and took up an hour of my time. I believe that one of my friends sent him to see me. My health is so precious. . . ."

"Well, what did he say?"

She inquired about his health and his work and asked him to take a rest and move to the country.

All this she said gaily, rapidly, and with a peculiar gleam in her eyes. But Aleksei Aleksandrovich did not see anything peculiar in this tone of hers. He heard only her words, and accepted them at face value. He replied to her frankly, though jokingly. There was nothing remarkable in this conversation, but later on Anna could never recall this short scene without painful and tormenting shame.

Seryozha came in, preceded by the governess. If Aleksei Aleksandrovich had allowed himself, he would have noticed the shy and confused look with which Seryozha glanced first at his father, then at his mother. But he did not want to see anything, and so he did not.

"Ah, young man! He's grown up. Looks like a man now. How are you, young man?"

He extended his hand to the frightened Seryozha. Seryozha had always been shy in his relationship with his father, but since Aleksei Aleksandrovich had begun calling him "young man," and since he himself had begun to wonder whether Vronsky was a friend or an enemy, he had avoided his father. As though seeking help, he looked up at his mother; he felt at ease only with his mother. In the meantime Aleksei Aleksandrovich exchanged a few words with the governess, holding his son by the shoulder, and Seryozha felt so painfully embarrassed that, as Anna noticed, he was on the verge of tears.

Anna had blushed at the moment when her son came in and, noticing Seryozha's embarrassment, she quickly rose, took Aleksei Aleksandrovich's hand from her son's shoulder, kissed her son, took him to the terrace, and returned immediately.

"Well, it's time," she said, glancing at her watch. "Why isn't Betsy here?"

"Yes," said Aleksei Aleksandrovich, and rising, he interlaced his fingers and cracked his knuckles. "I've brought you some money, since fair words butter no parsnips," he said. "You need the money, I believe."

"No, I don't . . . yes, I do . . ." she said without looking at him, blushing to the roots of her hair. "I hope you'll be back after the races."

"Oh, yes!" replied Aleksei Aleksandrovich. "And here is the belle of Peterhof, Princess Tverskoy," he added, looking through the window as a carriage rolled up. It was of English make, the harness without a collar and shaft bow, its tiny body set unusually high. "What elegance! How beautiful! Well, let us also go."

Princess Tverskoy did not come out of the carriage, and her

footman, in half-boots, cape, and black hat, jumped down as they reached the entrance porch.

"I'm leaving. Goodbye," said Anna, and she kissed her son and came over to Aleksei Aleksandrovich, extending her hand. "It was very kind of you to come."

Aleksei Aleksandrovich kissed her hand.

"Goodbye. I am glad that you'll be back for tea," she said and left, sparkling and gay. But as soon as he disappeared from view, she felt the spot where his lips had touched her hand and she shrank in disgust.

28

WHEN ALEKSEI ALEKSANDROVICH appeared at the races, Anna was already sitting next to Betsy in the pavilion in which the highest level of society gathered. She noticed her husband from afar. Two men, her husband and her lover, were the two centers of her life, and without seeing or hearing them she could feel their approach. While he was still some distance away, she sensed her husband's approach and involuntarily followed his movements in the sea of people. She saw that he was coming toward the pavilion, now condescendingly acknowledging the ingratiating bows, now amiably and absentmindedly greeting his equals, and now attentively seeking to catch the eyes of the powerful, raising his large round hat, which pressed on the tips of his ears. She knew all these gestures of his and she loathed them. Only ambition, she thought, only an urge to succeed, that's all that his heart contains. All the rest, lofty ideals, love of learning, religion, all these are but tools for success.

By his searching looks at the ladies' pavilion (he looked straight at her, but did not recognize her in the sea of muslins, ribbons, feathers, umbrellas, and flowers), she knew that he was looking for her, but she deliberately did not acknowledge his glance.

"Aleksei Aleksandrovich!" Countess Betsy called to him, "you are probably looking for your wife. Here she is."

He smiled his cold smile.

"The brilliance of this group is so overwhelming that I am completely dazzled," he said, and he entered the pavilion. He smiled to his wife, as a husband would smile on meeting a wife from whom he had just parted, and greeted the princess and other acquaintances, giving each one his due by exchanging jests with the ladies and salutations with the gentlemen. A gentleman whom Aleksei Aleksandrovich highly respected, an adjutant-general known for his great mind and learning, stood downstairs near the pavilion. Aleksei Aleksandrovich engaged him in conversation.

It was intermission time at the races, and nothing interfered with their conversation. The adjutant-general condemned racing. Aleksei Aleksandrovich objected, defending it. Anna listened to his thin, even voice without missing a single word, and each word of his sounded false and assaulted her ears.

When the three-mile steeplechase started, she leaned forward and, her eyes fixed on Vronsky, she watched him approach his horse and mount her. She could still hear the ceaseless, offensive sound of her husband's voice. She was tormented by anxiety for Vronsky's safety and even more tormented by what seemed to her to be the ceaseless sound of her husband's thin voice, with its familiar intonations.

I may be a wicked and lost woman, she thought, but I don't like to lie, I can't stand lies. But *he*, my husband, feeds on lies. He knows everything; he sees everything. What can he feel, if he talks so calmly? If he were to kill me, to kill Vronsky, I'd respect him. But no, all he needs are lies and decorum, Anna said to herself, not knowing what it was that she really expected of her husband, and what she would like him to be. Moreover, she did not understand that that day's unusual talkativeness on the part of Aleksei Aleksandrovich, which annoyed her so much, was only a sign of his inner anxiety and restlessness. Like a child who has hurt himself and hops about to bring his muscles into action and thereby lessen his pain, so Aleksei Aleksandrovich was in need of mental activity to suppress those thoughts about his wife which, in her presence, in the presence of Vronsky, and with the constant repetition of his name, demanded his attention. And, as it is natural for a child to hop, so it was natural for him to speak in a fluent and learned manner. He said, "Danger is an essential ingredient of cavalry racing. If, in her military history, England can point to some of the most brilliant performances of her cavalry, it is due to one fact only, to the power that during her history she developed in her men and their animals. Sport, in my opinion, is of great importance, but we, as usual, see only the superficial aspect of it."

"Not so superficial," said Princess Tverskoy. "They say that one officer broke two ribs."

Aleksei Aleksandrovich displayed a smile which showed his teeth, but expressed nothing.

"Let us concede, Princess, that this is not a superficial matter, but an internal one. But that's not the point," he said, and he turned again to the general, to whom he spoke in a serious manner. "Don't forget that the riders are military men who have chosen their careers, and you must agree that there is another side to the coin in every profession. This is a necessary part of military duty. The horrible sport of boxing or bullfighting is a sign of barbarism. But this refined sport is a sign of progress."

"Well, I'll never come again; it affects me too strongly," said Princess Betsy. "Don't you agree, Anna?"

"It's true, but you can't tear yourself away," said another lady. "If I were a Roman, I wouldn't miss a single circus."

Anna remained silent, and without lowering her binoculars, she kept looking at one spot.

At that moment a tall general passed through the pavilion. Aleksei Aleksandrovich, interrupting his speech, rose hurriedly, but with dignity, and greeted him with a low bow.

"You're not racing?" the officer asked him jokingly.

"My kind of race is more difficult," answered Aleksei Aleksandrovich respectfully.

And though the answer had no meaning, the officer pretended that he had heard a clever remark from a clever man and that he fully understood *la pointe de la sauce*.

"There are two sides," said Aleksei Aleksandrovich, resuming his interrupted speech, "performers and spectators. I admit that love of this kind of spectacle is the surest sign of the viewer's low standards, but—"

"Princess, a bet!" came the voice of Stepan Arkadievich from below. "Whom are you for?"

"Anna and I are for Prince Kuzovlev," replied Betsy.

"I am for Vronsky. A pair of gloves."

"Accepted!"

"It's wonderful, isn't it?"

Aleksei Aleksandrovich kept silent while the conversation continued around him, but then abruptly resumed his speech.

"I agree that manly games—" he tried to continue.

But at that moment the riders started, and the conversation stopped. Aleksei Aleksandrovich also fell silent, and everyone rose and turned his eyes toward the stream. Aleksei Aleksandrovich was not interested in the race and therefore did not look at the riders, but let his tired eyes wander absent-mindedly over the spectators. His eyes stopped on Anna.

Her face was pale and stern. Evidently she saw nothing and no one, save one person. Her hand convulsively clutched her fan; her breath stopped. He glanced at her and hurriedly turned away to watch other faces.

Look how tense this lady is, just like the others! Aleksei Aleksandrovich said to himself; It's quite natural. He did not want to look at her, but involuntarily his eyes were drawn toward her. He again looked at her face, trying to avoid reading what was so clearly written on it, but against his will he read what he did not want to know, and it terrified him.

Everyone was affected by the first accident, Kuzovlev's fall at the river, but Aleksei Aleksandrovich clearly saw the pale, triumphant face of Anna, happy that the man she watched had not fallen. When, after Makhotin and Vronsky had gone over the large barrier, another officer struck his head and fell dead on the spot, a feeling of horror gripped all the spectators. But Aleksei Aleksandrovich saw that Anna had not even noticed it and could scarcely understand the conversation around her. More and more frequently his eyes turned toward her, and his look grew more penetrating. Anna, absorbed in watching Vronsky, felt her husband's cold eyes fixed on her from the side.

She looked around for a moment, glanced at him questioningly, and turned back, frowning slightly.

"Oh! I don't care," she seemed to tell him; and she did not give him another glance.

It was an unlucky steeplechase, and of seventeen riders more than half fell and suffered injuries. At the end of the race everybody was upset, the more so because the Czar was not pleased.

29

ALL LOUDLY expressed their disapproval, and repeated the sentence pronounced by someone: "All we need now is a circus with its lions." Everyone felt so horrified that, when Vronsky fell and Anna cried out loudly, there seemed nothing unusual in it. But right after this, Anna's face showed a change that was definitely improper. She was completely distraught. She fluttered like a trapped bird. First she wanted to stand up and go anywhere at all, then she turned to Betsy.

"Let's go, let's go," she said.

But Betsy did not hear her. Bending over the rail, she was talking to a general who had come up to her.

Aleksei Aleksandrovich came up to Anna and courteously offered her his arm.

"Let us go, if you wish," he said in French, but Anna was listening to what the general said, and she did not notice her husband.

"They say he also broke his leg," said the general. "It's an outrage."

Without replying to her husband, Anna raised her binoculars and looked at the spot where Vronsky had fallen; but it was so far, and such a crowd had gathered, that she could not make anything out. She lowered the binoculars and was ready to leave, but at that moment an officer galloped up and reported something to the Czar. Anna strained forward to listen.

"Stiva! Stiva!" she called to her brother.

But her brother did not hear her. Again she was ready to leave.

"Once again I offer you my arm, if you wish to leave," said Aleksei Aleksandrovich, touching her with his hand.

She shrank from him with disgust, and without looking at his face, replied, "No, no. Leave me alone. I'll stay here."

She now saw an officer coming toward the pavilion from where Vronsky's mishap had taken place. Betsy waved her handkerchief at him.

The officer informed them that the rider had not been killed, but that the horse had suffered a broken spine.

On hearing this, Anna quickly sat down and covered her face with her fan. Aleksei Aleksandrovich saw that she was crying. She could not restrain either her tears or the sobs that convulsed her breast. Aleksei Aleksandrovich screened her to give her a chance to recover.

"For the third time I offer you my arm," he said after a while, turning toward her. Anna looked at him without knowing what to say. Princess Betsy came to her aid.

"No, Aleksei Aleksandrovich. I brought her and I promised to take her home," interjected Betsy.

"Excuse me, Princess," he said, smiling politely, but looking firmly into her eyes. "I see that Anna is not quite well, and I want her to come with me."

Anna looked about, frightened. Then she rose timidly and took her husband's arm.

"I'll find out how he is and let you know," Betsy whispered to her.

At the exit from the pavilion, Aleksei Aleksandrovich, in his usual way, exchanged a few words with acquaintances, and Anna, as always, had to take part and answer questions, but she did not know what she was doing, and in a daze she walked arm in arm with her husband.

Was he killed or not? Is it true? Will he come or not? Will I see him tonight? she wondered.

Without speaking, they took their seats in Aleksei Aleksandrovich's coach, and they were still silent when it emerged from the multitude of carriages. In spite of everything he had seen, Aleksei Aleksandrovich did not permit himself to think of the true circumstances surrounding his wife. He saw only the outward symptoms. He saw that she had behaved improperly, and considered it his duty to speak to her about it. But he found it very difficult to say only this to her and nothing more. He opened his mouth to tell her how improperly she had behaved, but involuntarily said something completely different.

"It's surprising how much interest these cruel spectacles have for us," he said. "I notice—"

"What? I don't understand," Anna said scornfully.

He felt offended and immediately began to tell her what he had wanted to say.

"I must tell you—" he said.

Here it is, the explanation, she thought fearfully.

"I must tell you that today you behaved improperly," he told her in French.

"In what way did I behave improperly?" she asked loudly, turning her head toward him with a quick movement and looking straight into his eyes. She faced him now not with her former mask of gaiety, but with an air of determination with which she strove to hide the fear she now felt.

"Don't forget," he warned, pointing to the open window behind the coachman.

He rose and closed the window.

"What did you find so improper?" she repeated.

"The despair, which you couldn't hide when one of the riders fell."

He waited for her to contradict him, but she kept silent, looking straight ahead.

"I had already asked you to behave in public in such a way that malicious gossipers would have nothing to say against you. There was a time when I spoke about our private relations; I'm not talking about them now. I'm talking now about our outward relations. You behaved improperly, and I would not like to see it repeated."

She did not hear half of what he said; she feared him, and her only thoughts were whether Vronsky was alive. Did they mean him when they said that he was safe and that the horse had a broken spine? She just feigned a derisive smile when he finished and said nothing because she had not heard what he had said. Aleksei Aleksandrovich had begun his speech bravely, but when he clearly understood what he was saying, the fear which she felt communicated itself to him. He saw her smile, and a strange delusion possessed him.

She smiles at my suspicions, he thought. Yes, she'll now repeat what she told me once before, that there was no foundation for my suspicions, that all this is ridiculous.

Now, with the impending revelation of the entire truth, there was nothing he wished more than to hear her say derisively, as before, that his suspicions were ridiculous and had no foundation. What he knew was so terrifying that he was ready to believe anything. But from the expression on her face, frightened and sullen, he knew that now he could hope for no lies from her.

"Perhaps I am mistaken," he said. "If that's the case, I ask your forgiveness."

"No, you are not mistaken," she said slowly, boldly looking at his cold face. "You are not mistaken. I was desperately frightened and still am. I am listening to you and thinking of him. I love him, I am his mistress. I cannot stand you, I fear you, I hate you. Do whatever you wish with me."

She flung herself into the corner of the coach, buried her face in her hands, and broke into sobs. Aleksei Aleksandrovich remained motionless, staring fixedly before him. But his face suddenly turned as solemnly immobile as the face of a dead man, and this expression did not change until they arrived at the dacha. As they neared their house, he turned to her with the same expression on his face.

"Well then! I demand that you observe the appearances of propriety until such time," he said in a trembling voice, "as I take measures to protect my honor, and I will inform you of them."

He alighted and helped her down. While the servants watched, he shook hands with her in silence, resumed his seat in the coach, and left for Petersburg.

A short while later, Princess Betsy's servant brought her a note:

"*I sent to Aleksei's to inquire about him. He writes that he is well and unharmed, but in despair.*"

Then he *will* come! she thought; How good it is that I told him everything.

She looked at the clock. There still remained three hours, and the recollection of the last meeting kindled her blood.

My God, how light it is yet! It's frightening, but I love to see his face, and I love this eerie light. . . . My husband! Ah, yes . . . thank God, I am through with him.

30

As usually happens in places where people congregate, in the small German spa where the Shcherbatskys were staying a kind of social crystallization occurred, assigning to each his own rigid, defined place. As a particle of water, when chilled, acquires the definite and unchangeable form of a crystal of snow, so each new person, on arriving at the spa, immediately settled in his proper place.

Fürst Shcherbatsky *samt Gemahlin und Tochter* took up a social position that had been defined and predestined by the apartment into which they had moved, by their name, and by their acquaintances.

A real German princess was visiting the spa that year; therefore the social crystallization proceeded with more than usual vigor. Princess Shcherbatsky was very anxious to present her daughter to the German princess, and she performed this ritual on the second day after her arrival. Kitty made a low and graceful curtsey in her Paris dress, a "very simple" one, meaning a very elegant summer dress. The German princess said, "I hope that the roses will soon return to this pretty face," and the Shcherbatskys' life now ran along a firmly outlined course from which it was impossible to deviate. The Shcherbatskys met an English lady and her family, a German countess and her son, who had been wounded in the last war, a Swedish scientist, and M. Canut and his sister. But the principal group to which the Shcherbatskys belonged now comprised a Moscow lady, Maria Evgenievna Rtishchev, and her daughter, whom Kitty did not like, for she, too, had fallen sick as a result of a love affair; also in the group was a Moscow colonel, whom Kitty had seen since childhood in his uniform and epaulettes, and who, with his small eyes, open neck, and colored tie, now seemed unusually ridiculous and boring; but it was hard to get rid of him. When all things had been firmly established, Kitty became very bored, especially since her father had gone to Karlsbad, and she remained alone with her mother. She was no longer interested in the people she knew, feeling that she could learn nothing new from them. Here in the spa she was now principally and intensely interested in observing and speculating about the people she did not know. It was Kitty's way to see the very best in people, particularly in those whom she did not know. And now, speculating on who was who, on the relationship that existed between them, and on the kind of people they were, Kitty created the most wonderful and admirable characters, and in her observations found that her speculations had been correct.

Of all such people she was most interested in a Russian girl who came to the spa in the company of a Russian lady, Madame Stahl, as everybody called her. Madame Stahl was a member of the highest social set, but she was so sick that she could not walk, and only rarely, when the weather was good, could she be seen in a wheel chair. But Madame Stahl, as the princess explained, did not associate with any of the Russians, not so much because of her sickness as because of her pride. The Russian girl attended Madame Stahl and, as Kitty noticed, was very friendly with all the gravely ill people, of whom there were a great number at the spa, and whom she looked after in the most unaffected way. The Russian girl, as Kitty had observed, was not related to Madame Stahl and at the same time was not a hired companion. Madame Stahl called her Varenka, and others addressed her as Mlle. Varenka. Kitty was not only interested in observing the relationship between this girl and Madame Stahl and with other people unknown to her; as so often happens, she felt an inexplicable sympathy for this Mlle. Varenka, and by the looks which the girl directed at her, she knew that the feeling was mutual.

It was not as though Mlle. Varenka had passed the bloom of youth, but rather that she had never experienced youth. She could have been nineteen or thirty. In spite of her sickly complexion, her features made her pretty rather than homely. She would have been considered well-formed but for her excessive leanness and for the disproportionate size of her head in contrast to her medium height; but she could hold little appeal for men. She was like a beautiful but fading flower, which still retains all its petals but has lost its fragrance. Moreover, she probably had no appeal for men because she lacked what Kitty exuded, the suppressed fire of life and the awareness of her own attractiveness.

She always seemed busy with obviously important things, and therefore could not be interested in anything trivial. This contrast with her own nature particularly attracted Kitty to the girl. Kitty felt that in herself and in her way of life, she would find the standard she was now so anxiously searching for: for life's goals and life's values beyond the confines of the social life, which Kitty abhorred, and where the relationship between a girl and men seemed to Kitty now but a shameful exhibition of a commodity waiting for a buyer. The more Kitty watched her unknown friend, the more she became convinced that this girl indeed was that most perfect creature she imagined her to be, and the more she wished to know her.

Both girls met several times a day, and at each meeting Kitty's eyes said, Who are you? What are you? Isn't it true that you are the delightful creature which I imagine you to be? But, for Heaven's sake, her look added, don't think that I permit myself to force my acquaintance upon you. It's just that I love and admire you. I also love you, and you are very, very sweet. And I would love you still more if I had the time, answered the look from the unknown girl. And, indeed, Kitty saw that she was always busy: either she would accompany the children of a Russian family from the spa, or she would carry a blanket to a sick lady and cover her, or she would try to entertain some peevish sick man, or for someone else she would select and buy pastry for his coffee.

Soon after the arrival of the Shcherbatskys, a new couple appeared at the morning water cure, attracting everyone's unfriendly attention. He was a tall, stooped man with huge hands, dressed in a short, ill-fitting old coat, his eyes black, naïve, and at the same time frightening; his companion was a slightly pockmarked, pretty lady, dressed in very poor taste. Assuming that this couple was Russian, Kitty's imagination began to create a moving and beautiful romance of their lives. But the princess, who had found out from the *Kurliste* that these were Nikolai Levin and Maria Nikolayevna, explained to Kitty what a wicked man this Levin was, and all Kitty's dreams about these two persons crumbled. And not only because of the information which her mother had given her, but because he was Konstantin's brother, she at once took a great dislike to these two people. By his usual habit of jerking his head, this Levin aroused in her an irrepressible feeling of abhorrence.

It seemed to her that in his large terrible eyes, which persistently followed her, there was an expression of hatred and derision, and she took pains to avoid him.

31

It was a cloudy day, rain had fallen all morning, and the patients, carrying umbrellas, crowded in the gallery.

Kitty walked with her mother and the Moscow colonel, who gaily paraded his European morning coat, bought in Frankfurt. They walked along one side of the gallery, trying to avoid Levin, who walked along the other. Varenka, in a dark dress and a black hat with its brim turned down, led a blind Frenchwoman the length of the gallery, and every time she met Kitty they exchanged friendly looks.

"Mama, may I talk to her?" asked Kitty, as she watched her unknown friend. She noticed that Mlle. Varenka was headed toward the spring, and that they might meet there by chance.

"Yes, if you are so eager to do so, but first I'll inquire about her and see her myself," answered her mother. "What do you see in her? A hired companion, probably. If you want, I'll meet Madame Stahl. I knew her *belle-soeur*," added the princess, proudly raising her head.

Kitty knew that the princess was hurt that Madame Stahl, it seemed, avoided meeting her. Kitty did not persist.

"She's so wonderful, so charming!" she said, looking at Varenka, who at that moment was helping a French lady to a glass of water. "Look how everything about her is simple and charming."

"Your *engouements* are ridiculous," said the princess. "No, let's turn back," she added, noticing Levin, who was coming in their direction, accompanied by his lady and a German doctor to whom he was speaking loudly and angrily.

As they were turning back, they suddenly heard shouting instead of the loud conversation. Levin stopped and shouted at the doctor, who also was greatly excited. A crowd gathered around them. The princess and Kitty left hurriedly, and the colonel joined the crowd to find out what had happened.

A few minutes later the colonel caught up with them.

"What happened?" asked the princess.

"It's a shame and a disgrace," replied the colonel. "To come across a Russian abroad is one thing you always fear. This tall gentleman quarreled with the doctor, reviled him, claiming improper treatment and threatening him with his cane. It's a disgrace!"

"Ah, how unpleasant!" said the princess. "Well, how did it end?"

"Luckily that lady stepped in, you know . . . in that mushroom hat. A Russian, I believe," said the colonel.

"Mlle. Varenka?" Kitty asked joyfully.

"Yes, yes. She alone knew what to do. She took the gentleman by the arm and led him away."

"You see, Mama," Kitty said to her mother. "And you are still surprised that I admire her."

The next day, observing her unknown friend, Kitty noticed that Mlle. Varenka was on the same terms with Levin and his lady as with her other *protégés*. She came over to them, talked to them, and served as interpreter for the woman, who spoke no foreign languages.

Kitty was still more persistent now in asking her mother's permission to meet Varenka. And though the princess greatly disliked taking the first step in meeting Madame Stahl, who allowed herself, for some unknown reason, to keep aloof, she inquired about Varenka. All the details which she learned proved that there would be neither anything wrong nor much good in making this acquaintance. She first went up to Varenka to introduce herself.

Availing herself of a moment when her daughter had gone over to the spring and Varenka had stopped at the bakery, the princess went over to her.

"Allow me to introduce myself," she said with a dignified smile. "My daughter is in love with you. Perhaps you don't know me. I—"

"The feeling is more than mutual, Princess," replied Varenka quickly.

"What a good deed you did yesterday for our poor compatriot!" said the princess.

Varenka blushed.

"I don't remember. I don't believe I did anything," she said.

"Don't you remember? You saved that Levin from trouble."

"Yes, *sa compagne* called me, and I tried to calm him. He is very sick, and he was dissatisfied with the doctor. And I am accustomed to taking care of sick people."

"Yes, I heard that you live in Mentone with your aunt, Madame Stahl, I believe. I knew her *belle-soeur*."

"She's not my aunt. I call her *Maman*, but I'm not related to her. I'm her ward," Varenka replied, blushing again.

She said it with such simplicity, the charming expression of her face was so frank and truthful, that the princess understood why Kitty was in love with Varenka.

"What about that Levin?" asked the princess.

"He's leaving," Varenka replied.

Just then, beaming with happiness because her mother had met her unknown friend, Kitty came up from the spring.

"Come here, Kitty. You've had such a great desire to meet Mademoiselle. . . ."

"Varenka," Varenka interjected, smiling. "Everyone calls me that."

Kitty blushed with happiness, and for a long while remained silent, holding her new friend's hand and squeezing it. Varenka's hand did not respond to this gesture, but lay motionless in Kitty's hand. Though the hand did not respond, Mlle. Varenka's face lit up with a quiet, joyful, yet somewhat sad smile, which showed her large but beautiful teeth.

"I myself have wished it for a long time," she said.

"But you're so busy. . . ."

"On the contrary, I'm not busy at all," Varenka replied. But at this moment she had to leave her new friends, for two little Russian girls, children of a patient, ran up to her.

"Varenka, Mama is calling you," they said.

And Varenka followed them.

32

FOLLOWING ARE THE details that the princess learned about
Varenka, about her relationship with Madame Stahl, and
about Madame Stahl herself.

Madame Stahl, of whom some said that she had driven her
husband to his death, and others that he had tormented her
by his immoral conduct, was always a sickly but zealous
woman. Her first child, born after her divorce from her husband, died right after birth, and Madame Stahl's relatives,
knowing how sensitive she was and fearing that the news
would kill her, replaced the dead child with another, born to
a court cook the same night and in the same house in Petersburg. That child was Varenka. Later, Madame Stahl found
out that Varenka was not her daughter, but she continued
her education, especially since soon after her birth Varenka
lost all her family.

Madame Stahl had lived in southern Europe continuously
for over ten years, never leaving her bed. Some said that
Madame Stahl, by being known as a virtuous and deeply
religious woman, had reached her high social standing. Others
said that she was indeed the truly virtuous person she claimed
to be, and that she lived only for the good of her fellow men.
None knew whether she was Catholic, Protestant or Orthodox.
One thing was certain—she was on friendly terms with the
most prominent members of all churches and denominations.

Varenka always lived with her when she was abroad, and
everyone who knew Madame Stahl knew and loved Mlle.
Varenka, as everyone called her.

All these details convinced the princess that there would be
nothing wrong in a friendship between her daughter and
Varenka, particularly since Varenka's manners and upbringing
were the best. She spoke French and English perfectly and,
most important, she had delivered a message from Madame
Stahl in which she expressed her regret that, on account of
her illness, she had been deprived of the pleasure of meeting
the princess.

After she met Varenka, Kitty's enchantment with her friend
grew still stronger, and with each day she found in her new
virtues.

When the princess heard that Varenka sang well, she asked her to visit them in the evening to sing for them.

"Kitty plays, we have a piano, though not a very good one, and it will be such a pleasure to have you," said the princess with her feigned smile, which Kitty now found particularly unpleasant, for she noticed that Varenka did not want to sing. However, Varenka came that evening, bringing her music. The princess invited Maria Evgenievna and her daughter, and the colonel.

It seemed that the presence of strangers did not disturb Varenka in the least, and she immediately went over to the piano. She could not accompany herself, but she sight-read freely. Kitty, who played well, accompanied her.

"You have an extraordinary talent," the princess told her after Varenka had sung the first piece.

Maria Evgenievna and her daughter thanked her and praised her.

"Look," said the colonel, pointing to the window. "What a large audience you have." Indeed, quite a large crowd had gathered under the windows.

"I am very glad that it gives you pleasure," Varenka said simply.

Kitty looked at her friend with pride. She admired her artistry, her voice, her face; but most of all she admired her poise, especially since Varenka evidently did not think much of her voice and did not care at all for compliments. It seemed that all she wanted to know was whether she should continue to sing or whether it was enough.

How proud I'd be in her place! thought Kitty. How happy I'd feel, watching that crowd under the windows. But she doesn't care. She's moved only by her desire to please *Maman* and not to refuse her request. What is there about her? What gives her the strength to ignore everything and remain so self-assured and calm? How much I'd like to know this and to learn from her! Kitty thought, looking into her calm face. The princess asked Varenka to sing some more, and Varenka sang another piece in the same even, clear and fine voice, standing erect and tapping the rhythm out on the piano with her slim, dark hand.

Her next piece of music was an Italian song. Kitty played the introduction and looked at Varenka.

"Let's skip this one," Varenka said, blushing.

Kitty looked at Varenka, startled and puzzled.

"All right, let's do another," she said hastily, turning the page. She immediately understood that there was something special about the piece.

"No," said Varenka, putting her hand on the page and smiling, "let's sing it." And she sang it as calmly, self-assuredly, and beautifully as the previous songs.

When she finished, everyone thanked her again, and they left to have tea. Kitty and Varenka went into the small garden next to the house.

"Have you some memory connected with that song?" asked Kitty. "Don't tell me about it, just tell me whether it's so," she added hurriedly.

"Why shouldn't I tell you?" Varenka said unaffectedly, and without waiting for an answer, she continued, "Yes, it brings back a memory, once very painful. I loved a man and sang this song for him."

Kitty, her large eyes wide, remained silent as she looked tenderly at Varenka.

"I loved him, and he loved me. But his mother was against it, and he married another. He now lives not far from us, and I see him occasionally. You didn't imagine that I, too, had had a romantic affair," she said, and in her beautiful face there flickered a faint flame which, Kitty felt, once had brightly lit the whole of her.

"Why not? If I were a man, I couldn't love anyone else after knowing you. But I can't understand how, to please his mother, he could forget you and make you unhappy. He had no heart."

"Oh no, he's a very good man, and I'm not unhappy. On the contrary, I'm very happy. Well, shall we sing any more tonight?" she added, turning toward the house.

"How good you are, how good!" exclaimed Kitty and, stopping her, she kissed her. "If I could only be even a little like you!"

"Why should you be like anyone? You are good as you are," Varenka said, smiling her gentle, tired smile.

"No, I'm not good at all. But tell me. . . . Wait, let's sit down," said Kitty, indicating a seat on the bench next to her. "Tell me, isn't it humiliating to think of a man who spurned your love, one who didn't want you?"

"But he didn't spurn it. I believe that he loved me, but he was an obedient son. . . ."

"But suppose he did it not to please his mother, but of his

own free will?" asked Kitty, feeling that she had revealed her secret, and that her face, flushed with shame, had already betrayed her.

"Then he would have acted wrongly, and I should have no pity for him," replied Varenka, evidently understanding that this no longer referred to her, but to Kitty.

"But the humiliation?" asked Kitty. "It's impossible to forget the humiliation; it's impossible," she said, remembering her look at the last ball, when the music had stopped.

"But why feel humiliated? You didn't do anything wrong, I'm sure."

"Worse than that. I'm now ashamed."

Varenka shook her head and put her hand on Kitty's.

"Why feel ashamed?" she asked. "You surely didn't tell a man who didn't care for you that you loved him?"

"Of course not. I never said a word, but he knew it. There were looks and gestures. If I live to be a hundred, I won't forget it."

"Why? I can't understand. What matters is whether you still love him or not," said Varenka with complete frankness.

"I hate him, and I can't forgive myself."

"Why not?"

"The shame, the humiliation."

"Oh, if all girls were as sensitive as you," said Varenka. "There isn't a girl who hasn't gone through it. And all this is so unimportant."

"But what is important?" asked Kitty, looking at her with a surprised and inquiring look.

"Oh, many things are important," said Varenka with a smile.

"What for example?"

"Oh, many things are more important," repeated Varenka, without knowing what to say. But at this moment the princess' voice could be heard from the window.

"Kitty, it's getting chilly. Either take a shawl or come inside."

"Really, it's time," said Varenka, rising. "I must still see Mademoiselle Berthe. She asked me to come."

Kitty held her hand, and her look, burning with curiosity and entreaty, asked, "What is it that's so important that it brings such peace? You know, tell me!" But Varenka simply did not understand what Kitty's look asked. She only remembered that today she had to visit Mme. Berthe and be back at twelve o'clock for tea with *Maman*. She entered the room, picked up her music and, saying good night to all, she was about to leave.

"Let me take you home," said the colonel.

"Indeed, how can you go alone in the darkness?" agreed the princess. "At least let Parasha go with you."

Kitty saw that Varenka could scarcely restrain her smile on hearing that someone must accompany her.

"No, I always walk alone, and nothing ever happens to me," she said, reaching for her hat. She kissed Kitty, and without telling her what was so important, she left, walking briskly, with the music under her arm. She disappeared in the semi-darkness of the summer night, taking away with her the secret of what it was that was so important and that had brought her her enviable composure and dignity.

33

KITTY MET MADAME STAHL too, and this acquaintance, in addition to her friendship with Varenka, had a deep influence upon her and brought her consolation in her misfortune. She found consolation in the totally new world that opened to her through this acquaintance, a world which had nothing in common with her past, a sublime, beautiful world, from the height of which this past could be calmly contemplated. She learned that, in addition to a life based on instinct, which Kitty had led heretofore, there was a spiritual life. Religion opened the door to this life, but a religion that had nothing in common with the one Kitty had known since childhood, which consisted of masses and vespers in the Home for Widows, where you could meet your friends, and of memorizing the Slavonic texts under a priest's instruction. This new religion was sublime and mysterious, a font of beautiful thoughts and feelings. It was a religion in which one could not only believe, because it was so ordained, but which one could love.

It was not from words that Kitty learned all this. Madame Stahl spoke to Kitty as to a lovely child whom you admire as a memory of your own youth, and only once did she mention that nothing but love and faith brought man consolation in his sorrows, and that there was no sorrow too insignificant for Christ's compassion. Then she changed the topic of conversation. But from each movement of hers, from each word, in each heavenly look, as Kitty called it, and particularly from the whole history of her life, which Varenka had told her, from all of these Kitty learned "what was important," which she had not known heretofore.

But no matter how sublime Madame Stahl's character, how moving the whole history of her life, how noble and kind her words, Kitty unconsciously noticed in her some traits that embarrassed her. She noticed that Madame Stahl smiled derisively when she inquired about her relatives, and this was against the principles of Christian charity. And once she was present when Madame Stahl received a Catholic priest, and noticed that she carefully kept her face within the shadow of the lampshade, smiling strangely. Though both these matters were trifling, they embarrassed her, and she had her doubts concerning Madame Stahl. But lonely Varenka, who had no friends or relatives, who lived with the memory of a sad disappointment, who demanded nothing and gave everything, seemed to Kitty the very model of perfection of which she could only dream. Varenka's example taught her that only by forgetting yourself and loving your fellow man can you become calm, happy, and good. And that was what Kitty desired. Now she understood clearly what it was that was "most important," but she was not satisfied only to delight in it. With all her heart she abandoned herself to this new life, now open to her. Varenka described to her the activities of Madame Stahl and others, and from these descriptions Kitty devised a plan for her new life. Like Madame Stahl's niece Aline, of whom Varenka had told her so much, wherever she might live she would seek out the unfortunate, help them as much as possible, distribute the Gospels, read the Gospels to the sick, to criminals, to the dying. The thought of reading the Bible to criminals, as Aline did, particularly delighted Kitty. But all these were secret dreams, which Kitty did not divulge either to her mother or to Varenka.

However, while waiting for the time when she would be able to fulfill her plans on a large scale, Kitty, following Varenka's example, easily found occasion to apply her principles even here at the spa, where there were so many who were sick and unfortunate.

At first, the princess noticed only how strongly Kitty was influenced by her *engouement*, as she called it, with Madame

Stahl, and particularly with Varenka. She saw that Kitty not only imitated Varenka in her activities, but unconsciously mimicked her manner of walking, speaking and blinking. But later the princess noticed that, aside from this enchantment, her daughter was going through a serious spiritual change.

The princess saw that in the evenings Kitty read the Gospels in French, a present from Madame Stahl, something that she had never done before; that she avoided her social acquaintances and drew close to those patients who were under Varenka's care, particularly the poor family of the sick painter Petrov. Kitty was obviously proud to serve as a nurse to that family. This was all very well, and her mother had no objection to it, especially since Madame Petrov was an honorable person, and the German princess, noticing Kitty's activities, praised her, calling her a ministering angel. Everything would have been fine had it not been overdone. But the princess saw that her daughter went to the extreme, and she told her so.

"*Il ne faut jamais rien outrer,*" she said.

But her daughter did not reply. In her heart she knew well that you cannot overdo Christian charity. How could one overdo when following a teaching that exhorts you to turn the other cheek when smitten on one, and to give your shirt when they take your cloak. But the princess did not like this excessive zeal, especially since she felt that Kitty did not want to open her heart to her. In fact, Kitty concealed from her mother her new views and feelings. She concealed them not because she did not respect or love her mother, but only because she was her mother. She would have revealed them to anyone rather than to her mother.

"Anna Pavlovna has not come to see us for quite a while," the princess remarked once, referring to Madame Petrov. "I invited her. She seems to be displeased about something."

"No, I haven't noticed anything, *Maman,*" said Kitty, flaring up.

"Hasn't it been quite a while since you were there?"

"Tomorrow we're going on an excursion to the mountains," replied Kitty.

"Go, then," said the princess, looking at her daughter's embarrassed face and trying to guess the cause of her embarrassment.

That same day Varenka came to dinner and announced that Anna Pavlovna had changed her mind about the excursion to the mountains, and the princess noticed that Kitty blushed again.

"Kitty, has anything come between you and the Petrovs?" asked the princess when they were alone. "Why does she no longer send the children or come herself?"

Kitty replied that nothing had happened between them and that she herself was completely at a loss to understand why, as it seemed, Anna Pavlovna was displeased with her. What Kitty said was completely truthful. She did not know the reason for Anna Pavlovna's change of heart, but she could guess. What she suspected she could not tell her mother, or even herself. It was one of those subjects of which you are aware, but which you cannot discuss even with yourself. It would be too terrible and shameful to be mistaken.

Again and again she recalled all the details of her relationship with this family. She remembered the genuine happiness that showed on Anna Pavlovna's good-natured, round face when they met; she recalled their secret conversations about the patient, their schemes to keep him away from his work, which he was forbidden to do, and to take him for walks; she recalled the attachment of their youngest boy, who called her "my Kitty" and who refused to go to sleep without seeing her. How good everything had been! Then she remembered the emaciated figure of Petrov, with his long neck, his brown suit, his thin curling hair, his questioning blue eyes which in the beginning had frightened Kitty, and his painful attempts to look cheerful and spirited in her presence. She recalled her early efforts to overcome the aversion she felt toward him, as toward all consumptives, and the pains she took to converse with him. She recalled the shy, tender look he always gave her, and her strange feeling of compassion and embarrassment and, at the same time, of awareness of her charity. How good all this had been! All this was true in the beginning. But a few days ago everything suddenly went wrong. Anna Pavlovna met Kitty with feigned kindness, and ceaselessly watched her and her husband.

Could it be that the touching joy with which he always met her was the cause of Anna Pavlovna's estrangement?

Yes, she recalled, it seemed so unnatural for Anna Pavlovna and so completely unlike her usual kindness, when two days ago she said with annoyance, "He kept waiting for you and refused to drink coffee without you, though he is terribly weak."

Yes, perhaps she was displeased that I handed him the wrap. It was such a simple act, but he took it so awkwardly and thanked me so profusely that I, too, became embarrassed. And that excellent portrait he made of me. And then, most important, that look, shy and tender! Yes, yes, it's true! Kitty repeated to herself in horror. No, it cannot, it must not be! He's so pitiful! she said to herself a moment later.

This doubt marred the charm of her new life.

34

TOWARD THE END of the season at the spa, Prince Shcherbatsky returned to his family. He had gone to Karlsbad and then to Baden and Kissingen to visit his Russian friends in order to soak up Russian atmosphere, as he put it.

The prince and princess held entirely contradictory views regarding life abroad. The princess found everything abroad beautiful, and in spite of her well-established position in Russian society, when abroad she tried to play the part of a European lady, which she was not, for she was a typical Russian noblewoman. She therefore assumed false airs, and this made her somewhat uncomfortable. To the prince, on the other hand, everything he saw abroad seemed unpleasant; the European way of life was a burden to him; he held on to his Russian habits, and when abroad, he did his best to show that he was less Europeanized than he actually was.

The prince returned, looking thinner than before, the baggy skin of his cheeks drooping, but he was in an excellent frame of mind. His good humor increased when he found Kitty fully recovered. The news about Kitty's friendship with Madame Stahl and Varenka, and the princess' remark about the change she had noticed in Kitty, troubled him. They aroused his usual jealousy toward everything that attracted his daughter away from himself, and he feared lest she withdraw from his influence into regions inaccessible to him. But these unpleasant reports were lost in his usual expanse of good will and cheer, which the Karlsbad waters had greatly augmented.

On the day after his arrival, the prince, dressed in his long coat, with his Russian wrinkles and puffed cheeks supported by his starched collar, went out with his daughter to the spring in the happiest frame of mind.

It was a beautiful morning. The neat, cheerful houses with their little gardens; the beery, happy German servant girls with their ruddy complexions and red hands; and the bright sun, gladdened the heart. But the nearer they came to the spring the more patients they met, their misery accentuated by this orderliness of everyday German life. Kitty was no longer affected by this contrast. The bright sun, the gaily sparkling verdure, and the sounds of music formed a natural frame in which she observed these familiar faces and their changes for better or worse. But to the prince, the bright light of the June morning, the sounds of the orchestra playing a gay popular waltz, and particularly the sight of the healthy servant girls, seemed indecent and ugly when set against these cheerlessly shuffling, half-dead men who had congregated here from all corners of Europe.

Though he had felt proud and, it seemed, rejuvenated when he walked arm-in-arm with his beloved daughter, his firm gait and his strong limbs, layered in fat, now made him feel embarrassed and guilty. He felt almost like a man who appears undressed in public.

"Introduce me to your new friends," he told his daughter, pressing her arm with his elbow. "I even took a liking to your horrible Soden because it cured you. But it's so sad here. Who is he?"

Kitty told him the names of the people they met, those she knew and those she didn't know. Just at the entrance to the garden they met the blind Mlle. Berthe and her guide, and the prince was struck by the expression of tenderness Kitty's voice evoked in the old Frenchwoman. With the usual excessive politeness of the French, she at once addressed him, praising him for having such a remarkable daughter, extolling Kitty to the heavens in her presence, calling her a precious treasure, a pearl, a ministering angel.

"Then she is angel number two," the prince said, smiling. "She calls Varenka angel number one."

"Oh! Mademoiselle Varenka is a true angel, *allez!*" echoed Madame Berthe.

They came across Varenka herself in the gallery. She walked briskly in their direction, carrying a handsome red handbag.

"Here's Papa!" Kitty said to her.

Simply and unaffectedly, as was her wont, Varenka made a gesture midway between a bow and a curtsey, and immediately engaged the prince in conversation, speaking to him with ease and without affectation, as she did with everyone.

"Of course I know you, I know you very well!" the prince told her with a smile that, to Kitty's happiness, proved that her father liked her friend. "And where are you going in such a hurry?"

"*Maman* is here," she said, turning to Kitty. "She didn't sleep at all last night, and the doctor advised her to take a ride. I'm taking her handwork to her."

"So that was the number one angel!" said the prince, when Varenka left.

Kitty saw that he wanted to make fun of Varenka but couldn't because he liked her.

"And now we'll meet all your other friends," he added, "even Madame Stahl, if she deigns to recognize me."

"Do you really know her, Papa?" asked Kitty fearfully, noticing the flame of derision kindling in the prince's eyes as he mentioned Madame Stahl's name.

"I knew her husband slightly, and her too before she turned pietist."

"What does 'pietist' mean, Papa?" asked Kitty. She was now afraid to learn that what she prized so highly in Madame Stahl had a name.

"I don't know for sure. I only know that she thanks God for everything, for every misfortune, and even thanks God that her husband died. It's ridiculous, for they had a terrible life."

"Who's that? What a pitiful face!" he asked, noticing a patient of short stature, seated on a bench in a brown coat and white trousers, which lay in strange folds on the fleshless bones of his legs.

The gentleman raised his straw hat above his thin curling hair, displaying his high forehead, sorely reddened by the pressure of the hat.

"It's Petrov, a painter," replied Kitty, blushing. "And there's his wife," she added, indicating Anna Pavlovna. As though on purpose, just as they approached she went after her child, who was running down the path.

"How pitiful he is, and what a kind face he has!" said the prince. "Why didn't you go over to him. Perhaps he wanted to tell you something."

"Then let's go over," Kitty said, turning resolutely. "How do you feel today?" she asked Petrov.

Petrov rose, leaning on his cane, and looked shyly at the prince.

"This is my daughter," said the prince. "Allow me to introduce myself."

The painter bowed and smiled, showing his extraordinarily shiny, white teeth.

"We waited for you yesterday, Princess," he told Kitty.

Saying this, he tottered, then repeated the same movement, trying to show that he did it deliberately.

"I wanted to come, but Varenka told me that Anna Pavlovna had let her know that you were not going."

"Not going?" said Petrov, blushing. He went into a fit of coughing, as his eyes searched out his wife. "Aneta, Aneta," he called loudly, the thick veins on his white neck swelling like cords.

Anna Pavlovna came up.

"Why was the princess told that we were not going?" he angrily whispered, his voice gone.

"How are you, Princess?" asked Anna Pavlovna with a false smile, addressing Kitty in a manner quite different from what it had been. "I am very glad to meet you," she said, turning to the prince. "You have been long awaited, Prince."

"Why was the princess told that we were not going?" the painter whispered again, hoarse and still angrier. His voice failed him, and he could not give his words the expression he wanted, and this evidently vexed him still more.

"Oh, dear! I thought we weren't going," replied his wife, annoyed.

"But, when . . ." he went into a fit of coughing and waved his hands.

The prince tipped his hat and left with his daughter.

"Ah, me," he sighed heavily. "Oh, what unfortunate people!"

"Yes, Papa!" replied Kitty. "And you should know that they have three children, no servants, and almost no means. He receives some help from the academy," she said with animation. She tried to suppress the uneasiness that had been aroused by the strange change in Anna Pavlovna's attitude.

"There's Madame Stahl," said Kitty, indicating a wheel chair in which something lay, shaded by a parasol, tucked among pillows, and wrapped in gray and blue.

It was Madame Stahl. Behind her stood a huge, somber German attendant who wheeled her chair. Next to her was a light-haired Swedish count whom Kitty knew by name only. A few patients lingered near the wheel chair, staring in wonder at the lady.

The prince went over to her, and at once Kitty noticed in his eyes a spark of derision, which embarrassed her. He approached Madame Stahl and spoke to her with exceeding kindness and politeness, in such an excellent French as few speak nowadays.

"I do not know whether you remember me, but I wish to present myself to thank you for your kindness to my daughter," he said, taking off his hat and holding it in his hand.

"Prince Aleksandr Shcherbatsky," said Madame Stahl, raising her heavenly eyes, in which Kitty read displeasure. "I'm happy to see you. I'm so fond of your daughter."

"Are you still not well?"

"I am used to it now," said Madame Stahl, and she introduced the prince to the Swedish count.

"You have changed very little," the prince told her. "I have not had the honor of seeing you for about ten or eleven years."

"Yes, God gives us our cross and the strength to bear it. Sometimes you wonder why life drags on. . . . On the other side!" she said with annoyance to Varenka, displeased by the way she had wrapped the blanket around her legs.

"Probably to do good," said the prince, his eyes laughing.

"It is not given to us to judge," said Madame Stahl, carefully watching the expression on the prince's face. "Then you will send me the book, my dear count? I thank you sincerely," she said, turning to the young Swede.

"Ah!" cried the prince, noticing the Moscow colonel who was standing nearby. He said goodbye to Madame Stahl and left with his daughter and the colonel, who joined them.

"Such is our aristocracy, Prince!" said the colonel, trying to sound derisive. He was offended by Madame Stahl's refusal to meet him.

"She's the same as she always was," replied the prince.

"Did you know her before she became an invalid?"

"Yes, she became an invalid while I knew her," said the prince.

"They say that she has not been on her feet for ten years."

"She hasn't, because her legs are too short. She had a very bad figure."

"Papa, it cannot be!" cried Kitty.

"Such is the gossip, my friend. But your Varenka does get in trouble," he added. "Ah, invalid women!"

"Oh, no, Papa!" Kitty objected heatedly. "Varenka adores her. And then she does so much good, as anyone will tell you. She and Aline Stahl are known to everyone."

"Perhaps," he said, pressing her arm with his elbow. "But it is better to do such deeds without public knowledge."

Kitty fell silent, not because she had nothing to say but because she was unwilling to reveal her secret thoughts even to her father. However, it seemed strange that, though she had resolved not to give in to her father's views and to grant him no admittance to her private thoughts, she felt that the heavenly image of Madame Stahl that she had carried for a whole month in her heart, vanished irretrievably, as a shape formed by a dress which has been tossed aside vanishes when one realizes that it was formed only by the way the dress fell. Only a woman with short legs remained, staying in bed because she was deformed, and tormenting meek Varenka for having adjusted the blanket incorrectly. And by no stretch of the imagination could she restore her former image of Madame Stahl.

35

THE PRINCE'S GOOD humor communicated itself to the members of the household, to his acquaintances, even to the Shcherbatskys' German landlord.

When he returned from the spring, accompanied by Kitty, he invited the colonel, Maria Evgenievna, and Varenka for coffee, and ordered a table and chairs to be brought into the garden under the chestnut tree and lunch served there. His cheerfulness was shared by the landlord and the servants. They were aware of his generosity, and half an hour later the sick doctor from Hamburg, who lived upstairs, looked through the window envying this gay Russian company of healthy people, assembled under the chestnut tree. A table, covered with a white cloth and laden with coffeepots, bread, butter, cheese, and cold cuts, was placed in the tremulous shadow formed by the leaves fluttering overhead. The princess, in a bonnet with a lilac ribbon, sat at the table, serving coffee and sandwiches. At the other end of the table was the prince, eating with gusto and talking loudly and cheerfully. The prince displayed the presents he had brought, little carved chests, gewgaws, and a variety of paper knives, of which he had bought quite a number at all the spas, which he now distributed to everyone, including Lischen, the servant girl, and the landlord, with whom he exchanged jokes in his broken, funny German. He assured him that it was not the waters that had cured Kitty, but his excellent meals, particularly his prune soup. The princess laughed at her husband for his Russian habits, but was more animated and gay than she had been all this time at the spa. The colonel, as always, smiled at the prince's jokes, but, concerning Europe, of which he considered himself a profound student, he sided with the princess. The good-natured Maria Evgenievna shook with laughter at all the prince's amusing remarks, and Varenka yielded to a weak but infectious laughter in response to the prince's jokes, in a way Kitty never had seen before.

Kitty enjoyed all this, but could not help worrying. She could not solve the problem her father had unwittingly created for her by his jocular attitude toward her friends and toward the life that she now loved so much. The change in her relationship with the Petrovs, which had so unpleasantly and clearly come into the open this morning, now added to her problem. Everybody was enjoying himself, but Kitty could not share in the general merriment, and this troubled her still more. She had a feeling resembling that of her childhood, when she had been punished by being locked in her room, from which she could hear the happy laughter of her sisters.

"Now, why did you buy all these things?" asked the princess, smiling and handing her husband a cup of coffee.

"Well, you walk around and come up to a small stall; the man asks you to buy something. '*Erlaucht, Excellenz, Durchlaucht.*' Well, as he says, '*Durchlaucht,*' I can resist no longer, and ten thalers are gone."

"This is all because you were bored," said the princess.

"Of course I was bored. And so bored, Mother, that I could scarcely stand it."

"How could you be bored, Prince? There are so many interesting things in Germany now," said Maria Evgenievna.

"I know all those interesting things of yours. I am familiar with the prune soup and pea sausage. I know everything."

"But Prince, you must admit that their public institutions are interesting," said the colonel.

"Interesting? They all shine with self-satisfaction, like copper coins; they have triumphed over everyone. What have I to be self-satisfied about? I have triumphed over no one. I take off my boots and even place them outside the door myself. I have to get up in the morning, dress right away, and then go to the dining room for that terrible tea. How different it is at home! You wake up unhurriedly; some trifle annoys you, you grumble, you calm down, you think everything over, you're in no hurry."

"But you forget that time is money," said the colonel.

"What time do you mean? There is a kind of time that you would sell at half a ruble a month, and there is another kind that you wouldn't sell—not even half an hour—at any price. Isn't that so, Katenka? Why do you look so unhappy?"

"I'm all right."

"Why are you in a hurry? Don't go yet," he said, turning to Varenka.

"I must go home," said Varenka. She rose and again burst into laughter.

She recovered, said goodbye, and went into the house for her hat. Kitty followed her. Even Varenka seemed different to her. She was not worse than she had been, but she was different from what she had imagined her to be.

"Oh, it's been a long time since I laughed so much," said Varenka, reaching for her parasol and handbag. "What a darling your father is."

Kitty remained silent.

"When will I see you?" asked Varenka.

"*Maman* is going to see the Petrovs. Will you be there?" asked Kitty, sounding out Varenka.

"I will," replied Varenka. "They're getting ready to leave, and I promised to help them pack."

"Then I'll also come."

"Why should you?"

"Why shouldn't I? Why? Why?" asked Kitty, her eyes wide. She took hold of Varenka's parasol to restrain her. "Wait, why shouldn't I?"

"Because your father has arrived, and furthermore, they don't feel at ease with you."

"No, tell me, why don't you want me to visit the Petrovs frequently? You don't want me to. Why?"

"I didn't say that," Varenka replied calmly.

"Please tell me!"

"Shall I tell everything?" asked Varenka.

"Everything, yes, everything!" echoed Kitty.

"Well, there is really nothing special, but Mikhail Alekseyevich" (the painter's name) "had been anxious to leave, but now he doesn't want to go," said Varenka, smiling.

"Well?" said Kitty, urging Varenka on with a gloomy expression on her face.

"Then, for some reason or other Anna Pavlovna said that he didn't want to leave because of you. Of course, this was entirely out of place, and it led to a quarrel. And you know how quarrelsome these patients are."

Kitty's frown deepened. She kept silent, and only Varenka spoke, trying to assuage and compose her. She anticipated the approach of an outburst, but whether it would erupt in words or tears she did not know.

"So it's better for you not to go. . . . You understand; you're not offended."

"It serves me right, it serves me right!" said Kitty quickly, seizing the parasol from Varenka's hands and avoiding her friend's eyes.

Varenka was tempted to smile at her friend's childish outburst, but she was afraid to offend her.

"Why do you say that? I don't understand," she said.

"It serves me right, because all this was nothing but pretense; all this was made up, it did not come from the heart. Why should I care about a stranger? The result is that I became the cause of a quarrel and did what nobody had asked me to do. All of this was pretense! Pretense! Pretense!"

"But what was the purpose of pretending?" Varenka asked softly.

"Ah, how foolish, how terrible! I had no right. . . . It was all pretense!" she said, opening and closing the parasol.

"But what was the purpose?"

"To appear better than you really are to other people, to yourself, to God; to deceive everyone. No, I won't be taken in by it any longer. One may not be good, but at least one may not be an impostor, or a deceiver."

"But who is a deceiver?" Varenka asked reproachfully. "You speak as though—"

But Kitty had lost her temper. She did not let Varenka finish.

"I'm not talking about you, not at all about you. You are perfect. Yes, I know that you are truly perfect. But can I help it if I'm not good? All this wouldn't have happened if I were good. But I'd rather remain as I am than pretend to be otherwise. What have I to do with Anna Pavlovna? Let them live their lives, and I mine. I can't be otherwise. And it's so different, so different. . . ."

"What's so different?" Varenka asked, puzzled.

"Everything. I can live only as my heart tells me, and you live by rules. I fell in love with you sincerely, but you, probably, only to save me, to enlighten me!"

"You are unjust," said Varenka.

"But I'm not talking about anyone else; I'm talking only about myself!"

"Kitty!" called her mother, "Come here and show your father your corals."

Kitty did not make up with her friend, and with a proud air she took the box with the corals from the table and went to her mother.

"What's the matter with you? Why is your face so red?" her father and mother asked in one voice.

"Nothing," she replied. "I'll be right back." And she ran back into the house.

She's still here, she thought. My God, what will I tell her? What have I done? What have I said? Why did I offend her? What shall I do? What will I tell her? Kitty thought before entering the room.

Varenka, her hat on, was sitting at the table, holding the parasol and examining one of its springs, which Kitty had broken. She raised her head.

"Varenka, forgive me," Kitty whispered, going over to her. "I don't remember what I said. I. . . ."

"Believe me, I didn't want to upset you," said Varenka with a smile.

They made peace. But with her father's arrival, all of the world in which Kitty had been living changed. She did not renounce everything that she had learned, but she understood that she had been deceiving herself by assuming that she could be what she wanted to be. As though she had suddenly awakened, she perceived how difficult it was to remain free from pretense and ostentation at that height to which she had aspired to rise. Moreover, she learned how oppressive was the world of affliction, sickness and death, in which she had lived. The efforts she had made to love it were too painful. She was anxious to breathe the fresh air of Russia, to go as soon as possible to Ergushovo, to which, she had learned from a letter, her sister Dolly and the children had already moved.

But her love for Varenka had not diminished. On taking leave of her, Kitty pressed her to visit them in Russia.

"I'll come when you get married," said Varenka.

"I'll never marry."

"Then I'll never come."

"Then for this reason alone I'll get married. Don't forget, you promised!" said Kitty.

The doctor's prognosis proved true. Kitty returned home to Russia fully recovered. She was no longer so carefree and gay as before, but she was calm. The Moscow misfortune became a memory.

PART THREE

1

SERGEI IVANOVICH KOZNYSHEV wanted to rest from his intellectual pursuits, and instead of going abroad, as he usually did, at the end of May, he went to visit his brother in the country. It was his conviction that the best life was country life. He had now come to his brother to enjoy this life. Konstantin Levin was very glad to have him, especially because he no longer expected his brother Nikolai that summer. But in spite of his love and respect for Sergei Ivanovich, the presence of his brother in the country somewhat embarrassed Konstantin Levin. He was embarrassed, even displeased by his brother's attitude toward the country. For Konstantin Levin the country was the seat of life, with its joys, sufferings, and toil. For Sergei Ivanovich the country was, on the one hand, a place of rest from work, and on the other, a useful antidote against corruption, which he took with pleasure and with an awareness of its usefulness. Konstantin Levin prized the country as a stage for performing work which was useful beyond any doubt. Sergei Ivanovich prized it because here one could and should perform no work. Moreover, Sergei Ivanovich's attitude toward the peasants irked Konstantin. Sergei Ivanovich insisted that he knew and loved the peasants and often conversed with them, which he could do easily and without affectation. The conclusions he drew from these conversations were always favorable to the peasants and also proved to himself how well he knew them. Konstantin Levin did not like this attitude of his brother's. To Konstantin the peasant was but the chief partner in their common undertaking, and in spite of all his respect and genuine love for the moujik, which, he said, he had probably imbibed together with the milk of his peasant nurse, he treated him as a partner. Sometimes he had a deep admiration for the strength, gentleness, and justice of the people, but very often, when their common undertaking called for other qualities, he was incensed by their carelessness, slovenliness, drunkenness, and deceit. If Konstantin Levin were asked whether he loved the peasants, he would be at a loss for an answer. He both loved them and did not love them, just as with people in general. Of course, being a good man, he loved people more often than not, and he felt the same way about the peasants. But he could have no special feelings for the peasants as such, for not only did he live with them, not only were his own interests bound with theirs, but he considered himself one of them. He found in them, and in himself, neither peculiar merits nor faults, and he could not visualize himself as set apart from them. Moreover, though he had long lived in the closest relationship with the moujiks as their master and arbitrator, and, more important, their adviser (the moujiks trusted him and they traveled as much as forty versts to seek his advice), he had no definite opinion about them, and he could not say whether he knew the peasants any more than he could say whether he loved them. To say that he knew them would be tantamount to saying that he knew people in general. He had always observed and studied all kinds of people, including the moujiks, whom he considered good and interesting, continuously discovering in them new traits, changing his former opinions and forming new ones. Sergei Ivanovich did the opposite. He loved and praised country life, contrasting it to the life he did not love. In just the same way he loved the peasants, in contrast to the class of people he did not love, and in just the same way he knew the peasants, contrasting them with people in general. In his methodical mind he formed a clear outline of peasant life, based partly on that life itself but mainly on the contrast to other forms of life. He never changed his opinion about the peasants or his sympathetic attitude toward them.

When the brothers discussed their differing opinions about the peasants, Sergei Ivanovich always had the upper hand, just because his opinion about the peasants, their nature, their traits and tastes, were definite. But Konstantin Levin held no definite or unchangeable opinions on this subject. Therefore, in their discussions, Konstantin was always caught contradicting himself.

Sergei Ivanovich considered his younger brother a fine

fellow, whose heart was set right (as he expressed it in French) but whose mind, though quite alert, was subject to the impressions of the moment and therefore full of contradictions. With the condescension of an elder brother, he sometimes explained to him the meanings of things, but could find no pleasure in arguing with him, because he found it too easy to defeat him.

Konstantin Levin considered his brother a man with a great mind and erudition, honorable in the loftiest meaning of the word, and endowed with a capacity of working for the common good. But deep in his heart, the older he grew and the better he got to know his brother, the more frequently it occurred to him that this capacity of working for the common good, of which he felt himself completely deprived, perhaps was not a merit of his brother but betrayed a want of something, not a want of good, honest, and noble aims and tastes but a want of that life force that is called the heart, that longing which makes a man choose and follow only one way of life out of a countless number offered to him. The better he knew his brother, the more he noticed that it was not their hearts that moved Sergei Ivanovich and many others like him to a love for the common good; they decided in their minds that it was right to work for the common good, and they did it for that reason alone. This assumption gained still more weight with Levin as he observed that his brother took no more to heart the problems of the common good, or of the immortality of the soul, than he did a game of chess or the ingenious construction of a new machine.

Moreover, Konstantin Levin did not feel quite at ease with his brother in the country, because in the country, particularly in the summer, he was always busy with his work, and the long summer days seemed too short to perform all that he had to do, whereas Sergei Ivanovich rested. But though he rested now, in other words he did not work on his book, he was so accustomed to intellectual activity that he loved to express beautifully and concisely the thoughts that came to his mind, and to have someone to listen. His brother was his usual and natural audience. Therefore, in spite of their frank and friendly relationship, Konstantin felt uneasy about leaving his brother alone. Sergei Ivanovich liked to lie down on the grass and, basking in the sun, talk leisurely.

"You would scarcely believe," he would say to his brother,

"how much I delight in this total indolence. My head is a complete void, with not one thought in it."

But Konstantin Levin was not interested in sitting and listening to him, especially since he knew that without his supervision the peasants would spread the manure on uncleared fields and they would do it God knows how, and that they would not attach the plowshares properly and then would say that these new-fangled plows were a foolish invention, and that the old simple Russian plow was much better, and so on.

"Haven't you run around in the heat long enough?" Sergei Ivanovich would ask him.

"I just have to go to the office for a minute," Levin would say, and he would rush into the field.

2

IN THE EARLY days of June an accident occurred. Agafia Mikhailovna, the nurse and housekeeper, was taking a jar of freshly pickled mushrooms into the cellar. She slipped, fell, and sprained her wrist. A recently graduated zemstvo doctor arrived, young and talkative. He examined the hand, said that it was not sprained, applied compresses, and remained for dinner, evidently enjoying his conversation with the famous Sergei Ivanovich Koznyshev. To display his enlightened views, he related all the country gossip, complaining of the poor state of the zemstvo. Sergei Ivanovich listened attentively, asked questions, and, inspired by his new audience, grew expansive and made a few pointed and weighty remarks, to which the young doctor listened with due respect. He had reached that enlivened state of mind so familiar to his brother, which usually followed a brilliant and lively conversation. After the doctor left, Sergei Ivanovich wanted to go fishing. He loved fishing and seemed proud that he could love such a foolish pastime.

Konstantin Levin, who had to go to the plowlands and to the meadows, offered to take him to the river in his cabriolet.

Summer was beyond its midpoint, a time when this year's crop already showed itself fully; when one began to think about next year's sowing; when the time for mowing was approaching; when the rye had brought forth its ears and, grayish-green, rippled in the wind, its unripened ears still light; when the green oats, sown late in the year, had grown up evenly and were sprinkled with tufts of yellow grass; when the early buckwheat had spread its leaves, screening the ground; when the fallow fields, hardened by the trampling of the cattle, with roadways through them still visible, proved too hard to be broken up by the old-fashioned plows and remained half-plowed; when in the evening twilight the dried piles of manure that had been brought here mingled their odors with the nectar-bearing grasses; when in the lowlands, awaiting the scythe, the immense expanse of land, which had been set aside as meadows, showed clumped, blackened stalks of uprooted sorrel.

It was a time for a short respite from agricultural labors, before the gathering of the harvest, an event that called for the peasants' utmost efforts. The harvest was rich, the days were clear and hot, the short nights dewy.

In order to reach the meadows, the brothers had to pass through a wood. All the way there, Sergei Ivanovich admired the beauty of the wood, overgrown with heavy foliage; he pointed out to his brother now an old linden tree looking dark on its shady side and ready to bloom, its yellow stipules glistening, now the young shoots of this year's trees, with their shining emerald verdure. Konstantin Levin did not like to speak about nature's beauty or to listen to a description of it. To him, words marred the beauty of what he observed. He listened to his brother without contradicting him, but his thoughts strayed in another direction. When they passed the wood, all his attention was drawn to a fallow hillock, here yellowing with grass, there trampled and crisscrossed with trenches, in some places the earth piled high, in others plowed. A row of carts rode over the fields. Levin counted the carts, was glad to see that everything was being done as required, and at the sight of the meadows he fell to thinking of the mowing. Haymaking always particularly aroused his spirits. When they reached the meadow, he halted his horse.

The morning dew still remained at the roots of the thick grass. Sergei Ivanovich did not want to get his feet wet, so he asked his brother to take him to the willow at the river, where perch were known to bite. Though Levin was sorry to trample the grass, he drove into the meadow. The tall grass softly entwined the wheels and the horse's legs, scattering its seed on the wet spokes and pasterns.

His brother sat under the willow and arranged his fishing tackle. Levin tied his horse and went into the vast, grayish-green expanse of the meadow, unrippled by the wind. In the swale the silky grass, its seeds ripened, now reached almost to his waist.

Levin crossed the meadow, emerged on the road, and came upon an old man with a swollen eye, who carried a basket with swarming bees.

"Did you catch them, Fomich?" he asked.

"Not at all, Konstantin Dmitrievich! I wish I were able to. This is the second time the swarm has left me. My thanks to the boys, your plowers—they unhitched a horse, galloped after the swarm and caught it."

"What do you say, Fomich, should we start mowing or wait?"

"Well, as we reckon, it's better to wait till St. Peter's Day. But you always start earlier. Well, with God's help, the grass is good. And it'll give more room to the cattle."

"And the weather, what do you think?"

"It's in God's hands. Perhaps it will be good."

Levin came over to his brother. The fish were not biting, but Sergei Ivanovich was not bored and seemed to be in the best of spirits. Levin saw that he was still under the influence of his conversation with the doctor and wanted to talk some more. Levin, on the other hand, was anxious to hurry home, to summon the mowers for the next day, and thus settle the matter of mowing the meadow, which preoccupied him.

"Well, let's go," he said.

"Why are you in a hurry? Let's sit here for a while. Look how wet you are. Even if the fish do not bite, fishing is a pleasure. Any hunt is a pleasure because it brings you in contact with nature. How beautiful this steely water is," he said. "These grassy banks!" he continued. "They always remind me of a riddle. Do you know it? The grass tells the water, 'We'll take a stroll, we'll take a stroll.'"

"I don't know the riddle," Levin answered dispiritedly.

3

"You know, I was thinking about you," said Sergei Ivanovich. "What's going on in your county, as I have heard it from the doctor, is a disgrace, and he's quite an intelligent fellow. I've told you in the past and I tell you now that it's wrong for you not to attend the meetings and, in general, to take no part in zemstvo affairs. If the best men stay away from them, then of course God knows what will happen. We pay our money, and it's spent on salaries; but there are no schools, no assistant surgeons, no trained midwives, no pharmacies, nothing."

"But I tried," Levin answered reluctantly. "I can't do it. It can't be helped."

"What do you mean you can't do it? I must say, I don't understand—I don't believe that you don't care, or that you're incompetent. Or is it sheer laziness?"

"None of the three. I tried, but I know that I simply can't do it," answered Levin.

He did not pay full attention to his brother's words. Scanning the plowland beyond the river, he noticed a black object, but he could not make out whether it was a horse or the steward on horseback.

"But why can't you do it? You tried, it didn't go your way, and you decided to give up. Have you no self-esteem?"

"I don't understand," said Levin, stung to the quick by his brother's words, "what self-esteem has to do with it. When I was in the university and was told that others understood integral calculus while I didn't, it was a matter of self-esteem. But here, first you must become convinced that you possess certain abilities to act in these matters, and what is more important, that all these matters are of great value."

"Well! Aren't they?" Sergei Ivanovich asked, deeply hurt that his brother ascribed no importance to something that interested him, and, particularly, that he seemed to be scarcely listening to him.

"It seems of no importance to me. It doesn't interest me, so what can I do?" answered Levin. He could now make out that the object he was watching was his steward, who evidently had dismissed the moujiks from the plowland, where they were now turning over their plows. Have they really finished plowing? he wondered.

"But listen to me," said the older brother, wrinkling his handsome, intelligent face. "Everything has its limits. It's all very well to be a strange and sincere person, and to hate falsehood. I understand this. But what you say has no meaning or has a very bad meaning. How can you consider it unimportant that the peasants whom, as you say, you love so dearly—"

I never said that, thought Konstantin Levin.

"That the peasants die without being helped, ignorant mid-wives are the cause of infant deaths, the people wallow in ignorance and are at the mercy of every government clerk; and you are given the means to help these people, but you don't because, in your opinion, it's not important?"

And this was the dilemma which Sergei Ivanovich posed to him: either you are so backward that you don't see all that you could accomplish, or you don't want to sacrifice your quiet life, your vanity, and I don't know what else.

Konstantin Levin felt that he had to give in and admit that he lacked interest in public affairs. He was hurt and troubled.

"Both," he said decisively. "I don't see how it could be done—"

"Why? Couldn't decent medical help be given, if the money were administered properly?"

"It couldn't, it seems to me. . . . Our county covers four thousand square versts, and with the blizzards, floods, and urgent seasonal work, I don't see how you could administer medical help everywhere. And in general, I don't believe in medicine."

"Wait, you are wrong—I can give you a thousand other examples. . . . Well, how about schools?"

"Why do you need schools?"

"How can you say that? Can anybody doubt that education is useful? If it's good for you, it's good for everybody."

Konstantin Levin, feeling that he was being pressed to the wall, grew excited and unconsciously revealed the main cause of his indifference to public affairs.

"Perhaps all this is good, but why should I care to establish dispensaries that I'll never visit, and schools I'll never send my children to, the peasants don't want to send their children to and that I'm not yet quite sure they should send them to?" he asked.

For a moment Sergei Ivanovich was taken aback by his brother's unexpected views, but he immediately conceived a new plan of attack.

He kept silent, picking up a fishing rod, threw his line in again and turned to his brother with a smile.

"But wait. First of all, there is a need for dispensaries. Didn't we send for the doctor to help Agafia Mikhailovna?"

"Yes, but I think that her hand will remain crooked."

"That remains to be seen. Then, a literate moujik is surely of more use and greater value to you as a worker."

"No, you may ask anyone," Konstantin Levin answered decisively. "Literate moujiks are very bad workers. You can't use them to mend roads, and after you've built a bridge, they steal it."

Sergei Ivanovich frowned. He disliked arguments, particularly those that ceaselessly shift from one point to another and bring up disconnected statements, so that one doesn't know which to refute first.

"But that's not the point. Tell me, do you believe that education is good for the peasant?"

"I do," said Levin inadvertently, and at once he felt that he had not said what he really thought. He knew that if he would really admit this, it could be proven to him that he had been talking nonsense. He didn't know how it would be proven, but he knew that without doubt it would be proven logically, and he waited for the proof.

The proof turned out to be simpler than Konstantin Levin had expected.

"If you admit that it is good," said Sergei Ivanovich, "you, as an honest man, can't do anything but love and sympathize with such a cause and want to work for it."

"But I still don't admit that it's good," Konstantin Levin said blushing.

"You don't? But you just said. . . ."

"What I mean is that I don't consider it either good or possible."

"This you can't know unless you try."

"Well, suppose it's so," said Levin, though he did not suppose it at all, "suppose it's so. I still don't see why I should be concerned about it."

"What do you mean?"

"Well, since we've gone so far, you explain it to me from a philosophical point of view," said Levin.

"I don't understand what philosophy has to do with it," said Sergei Ivanovich in a tone that, it seemed to Levin, showed that he did not accord his brother any right to discuss philosophy. This irked Levin.

"This is what I mean," he said excitedly. "I believe that in all our actions we are moved primarily by a concern for our own welfare. I, as a nobleman, find nothing in these zemstvo institutions that contributes to my welfare. The roads aren't better and can't be better. My horses will travel even on bad roads. I have no need of doctors and dispensaries, nor of a justice of the peace, whom I've never applied to and never will. I need no schools and even consider them harmful, as I've told you. I have no personal interest in the zemstvo institutions. All they mean to me is that I must pay a tax of eighteen kopecks a dessiatine, must travel to the city, spend nights with bedbugs, and listen to all kinds of nonsense."

"Hold on," interrupted Sergei Ivanovich with a smile. "We had no personal interest in the liberation of the peasants, but we worked for it."

"No," Konstantin interrupted, still more excited, "the liberation of the peasants was quite a different thing. We had a personal interest in it. We wanted to free ourselves of the yoke that oppressed all of us, all men of good will. But to be a deputy in the zemstvo, to discuss the number of sanitation men to be hired, or which way pipes should be laid in a city in which I don't live; to be a member of the jury to try a moujik who has stolen a ham, and for six hours to listen to lawyers and prosecutors droning all kinds of nonsense, and to the judge, asking my feeble-minded Alyosha, 'Mister defendant, do you confess to having carried off a ham?' Well?"

Levin now veered off the line of their discussion and went on mimicking the judge and the feeble-minded Alyosha, believing it was all relevant.

But Sergei Ivanovich shrugged his shoulders.

"What are you trying to say?"

"I just want to say that the rights that concern me—concern my own interest—I will always defend with all my power. When, in our college years, the gendarmes searched our apartments and read our letters, I was ready to defend these rights with all my power, my rights to education and freedom. I know that the problem of compulsory military service affects the fate of my children, of my brothers and myself. I am ready to discuss what concerns me. But to decide how to spend forty thousands rubles of the zemstvo's money, to try feeble-minded Alyosha, this I don't understand and can't do."

It was as though a dam had broken, and Konstantin Levin's words poured out. Sergei Ivanovich smiled.

"But some day you may be brought to trial. Would you like to be tried in the old criminal courts?"

"I'll not be brought to trail. I'll never cut a man's throat, and I have no need of courts. Now," he continued, again raising a completely irrelevant point, "our zemstvo institutions and all that are like the birch trees we used to stick in the ground on Trinity Sunday, to give the appearance of a European forest, which, however, grew up naturally. Even if I wanted to, I couldn't water those birch trees or have any confidence in them."

Sergei Ivanovich only shrugged his shoulders, showing how puzzled he was at the birch trees that had now been drawn into the conversation, but he quickly grasped his brother's point.

"Wait, you can't argue this way," he remarked.

But Konstantin Levin, anxious to vindicate the shortcoming he knew he was guilty of, namely, his indifference to the common good, continued:

"I believe that no activity can be sound unless it's based on personal interest. This is a general philosophical truth," he said, emphatically repeating the word "philosophical," as if to show that he, too, like anyone else, had the right to discuss philosophy.

Sergei Ivanovich smiled again. He, too, has some kind of philosophy to serve his purposes, he thought.

"Well, you'd better leave philosophy alone," he said. "For ages, it has been the main purpose of philosophy to find the necessary bond that exists between personal and common interests. But that isn't the point. What I have in mind is to correct the comparison you made. The birch trees were not just stuck into the ground, but either had been planted or were grown from seed, and they should be well cared for. Only those nations have a future and can be called historical that sense what is important and meaningful in their institutions and prize them."

Sergei Ivanovich transferred the discussion into the realm of philosophy and history, inaccessible to Konstantin Levin, and proved to him how entirely wrong his view was.

"And as for your dislike for it, I must tell you frankly that it is our Russian indolence and haughtiness. I'm sure it's a temporary aberration with you and will soon pass."

Konstantin Levin kept silent. He felt crushed on every point, but at the same time he knew that his brother had not understood what he wanted to say. But what he did not know was why his brother had not understood him: was it because he was unable to express clearly what he wanted to say, or because his brother did not want to or could not understand him? But he did not dwell on these questions and, making no reply to his brother, he turned his thoughts to something entirely different, a personal matter.

Sergei Ivanovich reeled in his last line, untied the horse, and they left.

4

THE FOLLOWING was the personal matter that preoccupied Levin during his conversation with his brother. The previous year he had on one occasion come to a meadow that peasants were mowing. Getting angry with his steward, he resorted to his usual way of calming himself. He took a scythe from one of the moujiks and began to mow.

This work pleased him so much that he repeated it several times. He mowed the whole meadow in front of his house and from early spring of this year he had been contemplating a plan to mow for whole days together with the moujiks. Since the arrival of his brother he was in doubt whether to do it. He felt uneasy about leaving him alone day after day, and he was afraid that his brother might laugh at him for it. But as he walked through the meadow and recalled the impression the mowing had made on him, he all but decided that he would do it. And after the argument with his brother, he again recalled his project.

I need some physical exercise; without it, my character will completely deteriorate, he thought, and he decided to mow, no matter how strange it might appear to his brother and to others.

That evening Konstantin Levin went to his office, gave his orders concerning the forthcoming work, and sent messengers to the villages to summon mowers for the following morning. He planned to mow Kalinov meadow, the largest and best.

"And please send my scythe to Titus; have him sharpen it and bring it tomorrow. Perhaps I will mow, myself," he said, trying to hide his embarrassment.

The steward smiled and said, "Very good, sir."

During tea that evening, Levin spoke to his brother on the same subject.

"The weather seems to have settled," he said, "and tomorrow I begin mowing."

"I'm very fond of that kind of work," said Sergei Ivanovich.

"I'm extremely fond of it. Several times I mowed, myself, together with the moujiks, and tomorrow I intend to work the whole day."

Sergei Ivanovich raised his head and looked inquiringly at his brother.

"What do you mean? Just as the moujiks, the whole day?"

"Yes, I really enjoy it," said Levin.

"It's a fine physical exercise, but you'll scarcely be able to stand it," said Sergei Ivanovich, without even a touch of irony in his voice.

"I've tried it. It's hard in the beginning, but then you get used to it. I don't think I'll fall behind."

"Well, well! But tell me, how do the peasants take it? Most likely they laugh at you, their queer master."

"No, I don't think so. And the work is so enjoyable and so hard it leaves no time for thinking."

"And will you have dinner with them? It would be embarrassing to send you wine and roast turkey."

"No. When they take their rest, I'll come home."

The next morning Konstantin Levin rose earlier than usual, but the affairs of the estate detained him, and when he reached the meadow, the mowers were already moving along their second row.

As far as the top of the hill, there opened to his view the shadowed part of the meadow that had already been mowed, with the graying swaths and the black heaps formed by the coats the mowers had left at the beginning of the first row.

As he approached, he sighted the peasants moving one after another in a long line, each swinging his scythe in his own way, some dressed in coats, others in shirtsleeves. He counted forty-two men.

They moved slowly along the uneven surface of the meadow near the old dam. Levin recognized some of his own men. There was old Ermil in his very long, white shirt, bending and swinging his scythe; there was young Vaska, Levin's coachman, cutting each swath with a great sweep. And there was Titus, Levin's instructor in mowing, a short, slender peasant; without bending, he moved onward, cutting his wide swath as if playing with the scythe.

Levin dismounted, tied his horse near the road, and approached Titus, who brought out from the bush another scythe and handed it to Levin.

"It's ready, master. It cuts by itself, like a razor," said Titus with a smile, removing his hat and handing him the scythe.

Levin took it and tried it out.

The gay, perspiring mowers who had finished their rows came up to the road one after another and smiled in greeting to their master. They all looked at him, but none said anything until a tall old man with a wrinkled, bearded face, dressed in a sheepskin jacket, came up to the road and addressed him.

"Look, master, once you tackle a job, stick it out," he said, and Levin heard a restrained laugh among the mowers.

"I'll try not to fail," he said, taking his place behind Titus and waiting to start.

"Remember," repeated the old man.

Titus made room for him, and Levin walked after him. As is usual near the road, the grass was low, and Levin, who had not mowed for a long time and was embarrassed by the looks directed toward him, mowed badly for the first few minutes, though he swung his scythe forcefully. He heard the peasants behind him talking.

"They didn't set it right; the handle is too high. See how he has to bend," said one.

"Press harder on your heels," said another.

"It's all right, he'll learn," continued the old man. "See how fast he is. You are making your swath too wide; you'll wear yourself out. Well, he's the master; he does it for himself. But look at his row. They used to slap us for such work!"

The grass turned softer, and Levin, listening but not replying to all these remarks, tried to mow as well as he could as he followed Titus. They took about a hundred steps. Titus kept moving, showing not the faintest sign of fatigue. But Levin was already fearful that he would not be able to carry on: he was so tired.

He felt that he was swinging the scythe with his final efforts and decided to ask Titus to halt. But at that very moment Titus himself stopped, bent down, took a handful of grass, wiped the scythe and began to sharpen it. Levin stretched, took a deep breath, and turned around. A moujik walked behind him. Evidently he, too, was tired, for even before reaching Levin he stopped and began to sharpen his scythe. Titus was through sharpening his own and Levin's scythes and they resumed their work.

The second stage was the same. Titus walked on, swinging his scythe rhythmically, not stopping nor seeming to tire. Levin followed him, trying not to fall behind. It became harder and harder for him. There were moments when it seemed that his strength would leave him entirely, but each time Titus would halt to sharpen the scythes.

In this way they completed the first row. And this long row seemed to Levin particularly difficult, but when they reached the end of it, and Titus, throwing his scythe over his shoulder, turned back and slowly followed the traces left by his heels on the cut grass, Levin walked the same way along his swath. Though his face was bathed in sweat, which dripped from his nose, and his back was thoroughly drenched, he felt very well. He knew now that he would stand the trial, and this made him particularly happy.

But the fact that his work was not done well marred his pleasure. I'll swing less with my hands and more with my whole body, he thought, comparing Titus' row, straight as a taut string, with his own, which was disordered and uneven.

The first row, Levin observed, Titus had covered with particular speed, evidently trying to test his master, and the first row happened to be a long one. The rows that followed were easier, but Levin still had to summon all his power not to fall behind the moujiks.

He did not think about anything and had only one wish: not to lag behind the moujiks and to perform his work in the best possible way. He heard only the clang of the scythes and saw before him the erect, retreating figure of Titus, the curved semicircle of the swath, the grass and flower tops slowly falling in waves at the touch of the scythe's blade, and ahead of him the end of the row, the place of rest.

He did not know what it was or where it came from, but in the middle of his work he suddenly felt a pleasant sensation of coolness on his hot, perspiring shoulders. While the scythes were being sharpened, he glanced at the sky. A low, dense cloud had moved up, and a heavy rain was falling. Some of the moujiks put on their coats; the others, Levin among them, felt pleasantly refreshed and just happily shrugged their shoulders.

Row followed row. There were long rows, short ones, good grass and bad. Levin lost all sense of time and was completely unaware of whether it was early or late. A change was now taking place in his work, one that brought him immense pleasure. During his work he passed through moments when he forgot what he was doing when the work was effortless, and at these moments the row of grass he cut was almost as straight

and as good as Titus'. But as soon as he recalled what he was
doing and tried to do it better, he immediately felt all the
hardship of his toil, and the row turned out badly.

After they had completed another row, he was ready to
turn back, but Titus halted, approached the old man, and said
something to him softly. Both of them looked at the sun. What
are they talking about—and why aren't they turning back
along the row? thought Levin. It did not occur to him that the
moujiks had already been working without a stop for more
than four hours and that it was time for breakfast.

"Breakfast time, master," said the old man.

"Is it? Well, let's have it."

Levin handed his scythe to Titus. The moujiks went over to
their coats for their bread, and Levin walked along with them
toward his horse, through the broad mowed area of the field,
sprinkled lightly by the rain. Only now did he understand that
he had guessed wrong about the weather, and that the rain
was soaking his hay.

"It will ruin the hay," he said.

"It's all right, master. Mow when it rains, and rake when it
shines," said the old man.

Levin untied his horse and rode home to have coffee.

Sergei Ivanovich had just risen. After coffee, Levin returned
to the meadow before Sergei Ivanovich had time to dress and
come into the dining room.

5

AFTER BREAKFAST, Levin did not resume his former place in
the line of the mowers. An old wag had invited him to take his
place between him and a young peasant who had married only
last fall, and for whom this was the first summer he had come
out to mow.

The old man, holding himself erect, walked in front of him,
spacing his steps evenly and widely with his feet turned out.
He moved his arms evenly and precisely and, it seemed, as
easily as he swung them while walking. And he laid down a
wide even swath as though it were a game. It seemed that the
sharp scythe alone, and not he, cut into the succulent grass.

Young Mishka walked behind Levin. He had tied his hair
with a plait of fresh grass, and his handsome young face mir-

rored his efforts, but as soon as one looked at him, he smiled. Evidently he would die rather than admit that the work was hard for him.

Levin walked between them. At the peak of the heat the work did not seem to him very hard. The sweat he was bathed in cooled him, and the sun, which scorched his back, head, and his arms, bare to the elbows, added vigor and tenacity to his exertion. And more and more often there were those moments when he lost awareness of his activities, when he could turn his thoughts away from what he was doing. The scythe moved by itself. Those were happy moments. And still happier were those moments when, coming up the river where the rows ended, the old man wiped the scythe with a tuft of thick wet grass, bathed its steel in the fresh water of the river, scooped some water with his cup and offered some to Levin.

"Well, how do you like my kvas?" he asked, winking.

And, in fact, Levin had never drunk anything like this tepid, greenish water, tasting of the rust of the tin cup. And right after this followed the blissful, slow walk, his hand on the scythe, when he could wipe the dripping sweat, breathe deeply, survey the whole extended line of mowers, and observe what was going on around him in the field and in the wood.

The longer Levin worked, the more often those moments of unawareness occurred when his arms no longer swung the scythe, but his whole body, fully conscious of itself, full of life, was drawn by the scythe and, as if under some spell, the work was done properly and accurately by itself, without his thinking of it. Those were the most blissful moments.

The work grew difficult only when he had to change from these motions, which had become automatic, and concentrate on how to mow around some tussock or unweeded clusters of sorrel. The old peasant did it without effort. When he came across a tussock, he altered his motions, and here with the point of the scythe, there with his heel, he struck a few times against its sides. While doing this, he examined it and observed what was revealed to him. Now he tore off a berry, ate it, or offered it to Levin, now with the point of his scythe he tossed aside a twig, now he examined a little quail's nest from which the hen flew out underneath the scythe. If he happened upon a snake crossing his path, he pierced it, raised it into the air with his scythe as with a fork, showed it to Levin, and tossed it aside.

But these changes of pace proved difficult for Levin and the young peasant behind him. Both of them were now adjusted to one set of motions, were completely taken up with their work, and were not strong enough to alter their movements and at the same time observe what was going on before them.

Levin did not notice how the time passed. If he were asked how long he had been mowing, he would have said half an hour, but it was near dinnertime. Walking along the swath, the old man called Levin's attention to the boys and girls who, scarcely visible, were coming toward the mowers from all directions, along the road or through the tall grass. They carried parcels of bread, as well as kvas in small jars stoppered with rags, their burdens pulling on their little hands.

"Look. The little ones are coming!" he said, pointing to the children and, shading his eyes, he looked at the sun.

They cut two more swaths, and then the old man stopped.

"Time for dinner, master!" he said decisively.

When they reached the river, the mowers moved through the mowed area toward their coats, where the children were waiting for them with their dinners. The moujiks congregated in groups, those that lived far beside the carts, others under the willow, where they strewed some grass. Levin sat down with them. He had no desire to leave. All the embarrassment caused by the master's presence had long since vanished. The moujiks made ready for dinner. Some of them washed; the young men bathed in the river; others arranged a place for rest, untied the little bags containing bread, and opened the kvas jars. The old man crumbled some bread into his bowl, mashed it with the handle of his spoon, poured some water from his drinking cup, cut off another slice of bread, put some salt on it, and turned to the East to say a prayer.

"Well, master, taste my dish," he said kneeling before his bowl.

The dish was so tasty that Levin decided not to go home. He had his dinner with the old man and engaged him in a conversation about his domestic affairs, showing a very lively interest in them, told him about his own affairs and about everything concerning his life that might be of interest to the old man. He felt closer to him than to his brother, and he unconsciously smiled at the tenderness that he felt toward the man. The old man rose again, prayed, and lay down right there under the bush, using some grass as a pillow. Levin did the same, and though the flies and gnats, persistent and tenacious in the sunshine, tickled his perspiring face and body, he immediately fell asleep and woke only when the sun passed over the bush and began to reach him. The old man had long since awakened and was sitting there, sharpening the young mowers' scythes.

Levin looked around and did not recognize the place, it had changed so much. An immense stretch of the meadow had been mowed and shone with a strange new brightness, the cut grass already fragrant in the slanting rays of the evening sun. The bushes at the river, with the grass mowed around them, the river itself, formerly screened but now shining like steel as it meandered, the people, rising and moving around, the steep wall of the unmowed meadow, and the hawks hovering over the denuded fields—all this was entirely new. Now fully awake, Levin began to calculate how much of the meadow had been mowed and how much could still be done that day.

An unusual amount of work had been accomplished, considering that there were only forty-two mowers. The large meadow, which in former times had taken thirty serfs two days to mow, was already completely mowed. Only small patches at the corners remained to be done. But Levin was eager to mow as much of the meadow as possible that day, and he was annoyed that the sun was setting so early. He was not tired at all; he was eager to get as much work done as quickly as possible.

"What do you think, will we get to mow Mashkin Hill?" he asked the old man.

"As God wills, but the sun is getting low. Some vodka for the boys, perhaps?"

During the late afternoon snack, while they took another rest and the smokers had their smoke, the old man announced to the men that there would be a reward of vodka if they mowed Mashkin Hill.

"Why not? Come on, Titus, start. We'll do it in no time! We can eat our fill tonight. Let's start!" they cried on all sides and, swallowing their bread, the mowers fell into line.

"Well, boys, watch out!" said Titus, the leader, almost trotting.

"Go ahead, go ahead!" said the old man, following him and easily overtaking him. "I'll cut you! Watch out!"

And young and old mowed as though vying with each other. But though they hurried, they did not ruin the grass, and the rows were straight and even as before. In five minutes they were through with the small area at the corner. While the last mowers were still coming up to the end of their rows, those ahead of them grabbed their coats, threw them over their shoulders and crossed the road toward Mashkin Hill.

The sun was setting behind the trees when, their drinking cups clanging, they entered the little wooded gully of Mashkin Hill. Inside, the grass was waist high, tender, soft, its blades wide, and in some places around the woods mottled with cow-wheat.

And after a short consultation whether to form the rows lengthwise or crosswise, Prokhor Ermilin, also an outstanding mower, a huge, swarthy moujik, led the way. He walked forward the length of the row, turned around, and began mowing. All the mowers fell in line behind him, moving downhill into the dell and uphill to the very fringe of the wood. The sun was setting behind the wood. The dew had already gathered, and only on one side of the hill did the mowers walk in the sunshine; as its foot, where the mist had risen, and on its other side, they walked in a fresh, dewy shade. The work was in full swing.

The aromatic grass, cut with a swishing sound, fell in wide swaths. The mowers crowded on all sides along the short rows, their drinking cups clanging. They filled the air with the sounds of clashing scythes, the whistle of whetstone on a scythe, and their gay shouts as they encouraged one another.

Levin still walked between the young fellow and the old man. The old man, now dressed in his sheepskin jacket, was as gay, jocular, and free in his movements as before. In the wood they constantly came upon swollen birch-mushrooms amidst the succulent grass. The mowers cut them down, but the old man, whenever he came across such a mushroom, bent down, picked it up, and put it in his bosom. "One more present for the old woman," he would say.

Though it was easy to mow the wet soft grass, it was hard to climb up and down the steep banks of the gully. But it did not trouble the old man. Steadily swinging his scythe, he climbed the steep bank, moving slowly in his large bast shoes, his steps short and firm. Though his whole body trembled, and his trousers slipped down below his shirt, he did not miss a single blade of grass or a single mushroom, and kept joking with the moujiks and with Levin. Levin walked behind him and often thought that he would surely fall, as, scythe in hand, he ascended a hillock so steep that it would be difficult to go up empty-handed. But he climbed up and did what was required. He felt that some external force moved him.

6

MASHKIN HILL had been mowed, the last rows completed. The mowers put on their coats and gaily left for home. Levin mounted his horse, regretfully said goodbye to the moujiks, and left for his home. On the hill he looked back. In the mist that had risen from the dell, he could not see the peasants, but he could hear their gay, coarse voices, their loud laughter, and the clang of the scythes.

Sergei Ivanovich had dined much earlier and now drank iced lemonade in his room, looking over the newspapers and magazines that had just arrived in the mail, when Levin burst into his room, talking gaily. His hair, matted and wet with perspiration, clung to his forehead, and his chest and back were dark and sweaty.

"We did the whole meadow. How good it was, how wonderful! And how've you been?" asked Levin. He had completely forgotten the unpleasant conversation of the previous day.

"Goodness! How terrible you look!" said Sergei Ivanovich, displeased with his brother for the moment. "But close the door, close the door," he exclaimed. "You've let in at least ten of them."

Sergei Ivanovich could not abide flies, and in his room he opened the windows only at night, carefully keeping his door closed.

"I swear, not a single one. And if I let any in, I'll catch them. You'd scarcely believe what a pleasure it was. How did you spend your day?"

"Very well. But did you really mow the entire day? You must be hungry as a wolf. Kuzma has prepared your meal."

"No, I'm not hungry. I had my meal there. I'll go and wash now."

"Go ahead. I'll see you soon," said Sergei Ivanovich, shaking his head as he looked at his brother. "Well, hurry up," he added, smiling and gathering his books, and he was about to leave. But suddenly he grew cheerful and did not wish to part with his brother.

"And where were you during the rain?"

"What rain? It was just a drizzle. Well, I'll be back in a minute. So you've had a good day? Excellent!" And Levin went up to change.

Within five minutes the brothers met in the dining room. Though Levin thought that he was not hungry and sat down to dinner only out of consideration for Kuzma, when he began to eat, the food tasted exceptionally good. Sergei Ivanovich looked at him with a smile.

"Oh yes, there's a letter for you. Kuzma, please bring it. It's downstairs. But don't forget to close the door."

The letter was from Oblonsky. Levin read it aloud. Oblonsky wrote from Petersburg. *"I received a letter from Dolly. She is in Ergushovo, and nothing goes well with her. Please go to see her, give her your advice; you are always so helpful. She will be so glad to see you. She is all alone, the poor thing. My mother-in-law and her family are still abroad."*

"Fine! I'll certainly go," said Levin. "But let's go together. She's such a darling. Isn't she?"

"How far is it?"

"About thirty versts. Perhaps forty. But the road is excellent. It'll be an easy trip."

"I'll be very glad to go," said Sergei Ivanovich, still smiling. His younger brother's appearance infected him with its cheerfulness.

"Well, you have some appetite," he said, looking at the deeply tanned face and neck of his brother, bent over his plate.

"It's wonderful! You'd scarcely believe how effective such exercise is against all kinds of foolishness. I want to enrich medicine with a new term: *Arbeitskur.*"

"But you don't seem to need it."

"No, but it's good for all kinds of nervous disorders."

"Yes, it must be given a trial. I was going to come over to you at the meadow, but the heat was so unbearable that I went no farther than the wood. I sat there for a while and then went through the wood to the village, where I met your old wet nurse and asked her about the moujiks' opinions of you. As I understand it, they don't approve of your working. 'It isn't a gentleman's job,' she said. In general, it seems to me that the peasants are very precise in defining what they call 'gentlemen's' activities, and they demand that the masters abide by this definition and do not exceed the limits they have set for them."

"Perhaps. But it was a pleasure such as I've never before had in my life. And I've done nothing wrong. Don't you agree?" asked Levin. "Can I help it if they don't like it? Well, I don't think it's very important. Eh?"

"In general," continued Sergei Ivanovich, "I see that you are pleased with your day."

"Very much so. We mowed the whole meadow. And I've struck up a friendship with such a grand old man. You can't imagine how delightful everything was."

"So you are pleased with your day. And I was too. First of all, I solved two chess problems, one of which is very interesting, as it opens with the pawn. I'll show it to you. Then I was thinking about our conversation of yesterday."

"What? Yesterday's conversation?" asked Levin, squinting contentedly, puffing after his dinner, and completely unable to remember what it was they had discussed the previous day.

"I admit that you are partly right. You assert that personal interest is man's only incentive, whereas I believe that every man with some degree of education should be interested in the common good. In this we disagree. But perhaps you are right in maintaining that activity that brings material reward would be more inviting. In general, your nature is too *prime-sautière*, as the French say. You are for all-absorbing, forceful activity, or nothing."

Levin listened to his brother and could not and would not understand him at all. He was only afraid that his brother might ask him a question that would prove he was not listening.

"And that's the way it is, my friend," said Sergei Ivanovich, patting him on the shoulder.

"Yes, of course! Why, I don't insist that I'm right," replied Levin with a childish, apologetic smile. What was it we argued about? he thought. Of course, both he and I are right, and everything is fine. But I must go to the office and see to things. He rose, stretched, and smiled.

Sergei Ivanovich also smiled.

"Let's go together," he said. He did not want to part with his brother, who exuded such freshness and vigor. "Let's go together. We'll stop at the office, if you have to."

"Oh, good heavens!" exclaimed Levin, so loudly that he frightened Sergei Ivanovich.

"What's the matter?"

"How is Agafia Mikhailovna's hand?" asked Levin, slapping his forehead. "I forgot about her."

"Much better."

"But I'll look in on her just the same. I'll be back before you have time to put on your hat."

And he ran down the stairs, his heels clattering like a rattle.

7

STEPAN ARKADIEVICH arrived in Petersburg to fulfill a most natural obligation, well known to officials, but incomprehensible to others; a most necessary act, without which one could not continue in government service, namely, reminding the ministry of one's existence. While fulfilling this obligation, he had a gay and pleasant time, visiting the races and the country villas, having taken almost all the money from the house. Dolly and the children had moved to the country to cut expenses as much as possible. She moved to the estate at Ergushovo, her dowry, that same estate where the timber had been sold in the spring. It was fifty versts from Levin's Pokrovskoe.

At Ergushovo, the large old house had been torn down a long time ago, and the smaller house had been restored and enlarged by the prince. Twenty years earlier, when Dolly was still a child, this house was spacious and comfortable, though, as all such houses, it had the driveway along its side and did not face south. But now this house was old and run-down. That spring, when Stepan Arkadievich had gone to the country to sell the timber, Dolly had asked him to inspect the house and to see that all the necessary repairs were made. Stepan Arkadievich, like all conscience-stricken husbands, zealous of his wife's comforts, inspected the house himself and ordered all changes which, in his opinion, were urgent. According to him, all the furniture had to be reupholstered with cretonne, the drapes hung, the garden cleared, a little pier at the pond built, and flowers planted. But he had forgotten many other urgent repairs, and this later caused Daria Aleksandrovna much grief.

No matter how much Stepan Arkadievich tried to be a thoughtful father and husband, he could by no means keep in his mind the fact that he had a wife and children. His tastes were those of a bachelor, and he followed those alone. On returning to Moscow, he proudly declared to his wife that everything had been prepared for her, that the house would be as pretty as a toy, and he advised her to move there. Stepan Arkadievich was in every respect pleased with the prospect of his wife's departure for the country: it would be good for the children's health, it would decrease expenses, and it would give him more freedom. Daria Aleksandrovna considered that moving to the country for the summer was most urgent for the children's sake, particularly for the little girl who could not recover from her attack of scarlet fever. It would at last relieve her of petty humiliations, and of petty and worrisome indebtedness to the firewood dealer, the fish dealer, and the shoemaker. Moreover, she wanted to go to the country because she dreamt of luring her sister into staying with her. Kitty was expected to return from abroad in the middle of the summer, and her doctor had prescribed bathing. Kitty wrote from the spa that nothing pleased her more than the prospect of spending the summer with Dolly in Ergushovo, which to both of them was so rich in childhood memories.

The first days of Dolly's life in the country were very difficult. She had lived in the country in her childhood, and the impression that remained was that country life was the salvation from all city ills, that though life in the country was not gracious (to which Dolly easily resigned herself), it was inexpensive and comfortable: everything was there, everything was inexpensive, everything was available, and it was good for the children. But now, when she arrived in the country as a housewife, she saw that everything was not at all the way she had thought.

A heavy rain fell on the day after their arrival. At night it rained into the hallway and the nursery, and they had to transfer the children's beds into the drawing room. They could not find a scullery maid. Out of nine cows, according to the cowherd, some were in calf, some had just calved, some were old, and others were hard-uddered; there was not sufficient butter or milk even for the children; there were no eggs. It was impossible to obtain a chicken; they cooked and roasted old, tough, purple-fleshed roosters. All the peasant women were busy digging potatoes, and it was impossible to hire one to wash the floors. They could take no rides, because one of the horses had grown restive and would strain itself

against the shaft. There was no place to bathe; the whole
river bank had been trampled by cattle and was exposed to
view from the road. It was impossible even to take a walk,
for cattle passed into the garden through a broken fence,
and there was one frightening bull who bellowed and therefore probably butted. There were no fit closets for their
clothes. Those that were, either did not close or opened by
themselves when someone passed by. There were neither iron
nor earthen pots, nor cauldron for the laundry, nor an ironing
board in the maidservants' room.

In the beginning Daria Aleksandrovna was in despair, as
instead of finding peace and rest, she was faced with what
she considered terrible calamities. She busied herself as best
she could; she felt how hopeless her situation was, and constantly fought to restrain the tears that came to her eyes.
The steward, a former cavalry sergeant-major and later a
doorman, whom Stepan Arkadievich liked for his handsome
and respectful appearance, was not in the least concerned
by Daria Aleksandrovna's misfortunes, courteously repeating,
"It is utterly impossible; these are mean people," and was of
no help at all.

The situation looked hopeless. But in the Oblonsky household, as in all households, there was one person, unnoticed,
but most important and most useful—Matriona Filimonovna.
She tried to compose her mistress, assured her that everything
would come out right in the end (these were her words, and
Matvei had taken them over from her), and she took matters
into her own hands in her calm and unhurried way.

She at once made friends with the steward's wife. On the
very first day she had tea with her and her husband under the
acacias, and they discussed the whole situation. There under
the acacias, a club was quickly formed, presided over by
Matriona Filimonovna, and through the effort of this club,
which comprised the steward's wife, the village elder, and
the office clerk, all the discomforts were gradually overcome,
and within a week everything, indeed, had *come out right*.
The roof was repaired, a cook was hired—she was a friend
of the village elder's—chickens were purchased, the cows
began to give milk, the garden was fenced, the carpenter
made a mangle, hooks were attached to the closets so that
they no longer opened by themselves, and the ironing board,
padded with soldier's cloth, now rested between the arm of

the chair and the dresser, and the odor of ironing came from the maidservants' room.

"See, and you had given up all hope," said Matriona Filimonovna, pointing to the ironing board.

They even built a bathing shed of straw mats. Lily began bathing, and Daria Aleksandrovna's hopes for a comfortable though not a tranquil life in the country had come true in part. With six children to care for, Daria Aleksandrovna's life could not be tranquil. One of them fell sick, another might get sick, a third needed something, a fourth showed signs of misbehavior, and so on. Short interludes of peace occurred very, very infrequently. But these preoccupations, these worries, were the only happiness Daria Aleksandrovna could have. Without them she would remain alone with her thoughts about a husband who did not love her. Moreover, no matter how much she dreaded possible illness in the children, how much she worried when they actually fell sick, and how much she was troubled by signs of their misbehavior, the children themselves now rewarded her with little joys. These joys were so little that they were unseen, as gold is unseen in sand, and in bad moments she saw only her worries, only the sand. But there also were good moments, when she saw her joys only, the gold.

Now, in the seclusion of the country, she more and more often became aware of these joys. Often, while watching her children, she tried hard to convince herself that she was mistaken, that like every mother, she was partial to them; nevertheless, she could not help telling herself that her children were delightful, all six of them, each in his own way, and all of them exceptional. They were a source of happiness and pride to her.

8

At the end of May, when everything had been more or less set right, she received from her husband an answer to her complaints about the discomforts of her life in the country. He wrote asking forgiveness for his thoughtlessness and promised to come at the first opportunity. This opportunity had not arrived, and until the beginning of June Daria Aleksandrovna lived alone in the country.

On the Sunday of St. Peter's Fast, Daria Aleksandrovna went to mass to have her children take the sacrament. In her intimate philosophical discussions with her sister, mother, and friends, she often surprised them with her liberal thoughts on religion. She professed her own strange religion of metempsychosis, in which she believed firmly, caring very little for the dogmas of the church. But within the family—and not only to provide an example, but in all sincerity—she strictly observed all the rites of the church. She worried because her children had not taken the sacrament for almost a year, and, with Matriona Filimonovna's full understanding and approval, she decided to have them take it now, in the summer.

For several days in advance, Daria Aleksandrovna was busy readying the children's wardrobe for this occasion. Dresses were sewn, altered, laundered, flounces and hems lowered, buttons sewn, and ribbons prepared. One dress, Tania's, which the English governess had undertaken to sew, caused Daria Aleksandrovich much concern. The English governess had made the tucks in the wrong places, had set the sleeves too low, and had almost ruined the dress. The dress was so narrow at Tania's shoulders that it was painful to look at her. But Matriona Filimonovna saved the day by setting in gussets and adding a cape. The damage was repaired, but this almost led to a quarrel with the English governess. In the morning, however, everything was set right, and about nine o'clock—she had asked the priest to postpone the mass until that time—the children, beaming with happiness and dressed in their finery, stood at the carriage near the porch, waiting for their mother.

Through Matriona Filimonovna's influence, the steward's Chestnut had been harnessed to the carriage instead of the restless Raven. Daria Aleksandrovna, delayed by attending to her toilette, now came out, attired in a white muslin dress, to take her seat in the carriage.

Daria Aleksandrovna had dressed and combed with much care and concern. In former years she had dressed for herself, to look beautiful and attractive. But the older she grew, the less she liked to dress up. She knew that she had lost her good looks. But now she again dressed with pleasure and care. She dressed now not to please herself, not to appear beautiful for her own sake, but so that she, the mother of these charming children, might not spoil the impression they made. Taking one last look in the mirror, she was satisfied with what she saw. She was attractive. Not as attractive as she had wanted to be in former times when going to a ball, but attractive enough for her present purpose.

There was no one in the church but the moujiks, the servants, and their wives. But Daria Aleksandrovna saw, or it seemed to her that she saw, the admiration with which they looked at her and the children. The children not only looked beautiful in their handsome attire, but were charming in their mannerly behavior. True, Alyosha did not stand quite properly and kept turning around, trying to see the back of his jacket, but he was a pleasure to look at. Tania stood like a grown-up, watching over the younger children. But the youngest one, Lily, was charming, with her look of innocent wonderment. One could scarcely suppress a smile when, after taking the sacrament, she said, in English, "Please, some more."

On the way home the children felt that a solemn event had taken place, and they were very quiet.

At home, too, everything was going well. But at lunch Grisha began to whistle and, what was worse, he did not obey the English governess. For this he went without dessert. Daria Aleksandrovna would not have allowed punishing him on such a day if she had been present, but she had to uphold the English governess' order, and she confirmed her decision that Grisha would go without dessert. The general good cheer was somewhat marred by this incident.

Grisha cried, saying that Nikolinka also had whistled but hadn't been punished, and that he was crying not on account of the dessert—he didn't care about that—but because they had been unjust to him. This became so grievous that Daria Aleksandrovna decided to forgive Grisha, after first consulting the English governess. As she passed through the dining room on her way to see her, she observed a scene which filled her heart with such joy that tears came to her eyes, and she herself pardoned the culprit.

The guilty boy was sitting on a window sill in the corner of the room. Next to him was Tania, with her plate. She had pretended that she wanted to give part of her dessert to her dolls and had asked permission to go to the nursery, taking it to her brother instead. He continued to cry over the injustice of his punishment, ate the dessert which Tania had brought him, and kept repeating through his sobs, "You eat too; let's eat together . . . together."

At first Tania was moved by pity for Grisha, then by the awareness of her own kind deed, and tears came to her eyes, too. However, she did not refuse to eat her portion.

They were frightened when they saw their mother, but from the expression on her face they understood that what they were doing was good. They laughed and, their mouths still full of dessert, they began wiping their smiling lips with their hands, smearing their beaming faces with jam and tears.

"Heavens! Your new white dress! Tania! Grisha!" exclaimed their mother, trying to save the dress, and smiling with a blissful, enraptured smile, her eyes full of tears.

The children were told to take off their new clothes, the girls to put on blouses, the boys old jackets. The carriage was made ready, again, to the steward's regret, with Chestnut in harness. They were going to gather mushrooms, and then to bathe in the river. Shrill shouts of happiness rose in the nursery and did not die down until their departure.

They gathered a full basket of mushrooms, and even Lily found one. Formerly Miss Hull would find a mushroom and point it out to her, but now she herself found a large mushroom, and the children shouted happily, "Lily found a mushroom!"

Then they rode up to the river, left the horses under the birch trees, and went into the bathing shed. The horses, flicking away gadflies with their tails, were tied to a tree by the coachman Terenti. He stretched out on the grass in the shade of a birch tree and smoked. From the bathing shed he could hear the incessant sound of childish merriment.

Though it was tiring to keep watch over all the children and to restrain their playfulness; though it was hard to keep straight all these little stockings, pants, shoes from various owners; to untie, unbutton, and fasten again all those laces and buttons; Daria Aleksandrovna, who herself loved bathing and considered it very beneficial for the children's health, enjoyed nothing more than these baths in the company of her children. To touch all these chubby little feet, to put them into their little stockings, to take into her hands and dip in water the naked bodies and to listen to their shouts, now happy, and now frightened; to watch them gasping, their eyes wide, happy and frightened, and to observe these splashing little angels of hers—all this was her greatest delight.

When half the children were already dressed, a few peasant

women in their holiday clothes, who had been gathering herbs, shyly came over to the bathing shed. Matriona Filimonovna called out to one of them and asked her to dry a sheet and shirt that had fallen into the water, and Daria Aleksandrovna engaged them in conversation. The women, who at first could not understand the words addressed to them and covered their smiles with their hands, soon gathered their courage and replied to Daria Aleksandrovna's questions, gaining her favor by their show of sincere admiration for the children.

"Look. What a beauty, white as sugar!" said one, admiring Tanechka and shaking her head. "But skinny. . . ."

"Yes, she's been sick."

"You probably bathed this one, too," said another woman, referring to the infant.

"No, he's only three months old," Daria Aleksandrovna replied proudly.

"Is that so?"

"And have you any children?"

"I had four, two are living, a boy and a girl. I weaned her before last Shrovetide."

"And how old is she?"

"In her second year."

"Why did you nurse her so long?"

"It's our custom: for three fasts. . . ."

To Daria Aleksandrovna the conversation was most interesting. She asked, "How was the childbirth? What was his illness? Where is your husband? Does he come home often?"

Daria Aleksandrovna did not want to leave the women, since she found their conversation so interesting and their interests so similar to hers. The women, as Daria Aleksandrovna clearly saw, admired her mainly for her large family and for their good looks, and this gave her the greatest pleasure. The women amused Daria Aleksandrovna and hurt the feelings of the English governess, for she was the uncomprehending butt of their laughter. One of the young women observed the Englishwoman, who was the last to dress and, as she watched her putting on her third petticoat, could not refrain from remarking, "She keeps putting them on, but she is still not finished," and they all burst into loud laughter.

9

DARIA ALEKSANDROVNA, a kerchief on her head, was surrounded by all her bathed children, their heads still wet. As they were approaching the house, the coachman said:

"There is a gentleman from Pokrovskoe, I believe."

Daria Aleksandrovna looked ahead and was happy to recognize the familiar figure of Levin, walking toward them, dressed in a gray hat and gray coat. She was always glad to see him and particularly now, when she appeared in all her glory. No one could appreciate her majesty better than Levin.

When he saw her, he came face to face with one of the pictures of his future family life, as he had created it in his imagination.

"You're just like a mother hen, Daria Aleksandrovna!"

"I'm so glad to see you!" she said, extending her hand.

"Perhaps you are, but I've had no word from you. My brother is visiting me. I received a note from Stiva telling me that you were here!"

"From Stiva?" asked Daria Aleksandrovna, surprised.

"Yes, he writes that you've moved here, and thinks that you will permit me to be of service to you," said Levin and, while saying this, he suddenly felt embarrassed, interrupted his speech, and walked silently alongside the carriage, breaking off linden tree shoots and chewing them. He was embarrassed, for he believed that Daria Aleksandrovna would be displeased by the help of an outsider in a matter in which her husband should have helped her. In fact, Daria Aleksandrovna disliked Stepan Arkadievich's habit of involving strangers in their family affairs. She saw at once that Levin understood this. And for this sensitiveness, for this understanding, Daria Aleksandrovna loved Levin.

"I understand, of course," said Levin, "that this only meant that you wanted to see me, which makes me very happy. Of course, I imagine that to you, a city matron, everything here is strange. If you need anything, I am at your service."

"Oh, no!" said Dolly. "We had trouble in the beginning, but everything has been set right, thanks to my old nurse," she said, indicating Matriona Filimonovna, who knew that they were talking about her and smiled at Levin gaily and amiably. She knew him, knew that he would make a good husband for the young lady, and hoped that they would marry.

"Sit down, please. We'll make room for you," she told him.

"No, I'll walk. Children—who wants to join me in a race against the horses?"

The children did not know Levin well. They did not remember ever having seen him, but they did not display toward him the feeling of strange embarrassment and aversion children often feel toward adults who are insincere with them, for which they are often punished. Pretense of any kind may deceive the cleverest, most clear-sighted person, but the least intelligent child will recognize pretense and will shrink from it, no matter how skillfully it may be concealed. Whatever Levin's shortcomings, he had not a trace of pretense. Therefore the children showed him the same friendliness which they observed on their mother's face. In response to his invitation, the two older children at once jumped off the carriage and ran alongside him as unaffectedly as they would in the company of their nurse, Miss Hull, or their mother. Lily also wanted to be with him, and her mother handed her over to him. He put her on his shoulder and they resumed the race.

"Don't worry, don't worry, Daria Aleksandrovna!" he said, smiling happily at their mother. "I couldn't possibly hurt or drop her."

And observing his skillful, vigorous, protectively careful and fully controlled movements, the mother allayed her fears and watched him with a happy and approving smile.

Here in the country, in the company of the children and the congenial Daria Aleksandrovna, Levin came into that childishly happy state of mind which he often experienced and which Daria Aleksandrovna particularly liked in him. While running with the children, he showed them some gymnastic stunts, amused Miss Hull with his poor English, and spoke to Daria Aleksandrovna about his work in the country.

After dinner, Daria Aleksandrovna, seated alone with him on the terrace, broached the subject of Kitty.

"Did you know that Kitty is coming to spend the summer with me?"

"Is she?" he snapped, and at once, to change the topic of conversation, he said, "Shall I send you the two cows? If you want to keep accounts with me, you may pay me five rubles a month, providing you're not ashamed to do so."

"No, thank you. We are already provided for."

"Then I'll look over your cows and, with your permission, I'll leave instructions about their feed. Feeding is most important."

And just to keep the conversation on safe ground, Levin expounded to Daria Aleksandrovna the theory of dairy farming which regards the cow as a machine for turning feed into milk, and so on.

He spoke of this, but was both anxious and afraid to hear detailed news about Kitty. He dreaded lest his composure, attained with such difficulty, would be disturbed.

"Yes, somebody has to take care of it, but who will do it?" Daria Aleksandrovna replied, reluctantly.

With the aid of Matriona Filimonovna, she had now put her affairs in order, and she was reluctant to make any changes. Moreover, she did not believe in Levin's competence in agriculture. She regarded with suspicion his opinion that a cow was a machine for manufacturing milk. It seemed to her that ideas of this kind could only hamper estate management. She believed that everything was much simpler: as Matriona Filimonovna explained, you just have to give Pestrukha or Belopakhaia more feed and more to drink and prevent the cook from taking away the kitchen scraps for the laundress' cow. This was obvious. But theories of flour and grass diets seemed to her vague and of little value. And, what was most important, she wanted to talk to him about Kitty.

10

"KITTY WRITES that she wants nothing so much as seclusion and calm," said Daria Aleksandrovna, after a silence.

"Does she feel better now?" Levin asked anxiously.

"Thank God, she has fully recovered. I never believed that her lungs were affected."

"Ah, I'm so glad to hear it!" said Levin, and Dolly saw a tender and helpless expression on his face as he said these words. Then he looked at her in silence.

"Listen, Konstantin Dmitrievich," said Daria Aleksandrovna, smiling her good-natured and slightly mocking smile.

"Why are you angry with Kitty?"

"I? I'm not angry," said Levin.

"No, you are angry. Why didn't you visit either us or them when you were in Moscow?"

"Daria Aleksandrovna," he said, blushing to the roots of his hair, "I'm really surprised that you, with all your kindness, don't understand. Haven't you any pity for me, when you know. . . ."

"What is it that I know?"

"You know that I proposed and was refused," said Levin, and all the tenderness which a moment ago he had felt toward Kitty was replaced in his heart by bitterness, caused by the insult he had suffered.

"Why did you think that I knew?"

"Because everybody knows."

"Here you are mistaken. I didn't know it, though I suspected it."

"Well, now you know."

"I only knew that something had happened that made her suffer terribly and that she asked me never to speak of. And if she didn't tell it to me, she didn't tell it to anyone. Well, what happened between you? Tell me."

"I told you what happened."

"When?"

"During my last visit to you."

"Let me tell you something," said Daria Aleksandrovna. "I feel terribly, terribly sorry for her. You are suffering because of your pride. . . ."

"Perhaps," said Levin, "but—"

She interrupted him.

"But I'm terribly, terribly sorry for her, the poor thing. Now I understand everything."

"You will forgive me, Daria Aleksandrovna," he said, rising. "Good day, Daria Aleksandrovna."

"No, wait," she said, holding his sleeve. "Wait, sit down."

"Please, let's not talk about it," he said, sitting down and feeling a hope which he had assumed was buried, stirring and rising in his heart.

"If I didn't love you," said Daria Aleksandrovna, tears welling in her eyes, "if I didn't know you as I do. . . ."

The feeling that had seemed dead revived now with more and more vigor, mounted, and began to take possession of Levin's heart.

"Yes, now I understand everything," continued Daria Aleksandrovna. "You cannot understand it. You men, who are free to choose, always know exactly with whom you are in love. But a girl, with her womanly and maidenly shyness, must wait to be asked. She sees you men only from afar and takes every word at face value, and sometimes she may feel that she doesn't know what to say."

"Yes, if the heart does not dictate. . . ."

"No, the heart does dictate, but think of it this way: you men choose a girl, you visit her family, you get to know her, you observe, you wait to see whether you will find in her qualities which you love, and then, when you are convinced that you love her, you propose. . . ."

"Well, that's not quite so."

"It doesn't matter. You propose when your love has ripened fully, or when the scales tip in favor of one rather than another. But the girl isn't consulted. She is expected to make her own choice; but she cannot choose, she may only answer yes or no."

"Yes, the choice was between me and Vronsky," thought Levin, and the spirit that had seemed to revive died again and lay heavily in his heart.

"Daria Aleksandrovna," he said, "that's the way you choose a dress or some other article, but not love. The choice was made, and it's for the better. . . . And it cannot be done over. . . ."

"Ah, pride, nothing but pride," said Daria Aleksandrovna, as if scornful of that feeling, so base in comparison with the other feeling, known only to women. "And when you proposed to Kitty, she was precisely in that state in which she could give no answer. She was hesitant. She hesitated in her choice between you and Vronsky. She saw him every day, but she had not seen you for a long time. I admit, were she older—I, for instance, in her place, would not have hesitated at all. I have always disliked him, and I was right."

Levin recalled Kitty's answer. She had said, *"No, this cannot be. . . ."*

"Daria Aleksandrovna," he said coldly, "I appreciate your confidence in me, but I think that you are mistaken. But right or wrong, my pride, of which you are so scornful, makes it impossible for me to entertain any thought about Katerina Aleksandrovna—you understand—entirely impossible."

"I'll add one more thing: you realize that I'm talking about my sister, whom I love as my own children. I'm not saying that she loves you; I only wanted to say that her refusal at that moment did not mean anything."

"I don't know," said Levin, jumping up. "If you could only know how much pain you are causing me. It's the same as if your child had died and you were being told how good he had been, how long he could have lived, how much joy he could have brought you. But he is dead, dead, dead. . . ."

"How ridiculous you are," said Daria Aleksandrovna. She smiled sadly, though she saw how disturbed Levin was. "Yes, now I understand it even better," she continued pensively. "Then you won't come to see us when Kitty is here?"

"No, I won't come. Of course, I won't avoid Katerina Aleksandrovna, but I'll do my best in every way to save her from the annoyance my presence may cause."

"You are being very, very ridiculous," replied Daria Aleksandrovna, looking at him tenderly. "Well, let's forget what we have been discussing. What's the matter, Tania?" asked Daria Aleksandrovna in French of the girl, who had come into the room.

"Where's my little shovel, mama?"

"Ask me in French, as I did."

The girl wanted to do so, but forgot the French word for "shovel." Her mother helped her and then told her in French where to find it. Levin was annoyed by this.

Everything about Daria Aleksandrovna's home and her children seemed much less charming than before.

Why does she speak French to the children? he thought. How unnatural and false! And the children feel it. Teach French and unlearn sincerity, he thought, unaware that Daria Aleksandrovna had pondered on this problem many times and had concluded that this was the proper method of educating her children, even if it might affect their frankness.

"But why should you leave? Stay for a while."

Levin remained for tea, but his good cheer had left him, and he was ill at ease.

After tea he went into the entrance hall to send for his carriage, and when he returned, he found Daria Aleksandrovna upset and in tears. While Levin was outside, something had happened which suddenly destroyed Daria Alexsandrovna's happy state and her pride in her children. Grisha and Tania had had a fight over a ball. Daria Aleksandrovna, hearing the children's shouts in the nursery, ran over to them and found them in a terrible state. Tania held Grisha by the hair and, his face viciously distorted, he was striking at her wildly with his fists. Daria Aleksandrovna's heart sank as she saw this. It seemed that darkness had enveloped her life. She realized that her children, of whom she was so proud, were really most ordinary, even bad and ill-bred, with coarse, bestial traits—wicked children.

She could not think or talk about anything else and she had to tell Levin about her misfortune.

Levin saw that she was unhappy and tried to console her, saying that if children fight, it does not prove that they are bad. But while saying this, Levin thought to himself, deep in his heart: No, I won't put on airs and won't speak French to my children, but then my children will be different. If only they aren't spoiled and their nature not distorted, they can be delightful. Yes, my children will be different.

He said goodbye and left. She did not try to restrain him.

11

In the middle of July, the elder of the village next to Levin's sister's estate, which was some fifteen miles from Pokrovskoe, came to see Levin with a report on the mowing. The grass in the swales was the primary source of income for his sister's estate. In former years, the moujiks had rented them at twenty rubles a dessiatine. When Levin took over the management of the estate, he inspected the meadows, decided that they were worth more, and demanded twenty-five rubles a dessiatine. The moujiks did not agree to this price and, as Levin suspected, kept others from bidding. Levin went there himself and ordered the meadows to be mowed, partly by hiring help, partly by sharing the yield. The moujiks of the village opposed this change in every way, but it was all worked out, and during the first year the income from the meadows almost doubled. During the third and the past years, the moujiks still showed the same resistance, but the mowing was done as in previous years. But this year the moujiks had rented all the meadows, sharing one third of the yield. The elder now had arrived to inform Levin that all the work had been done and that, fearing rain, he had invited the office clerk and in his presence had already set aside eleven haystacks as the master's share. From the vague answers of the elder to his question about the amount of hay from the main meadow; from the haste with which, without permission, he had divided the hay; from the general tone of the moujiks' words Levin understood that there had been something wrong in the division of the hay, and he decided to go himself to investigate the matter.

He arrived at the village toward dinnertime and left his horse with a friend, an old man, the husband of his brother's former wet nurse. Levin went into the apiary to see the old man, from whom he expected to get all the details about the hay mowing. Talkative, handsome old Parmenich gaily welcomed Levin, took him around the apiary, and gave him all the details about the bees and this year's swarms. But his answers became vague and reluctant when Levin asked him about the haying. This further confirmed Levin's suspicions. He went to the meadow and inspected the haystacks. He saw that no haystack contained fifty cartloads of hay and, to expose the moujiks, Levin at once called for the carts which had carried the hay, and he had one of the haystacks transferred to the barn. The haystack contained only thirty-two cartloads of hay. In vain did the elder assure him that the hay had been fluffy and that it had pressed down in the haystack; in vain did he swear that everything had been done honestly. Levin accused them of having divided the hay without his permission, and he therefore did not accept this hay at fifty cartloads per haystack. After lengthy arguments, it was decided that the moujiks would accept these eleven haystacks at fifty cartloads per haystack as part of their share, and that the master's share should be given anew. These arrangements and the division of the haycocks lasted until the early evening meal. When all the hay had been divided, Levin, leaving the rest of the business to the clerk, sat near a haycock marked off by a willow twig, looking fondly at the meadow teeming with people.

Before him, at the bend of the river beyond the small swamp, there moved a varicolored file of women, gaily chattering in their sonorous voices. The scattered hay was rapidly collected into gray wavy strips which meandered over the light-green, newly grown grass. The women were followed by moujiks carrying pitchforks, and from the strips there rose wide, tall, puffed haycocks. Over the left side of the meadow, now cleared, the carts clattered, and one after another, with pitchforks plunged deeply into them, the haycocks vanished, transformed into loads of sweet-scented hay, loaded onto the heavy carts and hanging over the horses' croups.

"We'll make it while the weather holds. It'll be fine hay!" said an old moujik, sitting down next to Levin. "Not hay, but tea. Look how fast they are, like ducklings after grain," he added, pointing at the moujiks loading the haycocks. "Since dinner a good half has been done!"

"Is this the last one?" he shouted to a young man who, standing on the fore part of the driver's seat and shaking the ends of the hemp reins, was riding by.

"It is the last, little father!" cried the young man, slowing his horse. With a smile he turned toward a rosy, smiling young woman who was sitting on the driver's seat, and then rode out.

"Who is he? Your son?" asked Levin.

"My youngest," said the old man with a tender smile.

"What a fine young man!"

"He's all right."

"Is he married?"

"He was two years ago last Philip's Fast."

"Any children?"

"None! The first year he didn't understand anything, and then he was shy," added the old man. "Some hay! Just like tea," he repeated, anxious to change the subject.

Levin watched Vanka Parmenov and his wife more closely. They were loading a haycock onto a cart not far from him. Ivan Parmenov was standing on the cart, treading and leveling the huge heaps of hay which his young, beautiful wife nimbly handed to him, first by the armful, then with a pitchfork. The young woman worked cheerfully, deftly, and without effort. The heavy, compressed hay did not yield at once to the pitchfork. First she leveled it and dug the pitchfork into it; then, by a supple and brisk movement, she put the whole weight of her body onto the pitchfork. She quickly straightened her back and, standing erect, her waist bound by a red belt, and showing her ample bosom underneath her white blouse, she nimbly adjusted her grasp on the pitchfork, raised it high, and tossed a forkful of hay onto the cart. Ivan, evidently eager to relieve her of even a moment of unnecessary exertion, hastily caught the raised forkful, spreading his arms wide, and flattened it on the cart. His wife lifted up the last bit of hay on a rake, brushed the haydust from her neck, straightened the red kerchief which had slipped from her white forehead, and crawled under the cart to tie the load down. Ivan told her how to tie the rope around the crossbar and laughed loudly at something she said. The expression on both their faces revealed a strong, young, recently awakened love.

12

THE LOAD WAS tied down. Ivan jumped down and led the strong, well-fed horse by the bridle. His wife tossed the rake onto the cart and, her arms swinging, she briskly walked over to the rest of the women, who were assembling to form a chorus. Ivan, on reaching the road, joined the line of carts. The women, their rakes over their shoulders, walked behind the carts. Their colorful dresses shone brightly, their chattering voices resounded happily. One of the women started a song in a coarse, harsh voice and sang the first verse, and then about fifty varied voices, coarse and thin, all full of vigor joined in and repeated the same song from the beginning.

The singing women were approaching Levin, and it seemed to him that this gaiety moved upon him like a thundering cloud. The cloud moved up, enveloped him and the haycock on which he lay, the other haycocks, the carts, the meadows, and the distant fields. And everything rocked and swung to the rhythm of this wild, happy song, with its shouts, whistles and exclamations. Levin envied this uninhibited merriment. He wanted to take part in this expression of the enjoyment of life. But he could do nothing of the kind; he had to lie there, watching and listening. When the singing women disappeared from view and earshot, a feeling of distress caused by his loneliness, by his physical idleness, by his hostility toward this world, took possession of Levin.

Some of the moujiks who had argued with him more than the others about the hay, those whom he had offended, or those who had wanted to cheat him, these same moujiks greeted him gaily, and seemingly did not and could not bear any grudge against him. They felt no regret that they had wanted to cheat him; they didn't even remember it. All this had drowned in the sea of common toil. God had given them this good day. God has given them the strength. The day and the strength were devoted to labor, which provided its own reward. But for whom was this labor? What would be the fruit of this labor? These were extraneous and worthless considerations.

Levin often had a feeling of love for this kind of life, often envied those who lived it, but today for the first time, particularly under the impression gained by watching Ivan Parmenov and his young wife, Levin saw clearly that it was within his power to change the burdensome, idle, artificial and selfish life he had been living for this life of labor, pure, beautiful and shared with others.

The old man who had been sitting next to him had long since left for home. The crowd had broken up. Those who lived nearby left for their homes; others made ready for supper and for an overnight stay on the meadow. Levin, unnoticed by the others, remained on the haycock, watching, listening, and thinking. Those who remained here did not sleep at all that short summer night. At first there could be heard the shouts of general gay conversation and laughter as they had their supper, then there were more songs and laughter.

That long day of labor had left in them nothing but a feeling of gaiety. Before dawn everything grew silent. All that could be heard were the incessant croaking of the frogs in the swamp and the snorts of the horses in the meadow in the rising early-morning mist. When he awoke, Levin climbed down from the haycock and, scanning the stars, understood that the night had passed.

Well then, what shall I do? How will I do it? he asked himself, trying to explain to himself all his thoughts and feelings of that short night. Everything he had thought and felt divided into three separate courses. One was the rejection of his former way of life, of his idle learning, his worthless information. He delighted in rejecting this, and it was so simple and easy to do. Other thoughts and visions concerned the life he wanted to live now. He saw clearly how simple, pure, and just this life was, and he was convinced that it would bring him contentment, peace, and dignity, the absence of which affected him so painfully. But his thoughts took a third course. How to make the transition from the old life to the new. And to this problem he found no clear answer. Should I have a wife? he thought. Shall I work and feel the need for work? Shall I leave Pokrovskoe? Shall I buy land? Shall I join a peasants' community? Shall I marry a peasant woman? How shall I do it? he asked himself again, and found no answer. Well, I didn't sleep all night and can't think clearly now, he said to himself. I'll see it clearly later. One thing is certain; this night has decided my fate. All my former dreams of family life are nonsense, not the real thing, he said to himself. All this is so much simpler and better.

How beautiful! he thought, looking at the cluster of fluffy, white, little clouds, resembling a strange mother-of-pearl shell, which hung just over his head in the middle of the sky. How wonderful everything is this lovely night. And when did this shell have time to form? Only a short while ago I looked at the sky and there was nothing there but two white bands. Yes, my views on life have changed as unnoticeably.

He left the meadow and walked along the highway toward the village. A breeze came up; everything was gray and somber. The dusky moment arrived that usually precedes sunrise, the total victory of light over darkness.

Shrinking with cold, Levin walked rapidly, his eyes fixed on the ground. What's that? Is somebody coming? he thought, hearing the sound of little bells. He raised his head. He saw a coach, forty paces away, drawn by four horses, with luggage on its top, moving in his direction on the grassy road on which he was walking. The wheel horses, trying to avoid the ruts, pressed against the shaft, but the skillful coachman, sitting sideways on the coach box, kept the shaft over the rut, so that the wheels rolled over a smooth surface.

That was all that Levin noticed and, without thinking who the passengers might be, he absent-mindedly glanced at the coach.

An old lady was dozing in the corner of the coach, and at the window there was a young girl who evidently had just awakened. With both her hands she held on to the ribbons of her white bonnet. Serene and pensive, lost in a gracious and complex inner life unknown to Levin, she looked past him at the sunrise.

At this very moment, when this vision began to disappear, her frank gaze fell upon him. She recognized him, and surprise and joy lit up her face.

He could not be mistaken. Those eyes could belong to only one person in this world. There was only one being on whom he could center all the world and all life's meaning. It was she. It was Kitty. He understood that she was coming from the railroad station to Ergushovo. And everything that had troubled Levin during the sleepless night, all the decisions he had made, suddenly vanished. With aversion he recalled his dream of marrying a peasant woman. Only there, only in the coach that was now fast drawing away and had moved to the other side of the road, only there could he find the key to the riddle of life that had lately oppressed him so deeply.

She no longer was looking about. The sounds of the rolling coach died down, and the jingle of the little bells could scarcely be heard. A dog's bark showed that the coach had passed the village, and here he was, surrounded by empty fields, with the village beyond, a stranger to all, walking alone along a deserted road.

He looked at the sky, hoping to find the shell he had admired, which had been the symbol of his thoughts and feelings of the previous night. There was nothing in the sky now that resembled the shell. There, in the unapproachable heights, the mysterious change had already taken place. There was not even a trace of the shell, and over half of the sky there spread a smooth carpet of fluffy clouds, growing smaller and smaller. The sky grew pale blue and brightened and gave to his questioning look an answer both tender and unattainable.

No, he said to himself, no matter how good that life of simplicity and toil is, I cannot turn back to it. I love *her*.

13

No ONE BUT the closest friends of Aleksei Aleksandrovich knew that this apparently frosty and rational man had one weakness, which contradicted the general bent of his character. Aleksei Aleksandrovich could not hear or see a crying child or woman without becoming upset. The sight of tears always disconcerted him and deprived him completely of his ability to reason calmly. His office manager and his secretary were aware of this weakness of his, and they warned women petitioners to refrain from crying by all means, if they did not want to harm their cases. "He will get angry and will not listen to you," they said. And in fact, on such occasions, the disturbing effect made on Aleksei Aleksandrovich by the sight of tears expressed itself in a burst of anger. "I can't, I can't do anything for you. Please get out!" he usually shouted when this occurred.

When, on their return from the races, Anna revealed to him her relations with Vronsky, and then, covering her face with her hands, had burst into tears, Aleksei Aleksandrovich, in spite of his rising anger toward her, was on the verge of the same emotional disturbance to which he was always subjected at the sight of tears. Aware of this, and knowing that the expression of his feeling would appear out of place in the present situation, he tried to suppress within himself every manifestation of life; therefore, he did not stir and did not look at her. This resulted in the strange, deathlike expression on his face that astonished Anna so profoundly.

When they reached the house, he helped her down from the carriage, forced himself to part from her with usual courtesy, and to utter words that did not commit him in any way. He declared that he would let her know his decision on the following day.

His wife's words, which confirmed his worst suspicions, had grievously wounded Aleksei Aleksandrovich. This feeling was intensified by the strange feeling of pain and pity for her that her tears had awakened in him. But when he remained alone in the coach, Aleksei Aleksandrovich, to his surprise and joy, felt complete relief from that feeling of pity, and from all the doubts and pangs of jealousy that had tormented him of late.

He felt like a man whose long-aching tooth had been extracted. After intense pain and a feeling that something immense, larger than his whole head, was being drawn out of his jaw, the patient, scarcely believing his good fortune, suddenly feels that what had long embittered his life and absorbed all his attention no longer exists, and that the tooth will no longer be the sole object of his thoughts and interests. Such was Aleksei Aleksandrovich's feeling. The pain had been unusual and extreme, but now it was gone. He felt that he could again live without thinking of his wife alone.

Without honor, without a heart, without religion; a depraved woman! I've always known and always seen it, though, out of pity for her, I've tried to delude myself, he said to himself. And he really believed that he had always seen it. He recalled the details of their past life, in which formerly he had seen nothing wrong; now these details proved clearly that she had always been an evil woman. I made a mistake by binding my life with hers, he thought. But there was nothing evil in my mistake, and therefore I cannot feel unhappy.

It's not I that am guilty, he said to himself, but she. But I'm not concerned about her. She no longer exists for me. . . .

He was no longer interested in anything that might happen to her or to his son, toward whom his feelings had changed as they had toward her. One thing concerned him now—how to cleanse himself of the filth with which she had bespattered him by her fall, how to do it in the best, most proper, most convenient for himself and therefore most honest way, and how to go on living an active, honest, and useful life.

I cannot feel unhappy because a contemptible woman committed a crime. I only need to find the best way out of the difficult situation she has put me in. And I'll find it, he said to himself, frowning more and more deeply. I'm not the first, nor the last. And in addition to recalling historical cases, beginning with Menelaus, whose story had been refreshed in general memory by the operetta, *The Beautiful Helène,* he recalled the long modern roster of society wives who had been unfaithful to their husbands. Darialov, Poltavsky, Prince Karibanov, Count Paskudin, Dram—yes, Dram too, such an honest, capable man—Semionov, Chagin, Sigonin, recalled Aleksei Aleksandrovich. True, they are objects of unreasonable ridicule, but I've always considered it a misfortune only, and I have always been sympathetic, Aleksei Aleksandrovich said to himself, though this was not true. He had never sympathized with this kind of misfortune, and the more frequently wives deceived their husbands the prouder he was of himself. This is a misfortune that may befall anyone. And this misfortune has befallen me. The only problem is how best to bear it. And he began to recall in detail the actions of those who were in the same situation as he.

Darialov fought a duel. . . .

In his youth, duels particularly attracted Aleksei Aleksandrovich precisely because physically he was a timid person, as he well knew. Aleksei Aleksandrovich could not think without dread that a pistol might be aimed at him, and he had never in his life used any firearms. In his youth, this dread had often made him think of duels and imagine himself in a situation in which he would have to endanger his life. But by the time he had reached his present successful position in life, he had long since forgotten the feeling. Yet the old feeling had left its mark, and the fear of his cowardice was even now so great that Aleksei Aleksandrovich for a long while pondered on the problem of a duel. He flattered himself with this thought, though he knew beforehand that he would not fight under any circumstances.

There is no doubt that our society is still so uncivilized (unlike England) that a great many people—and among them were those whose opinions Aleksei Aleksandrovich held in particular esteem—would look upon a duel with favor; but what will it achieve? Suppose I challenge him to a duel, continued Aleksei Aleksandrovich to himself. Visualizing vividly the night he would spend after the challenge, and the pistol aimed at him, he trembled and realized that he could never do it. Suppose I challenge him, suppose they instruct me, he continued thinking. They show me where to stand. I pull the trigger, he said to himself, closing his eyes; and it turns out that I have killed him, said Aleksei Aleksandrovich, shaking his head to rid himself of these foolish thoughts. Of what use would murdering a man be in solving the problem of my relationship with my depraved wife and my son? I'd still have to decide what to do with her. But more probably and even certainly, I'd be killed or wounded. I, an innocent man, a victim, killed or wounded! It makes still less sense. Moreover, challenging him to a duel would be a dishonest act on my part. Don't I know beforehand that my friends would never permit me to fight a duel? That they would not allow the life of a statesman so valuable to Russia to be exposed to danger? What would be the result? It would be that, well aware beforehand that the matter could never reach a dangerous stage, I would only be trying to bask in false glory. It would be dishonest, fraudulent, a lie to others and to myself. A duel is out of the question, and nobody expects it of me. My purpose is to protect my reputation, which I need to continue my work without impediment. His official duties, which had always seemed very important to Aleksei Aleksandrovich, seemed particularly important now.

Having considered and rejected a duel, Aleksei Aleksandrovich turned his mind toward the problem of a divorce, another solution chosen by some of the husbands whom he remembered. Turning over in his mind all the well-known cases of divorce (and there were many such cases in the highest circles so familiar to him), Aleksei Aleksandrovich could not find a single one that would serve the purpose he had in mind. In all these cases the husband surrendered or sold his unfaithful wife, and the parties who, by admitting their guilt, had lost the right to remarry, established fictitious, quasi-legal relations with their new spouses. But in his own case, Aleksei Aleksandrovich saw that it would be impossible to obtain a formal divorce, one that would put all the onus on his wife. He saw that the complex circumstances of his life would not permit the presentation of the offensive proofs the law required to condemn a guilty wife. He saw that the refined nature of his kind of life would not permit the use of such proofs, even if they existed, and if they were used, he would be lowered in public opinion more than she.

An attempt to get a divorce would only result in a notorious court case, which would be welcomed by his enemies, would cause malicious gossip, and would debase his social status. And the main purpose, the settling of this matter with the least disturbance, would not be achieved. Moreover, a divorce, or even an attempted divorce, as was well known, results in a complete rupture between wife and husband and in her joining her lover. And though Aleksei Aleksandrovich believed that he disdained his wife and was completely indifferent toward her, there still remained in his heart one feeling toward her: he was loath to see her free to join Vronsky and so benefit by her crime. This one thought so upset Aleksei Aleksandrovich that, as it came to his mind, he groaned with mental anguish, rose, and changed his seat in the coach. For a long time afterward he sat there frowning, wrapping the fluffy robe around his chilled, bony legs.

Besides a formal divorce, there is another way out. One may separate from his wife, as did Karibanov, Paskudin, and that good man, Dram, he continued thinking after he had calmed down. But this step would subject him to the same disgrace as a divorce, and, more important, would just throw his wife into Vronsky's arms in exactly the same way as a formal divorce. "No, this is impossible, this is impossible!" he said loudly, again busying himself with the wrap. I am not to be unhappy, he thought, nor must she and he be happy.

The feeling of jealousy that had tormented him in his state of uncertainty vanished at the moment when the tooth was so painfully extracted by his wife's words. But this feeling was now replaced by another; not only did he dislike to see her exulting in her crime, but he wanted her to suffer for it. He did not admit it, but deep in his heart he wished her to suffer for having disturbed his peace and sullied his honor. And again, after considering and once more rejecting the possibility of a duel, divorce, or separation, Aleksei Aleksandrovich became convinced that there was only one way out—to hold on to her, concealing from the world what had happened, take all measures to break this liaison, and also to punish her, which was most important, though he refused to admit it to himself. I must announce, he thought, that after having examined the difficult situation in which she has placed the family, I have decided that all other solutions would prove worse for both of us than maintaining an outward status quo. I agree to this, but under the inviolable condition that she, on her part, obeys my order, namely, that she breaks with her lover.

One more consideration reinforced Aleksei Aleksandrovich in this final decision. And only by such a decision do I follow the precepts of religion, he said to himself. With such a decision I do not repudiate a depraved wife; I give her a chance to reform, and even though it will be very hard for me, I will devote some of my efforts to reforming and saving her. Though Aleksei Aleksandrovich knew that he could have no moral influence over his wife, that nothing would result from all these attempts at reformation other than pretense, and though in these difficult moments it had not at all occurred to him to seek guidance in religion, now, when he believed that his decision followed the precepts of religion, this religious sanction gave him full satisfaction and some peace of mind. He was glad to think that no one would be able to say that in such a great crisis in his life he had not acted in accordance with the teachings of religion, whose banner he had always held high amidst general neglect and indifference. Reflecting upon further details, Aleksei Aleksandrovich was at a loss to see why his relationship with his wife might not continue almost as it had been before. No doubt she could never regain his respect; but there was not and could not be any reason why he should upset his own life and suffer on account of his wicked, unfaithful wife. Yes, time will pass, time which settles everything, and our former relationship will be restored, Aleksei Aleksandrovich said to himself. It will be restored to that state in which it will cause me no further worry during my lifetime. She should be unhappy, but I'm not at fault so I must not be unhappy.

14

ON APPROACHING PETERSBURG, Aleksei Aleksandrovich had set his mind on this decision; moreover, he had outlined in his mind a letter, which he would write to his wife. In the entrance hall he glanced at the letters and the papers from the ministry and ordered them brought to his room.

"Have the coach put in the stable and don't admit anyone," he replied to the doorman's question, accentuating with some pleasure the words *don't admit*, which showed that he was in a good frame of mind.

In his study he walked twice up and down the room, stopped at his huge writing desk with six candles on it, lit beforehand by his valet, cracked his knuckles, sat down, and arranged his writing implements. Setting his elbows on the table, he inclined his head sideways, thought for a moment, and began to write. He did not stop for a second; he began with no salutation and he wrote in French, using the plural pronoun "you," which in French does not sound so formal as in Russian.

During our last conversation, I informed you of my intention to let you know my decision concerning the subject of that conversation. After carefully considering the whole matter, I am writing to you in order to fulfill my promise. Here is my decision. Whatever you have done, I do not consider that I have the right to break the bonds with which we are bound by a Superior Power. The family cannot be destroyed by the whim, fancy, or even by the criminal act of one of the spouses, and our life must go on as before. This is essential for my sake, for yours, and for the sake of our son. I am fully convinced that you have repented and are repenting that which is causing me to write the present letter, and that you will co-operate with me in extirpating the cause of our discord and in forgetting what has happened. Otherwise you may yourself imagine what awaits you and your son. About all of this I hope to talk to you in detail in a personal interview. Since the summer is coming to an end, I would ask you to return to Petersburg as soon as possible, no

*later than Tuesday. All the necessary arrangements for
your moving will be made. Kindly note that I consider
your compliance with my request to be particularly
important.*

A. KARENIN

P.S. I am enclosing in this letter money for your expenses.

He read the letter and was pleased with it, particularly because he had remembered to send her money. The letter
contained no harsh words, no reproaches, but neither did it
show any forbearance. Most important, it formed a convenient
bridge for reconciliation. He folded the letter, smoothed it
with the large, heavy, ivory knife, placed it in an envelope
with the money, and with the feeling of pleasure that the
manipulation of fine writing implements always gave him,
he rang the bell.

"Have it delivered to Anna Arkadievna at the country house
by a messenger tomorrow morning," he said, and rose from his
chair.

"Yes, Your Excellency. Shall I serve tea in the study?"

Aleksei Aleksandrovich ordered tea served in the study
and, playing with the massive paper knife, he went over to
the armchair, where a lit lamp and an open French book on
the Eugubine tables awaited him. An oval, gold-framed
portrait of Anna, the beautiful work of a famous painter, hung
over the armchair. Aleksei Aleksandrovich glanced at it. Her
impenetrable eyes looked at him derisively and insolently,
as they had during their last conversation. The sight of the
black lace covering her head, masterfully painted by the
artist, of her black hair and her beautiful white hand with
its fourth finger covered with rings, affected Aleksei Aleksandrovich with their unbearable insolence and challenge.
After looking at the portrait for a moment, Aleksei Aleksandrovich shuddered so violently that his lips trembled, making
the sound "brr," and he turned away. He hurriedly sat in the
chair and opened the book. He tried to read, but could not
revive his former very lively interest in Eugubine tables. He
looked at the book, but his thoughts were elsewhere. He did
not think of his wife, but of a complicated problem that had
recently arisen in his official business, which had occupied all
his attention. He felt that he grasped all the complexity of
this matter now better than ever, and that in his mind there
was forming—he could say it without self-delusion—a mo-

mentous thought which would untangle this matter, advance
him in his career, humble his enemies, and therefore greatly
benefit the country. As soon as the servant who had brought
the tea left the room, Aleksei Aleksandrovich rose and walked
over to the desk. He placed a briefcase containing papers relating to his current affairs in the middle of the desk, and
with a faint, self-satisfied smile, reached for a pencil from
the stand. He engrossed himself in a paper he had had sent
from the office, which pertained to the present complex case.
These were the details of the case. Aleksei Aleksandrovich, as
a government official, possessed a distinctive trait, typical of
every ambitious official. This trait, combined with his per-
severing ambition, self-control, honesty, and self-confidence,
had helped to advance him in his career. It consisted of contempt for paperwork, a desire to curtail red tape, a direct
approach to life's problems whenever this was possible, and
a concern for economy. It happened that the famous Commission of the Second of June had discussed the irrigation of
the fields in Zaraisky Province. This case was under the juris-
diction of Aleksei Aleksandrovich's ministry and presented a
flagrant example of waste and red tape. Aleksei Aleksandrovich knew that the handling of this case had been justly
criticized. The case of the irrigation of the fields in Zaraisky
Province had been started by the predecessor of Aleksei
Aleksandrovich's predecessor. It was true that much money
had been and still was being spent unproductively, and it was
obvious that nothing would come of it. At the beginning of
his career, Aleksei Aleksandrovich had seen this clearly, and
he had wanted to take the matter into his own hands. But at
that time he was still not sure of his standing and he knew
that the interests of many people were involved in the case;
it would have been unwise on his part to interfere in it. Then,
busying himself with other matters, he quite forgot about this
one. But the case ground on by itself through sheer inertia. (It
was the source of income for many people, and particularly
for one family, strictly moral and musically inclined; all the
daughters played stringed instruments. Aleksei Aleksandrovich knew this family; he was the nuptial godfather of the
older daughter.) Aleksei Aleksandrovich considered it dishonest that an antagonistic ministry should raise this problem,
particularly when in each ministry there could be found even
worse cases, which, however, nobody mentioned out of a
sense of official propriety. Now, since they had flung down

the gauntlet, he took it up courageously and demanded the appointment of a special commission for the study and examination of the work done by the commission for the irrigation of the fields in Zaraisky Province. And he showed no mercy to those gentlemen. He demanded the appointment of another special commission, on the organization of the minorities. The issue of the organization of the minorities had been accidentally raised in the Committee of the Second of June with the strong support of Aleksei Aleksandrovich, who believed this problem brooked no delay because of the deplorable state of the minorities. In the committee it had caused a bitter wrangle between several ministries. The ministry that was hostile to Aleksei Aleksandrovich insisted that the minorities were thriving, that the projected change in their organization might destroy their prosperity, and that whatever was wrong in this case had come about because Aleksei Aleksandrovich's ministry had not taken all the necessary measures prescribed by law. Now Aleksei Aleksandrovich intended to demand: first, that one more commission be appointed to study, in the field, the state of the minorities; second, if it were proved that the state of the minorities was really such as appeared in the official data in the possession of the committee, one more commission should be appointed, a scientific commission for the study of the causes of this deplorable state of the minorities from the following points of view: (a) political, (b) administrative, (c) economic, (d) ethnographic, (e) material, (f) religious; third, that the antagnostic ministry be required to present information on all measures the ministry had taken during the last decade to avert the unfavorable conditions that had brought the minorities to their present state; and, fourth and last, that the ministry be required to explain why it had acted in direct contradiction to Article 18 and to the note to Article 36 of the Basic Organic Law, as could be seen from submitted Reports #17015 and #18308 of the 5th of December 1863 and of the 7th of June 1864. Aleksei Aleksandrovich's face flushed with excitement as he hastily outlined his ideas. After he had filled a sheet of paper he rose, rang, and sent a note to his office manager for additional information. He rose, paced the room, glanced again at the portrait, frowned, then smiled contemptuously. He read some of the book on Eugubine tables, his interest in them revived. At eleven o'clock

Aleksei Aleksandrovich retired; and when, in bed, he remembered the incident with his wife, it seemed much less dismal than before.

15

THOUGH ANNA DISAGREED with Vronsky obstinately and angrily when he told her that her situation was impossible and tried to persuade her to reveal everything to her husband, deep in her heart she knew that her situation was deceitful and dishonorable and with all her heart she wished to change it. On their way back from the races, in a moment of excitement, she had told her husband everything. In spite of the anguish which it caused her, she was glad that she had done it. After her husband left she told herself that she was glad that now everything would be settled, and that at least, there would be no more need for lies and deceit. She was sure that her situation would now become permanently clarified. It might be bad, this new situation, but it would be clarified; further ambiguity and falsehood no longer were possible. The anguish which she caused her husband and herself by her words would be rewarding now, when everything would become clear, she thought. That same evening she saw Vronsky, but she did not tell him what had happened between her husband and herself, though she should have told him if she really wanted her situation to be clarified.

When she awoke the next morning, the first thing she recalled was the words she had spoken to her husband, and they seemed so terrifying that she could not now understand how she could have brought herself to pronounce such strange, horrible words, and she could not imagine what would happen now. But the words had been uttered, and Aleksei Aleksandrovich had left without saying anything. I saw Vronsky, she thought, and didn't tell him. At the moment he was leaving, I still wanted to call him back and tell him, but I changed my mind because it seemed strange that I hadn't told him at the first opportunity. Why didn't I tell him, though I wanted to? In reply to this question a blush of shame burned her face. She knew what had restrained her; she knew that it was shame. Her situation, which had seemed clarified last night, now appeared not only unclear but hopeless. She was terrified by the disgrace which she had not even thought about before. When she thought of what her husband might do, the most terrible ideas occurred to her. She imagined that the manager would soon come to drive her out of the house, that her shame would become known to the whole world. She asked herself where she would go if she were driven from the house, and found no answer.

When she thought about Vronsky, it seemed to her that he did not love her, that he was already beginning to tire of her, that she could not throw herself upon him, and this aroused her animosity toward him. It seemed to her that she had told everyone, and that all had heard the words she had spoken to her husband and that she ceaselessly repeated in her mind. She could not bring herself to look into the eyes of those around her. She could not bring herself to call her maid, and still less to go downstairs and see her son and the governess.

The maid, who had been listening at the door for some time, came in without having been called. Anna looked into her eyes questioningly and blushed with fear. The maid apologized for intruding, saying that she thought that she had been called. She brought in a dress and a note. The note was from Betsy. Betsy reminded her that she was expecting guests that morning for a game of croquet: Liza Merkalov and Baroness Stolz, with their admirers, Kaluzhsky and old Stremov. *"Please come, if only to watch it as a commentary on mores! I am expecting you,"* she wrote at the end of the note.

Anna read the note and sighed heavily.

"No, I don't need anything," she told Annushka, who was arranging the bottles and brushes on her dressing table, "Go. I'll get dressed and come out. No, I don't need anything."

Annushka left, but Anna did not start dressing; she remained in the same position, her head and arms drooping. From time to time her entire body shuddered, then it quieted again, as if she were trying to make some gesture, to say something. She kept repeating, "My God! My God!" But neither the words "God" nor "my" meant anything to her. She had had a religious upbringing and had never doubted the teachings of religion, but in her present situation the thought of seeking aid in religion seemed to her as inconceivable as the thought of seeking aid from Aleksei Aleksandrovich himself. She knew beforehand that she could get aid from religion only under the condition that she give up everything that to her was the very purpose of life. She felt oppressed, and fright began taking possession of her, the fear of a new emotional state never before experienced. She felt that within her heart everything began to double, as sometimes things appear double to tired eyes. At times she did not know what she feared or what she wanted. She did not know whether she feared or she wanted what had been or what would be; neither did she know what it was that she really wanted.

Ah, what am I doing! she said to herself, suddenly feeling a pain on both sides of her head. When she came to her senses, she found herself clasping her hair, both hands pressing against her temples. She jumped up and began to pace the room.

"Coffee is served, and the mademoiselle and Seryozha are waiting," announced Annushka, who returned to find Anna again in the same state.

"Seryozha? What about Seryozha?" asked Anna, suddenly enlivened and, for the first time this morning, recalling the existence of her son.

"He misbehaved, I believe," answered Annushka, smiling.

"How?"

"There were some peaches in the corner room. It seems that he secretly ate one."

Reminded of her son, Anna suddenly felt released from her hopeless state. She recalled the partly sincere but highly exaggerated role of a mother, living only for her son, that she had assumed for the past few years. She was glad to feel that in her present state, whatever her relationship with Vronsky and her husband would be, she possessed a domain independent of it. Her son was that domain. In whatever situation she might find herself, she could not abandon her son. Even if her husband were to expose her to shame and drive her away, even if Vronsky were to grow cold toward her and continue to live his independent life (again she thought of him with bitter reproach), she could not abandon her son. She had a purpose in life. She must act, must act to make secure her bonds with her son, to feel sure that he would not be taken from her. She must act as quickly as possible, before they took him from her. She must go away with her son. This was now the only thing to do. She must compose herself and find a way out of this unbearable situation. The thought of an act directly connected with her son, the thought of going away somewhere with him, at once brought her the composure she sought.

She dressed hurriedly, went downstairs and, walking briskly, entered the dining room where, as usual, her coffee was ready, and Seryozha and the governess were waiting for her. Seryozha, all in white, stood at the table under the mirror, his back and head bent; with an expression of deep attention, which was so familiar to her and in which he resembled his father, he was busy with the flowers which he had brought.

The governess looked particularly stern. Seryozha shouted shrilly, as he often did, "Ah, Mama!" and stopped, undecided whether to go over to greet his mother or first to complete the garland and then take it to her.

The governess greeted Anna and then gave her a long and detailed account of Seryozha's offence, but Anna did not listen to her. She wondered whether to take her along. No, I won't, she decided. I'll just take my son.

"Yes, that was very wicked," said Anna and, holding her son's arm, she looked at him not sternly, but shyly, which embarrassed and pleased the boy. Anna kissed him. "Leave him with me," she told the surprised governess and, still holding her son's arm, she sat down at the table to have her coffee.

"Mama! I . . . I . . . didn't," he said, trying to guess by the expression of her face what awaited him for having eaten that peach.

"Seryozha," she said as soon as the governess had left the room, "it was wicked, but you won't do it again. Do you love me?"

She felt the tears coming to her eyes. Can I help loving him? she asked herself, staring at his frightened, yet delighted face. Could he possibly take his father's part and condemn me? Could he possibly have no pity for me? Tears rolled down her cheeks, and to hide them she rose abruptly and almost ran out onto the terrace.

After the thundershowers of the last few days, the weather had become cold and clear. The bright light of the sun glided through the cleansed leaves of the trees. The air was cold.

She shivered from the cold and from the terror within her, which here, in the fresh air, took hold of her with renewed force.

"Go, go to Mariette," she told Seryozha, who was coming up to her. She began to pace up and down the straw mat on the terrace. Couldn't they forgive me? Won't they understand that it could not have happened otherwise? she asked herself.

She stopped and looked at the aspen treetops swaying in the wind, their cleansed leaves shining brightly in the cold sun. She understood that she would not be forgiven, that everyone and everything would now have no pity on her, just as this sky, this verdure, had none. She felt again that within her heart everything began to double. I mustn't think, I mustn't think, she said to herself. I must get ready to go. Where? When? Whom should I take along? Yes, to Moscow, on the evening train, Annushka and Seryozha, and only the most necessary things. But first I must write to both of them. She quickly went into the house, entered her sitting room, sat down at the table, and wrote to her husband:

> *After what has happened, I cannot remain in your house any longer. I am leaving and taking our son. I do not know the law and therefore do not know with which of the parents the son must remain, but I am taking him along because I cannot live without him. Be magnanimous, leave him with me!*

Up to this point she wrote quickly and without effort, but the appeal to his magnanimity, of which, she believed, he was devoid, and the obligation to conclude the letter with some sort of moving sentence troubled her.

> *I cannot speak about my guilt and repentance, because. . . .*

She stopped again, having lost the thread of her thoughts. No, she said to herself, there is no need. She tore up the letter, rewrote it, omitting the appeal to his magnanimity, and sealed it.

She had to write another letter, to Vronsky. "*I have told my husband,*" she began, and then sat for a long while, lacking the strength to continue. It was so gross, so unwomanly. After all, what can I write to him? she asked herself. A blush of shame again covered her face. She recalled his composure and, in annoyance, she tore up the paper on which she had written the sentence. There is no need, she said to herself, and closing her writing pad, went upstairs. She announced to the governess and the servants that she was leaving that day for Moscow and at once started to pack.

16

PORTERS, GARDENERS, AND servants walked about all the rooms of the villa, carrying out the belongings. Closets and dressers stood open; twice a servant ran over to the store for some cord; newspaper littered the floor. Two chests, bags, and bundled wraps were taken down to the entrance hall. The coach and two hired carriages waited at the porch. Anna, her anxiety forgotten while she kept busy, was standing in front of the table in her sitting room, packing her traveling bag, when Annushka drew her attention to the sound of a carriage approaching the house. Anna looked through the window and saw Aleksei Aleksandrovich's messenger on the porch, ringing the doorbell.

"Go see what it is," she said calmly, ready to face anything, and she sat in a chair, her hands on her knees. A servant brought a thick envelope with Alexsei Aleksandrovich's handwriting on it.

"The messenger was told to bring an answer," he said.

"Very well," she said and, as soon as the servant left, she opened the letter with trembling hands. A packet of flat banknotes wrapped in a paper band fell out. She pulled out the letter and began to read the last part of it. *"All the necessary preparations for your moving will be made. . . . I consider your compliance with my request to be particularly important,"* she read. She hastily scanned the lines that followed, then read the whole letter, and reread it from the beginning. When she finished, she felt cold and knew that a terrible misfortune had befallen her, such as she could scarcely have expected.

In the morning she had repented the words which she had spoken to her husband and wished only that somehow those words had not been uttered. This letter now admitted that those words had not been spoken, and her wish was fulfilled. But now, of all the things she could imagine, this letter seemed to her the most terrifying.

He's right! He's right! she said to herself. Of course, he's always right, he is a Christian, he is magnanimous! Yes, a base, horrible man! And no one but I understands and will understand it, and even I cannot fully explain it. They call him a religious, upright, honest, intelligent man; but they don't see what I've seen. They don't know that for eight years he has oppressed my life, stifled everything that was alive in me, that it never occurred to him that I am a living woman, that I yearned for love. Nobody knows how often he insulted me and was pleased with himself. Haven't I used all my efforts to give some meaning to my life? Haven't I done my best to love him, to love my son when it was no longer possible to love my husband? But the time came when I understood that I could no longer deceive myself, that I was alive, that I was not guilty, that this is how God created me, that I must love and live. But what now? I could bear anything, could forgive anything, were he to kill me, or kill him; but no, he. . . ."

How could I have failed to guess what he would do? He acts in accordance with his base nature. He'll remain in the right, and though I'm already lost, he'll try to increase my disgrace. "*You may yourself imagine what awaits you and your son,*" she thought, recalling the words of the letter. This is a threat to take away my son and it's probably in accordance with their stupid laws. But don't I know why he says this? He doesn't believe that I love my son, or he scorns this feeling of mine (in fact, he always mocked it). But he knows that I wouldn't abandon my son, that I couldn't, that without my son there would be no life for me even with the man I love, that by abandoning my son and leaving my husband I would be acting like the most shameless, wicked woman. He knows it, and he also knows that I would not have the courage to do it.

"*Our life must go on as before,*" she recalled another sentence from the letter. It was a tormenting life before; it has been terrible lately. And what will happen now? He knows. He knows that I cannot regret what is my very life, my love. He knows that nothing will come of it but lies and deception, but he continues to torment me. I know him. I know that he delights as much in deceit as a fish in water. But no, I will not afford him this delight. I will tear apart the cobweb of deceit in which he wishes to entangle me, come what may. Anything would be better than lies and deceit.

But how? My God! My God! Was there ever a woman as unfortunate as I?

"I will tear it apart! I will tear it apart!" she cried, springing to her feet and restraining her tears. She walked up to the desk to write another letter to him. But deep within her heart she already felt that she hadn't the strength to tear the web, that she hadn't the strength to find a way out of her predicament, dishonorable and deceitful as it was.

She sat at the desk, but instead of writing, she put her hands on it, buried her head in them, and cried as children do, her breast convulsed with short sobs. She cried because her hope of clarifying and precisely defining her situation had been destroyed forever. She knew beforehand that everything would remain as before, or even much worse than before. She felt that her social position, which that morning had seemed unimportant, was precious to her, that she would not be able to exchange it for the shameful state of a woman who has left her husband and her son to join her lover. She felt that in spite of her efforts, she would prove no stronger than she was. She would never enjoy her love openly but always remain a sinful woman, living under the constant threat of detection, deceiving her husband by a shameful affair with a strange, independent man with whom she could not join her life. She knew that this was the way it would be, and at the same time it was so terrible that she could not even imagine how it would end. She cried without restraint, as children cry when punished.

She was interrupted by the sound of a servant approaching, and averting her face, she pretended to be writing.

"The messenger is asking for an answer," said the servant.

"An answer? Yes," said Anna, "tell him to wait. I'll ring."

What can I write? she thought. What can I decide by myself? What do I know? What do I want? What do I love? She felt again that within her heart everything appeared doubled. She was again alarmed by this feeling, and to rid herself of these thoughts about herself, she availed herself of the first pretext for action. I must see Aleksei. (This is what she called Vronsky in her thoughts). He alone can tell me what I must do. I'll go to Betsy's. Perhaps I'll see him there, she said to herself. She forgot completely that when she had told him yesterday that she would not be at Tverskoy's, he had replied that in that case he would not be there either. She went up to the table and wrote to her husband, "*I have received your letter. A.*" She rang and gave the note to the servant.

"We are not leaving," she told Annushka, who entered the room.

"Not leaving at all?"

"No, don't unpack until tomorrow. Let the coach remain. I'm going to the princess'."

"What dress shall I get out for you?"

17

AT THE CROQUET party to which Princess Tverskoy had invited Anna, the company was supposed to comprise two ladies and their admirers. These two ladies were prime representatives of a new Petersburg elite, which was called, in imitation of some imitation, *"les sept merveilles du monde."* These ladies belonged to a circle that although at the highest level, was extremely hostile to Anna's set. Moreover, old Stremov, one of the most influential persons in Petersburg and an admirer of Liza Merkalov, was Aleksei Aleksandrovich's opponent in the ministry. In view of all this, Anna did not want to go, and the hints in Princess Tverskoy's note referred to Anna's refusal. But now Anna, hoping to see Vronsky, decided to go.

Anna arrived at Princess Tverskoy's before the other guests.

As she was entering the house, Vronsky's servant, with well-groomed side whiskers and looking like a Gentleman of the Bedchamber, was also entering. He stopped at the door and, taking off his cap, let her pass. Anna recognized him and only then recalled that Vronsky had told her the day before that he would not be there. Most probably this was what he had written in this note,

While taking off her coat in the entrance hall, she heard the servant, who even pronounced his *r*'s as a Gentleman of the Bedchamber, say, as he delivered the note, "from the count to the princess."

She wanted to ask him where his master was. She wanted to return home and send Vronsky a letter asking him to come to see her, or to go to see him herself. But there was now no way to do any of these things. The bells had already sounded, announcing her arrival, and Princess Tverskoy's servant was already standing sideways at the open door, waiting for her to enter the inner rooms.

"The princess is in the garden. You will be announced. Would you like to go to the garden?" asked another servant in the other room.

Her state of hesitation and confusion remained the same as at home. It grew still worse because she could not do anything, could not see Vronsky, but had to remain here in the company of strangers so ill-suited to her present mood. But she knew she was dressed becomingly; she was not alone; she was in the midst of this familiar, festive display of idleness; and she felt easier here than at home. She did not have to think of what to do, everything was being done for her. As always, Anna smiled at Betsy who came out to meet her, looking strikingly elegant in her white dress. Princess Tverskoy was accompanied by Tushkevich and a young lady, her relative, who, to the enormous satisfaction of her provincial parents, was spending the summer with the famous princess.

Evidently there was something unusual about Anna, because Betsy noticed it at once.

"I didn't sleep well," said Anna, staring at a servant who came toward them bringing, as she believed, a note from Vronsky.

"I'm so glad that you've come," said Betsy. "I was tired and was going to have a cup of tea before the guests arrive. Why don't you and Masha go," she said, turning to Tushkevich, "and try out the croquet ground where the grass has been mowed? And at tea we'll have a cozy chat. All right?" she said, turning to Anna, smiling and pressing her hand, in which she held a parasol.

"But I cannot stay long. I must go to see old Vrede. For a century I have been promising to visit her," said Anna. Though deceit was alien to her nature, she practiced it when in public easily and naturally, even pleasurably.

She could by no means explain why she had said something on the spur of the moment. She said it only because Vronsky would not be there, and she needed some freedom of action to try to find him somewhere else. But why, of the many persons whom she had to visit, she mentioned the name of the lady in waiting, Vrede, she could not explain. Yet, as it turned out later, in her devious attempts to meet Vronsky, no better thought could have occurred to her.

"No, I absolutely will not let you go," replied Betsy, looking attentively at Anna's face. "Indeed, I'd be offended if I didn't love you so much. One would think that you fear that my company might compromise you. Please serve tea in the small drawing room," she said, screwing up her eyes as she always did when she addressed a servant. She took the note from him and read it. "Aleksei has disappointed me," she said in French. "He writes that he cannot come," she added in a natural, frank tone, as if she could never suspect that Vronsky had any more importance to Anna than just another partner in a game of croquet.

Anna knew that Betsy knew everything, but as she listened to the way Betsy spoke to her about Vronsky, she always felt momentarily convinced that she knew nothing.

"Oh!" said Anna indifferently, as if little interested, and continued to smile. "How can your company compromise anyone?" This play of words, this concealment of the truth, was a source of great delight to Anna, as to all women. Not the necessity to conceal it, not the purpose for which it was being concealed, but the very process of concealment itself delighted her. "I can't be more Catholic than the Pope," she said. "Stremov and Liza Merkalov are the cream of the cream of society. Futhermore, they are received everywhere, and I"—she deliberately emphasized the word I—"have never been strict and intolerant. I'm just pressed for time."

"Perhaps you don't want to see Stremov. Let him have his arguments with Aleksei Aleksandrovich in the committee; this doesn't concern you. But as a man of the world, he's the most courteous that I've ever known, and an ardent croquet player. You'll see. And though his love for Liza seems ridiculous, you have to see how the old man makes the best of this ridiculous situation. He's very charming. Have you met Sappho Stolz? She is of the new, completely new set."

While Betsy was saying all this, by her cheerful, intelligent look Anna felt that Betsy partly understood the state she was in and was planning some scheme to help her. They were seated in the small sitting room.

"I must, however, write to Aleksei," said Betsy. She sat at the table, wrote a few lines, and put the paper in the envelope. "I'm inviting him to come for dinner. I have one lady for dinner without an escort. See if I've been convincing enough. Excuse me for a moment. Please seal the letter and have it delivered," she said at the door. "I must go to see to things."

Without thinking for a moment, Anna sat at the table with Betsy's letter and, without reading it, added at the bottom, "*I must see you. Come to Vrede's garden. I'll be there at six o'clock.*" She sealed the letter, and Betsy, who had returned, in her presence gave it to be delivered.

And indeed, at the tea, which was served on a small table in the cool, small drawing room, the two women had the cozy chat Princess Tverskoy had promised to have before the guests arrived. They gossiped about those who were expected, and the conversation centered on Liza Merkalov.

"She is very lovely, and I have always liked her," said Anna.

"You should love her. She dreams about you. Yesterday she came over to me after the races and was deeply disappointed that she had missed you. She says that you are the veritable heroine of a novel, and were she a man she would perform a thousand foolhardy deeds for your sake. Stremov says that she does them anyway."

"But please tell me, I could never understand," said Anna after a short silence, in a tone that showed clearly that she was asking not an idle question, but one more important to her than it should have been. "Please tell me what her relationship is to Prince Kaluzhsky, the one called Mishka? I've met them only a few times. What is it about?"

Betsy smiled with her eyes and looked at Anna attentively.

"A new style," she said. "All of them have accepted this new style. They've discarded the old ways. But there are different ways of discarding them."

"Yes, but what is her relationship to Kaluzhsky?"

Betsy replied with a burst of gay, unrestrained laughter, something she seldom did.

"But you are usurping the privileges of Princess Miakhky. This is a question fit for the *Enfant Terrible*," and Betsy, against her will, again burst into the contagious laughter of people who seldom laugh. "You have to ask them," she said, with tears of laughter in her eyes.

"Yes, you're laughing," said Anna, involuntarily infected by Betsy's laughter, "but I never understood it. I cannot understand the husband's role."

"The husband? Liza Merkalov's husband brings her her wraps and is always at her service. And what is really going on there, nobody cares. You know that in proper society one does not speak or think of certain details regarding the toilette. The same holds true here."

"Will you be at Rolandako's party?" asked Anna, to change the subject.

"I don't think so," said Betsy, and without looking at her friend she began to pour the aromatic tea carefully into small transparent cups. She moved one cup over to Anna, reached for a cigarette, set it in a silver cigarette holder, and lit it.

"You see, I'm in a happy situation," she said, laughing no longer and reaching for her cup. "I understand both you and Liza. Liza is one of those naïve people who, like children, don't understand the difference between good and evil. At least she didn't understand it when she was very young. And now she knows that this naïveté is becoming to her. Now perhaps she deliberately doesn't understand," said Betsy with a subtle smile. "Nevertheless, it's becoming to her. You see, you can consider the same thing either a tragedy and a cause of torment, or look at it simply, even cheerfully. Perhaps you're inclined to look at things from the tragic point of view."

"How I would like to know others as I know myself," said Anna in a serious and pensive tone. "Am I worse than others or better? Worse, I think."

"You're a terrible, terrible child," repeated Betsy. "But here they are."

18

THEY HEARD the sounds of steps, of a man's voice, of a woman's voice and of laughter, and then the expected guests came in: Sappho Stolz and a young man known as Vaska, beaming with an overabundance of health. Obviously blood sausages, truffles, and burgundy did him good. Vaska bowed to the ladies, but glanced at them for a second only. He had followed Sappho into the drawing room and through the drawing room, as if tied to her, and kept his sparkling eyes fixed on her as though he wished to devour her. Sappho Stolz was a blonde with black eyes. She walked in, taking small brisk steps in her high-heeled shoes, and shook the ladies' hands firmly, like a man.

Anna had never met this new celebrity and was struck by her beauty, the extremity of her toilette, and the daring of her manners. Her coiffure was made up so high with her own and with false, soft, golden hair that in size it equaled her gracefully protruding and well-exposed bust. Her impetuous motions were such that at her every move forward her knees and the upper part of her legs showed their shapes underneath her dress, and one unconsciously asked himself where indeed in the back of all this fluttering structure was her actual small and shapely body itself, so naked above and so hidden below and and in the back.

Betsy hurriedly presented her to Anna.

"Can you imagine, we nearly ran over two soldiers," she began immediately, winking, laughing, and arranging her train, which she had tossed too far to one side. "I was riding with Vaska. Oh, yes, you haven't met yet," she said. Giving his last name, she introduced the young man, blushing and loudly laughing at her blunder of having referred to him as Vaska to a lady who had not met him.

Vaska again bowed to Anna, but said nothing. He turned to Sappho.

"You lost your bet. We arrived earlier. Pay, if you please," he said, smiling.

Sappho smiled still more gaily.

"But not now," she said.

"I don't care; I'll get it later."

"Very well, very well. Oh, yes," she said, suddenly turning to her hostess. "How gross of me! I almost forgot. I brought a friend with me. Here he is."

The unexpected young guest whom Sappho had brought and about whom she had forgotten, was, however, such an important person, that, in spite of his youth, both ladies rose to meet him.

He was Sappho's new admirer. Like Vaska, he too, followed her steps.

Soon Prince Kaluzhsky arrived, and Liza Merkalov with Stremov. Liza Merkalov was a slim brunette, with an Oriental, indolent face and beautiful eyes, impenetrable, as everyone described them. The style of her dark toilette (Anna immediately noticed and approved) fully harmonized with her beauty. Whereas Sappho was severe and trim, Liza was yielding and pliant.

But in Anna's eyes, Liza was the more attractive. Betsy had told Anna that Liza played the part of a naïve child, but when Anna saw her she knew that it was not so. True, she was a naïve and spoiled woman, but a very kind and meek one, too. True, her manner was the same as Sappho's; like Sappho, she was followed by two admirers who clung to her, devouring her with their eyes, one of them a young man, the other older. But there was something about her that elevated her above her milieu. She had the brilliance of a true diamond among beads of glass. This brilliance shone in her beautiful, truly inscrutable eyes. The weary and at the same time passionate look in those darkly circled eyes impressed one with their complete sincerity. As one looked into them, he felt sure that he knew all about her and, knowing her, could not help falling in love with her. At the sight of Anna her face lit up with a happy smile.

"Oh, how glad I am to see you!" she said, coming over to her. "Yesterday at the races I wanted to come over to you, but you had left. I particularly wanted to see you yesterday. It was terrible, wasn't it?" she said, directing at Anna a look that, it seemed, revealed her whole heart.

"Yes, I didn't expect that it would be so disturbing," said Anna, blushing.

At this time the company rose to go into the garden.

"I'm not going," said Liza, smiling, and sitting down next to Anna. "Will you stay too? Who cares for croquet?"

"But I like it," said Anna.

"Tell me, what do you do to avoid boredom? One is cheered just by looking at you. Your life is full, but I am bored."

"You, bored? But yours is the gayest circle in Petersburg," said Anna.

"Perhaps those who don't belong to our circle are even more bored. But we, particularly I, are not gay but terribly, terribly bored."

Sappho lit a cigarette and left for the garden in the company of her two young men. Betsy and Stremov remained at their tea.

"What do you mean, bored?" said Betsy. "Sappho says that last night they had the most wonderful time at your house."

"How wretched it was!" said Liza Merkalov. "We all came to our house after the races. It was the same thing, the same thing! It was all the same thing. We spent the evening sitting around on divans. What was so gay about it? Now, tell me, what do you do to avoid boredom?" she asked, turning again to Anna. "One look at you shows that here is a woman who may be happy or unhappy, but never bored. Tell me, how do you do it?"

"I do nothing about it," said Anna, blushing at the importunate questioning.

"That's the best way," said Stremov, entering the conversation.

Stremov was a man of fifty, graying, still vigorous, his face homely but displaying character and intelligence. Liza Merkalov was his wife's niece, and he spent all his free time with her. On meeting Anna Karenina, he, Aleksei Aleksandrovich's opponent in service, behaved as a man of the world and an intelligent person and strove to be particularly courteous to her, the wife of his enemy.

"Nothing," he interjected with a thin smile, "that's the best remedy. I've been telling you for a long time," he said, addressing Liza Merkalov, "to avoid boredom, you must not think that you are going to be bored, just as you must not fear that you will not fall asleep if you fear insomnia. That's exactly what Anna Arkadievna said."

"I would be very happy if I'd said that. It's so clever, and it's true," Anna said, smiling.

"But tell me why one should have trouble falling asleep, and why should it be hard to avoid boredom?"

"To fall asleep you must do some work, and to amuse yourself you must do some work."

"But why should I do work if nobody needs my work? And I cannot and will not pretend."

"You are incorrigible," said Stremov, without looking at her, and turned again to Anna.

He knew Anna very slightly, so he could talk to her about trifles only. But when he asked her when she was going to move to Petersburg, or told her how much Countess Lydia Ivanovna liked her, he spoke with an expression that showed that with all his heart and even more he wanted to please her and show his respect for her.

Tushkevich entered and announced that the whole company was waiting for the croquet players.

"Please don't go," asked Liza Merkalov, seeing that Anna was about to leave. Stremov joined Liza.

"It is too much of a contrast," he said, "to visit old Vrede after being in this company. Moreover, there you will cause her to indulge in malicious gossip, but here you will stir other feelings the best and the very opposite of malicious gossip," he told her.

For a moment Anna was undecided. The flattering words of this clever man, the naïve, childish sympathy shown to her by Liza Merkalov, and this familiar social atmosphere, all this seemed so easy, and the difficulties she was going to face so great that for a moment she was undecided whether to remain here and postpone a while longer the pain of the forthcoming conversation. But as she recalled what awaited her in the solitude of her home if she made no decision, and as she remembered how she had clutched at her hair with both hands, a gesture frightening even in retrospect, she said goodbye and left.

<h1 style="text-align:center">19</h1>

Vronsky, in spite of his seemingly frivolous social life, was a person who hated disorder. In his youth, while still in school, he once felt humiliated, when, his affairs in a tangle, he asked for a loan and was refused. Since then he had never again placed himself in a similar situation.

To keep his affairs in order, about five times a year, depending on the circumstances, he secluded himself and cleared up the state of his accounts. He called it straightening up accounts, or *faire la lessive*.

Waking late in the morning after the races, Vronsky, without shaving or bathing, put on his military jacket and, placing all his money, bills, and letters on the table, began to work. Petritsky knew that, while in such a state, Vronsky was easily angered. Therefore, when, on awakening, he saw his friend at his desk, he quickly dressed and left without disturbing him.

Every man who knows in great detail all the complexity of the circumstances which surround him, unconsciously assumes that the complexity of these circumstances and the difficulty of clarifying them are peculiar to him alone; it would never occur to him that others are surrounded by the same complexity of personal circumstances, And this is the way it appeared to Vronsky. He thought, not without an inner pride and not without reason, that another person would have grown confused a long time ago and would have been forced to act wrongly were he in similar difficulties. But Vronsky felt that this was the precise time to straighten all his accounts and to clarify his situation in order to avoid confusion.

The first problem Vronsky set about to solve was that of finances, the easiest one. In his small handwriting he entered all his debts on a sheet of notepaper, added them, and found that he owed seventeen-thousand rubles, plus a few hundred that he ignored for the sake of clarity. He counted his cash and bank accounts and found that he possessed eighteen hundred rubles, and until the New Year no receipts were forthcoming. Having reread the list of debts, he divided them into three groups. The first comprised those debts that had to be paid immediately or, at least, demanded that cash be ready for their payment at first notice. These debts amounted to four thousand: fifteen hundred for the horse and two thousand five hundred he had guaranteed for a young comrade, Venevsky, who in his presence had lost this amount to a sharper in a card game. Vronsky had wanted to pay the money on the spot (he had had it with him), but Venevsky and Yashvin had insisted that they would pay, and not Vronsky, who had taken no part in the game. All this was fine, but Vronsky knew that though his part in this sordid affair was limited to the guarantee he had given for Venevsky, he must have the two thousand five hundred on hand to fling at the sharper and to preclude any further discussion with him. Thus, for this first and most important group of debts he needed four thousand. The second group comprised less important debts, amounting to eight thousand. These were debts mainly connected with his racing stable: to the hay and oat contractor, the Englishman, the harness maker, and so on. About two thousand had to be paid on these accounts to have complete peace of mind. The last group of debts—to stores, hotels, and the tailor—were not worth thinking about. He therefore needed at least six thousand for his current expenses, but had only eighteen hundred. For a man with an income of a hundred thousand, as everybody thought, the payment of such debts would seem to present no difficulties. But the truth was that he was far from having an income of a hundred thousand. His father's enormous wealth, which alone brought a yearly income of two hundred thousand, remained undivided between the brothers. When his older brother, deep in debt, married Princess Varia Chirkov, the penniless daughter of a Decembrist, Aleksei yielded to his older brother all the income from his father's estates, leaving for himself only twenty-five thousand a year. Aleksei then told his brother that this income would be enough for him until he married, which probably would never happen. And his brother, who commanded one of the most expensive regiments and who had just married, could not refuse such a gift. In addition to the twenty-five thousand on which the brothers had agreed, Aleksei received about twenty thousand yearly from his mother, who had her own fortune, and Aleksei spent all of this money. Of late, his mother, angered by his love affair and by his departure from Moscow, had stopped sending him money. Consequently Vronsky, who was accustomed to spending forty-five thousand a year, received only twenty-five thousand and found himself in these difficulties. He could extricate himself only by applying for money to his mother, but he could not bring himself to do that. Her last letter, which he had received the day before, particularly vexed him, because she hinted at her readiness to help him in his social advancement and in his career but not in leading a life that had scandalized the whole of society. His mother's design to bribe him had insulted him deeply, and he felt still more estranged from her. But he could not withdraw his generous offer, although he vaguely foresaw some unexpected happenings connected with his affair with Karenina. He felt that he had made his generous offer without due thought, and that, though unmarried, he might need the whole hundred thousand. But he could not withdraw his offer. When he thought of his sister-in-law, recalled how that sweet and charming Varia reminded him on any convenient occasion that she remembered his magnanimity and appreciated it, he knew that he could not withdraw his offer. It would be as impossible as to hit a woman, steal, or tell a lie. There was only one possible and unavoidable solution, which Vronsky accepted without a moment's hesitation, and that was to borrow ten thousand rubles from a usurer, which was easy to do, to cut his expenses in general, and to sell his race horses. His mind made up, he at once wrote to Rolandaki, who had several times offered to buy his horses. Then he sent for the Englishman and for the usurer, and divided the money he had according to the bills to be paid. When he finished this business, he wrote a cold and curt reply to his mother. Then he reached for his wallet, took out three notes from Anna, reread them, burned them and, recalling the conversation they had had the day before, fell to thought.

20

VRONSKY'S LIFE was a particularly fortunate one in that he had a set of rules for defining beyond question everything that one should and should not do. Though this set of rules took in only a small area of circumstances, the rules were incontrovertible, and Vronsky, never emerging from that area, never for a moment hesitated in doing what he had to. These rules demanded absolutely that one is obliged to pay the cardsharp but not the tailor, that one should not lie to men, but could lie to women, that one should not deceive anybody but a husband, that one should not forgive an insult but could be the insulter, and so on. All these rules might be unreasonable and unjust, but they were incontrovertible, and by obeying them, Vronsky felt secure and he could hold his head high. But very recently, because of his relationship with Anna, Vronsky began to feel that his set of rules did not encompass all his circumstances and that the future held doubts and difficulties in which he could no longer define his guidelines.

His present relationship with Anna and her husband seemed to him simple and clear. It was clearly and precisely defined by the set of rules that guided him.

She was an honorable woman who had brought him the gift of her love, and he loved her. Therefore to him she was a woman worthy of the same respect as a legal wife and even more. He would rather have his arm cut off than permit himself, by a word or hint, to insult her or even deny her the greatest respect due a woman.

His relationships with society were also clear. Everyone might know, might suspect, but no one dared talk about it. If they did, he was ready to force the gossips to keep silent and respect the nonexisting honor of the woman he loved.

His relationship with the husband was the clearest. From the moment that Anna fell in love with Vronsky, he considered that he alone had an inalienable right over her. The husband was but a useless and obstructive person. No doubt he was in a miserable situation, but what could be done? The only right the husband had was to demand satisfaction with a weapon in his hand, and for this Vronsky had been ready from the first moment.

But lately a new, inner relationship had formed between him and her, one that frightened Vronsky by its vagueness. Only yesterday she had told him that she was pregnant. He felt that this information, and the part she expected him to play, demanded something not fully defined by the code that guided his life. And in fact, he was caught unawares; and at the first moment, on learning of her state, his heart demanded that she leave her husband. He had said it, but now, thinking it over, he saw clearly that it would be better to avoid the issue, and at the time he said this to himself he feared that perhaps he was doing something wrong.

When I told her to leave her husband, it meant that she should join me. Am I prepared for this? How can I go away with her now if I have no money? I admit that I could manage it. . . . But how can I go away with her, if I am in the service? If I said it, I must be prepared to do it; it means I must have money and retire from the service.

He began to think. The problem of whether to retire or not led him to think of another interest in his life, a secret one, known to him alone, and though secret, perhaps the most important in his life.

He had been moved by ambition since the days of his childhood and youth, though he refused to confess it even to himself; but this passion was so strong that now it did battle against his love. His first moves in society and in his career had been successful, but two years earlier he had committed a gross mistake. In his desire to show his independence and to hasten his advancement he had refused a position which had been offered to him, in the hope that his refusal would enhance his standing. But it turned out that he had overstepped himself, and he was bypassed. And thoughtlessly having assumed the part of an independent person, he stood up to it, acting subtly and cleverly and pretending that he was angry with no one, had been wronged by no one, and that the only thing he wished for was to be left alone, for he enjoyed his life. Actually he had not enjoyed himself since he went to Moscow last year. He felt that this reputation as an independent man who could attain anything but cared for nothing was beginning to wear thin, that many were beginning to believe that all he could attain was to remain a good and honest fellow. His affair with Karenina, which had created such a stir and had attracted so much attention, adding new luster to his position, for a while curbed the gnawing of unfulfilled ambition, but a week earlier this gnawing had resumed with new force. A childhood friend of his, a member of his group, his classmate Serpukhovskoy, a rival in school, in gymnastic contests, in pranks, in dreams of a career, had recently returned from Central Asia, where he had received two advancements and an award seldom given to such a young general.

As soon as he arrived in Petersburg, he began to be spoken of as a new rising star of the first magnitude. A classmate and contemporary of Vronsky, he was a general and was slated for an appointment that would affect the affairs of state, whereas Vronsky, though independent and brilliant, and loved by a beautiful woman, still remained a captain, and was allowed to remain independent as much as he pleased. Of course, he thought, I don't and can't envy Serpukhovskoy, but his advancement shows that it pays to be patient, and that success for a man like myself can come very quickly. Three years ago he was in the same position as I. If I retire, I burn my bridges. If I remain in service, I lose nothing. She herself said that she didn't want to make any changes. And having her love, I can't envy Serpukhovskoy. He slowly twirled his mustache, rose from the table and paced the room. His eyes shone with a singular brightness, and he was now in that calm, confident, cheerful frame of mind he always found himself in after he had clarified his situation. Everything was crystal clear, as it had been after he had set his accounts in order. He shaved, took a cold bath, dressed, and went outside.

21

"I've come to fetch you. Your work has lasted too long today," said Petritsky. "Well, have you finished?"

"I have," replied Vronsky, smiling with his eyes only and twirling the tips of his mustache carefully, as though if he moved too boldly and quickly he might upset the good order in which he had arranged his affairs.

"After something like this you always look as though you've just come from a bathhouse," said Petritsky. "I was sent by Gritska," (that was what they called the regimental commander) "they are waiting for you."

Vronsky looked at his friend without answering; he was thinking about something else.

"Is that music I hear over there?" he asked, listening to the familiar sounds of the band playing polkas and waltzes. "What sort of holiday is it?"

"Serpukhovskoy has arrived."

"Ah!" said Vronsky, "I didn't know."

His smiling eyes shone still more brightly.

Once he had really decided that he was happily in love, that he had sacrificed his ambition for its sake—at least he assumed such a role—Vronsky could neither envy Serpukhovskoy nor feel hurt that on a visit to the regiment he had not come to see him first. Serpukhovskoy was his good friend, and he would be glad to go to see him.

"Oh, I'm very glad to hear that."

The regimental commander, Demin, occupied a large manor house. All the guests assembled on its spacious porch. The first thing Vronsky saw in the yard was a group of singers in white military jackets, standing near a cask of vodka, and the healthy, happy regimental commander surrounded by his officers. The regimental commander ascended the first step to the porch, waved his hands, and shouted something to a group of soldiers standing to one side; he shouted over the sounds of the band playing an Offenbach quadrille. A group of soldiers, a sergeant-major, and a few other noncommissioned officers walked up to the porch together with Vronsky. The regimental commander turned back to the table and then emerged again on the porch with a goblet in his hand, and proposed a toast. "To the health of our former comrade, the brave General Serpukhovskoy. Hurrah!"

Behind the regimental commander, Serpukhovskoy himself came out, smiling, with a goblet in his hand.

"You're getting younger and younger, Bondarenko," he said, turning to the sergeant-major, who stood directly facing him, a dashing, red-cheeked soldier who was serving his second enlistment.

Vronsky had not seen Serpukhovskoy for three years. He had matured, let his side whiskers grow, but was still well-formed and impressive, not so much for his handsome features as for the gentleness and nobility of his face and figure. The only change Vronsky noticed in him was the constant, calm radiance which appears on the faces of those who are successful and are confident that their success is universally acknowledged. This kind of radiance was familiar to Vronsky, and he at once noticed it in Serpukhovskoy.

While going down the stairs, Serpukhovskoy noticed Vronsky. A happy smile lit Serpukhovskoy's face. He lifted his head sharply and raised his goblet, greeting Vronsky and showing him with this gesture that first he must go over to the sergeant who, standing at attention, was holding his lips ready for a kiss.

"Well, here he is!" shouted the regimental commander. "But Yashvin told me that you were in one of your bad moods."

Serpukhovskoy kissed the moist fresh lips of the dashing sergeant and, wiping his mouth with his handkerchief, he went over to Vronsky.

"I'm so glad to see you!" he said, shaking hands with him and taking him aside.

"Take care of him!" the regimental commander cried to Yashvin, pointing to Vronsky, and then he went over to the soldiers.

"Why weren't you at the races yesterday? I hoped to see you there," said Vronsky, looking at Serpukhovskoy.

"I was there, but I came late. Please," he added, turning to the adjutant, "distribute this among the men from me."

He hastily took from his wallet three one-hundred ruble bills and then blushed.

"Vronsky! Something to eat or drink?" asked Yashvin. "Bring something for the count. Here's your drink."

The revel at the regimental commander's lasted quite a while.

They drank a lot. They swung Serpukhovskoy about and tossed him into the air. Then they swung the regimental commander. The regimental commander himself and Petritsky danced in front of the singers. Then the regimental commander, somewhat winded, sat down on a bench in the yard and began to prove to Yashvin the superiority of Russia over Prussia, particularly in cavalry attacks. The revelry calmed down for a moment. Serpukhovskoy went into the house and entered the bathroom to wash his hands. There he found Vronsky, who was splashing himself with water. He had taken off his jacket, held his red hairy neck under the stream of water in the washstand, and was rubbing his neck and head with his hands. When he had finished washing, he went up to Serpukhovskoy. They both took seats here on a small divan and entered into a conversation that interested both of them.

"I knew all about you from my wife," said Serpukhovskoy. "I'm glad you've seen her so often."

"She is Varia's friend, and these are the only Petersburg women whom it gives me pleasure to meet," Vronsky replied with a smile. He smiled because he foresaw the subject to which the conversation was leading, and it pleased him.

"The only ones?" Serpukhovskoy repeated with a smile.

"I know all about you, but not only through your wife,"

said Vronsky, with a severe expression on his face, ignoring the hint. "I'm very happy about your success, but I'm not surprised. I expected still more."

Serpukhovskoy smiled. Evidently he was pleased to be thought of so highly, and saw no need to hide his pleasure.

"I, on the contrary, confess sincerely that I expected less. But I'm glad, very glad. I am ambitious; it's my weakness, I confess."

"Perhaps you wouldn't confess it if you weren't so successful," said Vronsky.

"I don't think so," said Serpukhovskoy, smiling again. "I wouldn't say that life would not be worth living without it, but I would be bored. Of course, I may be mistaken, but it seems to me that I possess some abilities that are appropriate to the kind of activity I've chosen, and that if power of whatever kind were given to me, I would wield it in a better way than some others I know," said Serpukhovskoy, beaming in awareness of his success. "Therefore the closer I get to it the happier I am."

"That may be true for you, but not for everyone. I used to think that way, but as time goes by, I realize that it doesn't pay to live for this alone," said Vronsky.

"Here it comes! Here it comes!" said Serpukhovskoy with a laugh. "I began by saying that I had heard about you, about your refusal. . . . Of course, I approved of it. But there's a way of doing things. I believe that you did the right thing, but you didn't do it the way you should have."

"What is done, is done, and you know that I never disavow what I've done. And I am pleased with my life."

"Pleased for a while. It won't satisfy you. I wouldn't tell this to your brother. He's a charming child, very much like our host. There he goes!" he added, listening to the hurrahs. "He's happy, but this wouldn't satisfy you."

"I don't say it would."

"But that's not all. People like you are needed."

"By whom?"

"By whom? By society. Russia needs men, needs a party, or else everything will go to the dogs."

"What do you mean? Bertenev's party opposing Russian communists?"

"No," said Serpukhovskoy. He wrinkled his face, annoyed that he could be suspected of such foolishness. "*Tout ça est une blague*. It always has been and always will be. It's not a problem of communists. But these intriguers always have to contrive an issue involving a harmful, dangerous party. It's an old trick. No, what is needed is a party that would wield power and would be made up of independent men such as you and I."

"But why?" asked Vronsky. He named some influential people and asked, "Why aren't they independent?"

"Only because they have no independent means or were born without them, possess no titles, and weren't born close to the sun as we were. They can be bought with money or with a favor. To keep their positions they must invent some sort of policy. They create a line of thought, a policy in which they themselves do not believe, and one that is harmful; and this policy is only a means to obtain a house supplied by the government and a given salary. *Cela n'est pas plus fin que ça,* as you watch them play their cards. Perhaps I'm worse or more stupid than they, though I don't see why I should be. But we surely have one important advantage over them: it isn't easy to buy us. And such people as we are needed now more than ever."

Vronsky listened to him attentively, but he was less interested in the content of his words than in the attitude of Serpukhovskoy, who was ready to struggle against the powerful ones and in this respect had his likes and dislikes, whereas all his own official interests centered on his squadron. Vronsky also understood how powerful Serpukhovskoy could be, thanks to his infallible ability to think things through and to understand them, and to his intelligence and eloquence, which were so rare in the milieu in which he lived. And he envied him, no matter how guilty it made him feel.

"But I still lack what is most important in this case," he answered. "I lack the desire for power. I've had it, but it has disappeared."

"If I may say so, that's not true," Serpukhovskoy said, smiling.

"No, it is true, it is true! . . . now," added Vronsky, trying to be sincere.

"Yes, *now,* this is something different; but this *now* will not last forever."

"Perhaps," replied Vronsky.

"You say perhaps," continued Serpukhovskoy as though guessing his thoughts, "but I say surely. And that is why I wanted to see you. You acted as you should have. I understand, but you must not persevere. All I want is a *carte blanche* from you. I'm not acting as your patron. . . . Though why shouldn't I? You acted as my patron often enough. I would hope that our friendship is above that. Yes," he said, smiling gently at him, like a woman, "give me *carte blanche*, retire from the service, and I will draw you in unnoticeably."

"But I want you to know that I don't need anything," said Vronsky. "I only want everything to be as it has been."

Serpukhovskoy rose and faced him.

"You say that you want everything to be the way it has been. I know what you mean. But listen to me: we are contemporaries, probably you have known more women than I." Serpukhovskoy's gesture and smile showed Vronsky that he need have no fear, and assured him that he would touch the painful spot tenderly and carefully. "But I'm married, and, truly, by knowing only the wife whom you love (as some writer has said), you understand all women better than if you have known thousands."

"We'll be there in a minute," cried Vronsky to an officer who looked into the room, calling them to the regimental commander.

Vronsky was now eager to hear what he was going to tell him.

"Here's my opinion. Women are the main obstacle to man in his pursuits. It's hard to love a woman and accomplish anything. There is one remedy for this, one that affords you the means to love without interference, and that is marriage. How can I explain to you what I mean," said Serpukhovskoy, who loved similes. "Wait, wait! If you carry a *fardeau*, you can have your hands free only when the *fardeau* is tied to your back; marriage is like that. And I learned this when I married. My hands have suddenly been freed. But dragging this *fardeau* without marriage keeps your hands so occupied that you can do nothing else. Look at Mazankov or Krupov. They ruined their careers because of women."

"But what women!" said Vronsky, recalling the Frenchwoman and the actress with whom these two men had been involved.

"The higher the social position of the woman, the worse it is. Now you not only carry the *fardeau* in your hands, you have to seize it from another person."

"You have never loved," said Vronsky, looking straight ahead and thinking of Anna.

"Perhaps. But remember what I told you. And another thing: all women are more materialistic than men. To us love is something sublime, but they are always *terre-à-terre*."

"Just a minute, just a minute," he said, turning to the servant who had come in. But the servant had not come to repeat the call, as he thought. The servant brought a note.

"A messenger brought it from Princess Tverskoy."

Vronsky opened the letter, and his face flushed.

"I have a headache; I'll go home," he said to Serpukhovskoy.

"Well, goodbye. May I have the *carte blanche?*"

"We'll talk about it some other time. I'll see you in Petersburg."

22

IT WAS already after five. To arrive on time, and also to avoid using his own horses, which were known to everyone, Vronsky took Yashvin's hired coach and told the coachman to go as fast as he could. The old four-passenger coach was spacious. He sat down in the corner, stretched his legs on the front seat and became lost in thought.

A vague awareness of the clear state to which his affairs had been brought, a vague sense of the friendliness and flattery with which Serpukhovskoy had treated him, considering him an indispensable person, and, most important, the expectation of the forthcoming rendezvous, all blended into a general enjoyment of life. This feeling was so intense that he smiled unconsciously. He put his feet down, crossed his legs, felt his firm calf, which had been bruised in yesterday's fall, leaned backward and took several deep breaths.

Good, very good! he said to himself. He had often felt such a happy awareness of his body, but he had never loved himself, his body, as he did now. It gave him pleasure to feel the slight pain in his strong leg, to feel the pull of his chest muscles as he breathed. The same clear and cold August day that had filled Anna with such despair, seemed to him stimulating and invigorating; it refreshed his face and neck, which still stung from the washing. The scent of his pomaded mustache seemed particularly pleasant in this fresh air. Everything he saw through the window of the coach, everything in this cold clear air, in this pale sunset, seemed as fresh, joyful, and vigorous as himself: the roofs of the houses, shining in the rays of the setting sun; the sharp outlines of the fences and building corners; the figures of the few pedestrians and carriages; the motionless verdure of the trees and grass; the fields with their regular rows of potato plants; and the slanting shadows cast by the houses, trees, bushes, and those very rows of potato plants. Everything looked beautiful, as in a lovely landscape painting just completed and varnished.

He leaned out the window and cried to the coachman, "Faster! Faster!" He reached into his pocket for a three-ruble note, which he thrust at the coachman, who had turned around. When the coachman's hand felt it at the lantern, he cracked his whip sharply and the coach bounded forward on the level road.

I need nothing, nothing but this happiness, he thought, looking at the bone knob on the bell in the space between the windows and visualizing Anna as he had seen her the last time. And as time goes on, my love for her grows greater. Here is the garden of Vrede's government villa. Where is she? Where? How? Why did she tell me to meet her here and why did she write in Betsy's letter? He hadn't thought of it until now, but it was too late. Before reaching the alley, he told the coachman to stop, opened the door, jumped down from the moving coach, and entered the alley leading to the house. There was no one in the alley, but he saw her off to the right. Her face was hidden under a veil, but his happy look took in the distinctive walk she alone possessed, the set of her shoulders, the carriage of her head, and at once he felt as if an electric current had run through his body. He was conscious, with renewed force, of his entire being, from the springy movements of his legs to the movements of his lungs in breathing. His lips tingled.

When they met, she pressed his hand firmly.

"Are you angry that I called you? I had to see you," she said, and the serious and stern set of her lips, which he could see under the veil, at once changed his mood.

"I angry? But how did you come? Where shall we go?"

"It doesn't matter," she said, taking him by the arm. "Come, I must talk to you."

He understood that something had happened, and that this rendezvous would not be a happy one. In her presence he had no will of his own. Without knowing the reason for her anxiety, he already felt that he, too, was disturbed by the same anxiety.

"What is it?" he asked, pressing her arm to him with his, and trying to read her thoughts on her face.

She walked a few steps in silence to gather courage and then suddenly stopped.

"I didn't tell you yesterday," she began, breathing heavily and quickly, "that on my return home with Aleksei Aleksandrovich, I disclosed everything to him. . . . I told him that I could not be his wife, that . . . I told him everything."

He listened to her, unconsciously leaning forward, as though desiring to lighten the burden she bore. But as soon as she said this, he at once straightened, and his face assumed a stern and proud expression.

"Yes, this is better, a thousand times better! I understand how hard it was," he said.

But she did not listen to his words. She read his thoughts by the expression of his face. She could not understand that this expression was produced by the first thought which had occurred to Vronsky, the thought of a duel, now inevitable. The thought of a duel had never occurred to her, and therefore she interpreted differently the momentary stern expression of his face.

When she had received her husband's letter, she already knew deep within her heart that everything would remain as before, that she would not be strong enough to renounce her social position, abandon her son and join her lover. The morning she had spent at Princess Tverskoy's further convinced her of this. But this meeting, nevertheless, was of great importance to her. She hoped that this meeting would change their situation and save her. If, on hearing this news, he would tell her resolutely, passionately, without a moment's hesitation, "Leave everything and come with me!" she would abandon her son and go away with her lover. But the news did not affect him the way she had expected; he only seemed to be resenting some offence.

"It was not hard at all. It came by itself," she said with annoyance. "Here . . ." and she reached into her glove for her husband's letter.

"I understand, I understand!" he interrupted, taking the letter, but not reading it and trying to calm her. "I wished only one thing, asked only for one thing: to put an end to this situation, to dedicate all my life to your happiness."

"Why do you tell me this?" she said. "Could I ever doubt it? If I had any doubts. . . ."

"Who is that coming?" Vronsky asked suddenly, pointing to two ladies who were heading in their direction. "Perhaps they know us," and he hurriedly turned into a side path, leading her along.

"Oh, I don't care!" she said. Her lips trembled. It seemed to him that her eyes looked at him from under the veil with strange resentment. "I repeat: that's not the problem. I've never doubted it. But here's what he writes. Read it." She stopped again.

Just as when she had told him of her break with her husband, Vronsky again, while reading the letter, submitted unconsciously to the natural reaction brought about by his attitude toward a wronged husband. Now, with the letter in his hands, he unconsciously thought of the *challenge* he certainly would receive today or tomorrow. He thought of the duel itself, how with the same cold and proud expression of his face as he had now, he would shoot into the air and face the shot of the insulted husband. And at the same time a thought flashed through his mind. He recalled what Serpukhovskoy had told him and what he himself had thought that morning—that it was better not to bind oneself—and he knew that this thought he could not share with her.

After he had read the letter, he raised his eyes toward her, and his glance lacked resolve. She understood immediately that he had pondered this matter earlier. She knew that whatever he would say, he would not reveal to her all his thoughts. And she understood that her last hope had been betrayed. This was not what she had expected.

"You see what kind of man he is," she said in a trembling voice, "he—"

"Forgive me, but I'm glad that it happened," Vronsky interrupted. "For God's sake, let me finish," he added, his look begging her to let him explain what he meant. "I am glad because it cannot, it can by no means remain as he expects."

"Why can't it?" said Anna, restraining her tears. Obviously she no longer gave any weight to what he would say. She felt that her fate had been sealed.

Vronsky wanted to say that after this duel, which he considered unavoidable, the present situation could not continue, but he said something else.

"It cannot continue. I hope that now you'll leave him. I hope," he said, confused and blushing, "that you'll allow me to plan and arrange our lives. Tomorrow—" he was going to begin.

She did not let him finish.

"And my son?" she cried. "Do you see what he writes? I must leave him, but I don't want to and I can't."

"But, for God's sake, what would you prefer? To leave your son or to remain in this humiliating situation?"

"Whom does it humiliate?"

"Everyone, and yourself most of all."

"You call it humiliating . . . don't say that. These words have no meaning for me," she said in a trembling voice. She did not want him to speak untruthfully now. All that remained for her was his love, and she wanted to love him. "Please understand that since the day when I fell in love with you everything has changed. There is one and only one thing for me—your love. If it is mine, I feel so elevated, so secure that nothing can humiliate me. I'm proud of my situation, for . . . I am proud because . . . am proud. . . ." She could not finish and say what it was that made her so proud. Tears of shame and despair choked her. She stopped and burst into sobs.

He, too, felt a lump in his throat and a tingle in his nose, and for the first time in his life he felt like crying. He could not have explained what it was that so moved him; he pitied her, but he felt that he could not help her, and at the same time, he knew that he was the cause of her misfortune, that he had done something wrong.

"Isn't a divorce possible?" he asked hesitatingly. She shook her head without answering. "Couldn't you take your son and still leave him?"

"Yes, but it all depends on him. Now I must go to him," she said coldly. Her premonition that everything would remain as before had not deceived her.

"On Tuesday I'll be in Petersburg, and everything will be decided."

"Well, let's not talk about it any more," she said.

Anna's coach rolled up. She had sent it away with orders to return to the fence around Vrede's garden. She said goodbye to him and left for her house.

THE USUAL meeting of the Committee of the Second of July took place on Monday. Aleksei Aleksandrovich entered the committee room, greeted the members of the committee and the chairman in his usual manner, took his seat, and laid his hands on the papers prepared for him. Among these papers were the memoranda which he needed and the outlines of the speech he was going to give. Actually, he needed no reference materials. He remembered everything and saw no necessity for rehearsing his speech in his mind. He knew that when the time came and he faced his opponent, who would vainly try to look unconcerned, his speech would flow more easily without preparation than if he reviewed it now. He felt that the content of his speech was of such great consequence that each word was important. In the meantime, listening to the regular report, he maintained his most innocent, harmless look. Looking at his white hands, their veins bulging, which so tenderly felt with their long fingers both edges of the sheet of white paper spread before him, and at his face, tired and inclined to one side, nobody would believe that from these lips would pour forth words that would stir such a terrible tempest that the members of the committee would be forced to shout and to interrupt each other and the chairman would have to call for order. When the report had been read, Aleksei Aleksandrovich declared in his thin, soft voice that he wished to express some of his opinions concerning the government of the minorities. Everyone's attention was drawn to him. Aleksei Aleksandrovich cleared his throat and began to propound his views. He did not look at his opponent, but at the first person whom he happened to face, something he always did when he delivered his speeches. It was a little, timid old man, who never expressed his opinions in the committee sittings. When he came to the Basic Organic Law, his opponent sprang to his feet, expressing his objection. Stremov, who was a member of the commission too, and was also hurt to the quick, began to defend himself, and a general uproar ensued. But Aleksei Aleksandrovich carried the day, and his proposition was accepted. Three new commissions were appointed, and the next day, in a certain Petersburg circle, the sitting of committee was the sole topic of conversation. Aleksei Aleksandrovich's success surpassed his expectations.

When he awoke the following morning, Tuesday, he recalled with pleasure his victory of the previous day. When his office manager, in his desire to flatter him, related the rumors he had heard about the committee sitting, Aleksei Aleksandrovich could not restrain a smile, though he tried to look indifferent.

Busy with his office manager, Aleksei Aleksandrovich completely forgot that this was Tuesday, the day appointed for Anna Arkadievna's return, and he was surprised and annoyed when the servant came in to announce her arrival.

Anna arrived in Petersburg early in the morning. She had sent a telegram ordering the coach, and therefore Aleksei Aleksandrovich might have known that she was coming. But when she arrived, he did not meet her. She was told that he had not yet come out of his study and was at work with his office manager. She ordered the servant to inform her husband of her arrival, went into her sitting room, and busied herself with arranging her belongings, expecting him to come to see her. But an hour passed, and he still had not come. She went into the dining room under the pretext of giving some orders, and she purposely spoke in a loud voice in the hope that he would come out to her; but he did not, though she heard him come up to the doorway of his study to see his office manager off. She knew that, as usual, he would leave for his office soon, and she wanted to see him before he left so that their relationship might be defined.

She crossed the drawing room and then resolutely made for his room. When she entered, he was sitting at a small table, leaning his elbows on it and looking straight ahead with a dejected air. He was dressed in his uniform, evidently ready to leave. She saw him before he could see her, and she understood that he was thinking of her.

On seeing her, he was about to rise, changed his mind, and then his face flushed, something Anna had never seen in him before. He quickly rose and went up to greet her, looking not into her eyes, but higher, at her forehead and headdress. He came up to her, took her hand, and asked her to sit down.

"I'm very glad that you've returned," he said, sitting down next to her. He obviously wanted to say something else, but he faltered. He began to say something several times, then stopped. Though in preparing herself for this meeting she had expected to rebuke him and show her contempt for him, she did not know what to say to him and pitied him. A long silence ensued. "How is Seryozha?" he asked, and without waiting for an answer, he added, "I'll not dine at home today and now I must go."

"I wanted to go to Moscow," she said.

"No, it was very, very good of you to have come here," he said, and again he fell silent.

Seeing that he could not gather the strength to begin the conversation, she began it herself.

"Aleksei Aleksandrovich," she said, looking at him without lowering her eyes under his steady gaze, directed at her coiffure. "I am a sinful woman, a wicked woman, and I am just what I told you I was at that time, and I have come to tell you that I can change nothing."

"I've not asked you about it," he said, suddenly looking straight into her eyes with hatred and resolution. "I expected this." Stirred by anger, he evidently regained control over his faculties. "But as I told you then, and as I wrote to you," he said in a harsh, thin voice, "and as I repeat now, I am not obliged to know it. I ignore it. Not all wives are so kind as you and are in such a hurry to give their husbands this *pleasant* news." He emphasized the word *pleasant*. "I'll ignore it until it becomes publicly known and my name is disgraced. Therefore I warn you that our relationship must remain as it has always been, and only when you *compromise* yourself will I be obliged to take measures to defend my honor."

"But our relationship cannot be as it has always been," said Anna, in a timid voice, looking at him fearfully.

When she again saw these calm gestures, heard this shrill, childlike, derisive voice, her repugnance toward him destroyed the feeling of pity she had. In spite of her fear, she was most anxious to have her situation clarified.

"I cannot be your wife, when I—" she began to explain.

He laughed coldly and spitefully.

"Probably the kind of life you have chosen has affected your concepts. I both respect and scorn. . . . I respect your past and scorn your present so deeply that I was far from implying the meaning which you have given my words."

Anna sighed and bowed her head.

"But I can't understand how, as independent as you are," he continued, getting excited, "after bluntly informing your husband of your unfaithfulness to him, in which you seem to see nothing reprehensible, you find it reprehensible to fulfill the duties of a wife to her husband."

"Aleksei Aleksandrovich! What do you want of me?"

"I demand that I never see that man here, that you behave in such a manner that neither *society* nor the *servants* could accuse you. . . . That you never see him again. It seems to me that I am not demanding much. In return, you will enjoy the privileges of an honest wife without fulfilling her duties. That's all I have to tell you. Now I must go. I will not dine at home."

He rose and went to the door. Anna also rose. He bowed in silence and let her pass.

24

The night Levin spent on the haycock had its effect upon him. He became disgusted with the work he was doing and lost all interest in it. In spite of a rich harvest, he had never met with so many failures and such enmity toward him on the part of the moujiks as he had this year, or so, at least, it seemed to him. The cause of the failures and the animosity was now quite clear to him. The pleasure he had found in the work itself; the closeness to the moujiks which had resulted from it; his envy of the moujiks and their life; his desire to live that life, which that night had turned from a dream into an intention; his reflections upon the ways of accomplishing that intention—all this had changed his opinion of his own farming to such a degree that by no means could he be interested in them as before and he could not help seeing that his relationship with the laborers, which was the foundation of his entire enterprise, was not a pleasant one. Herds of cows, all of improved stock like Pava, his fertilized and plowed lands, nine level fields hedged with willow bushes, ninety dessiatines of fields deeply plowed with manure, seed drills, and so on— all this would have been magnificent had he taken care of it himself, or with his friends, people who sympathized with him. But he now saw clearly (his work on the book on agriculture, in which the labor was regarded as the most important element, contributed much to the formation of this view), he now saw clearly that the farming enterprise he conducted was nothing but a stubborn, heartless contest between him and the laborers, in which one side, his, continually strove to change everything according to the highest accepted standards, whereas the other side wished to leave the natural order of things. And in this contest he saw that, with the greatest effort on his part and without any exertion or even attempt on the other, his farm was making no progress, that the excellent agricultural implements, the beautiful cattle, and the land, all were going to ruin. And, most important, not only was the energy spent on his farming utterly wasted, but its very purpose seemed to him totally unworthy. He could not help seeing it now, when the nature of his enterprise was so clear to him. Actually, what was the nature of this contest? He fought for every penny (and he had to fight for it, for if his energy slackened he would not have enough money to pay the laborers), and they persisted in doing their work casually and enjoyably in their accustomed manner. It was to his interest that each laborer perform as much work as possible, that he keep his mind on his work, that he be careful not to break the winnowing machine, the horse-drawn rakes, the threshing machine, and that he think of what he was doing. But the laborer wanted to work as enjoyably as he could, taking his rest and, most important, going along in a carefree, unconcerned way. That summer Levin had observed it on all sides. He had ordered his men to mow clover for hay, selecting for this purpose the inferior dessiatines that were overgrown with grass and wormwood and were unfit for seeding. But instead, they mowed rows of the best dessiatines of seed clover, claiming that the steward had told them to do so, and tried to comfort him with the thought that it would make excellent hay. But he knew that the reason they had done this was that it was easier to mow these dessiatines. He sent a tedder for the hay; they broke it on the first swaths, for the moujik was bored with sitting on a box under the rotating wings. And they told him, "Don't worry, the women will turn it in no time." The plows were unfit for use, because the worker never thought of raising the share when he turned, and by forcing it he wore out the horses and ruined the soil. Yet, he was asked not to worry. They did not keep the horses out of the wheatfields, because no peasant wanted to be a night watchman, and, against his orders, they took turns watching the fields at night, with the result that Vanka, after a day's work, would fall asleep and then repent his sins, saying, "I'm at your mercy." They overfed the three best calves by letting them eat the grass in the mowed clover field without first watering them, and he could not convince them that the calves were blown up by the clover. Instead, to comfort him, they told him that his neighbor had lost a hundred and twelve head of cattle within three days. All this was done not because anyone wished to do any harm to Levin or to his farm; on the contrary, he knew that they loved him, regarding him as a master devoid of guile (this was highest praise). But all this was done because they wanted to work in a gay and carefree manner, and considered his interests not only alien and incomprehensible, but inevitably contradictory to their own just interests. For a long time now Levin had felt dissatisfied with his work. He saw that his boat was leaking, but he had not looked for nor found the leak, perhaps intentionally deluding himself. But now he could no longer delude himself. He had not only lost interest in the work he was doing, it disgusted him, and he could do it no longer.

To all this was added the presence of Kitty Shcherbatsky within thirty versts. He did not want to and could not bring himself to see her. When he saw Daria Aleksandrovna Oblonsky, she asked him to visit them; to visit with the purpose of again proposing to her sister who, as she suggested indirectly, would now accept him. Levin himself, on seeing Kitty Shcherbatsky, felt that he had not stopped loving her, but he could not visit the Oblonskys knowing that she was there. The fact that he had proposed and been refused had placed an insurmountable obstacle between them. I cannot ask her to be my wife just because she could not be the wife of the one she wanted, he said to himself. This thought made him cold and hostile toward her. I wouldn't be able to talk to her without a feeling of reproach; I couldn't look at her without enmity; and she would only hate me more, as would be natural. And then, how could I visit them now, after what Daria Aleksandrovna has told me. Could I conceal the knowledge of what she said? And I would be the magnanimous one, ready to forgive and forget! I, forgive her and honor her with my love? . . . Why did Daria Aleksandrovna tell me this? I could have met her accidentally, and everything would have come out naturally; but now it's impossible, impossible.

Daria Aleksandrovna sent a note asking for a lady's saddle for Kitty. "*I've been told that you have such a saddle*," she wrote to him. "*I hope that you will bring it yourself.*"

This was more than he could endure. How could such an intelligent, sensitive woman so humiliate her sister! Ten times he tried to write a note, but each time he tore it up, and then he sent off the saddle without any reply. He could not write to her that he would go, because he could not go, but it would have been still worse to write that he was busy, or that he had to go on a trip. So he sent the saddle off without a note. He knew that what he had done was shameful, and the next day, after handing over to his steward the management of the farm, to which he now felt an aversion, he left for a remote county to visit his friend Sviazhsky. There were magnificent double-snipe marshes in his neighborhood, and his friend had written to him recently, reminding him of his long-standing promise to visit him. The double-snipe marshes in Surovsky County had long tempted Levin, but, being busy, he had kept postponing the trip. Now he was glad to get away from the vicinity of the Shcherbatskys, and even more so from the farm, particularly to go hunting, an activity in which he always found the greatest consolation for his troubles.

25

THERE WAS neither a railroad nor a post road to Surovsky County, and Levin traveled in a tarantas drawn by his own horses.

Halfway there he stopped for a meal at the home of a rich moujik. A bald, vigorous old man, with a wide red beard graying at the cheeks, opened the gates, pressing himself against the gatepost to let the troika in. Having pointed out to the coachman a shed in the large, clean, neat, new yard, in which there were some charred old-style plows, the old man invited Levin into the room. A neatly dressed young woman, with galoshes over her bare feet, was bent over, mopping the floor in the new entrance hall. She was frightened by Levin's dog, which ran in after him, and she cried out, but she quickly laughed at her own fright when told that the dog was harmless. Pointing with her bare arm, she showed Levin the door into the room and turned back to mopping the floor, again bending over and hiding her lovely face.

"Some tea?" she asked.

"Yes, please."

It was a large room, with a stove of Dutch tiles and a partition. Under the icons were a table decorated with colored designs, a bench and two chairs. There was a small dish closet near the entrance door. The shutters were closed, and there were few flies in the room. Everything was clean, and Levin saw to it that Laska, who had run along the road and had stepped in the puddles, did not soil the floor. Levin looked around the room and went out into the back yard. The pretty young woman in galoshes hurried to the well with two empty pails swinging on a yoke.

"Make it fast," the old man shouted gaily at her as he came over to Levin.

"Sir, are you going to visit Nikolai Ivanovich Sviazhsky? He stops here too," he started talkatively, leaning on the railing of the porch.

In the middle of the old man's story about his acquaintance with Sviazhsky, the gates creaked again and the laborers, who were returning from the field, drove the old-style plows and harrows into the yard. The horses, harnessed to the plows and harrows, were large and well fed. The laborers evidently were members of the household: two were youngsters in cotton shirts and caps; the other two, one an old man, the other a young lad, dressed in coarse linen shirts, were hired hands. The old man came over from the porch to the horses and began to unharness them.

"What have they been plowing?" asked Levin.

"We've been earthing potatoes. We also rent a little land. Fedot, don't take the gelding, but tie him to the log. We'll harness another horse."

"Well, father, have you brought the plowshares as I asked?" the huge, powerfully built young man asked. He evidently was the old man's son.

"They are in the sleigh," replied the old man, coiling the loose reins into a circle and tossing them on the ground. "Mount them while they have their dinner."

The good-looking young woman came through the entrance hall with two full pails, the weight of the pails pressing on her shoulders. From somewhere more women appeared, the young ones pretty, the middle-aged and old ones homely, with children or without children.

The samovar chimney hummed. The workers and members of the family, having attended to the horses, came in to dinner. Levin brought his lunch in from his carriage and invited the old man to have tea with him.

"We've already had ours today," said the old man, obviously pleased with the invitation. "Perhaps, for the sake of company."

At tea Levin learned the whole history of the old man's farming. Ten years ago the old man had rented from the landowner one hundred and twenty dessiatines, and last year he had bought it and had rented three hundred more from a neighboring landowner. A small part of the land, the poorest, he let, and his family plowed about forty dessiatines with the help of two hired hands. The old man complained that conditions were bad. But Levin understood that he complained for the sake of form, and that his farm was flourishing. If they really had been bad, he would not have bought the land at a hundred and five rubles, would not have married off three sons and a nephew, would not have rebuilt his houses after two fires, improving them each time. In spite of the old man's complaints, one could see that he was justly proud of his prosperity, proud of his sons, nephew, daughters-in-law, horses, and cows, and particularly that this entire undertaking remained a single unit. From his conversation with the old man Levin learned that he was not against innovations. He had planted a lot of potatoes, and his potato plants, as Levin had observed while on the way there, had already flowered and were beginning to set, whereas Levin's had just begun to flower. He earthed the potatoes with a new-style plow, which he had borrowed from the landlord. He sowed wheat. One small detail especially impressed Levin: after they had thinned the rye, they used the thinnings as fodder for the horses. How often, on seeing this excellent fodder go to waste, had Levin wanted to have it rescued, but it had always seemed impossible. But the moujik could do it, and he could not praise the fodder enough.

"What else do the women have to do? They carry the piles up to the road for the carts."

"But with us, the landowners, everything goes badly on account of the laborers," said Levin, offering him a glass of tea.

"Thank you," said the old man. He accepted the glass, but refused the sugar, showing the piece on which he had been nibbling.

"What can you accomplish with laborers?" he said. "They will ruin you. Take, for instance, Sviazhsky. We know that his land is the best, but he cannot boast of good harvests. It's all carelessness!"

"But you also employ hired labor."

"We moujiks are different. We watch every step. Those who don't do well, go. We can always manage by ourselves."

"Father, Finogen wants some tar," said the young woman in the galoshes, as she entered the room.

"That's how it is, sir," said the old man. He rose, crossed himself unhurriedly, thanked Levin, and left.

When Levin entered the back room to call his coachman, he found all the males of the family at the dinner table. The women stood about them, serving. An enormous young man, his mouth full of kasha, was telling a funny story, everyone laughed loudly, and the young woman in the galoshes, who was pouring some cabbage soup into a bowl, laughed with particular gaiety.

It was quite possible that the sight of the pretty woman in the galoshes helped greatly in creating the impression of good order which this peasant household made upon Levin. The impression was so strong that he could in no way rid himself of it. And all the way from the old man's to Sviazhsky's, again and again he recalled this household, as though there was something in this impression that required his particular attention.

26

Sviazhsky was marshal of the nobility for his county. He was five years older than Levin and had been married for a long time. A young sister-in-law, whom Levin liked very much, lived with them. Levin knew that Sviazhsky and his wife had their hearts set on his marrying this girl. He knew it for certain, as young men, the so-called bridegrooms, always do, though he never could bring himself to admit this to anyone. And he knew that though he wanted to get married, and though in all probability this very attractive girl would make an ideal wife, he, even were he not in love with Kitty Shcherbatsky, would as much be able to marry this girl as to fly into the sky. This awareness marred the pleasure he expected from his visit to Sviazhsky.

It was the first thought that occurred to him when he received Sviazhsky's letter inviting him to a hunt. However, he decided that he had no reason whatsoever to suspect Sviazhsky of harboring such thoughts about him, so he accepted the invitation. Moreover, deep within his heart he wanted to try himself, to test once more his feelings toward this girl. Life in Sviazhsky's household was most pleasant, and Sviazhsky himself, the best kind of a zemstvo member that Levin had ever known, always proved highly interesting to him.

Sviazhsky was one of those people who always aroused Levin's wonder. The reasoning of such men, very logical, though never independent, followed its own path, and their lives, unusually well defined and steadfast in direction, followed a totally independent course, almost always contradictory to their reasoning. Sviazhsky's opinions were unusually liberal. He despised the nobility and believed that most of the noblemen secretly favored serfdom, though out of fear they did not express their opinions openly. He considered Russia a lost land, like Turkey, and the government of Russia so bad that he did not even permit himself ever to criticize its acts seriously. But at the same time he held the position of marshal of the nobility, which he filled in an exemplary way, and when traveling he always put on the cap with its red band and cockade. He believed that a decent existence was possible only abroad, where he went at every opportunity, and at the same time he conducted in Russia a complex modern farming enterprise, and with the greatest interest followed and knew well everything that happened in Russia. He believed that the Russian moujik in his mental development was still in the transitional stage between ape and man, and at the same time at the zemstvo meetings he shook hands with the moujiks more willingly than anyone else and listened to their opinions. He was a freethinker, yet he was preoccupied with the problem of improving the state of the clergy and of decreasing the number of parishes, and at the same time he strove to have the church remain in his village.

On the feminine question he sided with the radical advocates of complete freedom for women and particularly for their right to work, yet his relationship with his wife was such that everybody admired their devoted, childless family life. And he arranged his wife's life in such a manner that she did not have to do anything, nor could she do anything but share her husband's efforts to spend their time in the most happy and enjoyable way.

Had it not been Levin's habit to see the best in every person, he would neither hesitate to define Sviazhsky's character nor would he have any difficulty in doing so. He would say to himself, He is either a fool or a knave, and everything would have become clear. But he could not use the word "fool," because Sviazhsky was not only a clever but a very learned man who regarded his learning with unusual modesty. There was no subject in which he was not versed, but he displayed his knowledge only when he was pressed to do so. Still less could Levin say that he was a knave because undoubtedly Sviazhsky was an honest, good, intelligent person who was always cheerful and active, whose work was highly esteemed by all those around him, and who never could or would consciously do anything wrong.

To Levin, Sviazhsky and his life always remained a living enigma. He tried to understand him but he could not.

They were friends, so Levin permitted himself to question Sviazhsky, trying to unearth his basic views on life; but his efforts were in vain. Every time Levin tried to penetrate beyond the open anteroom doors leading into Sviazhsky's mind, he noticed Sviazhsky's slight embarrassment. His face would betray a hardly noticeable anxiety, as if he feared that Levin might understand him, and he would rebuff Levin cheerfully and good-naturedly.

Now, after his disappointment in his work, the visit to Sviazhsky was giving Levin particular pleasure. The sight of these two happy doves, satisfied with themselves and everyone else, and of their cozy nest, affected him happily. Moreover, in his present state of dissatisfaction with his life, he was anxious to learn Sviazhsky's secret, the one that rendered his life so clear, so well defined, so cheerful. In addition, Levin knew that at the Sviazhsky's he would meet the landowners of the neighborhood, and he was now particularly eager to talk to them, to listen to their conversation about farming, harvesting, hiring help, and so on. These subjects, Levin knew, were looked upon as unworthy, but to Levin they alone seemed important. Perhaps this was not important, thought Levin, in the days of serfdom, or is not important in England. In both cases we deal with stable conditions for farming. But here in Russia, after all the profound changes, the single most important problem at present is in what way these conditions can be settled.

The hunt did not turn out as well as Levin had hoped. The marsh had dried up, and there were no double snipe at all. In a whole day's hunt he bagged only three birds, but, on the other hand, he developed a ravenous appetite, as he always did when hunting, and he found himself in excellent spirits and in the state of mental animation that always accompanied his vigorous physical exertions. During the hunt, when it seemed to him that he was not thinking about anything, he recalled several times the old man and his family, and this impression, it seemed, demanded not only his attention but the resolution of some problem connected with it.

Two landowners who had arrived on some guardianship business were present at the evening tea, and an interesting conversation ensued, as Levin had expected.

Levin was seated with the hostess at the tea table and had to converse with her and her sister-in-law, who was seated opposite him. The hostess was a round-faced, fair-haired lady of medium height, sparkling with dimples and smiles. Levin tried to find the key in her to the important enigma her husband represented to him. But his thoughts could not flow with complete freedom, for he was painfully embarrassed. This painful embarrassment was the result of his being seated opposite the sister-in-law, who was wearing a dress that, it seemed to him, she had put on especially for his benefit and had a trapezoidal décolletage exposing her white bosom. In spite of the fact that her bosom was very white, or perhaps because of it, this quadrangular décolletage prevented Levin from thinking clearly. He imagined, in all probability erroneously, that this décolletage had been made on his account. He considered that he had no right to look at it and tried not to look at it, but he felt guilty for the very fact that the décolletage had been made. It seemed to Levin that he was deceiving someone, that he had to explain something, which, however, in no way could be explained. He therefore kept blushing and felt uneasy and embarrassed. His embarrassment communicated itself to the pretty young lady. But the hostess, it seemed, did not notice it and deliberately drew her into the conversation.

"You believe," she said, continuing the conversation they had started, "that my husband can find no interest in anything Russian. On the contrary; he enjoys himself abroad but never as much as here. Here he feels that he's in his own milieu. He's so busy, and he has the gift of being interested in everything. By the way, have you visited our school?"

"I've seen it. . . . It's the little house covered with ivy, isn't it?"

"Yes, it is Nastia's enterprise," she said, indicating her sister.

"Do you yourself teach?" asked Levin, trying to look past the décolletage, but feeling that wherever he looked in her direction he would see it.

"I myself have taught and still do, but we have an excellent teacher. And we have introduced physical education."

"No, thank you, no more tea," said Levin. He felt that he was discourteous, but could no longer endure this conversation. He blushed and rose. "I hear a very interesting conversation there," he added, and he walked over to the host and the two landowners at the other end of the table. Sviazhsky was seated at the table sideways. One hand leaned on the table, toying with his cup; he gathered his beard in the other hand, raised it to his nose and released it, as if smelling it. His shining black eyes looked straight at the excited, gray-mustached landowner and, evidently, he was amused by his words. The landowner complained of the peasants. Levin saw clearly that Sviazhsky knew a reply to all the landowner's complaints, one that would at once demolish the substance of his speech. His position, however, did not permit him to give such an answer, and he listened to the landowner's ridiculous speech not without pleasure.

The gray-mustached landowner obviously was an inveterate advocate of serfdom, an old country dweller, and an enthusiastic gentleman farmer. Levin noticed signs of this in his dress—in his old-fashioned, shabby coat, which he evidently was not accustomed to wearing; in his clever, scowling look; in his flowing Russian speech; in his imperious tone, obviously acquired through long experience; and in the resolute movements of his large, handsome, tanned hands which displayed only one ring, a wedding ring on his fourth finger.

27

"IF ONLY I WEREN'T sorry to leave everything that had been built up . . . at the cost of so much toil, I would give up everything, sell out, and would go away, like Nikolai Ivanovich, to listen to *The Beautiful Helène*," said the landowner, a pleasant smile brightening his old intelligent face.

"But you don't do it," said Nikolai Sviazhsky. "There must be a reason."

"There is one reason: I live in a house, neither bought nor

rented. And there is still hope that the peasants will come to their senses. Otherwise, just think of it, this drunkenness and debauchery! All of them live apart now, have neither horse nor cow. They almost die of starvation, but try to hire them, and they will only damage everything, and even summon you to the justice of the peace."

"Then you yourself may complain to the justice of the peace," said Sviazhsky.

"I complain? Never in my life. It would create such an uproar that I would regret my complaint. Take, for instance, the mill. They took their advance and left. And what did the justice of peace do? He acquitted them. Our only hope is the volost court and the village elder. He'd give them a whipping as in the old times. If it weren't for that, you'd have to leave everything and run to the end of the world."

Obviously the landowner was provoking Sviazhsky, but Sviazhsky not only did not mind it, he apparently was amused by his words.

"But we do our farming without having recourse to such measures," he said with a smile. "Levin, I, and he."

He indicated the other landowner.

"Yes, Mikhail Petrovich is doing well, but ask him how he does it. Is this rational farming?" asked the landlord, ostentatiously displaying the word "rational."

"My method is simple," said Mikhail Petrovich. "Thank God, all I have to do is to have the money ready to pay the peasants' fall taxes. They come to me and beg me, 'Help us, little father.' Well, they are my neighbors, and I feel sorry for them. I pay the first third and tell them, 'Remember, lads, I have helped you and you must help me when I need you for oat sowing, hay making, and at harvest time,' and we settle how much each will have to do. Of course, some of them have no conscience."

Levin, who had long been aware of these patriarchal ways, exchanged looks with Sviazhsky and interrupted Mikhail Petrovich, turning again to the gray-mustached landowner.

"And what is your solution?" he asked. "How should we do our farming now?"

"It has to be done Mikhail Petrovich's way: either share half the crops with the moujiks or rent the land to them. This can be done, but in this way the general wealth of the country is being wasted. Whereas the land, when worked by the serfs and well-managed, yielded ninefold, now under the half-crop arrangement it yields threefold. Emancipation has ruined Russia."

Sviazhsky looked at Levin, his eyes smiling, yet with a hint of mockery. But Levin did not find the landowner's words ridiculous, for he understood them better than he had understood Sviazhsky. Many of the arguments that the landowner continued to expound, trying to show how emancipation had ruined Russia, seemed to him quite true, new, and incontrovertible. Evidently the landowner spoke his own thoughts—a rare occurrence—thoughts that had not been formed by him out of a desire to occupy his idle mind, but had ripened in the setting of his secluded country life and that he had pondered thoroughly.

"The fact is, if you please, that progress is always achieved by acts of authority," he said, evidently trying to show that he was not a stranger to learning. "Take the reforms of Peter, Catherine, Aleksandr. Take the history of Europe. It is even truer with the progress made in agriculture. Even the potato had to be introduced by force. Even the old-style plow was not always with us. It was introduced, perhaps, in the early ages of our history, and certainly by force. In our times, under serfdom, we, the landowners, introduced improvements into farming: drying kilns, threshing machines, and manure carting. We introduced these by our authority. At first the peasant resisted, then they followed our way. But now, with the emancipation, all authority has been taken away from us, and our farming, while it has reached a high level, is bound to sink to a most savage, primitive state. That's how I see it."

"But why? If it is done rationally, can't you still conduct it through hired help?"

"I have no authority. May I ask you through whom I will conduct it?"

There it is, the working force, the main element of agriculture, thought Levin.

"Through hired labor."

"The laborer doesn't want to work well, to use good equipment. The laborer knows only one thing—how to get roaring drunk—and then he will damage everything you put into his hands. He'll overwater the horses; he'll ruin the new harness; he'll steal your iron-rimmed wheel and sell it for a drink; he'll drop a bolt into a threshing machine and break it. Everything that isn't to his liking makes him sick. This is why the level of farming has sunk so low. The land is deserted, overgrown with weeds or distributed among the moujiks. Fields that produced a million measures now produce only a hundred thousand, and, in general, wealth has decreased. If they had done the same thing, but responsibly. . . ."

And again he began to expound his plan for emancipation, which could have avoided all the failures.

Levin was not interested in it, and when the landowner had finished, Levin reverted to his first statement, addressing Sviazhsky and trying to elicit from him a serious expression of his opinion.

"It is quite true that the level of farming is going down, and that with our existing relationship with the laborers it is impossible to conduct rational farming profitably," he said.

"I don't agree," answered Sviazhsky, now serious. "All I see is that we don't know how to farm, and that, on the contrary, under serfdom our methods of farming were far from being at the highest level; they were at the lowest. We have no machines, no good stock, no proper methods of management, no accounting system. Ask a landowner and he will be unable to tell you what brings him profit and what doesn't."

"Italian bookkeeping," the landowner said sarcastically. "But count as you will, if they damage everything, there will be no profits."

"Why should they do all this damage? True, they'll break your wretched threshing machine, your miserable Russian treadmill, but they will not break my steam threshing machine. They will ruin your Russian jade—what do you call that breed? The pull-the-tail breed—for you have to pull the jade by the tail, but if you bring in Percherons or other good breeds, they won't ruin them. The same goes for the rest. We must raise our standards for agriculture."

"But where does one get the money, Nikolai Ivanovich? It's good for you to talk, but I have to support a son in the university, and the smaller ones are still in school. Percherons are not for me."

"There are banks for this."

"To see my last possession go under the hammer? No, thanks."

"I don't agree that we must and can raise our standards for agriculture," said Levin. "I've been kept busy at it, I have the means for it, but I haven't been able to accomplish anything. I don't know of what use banks would be. I, for one, lost money on everything I invested in my estate: I lost money on the stock and I lost on the machines."

"That's true," confirmed the gray-mustached landowner, laughing with genuine satisfaction.

"And I'm not the only one," continued Levin. "I could mention all the landowners who use improved methods of farming. All of them, with rare exceptions, conduct their business at a loss. But tell me, is your farm profitable?" asked Levin, and at once he noticed the flash of fear he always saw when he tried to penetrate beyond the foyer of Sviazhsky's mind.

Actually, Levin did not ask this question in good faith. Only a short while ago, at tea, his hostess had told him that this summer they had invited a German from Moscow, a specialist in accounting, who for five-hundred rubles had examined their farm and found that they were losing over three-thousand rubles a year. She did not remember exactly how much, but the German evidently had figured it out to the last kopeck.

The landowner smiled at this question about Sviazhsky's profits, for he obviously knew how little profit the estate of his neighbor, a marshal of the nobility, was bringing him.

"Perhaps it isn't profitable," answered Sviazhsky. "This only proves that either I'm a bad manager, or that I spend too much capital on increasing the land's rental value."

"Oh, rental value!" Levin cried in horror. "Perhaps they have it in Europe, where the land improves with the amount of labor spent on it. But all our land deteriorates as it is worked; it's being used up, and therefore with us rental value does not exist!"

"No rental value? It's an economic law."

"Then we are exempt from the law. This rental value does not explain anything for us; on the contrary, it makes things more complicated. No, tell me, how can the theory of rental value—"

"Would you like to have some curdled milk? Masha, bring us some curdled milk and raspberries," he asked his wife. "The raspberries are lasting unusually long this year."

In the best frame of mind, Sviazhsky rose and stepped aside, evidently believing that at that point the conversation had come to an end, whereas Levin thought that it had only begun.

Left by his companion, Levin continued his conversation, addressing himself to the landowner. He tried to prove to him that all their difficulties stemmed from an unwillingness to learn the nature and the habits of the laborer. But, like everyone else who forms his own opinions in seclusion, the landowner was reluctant to share another person's views and was partial to his own. He insisted that the Russian moujik was a pig and loved his piggishness, and that only authority could bring him out of his piggishness, whereas no such authority existed.

"We should use the stick," he insisted, "but we have grown so liberal that instead of using the thousand-year-old stick we leave it to the lawyers. And when the worthless, stinking moujiks go to jail, there they are fed excellent soup, and the number of cubic feet of air for their use is carefully measured."

"Why," asked Levin, trying to return to the main problem, "do you think we couldn't find a relationship with the working force, under which work would be most productive?"

"You could never do it with the Russian people! You don't have the authority," replied the landowner.

"But how else could new conditions be created?" asked Sviazhsky. He had eaten the curdled milk; now he lit a cigarette and joined the disputants. "All possible relationships with the working force have been studied and defined," he said. "A relic of barbarism, the primitive community with mutual responsibility, is falling apart; serfdom has been abolished, and only free labor remains, with its definite and available forms, which we must accept. One cannot avoid using the hired man, the day laborer, and the farm hand."

"But Europe is dissatisfied with these forms."

"She's dissatisfied, looks for new ones, and probably will find them."

"That's what I am saying," said Levin. "Why shouldn't we, for our part, look for them?"

"Because it would be tantamount to seeking new methods of railroad building. The methods exist; they've already been worked out."

"But what if they don't suit us, if they are absurd?" asked Levin.

And again he saw the expression of fear in Sviazhsky's eyes.

"Yes, we like to brag that we've found what Europe is seeking. I know all this, but if you'll excuse my asking, are you aware of all that Europe has accomplished in the problem of the organization of workers?"

"No, I know very little about it."

"The best minds of Europe are now taken up with this problem. The Schultze-Delitsch view. . . . Then this immense literature on the labor problem, the most liberal Lassalle tendency—Mulhausen's system—this is already a fact, as you probably know."

"I know something about it, but only vaguely."

"No, you only say so. Most probably you know it as well as I. Of course, I'm not a professor of sociology, but I have been interested in these problems, and if they interest you, you should study them."

"Well, what was their conclusion?"

"I'm sorry. . . ."

The landowners rose, and Sviazhsky saw them to the door, once more checking Levin's unpleasant custom of attempting to pry behind the anteroom of his mind.

28

LEVIN WAS UNBEARABLY bored that evening in the company of the ladies. Never before had he been so disturbed by the thought that his present dissatisfaction with his work was the result not of his personal state of affairs but of the general conditions which existed in Russia. He realized that establishment of some sort of relationship with the laborers, under which they might work as they did for the moujik whom he had visited on the road, was not a dream but a problem that had to be solved. It seemed to him that these problems could be solved and that he was obliged to try to solve them.

He said goodbye to the ladies and promised to remain all next day in order to ride with them to the government forest to view an interesting landslide. Before retiring, Levin stopped in his host's study for some books on the labor problem which Sviazhsky had promised him.

Sviazhsky's study was an enormous room furnished with shelves of books, a heavy writing desk in the middle of the room, and a round table with a lamp surrounded by a star-shaped display of the latest newspapers and magazines in different languages. There was a filing cabinet next to the desk, with gold-colored labels on the drawers designating their various contents.

Sviazhsky reached for his books and sat down in the rocking chair.

"What are you looking at?" he asked Levin, who had stopped at the round table, browsing through the magazines.

"Oh yes, there's a very interesting article in that one," said Sviazhsky, referring to the magazine which Levin held in his hands. "As it turns out," he added with gay animation, "the chief perpetrator of the partition of Poland was not really Frederick the Great. As it turns out. . . ."

And with his usual clarity he related in brief these new, very important and interesting findings. Though Levin was now mostly preoccupied with his thoughts about his farm, he asked himself as he was listening to his host, What goes on inside him? And why is he interested in the partition of Poland? When Sviazhsky had finished, Levin unconsciously asked, "Well, what of it?" There was nothing to it. The only interesting thing was that something had "turned out." But Sviazhsky did not explain and found it unnecessary to explain why he was interested in it.

"Yes, I was very interested in the angry landowner," Levin said with a sigh. "He is clever, and there's a great deal of truth in what he says."

"Oh, you're mistaken. He favors serfdom secretly and inveterately, like all of them," said Sviazhsky.

"But you are their leader. . . ."

"Yes, but I lead them in another direction," Sviazhsky said, laughing.

"Here's what concerns me," said Levin. "He's right when he says that our kind of farming, rational farming, is a failure, and that only two kinds of farming prosper: that based on usury, as with that quiet one, or the most primitive. Whose fault is it?"

"Our own, of course. On the other hand, it isn't true that it's a failure. It's a success with Vasilchikov."

"The mill—"

"But I still don't know why you're so surprised. Both the material and moral levels of the peasants are so low that they are obviously bound to oppose anything that seems alien. In Europe, rational farming succeeds because there the peasants are educated. Therefore we have to educate our peasants, and that is the solution."

"But how will you educate them?"

"To educate them we need three things: schools, schools, and schools."

"But you yourself spoke of the low material level of the peasants. Then of what use would the schools be?"

"You know, you remind me of the story of the advice given to a sick man. 'You should try a laxative,' they told him. 'I have, and it made it worse.' 'Then leeches.' 'I have, and it made it worse.' 'Well, then pray to God.' 'I have, and it made it worse.' The same holds for you and me. When I speak of political economy, you say worse. When I mention socialism —worse. Education—worse."

"But how could schools help?"

"They could develop in him new demands."

"This I could never understand," Levin objected heatedly. "How could schools help the peasant improve his material conditions? You say that schools and education will develop in him new demands. It would be worse, because he wouldn't be able to satisfy them. And I could never understand how knowledge of addition, subtraction, and the catechism could help him to improve his material conditions. The other evening I met a peasant woman with a baby and asked her where she was going. 'I've been to the wise woman. My boy suffers from crying spells. I took him to be cured.' I asked her how the wise woman had treated the sickness. 'She set the baby on the hen roost and said some words.'"

"There you've said it yourself. To prevent her from taking the baby to be cured on the hen roost, you need—" Sviazhsky said with a gay smile.

"Oh, no!" Levin said with annoyance. "To me this cure is like curing the peasant with schools. The peasant is poor and ignorant. We see it as clearly as the woman sees that her child is sick, for it keeps crying. But how schools can cure the ills of poverty and ignorance is as incomprehensible to me as how hens on their perch can cure a sick child. You have to treat the cause of his poverty."

"Well, at least here you agree with Spencer, whom you dislike so much. He, too, claims that education may be a consequence of better standards of living, greater comforts and more frequent ablutions, as he says, but is not a result of learning to read and count."

"Well, I'm very glad or, on the other hand, very sorry that I've agreed with Spencer, but I've known something for a long time. Help will come not from schools, but from economic improvement, which will make the peasant richer and will give him more leisure; then he will have schools too."

"But all over Europe education is now compulsory."

"And do you yourself agree with Spencer on this point?" asked Levin.

But fear flashed in Sviazhsky's eyes, and he said with a smile:

"That's a great story about the crying spells. Did you really hear it yourself?"

Levin realized that he would never uncover the bond between this man's life and his thoughts. Evidently Sviazhsky was not at all concerned with the conclusions to which his reasoning might lead him. All that interested him was the process of reasoning itself. But he was displeased when this process of reasoning brought him to a dead end. This was the only thing that bothered him, and he avoided it by switching the conversation to some pleasant and cheerful topic.

Levin was very much moved by the impressions of that day, beginning with the impression made on him by the moujik whom he had visited on the road. That visit, it seemed, had served as a foundation for all his thoughts and impressions of that day. Some of the thoughts the charming Sviazhsky harbored were for public use only. And though he evidently held some other basic views on life, which he kept hidden from Levin, he took his place with the crowd whose name was legion and who led public opinion with expressions alien to his thoughts. That embittered landowner's opinions, painfully born out of his own life, were true, but he was wrong in his enmity toward a whole class of people, the best class in Russia. Levin himself was dissatisfied with his work and vaguely hoped to correct all that was wrong. All these impressions blended into a feeling of inner uneasiness and an expectancy of imminent solution.

Alone in his room, lying on the spring mattress, which bounced unexpectedly every time he moved his arms or legs, Levin did not fall asleep for a long while. Nothing of his conversation with Sviazhsky interested Levin, though many clever things had been said to him. But the landowner's arguments called for careful consideration. Unconsciously, Levin recalled all his words and in his mind corrected the replies which he had made.

Yes, I should have told him, "You say that our farming does not prosper because the moujik hates all new improvements, and that we need authority to introduce them. You would be in the right if farming could not go on at all without these improvements. But it does go on, and only where the laborer acts according to his habits, as at the old man's place on the road. Our general dissatisfaction with farming, yours and ours, proves that the fault lies either with us or with the laborers. We have long persisted in our way, the European way, without consideration of the nature of the labor force. Let us realize that we deal not with ideal labor, but with the *Russian moujik* and his instincts, and let us do our farming accordingly. Just imagine," I should have told him, "that you do your farming as the old man does, that you've devised means to get the laborers interested in the productivity of their labor, and have found the modicum of improvements which they will accept. Then, without exhausting the soil, you would reap twice or three times as much as before. Divide your gains in half, giving one half to the laborers; both your share and the laborers' will be bigger. But to accomplish this you must lower the standards of farming and get the laborers interested in the productivity of their work. How to do it is a matter of detail, but there's no doubt that it can be done."

Levin became greatly agitated by this thought. He could not sleep half the night, pondering the details required to realize his plan. He had not intended to leave the following day, but now he decided that he would go home early in the morning. In addition, the sister-in-law in her low-cut gown aroused in him a feeling akin to shame and repentance for some wrongdoing. And, most important, he had to leave without delay so as to have time to offer the moujiks his new plan before the winter sowing, and to sow under the new terms. He decided to make a complete change in all his former methods of farming.

29

THE FULFILLMENT OF Levin's plan presented many difficulties. But he did his utmost, and though he had attained only what he could rather than what he desired, he could now believe, without deceiving himself, that the effort was worth while. One of the chief difficulties was that work on his farm was already going on; it could not be stopped and begun anew, and this machinery had to be reshaped while in motion.

On the evening of his arrival he informed the steward of his plans. The steward, obviously pleased, agreed with him that what they had been doing until now was nonsense and a waste of money. The steward insisted that he had said the same thing a long time ago, but that nobody would listen. Yet, when it came to Levin's offer—to become a partner, together with the laborers, in the whole business of the estate, the steward looked very unhappy, gave no direct answer to the offer, and quickly turned to the urgent business of the morrow: they had to bring in the last sheaves of rye and had to send men to replow the fields. Levin felt that he had picked the wrong time.

When he approached the moujiks on the same subject, offering them land on new terms, he met the same principal difficulty. They were so busy with their daily work that they had no time to think over the advantages and disadvantages of his offer.

The simplehearted moujik Ivan, the cowherd, seemed to understand clearly what Levin was offering—that he and his family were to have a share in the gains from the cattle yard—and fully sympathized with this idea. But when Levin tried to impress him with the forthcoming profits from it, an expression of uneasiness and regret appeared on Ivan's face, and he apologized that he had no time to listen to him. He suddenly discovered that he had some urgent work to do: to toss the hay into the stall with the pitchfork, or to bring in water, or to clean out the stalls.

The other difficulty he met lay in the peasants' unshakable conviction that the landowner could have no other aim but to despoil them as neatly as possible. They were fully convinced that his real purpose (regardless of what he might say) would always be hidden in what he left unsaid. And they themselves, in their discussions, spoke a great deal without ever revealing their main purpose. Moreover (Levin felt that the choleric landowner was right), in any agreement into which they entered, the peasants' first and unchangeable demand was that they must not be forced to accept any new, improved methods of farming and the use of new implements. They admitted that the new-style plow was better than the old one, that the scarifier did the work more quickly, but they found thousands of reasons why neither of them should be used. And though Levin was certain that the standards of farming had to be lowered, he regretted giving up improvements that were so obviously advantageous. In spite of all these difficulties, he had achieved his aim, and by the fall his plan was working, or so it seemed to him.

At first, Levin thought of handing over the whole farm, as it was, to the moujiks, laborers, and the steward on the new partnership terms, but he soon became convinced that this was impossible, and he decided to divide up the farm. The cattle yard, orchard, vegetable garden, meadows, and fields he divided into several parts, each division forming a separate unit. The simplehearted Ivan, the cowherd, seemed to Levin to understand the plan best of all. He organized an artel, consisting chiefly of members of his family, and became a partner in the cattle yard. The distant field, which for eight years had lain fallow, was taken over on the new terms by six moujik families with the help of the clever carpenter, Fyodor Rezunov, and the moujik Shuraev took over all the vegetable gardens on the same terms. The rest was still managed as before, but these three units formed the beginning of a new system, and Levin was fully absorbed in them.

True, in the cattle yard the work did not proceed any better than before, and Ivan was strongly opposed to keeping the cows in warm sheds or to making butter of cream, insisting that cows kept in the cold required less fodder, and that butter made of sour cream brought more profit. He asked for wages, as under the old system, and was not concerned at all that the money he received was actually not wages, but advance payments on his share of the profits.

True, Fyodor Rezunov's group did not plow the field twice with the new-style plows, as had been agreed, under the pretext that time did not permit it. True, the moujiks of this group referred to their land not as partnership land but as land rented for half the crop, though they were holding it under the new terms. And many a time the moujiks of this artel and Rezunov himself told Levin, "Why don't you take your rent money? It would be better for you and for us." In addition, these moujiks, under different pretexts, delayed building a cattle yard and threshing barn on this land, as had been agreed, and procrastinated until winter arrived.

True, Shuraev intended to sublet the vegetable gardens to the moujiks in small lots. Evidently he completely and, it seemed, deliberately misunderstood the terms on which the land had been given to him.

True, when he was talking to the moujiks, explaining all the advantages of this enterprise, Levin often felt that the moujiks listened only to the sound of his voice and that they firmly believed that whatever he said they would not let him deceive them. He felt it particularly when he spoke to the shrewdest of the moujiks, Rezunov, and he noticed a twinkle in Rezunov's eye, which showed clearly that he was ridiculing Levin and was fully confident that if anybody was going to be fooled, it would not be he, Rezunov.

In spite of all this, Levin thought that the enterprise was succeeding, and that by keeping strict accounts and remaining persistent in his demands, he would prove to them the eventual advantages of this arrangement, and that then the enterprise would go on its own.

These matters, combined with the management of the rest of the farm, which still remained in his hands, and his work in his study on his book, kept Levin so busy the entire summer that he had almost no time for hunting. At the end of August he heard that the Oblonskys had left for Moscow; he learned it from the man who brought back his saddle. He felt that by his discourtesy in not responding to Daria Aleksandrovna's letter, something he could not think of without blushing, he had burned his bridges and would never visit them again. He had done the same to Sviazhsky, leaving without saying goodbye. Nor would he visit him again. It did not matter to him now. Nothing in his life had ever occupied him so much as his present work on the reorganization of his farm. He read all the books Sviazhsky had given him and ordered the ones he did not have. He read books on political economy and on socialism as they related to this subject and, as he had expected, found nothing in them bearing on his present enterprise. In books on political economy, in Mill, for instance, the first book that he studied with great zeal, hoping at any moment to find the answer to his question, he found laws based on the state of European economy. But he could in no way see why these laws should be considered universal, since they could not be applied to Russia. He found the same in books on socialism: either beautiful but unrealistic fantasies, which had attracted him during his college years, or corrections and repairs to be made in the state of affairs that existed in Europe, but with which Russian agriculture had nothing in common. Political economy taught that the laws governing the growth of European wealth were universal and incontrovertible. The theory of socialism asserted that the development of economy in accordance with these laws led to disaster. But neither the one nor the other gave any answer, not even the faintest hint of one, to the question of how he, Levin, and all the Russian moujiks and landowners might employ the millions of their working hands and dessiatines of land most productively for the common welfare.

But once he had tackled this job, he conscientiously read everything relating to it, and he intended to go abroad in the fall to study it at first hand, so that the same thing might not happen to him in dealing with this problem as had happened so often with other problems. No sooner would he begin to understand someone else's ideas and express his own than he would suddenly be told, "And what about Kaufmann, Jones, Dubois, Micelli? You haven't read them? Read them. They've worked out this problem."

He now saw clearly that he had nothing to learn from Kaufmann and Micelli. He knew what he wanted. He knew that Russia had excellent land, excellent laborers, and that in some cases, as with the moujik on the road, the laborers and the land were very productive. But in most cases little was accomplished by investing capital in farming, as they did in Europe, and the only reason for this was that the laborers liked to work and worked well when they did it in their own way, that their resistance was not accidental but constant, and was based on the peasant's nature. He believed that the Russian nation, whose destiny was to people and till the immense, unoccupied stretches of land until all of it was settled, used methods fit for this purpose, and that these methods were not so bad as they were usually considered. And he wished to prove it theoretically in his book and in practice on his farm.

30

BY THE END of September, the timber for building the cattle yard on the land allotted to the artel had been carted in, the butter had been sold, and the profits divided. In practice the work on the farm proceeded successfully or, at least, so it seemed to Levin. But he also had to clarify the problem theoretically and to finish his book, which, according to Levin's dreams, would not only revolutionize political economy but would completely demolish it and lay the foundation for a new science—one that dealt with the peasant's relationship to the land. To do this he had only to travel abroad to study at first hand everything that had been done there on the subject and to find convincing proof that everything done there was inappropriate. Levin was waiting only for the wheat to be delivered, to get the money and to go abroad. But rainy weather had set in, and this prevented the bringing in of the grain and potatoes still remaining on the field and stopped all the other work, even the delivery of the wheat. The roads turned into quagmires, two mills were washed out, and the weather was growing still worse.

On the morning of September 30th, the sun appeared, and Levin, hoping that the weather had settled, began to make final preparations for his trip. He ordered the wheat put into sacks, sent the steward to the merchant to fetch the money, and he himself went around the farm to give his final orders before departing.

After he had attended to all his affairs, Levin returned home in the evening. Soaked by streams of water, which trickled from his leather coat down his neck and into his boots, he still felt most vigorous and animated. The bad weather had grown worse toward evening. His horse, thoroughly soaked and shaking his ears and head, was so painfully lashed by the sleet that he walked sideways. But Levin, wrapped in his bashlyk, felt comfortable, and looked around happily at the muddy streams running along the ruts, at the drops hanging from every bare branch, at the white blotch of sleet remaining unmelted on the boards of the bridge, and at the succulent, still fleshy leaves of the elm, fallen in a thick layer around the bare tree. In spite of the gloom of the surroundings, he felt particularly animated. His conversation with the moujiks in the remote village proved that they had begun to get used to the new system. The old innkeeper, in whose house he stopped to dry off, evidently approved of Levin's plan and offered to join the partnership in cattle buying.

I've only to be persistent in striving for my goal, and I'll attain it, thought Levin, and the goal is worth the work and toil. This isn't something personal; it's a matter of the general welfare. All the economy and, most important, the state of all the people must change completely. In the place of poverty —general wealth and prosperity; in the place of discord— harmony and community of interests. In a word, a bloodless revolution, the greatest revolution, first on a small scale in our country, then in the province, in Russia, in the whole world. For a just idea can't help but bring forth fruit. Yes, it's a goal that's worth the effort. And it doesn't matter that I'm only Kostia Levin, who, in a black tie, came to a ball, was refused by Princess Shcherbatsky, and now seems to himself so miserable and worthless. That proves nothing. I'm sure that Franklin felt as worthless and had as little confidence when he thought about himself. That doesn't matter. And he, too, probably had his Agafia Mikhailovna in whom he confided his plans.

It was already dark when Levin, engrossed in these thoughts, approached the house.

The steward had gone to the merchant and had returned with part of the money for the wheat. The agreement with the innkeeper was concluded, and on his way the steward had learned that the harvested grain remained in the fields everywhere, and their own ungathered hundred and sixty shocks were as nothing when compared with others.

After dinner Levin, as usual, sat in an armchair with a book, and while reading, continued to think about the trip he was going to make in connection with his book. That day all the meaning of his undertaking had seemed particularly clear to him, and in his mind he formed whole paragraphs, which expressed the essence of his thoughts. I must write it down, he thought. This should form the short introduction, which I considered unnecessary earlier. He rose to go over to the desk, and Laska, who had been at his feet, also got up, stretched, and looked at him as though asking where to go. But there was no time to write now, for the foremen came for their orders, and Levin went into the entrance hall to see them.

After he had given them his instructions concerning the next day's work and received all the moujiks who had come to see him on business, Levin returned to his study and sat down to work. Laska lay under the table. Agafia Mikhailovna sat at her usual place with her knitting.

After writing for a while, Levin, with sudden and unusual vividness, recalled Kitty, her refusal, and their last meeting. He rose and began to pace the room.

"Cheer up," said Agafia Mikhailovna. "Why do you stay at home? Why don't you go to the spa, as you decided to do?"

"I'm going the day after tomorrow, Agafia Mikhailovna. I have to finish my work."

"What work? Haven't you done enough for the moujiks? Even now they say, 'Our master will be rewarded by the Czar!' It's strange that you care so much for the moujiks."

"I don't care for them. I do everything for myself." Agafia Mikhailovna knew all the details of Levin's farming projects. Levin often expounded to her all the fine points of his ideas and frequently argued with her and disagreed with her views. But now she completely misunderstood his words.

"Of course, you must first of all think of your soul," she said with a sigh. "Parfin Denisich, for instance, though illiterate, died a death anyone would envy," she said, referring to a house servant who had died recently. "He received communion and extreme unction."

"I'm not talking about that," he said. "What I mean is that I do it for my own gain. I profit more when the moujiks work harder."

"Yet no matter what you do, you can get nothing from an idle fellow. If he has a conscience, he'll work; if not, nothing will help."

"But you yourself say that Ivan has been tending the cattle with more care."

"I must say," replied Agafia Mikhailovna, and her words evidently were not accidental but closely followed her line of thought, "I must say that you have to get married, that's what you have to do!"

Agafia Mikhailovna mentioned the same thing he had been thinking just a while ago, and it upset and offended him. Levin frowned and without replying, resumed his work, turning over in his mind all this thoughts regarding the significance of his work. Only occasionally did he hear, in the silence, the sound of Agafia Mikhailovna's knitting needles, and again he frowned as he recalled what he did not wish to recall.

At nine o'clock there was the sound of a bell and of a carriage thudding along the muddy road.

"Here are some visitors. You won't be lonesome any longer," said Agafia Mikhailovna, rising and going over toward the door. But Levin ran out ahead of her. His work had stalled, and he was glad to have any guest at all.

31

WHEN LEVIN HAD run halfway down the staircase, he heard a familiar slight cough in the entrance hall, but his steps muffled the sound, and he hoped that he was mistaken. Then he saw the gaunt, raw-boned, familiar figure in full view, and though it seemed that he could not be mistaken, he still hoped that he was, and that this gaunt man, who was taking off his fur coat and clearing his throat, would not be his brother Nikolai.

Levin loved his brother, yet his presence always distressed him. And now, under the influence of the thoughts that had been occupying him, and of Agafia Mikhailovna's remark, he was in a hazy, confused state of mind, and his brother's visit seemed to him all the more oppressive. Instead of a cheerful, healthy stranger who, he hoped, would distract him from his present state of confusion, he had to welcome his brother, who understood him thoroughly and who would make him reveal his most intimate thoughts and open his heart. And this he did not like to do.

Angry with himself for such base thoughts, Levin hurried into the entrance hall. As soon as he came close to his brother, the feeling of personal disappointment vanished immediately and changed into a feeling of pity. Though his brother Nikolai had earlier looked frightfully sick and haggard, he had grown still thinner and looked even worse now. He was a skeleton covered by skin.

He stood in the entrance hall, pulling his muffler off his long, thin, twitching neck, all the while smiling a strange, pitiful smile. On seeing this humble and meek smile, Levin felt a lump rise in his throat.

"Here I am, come to visit you," said Nikolai in a hollow voice, without taking his eyes off his brother for a moment. "I've wanted to come for a long time, but I wasn't well. But now I feel much better," he said, smoothing his beard with his long, thin hands.

"Yes, of course," replied Levin. And he grew still more frightened when, as he kissed his brother, his lips felt the dryness of his body and he saw, from close up, his large eyes, sparkling strangely.

A few weeks earlier Levin had written to his brother that he had sold the small part of their patrimony that had still remained undivided, and that his brother could now receive his share, about two thousand rubles.

Nikolai said that he had come to get this money, but mainly to visit the ancestral nest and, like the hereos of old, by touching the ground to regain his strength, which he needed for the work he had to do. In spite of his more pronounced stoop, in spite of his unusual thinness, accentuated by his height, his movements were quick and abrupt as always. Levin took him to his study.

Nikolai changed clothes with particular care, something that had not been his custom, then combed his thin, straight hair and, smiling, came upstairs.

He was in the kindest and gayest mood, such as Levin had often seen in him in childhood. He even mentioned Sergei Ivanovich without rancor. He exchanged a few joking remarks with Agafia Mikhailovna and inquired about the old servants. The news of Parfin Denisich's death affected him strongly. An expression of fear appeared on his face, but he soon recovered.

"Well, he was quite old," he said, and then changed the subject. "Look, I'll stay with you a month or two, and then back to Moscow. You know, Miakhkov promised me a position, and I'm going to work. I'll now arrange my life quite differently," he continued. "You know, I've parted with that woman."

"With Maria Nikolayevna? Why?"

"She was a horrible woman! She caused me a great deal of trouble." But he did not relate what that trouble was. He could not tell him that he had driven Maria Nikolayevna away because she made weak tea and chiefly because she had treated him as a sick man. "And then, in general, I intend to change my life completely. Of course, I, like everyone else, have done many foolish things, but my lost fortune is the least of my regrets. The main thing is to be well, and my health, thank God, has improved."

Levin listened, vainly searching for something to say. Evidently Nikolai felt the same way. He began to ask his brother about his affairs, and Levin was glad to talk about himself, for he could do so without pretense. He told his brother of his plans and of his work.

His brother listened, but evidently he was not interested.

The closeness, the affinity of these two men was so great that their slightest movements, the tone of their voices, communicated more than their words.

They both, now, were occupied with one thought alone, overshadowing all else—Nikolai's sickness and approaching death. But neither of them dared speak about it, and since they did not speak about the only thing that preoccupied them, everything they said was false. Never had Levin felt so happy as when the evening ended and it was time to go to sleep. With no stranger, at no official visit, had he ever been so artificial and insincere as he had been that evening. And his awareness of this artificiality and his repentance for it caused him to be still more artificial. He wanted to cry over the approaching death of his beloved brother, but he had to listen to and take part in a conversation about how he would live.

It was damp in the house, and only one room was heated. Levin, therefore, placed his brother in his own bedroom, behind a partition.

His brother lay down, and whether he slept or not, he tossed like a sick man, coughed, and when he could not expectorate, he grumbled. Sometimes he sighed heavily and said, "Oh, my God!" At other times, when the phlegm choked him, he protested, "Oh, hell!" Levin was long in falling asleep, listening to his brother. His thoughts were most diverse, but they all had one ending—death.

For the first time, death, the unavoidable end to everything, confronted him with irresistible force. Death was not now as remote as it had appeared to him before. It was present here, in his beloved brother, who moaned in his sleep and, according to his habit, invoked indifferently God and the devil. Death was in himself, too; he felt it. Whether it would come today, tomorrow, or within thirty years, what did it matter? And what this inevitable death was, he not only did not know, not only had never contemplated, but could not and dared not contemplate.

"Here I am, working, striving to accomplish something, but forgetting that everything will come to the same end—death."

He sat on the bed in the darkness, crouching and hugging his knees. He kept thinking, his breath labored under the pressure of his thoughts. But the more he became engrossed in his thoughts, the more clearly he saw that it was undoubtedly true that he really had overlooked, in life, one small circumstance; he had forgotten that death would come; everything would end; that it was not worth while undertaking anything; and all this could not be helped. Yes, it was terrible, but it was true.

But I'm still alive. Then what must I do now? What must I do? he asked in despair. He lit a candle, rose gently, went up to the mirror, and began to examine his face and hair. Yes, there were gray hairs around his temples. He opened his mouth. His back teeth had begun to decay. He bared his muscular arms. Yes, there was much strength in them. But even Nikolinka's body had once been healthy, and now he was breathing there only with the remnants of lungs. He suddenly recalled how in childhood they had gone to sleep together, and had waited for Fyodor Bogdanych to leave the room. Then they tossed pillows at one another and laughed so loudly and unrestrainedly that even fear of Fyodor Bogdanych could not suppress the overflowing, bubbling consciousness of life's happiness. "And now this sunken, hollow chest . . . and here am I, blind to what will happen to me and why. . . ."

"Kha! Kha! Oh, hell! Why are you fussing? Why don't you sleep?" his brother's voice called to him.

"I don't know. Insomnia."

"But I slept well, and I no longer perspire. Here, feel the shirt. Isn't it dry?"

Levin felt it, went back behind the partition, and blew out the candle, but it was a long time before he fell asleep. Now that the problem of how to live had become somewhat clearer, he was confronted with the new, insoluble problem of death.

Yes, he's dying, he thought, and will die by spring, but how can he be helped? What can I say to him? What do I know of it? I had even forgotten its existence.

32

LEVIN HAD LONG observed that those whose presence was embarrassing on account of their excessive deference and meekness very soon become unbearable because of their excessive demands and nagging. He felt that such would be the case with his brother. Indeed, Nikolai's gentle mood did not last long. On the very next morning he turned irritable and nagged his brother unceasingly, hitting at his most sensitive spots.

Levin felt guilty, but he could not help it. He knew that if they were to cease pretending and to talk, so to say, heart-to-heart, saying only what they really felt and thought, then they would just look into each other's eyes, and Konstantin would simply say, "You're going to die, you're going to die, you're going to die," and Nikolai would just reply, "I know that I'm going to die, but I'm afraid, I'm afraid, I'm afraid." That is all they would say if they talked heart-to-heart. But they could not behave in this way. Therefore Konstantin tried to do what he had tried to do all his life and could not, something that, as he had observed, others did well, and without which life could not go on. He tried to say not what he really thought, and each time he felt that his words sounded false, that his brother was aware of it, and that it irritated him.

On the third day, Nikolai provoked his brother into revealing his plans, and not only set about to condemn them but deliberately confused them with communism.

"You've just borrowed the ideas of others, distorted them, and now try to apply them where they are inappropriate."

"But I assure you that my theory has nothing in common with them. They reject the principle of private property, capital, or inheritance, and I, without rejecting this primary stimulus," (Levin hated himself for using such words, but since he had become engrossed in his work, he unconsciously began to use foreign words more frequently) "I aim only to regulate labor."

"That's just the point. You've borrowed somebody else's idea, taken away its substance, and want to assure us that it's something new," said Nikolai, jerking his head angrily.

"But my idea has nothing in common—"

"They at least," interrupted Nikolai, with a sarcastic smile, his eyes flashing angrily, "fascinate you with their, I might say, geometrical clarity and certitude. Perhaps it is a utopia. But let us assume that all the past may be turned into a *tabula rasa:* private property and family are abolished, and labor prevails. But your theory has nothing—"

"Why do you confuse the two? I never was a communist."

"But I was, and I find that though it's premature, it's rational and has a future, as was the case with early Christianity."

"I only believe that the labor force should be examined

from a naturalist's point of view, that it should be examined, its nature studied, and—"

"That's entirely unnecessary. This force itself finds proper forms of activity in accordance with the state of its development. We had slavery everywhere, then the metayer system, we have the half-share system, the lease, farm laborers; what else do you want?"

These words suddenly chafed Levin, for deep in his heart he feared that they were true, that he indeed wanted to maintain a balance between communism and the established forms, and that this was scarcely possible.

"I'm seeking a means for making the laborer work productively, both for himself and for me," he replied heatedly. "I want to arrange—"

"You don't want to arrange anything. Just as you've done all your life, you want to show that you are different, that though you exploit the moujik, you do it in accordance with an ideal."

"Well, if that's what you think, then let's stop here," replied Levin, feeling the muscle of his left cheek twitch uncontrollably.

"You have no convictions and never had any. All you wish is to appease your vanity."

"All right, leave me alone."

"I will, and none too soon. The devil take you! I'm sorry I came."

Levin's efforts to calm him were in vain. Nikolai did not want to listen to him and obdurately insisted that it would be better for them to part; and Konstantin saw that his brother simply could not endure his life any longer.

Nikolai was almost ready to leave when Konstantin once again came over to him and awkwardly asked to be forgiven if he had insulted him in any way.

"Ah, magnanimity!" said Nikolai with a smile. "I'll give you the satisfaction of knowing that you're right, if you wish to have it. You're right, but I'm leaving just the same."

Just before leaving, Nikolai kissed him, and suddenly, with a strangely serious look at his brother, said, "Just the same, bear no grudge against me, Kostia." His voice trembled.

These were his only sincere words. Levin understood that these words meant, "You see and know that I'm very sick, and perhaps we'll never see each other again." Levin understood and tears sprang to his eyes. He kissed his brother again, but he could not speak, nor did he know what to say.

The third day after his brother's departure, Levin went abroad. During the trip he met Shcherbatsky, Kitty's cousin, who was surprised to find Levin so depressed.

"What's the matter?" Shcherbatsky asked.

"Nothing, there is just so little joy in life."

"Little joy? Here, come with me to Paris instead of going to your Mulhausen. You'll see how gay it can be there."

"No, for me it's all over. For me it's time to die."

"How strange!" Shcherbatsky said with a laugh. "I'm just beginning to live."

"I myself thought so, not so long ago, but now I know that I'll soon die."

Levin expressed what he had recently come to believe sincerely. Everywhere he saw only death or the approach of death. But this only increased his interest in the work he had undertaken. Somehow he had to live through his life until death arrived. Darkness hid everything from his sight. But precisely because of this darkness, he felt that his work was his only guideline through the darkness, and he clutched at it and held on to it with all his might.

PART FOUR

═══════════════════════════════════════

1

THOUGH THE KARENINS, husband and wife, continued to live under the same roof and met every day, they were total strangers. Aleksei Aleksandrovich had established a rule: to see his wife every day so as to give the servants no cause for suspicion, but he avoided dining at home. Vronsky never visited Aleksei Aleksandrovich's home, but Anna met him elsewhere, and her husband knew it.

The situation was painful for all three, and none of them could have endured even one day of this situation but for the hope that it would change and that this was but a temporary, painful difficulty which would pass. Aleksei Aleksandrovich expected that this passion would pass, as everything else does, that all this would be forgotten, and that his name would remain undisgraced. Anna, on whom this situation centered, and who suffered most of all, endured it because she not only expected but was fully convinced that all this would soon straighten out and become resolved. She had no idea at all how the situation would be resolved, but she was convinced that it would happen very soon. Vronsky, unconsciously yielding to her, also waited for something that, independent of him, would resolve all these difficulties.

In the middle of the winter, Vronsky spent a very boring week. He had been selected to attend a visiting foreign prince and had to show him all the sights of Petersburg. Vronsky himself was a person of imposing presence; moreover, he was skilled in the art of dignified courtesy and was accustomed to the company of such people. For these reasons he was selected to attend the prince. But to Vronsky the assignment seemed very burdensome. The prince did not want to omit anything in Russia that he might be questioned about on his return home. In addition, he was eager to enjoy the pleasures of Russia as fully as possible. Vronsky had to guide him in both these pursuits. In the morning they saw the sights of the city, in the evenings they enjoyed the national pastimes. The prince enjoyed a good health that was unusual even for a prince. Through exercise and good care of his body, he had acquired such vitality that, in spite of the excesses in which he indulged, he looked fresh as a large, shiny, green Dutch cucumber. The prince traveled a great deal and believed that access to national pastimes was one of the main advantages of the speed of present-day travel. He visited Spain and there he serenaded and became familiar with a damsel who played the mandolin. In Switzerland he killed a mountain goat. In England, dressed in a red coat, he galloped over fences and, to make good a bet, he killed two hundred pheasants. In Turkey he visited a harem, in India he rode an elephant, and now in Russia he wanted to taste the genuine Russian pleasures.

Vronsky, who was, in a manner of speaking, his chief master of ceremonies, found it very hard to choose among all the various kinds of pleasures offered to him by the Russians. These included trotting horses, Russian pancakes, bear hunting, troikas, gypsies, and revelries accompanied by the Russian custom of smashing dishes. The prince became imbued with the Russian spirit with unusual ease; he smashed traysful of dishes, held gypsy girls on his knee and, it seemed, kept asking, "Is there still something else, or does the Russian spirit consist only of this?"

Actually, of all Russian pleasures the prince most loved French actresses, a ballet dancer, and white-label champagne. Vronsky was accustomed to the company of princes, but whether because he himself had changed of late, or because he was too close to this prince, the week seemed to him terribly burdensome. All this week he constantly felt like a man who had been selected to attend a dangerous madman, feared this madman, and at the same time, because of his closeness to him, feared for his own sanity. Vronsky always felt compelled to maintain constantly the tone of strict official courtesy, so as to avoid being insulted. The prince treated with scorn those very people who, to Vronsky's surprise, did their utmost to offer him the pleasures of Russia. Vronsky blushed more than once with indignation when he heard the prince's opinions of the Russian women whom he wished to study. But the main reason that the prince seemed to him particularly offensive was that in the prince Vronsky unconsciously saw himself. And what he saw in that mirror he did not find flattering. It was a very stupid, very self-assured, very healthy, immaculately groomed man, and nothing else. True, he was a gentleman, and Vronsky could not deny it. He was poised with his superiors and did not court their favor, felt free and easy with equals, and with those below him he was contemptuously good-natured. Vronsky himself was such and considered it a great virtue, but his status was lower than the prince's, and he resented the latter's contemptuously good-natured attitude toward him.

A stupid ox! Am I really like him? he thought.

So, a week later, before the prince's departure for Moscow, when Vronsky came to say goodbye to him and to receive his thanks, he was happy that he had been relieved of this unpleasant situation and of this unflattering mirror. They parted at the railroad station after returning from a bear hunt, where for a whole night they had watched an exhibition of Russian daredeviltry.

2

WHEN HE returned home, Vronsky found a note from Anna. It read, "I am ill and unhappy. I cannot leave the house, nor can I bear any longer not seeing you. Come in the evening. At seven o'clock Aleksei Aleksandrovich leaves for the council meeting and will stay there until ten." For a moment he was surprised that she had asked him to come to her house in spite of her husband's prohibition, but he decided that he would go.

That winter Vronsky had been promoted to colonel, was no longer quartered with the regiment, and lived by himself. After breakfast, he lay down on the divan and within five minutes the memories of the vile scenes he had witnessed the last few days jumbled and intermixed with images of Anna and of the moujik who had located the bear and who had played such an important part in the bear hunt. Vronsky fell asleep. When he woke up, it was dark, and trembling with fear, he hurriedly lit a candle. What was it? he thought. What? What was the dreadful thing I saw in my dream? Oh, yes. That moujik, the bear hunter, small, dirty, with an unkempt beard. I believe he was bending over and doing something, and suddenly he said some strange words in French. Yes, that's all I saw in my dream, he said to himself. But why was it so frightening? He again vividly recalled the moujik and the incomprehensible French words he had uttered, and a chill of terror ran down his spine.

What nonsense! thought Vronsky and he glanced at the clock.

It was already half-past eight. He rang for his servant, dressed in a hurry, and went out on the porch. He completely forgot about his dream and was troubled only because he was late. Approaching the entrance to the Karenins', he looked at his watch and saw that it was already ten minutes to nine. A tall, narrow coach, with a pair of gray horses, stood near the entrance. He recognized Anna's coach. She's about to leave for my house, thought Vronsky. It would have been better. I don't like to go into this house. But it doesn't matter. I'm not one to hide, he said to himself and, with the manner of a man who in childhood learned that he had no reason to be ashamed, Vronsky alighted from his sleigh and approached the door. The door opened, and the doorman, holding a wrap, hailed the coach. Vronsky, who did not usually notice details, this time observed the surprise with which the doorman glanced at him. In the doorway itself, Vronsky almost collided with Aleksei Aleksandrovich. The light from the gas bracket fell directly upon the bloodless, worn face under the black hat, and upon the white tie, sparkling from underneath the beaver coat. Aleksei Aleksandrovich fixed his motionless, dull eyes upon Vronsky. Vronsky bowed, and Aleksei Aleksandrovich, compressing his lips, tipped his hat and passed. Vronsky saw that he sat down in the carriage without turning around, accepted his wrap and the binoculars through the window, and disappeared. Vronsky went into the entrance hall. He frowned, and his eyes flashed with anger and disdain.

What a situation! he thought. If he would only show some fight, defend his honor, I could act, I could express my feelings; but this weakness or baseness. . . . He makes me feel like a cheat, something I've never wanted to be and don't want to be.

Since his conversation with Anna in Vrede's garden, Vronsky's thoughts had profoundly changed. He had unconsciously submitted to Anna's weakness. She, yielding all of herself to him, expected him alone to decide their fate and agreed in advance to any decision. He, therefore, had long since given up the idea that this love affair might end as he had first thought it would. His ambitious plans again had lost their importance, and knowing that he had departed from that area of his activities where everything was clearly defined, he completely yielded to his emotion, and this emotion bound him to her more and more closely.

While still in the entrance hall, he heard her retreating steps. He understood that she had been waiting for him and listening, and now she had returned to the drawing room.

"No!" she exclaimed, seeing him, and with the first sound of her voice, tears appeared in her eyes. "If it continues like this, it will happen much, much sooner."

"What, my friend?"

"What? Here I am waiting, suffering, an hour, two. . . . No, I won't. . . . I cannot quarrel with you. I'm sure you couldn't come. No, I will not. . . ."

She put both her hands on his shoulders and gave him a long, deep, enraptured, and at the same time searching look. She studied his face to make up the time since she last had seen him. As at every meeting with him she blended the picture of him she had created in her imagination (incomparably superior, but in reality impossible) with what he actually was.

3

"Did you meet him?" she asked, as they sat down at the table under the lamp. "It was your punishment for being late."

"But how could it happen? He was supposed to be in the council."

"He went there, but he came back, and now he's left for somewhere else. But it's all right. Don't talk about it. Where were you? Still with the prince?"

She knew all the details of his life. He wanted to tell her that he had not slept all night and had fallen asleep only in the morning, but looking at her happy and animated face, he felt ashamed. And he told her that he had had to go somewhere and submit a report about the prince's departure.

"But is it all over now? Has he left?"

"Thank God, it's all over. You'd scarcely believe how unbearable it was."

"But why? This is the usual life for you young men," she

said, with a frown. And without looking at Vronsky, she reached for her crocheting on the table and began to disentangle the crochet hook.

"I've long since given up that kind of life," he said, surprised at the changed expression on her face and trying to understand what it meant. "And I confess," he added, his smile displaying his even white teeth, "that this whole week I've been observing this life as in a mirror, and I wasn't pleased with what I saw."

She held the crocheting in her hands, but did not crochet, and looked at him with a strange, unfriendly luster in her eyes.

"This morning Liza came to see me—they're still not afraid to visit me, in spite of Lydia Ivanovna," she interjected, "and she told me about your Athenian party. How vile!"

"I just wanted to say that—"

She interrupted.

"Was it Thérèse, whom you knew before?"

"I wanted to say—"

"How vile you men are! Can't you understand that a woman can't forget this kind of thing," she said, growing more excited and thus revealing the cause of her anger. "And particularly a woman who is not given to know your life. What do I know? What have I known?" she asked. "Only what you tell me. And how do I know that you're telling me the truth?"

"Anna, you are insulting me. Don't you believe me? Haven't I told you that I have no thoughts that I wouldn't reveal to you?"

"Yes, yes," she said, evidently trying to rid herself of her jealous suspicions. "But if you only knew how hard it is for me. I believe you, I believe you. . . . What were you saying?"

But for the moment he could not recall what he had wanted to say. These fits of jealousy, into which she was falling more and more often of late, frightened him, and, though he tried to conceal it, they alienated him from her, though he knew that the cause of her jealousy was her love for him. Many times he told himself that her love was his happiness, that she loved him as only a woman can for whom love outweighs all the other blessings of life, and yet he was much farther from happiness now than when he had followed her on her journey from Moscow. Then he had thought that he was unhappy, but that happiness lay before him. But now he felt that his greatest happiness was already behind him. She was not at all as she had been when he first saw her. Both spiritually and physically she had changed for the worse. Her figure had thickened, and when she spoke about the actress, her face became distorted with spite. He looked at her as a man looks at a flower he has plucked; the flower is now withered, and he can scarcely see in it the beauty for which he had plucked and wasted it. Nevertheless, he felt that when his love for her had been greater, he could have torn it from his heart if he had strongly desired to do so, but now, as at this moment, when it seemed to him that he did not love her, he knew that his bond with her was unbreakable.

"Well, what were you going to tell me about the prince? I've driven away the devil, I've driven him away," she added. The devil was their name for jealousy. "What were you going to tell me about the prince? Why was it so hard on you?"

"Oh, it was unbearable," he said, trying to recover the thread of his thoughts. "He doesn't improve much, as you get to know him better. He could be described as nothing but a well-cared-for animal, one of those that receive prizes at exhibitions," he said, with an air of annoyance which aroused her curiosity.

"But why?" she objected. "After all, he has traveled a great deal, and he is well educated."

"This is a completely different kind of education. It is their own kind. He evidently received his education just so he could scorn it as they scorn everything except animal pleasures."

"But all of you love these animal pleasures," she said, and again he noticed her gloomy look, which avoided his eyes.

"Why are you defending him?" he asked, smiling.

"I'm not defending him, and it doesn't concern me at all. But I think that if you disliked these pleasures, you could avoid them. But it gives you pleasure to gaze at Thérèse, dressed as Eve. . . ."

"Again, again the devil!" said Vronsky, taking her hand, which she had placed on the table, and kissing it.

"Yes, I can't help it! You don't know how worn out I was, waiting for you. I believe that I'm not jealous. I trust you when you are here with me, but when you are away from me and live your own unknown life. . . ."

She turned aside, at last managed to disentangle the crochet hook, and with her index finger began to throw over, one after the other, loops of white wool which sparkled in the light of the lamp. Her slender wrist, in its embroidered cuff, bent quickly and nervously.

"Well, where did you meet Aleksei Aleksandrovich?" she suddenly asked in a forced tone.

"We came face to face in the doorway."

"Did he greet you like this?"

She pulled a long face, her eyes half-closed, quickly changed her expression, folded her hands, and Vronsky suddenly saw on her beautiful face the same expression with which Aleksei Aleksandrovich had greeted him. He smiled, and she laughed gaily with the pleasant, throaty laugh that was one of her greatest charms.

"I absolutely refuse to understand him," said Vronsky. "If only after your confession at the country house he had broken up with you, challenged me to a duel . . . but this I cannot understand. How can he endure this situation? It's obvious that he's suffering."

"He?" she said derisively. "He's completely content."

"Why do we all have to suffer when everything could be so fine?"

"All but he. Don't I know him? Don't I know how thoroughly false he is? Could anyone who had any feelings live as he lives with me? He neither understands nor feels anything. Could any man with any feelings live under the same roof with his depraved wife? Could he talk to her? Address her as 'thou'?"

And unconsciously she mimicked him again. " 'Thou, *ma chère*, thou, Anna!' "

"He's not a man, he's not a human being, he's a puppet. No one but I know that. Oh, were I in his place, I long since would have killed a wife like me, would have torn her to pieces instead of repeating, 'Thou, *ma chère*, Anna.' He's not a man, he's a bureaucratic machine. He doesn't understand that I'm your wife, that he's a stranger, that he's not wanted. . . . But let's not talk about him any longer."

"You're wrong, my dear, you're very wrong," said Vronsky, trying to calm her. "But it doesn't matter. We'll not talk about him. Tell me, what have you been doing? How do you feel? What hurts you, and what did the doctor say?"

She looked at him with ironic gaiety. Evidently she had recalled some more ridiculous and preposterous traits of her husband's, and was waiting to demonstrate them.

But he continued:

"I imagine you're not ill; it's just your condition. When will it be?"

The ironic gleam in her eyes suddenly died, and her previous expression was replaced by a different smile—an awareness he did not share, and a gentle sadness.

"Soon, soon. You said that our situation is unbearable, and that it must be resolved. If you could only know how hard it is on me, how much I would give to love you openly and without fear! Then I would no longer suffer nor would I torment you with my jealousy. And it will happen soon, but not the way we think."

And at the thought of how it would happen, she felt such pity for herself that tears appeared in her eyes, and she could not go on. She put her hand on his sleeve. The white hand and its rings gleamed under the lamp.

"It won't happen as we think. I didn't want to tell you, but you made me. Soon, soon, everything will be settled, we will all find our peace and will suffer no longer."

"I don't understand," he said, although he did.

"You asked me when? Soon. And I won't survive it. Don't interrupt me," she continued hurriedly. "I know it, I'm sure of it. I'll die, and I'm glad that I'll die and bring relief both to you and to myself."

Tears flowed from her eyes. He bent toward her hand and began to kiss it, trying to hide his agitation which, he knew, was entirely without foundation, but which he could not control.

"It's the best way out," she added, pressing his hand firmly. "It's the only way left for us."

He collected himself and raised his head.

"What nonsense! What utter nonsense you are talking!"

"No, it's true."

"What is true?"

"That I'll die. I dreamt about it."

"You did?" asked Vronsky and at once he recollected his dream about the moujik.

"Yes, I had a dream," she said. "I had it a long time ago. I dreamt that I ran into my bedroom to get something or to find out about something, you know how it happens in a dream," she continued, her eyes wide with fright, "and I saw something standing there, in the corner of the bedroom."

"What nonsense! How can you believe—"

But she did not let him interrupt. What she was saying was too important to her.

"And that something turned around, and I saw that it was a

moujik, with an unkempt beard, a little, frightful moujik. I wanted to run away, but he bent over his bag, fumbling in it with his hands. . . .'"

She imitated the moujik, rummaging in his bag. Terror was written on her face. And Vronsky, remembering his own dream, felt the same terror filling his heart.

"He searched and muttered in French very rapidly, you know, with the French r, '*Il faut le battre le fer, le broyer, le petrir.* . . .' I was frightened, and I wanted to wake up, and I did . . . but I woke up in my dream. And I began to think of what this meant. And Kornei said to me, 'You'll die in childbirth, in childbirth, little mother. . . .' And I woke up."

"What nonsense, what nonsense!" said Vronsky, but he realized how completely unconvincing his voice sounded.

"But let's not talk about it. Ring the bell and I'll order tea. Wait, it won't take long, I—"

She stopped abruptly. Instantaneously, the expression on her face changed. Terror and agitation suddenly gave way to an expression of calm, serious, and blissful attention. He could not understand what that change meant. She had felt new life stirring within her.

4

AFTER MEETING Vronsky on the entrance porch, Aleksei Aleksandrovich left for the Italian opera, as he had intended. He sat through two acts and saw everyone whom he had to see. When he returned home, he carefully examined the coat rack and, finding no military coat there, went to his room, as usual. But contrary to his habit, he did not go to sleep; instead he paced up and down his study until three o'clock in the morning. Indignant with his wife, who refused to observe propriety and to comply with his only provision—not to receive her lover in her house—he could find no rest. She had not complied with his demand and he had to punish her and carry out his threat—to demand a divorce and to take her son from her. He knew all the difficulties that would be involved in this matter, but he had said he would do it, and now he had to carry out his threat. Countess Lydia Ivanovna hinted to him that this would be the best way out of his situation, and of late the practice of divorce suits had been so perfected that Aleksei

Aleksandrovich believed that he could surmount all the difficulties. And, as misfortunes never come singly, Aleksei Aleksandrovich's project concerning the organization of the minorities and the irrigation of Zaraisky Province had caused him so much trouble in the office of late that he had become extremely irritable.

He did not sleep at all that night, and his indignation, growing stronger all the time, reached its absolute limit toward morning. He dressed in a hurry. As though carrying a full vessel of indignation that he feared to spill lest, with the loss of it, he might lose the energy he needed for his interview with his wife, he went to her room as soon as he knew that she was up.

Anna, who thought that she knew her husband so well, was struck by his appearance as he entered the room. His forehead was wrinkled; his eyes stared gloomily straight ahead, avoiding her look; his lips were compressed tightly and scornfully. There was an air of determination and assurance in his walk, his movements, and in the tone of his voice, one that his wife had never known before. He entered the room without greeting her, walked up directly to her desk, and, taking the keys, opened the drawer.

"What do you want?" she cried.

"Your lover's letters," he answered.

"They're not there," she said, closing the drawer. But by this motion he understood that his guess was correct and, brusquely pushing aside her hand, he seized the folder in which, he knew, she kept all her important papers. She wanted to wrest it from him, but he pushed her away.

"Sit down! I want to talk to you," he said, putting the folder under his arm and holding it so tightly with his elbow that his shoulder rose.

Surprised and afraid, she looked at him in silence.

"I told you that I would not allow you to receive your lover in this house."

"But I had to see him for. . . ."

She stopped, for she could not invent any excuse.

"I'm not going into the details of why a woman must see her lover."

"I wanted; I just . . ." she said, flaring up. His rudeness provoked her and roused her courage. "Don't you realize how easy it is for you to insult me?" she asked.

"One can insult only an honest man or an honest woman, but

to tell a thief that he's a thief is only *la constantation d'un fait.*"

"This new trait—cruelty—I have not known in you until now."

"Do you call it cruelty when a husband gives his wife freedom and the continued protection of his name with the sole condition that she observe propriety? Is that cruel?"

"It's worse than cruel; it's vile, if you want to know," cried Anna, exploding with anger. She rose, ready to leave.

"No," he shouted in his shrill voice, which now rose a note higher than usual. Clutching her hand in his large fingers with such force that the bracelet left a red imprint, he forced her to sit down.

"Vile? If you want to use that word, it is vile to abandon a husband and a son for a lover and still eat the husband's bread!"

She bowed her head. Not only did she not tell him what she had told her lover yesterday, that *he* was her husband and that her husband was not wanted, but she did not even think about it. She realized how true his words were and only said softly:

"You cannot paint my situation any blacker than I myself see it, but why are you telling me all this?"

"Why am I telling it? Why?" he continued, still indignant. "Because I want you to know that since you did not comply with my wishes and did not observe propriety, I will take measures to bring this situation to an end."

"It will soon, very soon, come to an end anyway," she said, and at the thought of her approaching death, now so desirable, tears appeared in her eyes.

"It will end sooner than you and your lover think. You seek to satisfy your carnal passion—"

"Aleksei Aleksandrovich, it is not only ungenerous, it is even ignoble to hit someone when he is down."

"Yes, you think only of yourself, but the sufferings of the man who was your husband do not trouble you. It's of no concern to you that his whole life has been ruined, that he suffels . . ."

Aleksei Aleksandrovich spoke so rapidly that he stuttered and could not pronounce this word. At last he pronounced it *suffels.* This sounded funny to her and immediately she felt ashamed that anything should seem funny at such a moment. And for the first time, for an instant, she sympathized with him, put herself in his place, and pitied him. But what could she say or do? She bowed her head and remained silent. He, too, was silent for a while and then he spoke again, this time in a cool, less shrill voice, accenting his words, which he selected at random and which had no particular meaning.

"I have come to tell you . . ." he said.

She looked at him. No, I only imagined it, she thought, recalling the expression on his face when he struggled with the word *suffels*. Is it possible that a man with such dull eyes, so self-satisfied and composed, could feel anything?

"I can't change anything," she whispered.

"I've come to tell you that tomorrow I am leaving for Moscow and shall not return to this house. You will hear about my decision from my lawyer, to whom I will entrust the suit for divorce. My son will move to my sister's," said Aleksei Aleksandrovich, recalling with an effort what he wanted to say about his son.

"You need Seryozha to cause me pain," she said, looking at him with sullen eyes. "You don't love him. . . . Don't take Seryozha!"

"Yes, I have lost even my love for my son, because my loathing for you affects my feeling for him. Nevertheless, I will take him. Goodbye!"

He was about to leave, but she restrained him.

"Aleksei Aleksandrovich! Don't take Seryozha!" she whispered once more. "I have nothing else to say. Leave Seryozha until. . . . I will soon give birth to a child. Leave Seryozha with me!"

Aleksei Aleksandrovich's anger increased, and pulling his arm from her grasp, he left the room in silence.

5

THE WAITING room of the renowned Petersburg lawyer was crowded when Aleksei Aleksandrovich entered. There were three ladies: an old one, a young one and a merchant's wife, and three gentlemen: a German banker with a ring on his finger, a bearded merchant, and an angry official in uniform, with a decoration around his neck. To all appearances, they had been waiting for a long time. Two assistants were busy writing at their desks, their pens scratching. The writing implements, of which Aleksei Aleksandrovich was such a great admirer, were unusually fine. Aleksei Aleksandrovich could not help noticing this. One of the assistants, without rising, squinted and sullenly asked Aleksei Aleksandrovich:

"What can I do for you?"

"I want to see the lawyer."

"The lawyer is busy," the assistant answered sternly, pointing with his pen to the waiting people, and he continued to write.

"Couldn't he find time to see me now?" asked Aleksei Aleksandrovich.

"He has no time; he is always busy. Be kind enough to wait."

"Will you please give him my card," said Aleksei Aleksandrovich gravely, seeing that he was forced to reveal his identity.

The assistant took the card and, evidently disapproving of its contents, went through the doorway.

Aleksei Aleksandrovich approved of open courts in principle, but for some reasons, known to him as a high-ranking official, he did not approve of some of the details of their practice in Russia. He criticized them, but within the limits he had set for criticizing anything established by high authority. All his life he had spent in administrative posts; therefore, when he disapproved of something, his disapproval was tempered by his awareness that in general, mistakes are unavoidable and can be corrected. He disapproved of the conditions under which the lawyers were placed in the new courts. But until now he had had no dealings with lawyers and therefore his disapproval was only theoretical. Now, however, his disapproval gained strength through the unfavorable impression the lawyer's waiting room had made upon him.

"He will come out in a moment," said the assistant. And, indeed, within two minutes there appeared in the doorway the lean figure of an old jurist, who had been consulting with the lawyer, and the lawyer himself.

The lawyer was a small, thickset, bald man, with a dark reddish beard, light, bushy eyebrows, and a protruding forehead. He was as spruce as a bridegroom, from his necktie and double watch chain to his patent leather shoes. His face had a peasant cleverness, but his apparel was dandified and in bad taste.

"Come in, please," said the lawyer, turning to Aleksei Aleksandrovich. With a grave expression he let Karenin in and closed the door.

"Take a seat, please," he said, pointing to an armchair

alongside a desk laden with papers. He himself sat at the desk, rubbed his small hands together, their short fingers covered with white hair, and inclined his head sideways. But no sooner had he settled down when a moth flew over the desk. With an alacrity one would not expect of him, he spread his hands, brought them together to catch the moth, and resumed his former posture.

"Before I begin explaining my case," said Aleksei Aleksandrovich after he had observed the lawyer's movements with surprise, "I must stipulate that the case I must discuss with you will have to be kept confidential."

A faint smile stirred the lawyer's yellowed, drooping mustache.

"I wouldn't be a lawyer if I couldn't keep the secrets entrusted to me. But if you want to be convinced. . . ."

Aleksei Aleksandrovich glanced at his face and saw that the clever, gray eyes were laughing and already seemed to know all.

"Do you know my name?" continued Aleksei Aleksandrovich.

"I know you and, like all Russians," (he caught another moth) "I know of the great work you do," said the lawyer, bowing.

Aleksei Aleksandrovich sighed, gathering his courage. But once he had started, he continued in his squeaking voice, without embarrassment or hesitation, accentuating some of his words.

"I have the misfortune," began Aleksei Aleksandrovich, "of being a betrayed husband, and I wish to break legally my bonds with my wife. In other words, I wish to divorce her, but with the provision that our son does not remain with his mother."

The lawyer's gray eyes tried to refrain from laughing, but they danced with unrestrainable joy. Aleksei Aleksandrovich knew that he was witnessing not only the joy of a man who is about to engage in a profitable deal, but also his triumph and rapture; he saw a glitter in his eyes like the ominous glitter he had seen in the eyes of his wife.

"You want my help in getting a divorce?"

"Yes, exactly. But I want to inform you that perhaps I'm taking advantage of your kindness. I've come only for a preliminary conversation with you. I want a divorce, but I consider of great importance the way in which it may be obtained. It's very possible that if the method does not suit my requirements, I will refrain from any legal action."

"Oh, this is always the case," said the lawyer, "and everything will be done as you wish."

The lawyer lowered his gaze to Aleksei Aleksandrovich's legs, conscious that by his show of unrestrained glee he might offend his client. He glanced at a moth which flew past his nose, started after it, but restrained himself out of consideration for Aleksei Aleksandrovich's status.

"Though in general I am acquainted with the laws concerning these matters," continued Aleksei Aleksandrovich, "I would like to know the usual methods by which such cases are conducted in practice."

"Your wish is," replied the lawyer, without raising his eyes and not without pleasure entering the spirit of his client's proposal, "that I explain to you the methods by which your desire may be fulfilled."

And in reply to Aleksei Aleksandrovich's affirmative nod, he continued, only occasionally glancing at Aleksei Aleksandrovich's flushed face.

"According to our laws," he said in a tone indicating some disapproval of these laws, "a divorce, as you know, is permitted in the following cases. . . . Let them wait!" he said to his assistant, who showed his face in the doorway, but then he rose, said a few words to him, and resumed his seat. "In the following cases: physical defects of the spouses, then five-year desertion without communication," he said, counting them off on his short, hairy fingers, "then adultery." (This he pronounced with obvious pleasure.) "Following are the subdivisions," (he continued counting on his thick fingers, though obviously the cases and their subdivisions could not be classified together) "physical defects of the husband or the wife, then adultery committed by the husband or by the wife." Since he had used up all his fingers, he started over again and continued, "This is the theoretical aspect, but I presume that you've done me the honor of seeking my advice in order to learn of the practical application of the law. Therefore, on the basis of precedent, I must inform you that divorce cases are reduced to the following: I believe there are no physical defects? and this is not a case of desertion? . . ."

Aleksei Aleksandrovich inclined his head affirmatively.

"Then they are reduced to the following: adultery committed by one of the spouses and exposure of the guilty party by mutual consent, or, in the absence of such consent, involuntary exposure. I must tell you that the latter case occurs in practice very infrequently," said the lawyer and, glancing at Aleksei Aleksandrovich, he fell silent. He was like a pistol merchant who, having described to the buyer the advantages of each kind of weapon, leaves it to the buyer to make his choice. But Aleksei Aleksandrovich kept silent and therefore the lawyer continued, "The most usual, simple, and reasonable method, in my opinion, is adultery by mutual consent. I would not have allowed myself to say this were I speaking to an unenlightened person," said the lawyer, "but I presume that we understand such things."

Aleksei Aleksandrovich, however, was so disturbed that he could not at once understand the reasonableness of adultery by mutual consent, and his face mirrored his puzzlement. But the lawyer immediately came to his aid.

"Suppose two persons can no longer live together. If they both accept this fact, then the details and formalities are of no importance. And this is the simplest and most reliable method."

Aleksei Aleksandrovich now understood it clearly. But he had religious scruples that prevented him from accepting this method.

"This is out of the question in our case," he said. "One method only is admissible here: accidental detection, confirmed by letters which I have in my possession."

At the mention of letters, the lawyer compressed his lips and emitted a thin, condoling, yet contemptuous sound.

"If you please," he began, "cases of this kind are decided, as you know, by the department of religion. But the reverend fathers who decide these cases are eager to know all the particulars," he said, his smile showing that he approved of the priests' taste. "Letters, of course, can give partial confirmation; but proof must be obtained by direct means—by witnesses. And in general, if you will honor me with your confidence, then allow me to choose the necessary means. If you want results, you must accept the means."

"In that case . . ." began Aleksei Aleksandrovich, suddenly pale, but at this moment the lawyer rose and walked over to the door to talk to his assistant, who again had interrupted him.

"Tell her that we do not deal in cheap goods!" he said, and he returned to Aleksei Aleksandrovich.

On the way back to his seat, he deftly caught another moth. The upholstery will be in fine shape by summer! he thought with a frown.

"And so, you were pleased to say. . . ."

"I shall inform you in writing of my decision," said Aleksei Aleksandrovich, rising and leaning on the desk. After a short silence, he said, "From what you have told me I may then conclude that it's possible to obtain a divorce. I would also like you to let me know your fee."

"Everything is possible, if you give me full freedom of action," said the lawyer without replying to his question. "When may I expect to hear from you?" the lawyer added, moving toward the door, both his patent leather shoes and his eyes sparkling.

"In a week. And you will be good enough to advise me whether you will accept my case and let me know your fee."

"Very good, sir."

The lawyer bowed respectfully, escorted his client to the door and, when alone, abandoned himself to his feeling of joy. He felt so gay that, contrary to his rule, he made a concession to the lady who had bargained with him, and he stopped pursuing the moths, for he decided that the following winter his furniture would have to be redone in velvet, as at Sigonin's.

6

ALEKSEI ALEKSANDROVICH had gained a brilliant victory at the meeting of the commission on August 17th, but the results of the victory backfired. A new Commission for the Thorough Examination of the Life of the Minorities had been formed and, thanks to Aleksei Aleksandrovich's prompting, was dispatched to its destination with speed and vigor. Within three months their report was presented. The life of the minorities was examined from the political, administrative, economic, ethnographic, material and religious points of view. To every question the proper answer was given, and these answers left no room for doubt, for they had not been developed by human thought, always fallible, but each one was the product of official activity. All the answers resulted from official data and reports of governors and bishops, which were based on reports of county chiefs and county priests, which, for their part, were based on reports of volost offices and parish priests; therefore, all these answers left no room for doubt. For instance, all questions of why poor crops occur, why people cling to their creeds, and such questions, which could not be solved and would not be solved for centuries without the help of the official machinery, now received clear and positive answers. And the answers favored Aleksei Aleksandrovich's ideas. But Stremov, having been cut to the quick at the last meeting, on receipt of the commission's report, resorted to tactics which Aleksei Aleksandrovich had not anticipated. Stremov, carrying along with him several other members, suddenly switched to Aleksei Aleksandrovich's side, and not only ardently advocated that Karenin's propositions be carried out, but offered others of the same nature. These propositions, more extreme than had been anticipated in Aleksei Aleksandrovich's basic plan, were accepted, and only then did Stremov's tactics become obvious. The extreme nature of these propositions suddenly made them appear so foolish that at one and the same time statesmen, public opinion, clever ladies, and newspapers all attacked them, expressing their indignance at the propositions themselves and at their acknowledged author, Aleksei Aleksandrovich. Stremov stepped aside, pretending that he had but blindly followed Karenin's plan, and now he himself was surprised and indignant at what had been done. This undercut Aleksei Aleksandrovich. But, in spite of his failing health, in spite of his family troubles, Aleksei Aleksandrovich did not yield. The commission split. Some members, led by Stremov, claimed that they had been misled by the report of the investigating commission guided by Aleksei Aleksandrovich, and insisted that this report was nothing but nonsense and just a piece of paper. Aleksei Aleksandrovich and the other group, sensing danger in such a revolutionary attitude toward official papers, continued to uphold the findings of the investigating commission. This created confusion in the highest circles and even in society, and though this matter had aroused the interest of everyone, no one could understand whether the minorities actually lived in misery and faced ruin, or whether they were flourishing. This, and the contempt in which he was held on account of his wife's unfaithfulness, made Aleksei Aleksandrovich's position very precarious. In this situation, Aleksei Aleksandrovich made an important decision. To the surprise of the commission, he stated that he would ask permission to make a personal investigation in the field. On receipt of the permission, Aleksei Aleksandrovich left for the remote provinces.

Aleksei Aleksandrovich's departure caused a sensation, the more so because just before leaving, he officially returned his allowance for twelve horses, given him for the trip, along with the proper document.

"I find this very honorable on his part," Betsy remarked to Princess Miakhky. "Why should allowances be given for post horses, when, as everyone knows, there are now railroads everywhere."

But Princess Miakhky did not agree, and she was even annoyed by Princess Tverskoy's remark.

"It's all right for you to talk, with your untold millions," she said, "but I'm very pleased when, in the summer, my husband is sent on an inspection tour. The journey is good for his health and enjoyable, and I've made it a rule that this money pays for the upkeep of a carriage and coachman."

On his way to the remote provinces, Aleksei Aleksandrovich stopped in Moscow for three days.

On the day following his arrival, Aleksei Aleksandrovich started out on a visit to the governor-general. At the crossing of Gazetny Lane, where there is always a jam of coaches and cabs, Aleksei Aleksandrovich suddenly heard someone calling his name in such a loud and happy voice that he could not help but look around. On the corner of the sidewalk, in a short, stylish coat, with a small, stylish hat askew, his white teeth gleaming between his smiling red lips, gay, young and sparkling, stood Stepan Arkadievich, calling him with determination and persistence and demanding that he stop. Holding on with one hand to the window of a coach, which had stopped at the corner, and from which appeared a woman's head in a velvet hat and the little heads of two children, he smiled and waved the other hand at his brother-in-law. The lady smiled gently and also waved her hand to Aleksei Aleksandrovich. It was Dolly and her children.

Aleksei Aleksandrovich did not want to see anyone in Moscow, least of all his wife's brother. He tipped his hat and was about to continue on his way, but Stepan Arkadievich told his coachman to stop and ran up to him over the snow.

"Aren't you ashamed that you sent no word? When did you arrive? Yesterday I was at Dussot's and saw on the board

'Karenin,' but it didn't occur to me that it was you," said Stepan Arkadievich, pushing his head through the open window of the coach. "Otherwise I would have gone in. I'm so glad to see you!" he said, hitting one foot against the other to shake off the snow. "It's a shame not to let us know!" he repeated.

"I haven't had time; I'm very busy," Aleksei Aleksandrovich replied coldly.

"Come on over to my wife; she is so anxious to see you."

Aleksei Aleksandrovich removed the wrap which was tucked around his chilled feet and, alighting from the coach, made his way through the snow to Daria Aleksandrovna.

"What's the matter, Aleksei Aleksandrovich, why do you avoid us?" asked Dolly with a smile.

"I've been very busy. I'm very glad to see you," he said in a tone which plainly showed that he was sorry to see them. "How are you?"

"And how is my dear Anna?"

Aleksei Aleksandrovich muttered something and was about to leave. But Stepan Arkadievich stopped him.

"Here's what we'll do tomorrow. Dolly, invite him to dinner. We'll invite Koznyshev and Pestzov and will treat him with our Moscow intelligentsia."

"Please come," said Dolly. "We'll expect you at five or six o'clock, if you wish. How is my dear Anna? How long—"

"She is well," muttered Aleksei Aleksandrovich, frowning. "It was good to see you," he added, and he proceeded to his own coach.

"Will you come?" cried Dolly.

Aleksei Aleksandrovich said something, but Dolly could not hear it over the noise of the carriages.

"I'll drop in to see you tomorrow!" Stepan Arkadievich called after him.

Aleksei Aleksandrovich took his seat deep within the coach, so that he would not see or be seen.

"A queer person!" said Stepan Arkadievich to his wife and, glancing at his watch, he made a gesture in front of his face indicating his tender feelings for his wife and children, and then proceeded along the sidewalk with a youthful gait.

"Stiva! Stiva!" cried Dolly, blushing.

He turned around.

"You know that I have to buy coats for Grisha and Tania. Give me some money!"

"Never mind, tell him that I'll pay," and saying this he disappeared, cheerfully nodding to an acquaintance who rode by.

7

THE NEXT day was Sunday. Stepan Arkadievich dropped in at the Bolshoi Theater for the ballet rehearsal and handed Masha Chibisov the coral necklace he had promised her the day before. She was a pretty dancer who had recently joined the ballet with his help, and in the semidarkness behind the wings he managed to kiss her lovely face, which had brightened at the sight of the present. Besides giving her the coral necklace, he had to arrange to see her after the performance. He told her that he could not come at the beginning of the performance but promised to arrive toward the end of the last act and take her to supper. On the way back from the theater, Stepan Arkadievich stopped at the Okhotny Market and personally selected the fish and the asparagus for the dinner and by twelve o'clock he was at Dussot's, where he had to visit three people who, to his good fortune, were staying in the same hotel. They were Levin, who had stopped here after his recent arrival from abroad; his new chief, who had just been appointed to this high position and who was inspecting the Moscow office; and his brother-in-law Karenin, whom he wanted to bring home to dinner without fail.

Stepan Arkadievich enjoyed a good dinner, but he enjoyed even more giving a dinner party, small, but distinguished by the food, drinks and the selection of guests. He was greatly pleased by the prospect of that day's dinner. For food and drink there would be fresh-caught perch, asparagus, and, *la pièce de résistance*, excellent but simple roast beef, and appropriate wines. The list of guests comprised Kitty and Levin, and, to make it less obvious, a female cousin and the young Shcherbatsky in addition, and, *la pièce de résistance* among the guests, Sergei Koznyshev and Aleksei Aleksandrovich. Sergei Ivanovich was a Muscovite and philosopher, and Aleksei Aleksandrovich a practical man from Petersburg. And he also intended to invite the famous eccentric enthusiast, the liberal, garrulous musician and historian, a most charming youth of fifty, Pestzov, who would serve as sauce and garnish for Koznyshev and Karenin. He would provoke them and set them against each other.

The money he had received from the merchant as the second payment for the timber had not been spent yet. Of late, Dolly had been very good and kind, and the prospect of this dinner gladdened him in every respect. He was in the happiest frame of mind. But there were two somewhat unpleasant circumstances, both of them, however, drowned in the sea of good-natured gaiety which overflowed Stepan Arkadievich's heart. These two circumstances were as follows. First, when he had met Aleksei Aleksandrovich in the street on the previous day, he noticed that he was cold and stern with him. This expression on Aleksei Aleksandrovich's face, the fact that he had not informed them of his arrival, combined with rumors which he had heard concerning Anna and Vronsky, made Stepan Arkadievich believe that there was something wrong between husband and wife.

This was the first unpleasantness. The other cause for slight worry was his new chief. Like all new chiefs, he had already acquired the reputation of a terrible man, up at six o'clock in the morning, working like a horse, and demanding that his subordinates do likewise. Moreover, the new chief also had the reputation of having the manners of a bear, and, according to rumors, his opinions were entirely opposite to those of the former chief, which until now had also been Stepan Arkadievich's. On the previous day Stepan Arkadievich had come to work dressed in his uniform, and the new chief was very kind to him and spoke to him as to an old acquaintance. Therefore, Stepan Arkadievich considered it his duty to pay him a visit dressed in his morning coat. The thought that the new chief might not receive him kindly was that second unpleasant circumstance. But Stepan Arkadievich instinctively felt that everything would come right in the end. All of us are human; we're all sinners; then why be angry and quarrel? he thought as he entered the hotel.

"How are you, Vasili?" he asked as he walked through the hall, his hat askew, addressing a servant whom he knew. "Have you let your side whiskers grow? Is Levin in Number Seven? Show me the way please. And find out whether Count Anichkin" (the new chief) "will receive me."

"Very good, sir," replied Vasili with a smile. "It has been a long time since you favored us with a visit."

"I was here yesterday, but at the other entrance. Is this Number Seven?"

When Stepan Arkadievich entered, Levin and a moujik from Tver were standing in the middle of the room, measuring a new bearskin with a yardstick.

"Ah, did you kill it?" cried Stepan Arkadievich. "An excellent specimen. A she-bear? How are you, Arkhip?"

He shook hands with the moujik and sat at the edge of the chair without taking off his coat or hat.

"Take off your coat. Stay a while," said Levin, taking his hat.

"No, I have no time. I dropped in only for a second," replied Stepan Arkadievich. He opened his coat, then took it off, and spent a whole hour talking to Levin about hunting and on subjects of the most personal nature.

"Well, tell me, please, what did you do abroad? Where were you?" asked Stepan Arkadievich, when the moujik had left.

"I was in Germany, Prussia, France, and England, not in their capitals, but in the industrial cities, and I saw much that was new to me. And I'm glad that I was there."

"Yes, I know your project of organizing labor."

"That's not it. There's no labor problem in Russia. In Russia we have a problem of labor's attitude toward the land. It exists over there too, but there it's a matter of repairing what has been damaged, whereas with us. . . ."

Stepan Arkadievich listened to Levin attentively.

"Yes, yes!" he said. "Most probably you are right. But I'm glad that you're in good spirits. You hunt bears, work, and are full of enthusiasm, and yet Shcherbatsky told me—he saw you—that you are in some kind of depression, constantly talking about death. . . ."

"It's true; I keep thinking of death," said Levin. "It's indeed time to die. And all this is nonsense. I'll tell you the truth. I prize highly my ideas and my work, but actually, just think of it, our entire world is nothing but a speck of mold on a tiny planet. And we imagine that something great can be accomplished here—our ideas, our work! These are but grains of sand."

"But this, my friend, is as old as the world."

"It's true that it's old, but when you see it clearly, somehow everything becomes meaningless. When you realize that any one of these days you may die and that nothing will remain, how meaningless everything becomes! I consider my ideas to be of great importance, but they become, even if realized, as meaningless as it was meaningless to hunt down this bear. And so you spend your life diverting yourself by hunting, by working, just to keep your mind off the thought of death."

Stepan Arkadievich smiled subtly and gently as he listened to Levin.

"Well, of course! Now you've come to my point of view. Remember how you used to attack me for seeking life's pleasures? 'Oh, moralist, do not be so stern.'"

"No, there's still something good in life," said Levin in confusion. "I don't know. I only know that we will die soon."

"But why soon?"

"Well, you know, when you think of death, there may be less charm in life but more peace of mind."

"On the contrary, there's more pleasure toward the end. But I must go," said Stepan Arkadievich, rising for the tenth time.

"No, don't go!" said Levin, restraining him. "When will we meet again? I'm leaving tomorrow."

"What a dolt I am! I purposely came to. . . . You must have dinner with me today. Your brother will be there, and Karenin, my brother-in-law!"

"Is he here?" asked Levin, and he was about to inquire about Kitty. He had heard that early in the winter she had stayed in Petersburg with her sister, a diplomat's wife, and he did not know whether she had returned or not, but he decided not to inquire. It doesn't matter whether she will be there or not, he thought.

"Will you come?"

"Of course."

"At five o'clock then, in a morning coat."

Stepan Arkadievich rose and went downstairs to see his new chief. Stepan Arkadievich's instinct had not deceived him. The terrible new chief turned out to be a very courteous person. Stepan Arkadievich had lunch with him and stayed so late that it was after three o'clock before he saw Aleksei Aleksandrovich.

8

AFTER RETURNING from mass, Aleksei Aleksandrovich spent the rest of the morning indoors. He had two matters to attend to that morning: first, to receive and instruct a deputation from the minorities, which was heading for Petersburg, and which was now staying in Moscow; second, he had to write the lawyer the letter, as he had promised. Though the deputation had been summoned at Aleksei Aleksandrovich's initiative, it caused him much annoyance and even presented a danger, and Aleksei Aleksandrovich was very glad to find it in Moscow. The members of this deputation had no idea of the part they were supposed to play or of their duties. They were naïvely convinced that all they had to do was to present their needs and the actual state of their affairs and to ask for the government's help. They absolutely could not imagine that their declarations and demands were going to give aid to a hostile party and therefore ruin the whole case. Aleksei Aleksandrovich spent much time with them, wrote out a program from which they were not supposed to deviate, and, after dismissing them, he wrote some letters to Petersburg concerning the guidance to be given to the deputation. His chief assistant in this matter was supposed to be Countess Lydia Ivanovna. She was a specialist in deputations, and no one could compare with her when it came to publicizing a deputation and guiding it properly. After attending to this matter, he wrote to his lawyer. Without any hesitation he allowed him to act at his own discretion. He enclosed in the letter three notes from Vronsky to Anna, which he had found in the folder he had taken.

Ever since Aleksei Aleksandrovich had left his home with the intention not to return to his family, and since he had visited the lawyer and thereby had told the first person of his intention, and particularly since the time when he had transformed this affair of life into an affair of documents, he grew more and more accustomed to his intention and now saw clearly that it could be realized.

He was sealing the letter to the lawyer when he heard the loud voice of Stepan Arkadievich. Stepan Arkadievich was arguing with Aleksei Aleksandrovich's servant and was insisting that he be announced.

It doesn't matter, thought Aleksei Aleksandrovich. It's better this way. I'll reveal to him the state of my relationship with his sister and explain to him why I cannot accept his invitation to dinner.

"Ask him to come in," he said loudly, gathering the papers and putting them into the case.

"You see what a liar you are; he's at home," Stepan Arkadievich's voice could be heard, addressing the servant who had not let him in. Taking off his coat while he walked, he entered the room. "Well, I'm very glad to find you at home. I hope——" Stepan Arkadievich began happily.

"I can't go," Aleksei Aleksandrovich said coldly as he stood there without inviting his visitor to sit down.

Aleksei Aleksandrovich wanted to establish at once the formal relationship which should exist between him and the brother of his wife, against whom he had instituted divorce proceedings. But he had not taken into account that expanse of good will that overflowed Stepan Arkadievich's heart.

Stepan Arkadievich opened wide his clear, shining eyes.

"Why can't you? What are you trying to say?" he said in French, puzzled. "But you promised. And we're all counting on you."

"I want to say that I cannot be in your house because the family relationship that has existed between us must come to an end."

"What? How can this be? Why?" said Stepan Arkadievich with a smile.

"Because I'm instituting divorce proceedings against your sister, my wife. I must——"

Before Aleksei Aleksandrovich could finish what he was saying, Stepan Arkadievich did something unusual. Stepan Arkadievich groaned and sat down in a chair.

"No, Aleksei Aleksandrovich, that's impossible!" cried Oblonsky, and pain was visible on his face.

"It's true."

"I'm sorry, but I can't believe it."

Aleksei Aleksandrovich sat down, seeing that his words had not produced the desired effect, that he would have to go into an explanation, and that whatever the explanation would be, his relationship with his brother-in-law would remain as it had been.

"Yes, I've been put in the unfortunate position of having to sue for divorce."

"One word, Aleksei Aleksandrovich. I know that you are an admirable, upright man. I know that Anna is—forgive me, but I cannot change my opinion of her—an outstanding, admirable woman, and, therefore, forgive me, I cannot believe it. There must be some misunderstanding," he said.

"Yes, I wish it were only a misunderstanding. . . ."

"But wait, I understand," interrupted Stepan Arkadievich. "But, of course. . . . One thing only: you mustn't be in a hurry! You mustn't, mustn't be in a hurry!"

"I have not rushed things," said Aleksei Aleksandrovich coldly, "and in such a case one can ask no one's advice. My decision is firm."

"This is terrible!" said Stepan Arkadievich with a heavy sigh. "But I would do one thing, Aleksei Aleksandrovich. I beg you, do it!" he said. "You've not yet started the proceedings, I believe. Before you do, see my wife, speak to her. She loves Anna as her own sister; she loves you, and she is a wonderful woman. For God's sake, speak to her. Do me this favor, I beg of you!"

Aleksei Aleksandrovich was lost in thought, and Stepan Arkadievich looked at him with sympathy, without breaking the silence.

"Will you see her?"

"I don't know. This is why I didn't come to see you. I believe that our relationship must change."

"But why? I can't see it. I would like you to believe that our relationship has not been based solely on your marriage, and that you have for me at least some of the friendly feelings which I have for you . . . and genuine respect," added Stepan Arkadievich, shaking his hand. "Even if your worst conjectures are correct, I do not and will never dare to judge either side, and I see no reason why our relationship should change. But now do it; please come to see my wife."

"I see that we view this matter differently," Aleksei Aleksandrovich said coldly. "But let's not talk about it."

"But why shouldn't you come? At least today, to dinner. My wife is expecting you. Please come. And, most important, talk this matter over with her. She's a wonderful woman. For God's sake, I'm on my knees before you!"

"If you wish it so much I'll come," said Aleksei Aleksandrovich with a sigh.

And, to change the subject, he asked him about a matter which was of interest to both of them, about Stepan Arkadievich's new chief, who, though still young, had been suddenly appointed to such a high position.

Aleksei Aleksandrovich never had liked Count Anichkin and had always differed with him, and now he could not suppress the feeling of hatred, familiar to officials, that a man who has suffered a setback in his career has toward one who has been promoted.

"Well, have you seen him?" asked Aleksei Aleksandrovich with a sarcastic smile.

"Yes, he visited our council chamber yesterday. He seems to be very competent and energetic."

"Yes, but what is the purpose of his energy?" asked Aleksei Aleksandrovich. "Is it to do something or to rehash things that have already been done? This paper bureaucracy, of which he is a worthy representative, is the bane of our state."

"Truly, I don't know what can be held against him. I'm not acquainted with his views, but I know one thing—he's a fine fellow," replied Stepan Arkadievich. "I've just visited him and, really, he's a fine fellow. We had lunch together, and I taught him how to prepare that drink, you know, of wine and oranges. It's very refreshing. And it's strange that he didn't know it. He liked it very much. No, truly, a fine fellow."

Stepan Arkadievich glanced at his watch.

"Good heavens, it's after four and I still must see Dolgovushin! Well, then, come to dinner, please. You can't imagine how sorry my wife and I would be if you didn't."

The parting of Aleksei Aleksandrovich and his brother-in-law was quite different from their greeting.

"I've promised, and I'll be there," he said dejectedly.

"Please believe that I appreciate it, and I hope that you'll not regret it," replied Stepan Arkadievich with a smile.

He put on his coat as he walked, brushing his hand against the servant's head, laughed and left.

"At five o'clock, in a morning coat, please!" he cried once more at the door.

9

IT WAS AFTER five, and some of the guests had already assembled when the host himself arrived. He entered together with Sergei Ivanovich Koznyshev and Pestzov, who had bumped into each other at the entrance. They were, in Oblonsky's words, the two foremost representatives of the Moscow intelligentsia. Each of them was held in esteem both for his character and his intelligence. They respected each other but disagreed completely and hopelessly on almost every point, not because they belonged to opposing schools of thought but exactly because they were members of the same camp (their enemies failed to distinguish between them), and in this camp each one had his own shade of opinion. And since nothing is so difficult to conciliate as hair-splitting disagreements, they not only never agreed in their opinions but had long since become accustomed to ridiculing each other's incorrigible delusions in a good-natured way.

They were coming into the doorway, talking about the weather, when Stepan Arkadievich caught up with them. Oblonsky's father-in-law, Prince Aleksandr Dmitrievich, the young Shcherbatsky, Turovtzin, Kitty, and Karenin were already in the drawing room.

Stepan Arkadievich immediately noticed that, without him, things in the drawing room were not going well. Daria Aleksandrovna, in her festive, gray silk dress, evidently was worrying about her children, who had to dine separately in the nursery, and about her absent husband and could not sort out the guests properly without his help. They all sat like priest's daughters at a party (as the old prince said), evidently wondering why they were there, and forced themselves to say something just to avoid silence. The good-natured Turovtzin obviously felt out of place. When he saw Stepan Arkadievich, the smile on his thick lips seemed to say, "Well, my friend, you've put me with a group that's too smart for me! To have a drink, and the *Château des Fleurs*, that's my speed." The old prince kept silent, his shining eyes looking sideways at Karenin, and Stepan Arkadievich understood that he had already devised some pithy word with which to brand

403

this great statesman, who was the delicacy to be served to the guests.

From time to time Kitty glanced at the door, gathering courage to meet Konstantin Levin without blushing. The young Shcherbatsky, who had not been introduced to Karenin, tried to show that this did not embarrass him in the least. Karenin himself, as was his Petersburg custom when dining with ladies, was dressed in a swallow-tailed coat and white tie. From his look, Stepan Arkadievich understood that he had come only to keep his promise, and that by being present in this company he was performing a painful duty. He was the main cause of the chill that held all the guests in its grip prior to Stepan Arkadievich's arrival.

On entering the drawing room, Stepan Arkadievich apologized, explaining that he had been detained by the prince, the usual scapegoat for his tardiness and absences. Within a moment he had introduced the guests all around. He brought Aleksei Aleksandrovich and Sergei Koznyshev together and suggested to them the subject of the Russification of Poland, about which they immediately entered into a heated argument with Pestzov. He patted Turovtzin on the shoulder, whispered a funny remark to him, and placed him next to his wife and the prince. He told Kitty that she looked very pretty and introduced Shcherbatsky to Karenin. In one moment he had so thoroughly kneaded the dough of this company that the drawing room was completely transformed and lively conversation filled the air. Only Konstantin Levin was missing. But this was just as well, for when Stepan Arkadievich came into the dining room he noticed, to his dismay, that the port and the sherry had been obtained from Depret and not from Levé. He ordered his coachman to ride to Levé at top speed and turned back toward the drawing room.

On the way he met Konstantin Levin.

"Am I late?"

"Have you ever been on time?" asked Stepan Arkadievich, taking his arm.

"Have you many guests? Who are they?" asked Levin, blushing unconsciously and brushing the snow from his hat with his glove.

"You know most of them. Kitty is here. Come, I'll introduce you to Karenin."

In spite of his liberal views, Stepan Arkadievich knew that an introduction to Karenin could be only flattering, and therefore offered it to his best friends. But at this moment Konstantin Levin was in no position to be fully gratified by the favor of this introduction. He had not seen Kitty since that memorable evening when he had met Vronsky, except for the moment when he caught a glimpse of her on the highway. Deep in his heart he knew that he would see her here today. But giving free rein to his thoughts, he had tried to convince himself that he did not really know this. Now that he had heard that she was present, he suddenly felt such joy, and at the same time such fear, that it made him catch his breath, and he could not express what he wanted to say.

Which one is she now? Is she as she was earlier or as she was in the coach? Suppose what Daria Aleksandrovna said is true? And why shouldn't it be true? he thought.

"Oh, please, introduce me to Karenin," he said with effort, and after entering the drawing room with desperate determination, he caught sight of her.

She was neither as she had been before nor as she was in the coach. She was entirely different.

She was frightened, shy, shamefaced, and therefore all the more charming. She saw him the moment he entered the room. She had been waiting for him. She was filled with joy, and her joy embarrassed her so deeply that at one moment—the moment when he came up to the hostess and looked at her again—it seemed to her, to him, and to Dolly, who noticed everything, that she would not be able to control herself and would burst into tears. She blushed, paled, then blushed again and remained still, and, her lips quivering, she waited for him. He came over to her, bowed and, in silence, extended his hand. Except for the faint quiver of her lips and for the moistness of her eyes, which enhanced their luster, her smile was almost calm as she said:

"How long it has been since we saw each other!" and with an air of desperate determination she pressed her cold hand into his.

"You've not seen me, but I've seen you," said Levin, smiling and beaming with happiness. "I saw you on your way from the railroad station to Ergushovo."

"When?" she asked in surprise.

"You were riding to Ergushovo," said Levin, overwhelmed with a happiness which overflowed his heart. And how could I have dared to associate anything not innocent with this touching creature? Yes, it seems that what Daria Aleksandrovna told me is true, he thought.

Stepan Arkadievich took his arm and brought him over to Karenin.

"I would like you to meet," he said, giving their names.

"I am glad to meet you again," said Aleksei Aleksandrovich coldly, shaking hands with Levin.

"Have you met before?" asked Stepan Arkadievich, surprised.

"We traveled together for three hours," said Levin, smiling, "and we left the railroad car mystified, as though after leaving a masked ball, at least in my case."

"Well, well! If you please," said Stepan Arkadievich, indicating the dining room.

The men left for the dining room and went up to the *zakuska* table laden with six kinds of vodka and as many kinds of cheese, some with tiny silver scoops and some without, caviar, herring, a variety of canned food, and plates with small slices of French bread.

The men crowded around the aromatic vodkas and *zakuskas*, and the conversation between Sergei Ivanovich, Karenin, and Pestzov about the Russification of Poland gradually flagged in anticipation of dinner.

Sergei Ivanovich, better than anyone else, could bring to an end the most abstruse and serious discussion by abruptly seasoning it with some Attic salt, thus changing the mood of the company. He did so now.

Aleksei Aleksandrovich argued that the Russification of Poland could be achieved only if the Russian administration adhered to the highest principles.

Pestzov maintained that one nation assimilated another only when its population was greater.

Koznyshev accepted both points of view, but with qualifications. As they were leaving the drawing room, Koznyshev, to bring the conversation to an end, added with a smile:

"Then there remains only one remedy for the Russification of the minorities—to beget as many children as possible. In this respect my brother and I are the worst of all. But you married gentlemen, and particularly you, Stepan Arkadievich, you behave like true patriots. How many have you?" he asked, turning to his host with a kind smile and extending his tiny glass.

Everyone laughed, Stepan Arkadievich heartiest of all.

"Yes, that's the best remedy!" he said, chewing a piece of cheese and pouring a special brand of vodka into the proffered glass. The conversation indeed ended with this joke.

"This cheese isn't bad. Would you like some?" asked the host. "Have you really taken up exercising again?" he asked Levin, feeling the muscle of his arm with his left hand. Levin smiled, flexed his arm, and from underneath the thin cloth of his morning coat there rose a steely knob, like a round loaf of cheese, under Stepan Arkadievich's fingers.

"Some biceps! A Samson!"

"I think that bear hunting requires great physical strength," said Aleksei Aleksandrovich, who had only the vaguest idea about hunting, as he spread cheese on a slice of bread which was thin as a cobweb, crumbling it.

Levin smiled.

"Not at all. On the contrary, even a child can kill a bear," he said, bowing slightly and making way for the ladies, who had been invited by the hostess to the *zakuskas*.

"And you have killed a bear, I was told," said Kitty, vainly trying to spear an unyielding slippery mushroom with her fork and fluttering the lace of her dress through which her white arm shone. "Are there many bears in your neighborhood?" she added, partly turning her charming little head toward him and smiling.

Obviously there was nothing remarkable in what she had said, but what meaning, inexpressible in words, he found in each sound, in each movement of her lips, eyes, arms, which accompanied her words! They expressed entreaty for forgiveness, trust in him, gentle, timid tenderness, promise, hope, and love for him, in which he could not help believing and which overwhelmed him with happiness.

"No, we went to Tver Province. On the way back I met your brother-in-law in the railroad car, or rather your brother-in-law's brother-in-law," he said with a smile. "It was an amusing incident."

And with gaiety and amusement he began to describe how he, after a sleepless night, dressed in a sheepskin coat, had forced his way into Aleksei Aleksandrovich's compartment.

"The conductor, contrary to the proverb, wanted to put me out, on account of my clothes. But I began at once to express myself in refined language, and . . . you too," he said, turning to Karenin, but failing to recollect his name, "judged me by my sheepskin and at first wanted to throw me out, but then you took my part and for that I am grateful to you."

"In general, the passengers' right to choose their seats is very uncertain," said Aleksei Aleksandrovich, wiping the tips of his fingers with a napkin.

"I noticed that my appearance puzzled you," said Levin, smiling good-naturedly, "but I hastened to start a learned conversation to make up for my sheepskin."

Sergei Ivanovich continued his conversation with the hostess, and with one ear listened to the words of his brother, looking at him askance. What's the matter with him today? he thought. Such a triumphant tone! He did not know that Levin felt as though he had wings. Levin knew that she heard his words and that she liked to hear him. This was the only thing that interested him. For him there existed not only in this room but in the whole world only himself, who had acquired such great importance and significance, and she. He soared to a dizzying height, with all these good and dear Karenins, Oblonskys, and the whole world, somewhere far below.

Quite casually, without looking at them, as though he could find no other seats for them, Stepan Arkadievich placed Levin and Kitty next to each other.

"Well, you might as well sit down here," he said to Levin.

The dinner was as good as the china, of which Stepan Arkadievich was a connoisseur. The Marie-Louise soup turned out to be excellent. The tiny patties were irreproachable and melted in the mouth. Two servants and Matvei, in white ties, served the food and the wines without being noticed, softly and skillfully. With regard to food the dinner was a success, nor was it any less successful in other respects. The conversation, both general and in groups, never flagged, and toward the end of the dinner grew so animated that the men rose from the table without interrupting their talk, and even Aleksei Aleksandrovich cheered up.

10

PESTZOV LIKED to bring an argument to its conclusion and was not satisfied with Sergei Ivanovich's remark, the more so because he felt that his own view was wrong.

"I have never meant," he said over the soup, addressing Aleksei Aleksandrovich, "to consider the density of population alone as a matter of general principle, but only in conjunction with particular basic facts."

"It seems to me," Aleksei Aleksandrovich replied casually and unenthusiastically, "that it amounts to the same thing. In my opinion, the only nation that can influence another is one at a higher state of development, which—"

"But that's exactly the problem," Pestzov interrupted in his bass voice—he always was in a hurry to speak and, it seemed, he always put his whole heart into what he said. "How are we to define this higher development? The English, the French, the Germans—whose development is the highest? Who will assimilate whom? We see that the Rhine provinces have become French, but the Germans are not lower than the French," he cried. "There must be another criterion."

"It seems to me that influence is always exerted by those who are genuinely cultured," said Aleksei Aleksandrovich, raising his eyebrows slightly.

"But what must we assume as the sign of genuine culture?" asked Pestzov.

"I believe that these signs are known," replied Aleksei Aleksandrovich.

"Are they fully known?" Sergei Ivanovich interjected with a subtle smile. "It's now accepted that only the classical is the true education. But we hear heated arguments on both sides, and it cannot be denied that the opposite side has weighty arguments in its favor."

"You are a classicist, Sergei Ivanovich. Would you like some red wine?" asked Stepan Arkadievich.

"I'm not expressing an opinion concerning either type of education," said Sergei Ivanovich, condescendingly smiling at Stepan Arkadievich as at a child and holding out his glass. "I only say that both sides have weighty arguments," he continued, turning to Aleksei Aleksandrovich. "I'm a classicist by education, but in this argument I personally cannot take a stand. I see no convincing reason why classical studies should be preferred to the scientific."

"Natural science contributes as much to the education of the student," interjected Pestzov. "Take astronomy, take botany, or zoology, with their systems of universal laws!"

"I cannot fully agree with that," replied Aleksei Aleksandrovich. "It seems that it cannot be denied that the very process of studying the morphology of languages is beneficial to spiritual education. Moreover, it cannot be denied that the classical writers exert a very great moral influence, whereas, unfortunately, the teaching of natural science leads to the harmful and false theories that are the bane of our age."

Sergei Ivanovich wanted to say something, but Pestzov's deep bass interrupted him. He began heatedly to prove the fallacy of this opinion. Sergei Ivanovich waited calmly for his turn, evidently ready with a crushing repartee.

"But," said Sergei Ivanovich, smiling slightly and turning to Karenin, "we can't deny that it's hard to weigh exactly the advantages and disadvantages of either branch of learning. And the problem of which of them is preferable would not have been solved so quickly and with such finality but for the advantage of classical education which you have just mentioned: it has a moral—*disons le mot*—antinihilistic influence."

"No doubt!"

"If classical studies hadn't had the advantage of an antinihilistic influence, we would have reflected longer, would have weighed the arguments on either side more carefully," said Sergei Ivanovich with his subtle smile. "We would have left room for both schools. But now we know that these pills of classical education are a cure for nihilism, and we unhesitatingly offer them to our patients. . . . But what if they didn't possess this curative power?" he concluded with this dash of Attic salt.

Sergei Ivanovich's pills aroused everyone to laughter, and Turovtzin, who at last was rewarded with some amusement, for which he obviously had been waiting throughout the conversation, laughed most loudly and happily.

Stepan Arkadievich had made no mistake in inviting Pestzov. With Pestzov a clever conversation could not stop even for a minute. As soon as Sergei Ivanovich concluded one discussion with his joke, Pestzov began another.

"One can't even agree," he said, "that this was the government's aim. The government evidently is moved by general considerations, remaining indifferent to the effects its reforms may produce. For instance, women's education could certainly be considered potentially harmful, but the government establishes women's schools and universities."

And the conversation instantly turned to the new topic of women's education.

Aleksei Aleksandrovich expressed an opinion that the education of women is usually confused with their emancipation, and only for this reason could it be considered harmful.

"I, on the other hand, believe that the two are indissolubly bound," said Pestzov. "It's a vicious circle. Woman is deprived of her rights because she lacks education, and this lack of education results from her being deprived of her rights. We mustn't forget that the oppression of women is so heavy and has existed for so long that often we refuse to see the chasm that divides them from us," he said.

"When you talk about rights," said Sergei Ivanovich, waiting for Pestzov to stop, "do you mean the right to serve on juries, as town councilors, council heads, government employees, members of parliament? . . ."

"Certainly."

"But if, as a rare exception, some women can fill these positions, then it seems to me you are wrong in using the term 'rights.' It would be more correct to say 'duties.' Everyone will agree that when we are employed as jurymen, town councilors, telegraphers, we feel that we are performing our duty. Therefore, it is more correct to say that women seek to assume new duties, and on lawful grounds. And one can only sympathize with their desire to relieve the men of some of their burdens."

"Quite true," confirmed Aleksei Aleksandrovich. "The question is only whether they are capable of these duties."

"Probably they will be," interjected Stepan Arkadievich, "when their level of education rises. We see it—"

"And what about the saying?" said the prince, who for a long time had been listening to the conversation, his small eyes sparkling derisively. "We can say it in the presence of our daughters: 'a woman's hair is long, but her wit, well—' "

"They thought the same of the Negroes before the emancipation," Pestzov said angrily.

"It seems strange to me that women look for new duties," said Sergei Ivanovich, "whereas we see, to our misfortune, that men usually shun them."

"Duties lead to privileges of authority, money, honors. That's what women seek," said Pestzov.

"It's the same as if I were to seek the right to become a wet nurse and would feel slighted that, though women are paid for it, I am not wanted," said the old prince.

Turovtzin burst into loud laughter, and Sergei Ivanovich

regretted that he had not said it. Even Aleksei Aleksandrovich smiled.

"But a man cannot suckle a child," said Pestzov, "whereas a woman—"

"But there was an Englishman who reared his infant on board his ship," said the old prince, allowing himself this license in the presence of his daughters.

"We'll have as many women officials as there were such Englishmen," said Sergei Ivanovich.

"But what can a girl do if she has no family?" interjected Stepan Arkadievich, remembering Mlle. Chibisov, whom he had had in mind all this time, which made him sympathize with Pestzov and take his part.

"If you examine thoroughly the history of this girl, you will find that she has abandoned her own family, or her sister's, where she could do her part as a woman," said Daria Aleksandrovna angrily, suddenly entering into the conversation and evidently knowing which girl Stepan Arkadievich had in mind.

"But we are defending a principle, an ideal," Pestzov retorted in his sonorous bass. "Women want to become independent and educated. And because they know that this is impossible, they feel deprived and oppressed."

"And I feel deprived and oppressed because they refuse to employ me as a wet nurse in a home for children," the old prince said again, to the great amusement of Turovtzin, who, in a fit of laughter, dropped a spear of asparagus into the sauce, its thick end down.

11

EVERYONE TOOK PART in the general conversation except Kitty and Levin. At first, when they spoke about the influence of one nation or another, Levin unconsciously thought of what he would say on the subject. But these thoughts, formerly of such importance to him, now flashed through his mind as in a dream, without arousing the slightest interest. It even seemed strange to him that they were so anxious to speak about entirely pointless matters. And one would think that Kitty also would have been interested in the subject under discussion, the rights and education of women. How many times she had thought about the subject, recalling Varenka, her friend from abroad, and her difficult state of dependence! How many times she had thought about herself and what would happen to her if she did not marry! And how many times she had argued on this subject with her sister! But now it did not interest her at all. There was a conversation between herself and Levin. Yet it was not a conversation but some sort of mystic communion, which, with each passing moment, drew them closer to each other and aroused in both of them a feeling of joyous fear of the unknown into which they were entering.

At first, when Kitty asked him how he had happened to see her last year in the coach, Levin replied that it was while he was walking along the highway on his return from the meadow.

"It was very early in the morning. You probably had just awakened. *Maman* was asleep in the corner. It was a beautiful morning. I walked and wondered who that was in the coach and four. It was a beautiful team of four with bells. In a moment you flashed by, and I saw you at the window— you were sitting like this, holding the strings of your bonnet with both hands, completely lost in thought," he said with a smile. "How much I'd like to know what you were thinking of then. Was it important?"

I hope my hair wasn't a sight, she thought. But seeing his rapturous smile, brought forth by his remembrance of these details, she felt that, on the contrary, she had made a very good impression. She blushed and laughed gaily.

"Really, I don't remember."

"What a pleasure it is to watch Turovtzin laugh," said Levin, looking with admiration at his moist eyes and shaking body.

"Have you known him long?" asked Kitty.

"Who doesn't know him?"

"I can see that you don't approve of him."

"He is not bad, just worthless."

"That isn't true. You mustn't think that way," said Kitty. "I, too, had a low opinion of him, but he's a most gentle and remarkably good-natured man. He has a heart of gold."

"How could you have learned about his heart?"

"We are great friends. I know him very well. Last winter, soon after . . . after your visit to us," she said, with an apologetic and at the same time trusting smile, "all of Dolly's children were sick with scarlet fever, and he happened to look in. And, would you believe it," she said in a whisper, "he felt so sorry for her that he remained to help her care for the children. Yes, he stayed with her three weeks, looking after the children like a nurse.

"I'm talking to Konstantin Dmitrievich about Turovtzin and the scarlet fever," she said, leaning over toward her sister.

"Yes, a wonderful man, a darling," said Dolly, looking with a gentle smile at Turovtzin, who felt that they were talking about him. Levin glanced at Turovtzin once more and wondered why he could not have earlier perceived the wonderful qualities of this man.

"I'm sorry. I'll never again think ill of people," he said gaily, expressing his genuine feeling of the moment.

12

THE CONVERSATION THEY had started regarding the rights of women touched on one subject, delicate if discussed in the presence of ladies, that of unequal rights in marriage. At dinner, Pestzov attempted to attack it several times, but Sergei Ivanovich and Stepan Arkadievich carefully checked him.

But when they rose from the table and the ladies had left, Pestzov did not follow them, but turned to Aleksei Aleksandrovich and began to expound on the main cause of this inequality. In his opinion, this inequality was based on the fact that neither the law nor public opinion punished alike the unfaithfulness of a husband and unfaithfulness of a wife.

Stepan Arkadievich came over to Aleksei Aleksandrovich, inviting him to join him in a smoke.

"I don't smoke," Aleksei Aleksandrovich replied calmly, and as though wishing deliberately to prove that he did not fear this conversation, he turned to Pestzov with a cold smile.

"I believe that this attitude is based on the very nature of things," he said, and he was about to pass to the drawing room when Turovtzin suddenly addressed him.

"Have you heard about Priachnikov?" said Turovtzin who, enlivened by the champagne, had been waiting some time for the opportunity to break the silence under which he had been laboring. "Vasia Priachnikov," he said, smiling good-naturedly with his moist, rosy lips and addressing his remarks primarily to the guest of honor, Aleksei Aleksandrovich, "I was told recently, fought a duel in Tver with Kvytsky and killed him."

It seems that a sore spot is always bumped, as though on purpose, and, to his regret, Stepan Arkadievich noticed that that day the conversation constantly touched on Aleksei Aleksandrovich's sore spot. He again tried to draw his brother-in-law aside, but Aleksei Aleksandrovich himself asked inquisitively:

"Why did Priachnikov fight?"

"For his wife. He acted like a man! Challenged and killed him!"

"Ah," said Aleksei Aleksandrovich indifferently and, his eyebrows raised, he went toward the drawing room.

"I'm so glad that you've come," Dolly said to him with a frightened smile, as she met him in the anteroom. "I must talk to you. Let's sit down here."

Aleksei Aleksandrovich, still wearing the expression of indifference provided by his raised eyebrows, sat next to Daria Aleksandrovna with a forced smile.

"But," said Aleksei Aleksandrovich, "I was going to ask your permission to leave now. I have to start early tomorrow."

Daria Aleksandrovna was fully convinced of Anna's innocence and felt that she was growing pale and that her lips were trembling with indignation at this cold, unfeeling man, who so calmly intended to destroy her innocent friend.

"Aleksei Aleksandrovich," she said, looking at his eyes with reckless determination, "I asked you about Anna, but you didn't answer. How is she?"

"She seems to be well, Daria Aleksandrovna," answered Aleksei Aleksandrovich, without looking at her.

"Aleksei Aleksandrovich, forgive me, I have no right . . . but I love and respect Anna as my own sister. I beg you, I beseech you, tell me what happened between you? Of what are you accusing her?"

Aleksei Aleksandrovich frowned and, half-closing his eyes, he bowed his head.

"I believe that your husband has told you of the reasons which made me change my former relationship with Anna Arkadievna," he said, without looking at her, and watching with displeasure as Shcherbatsky walked through the room.

"I don't believe it, I can't believe it!" Dolly said with an agitated gesture, clasping her bony hands in front of her.

She rose quickly and put her hand on Aleksei Aleksandrovich's arm. "We'll be disturbed here. Follow me, please."

Dolly's agitation affected Aleksei Aleksandrovich. He rose and meekly followed her into the children's classroom. They sat at a table covered with oilcloth, which had been marked by a penknife.

"I don't, I don't believe it," said Dolly, trying to meet his look, which avoided her.

"One cannot disbelieve facts, Daria Aleksandrovna," he said, emphasizing the word *facts*.

"But what has she done?" asked Daria Aleksandrovna. "What has she actually done?"

"She rejected her duties and betrayed her husband. That is what she's done," he said.

"No, it cannot be. No, for God's sake, you are mistaken!" said Dolly, pressing her hands against her temples and closing her eyes.

Aleksei Aleksandrovich smiled coldly with his lips only, trying to prove to her and to himself how firm his conviction was. Though her ardent defense had left him unshaken, it added salt to his wound. He began to speak with great agitation.

"It's very hard to be mistaken when the wife herself declares it to her husband. She declares that eight years of her life and her son—all that was a mistake, and that she wants to begin life anew," he said angrily, his breathing labored.

"Anna and vice—I cannot see them together; I can't believe it."

"Daria Aleksandrovna," he said, now looking straight at Dolly's kind, agitated face and feeling that unconsciously he was giving free rein to his words. "I would give much to be able still to doubt. While I doubted, I suffered, but not as much as now. While I doubted, there was hope. But there's no hope now, and yet I still doubt everything. I am in such doubt about everything that I hate my son and sometimes don't believe that he is my son. I'm very unhappy."

He did not need to say this. Daria Aleksandrovna understood it as soon as he looked at her face. She pitied him, and her confidence in the innocence of her friend was shaken.

"Oh! It's terrible, terrible! But is it really true that you've decided on a divorce?"

"It's my last resort. I can do nothing else."

"Nothing else, nothing else . . ." she repeated with tears in her eyes. "No, nothing else!" she said.

"And the horror of this kind of misfortune is that though in other kinds, like loss or death, you bear your cross—here you must act," he said, as though divining her thought. "You have to put an end to the humiliating situation in which you are placed: the three of us cannot continue together."

"I understand, I understand completely," said Dolly and she bowed her head. She fell silent, thinking of herself, of her unhappy family life and suddenly, in agitation, she raised her head and folded her hands imploringly. "But wait! You are a Christian. Think of her. What will happen to her if you forsake her?"

"I have thought about it, Daria Aleksandrovna, I have given it much thought," said Aleksei Aleksandrovich. Red spots appeared on his face, and his dull eyes looked directly at her. Daria Aleksandrovna now pitied him with all her heart. "I did that very thing after she had revealed to me my disgrace. I kept everything as it was. I gave her a chance to repent, I tried to save her. And what was the result? She did not accede to my least demand—to observe propriety," he said, growing excited. "You can save only him who does not wish to perish, but if his nature is so depraved, so corrupt, that in his very corruption he sees his salvation, what can you do?"

"Anything but a divorce!" replied Daria Aleksandrovna.

"What else is there?"

"No, it's awful. She'll be no one's wife and she'll be lost."

"But what can I do?" Aleksei Aleksandrovich said, shrugging his shoulders and lifting his eyebrows. At the memory of his wife's last wrongdoing he felt so upset that he again turned cold as he had been at the beginning of the conversation. "I thank you deeply for your concern, but I must go," he said, rising.

"Please wait! You mustn't destroy her. Let me tell you about myself. I married, and my husband deceived me. I was angry and jealous; I wanted to leave everything. I myself wanted to. . . . But I returned to my senses, and who saved me? Anna. And here I am. The children are growing up, my husband has returned to us; he fully recognized his guilt; he is becoming more honorable and better behaved; and I carry on. I have forgiven, and you must forgive."

Aleksei Aleksandrovich listened to her, but her words no longer moved him. All the anger of the day when he had de-

cided on a divorce stirred within his heart anew. He straightened and spoke in a shrill, piercing voice.

"I cannot forgive, I don't want to, and I consider it unjust.
I have done everything for this woman, but she has trampled
everything in the filth which has become a part of her. I'm
not a vengeful man and I have never hated anyone, but I
hate her with all my heart and I cannot forgive her because
I hate her too much for all the evil she has caused me," he
said, tears of rage in his voice.

"Love them that hate you . . ." Daria Aleksandrovna
whispered shyly.

Aleksei Aleksandrovich smiled scornfully. He knew this
phrase well, but it could not apply to his case.

"Love them that hate you, but you cannot love them whom
you hate. Forgive me for having disturbed you. Everyone has
enough of his own worries!" And having regained his composure, Aleksei Aleksandrovich calmly said his farewells and
departed.

                        13

WHEN EVERYONE ROSE from the table, Levin wanted to follow
Kitty into the drawing room, but he was afraid that she would
be displeased with this obvious show of courtship. He remained with the men, taking part in the general conversation,
and without looking at Kitty, he was aware of her movements,
her glances, and of her location in the drawing room.

Without any effort, he was already keeping the promise he
had given her—always to think well of everyone and always
to love everyone. The conversation touched upon the peasant
commune in which Pestzov saw some special principle—a
"choral" principle, as he called it. Levin did not agree either
with Pestzov or his brother who, in his own way, both accepted and rejected the importance of the Russian commune.
But he spoke to them only to conciliate them and mitigate
their differences. He was not at all interested in what he
himself was saying and still less in what they were saying; he
wished for only one thing—that they and everyone else should
be pleased and contented. He was aware now that only one
thing was important. And that first stayed there in the drawing room, then began moving, and stopped at the doorway.

Without turning, he felt her look and smile directed at him and could not help turning around. She stood in the doorway with Shcherbatsky and looked at him.

"I thought you were going toward the piano," he said, going over to her. "Music is what I miss in the country."

"No, we've come here to look for you. I thank you for coming," she said, rewarding him with a smile as with a gift. "What's the use of arguing. Everyone will remain with his own opinions anyway."

"Yes, it's true," said Levin. "In most cases you argue heatedly only because you absolutely cannot understand what your opponent is trying to prove."

Levin often observed that in their discussions even the cleverest people spent enormous efforts and used an endless number of logical subtleties and words only to realize in the end that they had known, long before the beginning of their discussion, what it was that they took such pains to prove to each other. But their tastes varied and they were reluctant to reveal them lest they be attacked by their opponents. He often felt that in some discussions you understand what your opponent likes, and suddenly you yourself conceive a liking for the same thing, agree with your opponent, and then all arguments are superfluous. And sometimes he experienced the opposite: after finally explaining what you yourself like and why you have brought up all these arguments, if you happen to express it clearly and sincerely, your opponent suddenly agrees with you and drops the argument. This was what he was trying to explain to her.

She wrinkled her forehead, trying to understand. But as soon as he started to explain it, she understood.

"I understand: you must find out why he is arguing, what he likes, and then you can. . . ."

She grasped his thought completely and expressed it better than he had. Levin smiled happily: he was so deeply impressed by this change from the involved verbose argument with Pestzov and his brother to this laconic and clear, almost wordless, expression of the most complex thoughts.

Shcherbatsky left them, and Kitty went over to the card table that had been set up, sat down and, reaching for the chalk, began to draw winding circles on the new green cloth.

They resumed the conversation they had had during dinner —on women's freedom and their occupations. Levin agreed with Daria Aleksandrovna's opinion that a girl who remained unmarried would find her occupation as a woman in a family. He supported this opinion with a statement that no family could get along without help, and that each family, rich or poor, must have nurses, either hired or in the family.

"No," said Kitty. She blushed, but her frank gaze was still fixed boldly on him. "A girl may find herself in a situation which does not permit her to be taken into a family without humiliation, and she herself. . . ."

He understood her allusion.

"Oh, yes!" he said, "Yes, you are right, absolutely right."

And just from a glimpse of the fear in Kitty's heart, fear of spinsterhood and humiliation, he understood everything that Pestzov had said at dinner in favor of the emancipation of women. Loving her, Levin shared her fear and humiliation and forthwith renounced his own views.

They were silent. She kept drawing with the chalk on the table. A quiet light shone in her eyes. Submitting to her mood, he felt throughout his whole being the growing intensity of his happiness.

"Oh, I've scribbled over the whole table!" she said, and putting down the chalk, she made as though to rise.

How can I remain without her? he thought, terrified, and he reached for the chalk.

"Please wait," he said, sitting down at the table. "I've wanted to ask you something for a long time."

He looked straight into her affectionate though frightened eyes.

"Ask me, please."

"Here," he said, and he wrote the following letters: *w, y, t, m, i, c, b, d, y, m, a, t, t, o, o, n.* These letters meant: "When you told me, 'it cannot be,' did you mean at that time only, or never?" It seemed extremely improbable that she should understand this complicated sentence, but he stared at her as though his life depended on whether she would understand the meaning of those letters.

She glanced at him gravely, then leaned her frowning brow on her hand and began to read. She looked at him from time to time, as though asking, "Am I guessing right?"

"I understand," she said, blushing.

"What's this word?" he said, pointing at the *n*, which stood for "never."

"It means 'never,'" she said, "but it's not true."

He hurriedly rubbed off what he had written, gave her the chalk, and rose. She wrote: *a, t, t, I, c, n, r, o.*

Dolly felt completely relieved of the distress caused by her conversation with Aleksei Aleksandrovich when she saw these two figures: Kitty, with the piece of chalk in her hand, smiling shyly and happily and looking upward at Levin; and his handsome figure, bent over the table, his ardent look directed now at the table and now at her. He beamed suddenly: he understood. It meant: "At that time I could not reply otherwise."

He looked at her shyly and questioningly.

"Just at that time?"

"Yes," her smile told him.

"And . . . and now?" he asked.

"Well, read this, I'll say what my wish is. What I wish sincerely." She wrote the letters: *t, y, f, a, f, w, h.* It meant: "that you forget and forgive what happened."

He grasped the chalk with his tense, trembling fingers, broke it, and wrote the first letters of the following words: "I have nothing to forget and forgive; I never ceased loving you."

She looked at him with a lingering smile.

"I understood," she whispered.

He sat down and wrote out a long sentence. She understood, and without asking him whether she was right, she took the chalk and replied at once.

For a long while he could not understand what she had written, and he repeatedly looked into her eyes. His happiness threw him into confusion. He could by no means find the proper words, but in her eyes, sparkling with happiness, he read all that he needed to know. Then he wrote three letters. But even before he completed the question, she read it by following his hand, finished the question herself, and wrote her answer: "Yes."

"Are you playing *secrétaire?*" asked the old prince, coming over to them. "Well, let's go, if you want to get to the theater on time."

Levin rose and saw Kitty to the door.

Everything had been said in this conversation: that she loved him, that she would tell her father and mother about it, and that he should come to see her the next day.

14

WHEN KITTY LEFT and Levin remained alone, he felt so troubled without her and so impatient for the next morning to arrive, when he would see her again and join her forever, that he was in deadly fear at the prospect of spending fourteen hours without her.

He felt the need to be and speak with someone so as not to be alone and to help pass the time. Stepan Arkadievich would have been a most pleasant companion but he was leaving for a party, he said, although actually for the ballet. Levin just managed to tell him that he was happy, that he loved him, and that he never, never would forget what Stepan Arkadievich had done for him. Stepan Arkadievich's smile and his look showed Levin that he correctly understood his feelings.

"Well, isn't it already time to die?" said Stepan Arkadievich tenderly, shaking Levin's hand.

"N-n-no!" said Levin.

On parting with him, Daria Aleksandrovna also said, as though congratulating him, "I'm so glad that you've seen Kitty again. One should prize old friendships."

But Levin did not like these words of Daria Aleksandrovna. She could not understand how sublime and inaccessible to her all this was and she should not have dared to speak of it.

Levin took his leave of them, but in order not to remain alone, he caught his brother.

"Where are you going?"

"To a meeting."

"Well, I'm going with you. May I?"

"Why not? Let's go," said Sergei Ivanovich with a smile. "What's the matter with you today?"

"With me? I'm happy!" said Levin, opening the window of the coach in which they were riding. "You don't mind? It's stuffy in here. I'm happy! Why have you never married?"

Sergei Ivanovich smiled again.

"I'm very happy for you. She seems to be a fine—" began Sergei Ivanovich.

"Don't talk, please don't talk!" cried Levin, seizing with both hands the collar of his brother's coat and pulling it

422

closed. "She's a fine girl" were such common, cheap words, so ill-suited to his present feelings.

Sergei Ivanovich laughed gaily, something he rarely did. "But I still may say that I'm happy for you."

"You may say it tomorrow, only tomorrow, but nothing now! Nothing at all, silence!" said Levin, tugging again at his fur collar, and he added, "I love you very much. Well, may I go to the meeting?"

"Of course you may."

"What's today's topic?" asked Levin, continuing to smile.

They arrived at the meeting. The secretary read the minutes in a hesitant voice. Levin listened to him, and it was apparent that the secretary himself did not understand what he was reading. But by the expression on the secretary's face Levin saw what a friendly, good-natured and amiable person he was. This could be seen from his embarrassment and confusion when he read the minutes. Speeches followed. They argued about some appropriations and about laying some pipe, and Sergei Ivanovich made stinging remarks at two members and spoke at length about something triumphantly. Another member, after he had jotted something down on a piece of paper, first lost heart, but then replied with bitter, though polite, sarcasm. And then Sviazhsky (he, too, was there) said something, which sounded beautiful and noble. Levin listened to them and saw clearly that neither the appropriations of money nor the pipe really existed, and that these people were not at all angry with each other but were all very kindhearted and amiable and so good and friendly toward each other. They were in no one's way, and everyone was pleased. It seemed remarkable to Levin that now he could see through them, and by small signs which he had never noticed before, he could look into their hearts and see clearly that all of them were kind. That day all of them particularly loved Levin. This he could see by the way they spoke to him, by the gentle and friendly way in which even people whom he did not know looked at him.

"Well, are you pleased?" asked Sergei Ivanovich.

"Very much. I never thought it would be so interesting. It was fine, splendid!"

Sviazhsky came over to Levin and invited him to his house for tea. Levin was utterly unable to understand and remember what had displeased him about Sviazhsky, and what he had been seeking in him. He was a clever and unusually kind man.

"Thank you very much," he said, and he inquired about his wife and sister-in-law. By a strange association, in his imagination the thought of Sviazhsky's sister-in-law was connected with marriage. He therefore believed that no one was more befitted to listen to the story of his happiness than Sviazhsky's wife and sister-in-law, and he was very glad to go to see them.

Sviazhsky asked him about his farm, believing, as always, that he could not hear anything from him that had not previously been done in Europe, but now it did not displease Levin in the least. On the contrary, he felt that Sviazhsky was right, that all this was insignificant, and he noticed the remarkable gentleness and kindness with which Sviazhsky avoided pressing his point. The Sviazhsky ladies were particularly kind. It seemed to Levin that they already knew everything and were happy for him but were too considerate to talk about it. He spent about three hours with them, talking on different topics but always conscious only of what filled his heart. He did not notice that he had completely worn them out, and that it was long past their bedtime. Sviazhsky saw him to the entrance hall, yawning and wondering at his friend's strange state. It was after one o'clock. Levin returned to the hotel and was alarmed at the prospect of having to get through the next ten hours alone with his impatience. The servant on duty was awake. He lit the candles and was about to leave, but Levin restrained him. The servant Yegor, whom Levin had not noticed before, turned out to be a very clever, good, and, most important, a kindly man.

"Well, Yegor, is it hard to stay awake?"

"What can you do? It's part of the job. A family servant's job is easier, but there's more money in this."

It turned out that Yegor had a family of three boys and a girl. She was a seamstress whom he wanted to marry off to a saddler's clerk.

At this point Levin informed Yegor that love is what counted most in marriage, that love would ever make one happy, for happiness is found only within oneself.

Yegor listened to him attentively and apparently understood fully what Levin meant, but to confirm this he made a remark which surprised Levin. He said that when he served good masters, he was always pleased with them and now he was well pleased with his present master, though he was a Frenchman.

A remarkably kindhearted man, thought Levin.

"And when you married, Yegor, were you in love with your wife?"

"Of course I was," answered Yegor.

And Levin saw that Yegor was in a state of rapture, as he was, and was going to reveal to him his innermost feelings.

"My life also is wonderful. From early childhood . . ." he began, his eyes sparkling. Evidently he was affected by Levin's rapture, as one is affected by other people's yawns.

But at that moment the bell rang. Yegor left and Levin remained alone. He had eaten almost nothing at dinner and had refused tea and supper at the Sviazhsky's, but he could not think of supper. He had not slept the previous night, but could not even think of sleep. It was cool in the room, but the heat stifled him. He opened the small panes of both windows and sat at the table facing one of them. From above the snow-covered roof one could see a cross ornamented with chains and above it the triangle of the Charioteer with bright-yellow Capella. He looked now at the cross, now at the star, inhaled the fresh, frosty air, which was pouring steadily into the room, and as if in a dream, he followed the visions and memories shaped by his imagination. It was after three when he heard the sound of steps in the hall and looked out the door. It was the gambler Miaskin, whom he knew, returning from the club. He walked gloomily, frowning and clearing his throat. Poor, unhappy man, thought Levin, and tears of love and pity for this man sprang to his eyes. He wanted to talk to him, to comfort him. But remembering that he was in his shirtsleeves, he changed his mind and resumed his seat at the window to bathe in the cold air and to gaze at the wonderfully shaped, silent cross, full of meaning for him, and at the rising bright-yellow star. After six o'clock the floor polishers arrived noisily, a church bell rang, and Levin felt that he was getting chilly. He closed the windows, washed, dressed, and went out into the street.

15

THE STREETS WERE still deserted. Levin went to the Shcherbatsky house. The front doors were closed and everyone was
asleep. He turned back, returned to his room and ordered
coffee. The day servant, who had relieved Yegor, brought it.
Levin wanted to enter into a conversation with him, but the
bell rang, and he had to leave. Levin tried to take a sip of
coffee and a bite of bread, but his mouth was completely unable to cope with the bread. Levin spat out the bread, put
on his coat and went out once again. It was after nine when
he came to the Shcherbatsky house for the second time. They
had just arisen, and the cook had left to make his purchases.
He would still have to wait at least two hours.

All that night and morning Levin had been completely unaware of his surroundings as though totally removed from
the circumstances of his material life. He had not eaten at
all, had not slept for two nights, had spent a few hours undressed in the frosty air, and not only was more vigorous
and healthy than ever before but felt completely independent
of his body: he moved without exerting his muscles and
sensed that he could do anything. He was sure that he could
rise into the air or move the corner of the house if it were
required. All the remaining time he walked the streets, repeatedly glancing at his watch and looking around.

And what he saw then, he never saw again. He was particularly moved by the sight of children going to school, of
dark blue pigeons which had flown from the roof to the sidewalk, and of flour-covered loaves exhibited by some unseen
hand. The loaves, pigeons and the two boys were unearthly
creatures. All this happened simultaneously: one of the boys
ran up to the pigeon and, smiling, glanced at Levin; the
pigeon, fluttering its wings, glittered in the sunlight in the
midst of particles of snow which quivered in the air; and the
loaves, which were exhibited in the window, spread an aroma
of freshly baked bread. All this was so unusually fine that
Levin laughed and cried with joy. He made a large circle
around Gazetny Lane and Kislovka, returned again to the
hotel, and putting his watch in front of him, he sat down to
wait until twelve. In the next room, people spoke about

machines and about a fraud and coughed as people cough in the morning. They did not understand that the hands were nearing twelve. They reached it. Levin went out on the porch. The cabbies evidently knew everything. With happy faces they crowded around Levin, arguing with each other and offering him their services. Trying not to offend the other cabbies, and promising to hire them some other time, Levin engaged one and told him to take him to the Shcherbatskys'. The cabby was a fine fellow in a white shirt; its collar stuck out above his coat and was tight around his thick, red, firm neck. His sleigh was tall and neat, of a kind Levin never had the opportunity to ride in again. The horse was good, but though he tried to run rapidly, he remained in the same place. The cabby knew the Shcherbatsky house and, holding his elbows out in gesture of particular respect for his fare, he said, "pproo" and stopped the horse at the entrance. The Shcherbatsky doorman most probably knew everything. This could be seen in his smiling eyes and by the way he said, "You have not visited us for a long time, Konstantin Dmitrievich."

Not only did he know everything but evidently he was elated and forced himself to conceal his joy. Looking at his kind, senile eyes, Levin felt yet another new aspect to his happiness.

"Are they up?"

"Yes, come in, please! But leave it here," he said with a smile, as Levin started to reach for his hat. That meant something.

"To whom shall I announce you?" asked a servant.

Though the servant was young and a dandy, of the new breed of servants, he was a very fine and kindhearted man, one who understood everything.

"To the princess . . . prince . . . young princess," said Levin.

The first person he saw was Mlle. Linon. She walked through the dining room, her curls and her face sparkling. He had just said a few words to her when the rustle of a dress could suddenly be heard from behind the door. Mlle. Linon disappeared from Levin's vision, and he was seized with overpowering joy at his approaching happiness. Mlle. Linon hastily left him and walked over to another door. As soon as she left, brisk light steps sounded on the parquet floor, and his happiness, his life, he himself—the best that was in him—what he had so long desired and sought, rapidly approached him. She did not walk, but some invisible force carried her toward him.

He saw only her clear, sincere eyes, overcome by the same joy of love which filled his own heart. Those eyes shone closer and closer, blinding him with their light of love. She stopped right near him, touching him. Her hands rose and descended upon his shoulders.

She had done all she could; she had run up to him and, shy and happy, yielded all of herself. He embraced her and pressed his lips against her mouth which sought this kiss.

She, too, had not slept at all that night and had been waiting for him all morning. Her father and mother had assented wholeheartedly and rejoiced in her happiness. She had been waiting for him. She wanted to be the first to announce to him his and her happiness. She had readied herself to meet him alone and felt happy at the thought, then afraid and embarrassed, and did not herself know what she would do. She heard his steps and voice and waited behind the door for Mlle. Linon to leave. Mlle. Linon left. Without thinking, without asking herself how and what, she came over to him and did what she did.

"Let's go to Mama," she said, taking his hand. For a long while he could not say anything, not so much because he feared lest his words impair his sublime feeling, as because every time he wanted to say something, he felt that not words but tears of happiness would come forth. He took her hand and kissed it.

"Can it really be true?" he asked at last in a subdued voice. "I cannot believe that you love me!"

She smiled at his use of the familiar form and at the shyness with which he looked at her.

"Yes," she said, slowly and gravely. "I'm so happy!"

She entered the drawing room without releasing his hand. When she saw them, the old princess's breathing quickened, she burst into tears, then into laughter, and she ran up to them with a brisk step that Levin could not have expected, embraced Levin, kissed him, and moistened his cheeks with her tears.

"At last! I'm so happy! Love her. I'm so happy. . . . Kitty!"

"That was quick!" said the old prince, feigning indifference. But Levin noticed that his eyes were moist when he turned toward them.

"I've wanted this for a long time—always!" he said, taking

Levin's arm and drawing him to himself. "Even when that featherbrain fancied—"

"Papa!" cried Kitty, and she covered his mouth with her hands.

"Well, all right!" he said. "I'm very, very happy. Oh, how stupid I am! . . ."

And he embraced Kitty, kissed her face, her hand, and once again her face, and he made the sign of the cross over her.

Levin was possessed with a new feeling of love for the old prince, previously a stranger to him, as he watched Kitty kiss his fleshy hand long and tenderly.

16

THE PRINCESS WAS sitting in the armchair, silent and smiling. The prince sat down near her. Kitty stood by her father's chair, still holding his hand. All were silent.

The princess was the first to express everything in words and to transfer all thoughts and feelings into the realm of practical life. At first this seemed equally strange and painful to all.

"When will it be? We will have to bless them and announce their engagement. And when will the wedding be? What do you think, Aleksandr?"

"Ask him," said the old prince, indicating Levin. "He is the most important one here."

"When?" asked Levin, blushing. "Tomorrow. If you ask me, I say let us be engaged today and married tomorrow."

"Come now, no nonsense, *mon cher!*"

"Then in a week."

"He speaks as if he's lost his wits."

"But why not?"

"Good heavens," the mother said, smiling happily at this impatience. "And the trousseau?"

Is there really going to be a trousseau and all that? Levin thought in horror. But then could a trousseau, a betrothal, and all of that really mar my happiness? Nothing could do that. He looked at Kitty and noticed that the thought of the trousseau had not offended her in the least. It seems that it must be, he thought.

"I really don't know about such things and have only expressed my own preference," he said apologetically.

"Then we will decide. Now we may bless you and announce your engagement. That's how it's done."

The princess went over to her husband, kissed him and was about to leave. But he restrained her, embraced her tenderly like a young lover, and smiling, he kissed her several times. The old couple evidently had grown confused for a moment and did not fully realize whether it was they who were again in love or their daughter. When the prince and princess left, Levin came over to his fiancée and took her hand. He was now in control of himself and could speak, and there was much he had to tell her. But he did not at all say what he should have.

"How well I knew that it would be this way. I never hoped, yet deep in my heart I was always sure," he said. "I believe that it was fated."

"And I?" she said. "Even then . . ." she stopped and then continued, her sincere eyes looking at him with determination, "even then, when I rejected my happiness. I've always loved you alone, but I was carried away. I must tell you. . . . Can you forget it?"

"Perhaps this is for the best. There's much for you to forgive. I must tell you. . . ."

This was one of the confessions which he had decided to make. From the first day he had decided to confess to her two things—that, unlike her, he was not chaste, and that he was an unbeliever. It was painful to do it, but he had decided that he must confess to both things.

"No, not now, later!" he said.

"All right, later, but you must tell me. I'm not afraid of anything. I must know all. Everything is settled now."

"Is it settled then," he added, "that you'll take me as I am, that you'll not reject me? Is it?"

"Yes, yes."

Their conversation was interrupted by Mlle. Linon, who came with a tender though insincere smile to congratulate her dear pupil. She was still there when the servants came in with their congratulations. Then the relatives arrived, and a blissful confusion ensued from which Levin did not emerge until the day after his wedding. Levin was constantly embarrassed or bored, but the intensity of his happiness continued to grow stronger. He always felt that much was being demanded of him of which he was ignorant, and he did everything he was told to, and this made him happy. He thought that his courting would be completely unlike that of others, that the ordinary ways of courtship would not suit his singular happiness. But in the end he did as others do, and this intensified his happiness, making it so unusual as to be beyond compare.

"Now we'll have some candy," said Mlle. Linon, and Levin rode out to buy candy.

"Wonderful news!" said Sviazhsky. "I'd advise you to buy your bouquets at Fomin's."

"Must I?" and he rode over to Fomin's.

His brother told him to borrow money, that he would need it for expenses, presents. . . .

"Presents too?" and he dashed over to Fulde's.

And at the confectionery, at Fomin's and at Fulde's, he saw that everyone was waiting for him, that they were glad to see him, and that they rejoiced in his happiness, as everyone else did with whom he dealt those days. It was remarkable that not only did everybody like him but all those who formerly had been unfriendly, cold or indifferent, admired him and yielded to him in every way, treating his feelings gently and delicately. They shared his opinion that he was the happiest man in the world, for his fiancée was the apex of perfection. Kitty felt the same way. When Countess Nordston permitted herself to hint that she would prefer a better match, Kitty became so aroused and so persuasively proved that none in this world could be better than Levin, that Countess Nordston had to agree and, when Kitty was present, she no longer met Levin without a smile of admiration.

The only painful experience of those days was the confession he had promised to make. He consulted the old prince and, with his permission, he handed Kitty his diary, in which he had entered everything that had troubled him. He had actually written this diary with his future fiancée in mind. Two things troubled him: he was unchaste and an unbeliever. The confession of his unbelieving passed unnoticed. She was religious and never doubted the religious tenets, but she was entirely unconcerned about his outward skepticism. By loving him she knew his whole soul, and in it she found what she wished and it did not matter to her that a man with such a soul was called an unbeliever. But the other confession made her cry bitterly.

It was not without an inner struggle that Levin handed her his diary. He knew that there should be no secrets between him and her, and he therefore decided that this was the right thing to do. But he did not think of the possible effects of his confession; he had not put himself in her place. Only that evening, when he had come to visit them before the theater and, on entering her room, saw her tear-stained, pitiful, dear face, overcome by the irremediable sorrow he had caused her, did he see the bottomless chasm that separated his shameful past from her dovelike purity, and he was horrified by what he had done.

"Take away these horrible books!" she said, pushing aside the notebooks that lay in front of her. "Why did you give them to me? No, it's better that you did," she added, taking pity on his despair. "But it's horrible, horrible!"

He bowed his head and remained silent. He had nothing to say.

"You'll not forgive me," he whispered.

"No, I've forgiven you, but it's horrible."

His happiness, however, was so great that this confession did not mar it, but added a new nuance to it. She forgave him. But from that time on he considered himself still less worthy of her bowed more deeply to her morally, and valued his unmerited happiness still more highly.

17

UNCONSCIOUSLY reviewing the impressions of the conversation held during and after dinner, Aleksei Aleksandrovich was returning to his lonely hotel room. Daria Aleksandrovna's words about forgiveness had only annoyed him. Whether or not to follow the Christian precept in this matter was a problem that was too difficult to decide, which could not be discussed lightly; and this problem had long since been decided by Aleksei Aleksandrovich in the negative. Of all that had been said, he most vividly remembered the words of the foolish, good-natured Turovtzin: "He acted like a hero; he challenged him to a duel and killed him." Evidently everyone approved of this, though, out of politeness, no one said so.

This matter, however, is already settled, and there is no use in thinking about it, said Aleksei Aleksandrovich to himself. And thinking only about his forthcoming trip and the matter of the inspection, he entered his room and asked the doorman who accompanied him where his servant was. The doorman said that the servant had just gone out. Aleksei Aleksandrovich ordered tea, sat down at a table and, taking a railway time-table, began to plan his itinerary.

"Two telegrams," said the servant, who returned to the room. "Forgive me, your excellency. I left just for a minute."

Aleksei Aleksandrovich took the telegrams and opened them. The first informed him that Stremov had been appointed to the very position to which Karenin had aspired. Aleksei Aleksandrovich threw down the telegram, his face flushed, and began pacing up and down the room. "*Quos vult perdere dementat!*" he said, by "*quos*" referring to those who had furthered this appointment. It was not the fact that he had missed this appointment and evidently had been passed over that annoyed him. He wondered and could not understand how they failed to see that this blabbermouth and phrase-monger Stremov was totally unfit for the position. Didn't they see that by this appointment they were injuring themselves and their prestige?

Probably another one of the same kind, he said to himself bitterly as he opened the second telegram. This one was from his wife. The first thing he saw was the signature "ANNA" in blue pencil. "*I am dying. I beg you, I beseech you, to come. With your forgiveness I will die more peacefully,*" he read. He smiled scornfully and threw the telegram down. At first it seemed to him that there could be no doubt whatever that it was nothing but deceit and cunning. She'll stop at no decep-tion. She's going to give birth to a child. Perhaps she is sick as a result of the childbirth. But what are they up to? To have me legalize the child, to compromise me, and to hamper the divorce proceedings, he thought. But what about the words: "*I am dying*"? He reread the telegram and was struck by the directness of what was said. But suppose it's true? he said to himself. Suppose that at the moment of suffering and ap-proaching death she sincerely repents, and I, mistaking it for deception, refuse to go? It would not only be cruel; everyone would condemn me, and it would be stupid on my part.

"Piotr, arrange a coach. I've going to Petersburg," he told the servant.

Aleksei Aleksandrovich decided to go to Petersburg to see his wife. If her sickness were a sham, he would say nothing and leave. But if she were really sick and on her deathbed asked to see him, he would forgive her if he found her alive or would perform his last duty to her if he came too late.

On the way home he no longer thought of what had to be done.

Tired and dirty after spending a night in the railroad car, Aleksei Aleksandrovich rode in the early morning fog along the deserted Nevsky and looked straight ahead without thinking of what awaited him. He could not think about it because, as he tried to foresee what was going to happen, he could not rid himself of the notion that her death would immediately resolve all the difficulty of his situation. He watched the procession flash by him: bakers, closed stores, night cabbies, porters sweeping the sidewalks. He tried to suppress the thoughts of what awaited him, of what he dared not wish but wished nevertheless. He rode up to the entrance porch. A hired cab and a coach with a sleeping coachman were at the entrance. On entering the house, Aleksei Aleksandrovich brought out a decision as though from a remote corner of his mind, and examined it. It ran: If it is a fraud, show calm contempt and depart. If it is true, then observe propriety.

The doorman opened the door even before Aleksei Aleksandrovich rang. The doorman Petrov, also called Kapitonych, looked strange in his old coat, tieless and in slippers.

"How is the mistress?"

"Yesterday she gave birth safely."

Aleksei Aleksandrovich stopped and grew pale. He now understood clearly how strongly he wished her death.

"And how is her health?"

Kornei, in his morning apron, ran down the stairs.

"She is very sick," he replied. "Yesterday there was a doctors' consultation, and the doctor is here now."

"Take care of my luggage," said Aleksei Aleksandrovich and, feeling somewhat relieved that there still was hope for her death, he went into the hall.

There was a military coat on the coat rack. Aleksei Aleksandrovich noticed it and asked:

"Who is here?"

"The doctor, the midwife, and Count Vronsky."

Aleksei Aleksandrovich went into the inside rooms.

There was no one in the drawing room. On hearing the sound of his steps, the midwife, in a bonnet with lilac ribbons, emerged from his wife's sitting room.

She came over to Aleksei Aleksandrovich and, with a

familiarity brought about by the approach of death, she took his arm and led him toward the bedroom.

"Thank God you've arrived. She speaks only of you," she said.

"Make haste with the ice," came the doctor's commanding voice from the bedroom.

Aleksei Aleksandrovich entered her sitting room. At her table, on a low chair, was Vronsky, sitting sideways. His face was in his hands and he was crying. He jumped up on hearing the doctor's voice, dropped his hands from his face, and saw Aleksei Aleksandrovich. At the sight of her husband he grew so confused that he sat down again, drawing his head into his shoulders as though trying to disappear. But he forced himself to rise and said:

"She is dying. The doctors said there is no hope. I am here at your mercy, but let me stay here . . . but do what you will, I. . . ."

Seeing Vronsky's tears, Aleksei Aleksandrovich felt the approach of that state of emotional tension to which he was always brought by the sight of other people's sufferings. He avoided his face and, without listening to his words, hurriedly moved toward the door. From the bedroom came the voice of Anna, saying something. Her voice was cheerful and animated and her speech unusually clear. Aleksei Aleksandrovich entered the bedroom and went over to her bed. She lay there, her face turned toward him. Her cheeks were flushed, her eyes glistened, and her small white hands, protruding from the cuffs of her bedjacket, toyed with the corner of the blanket, twisting it. It was almost as though she were not only well and vigorous but also in excellent spirits. She spoke rapidly in a sonorous voice, her speech unusually clear and full of emotion.

"Because Aleksei, I mean Aleksei Aleksandrovich (what a strange, terrible fate that both of them should be called Aleksei), Aleksei would not refuse it to me. I would forget, he would forgive. . . . Why doesn't he come? He's kind, he himself doesn't know how kind he is. Oh, my God! Woe is me! Water, please! Oh, it will harm her, my little girl. Well, then, hire a wet nurse for her. Well, all right, that would be even better. He'll come, it will pain him to see her. Give her away."

"Anna Arkadievna, he has arrived. Here he is!" said the

midwife, trying to draw her attention to Aleksei Aleksandrovich.

"Oh, what nonsense!" continued Anna, still not seeing her husband. "But give her to me, my little girl, give her to me. He hasn't arrived yet. You say that he wouldn't forgive, because you don't know him. No one did. Only I, and it had become hard for me too. Seryozha, you know, has his eyes, and that's why I can't look into them. Did you give Seryozha his dinner? I know that everybody will forget. He wouldn't forget. You must transfer Seryozha to the corner room, and ask Mariette to stay with him."

Suddenly she shrank, fell silent and frightened, as though waiting for a blow, and she raised her hands to her face as though to defend herself. She saw her husband.

"No, no," she said, "I'm not afraid of him, I'm afraid of death. Aleksei, come here. I'm in a hurry because I have no time, I haven't long to live, I'll soon become feverish, and will no longer understand anything. I understand now, I understand everything, I see everything."

An expression of suffering appeared on Aleksei Aleksandrovich's drawn face. He took her hand and wanted to say something, but he could not utter a sound. His lower lip trembled, he still struggled to control his emotions and looked at her only occasionally. And every time he glanced at her, he saw her eyes, which gazed at him with such rapturous tenderness and kindness as he had never before seen in them.

"Wait, you don't know. Wait, wait," she said, and she stopped, as though collecting her thoughts. "Yes," she began. "Yes, yes. This is what I wanted to say. Don't be surprised at me. I'm still the same. . . . But there is someone else within me whom I fear—she fell in love with him, and I wanted to hate you and I couldn't forget her who had been before. She's not I. I'm the real one now, the whole one. I'm dying now, I know that I'm dying—ask him. I feel it now. Here they are, weights on my hands, my feet, my fingers. How huge my fingers are! But all this will end soon. . . . I want only one thing: forgive me, forgive me completely! I'm wicked, but my nurse told me, 'A holy martyr'—what was her name?— 'was still worse.' And I'll go to Rome. There's a desert there, and I'll bother no one. I'll take along only Seryozha and the little girl. . . . No, you cannot forgive me! I know that this cannot be forgiven. No, no, leave me, you are too good."

With one of her feverish hands she held his hand, with the other she pushed him away.

Aleksei Aleksandrovich grew more and more disturbed until his agitation reached a stage when he ceased struggling against it. He suddenly felt that what he had regarded as emotional agitation was actually a state of emotional bliss which unexpectedly brought him a new happiness such as he had never before felt. He did not think of the Christian precept, which he had wanted to follow all his life, that commanded him to forgive and love his enemies; nevertheless, a joyous feeling of love and forgiveness toward his enemies filled his heart. He knelt there, his head on the crook of her arm, its heat searing him through the bedjacket. He sobbed like a child. She embraced his balding head, moved over to him and, with an air of defiant pride, she raised her eyes.

"Here he is, I knew it! Now, farewell everyone, farewell! . . . They have come again. Why don't they leave? Take these fur coats off me!"

The doctor took her hands, and carefully moved her onto the pillow and covered her shoulders. She lay on her back meekly and looked straight ahead, her eyes radiant.

"Remember only that all I needed was forgiveness, and I want nothing else. . . . Why doesn't *he* come?" she said, turning toward Vronsky at the door. "Come here, come here! Give him your hand."

Vronsky came over to the edge of the bed and, at the sight of her, again covered his face with his hands.

"Uncover your face; look at him. He's a saint," she said. "Yes, uncover, uncover your face!" she said angrily. "Aleksei Aleksandrovich, uncover his face. I want to see him."

Aleksei Aleksandrovich took Vronsky's hands from his face, terribly distorted by shame and suffering.

"Give him your hand. Forgive him."

Aleksei Aleksandrovich gave him his hand without restraining the tears which poured from his eyes.

"Thank God, thank God!" she said. "I'm ready now. If I could only stretch my legs a little. That's it, that's fine. How badly done these flowers are; they don't look at all like violets," she said, indicating the wallpaper. "My God! My God! When will it end? Give me morphine. Doctor, give me morphine. Oh, my God! Oh, my God!"

And she thrashed about in the bed.

This doctor, as well as the other doctors, said that it was a case of puerperal fever, from which ninety-nine out of a hundred died. Fever, delirium, and unconsciousness continued the entire day. Toward midnight the patient fell into a coma, her pulse almost gone.

The end was expected at any moment.

Vronsky left for his home, but he came back in the morning, and Aleksei Aleksandrovich, meeting him in the entrance hall, told him:

"Don't leave, she may ask for you," and he himself took him to his wife's sitting room.

Toward morning there returned the same animation, vivacity, and rapid flow of thoughts and words, which again ended in a coma. The same happened on the third day, and the doctor declared that there was hope. That day Aleksei Aleksandrovich went into the study where Vronsky was sitting, closed the door, and sat opposite him.

"Aleksei Aleksandrovich," said Vronsky, feeling that the time for an understanding between them was approaching, "I can say nothing, I understand nothing. Have compassion for me. However much you suffer, believe me, my suffering is still greater."

He was about to rise, but Aleksei Aleksandrovich took his hand and said:

"I ask you to hear me out. It is urgent. I must explain to you the feelings which have governed and will govern me so that you may not be mistaken about me. You know that I've decided on a divorce and have even started the proceedings. I'll not hide from you the fact that when I began, I was tormented by doubts. I confess that the desire of wreaking vengeance on you and her pursued me. When I received the telegram, I came here with the same feeling. I'll say even more: I wished her death. But . . ." he fell into silence, hesitating whether or not to reveal to him his feelings. "But I saw her and forgave. And the happiness of this forgiveness revealed to me my duty. I have forgiven completely. I wish to offer my other cheek; I want to give my shirt when they take away my cloak, and only pray to God that he may not take away from me this happiness of forgiveness." Tears stood in his eyes, and Vronsky was struck by his serene, calm look. "This is my position. You may trample me into mire, may turn me into a laughingstock, but I'll not forsake her and will never utter a word of reproach against you," he continued. "My duty is clearly indicated. I must be with her and shall be. If she wants to see you, I'll let you know, but now, I believe, it's better that you leave."

He rose, and sobs disrupted his speech. Vronsky also rose and, stooped and bent, he looked up toward him. He did not understand Aleksei Aleksandrovich's feeling. But he felt that it was something sublime, and for him, with his views, even inaccesible.

18

AFTER HIS conversation with Aleksei Aleksandrovich, Vronsky went out on the porch of the Karenin house and stood there, remembering with difficulty where he was and where he had to go. He felt ashamed, humiliated, guilty, and deprived of the chance to wash off the stain of his humiliation. He felt that he had been forced out of the path he had so proudly and easily walked until now. Everything that had seemed to him so solidly established, his habits and his code of conduct, suddenly turned out to be false and inapplicable. The betrayed husband, who until now had been considered a miserable creature, an accidental and somewhat comical impediment to his happiness, was suddenly called back by her and exalted to a height that inspired humility, and at this height the husband appeared not malicious, not hypocritical, not ridiculous, but kindhearted, frank and noble. Vronsky could not help feeling this. Their roles had suddenly changed. Vronsky became aware that the husband was exalted and right, and he humiliated and wrong. He felt that the husband was magnanimous even in his misfortune, but he was base and petty in his deceit. But the awareness of his inferiority to the man whom he had unjustly despised was the lesser cause of his distress. He felt utterly miserable because his passion for Anna, which, it seemed to him, had cooled of late, had grown stronger than ever before now that he knew that he had lost her forever. He had seen all of her during her illness, come to know her heart, and it seemed to him that until then he had never loved her. And now, when he came to know her, and loved her as one ought to love, he was humiliated in her eyes and had lost her forever, leaving only a shameful memory. Most horrifying was his ridiculous, humiliating situation when

Aleksei Aleksandrovich had removed his hands from his shame-ridden face. He stood on the porch of the Karenin house, lost, not knowing what to do.

"A cab?" asked the doorman.

"Yes, a cab."

When he returned home after three sleepless nights, Vronsky, without undressing, lay down on the divan, his face downward, resting his head on his folded hands. His head felt heavy. The strangest images, memories, and thoughts followed one another with great speed and clarity: now it was the medicine, which he poured for the patient and spilled over the spoon, now the white hands of the midwife, now the strange posture of Aleksei Aleksandrovich on the floor at the side of the bed.

Sleep! Forgetfulness! he said to himself with a healthy man's calm confidence that if he was tired and sleepy, he would fall asleep at once. And, indeed, within a moment his thoughts grew confused and he began to sink into the abyss of oblivion. The sea of unconsciousness had already begun to sweep over his head when suddenly, as though shocked by a powerful electric current, he started with such force that his entire body bounced on the springs of the divan, and pushing down on his hands, he jumped to his knees in fright. His eyes were opened wide, as though he had not slept at all. The weight of his head and the weariness of his limbs, which he had felt a moment ago, suddenly vanished.

"You may trample me in the mire," he heard Aleksei Aleksandrovich say and he saw him standing before him. He saw Anna's face flushed with fever, her eyes shining, looking with love and tenderness not at him but at Aleksei Aleksandrovich. He saw himself, looking foolish and ridiculous, it seemed to him, when Aleksei Aleksandrovich took his hands from his face. He stretched out his legs again, flung himself upon the divan in his former position, and closed his eyes.

Sleep! Sleep! he repeated to himself. But with closed eyes he saw Anna's face still more clearly, as he had seen it on that memorable evening before the races.

"That's gone forever, and she wants to erase it from her memory. But I can't live without it. How can we be reconciled, how can we?" he said aloud and he unconsciously began to repeat these words. The repetition hampered the cropping up of new images and memories, which, he felt, thronged in his head. But the repetition of the words did not restrain his imagination for long. The best moments of his life, following one another with unusual speed, as well as his recent humiliation, again began to crowd into his mind. "Put your hands down," says Anna's voice. He removes his hands and feels the shame-filled and foolish expression on his face.

He continued to lie there, trying to fall asleep, but he felt that there was not the slightest hope for it, and he kept repeating in a whisper incidental words from scattered thoughts, trying in such a manner to block new images from forming. He listened and heard words repeated in a strange, insane whisper, "You failed to appreciate your opportunities; you failed to make use of them."

What is it? Am I losing my mind? he asked himself. Perhaps. Isn't this why people lose their minds, why they shoot themselves? he asked himself and, opening his eyes, he was surprised to see next to his head the embroidered pillow, the work of Varia, his brother's wife. He felt the tassel of the pillow and tried to think of Varia and to recall when he had seen her last. But it was painful to think of something else. No, I must fall asleep! He moved the pillow and pressed his head against it, but he had to force himself to keep his eyes closed. He sat up abruptly. It's all over for me, he said to himself. I must think over what I must do. What is left? In his mind he rapidly surveyed his life apart from his love for Anna.

Ambition? Serpukhovskoy? Society? The court? He could not decide anything. All this had had its meaning before, but not now. He rose from the divan, took off his coat, loosened his belt, and uncovering his hairy chest to breathe more freely, he walked up and down the room. This is how people lose their minds, he repeated, and this is how they shoot themselves . . . so as to feel no shame, he added slowly.

He went up to the door and closed it. Then, with a fixed look and tightly clenched teeth, he went to the table, took his revolver, looked it over, turned it to a loaded chamber and remained lost in thought. For a few moments he stood motionless, his head bowed with an expression of intense mental effort, the revolver in his hand, and he thought. Of course, he said to himself, as though a protracted, logical and clear course of thought had brought him to an incontrovertible conclusion. But actually, these words, "of course," which seemed so convincing to him, had resulted only from retracing the same circle of memories and impressions he had already gone over innumerable times during the past hour. The same memories of his happiness, now lost forever; the same awareness of the meaninglessness of what awaited him; the same realization of his humiliation. Even the sequence of these impressions and feelings was the same.

Of course, he repeated, when, for the third time, his thoughts followed the same vicious circle of memories and impressions. He put the revolver against the left side of his chest, and with a spasmodic movement of his whole hand, as though suddenly making a fist, he pulled the trigger. He did not hear the sound of the shot, but a violent blow to his chest knocked him down. He tried to hold on to the edge of the table, dropped the revolver, tottered and sat on the floor, looking around in bewilderment. He did not recognize his room as he looked from below at the curved legs of the table, at the waste basket, at the tiger rug. The rapid squeaking steps of his servant walking through the drawing room brought him to his senses. With effort he realized that he was on the floor and, noticing blood on the tiger rug and on his hand, he understood that he had shot himself.

"How stupid! I missed," he said, searching for his revolver with his hand. The revolver was next to him, but he searched beyond it. Continuing his search, he leaned toward the other side and, too weak to maintain his balance, he fell, bleeding profusely.

The elegant, side-whiskered servant, who often complained to his friends about his sensitive nerves, was so frightened when he saw his master lying on the floor that he left him there bleeding and ran for help. Within an hour Varia, his brother's wife, arrived and with the help of three doctors whom she had summoned from all over, and who had arrived at the same time, she put the patient in bed and remained to take care of him.

19

ALEKSEI ALEKSANDROVICH had committed an error. In preparing himself to see his wife, he had failed to consider the possibility that her repentance might be sincere, that he might forgive her, and that she might not die. He saw the full impact of this mistake two months after his return from

Moscow. But his mistake stemmed not only from his failure
to consider that possibility but also from the fact that prior
to the day of his meeting with his dying wife he had not known
how his heart would behave. At the bedside of his sick wife,
for the first time in his life, he abandoned himself to that feeling of tender compassion the suffering of others always
aroused in him, and of which he formerly had been ashamed,
as of a damaging weakness. Compassion for her, repentance
for having wished her death, and especially the very joy of
forgiving had brought him not only quick relief from all his
suffering, but also a peace with himself such as he had never
experienced before. He suddenly felt that what had been the
cause of his suffering became the source of his inner joy, and
what had appeared to him impossible when he censured, reproached, and hated, became simple and clear when he forgave and loved.

He forgave his wife and pitied her for her suffering and
repentance. He forgave Vronsky and pitied him, particularly
after rumors had reached him about his desperate act. He also
pitied his son more than before and reproached himself now
for having paid so little attention to him. But for the newborn
infant girl he had a particular feeling not only of pity but
also of tenderness. At first only a feeling of pity had moved
him to occupy himself with the helpless child, who was not
his daughter and who was neglected at the time of her
mother's illness, and who probably would have died without
his care, but he himself did not notice how he came to love
her. He visited the nursery several times a day and spent so
much time there that the wet nurse and the nurse, whom at
first he made uncomfortable, now grew accustomed to him.
Sometimes he would look silently for half an hour at the
saffron-red, downy, wrinkled little face of the sleeping baby,
and would watch her frowning forehead and plump little
hands with their curled fingers as she rubbed her little eyes
and the bridge of her nose with the back of her hands. Particularly at such moments, Aleksei Aleksandrovich felt fully
composed and at peace with himself, and he did not see anything unusual in his situation, nothing that should be
changed.

But as time passed, he saw more clearly that no matter how
natural he found his present situation, he would not be
allowed to remain in it. He felt that besides the benevolent
spiritual force that guided his soul, there was another rude

force, as powerful or more so, which directed his life, and that this force would not grant him the humble peace for which he longed. He felt that everyone looked at him with questioning surprise, that they did not understand him and expected something of him. He particularly felt how insecure and unnatural was his relationship with his wife.

When the mellowness that the approach of death had brought about in her had worn off, Aleksei Aleksandrovich began to notice that Anna feared him, that his presence embarrassed her, and that she could not look him straight in the eye. It seemed that she wanted something but did not dare to tell him, and that as though anticipating that their present relationship could not continue, she expected something of him.

At the end of February it happened that Anna's new baby, who also was named Anna, fell ill. In the morning Aleksei Aleksandrovich went into the nursery, ordered that a doctor be called, and left for the ministry. Having finished there, he returned home after three o'clock. As he came into the entrance hall, he noticed a handsome servant, dressed in his braided uniform and bearskin cape, holding a white raccoon fur cloak.

"Who is here?" asked Aleksei Aleksandrovich.

"Princess Elizaveta Fyodorovna Tverskoy," the servant answered, with what seemed to Aleksei Aleksandrovich to be a smile.

During this troubled time Aleksei Aleksandrovich noticed that his social acquaintances, especially the women, took particular interest in his wife and himself. In all these acquaintances he observed a feeling of joy, which they could scarcely conceal, the same joy that he had observed in the eyes of the lawyer and now in the eyes of the servant. It was as though everyone was delighted, as though they were marrying off someone. When they met him, they inquired about his health with a scarcely concealed joy.

Aleksei Aleksandrovich, displeased by Princess Tverskoy's presence both because of the memories associated with her and because of his dislike of her in general, went directly into the nursery. In the first room Seryozha, sprawled out on the table with his legs on a chair, was drawing something, chattering happily. The English governess, who during Anna's illness had replaced the French one, sat next to the boy with her needlework. She hurriedly rose, curtsied, and tugged at Seryozha.

Aleksei Aleksandrovich stroked his son's hair, replied to the governess's inquiry about his wife's health, and asked what the doctor had said about the baby.

"The doctor said that it was nothing serious, sir, and prescribed baths."

"But she is suffering," said Aleksei Aleksandrovich, listening to the baby crying in the next room.

"I believe that the fault lies with the wet nurse," the English governess said firmly.

"What makes you think so?" he asked her, stopping abruptly.

"Because the same thing happened at Countess Paul's. The baby was treated by the doctors, but it turned out that the baby was just hungry. The nurse had no milk, sir."

Aleksei Aleksandrovich thought it over for a few moments and then went into the other room. The baby lay in the arms of the wet nurse, struggling and turning her head away. She refused either to take the plump breast offered to her or to calm down, though both the wet nurse and the nurse, bent over her, tried to quiet her.

"Still no better?" asked Aleksei Aleksandrovich.

"Very restless," whispered the nurse.

"Miss Edward says that perhaps the nurse has no milk," he said.

"I think so too, Aleksei Aleksandrovich."

"Then why didn't you tell us?"

"Whom could I tell? Anna Arkadievna is always ill," said the nurse with displeasure.

The nurse was an old house servant. And these frank words, it seemed to Aleksei Aleksandrovich, hinted at his situation.

The baby cried still louder, frantically and hoarsely. The nurse threw up her hands, went over to the baby, and began to rock her to sleep as she walked.

"We must ask the doctor to examine the wet nurse," said Aleksei Aleksandrovich.

The healthy looking, smartly dressed wet nurse, fearing that she would be discharged, muttered something, covered her large breast and smiled scornfully at these doubts concerning her ability to suckle the baby. And in this smile Aleksei Aleksandrovich also saw a sneer at his situation.

"Poor child!" said the nurse, hushing the baby and continuing to walk.

Aleksei Aleksandrovich sat down on a chair and with an expression of suffering and dejection on his face watched the nurse pacing up and down.

When the baby finally calmed down and was placed in the deep cradle, and the nurse had arranged her pillow and stepped aside, Aleksei Aleksandrovich rose, and walking on tiptoe with difficulty, went over to the baby. He remained silent and with the same air of dejection watched the baby. But suddenly a smile appeared on his face, creasing his forehead so that his hair moved, and he quietly left the room.

In the dining room he rang and told the servant who came in to send for the doctor again. He was annoyed that his wife had not taken care of this sweet baby, and in his annoyance he felt no desire to see her or Princess Betsy. But his wife might wonder why, contrary to his habit, he had not come to see her. So he forced himself to go toward the bedroom. When he came up to the door on the soft rug, he involuntarily overheard a conversation which he did not want to hear.

"If he weren't leaving, I would understand your refusal and his, too. But your husband should be above this," said Betsy.

"It's not for my husband's sake but for my own that I don't want it. Don't talk to me about it!" Anna replied in an excited voice.

"But it's hard to believe that you don't wish to say goodbye to a man who has shot himself because of you."

"That's the very reason I don't wish it."

Aleksei Aleksandrovich stopped, a frightened and guilty expression on his face, and was about to withdraw without being noticed. But he changed his mind, considering that it would be undignified to do so, turned again, and, with a cough, went toward the bedroom. The voices fell silent as he entered.

Anna, dressed in a gray robe, sat on the couch, a thick brush of closely cropped hair on her shapely head. As always at the sight of her husband, her animation vanished at once. She lowered her head and cast an anxious look at Betsy. Betsy was dressed in the latest fashion, in a hat that floated somewhere over her head like a chimney cap over a lamp, and a dove-colored dress with sharply outlined diagonal stripes running across the bodice in one direction and across the skirt in the opposite. She sat next to Anna, her tall, flat body erect, and, inclining her head, she met Aleksei Aleksandrovich with a mocking smile.

"Oh," she said, as though in surprise. "I'm very glad to find you at home. You don't show yourself anywhere and I haven't seen you since Anna was taken ill. I've heard of everything—of your thoughtfulness. Yes, you're a wonderful husband!" she said with a meaningful and gracious air, as though awarding him the Order of Magnanimity for his behavior toward his wife.

Aleksei Aleksandrovich bowed coldly, kissed his wife's hand, and inquired about her health.

"I believe that I'm better," she said, avoiding his look.

"But you look feverish," he said, accentuating the word "feverish."

"Our conversation was too much for her," said Betsy, "and I think that I'm being too selfish. I had better go."

She rose, but Anna, suddenly blushing, grasped her hand.

"Don't go, please. I have to tell you . . . no, you," she said, turning to Aleksei Aleksandrovich, a blush spreading over her face and neck. "I don't want to and cannot hide anything from you."

Aleksei Aleksandrovich cracked his knuckles and bowed his head.

"Betsy told me that Count Vronsky wishes to visit us to say goodbye before leaving for Tashkent." She did not look at her husband and evidently was hurrying to tell him everything, however difficult it was to do so. "I answered that I couldn't receive him."

"You said, my friend, that it would depend on Aleksei Aleksandrovich," Betsy corrected her.

"No, I can't receive him, and this would not lead . . ." she continued, then stopped abruptly and glanced inquiringly at her husband (he was not looking at her). "In short, I don't want to. . . ."

Aleksei Aleksandrovich moved toward her and was about to take her hand. Her first impulse was to draw her hand back from his moist, seeking hand, with its large, bulging veins. But she restrained herself with obvious effort and pressed his hand.

"I'm very grateful for your trust, but . . ." he said. He was embarrassed and annoyed, feeling that what he could decide by himself so easily and so sensibly, he could not discuss in the presence of Princess Tverskoy. To him she was the embodiment of the rude force that society believed should govern his life and that prevented him from abandoning himself to his feeling of love and forgiveness. He stopped, staring at Princess Tverskoy.

"Well, goodbye, my dear," said Betsy, rising. She kissed Anna and left. Aleksei Aleksandrovich accompanied her.

"Aleksei Aleksandrovich! I know that you are a truly magnanimous person," said Betsy, stopping in the small drawing room and shaking his hand once again with particular firmness. "I'm an outsider, but I love her and respect you so much that I permit myself to give you my advice. Please receive him. Aleksei Vronsky is the embodiment of honor, and he is leaving for Tashkent."

"I thank you, Princess, for your concern and advice. But my wife herself will decide whom she will or will not receive."

He said this with his usual dignity, raising his eyebrows, and then he quickly realized that no matter what he would say there could be no dignity in his situation. This he saw in the controlled, wicked, derisive smile with which Betsy looked at him after he spoke.

20

ALEKSEI ALEKSANDROVICH took leave of Betsy in the hall and returned to his wife. She had been lying down, but on hearing his step, she hurriedly sat up, resumed her former position, and looked at him with fear. He saw that she had been crying.

"I'm very grateful to you for your trust in me," he said, repeating gently in Russian the sentence that, in Betsy's presence, he had said in French, and he sat next to her. When he spoke Russian, he addressed her as "thou," but this "thou" Anna found unbearably irritating. "And I'm grateful to you for your decision. I, too, believe that since Count Vronsky is leaving, there is really no need for him to come here. However—"

"I've already said it. Why repeat it?" Anna quickly interrupted with an annoyance that she failed to control. Surely there is no need, she thought, for a man to come to say goodbye to the woman whom he loves, for whose sake he was ready to destroy himself, to perish, and who cannot live without him. No, no need at all! She compressed her lips and lowered her shining eyes to his stiff-veined hands, which he was rubbing together slowly.

"We'll never talk about it again," she added, calming herself.

"I left the decision to you, and I'm glad to see—" Aleksei Aleksandrovich began.

"That my desire conforms to yours," she added, completing the sentence hurriedly, annoyed that he spoke so slowly when she knew beforehand everything he was going to say.

"Yes," he agreed, "and Princess Tverskoy's meddling in the most delicate of family matters is completely out of place. Particularly she—"

"I don't believe anything they say about her," said Anna hastily. "I know that she loves me sincerely."

Aleksei Aleksandrovich sighed and fell silent. She toyed nervously with the tassels of her robe and looked at him with a disturbing feeling of physical aversion, which she reproached herself for, but could not overcome. She wished now for one thing only—to be relieved of his hateful presence.

"I've just sent for the doctor," said Aleksei Aleksandrovich.

"I'm well. Why do I need a doctor?"

"You don't, but the baby keeps crying. I understand that the baby hasn't had enough milk."

"Then why didn't you let me nurse her when I begged to. In spite of everything," (Aleksei Aleksandrovich understood what she meant by "in spite of everything") "she's a baby, and they'll starve her to death." She rang and asked that the baby be brought in. "I wanted to nurse her but I wasn't permitted to, and now I'm being reproached."

"I'm not reproaching you. . . ."

"Yes you are! My God, why didn't I die?" she said, breaking into sobs. "Forgive me, I'm upset. I'm unjust," she said, recovering. "But leave me. . . ."

No, it can't go on like this, Aleksei Aleksandrovich said resolutely to himself as he left his wife.

Never before had he visualized so clearly as that day the hopelessness of his situation, in the eyes of society, in view of his wife's hatred for him, and generally as a result of the power of the mysterious rude force, which, in opposition to his emotional state, governed his life, demanded obedience to its will and a change in his relationship with his wife. He saw clearly that both society and his wife demanded something of him, but what it was exactly he did not know. He was conscious of a feeling of malice rising in his heart as a result of this, destroying his composure and all the merit of his achievements. He believed that it would be better for Anna to break off with Vronsky, but if everyone thought this impossible, he was ready even to permit the renewal of their relationship as long as the children were not disgraced, he was not deprived of them, and his way of life remained unchanged. No matter how wrong this might be, it was better than a complete break, which would put her in a hopeless shameful situation and would deprive him of everything that he loved. But he felt helpless. He knew beforehand that everyone was against him, that they would not allow him to do what now seemed to him so natural and good, and would force him to do what was wrong but what they deemed proper.

21

BEFORE BETSY had time to leave the drawing room, she met Stepan Arkadievich at the doorway. He had just arrived from Eliseyev's, where a shipment of fresh oysters had just arrived.

"Ah! Princess! What a pleasure!" he said. "I was at your house."

"I have only a minute, for I'm about to leave," Betsy said, smiling and pulling on her glove.

"Wait, Princess. Before you put on your glove, let me kiss your hand. Nothing pleases me so much in the return of old-fashioned manners as hand kissing." He kissed Betsy's hand. "When will I see you?"

"You don't deserve to," said Betsy, smiling.

"I certainly do, for I've become a most serious person. I settle not only my own family matters but others as well," he said, with a meaningful expression on his face.

"Oh, I'm delighted," replied Betsy, immediately grasping that he was referring to Anna. And turning back, they stopped in a corner of the room. "He'll drive her to her death," Betsy whispered importantly. "It can't go on; it can't go on."

"I'm very glad that you think so," said Stepan Arkadievich, shaking his head, a serious, anxiously sympathetic expression on his face. "That's why I came to Petersburg."

"It's the talk of the town," she said. "This is an impossible situation. She's wasting away. He doesn't understand that she is one of those women who can't take their feelings lightly. He should either make a bold decision and take her away or he should divorce her. But this is killing her."

"Yes, yes, that's it . . ." Oblonsky said with a sigh. "That's why I came. But, to be exact, it's not the only reason. I've been appointed Gentleman of the Bedchamber, and of course, I had to express my thanks. But most important, this matter has to be settled."

"May God help you!" said Betsy.

After seeing Betsy to the entrance hall, kissing her hand again above the glove, where the pulse beats, and filling her with so much improper nonsense that she no longer knew whether to be angry or to laugh, Stepan Arkadievich went to his sister. He found her in tears.

Though himself brimming over with happiness, Stepan Arkadievich immediately and effortlessly assumed a sympathetic, poetically animated air which fitted her present state. He asked her how she felt and how she had spent the morning.

"Terrible, simply terrible. The day, the morning, and all past and future days," she said.

"It seems to me that you are letting it get the best of you. You must pull yourself together; you must face life. I know it's hard, it's hard, but—"

"I've heard that women love some even for their vices," Anna began suddenly, "but I hate him for his virtue. I can't live with him. You see, even the sight of him affects me physically; I lose control of myself. I can't, can't live with him. What shall I do? I was unhappy and I thought that no one could be more unhappy, but I could never have visualized the horrible state I'm in now. Would you believe it— though I know he's a good and excellent man, that I'm absolutely unworthy of him, yet I hate him. I hate him for his magnanimity. And I have nothing left but—"

She wanted to say death, but Stepan Arkadievich did not let her finish.

"You're ill and upset," he said. "I assure you that you're exaggerating dreadfully. It's not so terrible as you seem to think."

And Stepan Arkadievich smiled. No one else in Stepan Arkadievich's place, dealing with such a desperate situation, would permit himself to smile (a smile would seem unfeeling), but there was so much kindness and almost womanly tenderness in his smile that it did not offend but soothed and calmed. His soft, reassuring words and smile were as soothing as almond oil. Anna soon felt it.

"No, Stiva," she said, "I'm lost, lost! Worse than lost. I'm not lost yet; I can't say that it's all over. On the contrary, I feel that it's not over yet. I'm like a taut string which must break. But it's not over yet . . . and it will end in disaster."

"No, a string can be gently loosened. There's a way out of every dilemma."

"I've thought and thought. There's only one—"

By her frightened look he again surmised that this way out, she believed, was death, and he did not let her finish.

"Not at all," he said. "You can't see your situation as I do. Let me give you my frank opinion." Again he cautiously smiled his almond-oil smile. "I'll start from the beginning. You married a man who is twenty years your senior. You married without love and without knowing what love was. Let's admit that was a mistake."

"A terrible mistake!" said Anna.

"But I repeat: this is an established fact. Then you had, shall we say, the misfortune to fall in love with a man not your husband. This was unfortunate, but this is also an established fact. Your husband accepted it and forgave you." He stopped after each sentence, waiting for her objections, but she did not reply. "That's the way it is. Now the question is: can you continue to live with your husband? Do you want to? Does he?"

"I don't know. I don't know anything."

"But you yourself told me that you can't stand him."

"No, I didn't. I take it back. I know and understand nothing."

"Yes, but—"

"You couldn't understand. I feel that I'm plunging headlong into an abyss, but must try to save myself. And I can't—"

"Then we'll spread a net and catch you. I understand you. I understand that you can't take it upon yourself to express your desire, your feeling."

"I desire nothing, nothing at all . . . only that all this come to an end."

"But he sees and knows it. And don't you think that it oppresses him no less than you? It distresses you, and him too, and what will it lead to? But a divorce would solve everything," Stepan Arkadievich said. It was not without an effort that he brought out this main point, and he looked at her meaningfully.

She made no reply but shook her head, with its cropped hair, in disagreement. But by the expression on her face, suddenly brightened with her former beauty, he saw that the only reason she did not wish it was because it seemed to her unattainable happiness.

"I feel terribly sorry for both of you. And how happy I would be to arrange this!" said Stepan Arkadievich, now smiling with more assurance. "Don't speak, don't say anything. If God would only help me express my feelings. I'll go to see him."

Anna looked at him with her pensive, shining eyes and said nothing.

22

WITH THE SAME somewhat solemn air which he wore when he took his chairman's seat in the council chamber, Stepan Arkadievich entered Aleksei Aleksandrovich's study. Aleksei Aleksandrovich, his hands behind his back, was pacing up and down the room, thinking of the same matter Stepan Arkadievich had just spoken about to his wife.

"I'm not intruding?" asked Stepan Arkadievich, feeling an unaccustomed embarrassment. To conceal his embarrassment he reached for his cigarette case, which he had just bought and which opened in a novel manner, smelled the leather and took a cigarette.

"No. What can I do for you?" Aleksei Aleksandrovich replied reluctantly.

"I would like to . . . I have to . . . yes, I have to talk to you," Stepan Arkadievich said, surprised at his unaccustomed shyness.

This feeling was so unexpected and so strange that Stepan Arkadievich would not believe that it was the voice of his conscience, which told him that what he was going to do was evil. Stepan Arkadievich had to make an effort to overcome his shyness.

"I hope that you trust my love for my sister and my affection and respect for you," he said, blushing.

Aleksei Aleksandrovich stopped without replying, but his face struck Stepan Arkadievich by its expression of submissive martyrdom.

"I've intended, I've wanted to talk to you about my sister and about the situation in which you both find yourselves," said Stepan Arkadievich, still struggling against his unaccustomed shyness.

Aleksei Aleksandrovich smiled sadly, glanced at his brother-in-law, and without answering, went over to the table. He picked up a letter he had started to write and handed it to his brother-in-law.

"I think about that same thing constantly. And here is what I have begun to write, believing that I would express myself more clearly in writing, and that my presence would irritate her," he said as he handed him the letter.

Stepan Arkadievich took the letter, puzzled and surprised, glanced at the lackluster eyes fixed upon him, and began to read:

I see that my presence oppresses you. No matter how hard it has been for me to convince myself of it, I see that it is so and that it cannot be otherwise. I am not blaming you and, as God is my witness, when I saw you as you lay ill, I decided with all my heart to forget everything that had happened between us and to start a new life. I do not regret and shall never regret what I have done. I have wished only for your good and for the good of your soul, but now I see that I have not attained it. Tell me yourself what will give you true happiness and peace of mind. I submit myself completely to your will and to your sense of justice.

Stepan Arkadievich gave the letter back. He continued to look at his brother-in-law with the same puzzled air as before and did not know what to say. This silence was so awkward to both of them that Stepan Arkadievich's lips twitched painfully as, in silence, he kept his eyes fixed upon Karenin.

"That's what I wanted to tell her," Aleksei Aleksandrovich said, turning aside.

"Yes, yes," said Stepan Arkadievich, and, choking with tears, he was unable to continue. "Yes, yes. I understand," he said at last.

"I want to know what her wish is," said Aleksei Aleksandrovich.

"I'm afraid that she herself doesn't understand her situation. She's not the one to judge," Stepan Arkadievich said, regaining control of himself. "She's crushed, actually crushed by your magnanimity. If she reads this letter, she'll not be able to say anything. She'll only hang her head still lower."

"But what else then? How can I explain . . . how can I find out what she wants?" asked Aleksei Aleksandrovich.

"If you permit me to express my opinion, I believe that it's within your power to point out directly what measures you believe must be taken to bring this situation to an end."

"Then you believe that it must be brought to an end?" Aleksei Aleksandrovich interrupted. "But how?" he added, making an uncharacteristic gesture with his hands before his eyes. "I don't see any possible way out."

"There's a way out of any situation," said Stepan Arkadievich. He rose with growing excitement. "There was a time when you wanted to break up. If you become convinced now that you cannot bring each other happiness. . . ."

"Happiness may have different meanings. But suppose I agree to everything, that I demand nothing. What is the way out of our situation?"

"If you want my opinion," replied Stepan Arkadievich with the same soothing, tender, almond-oil smile with which he had spoken to Anna. This good-natured smile was so persuasive that Aleksei Aleksandrovich, knowing his weakness and yielding to it, was unconsciously ready to believe whatever Stepan Arkadievich said. "She'll never say it. But it's entirely possible that she may have but one wish," continued Stepan Arkadievich, "and that is to bring to an end her relationship with you and all the memories connected with it. I believe that in your situation, your new relationship must be clarified, and this can happen only when both parties become free."

"A divorce," Aleksei Aleksandrovich interjected with disgust.

"Yes, in my opinion, a divorce. Yes, a divorce," Stepan Arkadievich repeated, blushing. "In every respect it's the most sensible way out for husband and wife who are in such a situation as yours. What else can they do if they find that they can no longer live together? This could happen to anyone." Aleksei Aleksandrovich sighed heavily and closed his eyes. "Only one thing must be considered here: does one of the spouses intend to remarry? If not, then it's very simple," said Stepan Arkadievich, his shyness disappearing rapidly.

Aleksei Aleksandrovich, his face drawn with emotion, muttered something to himself, but made no reply. Everything, which seemed so simple to Stepan Arkadievich, Aleksei Aleksandrovich had reflected upon a thousand times. And to him all this not only seemed far from simple but completely impossible. A divorce, the nature of which he already knew in detail, now seemed to him impossible because his feeling of personal dignity and his reverence for religion did not permit him to take upon himself the guilt of a fictitious act of adultery and still less to agree that his wife, whom he had forgiven and whom he loved, be exposed and disgraced. And there were still other, more important reasons which made a divorce unacceptable to him.

What would happen to their son if they were divorced? He could not be given to his mother. The divorced mother would have her own illegitimate family in which a stepson's situation and his bringing up would most likely be unfortunate. Keep the boy with him? He knew that this would be an act of vengeance on his part, and he did not wish it. Moreover, the main reason why Aleksei Aleksandrovich considered a divorce unacceptable was that by agreeing to it he would cause Anna's ruin. He remembered well what Daria Aleksandrovna had told him in Moscow. She had reminded him that if he decided on a divorce, it would prove that he thought about himself and not about the irremediable ruin this decision would bring upon her. And relating these words to his deed of forgiveness, to his affection for the children, he now had his own understanding of what she meant. To agree to a divorce, to give her freedom meant, he believed, to deprive himself of his only bond with the life of the children whom he loved, to deprive her of the only support she had on the path of virtue, and to bring on her ruination. He knew that if he divorced her, she would join Vronsky, and this union would be illegitimate and sinful, for according to the laws of the church, a wife was not allowed to remarry while her husband remained alive. She will join him and in a year or two either he will leave her or she will form a new liaison, thought Aleksei Aleksandrovich, and I, having agreed to such an unlawful divorce, will be the cause of her perdition. He had pondered this a hundred times and he was convinced that divorce was not only not so simple as his brother-in-law said but utterly unacceptable. He did not believe a single word of what Stepan Arkadievich was saying, he could a thousand times disprove each of his arguments, but he listened to him, feeling that his words were the voice of that powerful, rude force that directed his life and to which he would have to submit.

"The only question is under what conditions you would agree to a divorce. She wants nothing; she dares not ask for anything; she leaves everything to your magnanimity."

My God! My God! Why? thought Aleksei Aleksandrovich, remembering the details of a divorce where the husband takes upon himself the guilt, and in shame he covered his face with the same gesture with which Vronsky had covered his.

"You're upset. I understand. But if you'd think it over. . . ."

Whosoever shall smite thee on thy right cheek, turn to him the other also, and if any man will take away thy coat, let him have thy cloak also, thought Aleksei Aleksandrovich.

"Yes, yes!" he cried in a shrill voice. "I take upon myself the disgrace, I even surrender my son, but . . . hadn't we better stop all this? On the other hand, do as you please. . . ."

And turning away from his brother-in-law so that he might not see his face, he sat in a chair at the window. He felt embittered and ashamed, but in this bitterness and shame he experienced a sense of joy, and he was tenderly moved by the greatness of his resignation.

Stepan Arkadievich was moved. He remained silent for a moment.

"Aleksei Aleksandrovich, believe me, she will treasure your generosity," he said. "But evidently such is God's will," he added, and as he said this he felt that it was stupid and he could scarcely restrain a smile at his own stupidity.

Aleksei Aleksandrovich was about to answer, but tears choked him.

"It's a fatal misfortune, and it must be recognized as such. I accept this misfortune as an accomplished fact and I am trying to help both her and you," said Stepan Arkadievich.

When Stepan Arkadievich left his brother-in-law's room, he was moved, but this did not prevent him from feeling pleased with the success of his mission, since he was sure that Aleksei Aleksandrovich would not go back on his promise. And in this pleasurable state the thought occurred to him than when the matter was concluded he would ask his wife and friends a riddle. What is the difference between me and the Czar? A division created by the Czar profits no one, but a division of two persons created by me profits three. Or, what do I have in common with the Czar? Well, I'll fix it up later, he said to himself with a smile.

23

VRONSKY'S WOUND WAS serious, though the bullet had missed his heart. For several days he hovered between life and death. When he was able to speak for the first time, only Varia, his brother's wife, was in the room.

"Varia," he said, looking at her sternly. "I shot myself accidentally. And please, never talk about it, but just tell that to the others. Otherwise it'll look so foolish!"

Without replying to his words, Varia bent over him and looked at him with a happy smile. His eyes were clear, not feverish, but their expression was stern.

"Well, thank God!" she said. "Have you any pain?"

"Some here." He pointed to his chest.

"Then let me change your dressing."

He clenched his jaw and looked at her in silence while she changed the dressing. When she had finished, he said:

"I'm not delirious. Please see to it that there are no rumors that I deliberately shot myself."

"There are no such rumors anyway. But I just hope that you'll never again shoot yourself accidentally," she said with a questioning smile.

"I probably won't, but it would have been better. . . ."

And he smiled unhappily.

These words and smile frightened Varia, but in spite of them, when the inflammation had run its course and he began to recover, he felt that he had completely freed himself from one aspect of his misfortune. He felt as though he had cleansed himself of the shame and humiliation he had experienced earlier. He could think calmly of Aleksei Aleksandrovich now. He realized how magnanimous he was, but he himself no longer felt humiliated. Moreover, he reverted to the ways of his former life. He saw that he could again look people in the face and live following his habits. The only feeling he could not tear from his heart, though he never stopped struggling to do so, was his regret, verging on despair, that he had lost her forever. He had firmly decided within his heart that now, after he had atoned for the wrong which he had caused her husband, he had to renounce her and never again could come between her, in her repentance, and her husband. But he could not tear from his heart the feeling of regret that he had lost her love; he could not erase the memories of the moments of happiness he had known with her, which he had valued so little then, and which, with all their delights, haunted him now.

Serpukhovskoy had secured his appointment to Tashkent, and Vronsky accepted the offer without the slightest hesitation. But as the time for his departure grew closer, the sacrifice he had made seemed to him so much greater.

His wound had healed, and by now he could leave the house to ready himself for his departure for Tashkent.

Just to see her once, then to bury myself, to die, he thought, and during his farewell visits he expressed this thought to Betsy. With this request Betsy went to see Anna and brought back a negative reply.

So much the better, thought Vronsky when he heard this. It was a fit of weakness, which would have consumed my last bit of strength.

On the morning of the next day Betsy herself came to him and declared that she had received from Oblonsky the definite news that Aleksei Aleksandrovich had agreed to a divorce and that he therefore could go to see her.

Without even thinking of seeing Betsy off, and forgetting all his decisions, Vronsky did not inquire when he could see her or where her husband was but immediately drove over to the Karenins'. He ran up the stairs without seeing anyone or anything, and with a brisk step, scarcely able to keep from breaking into a run, he entered the room. Without caring or noticing whether anyone was in the room or not, he embraced her and covered her face, hands, and neck with kisses.

Anna had been preparing herself for this meeting, had thought of what she would say to him, but she failed to say any of it: his passion enveloped her. She wanted to calm him, calm herself, but it was too late. His feeling communicated itself to her. Her lips trembled so that for a long time she could say nothing.

"Yes, you've taken me and I'm yours," she said at last, pressing his hand to her heart.

"That's how it should be," he said. "While we are alive, it should be thus. Now I know it."

"It's true," she said, growing paler as she held his head. "But there is something terrible about this, after all that has happened."

"Everything will pass, everything will pass, and we'll be so happy. If our love is still capable of increasing, it will do so because there's something terrible in it," he said, raising his head and in his smile revealing his strong teeth.

She could not help but smile, replying not to his words but to his loving glance. She took his hand and passed it over her cool cheeks and cropped hair.

"I scarcely recognize you in your short hair. It's very becoming to you. A boy! But how pale you are!"

"Yes, I'm very weak," she said, smiling. And her lips began to tremble again.

"We'll go to Italy. You'll recover there," he said.

"Is it really possible that we'll be as husband and wife, alone, with our family?" she said, looking intently into his eyes.

"I only wonder how it ever could be otherwise."

"Stiva says that *he* agrees to everything, but I cannot accept his generosity," she said, looking thoughtfully past Vronsky. "I don't want a divorce, I don't care about it now. But I don't know what he'll decide about Seryozha."

He was at a loss to understand how at this moment of their reunion, thoughts of her son and the divorce should come to her mind. Did they really matter?

"Don't talk about it, don't think of it," he said, turning her hand over in his and trying to draw all her attention to himself. But she was not looking at him.

"Oh, why didn't I die? It would have been better!" she said, crying silently, tears rolling down both cheeks. She tried to smile so as not to upset him.

According to Vronsky's former beliefs, it would have been disgraceful and impossible to decline the flattering offer of a dangerous post in Tashkent. But now without a moment's hesitation he refused it, and noticing that his superiors disapproved of his act, immediately resigned his commission.

A month later, Aleksei Aleksandrovich remained in his apartment alone with his son, and Anna and Vronsky went abroad, without the divorce, having resolutely refused it.

PART FIVE

1

PRINCESS SHCHERBATSKY BELIEVED that it would be impossible to have the wedding before Lent, which was still five weeks off, for half the trousseau would not be ready by that time. But she could only agree with Levin that to wait until after Lent would be to wait too long, since Prince Shcherbatsky's old aunt was very ill and was expected to die soon, and then the period of mourning would delay the wedding still longer. Therefore, having decided to divide the trousseau into two parts, a large and a small trousseau, the princess agreed to have the wedding before Lent. She decided that the smaller portion of the trousseau she would prepare in its entirety now, the larger to be sent later, and she was very angry with Levin because he could not bring himself to answer her seriously whether he agreed to this or not. This decision was all the more convenient because the young couple was to leave right after the wedding for the country, where the contents of the large trousseau would not be needed.

Levin continued to be in the same irrational state in which it seemed to him that he and his happiness were the chief and only purpose of the whole world, that there was no need for him to think or to attend to anything, and that everything was and would be done for him by others. He did not even have any plans or goals for his future. He let others devise them, knowing that everything would be perfect. His brother Sergei Ivanovich, Stepan Arkadievich and the princess guided him in performing what was expected of him. All he did was to agree completely with everything they proposed. His brother borrowed money for him, the princess advised him to leave Moscow after the wedding. Stepan Arkadievich advised him to go abroad. He agreed to everything. Do as you wish if it gives you pleasure. I'm happy and my happiness can neither increase nor decrease, no matter what you do, he thought. When he told Kitty of Stepan Arkadievich's advice to go abroad, he was greatly surprised that she did not agree with it but had some definite ideas of her own concerning their future. She knew that in the country Levin had an occupation that he liked. He saw that she not only did not understand this occupation but did not care to. This, however, did not prevent her from considering it a very important matter. Therefore she knew that their home would be in the country and she did not want to go abroad, where she did not intend to live, but rather to where their home would be. This precisely expressed intention surprised Levin. But since it did not matter to him, he immediately asked Stepan Arkadievich, as though it were his duty, to go to the country and to arrange everything there, as he pleased and according to his taste, which he knew to be excellent.

"By the way," Stepan Arkadievich once said to Levin on his return from the country where he had made everything ready for the arrival of the young couple, "have you a certificate to prove that you've been to confession?"

"No, why?"

"They won't marry you without it."

"For Heaven's sake!" cried Levin. "I don't believe I've been to communion for about nine years. I never gave it a thought."

"You're a fine one!" Stepan Arkadievich said, laughing. "And you still dare to call me a nihilist. But you can't help it. You must prepare yourself for the sacrament."

"But when? There are only four days left."

Stepan Arkadievich arranged this too. Levin began to prepare himself. It was very hard for him, who did not believe but respected the beliefs of others, to be present at any religious ritual and take part in it. And in his present state of mind, when he felt for everything deeply and tenderly, Levin believed that it would be not only difficult but utterly impossible to submit to such hypocrisy. Now, at the height of his glory, at the flowering of his happiness, he would be forced to lie or to blaspheme, neither of which he could do. But to each of his persistent inquiries as to whether it was possible to obtain a certificate without performing the prescribed rites, Stepan Arkadievich replied that this was impossible.

"But what difference does it make to you? It takes only two

days, and he's a very kind and clever old man. He'll pull your
tooth in such a way that you won't even notice it."

At the first mass Levin tried to recall from his youth memories of the deep religious feeling he had felt between the
ages of sixteen and seventeen. But he quickly became convinced that this was quite impossible. He tried to look upon
all of this as an empty, meaningless custom, like the custom
of exchanging visits. But he felt that he could not even do this.
Levin's attitude toward religion, like the majority of his
contemporaries, was the vaguest. He could not believe, yet
at the same time he was not fully convinced that all this was
wrong. Therefore he was unable either to believe in the
importance of what he was doing or to look at it indifferently,
as at a meaningless formality. During all this preparation for
the sacrament he felt uncomfortable and ashamed, since he was
doing something he himself did not understand and that therefore, his inner voice told him, was false and wrong.

During the service he sometimes listened to the prayers,
trying to ascribe to them a meaning that would not contradict
his views, and sometimes, feeling that he could not understand
them and would have to reject them, he did not listen. Instead,
he busied himself with his thoughts, observations, and memories, which with unusual vividness crossed his mind as he
stood idly in the church.

He attended mass, vespers, and complin, and the next day
he rose earlier than usual and, without having his tea, he came
to the church at eight o'clock in the morning to listen to the
morning prayers and to confess.

The church was empty except for a begging veteran, two
old women, and the clergy.

The young deacon, the two sides of his long back clearly
outlined under his thin, short cassock, met him, went over to a
table at the wall, and at once began to read the prayers.

As he read, particularly in the frequent and rapid repetition,
of "Lord have mercy upon us," which sounded like "Lavmercipons, Lavmercipons," Levin felt that his mind was locked
and sealed and that it must not now be touched or stirred
lest this cause confusion. Therefore, as he stood behind the
deacon without listening to or trying to understand his words,
he kept thinking his own thoughts. How wonderfully expressive her hand can be! he thought, recalling the previous
evening when they were seated at the table in the corner of the
room. As was nearly always true at that time, they had nothing

to say to each other. Keeping her hand on the table, she kept opening and closing it, laughing outright at the sight of her actions. He recalled that he had kissed her hand and then had examined the converging lines on her rosy palm. Again, "Lav-mercipons," thought Levin, crossing himself, bowing, and watching the ease with which the deacon bent his back when he bowed. Then she took my hand and examined its lines. "You have a fine hand," she said.

And he looked at his hand and at the stubby hand of the deacon. Now it will end soon, he thought. No, he seems to be starting again from the beginning, he reflected as he listened to the prayers. No, it's coming to an end. He's already bowing to the ground. That's always done before the end.

Holding his hand under his velveteen cuff, the deacon discreetly accepted a three-ruble note, promised to enter his name in the register, and, his new boots resounding loudly against the tiles of the empty church, walked into the chancel. A moment later he reappeared and beckoned to Levin. A thought stirred within his mind, which had been locked until now, but he hurried to rid himself of it. It'll come right somehow, he thought, and he went toward the altar. After ascending the narrow steps and turning to the right, he saw the priest. The little old priest, with a thin, graying beard and kind, tired eyes, stood at the lectern turning the pages of the prayer book. He bowed slightly to Levin and at once began to read the prayers in his usual manner. When he finished, he bowed to the ground and turned toward Levin.

"Christ, who, unseen, is present here, accepts your confession," he said, indicating the crucifix. "Do you believe in all the teachings of our Holy Apostolic Church?" continued the priest, turning his face away from Levin and folding his hands under his stole.

"I have doubted and still doubt everything," said Levin in a voice which he himself found unpleasant. Then he was silent.

The priest waited for a few moments to see whether Levin would add anything, then closed his eyes and said, in a quick Vladimir dialect, accentuating the o:

"It is inherent in man's weakness that he doubt, but we must pray to merciful God to give us strength. What are your particular sins?" he added without the slightest pause, as if trying to waste no time.

"Doubt is my chief sin. I doubt everything and most of the time am in a state of doubt."

"It is inherent in man's weakness that he doubt," said the priest, repeating his words. "And what do you doubt mostly?"

"I doubt everything. Sometimes I even doubt the existence of God," Levin blurted out, and he was frightened by the impropriety of his words. But evidently Levin's words made no impression on the priest.

"What doubts can there be concerning God's existence?" he asked, with just a trace of a smile.

Levin kept silent.

"What doubts can you have about the Creator when you behold his handiwork?" continued the priest, speaking rapidly as was his custom. "Who adorned the heavens with their heavenly bodies? Who clothed the earth in its beauty? How could this come about without a creator?" he said, looking at Levin inquiringly.

Levin felt that it was improper to enter into a philosophical disputation with the priest and therefore answered the question directly.

"I don't know," he said.

"You don't. Then how can you doubt that God created everything?" the priest said in good-natured bewilderment.

"I don't understand anything," said Levin, blushing and feeling that his words were foolish and that in this situation they could not but be foolish.

"Pray to God and entreat him. Even the Holy Fathers had their doubts and prayed to God to strengthen them in their faith. The devil is very powerful, and we must not submit to him. Pray to God, entreat him. Pray to God," he repeated hastily.

The priest remained silent for a while, as if engrossed in a thought.

"I understand that you are going to marry the daughter of my parishioner and spiritual son, Prince Shcherbatsky," he added with a smile. "A fine young lady."

"Yes," replied Levin, blushing for the priest. Why ask about this at confession? he thought.

As if to reply to his thought, the priest told him:

"You are about to contract marriage, and perhaps God will award you progeny, isn't that so? What kind of rearing can you give your children if you do not conquer within yourself the temptations of the devil who incites you to disbelieve?"

he asked with gentle reproach. "If you love your child, as a good father you will not wish him only riches, luxury and honors. You will also wish him his salvation, his spiritual enlightenment through the light of truth. Isn't that true? What will you reply when the innocent little one asks you, 'Father, who created everything that delights me in this world—the land, the waters, the sun, the flowers, the grass?' Can it be possible that you will answer, 'I don't know?' You cannot but know, since the Lord our God, in his great loving kindness, has revealed it to you. Or your child will ask you, 'What awaits me in the life beyond?' What can you tell him if you really know nothing? What answers will you give him? Will you expose him to worldly pleasures and the works of the devil? That would not do," he said, and then he stopped inclining his head sideways and looking at Levin with his kind gentle eyes.

Levin made no reply at this point, not because he did not want to enter into an argument with the priest but because no one had ever asked him such questions. And there was quite enough time to think of how to answer the little ones when they would ask such questions.

"You are entering a period of your life," continued the priest, "in which you must choose a path and follow it. Pray to God that in His goodness He may help you and forgive you," he concluded. "May God, our Lord Jesus Christ, in His grace and in the bounty of His love for mankind, forgive you, my child. . . ." And having finished the prayer of absolution, the priest blessed him and released him.

On his return home that day, Levin was glad that the uncomfortable situation had come to an end, and in such a manner that he had not been obliged to lie. In addition, he was left with the vague recollection that what that kind hearted, gentle, little old man had said was not at all as foolish as it had at first seemed, but that it contained something that needed to be thought out.

Of course not now, thought Levin, but sometime in the future. More than ever before, Levin felt now that there was something unclear and impure in his heart, and that his attitude toward religion was the same as the one he had so clearly observed and disliked in others and for which he had reproached his friend Sviazhsky.

After he had spent that evening with his fiancée at Dolly's Levin was particularly cheerful. Describing to Stepan Arkadie vich his state of exhilaration, he said that he was as happy as a dog that, having been trained to jump through a hoop, at last understands and performs what has been demanded of it, and aroused by joy, barks, wags its tail, and in its joy jumps onto tables and window ledges.

2

ON THE DAY of the wedding, according to custom (the princess and Daria Aleksandrovna demanded strict observance of all the customs), Levin did not see his fiancée but dined at his hotel with three bachelors who congregated by chance: Sergei Ivanovich, Katavasov, a college classmate and now a professor of natural science whom Levin had met on the street and had brought to his hotel, and Chirikov, his best man, a Moscow justice of the peace, Levin's companion when bear hunting. It was a very gay dinner. Sergei Ivanovich was in the best frame of mind and was amused by Katavasov's original ideas. Katavasov, feeling that his originality was appreciated and enjoyed, paraded it. Chirikov took part in any conversation gaily and good-naturedly.

"Look," said Katavasov in a drawl, a habit he had acquired in his professorial duties, "what an able fellow our Konstantin Dmitrievich was. I speak of the absent, for he exists no longer. After graduating from the university he was a lover of science, and mankind was his interest. But now one half of his abilities he devotes to self-deception, and the other to justify this deception."

"I've never seen a more resolute enemy of marriage," remarked Sergei Ivanovich.

"No, I'm not its enemy. I'm a champion of the division of labor. Those who are not capable of doing anything else should produce human beings; the rest should contribute to their enlightenment and happiness. That's the way I see it. But those who are eager to engage in both occupations are legion, and I'm not one of their number."

"How happy I'd be to learn that you'd fallen in love," said Levin. "Please invite me to the wedding."

"I'm already in love."

"Yes, with a cuttlefish. You know," said Levin, turning to

his brother, "Mikhail Semionovich is writing a paper on the feeding and—"

"No, you're all confused. But it doesn't matter what I'm writing. The fact is that I'm really in love with the cuttlefish!"

"But the cuttlefish will not keep you from loving a wife."

"The cuttlefish will not, but a wife will interfere with my love for the cuttlefish."

"Why is that?"

"You'll see. You, as we know, love farming, hunting—well, you'll see!"

"Arkhip was here today. He said that there are elk without number in Prudno, as well as two bears," said Chirikov.

"You won't have my company for the hunt."

"There's the proof," said Sergei Ivanovich. "And say good-bye to your bear hunting now. Your wife will forbid it."

Levin smiled. The thought that his wife might forbid it was so delightful that he was ready to surrender forever the pleasure of seeing a bear again.

"But just the same, it's a pity that they will get the two bears without you. Remember how it was last time in Khapilov? That was a wonderful hunt," said Chirikov.

Levin did not want to destroy Chirikov's illusion that there could be anything good anywhere without her and therefore said nothing.

"No wonder the custom has been established to say farewell to one's bachelor days," said Sergei Ivanovich. "No matter how happy one is, he regrets the loss of his freedom."

"Tell us the truth, don't you feel a little like the bridegroom in Gogol's play, who escaped by jumping through a window?"

"He must, but he won't admit it," said Katavasov, breaking into loud laughter.

"Well, the window is open. . . . Let's go to Tver right now. There's a she-bear there. We can get her in her den. Joking aside, let's take the five o'clock train. And here let them do as they like," said Chirikov with a smile.

"But I swear to God," Levin said with a smile, "that I can't find in my heart a feeling of regret for my lost freedom."

"Yes, there's such chaos now in your heart that you can't find anything there," said Katavasov. "Wait until you settle down a bit, then you'll find it."

"No, in spite of my feeling" (he did not want to say "love" in their presence) "and my happiness, I should be regretful, even if only a little, of the loss of my freedom. . . . On the contrary, I'm actually glad that I'm losing it."

"That's bad! A hopeless case!" said Katavasov. "Well, let's drink to his recovery and let's wish him that at least a hundredth part of his dreams comes true. And that will be such happiness as the world has never seen!"

Soon after dinner the guests left to change for the wedding.

Remaining alone and recalling the conversation of these bachelors, Levin again asked himself whether he felt within his heart the regret for his lost freedom of which they had spoken. He smiled at this question. Freedom? What for? he thought. Happiness consists of loving and wishing; wishing her wishes, thinking her thoughts, giving up all freedom—that's happiness!

But how do I know her thoughts, her wishes, her feelings? a voice suddenly whispered to him. The smile vanished from his face, and he grew thoughtful. A strange feeling suddenly took possession of him. He was seized by fear and doubt, doubt about everything.

But what if she doesn't love me? What if she marries me only to get married? What if she herself doesn't know what she's doing? he asked himself. She may come to her senses after the marriage and only then will she understand that she does not and cannot love me. And strange, exceedingly wicked thoughts about her crept into his mind. He was as jealous of Vronsky as he had been a year earlier, as though the evening when he had seen her with Vronsky had been only yesterday. He suspected that she had not told him everything.

He leaped to his feet. No, this can't be, he said to himself in despair. I'll go to her, I'll ask her; I'll tell her for the last time, "We are still free. Isn't it better to break up now?" Anything would be better than permanent unhappiness, disgrace, unfaithfulness! With despair in his heart and hatred for everyone, for himself, for her, he left the hotel and drove to her house.

He found her in one of the rooms in the rear of the house. She was sitting on a trunk, sorting, with the help of a servant girl, a multitude of varicolored dresses which were laid out on the backs of the chairs and on the floor.

"Ah," she cried, beaming with joy at the sight of him. "Is that you?" (To this very day she still addressed him both as "thou" and as "you") "What a surprise. I'm disposing of my girlhood dresses. . . ."

"Oh! How nice!" he said, looking gloomily at the servant girl.

"Go, Duniasha, I'll call you later," said Kitty. "What's the matter?" she asked as soon as the girl had left, now addressing him unhesitatingly as "thou." She noticed the strange, troubled and gloomy expression on his face and became frightened.

"Kitty! I'm troubled. I cannot bear my suffering alone," he said with despair in his voice, stopping before her and looking into her eyes beseechingly. By the expression of her loving, sincere face he already knew that nothing would be accomplished by what he intended to say, but he still wanted her to undeceive him herself. "I've come to tell you that there's still time. All this can be undone and corrected."

"What? You confuse me. What's the matter?"

"I've said it a thousand times and can't help thinking . . . I'm not worthy of you. You shouldn't have agreed to marry me. Think about it. You made a mistake. Think it over carefully. You couldn't love me. If . . . please tell me," he said without looking at her. "I'll be unhappy. Let people say what they will. Anything would be better than unhappiness. . . . And it would be better to do it now, while there still is time. . . ."

"I don't understand," she answered in a frightened voice. "Does this mean that you want to part with me . . . that we shouldn't marry?"

"Yes, if you don't love me."

"You have lost your mind!" she cried, flushed with annoyance.

But his face was so pitiful that she suppressed her annoyance and, throwing the dresses from the chair, sat down next to him.

"What are you thinking of? Tell me everything."

"I think that you couldn't love me. Why should you love me?"

"My God! What can I do? . . ." she said, and she broke into tears.

"Ah! What have I done!" he cried and, kneeling before her, began to kiss her hands.

Five minutes later, when the princess came into the room, they were completely reconciled. Not only did Kitty assure him that she loved him but in reply to his question she even explained why she loved him. She said that she loved him because she understood everything about him, because she knew what he loved, and because everything that he loved was good. And this seemed to him quite clear. When the princess entered, they were seated on the trunk side by side, sorting the dresses and arguing whether to give Duniasha the brown dress as Kitty wanted to do, the dress that she had worn when Levin had proposed to her, or not to give that dress away, as he insisted, but to give Duniasha the blue one.

"Can't you understand? She is a brunette and it wouldn't be becoming. . . . I took everything into account."

When the princess discovered why he had come, she scolded him half in earnest and sent him home to change his clothes and to get out of Kitty's way while she had her hair done— Charles was expected momentarily.

"As it is, she hasn't been eating anything lately and has lost her looks, and here you come to upset her with your foolishness," she told him. "Off with you, my friend."

Levin, feeling guilty and ashamed but reassured, returned to his hotel. His brother, Daria Aleksandrovna, and Stepan Arkadievich, all in evening dress, were waiting to bless him with an icon. There was little time left. Daria Aleksandrovna still had to stop at her home to pick up her son. His hair curled and pomaded, he was to carry the bride's icon. Then one coach had to be sent for the best man and another one, which would bring Sergei Ivanovich, was to be sent back. . . . In general, there were many complicated matters to attend to. One thing was certain: they could waste no time, for it was already half-past six.

The ritual of the blessing fell through. Standing in a ridiculously solemn pose next to his wife, Stepan Arkadievich held the icon, told Levin to bow to the ground, blessed him with a kind, amused smile, and kissed him thrice. Daria Aleksandrovna did the same and was anxious to leave immediately, but once again she confused the destination of the carriages.

"Well, here's what we'll do: you go to fetch him in our coach, and perhaps Sergei Ivanovich will be kind enough to go along and then send back the coach."

"Of course, I'd be happy to."

"And we'll be there shortly. Have your things been sent off?" asked Stepan Arkadievich.

"They have," replied Levin, and he told Kuzma to help him dress.

3

A CROWD, mostly women, had gathered outside the church, which was lit up for the wedding. Those who had not managed to get inside crowded at the windows, jostling, arguing, and peering through the grating.

Over twenty coaches had already been lined up by the gendarmes along the street. A police officer, disregarding the frost, stood at the entrance, resplendent in his dress uniform. The carriages continued to roll up ceaselessly, and now ladies, adorned with flowers and holding their trains, now gentlemen, taking off their caps or black hats, entered the church. Inside the church both chandeliers were already lit, as well as all the candles at the icons. The golden luster on the red background of the iconostasis, the gilt designs of the icons, the silver of the chandeliers and candlesticks, the floor tiles, the rugs, the standards up in the choir loft, the narrow steps to the pulpit, the books darkened with age, the cassocks and the surplices—all were bathed in light. On the right side of the well-heated church, in the expanse of swallow-tail coats, white ties, uniforms and brocade, velvet, satin, coiffures, flowers, bare shoulders and arms, and long gloves, there hummed a restrained but lively conversation which echoed strangely in the high dome. Every time the door opened it squeaked, the conversation stopped, and everyone turned around, expecting the entrance of the bride and bridegroom. But the door had already opened more than ten times, and every time it was either some late guest who joined the circle of the invited to the right, or it was a spectator who had entered by deception or by having gained the favor of the police officer and who joined the group of the strangers to the left. Both the guests and the strangers had already passed through all the stages of a long wait.

At first they believed that the bridegroom and bride would arrive any minute, and they considered the delay of no importance. Then they began to glance at the door more and more frequently, wondering whether something had happened. Then the delay became embarrassing, and the relatives and guests tried to pretend that they were not concerned about

472

the bridegroom and that they were engrossed in their conversation.

The archdeacon, as a reminder that his time was precious, coughed slightly with impatience, making the windowpanes tremble. From the choir could be heard the sound of the choristers, now warming up, now blowing their noses. The priest repeatedly sent either the beadle or the deacon to find out whether the bridegroom had arrived, and he himself, in his violet cassock and embroidered sash, came over more and more frequently to the side doors to await the bridegroom. At last, one of the ladies looked at the clock and said, "How peculiar!" and all the guests grew restless and began to express in loud terms their surprise and displeasure. The best man went to find out what had happened. During that time Kitty, long since ready, in her white dress, long veil and a chaplet of orange flowers, stood in the dining room of the Shcherbatsky home together with her nuptial godmother, her sister Lvov, and looked through the window for more than half an hour, expecting to hear from the best man that the bridegroom had arrived at the church.

In the meantime Levin, wearing trousers but without his vest and swallow-tailed coat, paced up and down his hotel room, ceaselessly peering out the doorway and surveying the hall. But the man for whom he had been waiting did not appear, and in despair he turned back, waving his hands and addressing Stepan Arkadievich, who smoked unperturbed.

"Was there ever anyone in such a terrible and preposterous situation?" he asked.

"Yes, it's silly," echoed Stepan Arkadievich, smiling gently. "But calm down, they'll bring it soon."

"Of course!" said Levin, restraining his fury. "And those absurd open vests! They are impossible!" he said, looking at the crumpled front of his shirt. "And what if they've already sent my trunks to the railroad station!" he cried in despair.

"Then you'll put on mine!"

"I should have done that long ago!"

"It's better not to look ridiculous. . . . Wait, *everything will come out right in the end.*"

What happened was that when Levin was about to dress, Kuzma, his old servant, brought him his swallow-tailed coat, vest, and all the other necessary objects.

"And the shirt?" asked Levin.

"It's on you," Kuzma said, smiling calmly.

It had not occurred to Kuzma to leave a clean shirt out, and when he had been ordered to pack all the luggage and take it over to the Shcherbatsky home, from which the young couple was to leave that same evening, he did so, packing everything but the coat and the trousers. The shirt, which Levin had been wearing since that morning, was crumpled and could not be worn with the new-style open vest. It was too far to the Shcherbatskys'. A servant was sent to buy a shirt. He returned; everything was closed—it was Sunday. The servant was sent to Stepan Arkadievich's and brought his shirt, but it proved to be too wide and short. At last they sent him to the Shcherbatskys' to open the trunks. They were waiting for the bridegroom in the church, but he, like a wild animal locked in a cage, paced up and down the room, peered into the hall, and in horror and despair recalled what he had said to Kitty and what she might now be thinking.

At last Kuzma, shamefaced and scarcely able to catch his breath, burst into the room with the shirt.

"I got them just in time. They were already loading the things on the cart," said Kuzma.

Within three minutes, without looking at the clock so as to be spared the pain, Levin was running down the hall.

"That won't help," said Stepan Arkadievich, smiling and trying to catch up with him without undue haste. "I'll say it again: *everything will come out right in the end.*"

4

"THEY'VE ARRIVED! There he is! Which one? The younger one? And she, the poor soul, half dead!" could be heard in the crowd when Levin, who had met the bride at the entrance, entered the church with her.

Stepan Arkadievich explained to his wife the cause of the delay, and the guests, smiling, whispered one to another. Levin did not notice anything or anyone. He did not take his eyes off his bride.

All agreed that she had lost much of her beauty recently and that at the wedding she was far from looking as beautiful as she usually did. But Levin did not find it so. He looked at her tall coiffure with the long white veil and white flowers, at the high tucked collar, which, with singular grace, covered her long neck on the sides, leaving it open in front, and at her strikingly slender waist. It seemed to him that she looked more beautiful than ever, not because the flowers, the veil, or the Paris dress added anything to her beauty but because in spite of the splendor of all these artifices, the expression of her lovely face, of her look, of her lips, remained unchanged —it was her own unique expression of innocent truthfulness.

"I almost believed that you wanted to run away," she said, and she smiled.

"What happened to me is so silly I'm ashamed to talk about it," he said, blushing, and he had to avert his gaze toward Sergei Ivanovich, who had come up to them.

"That was some adventure with the shirt!" said Sergei Ivanovich, shaking his head and smiling.

"Yes, yes," replied Levin, without understanding what was being said to him.

"Well, Kostia, now you must make a vital decision," said Stepan Arkadievich, looking at him with mock concern. "Now, you are particularly well qualified to see how important it is. I've been asked whether you would prefer used candles or new ones. The difference is ten rubles," he added, curving his lips into a smile. "I made the decision, but I'm afraid you might not agree with me."

Levin understood that it was a joke, but he could not smile.

"Well, used or new? That is the question."

"Yes, yes! The new."

"Well, I'm very happy. The problem is solved!" said Stepan Arkadievich with a smile. "But how silly one becomes in this situation," he said to Chirikov when Levin, giving him an embarrassed look, moved closer to the bride.

"Look, Kitty, be the first one on the rug," said Countess Nordston, coming over to them. "You're a fine one!" she said, turning to Levin.

"Are you frightened?" asked Maria Dmitrievna, an old aunt.

"Are you chilly? You look pale. Wait, bend down!" said Kitty's sister, Madame Lvov, with a smile, and making a circle of her lovely, full arms, she arranged the flowers on Kitty's head.

Dolly came over, wanted to say something, but could not, broke into tears, and then forced a smile.

Kitty looked at everyone with the same absent look as Levin. To all the words addressed to her she could respond only with a happy smile, which now looked so natural on her.

In the meantime the clergy put on their robes, and the priest, followed by the deacon, came up to the lectern at the entrance of the church. The priest turned toward Levin and said something to him. Levin could not make it out.

"Take the bride's hand and lead her," the best man said to Levin.

For some time Levin could not understand what they wanted him to do. They corrected him several times and were going to give up because again and again he used the wrong hand, when at last he understood that he was supposed to use his right hand and, without changing his position, to take her right hand. When, at last he took his bride's hand in the proper way, the priest was already a few steps ahead of him and had stopped at the lectern. A crowd of relatives and friends, murmuring and rustling their trains, followed behind them. Someone bent down and adjusted the bride's train. The church grew so silent that one could hear the sound of dripping wax.

The little, old priest, in a kamelaukion, his silvery-gray hair parted behind his ears, freed his small wrinkled hands from under his heavy silver-cloth chasuble with its gold cross on the back, and righted something at the lectern.

Stepan Arkadievich came over softly to him, whispered something, and winking at Levin, turned back.

The priest lit two flower-adorned candles, holding them obliquely in his left hand, so that their wax dripped slowly, and turned his face toward the bride and bridegroom. It was the same priest who had confessed Levin. He glanced at the bridegroom and the bride with his tired, sad eyes, sighed, and having freed his right hand from under the chasuble, he used it to bless the bridegroom and in the same way, but with a shade more consideration and tenderness, touched Kitty's bowed head with his joined fingers. Then he handed them the candles, and reaching for the censor, slowly walked away.

Is it really true? thought Levin, glancing at his bride. He could barely see her profile from above, and from the slight movement of her lips and eyelashes he knew that she was conscious of his look. She did not return the look, but the tall, tucked collar stirred as it reached up to her tiny, rosy ear. He saw that a sigh stopped within her breast, and that her little hand trembled as, in its long glove, it held the candle.

All the fuss about the shirt, about his late arrival, the conversation with his relatives and friends, their displeasure, his ridiculous situation—all this suddenly vanished and he felt happy and frightened.

The tall, handsome archdeacon, in an alb of silver cloth, his combed and curled locks protruding along the sides of his head, stepped forward briskly and, raising his stole with two fingers in a practiced gesture, stopped in front of the priest.

"Bless, Master!" The solemn sounds, slowly following one after another, vibrated through the air.

"Blessed is our God, always, now, and ever, and unto ages of ages," the old priest intoned humbly in response, continuing to right something at the lectern. Filling the whole church from the windows to the vaulted ceiling, the full chords of the invisible choir rose, broad and harmonious, increased in volume, stopped for a moment, and softly died away.

They prayed, as always, for peace on high, for salvation, for the synod, for the Czar. They prayed for God's servants, Konstantin and Ekaterina, now joining in wedlock.

"That He will send down upon them perfect and peaceful love and succor, let us pray to the Lord." The archdeacon's voice seemed to suffuse the entire church.

Levin listened to the words and was struck by them. How did it occur to them to pray for help, particularly for help? he thought, recalling his recent fears and doubts. What do I know? What can I do in this awesome matter without help? he thought. Help, indeed, is what I need now.

When the deacon finished the litany, the priest turned to the couple, the book in his hand.

"Oh, Eternal God, who hast brought into unity those who were sundered," he intoned in his humble and sonorous voice, "and hast ordained for them an indissoluble bond of love; who didst bless Isaac and Rebecca; and didst make them heirs of thy promise: Bless also thy servants, Konstantin and Ekaterina, guiding them unto every good work. For thou art a merciful God, who lovest mankind, and unto thee do we ascribe glory, to the Father, and to the Son, and to the Holy Spirit, now, and ever, and unto ages of ages."

"Amen," the sound of the invisible choir again spread through the air.

"Who hast brought into unity those who were sundered and hast ordained for them an indissoluble bond of love"—how profound are these words and how well they suit one's feelings at this moment, thought Levin. Does she feel the same as I?

He glanced at her and met her look.

And from her expression he concluded that she felt the same way. But it was not so. She could scarcely understand the words of the service, and during the ceremony she did not even listen to them. She could not listen and understand them, so strong was the single emotion which overflowed her heart, and which grew more and more intense. It was the feeling of joy at the fruition of what had been ripening in her heart for the last month and a half and had brought her joy and suffering during those six weeks. On that day in their Arbat house, when in her brown dress she came over to him and silently surrendered herself to him, on that day and hour there occurred in her heart a complete break with her former life. A completely different, new, entirely unknown life began, but actually the former life continued. Those six weeks were most blissful and most tormenting. All her life, all her wishes and hopes focused on this one man, still unknown to her, to whom she was bound by a feeling still less understandable than the man himself, sometimes drawing her to him and sometimes repelling her, but with all this she continued to live in the conditions of her former life. Continuing to live her former life, she was deeply troubled about herself—by her complete and unbounded indifference to her past: to things, to habits, to people who had loved and still loved her, to her mother, who was hurt by this indifference, and to her dear father, until then beloved beyond anyone else in this world. Sometimes she was deeply troubled by this indifference and sometimes she rejoiced in what had caused the indifference. She could not think of anything nor wish for anything that lay outside her life with this man. But that new life did not exist yet, and she could not even imagine it clearly. It was only anticipation, a fear and joy in the unknown. And now at any moment the anticipation, the uncertainty, the remorse over renouncing her former life—all this would come to an end, and something new would begin. It could not but be terrifying in its uncertainty; but whether terrifying or not, it had already happened within her heart six weeks ago. And what was happening now was only the consecration of what had long since occurred in her heart.

Turning again toward the lectern, the priest took Kitty's tiny ring with difficulty, and telling Levin to extend his hand, he slipped the ring on the first joint of his finger. "The servant of God, Konstantin, plights his troth to the servant of God,

Ekaterina." And slipping the large ring on Kitty's tiny, pink finger, pathetic in its fragility, the priest pronounced the same words.

Several times the young couple tried to guess what they were supposed to do, but they were wrong each time, and the priest corrected them in a whisper. At last, after he had done all that was required, he crossed them with their rings and again handed Kitty the large one and Levin the small one. They again became confused, twice exchanged rings from hand to hand, and still the result was not satisfactory.

Dolly, Chirikov, and Stepan Arkadievich came forward to help them. Confusion ensued, with whispering and smiles, but the solemn and tender expressions on the faces of the young couple did not change. On the contrary, with their hands entangled they looked more serious and more solemn than before, and the smile with which Stepan Arkadievich whispered to them that now they should put on their own rings involuntarily died on his lips. He felt that a smile would offend them.

"For thou, in the beginning, didst make them male and female," the priest read after the exchange of rings, "and by thee is the woman joined unto the man as a helpmeet, and for the procreation of the human race. Wherefore, oh Lord our God, who hast sent forth thy truth upon thine inheritance, and thy covenant unto thy servants our fathers, even thine elect, from generation to generation: Look thou upon thy servant, Konstantin, and upon thy handmaid, Ekaterina, and establish and make stable their betrothal in faith, and in oneness of mind, in truth and love. . . ."

Levin became increasingly conscious that all his thoughts about marriage, his dreams of how he would arrange his life, all that had been childish, and that this was something he had not understood until now and understood still less at the moment although it was happening to him. He felt a choking sensation rise higher and higher in his chest, and uncontrollable tears came to his eyes.

5

ALL OF MOSCOW, relatives, and acquaintances, were in the church. Even during the ritual of the betrothal, a politely subdued conversation continued ceaselessly in the brilliantly lit church among the crowd of elegantly attired ladies, young girls, and men wearing white ties, swallow-tailed coats and uniforms. The conversation was carried on mostly by the men, while the women were engrossed in watching all the details of the ceremony, something which always moves them.

The group nearest the bride included her two sisters—Dolly and her older sister, the poised beauty Madame Lvov, who had arrived from abroad.

"Why did Maria put on a violet, practically black dress for the wedding?" asked Madame Korsunsky.

"With her complexion, it's her only salvation," replied Madame Drubetzkoy. "I wonder why they arranged the wedding for the evening. Like shopkeepers. . . ."

"It's more beautiful. I was married in the evening, too," replied Madame Korsunsky, sighing at the recollection of how lovely she had been that day, how ridiculously enamoured of her her husband had been, and how completely different everything was now.

"They say that whoever is a best man more than ten times will never marry. I wanted to be one the tenth time to insure myself, but the place was taken," Count Sinyavin told the pretty Princess Charsky, who had designs on him.

Mlle. Charsky replied only with a smile. She watched Kitty, thinking of the day when she, too, would stand as Kitty did now, with Count Sinyavin, and when she would remind him of the joke he had just made.

Shcherbatsky told the old lady in waiting, Nikolayev, that he intended to put the crown on Kitty's chignon to bring her happiness.

"She shouldn't have worn a chignon," answered Madame Nikolayev, who had long since decided that if the old widower whom she was pursuing would marry her, they would have the simplest kind of wedding. "I don't like such pomp."

Sergei Ivanovich spoke to Daria Dmitrievna, jokingly assuring her that the custom of honeymoon trips had become popular because newlyweds always feel somewhat shamefaced.

"Your brother should be proud. She is incredibly lovely. You must be envious."

"I am beyond that stage, Daria Dmitrievna," he replied, and his face suddenly assumed a sad and serious expression.

Stepan Arkadievich was telling his sister-in-law his joke about divorce.

"The chaplet must be adjusted," she said without listening to him.

"What a pity that she has lost her looks," Countess Nordston said to Madame Lvov. "But still he's not worth her little finger. Don't you agree?"

"No, I like him very much, and not just because he is my future *beau-frère*," replied Madame Lvov. "And how well he carries himself. It's so difficult to carry oneself well under these circumstances and avoid looking ridiculous. But he's not ridiculous, not tense, and one can see that he's moved."

"It seems that you've been expecting this."

"Just about. She always loved him."

"Well, let's see who'll step on the rug first. I advised Kitty to do it."

"It doesn't matter," replied Madame Lvov. "We're all meek wives; it's in our blood."

"But I deliberately stepped on it before Vasili. How about you, Dolly?"

Dolly stood near them, listening to their conversation, but she did not reply. She was moved. Tears stood in her eyes, and she would not have been able to say anything without breaking down. She was happy for Kitty and Levin. Recalling her own wedding, she glanced from time to time at her beaming husband, Stepan Arkadievich, oblivious to her present circumstances and recalling only her innocent first love. She remembered not herself alone but all her women friends and acquaintances; she remembered them in their uniquely solemn hour, when they stood as Kitty did now at their weddings, with love, hope, and fear in their hearts, renouncing the past and entering a mysterious future. Among those brides who came to her mind, she recalled her dear Anna—the news of her expected divorce had recently reached her. She, too, had stood there in her innocence, bedecked with orange flowers and a veil. And now?

"How terribly strange!" she said.

Not only did sisters, friends, and relatives witness every detail of the ceremony; there were strangers too. The women spectators, in their excitement, held their breath and watched, fearful lest they miss the slightest movement or expression on the face of bridegroom and bride. Annoyed, they did not reply to and often did not listen to the unimpressed men, who were making jests and side remarks.

"Why is she so tearful? Is she being forced into it?"

"Forced to marry such a fine man? Probably a prince."

"Is that her sister in the white satin? Now listen to the deacon shout, 'Wife, obey your husband!'"

"Is it the Chudov Monastery choir?"

"No, the Synodical."

"I asked a servant. He said he's taking her straight to their country place. He's terribly rich, they say. That's why they married her off to him."

"No, a fine couple."

"And, you, Maria Vlasievna, kept saying that they aren't wearing hoop skirts that stick out to the sides any more. Look how it sticks out on that one in puce. An ambassador's wife, they say. You can really see it . . . on both sides."

"But how darling the bride looks! Like a little lamb. Say what you want, we women are to be pitied."

Such was the conversation in the crowd of women spectators who had managed to squeeze through the church doors.

6

WHEN THE RITUAL of betrothal was over, an acolyte spread a pink silk cloth before the lectern in the middle of the church, the choir began singing a psalm set to elegant and complex music in which the tenor and the bass responded to each other, and the priest turned and indicated to the betrothed the pink silk cloth, which was spread on the floor. Though they had often heard about the belief that whoever stepped first on this cloth would be the master of the family, neither Levin nor Kitty could remember it when they took the few steps. Neither did they hear the loud remarks and the arguments on the part of some observers that he had stepped first or on the part of others that they had done it together.

After the usual questions about whether they desired to enter into matrimony and whether they had promised to marry someone else, and after they had given answers which sounded strange to themselves, a new service began. Kitty listened to the prayers and tried to understand their meaning, but she could not. As the ritual was being performed, a feeling of solemnity and serene joy filled her heart to overflowing and distracted her attention.

They prayed "that He will grant unto them chastity and of the fruit of the womb as is expedient for them: that He will make them glad with the sight of sons and daughters." They recalled that God had created woman from Adam's rib "for which cause a man shall leave his father and his mother and cleave unto his wife, and the two shall be one flesh," and "that this mystery is great." They prayed that God make them fruitful and bless them as He had Isaac and Rebecca, Joseph, Moses and Zipporah, and that he let them see the sons of their sons. All this is beautiful, thought Kitty, listening to these words, and it cannot be otherwise. A smile of joy, which communicated itself unconsciously to all who watched her, shone on her serene face.

"Put it on her head," was the advice given when, after the priest had put the crowns on the young couple, Shcherbatsky's hand in its three-button glove trembled as he lifted the crown high above Kitty's head.

"Put it on," she whispered, smiling.

Levin looked at her and was struck by the joyous radiance of her face. Involuntarily he was infected by her feeling and, like her, felt serene and joyous.

They enjoyed listening to the reading of the Epistle and to the thunder of the archdeacon's voice as he read the last verse, which the spectators had waited for with such impatience. They enjoyed drinking from a shallow bowl the warm, red wine mixed with water, and were still more pleased when the priest, opening his chasuble and taking both their hands in his, led them around the lectern while the basso burst forth with "Rejoice, Oh Isaiah!" Holding up the crowns, Shcherbatsky and Chirikov also smiled happily and, entangled in the bride's train, either fell behind or bumped against the bride and the bridegroom whenever the priest stopped. The spark of joy that had been kindled by Kitty seemed to affect all who were present in the church. It seemed to Levin that both the priest and the deacon, like himself, were tempted to smile.

The priest took the crowns from their heads, read the last prayer, and congratulated the newlyweds. Levin glanced at Kitty; he had never before seen her as she was now. She was beautiful, her face radiating new happiness. Levin wanted to say something to her, but he did not know whether the ritual was over. The priest came to his help. He said softly and with a gentle smile, "Kiss your wife, and you kiss your husband," and he took the candles from their hands.

Levin tenderly kissed her smiling lips, gave her his arm, and with the feeling of a new, strange closeness to her, led her from the church. He did not, he could not believe that it was true. Only when their wondering and shy looks met did he believe it, for he felt that they were now really one.

That same night, after supper, the newlyweds left for the country.

7

BY THIS TIME Vronsky and Anna had been traveling together in Europe for three months. They had visited Venice, Rome, Naples, and had just arrived in a small Italian city, where they intended to stay for some time.

The handsome headwaiter, the part in his thick, pomaded hair starting from his neck, in his swallow-tailed coat and the broad expanse of his white batiste shirt, a bundle of charms on his rotund belly, his hands in his pockets, squinting sternly and contemptuously, was replying to a gentleman who had stopped him. From the other side of the entrance the head-waiter heard the sound of steps ascending the stairs. He turned around and, seeing the Russian count who occupied the best suite in the hotel, he respectfully removed his hands from his pockets, bowed slightly, and reported that a messenger had come and that the matter of renting the *palazzo* had been settled. The manager was ready to sign the contract.

"Ah! That's good!" said Vronsky. "Is the lady in?"

"She went for a walk, but she is back now," replied the waiter.

Vronsky took off his soft, wide-brimmed hat and with his handkerchief mopped his perspiring forehead and hair, which he had let grow halfway down to his ears and combed back to hide his bald spot. And with an absent-minded glance at the gentleman who was still standing there and now stared at him, he was about to leave.

"This gentleman is a Russian and he asked for you," said the headwaiter.

With mixed feelings of annoyance at being nowhere able

to escape from his acquaintances, and of longing for some distraction from the monotony of his life, Vronsky took another look at the gentleman, who walked a few steps away and then stopped, and at one and the same moment the light of recognition kindled in both their eyes.

"Golenishchev!"

"Vronsky!"

Indeed, it was Golenishchev, Vronsky's classmate in the School of Pages. In school Golenishchev belonged to the liberal party, and on graduating he received a civilian rank and never saw service. They had become completely estranged after graduation and had met only once afterward.

At that meeting Vronsky had learned that Golenishchev had chosen some high-sounding liberal occupation and, as a result, was inclined to disdain Vronsky's interests and career. Therefore at that meeting Vronsky looked at Golenishchev with that cold and haughty air which he knew so well how to assume, and which meant: "You may like or dislike my way of life, but it doesn't concern me at all. You must respect me if you want to associate with me." But Golenishchev was contemptuously indifferent toward Vronsky's attitude. The present meeting, it would seem, should have estranged them still further. But they lit up and cried out with pleasure on recognizing each other. Vronsky would never have expected to be so glad to see Golenishchev, but he himself probably did not realize how bored he was. He forgot the unpleasant impression of their last meeting, and with an unconcealed expression of pleasure, he extended his hand to his former comrade. The same show of pleasure supplanted the expression of uneasiness on Golenishchev's face.

"I'm so glad to see you!" said Vronsky, his friendly smile displaying his firm, white teeth.

"They told me there was a Vronsky here, but I didn't know which one. I'm very, very glad to see you."

"Let's go in. Well, what are you doing?"

"I've been here for two months. I'm working."

"Ah!" Vronsky said understandingly. "Well, let's go in."

And following the custom of Russians, instead of speaking Russian, whereby he really could conceal from the servants what he was saying, he spoke French.

"Have you met Karenina? We are traveling together. I am going to see her," he said in French, looking keenly into Golenishchev's eyes.

"Oh! I didn't know," (though he really did) Golenishchev said indifferently. "When did you arrive?"

"I? Three days ago," Vronsky replied, with another keen look into his comrade's eyes.

Yes, he's an honorable man and sees things as one should, said Vronsky to himself, understanding what the expression on Golenishchev's face meant and why he had changed the topic of conversation. I can introduce him to Anna—he sees things as one should.

During the three months he had spent with Anna abroad, whenever he met someone new, Vronsky always asked himself how they would view his relationship with Anna, and in most cases he found in men a *proper* understanding. But if he or those who had the *proper* understanding were asked what this understanding consisted of, both he and they would have found it difficult to explain.

Actually, those who in Vronsky's opinion had the *proper* understanding had no such understanding at all but behaved as all well-brought-up people behave when faced with the complex and insoluble problems that beset the lives of all of us—they behaved decently, avoiding hints and unpleasant questions. They pretended to understand fully the meaning and significance of the situation, even to approve of it, yet they considered it improper and unnecessary to explain all this.

Vronsky saw immediately that Golenishchev was one of these and therefore was doubly glad to see him. And, indeed, Golenishchev behaved toward Karenina, when he was brought to her, just as Vronsky wished. Evidently without the slightest effort, he eschewed those topics of conversation that might have created any kind of embarrassment.

He had not met Anna before and was struck by her beauty and still more by the artlessness with which she accepted her situation. She blushed when Golenishchev was introduced to her by Vronsky, and he found the childish blush that spread over her friendly and beautiful face most attractive. But he particularly liked the manner in which, to avoid any misunderstanding that might arise in the presence of a stranger, she at once and, it seemed, intentionally addressed Vronsky as Aleksei and told the guest that they were moving to a newly rented house, known here as a *palazzo*. This simple and straightforward attitude toward her situation pleased Golenishchev. Watching her good-natured gaiety and liveliness, and knowing both Aleksei Aleksandrovich and Vronsky, Golenishchev believed that he understood her fully. It seemed to him that he understood what she could not understand at all, namely, how it could be that she could feel lively, gay and happy after having brought misfortune to her husband, abandoning him and her son, and losing her good name.

"It is mentioned in the guidebook," said Golenishchev, referring to the *palazzo* Vronsky was about to rent. "There's a beautiful Tintoretto there. One of his later works."

"I have an idea! The weather is fine. Let's go there and look at it again," said Vronsky, turning to Anna.

"I'd love to. I'll just put on a hat. Is it hot?" she asked, stopping at the door and looking at Vronsky inquiringly. And again a bright blush covered her face.

By her look Vronsky understood that she did not know on what terms he wanted to be with Golenishchev, and that she was not sure that she was behaving as he wanted her to.

He looked at her long and tenderly.

"No, not very," he said.

And it seemed to her that she understood completely, especially that he was pleased with her. She smiled at him and left the room with a brisk step.

The friends looked at each other and their faces showed embarrassment, as though Golenishchev, who obviously admired her, wanted to say something about her but did not know what to say. And Vronsky shared his embarrassment.

"Well, then," began Vronsky, just to start a conversation. "So you have settled here? Are you still busy with the same project?" he continued, remembering that he had been told that Golenishchev was writing a book.

"Yes, I'm writing the second part of *Two Principles*," said Golenishchev, flushing with pleasure at this question, "or, to be more exact, I'm not writing it yet, but preparing and collecting material. It will be much more comprehensive, and encompass almost all problems. We in Russia refuse to recognize that we are the heirs of Byzantium . . ." and he went into a long and vehement discourse.

At first Vronsky felt awkward, for he was not acquainted even with the first part of *Two Principles*, which the author had referred to as if to something well known. But later, when Golenishchev began to expound his ideas and Vronsky could follow him, he listened to him not without interest, even though he did not know the *Two Principles*, for Golenishchev talked well. But Vronsky was surprised and troubled by the vehemence with which Golenishchev spoke on the subject that occupied him. The longer he spoke, the brighter his eyes burned, the quicker he was in his objections to imaginary opponents and the more alarmed and offended he seemed. Remembering Golenishchev as a thin, active, good-natured and generous boy, always first in his class, Vronsky was at a total loss to understand the cause of his agitation and did not approve of it. He particularly disliked seeing Golenishchev, a man of good upbringing, put himself on the same level with the obscure hacks who angered him by their provocations. Was it worth while? Vronsky did not like it, but in spite of that he felt that Golenishchev was not happy and he pitied him. His mobile, still-handsome features betrayed unhappiness, almost insanity, as he continued to expound his ideas rapidly and vehemently, without even noticing Anna's entrance.

When Anna entered, she was wearing a hat and cape, her beautiful hand toyed with her parasol with a rapid movement, and she stopped beside Vronsky. He felt relieved at the opportunity to withdraw from Golenishchev's plaintive look, which was fixed upon him, and with renewed love he looked at Anna, beautiful and full of life and joy. Golenishchev collected himself with difficulty and at first was dispirited and gloomy, but Anna, kindly disposed toward everyone (as she had been lately), soon enlivened him with her simple, gay manner. After trying various subjects of conversation, she led him to a discussion of paintings, on which he spoke with competence, and she listened to him attentively. They walked to the house they had rented, and inspected it.

"One thing particularly pleases me," Anna said to Golenishchev on their way back. "Aleksei will have a good atelier. By all means take that room," she said to Vronsky in Russian, addressing him as "thou," for she already understood that in their isolation Golenishchev would become close to them and that there was no need for dissembling in his presence.

"Do you paint?" Golenishchev asked, quickly turning to Vronsky.

"I used to a long time ago, and now I've begun to do a little again," answered Vronsky, blushing.

"He's very talented," Anna said with a happy smile. "Of course I'm not the one to judge. But those who know have said the same thing."

8

DURING THIS first period of her freedom and rapid recovery, Anna felt inexcusably happy and full of the joy of life. The memory of her husband's misfortune did not mar her happiness. On the one hand, this memory was too frightening to think about. On the other, she could feel no remorse for being the cause of her husband's misfortune—so great was the happiness that it had brought to her. The memories of everything that had happened to her after her illness, of her reconciliation with her husband, their break, the news of Vronsky's injury, his reappearance, the preparations for the divorce, departure from her husband's home, parting with her son— all this seemed like a nightmare to her, one from which she had awakened abroad, alone with Vronsky. The memory of the wrong she had done her husband aroused in her a feeling akin to disgust and resembled the feeling of a drowning man who frees himself from the clutches of another, who drowns. Of course it was bad, but it was the only way to save herself, and it was better not to think of these frightening details.

One reassuring thought about the step she had taken had occurred to her at the first moment of their final break, and when she now dwelt on what had happened, she recalled that thought: I have unavoidably brought misfortune to this man, she thought, but I don't want to take advantage of his misfortune. I, too, suffer and will suffer, I've been deprived of everything that is dearest to me—my good name and my son. I acted badly, therefore I don't seek happiness; I will not accept the divorce and will suffer in my disgrace and in the separation from my son.

But she did not suffer, however sincerely she wished it. There was no disgrace. With that tact in which both of them abounded, they never put themselves in a false situation while they were abroad, avoiding the company of Russian ladies and always meeting people who pretended that they understood their relationship much better than they did themselves. In the beginning she did not even suffer because of her separation from her son. The baby, *his* child, was so sweet and had bound Anna so closely to her since the time that she alone remained with her, that Anna seldom remembered her son.

The urge to live, intensified by her recovery, was so strong and the conditions of life so new and pleasant that Anna felt inexcusably happy. The better she knew Vronsky, the more she loved him. She loved him for his own sake and for his love for her. Her complete possession of him was her constant joy. His closeness to her was always a delight. All of his traits, with which she became more and more familiar, were to her inexpressibly dear. His appearance, different now that he wore civilian dress, was as attractive to her as to a young girl in love. In everything he said, thought, or did she saw something unusually noble and sublime. Her admiration for him often frightened her; she sought but could not find in him anything that was not excellent. She dared not display to him her awareness of her own insignificance compared with him. It seemed to her that if he knew it, he might cease loving her sooner, and nothing frightened her so much now, though her fears were groundless, as that she might lose his love. But she could not help being grateful to him for his behavior toward her and showing him how highly she prized it. He, whose calling in her opinion unmistakably lay in government, in which he should have played a great part, had sacrificed his ambition for her without the least regret. More than ever he was tender and respectful toward her, and at every moment watchful lest her situation cause her embarrassment. He, who was so manly, not only never contradicted her but in his relationship with her had no will of his own, and it seemed his only concern was to anticipate her wishes. She could not but appreciate it, though this very excessive attention that he paid her, this atmosphere of care with which he surrounded her, sometimes oppressed her.

In the meantime Vronsky, in spite of the complete fulfillment of what he had so long desired, was not entirely happy. He soon saw that the fulfillment of his desire had brought him only a grain of sand out of the mountain of happiness he had expected. It showed him the eternal mistake men make by believing that happiness consists of the fulfillment of desire. In the beginning, after they had joined their lives together and he had changed to civilian clothes, he tasted the joys of a general freedom he had not known before, as well as the freedom of their love. He was content, but not for long. He soon felt that in his heart there arose a longing for new desires; he was bored. Independently of his will, he grasped at each of his fleeting whims, mistaking them for desires and goals.

He had to occupy in some way sixteen hours of each day, since they lived abroad in full freedom, not confined by those conventions of social life that had filled his time in Petersburg. He could not even think of the pleasures of bachelor life, which had diverted him during his former visits abroad. One such attempt, a late supper with friends, had an unexpectedly depressing effect on Anna, out of proportion to the pleasure he had received. Because of the equivocal nature of their situation, they could have no connections either with local gentry or the Russian group. As for sight-seeing, aside from the fact that they had already seen everything, he, as a Russian and as an intelligent person, did not ascribe to it the importance the English are so unreasonably apt to do.

And as a hungry animal grasps at every object it happens on in the hope of finding food, so did Vronsky blindly seize upon politics, upon new books, upon paintings.

Since he had, from childhood, shown abilities as a painter, and in later years, not knowing how to spend his money, had begun to collect engravings, he chose to concentrate on painting, seeking to find in it the fulfillment of all those wishes that had accumulated and demanded satisfaction.

He had a gift for understanding art and for copying paintings faithfully and in good taste, and he thought that he possessed the requisites of a painter. After some hesitation about what school of painting to select, religious, historical, genre, or realist, he began to paint. He understood all types and could be inspired by any of them. But he could not imagine that one might be completely ignorant of what schools of painting existed and be inspired directly by what was in his heart, regardless of whether what he painted would belong to some definite school. Since he did not know this and received his inspiration not directly from life but indirectly, from life as already represented in art, his inspiration came upon him with great speed and without effort, and just as quickly and effortlessly he succeeded in making his painting resemble those of the school he wanted to imitate.

Of all the schools he preferred the French, finding it graceful and effective, and in this style he began to paint a portrait of Anna in an Italian costume. To him and to everyone who saw it, the portrait appeared to be a great success.

9

THE OLD NEGLECTED *palazzo*, with its high, sculptured ceiling and wall frescoes, mosaic floors, heavy yellow damask drapes on tall windows, vases on consoles and mantelpieces, carved doors and somber halls hung with paintings—this *palazzo*, after they had moved into it, by its very appearance sustained in Vronsky the pleasant illusion that he was not so much a Russian landowner and retired master of the hunt as an enlightened connoisseur and patron of the arts, and in his own way, a modest painter who had renounced social position, connections and ambition for the woman he loved.

The role Vronsky had assumed after moving to the *palazzo* he filled very well, and having become acquainted through Golenishchev with a few interesting people, for a while he enjoyed peace of mind. Under the direction of an Italian professor of painting, he did landscapes and studied medieval Italian life. Most recently Vronsky had been so taken up with medieval Italian life that he even began to wear his wrap over his shoulder and his hat in the medieval style, which very much suited him.

"We live here and know little," Vronsky said one morning to Golenishchev, who had come to see him. "Have you seen Mikhailov's painting?" he asked, handing him a Russian newspaper he had received that morning, and pointing to an article about a Russian painter who lived in the same city and who had finished a painting that had long been discussed and had been bought in advance. The article criticized the government and the academy for failing to give any encouragement and help to an outstanding painter.

"I've seen it," replied Golenishchev. "Of course, he's not without talent, but he's moving in the wrong direction. It's the same Ivanov-Strauss-Renan attitude toward Christ and religious painting."

"What is the subject of the picture?" asked Anna.

"Christ before Pilate. Christ is presented as a Jew, with the full realism of the new school."

The question about the content of the picture led Golenishchev to a discussion of his favorite subject and he began to expound his views.

"I don't understand how they can be so grossly mistaken. Christ has already been definitely represented in the art of the great old masters. Therefore, if they want to represent a revolutionary or a wise man, and not God, let them select such historical figures as Socrates, Franklin, Charlotte Corday, but definitely not Christ. They take a subject that should not be used in art and then. . . ."

"Is it true that this Mikhailov lives in such poverty?" asked Vronsky, believing that he, as a Russian Maecenas, should help the painter whether his picture was good or bad.

"I doubt it. He's an outstanding portraitist. Have you seen his portrait of Madame Vasilchikov? But it seems that he doesn't want to paint portaits any longer, so his life may be difficult. I would like to say that—"

"Couldn't we ask him to do a portrait of Anna Arkadievna?" asked Vronsky.

"Why me?" asked Anna. "After yours I want no other portrait. Better to do Annie's—" (as she called her daughter) "there she is," she added, looking through the window at the beautiful Italian wet nurse who had brought the child out into the garden, and she quickly and unnoticeably glanced at Vronsky. The beautiful nurse, whose head Vronsky had used in his painting, was the only secret worry in Anna's life. While painting her, Vronsky admired her medieval-style beauty, and Anna did not dare to admit to herself that she feared she would be jealous of the nurse and therefore was particularly kind and indulgent to her and her little son.

Vronsky also looked through the window and into Anna's eyes and, turning quickly to Golenishchev, said:

"And do you know this Mikhailov?"

"I've met him. He's an odd person and completely uneducated. One of those new, wild men, you know, whom you so often meet nowadays; one of those freethinkers, you know, who *d'emblée* embrace the ideas of atheism, nihilism, and materialism. In former times," said Golenishchev without noticing or without wishing to notice that Anna and Vronsky wanted to say something, "in former times a freethinker was a man who had been brought up in the teachings of religion, law, and morality, and only after a difficult struggle with himself did he arrive at his convictions as a freethinker. But nowadays there has appeared a new type, a born freethinker. They grow up without even having heard that there are laws of morality and religion, that there are authorities; they grow up with negative ideas on everything. In other words, they are savages. He is one of them. I've heard that he's the son of a Moscow valet and that he's had no education. When he entered the academy and became famous, he, as a clever man, decided to educate himself. He turned to what seemed to him the source of education—the journals. In the old times, you know, if someone, let's say a Frenchman, looked for education, he would study all the classics, the theologians, the tragedians, the historians, the philosophers, and you know yourself what intellectual labors that involves. But with us nowadays he begins directly with nihilistic literature, learning very quickly the essence of the teachings of nihilism, and that's it. Moreover, twenty years ago he would have found in this literature signs of a struggle against authority, against time-honored opinions, and from this struggle he would understand that other ideas exist. But now he happens directly upon writings that don't even deign to argue against old views but tell you without hesitation that there exists nothing but evolution, natural selection, struggle for survival, and that's all. In my article I—"

"I have an idea," said Anna, who had already long since exchanged cautious glances with Vronsky, knowing that he was not interested in the education of this painter and only wanted to find out how he could help him and to order a portrait from him. "I have an idea," she said, resolutely interrupting the garrulous Golenishchev. "Let's go to his place."

Golenishchev collected himself and agreed readily. But since the painter lived in a distant part of the city, they decided to engage a carriage.

An hour later, Anna, seated next to Golenishchev, with Vronsky in the front seat of the carriage, rode up to a beautiful new house in a remote part of the city. They learned from the porter's wife, who came out to them, that Mikhailov admitted visitors to his studio but that at present he was in his apartment a short distance away. They sent him their cards, with a request to be allowed to view his paintings.

10

WHEN THEY BROUGHT him Count Vronsky's and Golenishchev's cards, the painter Mikhailov was at work as usual. That morning he had been working in his studio on a large painting. When he came home, he became angry with his wife for her failure to deal successfully with the landlady, who had demanded money.

"I've told you a thousand times not to try to explain. You're a fool anyway, but when you begin using your Italian, you're a fool three times over," he said to her after a long argument.

"Then pay your debts. It's not my fault. If I had the money—"

"For Heaven's sake, leave me alone!" Mikhailov cried tearfully, and covering his ears, ran into his workroom behind a partition and shut the door. What a simpleton! he said to himself. He sat down at the table and, opening the folder, at once eagerly resumed work on a drawing he had begun.

He never worked so eagerly and so well as when his life went badly, and particularly when he had quarelled with his wife. Ah, if only I could get away from all of this, he thought as he continued to work. He was working on a sketch of a man who was in a fit of anger. He had made a sketch earlier but it did not satisfy him. No, the other was better. . . . Where is it? He walked to his wife's room and, frowning and ignoring her, asked his older daughter where the paper was that he had given them. The paper with the rejected drawing was found, but it was soiled and spotted with drops of paraffin. Nevertheless he took the paper, put it on his table and, moving back from it and squinting, he began to examine it. Suddenly he smiled and waved his arms joyfully.

"That's it!" he said, and snatching a pencil, he began to draw rapidly. The paraffin spot had lent the man a new expression.

He was drawing this new expression when he suddenly recalled the energetic face and prominent chin of the shopkeeper from whom he bought his cigars, and he provided the individual he was drawing with this very face and chin. He laughed gleefully. Dead and artificial until now, the figure suddenly sprang to life and could not be altered further. The figure was alive, and was clearly and unmistakably distinct. The sketch could be corrected to fit the figure; the position of the legs could and even should be changed; the position of the left arm had to be changed completely and the hair thrown back. But while making these corrections, he did not change the figure but simply discarded what concealed it. It seemed to him that he was removing the covers that prevented the figure from being seen in its entirety. Each new stroke revealed all the more clearly the whole figure in its full power, just as it had suddenly appeared to him when he had seen the paraffin spots. He was carefully finishing his sketch when they brought him the visitors' cards.

"Just a minute, just a minute!"

He walked over to his wife.

"Come, Sasha, don't be angry!" he said to her, smiling shyly and tenderly. "You were wrong; I was wrong. I'll take care of everything." And having made up with his wife, he put on his hat and his olive-colored coat with a velvet collar and went to his studio. He had already forgotten about the figure he had drawn so successfully. Now he felt pleased and excited by the visit of these distinguished Russians who had arrived in a carriage.

Deep within his heart he had a definite opinion of the painting that now rested on his easel: he believed that no one had ever created such a painting. He did not think that his painting was better than all of Raphael's but he knew that what he wanted to express and had expressed in this painting, no one had ever done before. He had been convinced of this for a long time, ever since he had begun to paint it. But the opinions of others, whoever they might be, he considered of great importance; and they affected him deeply. Every remark, even the most insignificant, that showed that his critics saw even a small part of what he saw in this painting, moved him deeply. He always ascribed to his critics a greater depth of understanding than he himself possessed, and he always expected them to see something in his picture that he himself had not seen. And it seemed to him that he often found this in the remarks of viewers.

As he walked with a rapid step to the door of his studio, he was struck, in spite of his agitation, by the soft radiance of Anna, who stood in the shade of the entrance porch. She was listening to Golenishchev, who was speaking to her with animation, and at the same time she evidently wanted to observe the painter as he approached. He himself did not notice how he gained and absorbed this impression while he was coming over to them, and how, like the impression of his tobacconist's chin, he tucked it away into a place from which it could be recovered when needed. The visitors, who had been unfavorably impressed by the painter in advance, thanks to Golenishchev's report, were still more disappointed by his appearance. Thickset, of medium height, with a rocking gait, Mikhailov wore a brown hat, olive coat, and narrow pants, though wide pants had already long been in style, and he made an unpleasant impression, particularly because of his common, broad face, which expressed both shyness and a desire to preserve his dignity.

"Do come in," he said, trying to appear unconcerned, and as he entered the hall he reached into his pocket for the key and opened the door.

11

ON ENTERING THE studio, the painter once again scrutinized his visitors, and made a mental note of Vronsky's face, particularly of his jawline. Though his artistic imagination was constantly active, gathering material for his work, and though he grew more and more anxious as the moment approached when his painting would be judged, he was creating rapidly and precisely a mental picture of these three persons from just a few traits. That one (Golenishchev) was a Russian who lived here. Mikhailov did not remember his name or where he had met him or what they had talked about. He remembered only his face, as he remembered all the faces he had ever seen, but he also remembered that it was one of those faces his mind had stored away in a large compartment with other, similar faces, deceptively impressive, and lacking in expression. His thick hair and very high forehead gave a false depth to his face, in which was mirrored only a petty, childish, restless expression, centered on the narrow bridge of his nose. Vronsky and Karenina, Mikhailov believed, were distinguished and wealthy Russians who did not know anything about art, but, like all wealthy Russians, pretended to love and appreciate it. Most likely, he thought, they have already seen all the old stuff and now they visit the studios of the new painters, of the German charlatan and that English fool of a pre-Raphaelite, and have come here only to complete the tour. He was very familiar with the habits of the dilettantes (the cleverer they were the worse they were), their visits to the studios of modern painters with the sole purpose of being able to say that art had declined and that the more you see the works of new painters the more you are convinced that the old masters remain inimitable. He expected all this, saw all this in their faces, in the careless indifference with which they conversed, in the way they looked at the lay figures and busts, and the ease with which they walked around waiting for him to unveil the painting. In spite of this, while he was arranging his sketches, pulling up the shades, and removing the sheet from the painting, he felt deeply agitated, the more so because—though he believed that all notable and wealthy Russians were brutish and stupid—he liked Vronsky and was particularly taken with Anna.

"Here, if you please," he said, indicating the painting and stepping aside with his rocking gait. "It is *Pilate's Admonition*, Matthew, chapter twenty-seven," he said, feeling his lips begin to tremble with excitement. He walked away and stood behind them.

For the few moments when the visitors viewed the painting in silence, Mikhailov also looked at it, assuming the indifferent view of an outsider. During these few moments he believed beforehand that the most authoritative and valid judgment of his painting would be pronounced by these very visitors for whom he had felt such contempt only a moment earlier. He forgot all that he had thought of his painting during the three years he had worked on it. He forgot all its merits, of which he had been convinced; he viewed the painting with their new, indifferent look, the look of an outsider, and he did not see anything good in it. He saw in the foreground Pilate's annoyed expression and the calm face of Christ, and in the background the figures of Pilate's attendants and the face of John observing all that was happening. Each face, which had developed within him and acquired its particular expression after such intense search, after so many errors and corrections; each face, which had brought him so much suffering and so much joy; and all these faces, so often moved from place to place to harmonize with the whole, all these shadings of color and tone which he had attained with such difficulty—all this, as he looked at it through their eyes, seemed to him a vulgarity done for the thousandth time. The dearest face of all, the focus of the picture—Christ's face—which had filled him with such delight when it had revealed itself, lost everything as he looked at the picture through their eyes. He saw a well-executed (not even well, for he saw clearly now the multitude of its defects) copy of those innumerable Christs of Titian, Raphael,

Rubens, as well as of the soldiers and Pilate. All this was vulgar, old-fashioned, and in poor taste; and even badly executed—motley and weak. They would be right if they spoke hypocritically and courteously in the painter's presence but laughed at him and pitied him when alone.

The silence oppressed him too heavily (though it lasted no longer than a minute). So as to break it and show them that he was not upset, after some effort he addressed Golenishchev.

"I believe that I've had the pleasure of meeting you," he said, casting restless looks now at Anna and now at Vronsky, so as not to miss the slightest flicker in their expressions.

"Of course! We met at Rossi's on that evening, if you recall, when the young Italian lady, the new Rachel, recited poetry," Golenishchev replied eagerly, turning from the painting to the painter without the slightest regret.

He, however, noticed that Mikhailov was waiting for his opinion of the picture and said:

"Your picture has really come along since I saw it last. And now, just as then, I am deeply impressed by the figure of Pilate. It is so easy to understand this man, kindhearted and a fine fellow, but an official through and through, one who didn't know what he was doing. But it seems to me. . . ."

All of Mikhailov's mobile face quickly lit up. His eyes brightened. He attempted to say something, but in his excitement he failed to do so and he pretended to clear his throat. No matter how little he valued Golenishchev's ability to understand art, how insignificant was the correct remark that Pilate's face bore the expression of an official, how offensive it might seem to him that this remark had been expressed first, whereas the most important points had not been mentioned, Mikhailov was overjoyed by his remark. His own opinion of the figure of Pilate was the same as Golenishchev's. The fact that this judgment was one of a million others, which, as Mikhailov well knew, were all true, did not lessen the importance of Golenishchev's remark. He loved Golenishchev for this remark, and from a state of dejection he was suddenly transported to a state of rapture. At once he saw the whole picture revive with all the inexpressible complexity of life. Mikhailov again attempted to explain how he understood Pilate, but his lips trembled uncontrollably, and he could not speak. Vronsky and Anna also spoke, in those soft voices which visitors normally use at painting exhibitions, partly to avoid offending the painter and partly to avoid saying aloud something foolish, so easy to do when discussing art. It seemed to Mikhailov that they were impressed by the painting. He came over to them.

"What a wonderful expression Christ has!" said Anna. Of everything that she saw she liked best this expression, and she understood that this was the focus of the painting and that therefore, praising it would please the painter. "He apparently pities Pilate."

This, too, was one of the million correct judgments one could express concerning his painting and the figure of Christ. She said that He pitied Pilate. And really, Christ's expression should show pity, for it was an expression of love, of unearthly peace, of readiness to die, of awareness of the vanity of words. Of course, there was the expression of an official on Pilate's face and of pity on Christ's, for one was the embodiment of a life of the flesh, the other of the spirit. All this and many other thoughts flashed through Mikhailov's mind. And again his face lit up with delight.

"Yet, how well this figure is done! What transparency! One can walk around it," said Golenishchev, evidently showing by this remark that he did not approve of the nature of this figure and the idea it represented.

"Yes, wonderful artistry!" said Vronsky. "How well those figures in the background stand out! That's what I call technique," he said, addressing Golenishchev and evidently referring to the conversation they had had about Vronsky's despair of ever acquiring such a technique.

"Yes, yes, it's wonderful!" confirmed Golenishchev and Anna. In spite of his state of elation, Mikhailov was pained by their remark about technique and, glancing angrily at Vronsky, he suddenly frowned. He had often heard this word "technique," and was at a loss to understand what was meant by it. He knew that the word referred to the mechanical ability to draw and paint, without any regard for content. He had often noticed, as he did in these words of praise, that technique was contrasted with intrinsic worth, as though, as a good painting could be made of a bad subject. He knew that much attention and care had to be given by the painter lest he impair his painting while removing the covering that conceals its essential content, but this was performed neither by the painter's art nor his technique. If what he saw were revealed to a little child or to his cook, they, too, could bring to light what they had seen. And a painter who was most able and skilled in technique could not, by his mechanical abilities alone, create a picture, unless the full meaning of its content were first revealed to him. Moreover, he felt that as far as technique was concerned, he deserved the least praise for it. In everything that he was painting and had painted he saw glaring defects, which had resulted from his lack of care in removing the covering, and which he could not correct now without spoiling the entire work. And almost in all these figures and faces he still found remains of the coverings that had not been completely removed and that spoiled the painting.

"If you will permit me, I would like to say something . . ." said Golenishchev.

"Oh, please. I'd be very glad to hear it," said Mikhailov with a forced smile.

"He is represented by you as man who has become God, and not as God who has become man. I know, however, that that's what you meant."

"I couldn't paint a Christ whom I didn't have in my heart," Mikhailov said gloomily.

"Yes, but in that case, if you allow me to express my opinion. . . . Your painting is so good that my remark can do it no harm, and also it's my personal opinion. With you it's different. Your very motif is different. Let us take, for example, Ivanov. I believe that if Christ had to be brought down to the level of a historical figure, it would have been better for Ivanov to select another historical theme, a fresh one, untouched."

"But what if this is the greatest theme available to art?"

"If you search you will find others. But the fact is that art tolerates no arguments or discussions. As they look at Ivanov's painting, both the believer and unbeliever will ask, 'Is it God or isn't it God?' And this ruins the totality of the impression."

"Why do you say that? It seems to me that educated people can no longer disagree on this subject," said Mikhailov.

Golenishchev did not agree with this and, adhering to his initial idea of art demanding a totality of impression, he refuted Mikhailov's views.

Mikhailov was troubled, but could say nothing in defense of his idea.

12

ANNA AND VRONSKY, unhappy about the learned loquacious-
ness of their friend, had long been exchanging glances and,
at last, without waiting for their host, Vronsky went over to
another painting, a small one.

"Ah, what a beautiful picture! How wonderful! Marvelous!
How beautiful!" they cried out in a single voice.

What is it that they like so much? thought Mikhailov. He
had forgotten about this picture, one he had painted three
years before. He had forgotten all the suffering and joy he
had experienced with that painting when he had been constantly occupied with it, day and night, for several months.
He had forgotten about it as he usually forgot his completed
paintings. He did not even like to look at it, and exhibited it
only because he was waiting for an Englishman who wanted
to buy it.

"Just an old study," he said.

"How beautiful!" said Golenishchev, who also, it seemed,
was fascinated by this picture.

Two boys were fishing in the shadow of a willow tree. The
older one had just cast his line and was cautiously pulling out
the float from behind a willow, concentrating deeply on this
activity. Another boy, slightly younger, lay on the grass, leaning his head, with its rumpled fair hair, on his hand and
looking at the water with thoughtful blue eyes. What was
he thinking of?

Their admiration for the picture stirred within Mikhailov
his former agitation, but he feared and disliked this idle feeling for the past and therefore, although overjoyed at their
praise, he was eager to draw the visitors' attention to a third
painting.

But Vronsky asked him whether this painting was for sale.
To Mikhailov, who was elated by the visit, the question of
money seemed offensive.

"It was put out to be sold," he said, frowning gloomily.

When the visitors had left, Mikhailov sat down before the
painting of Pilate and Christ and recalled what the visitors
had said and what they had not said but meant. It was
strange: what had carried so much weight for him while they

were there and while he was judging from their point of view suddenly lost all its importance. He began to view his painting from his own point of view, as an artist, and he regained full confidence in the perfection and consequently in the significance of his painting. He needed this confidence to sustain the state of concentration that excluded all other interest and was the only state in which he could work.

He was still not completely satisfied with the foreshortening of Christ's leg. He reached for the palette and began to work. While correcting the leg, he looked frequently at the figure of John in the background. The visitors had not noticed it, but he knew that it had not been perfectly executed. When he finished the leg, he was going to work on that figure, but he was still too excited. He was equally unable to work either when unmoved or when moved too deeply and able to see everything too distinctly. In this transition from indifference to inspiration, there was only one stage at which work could be performed. But that day he was too agitated. He was about to cover the painting, but he stopped, and holding the sheet in his hand and smiling blissfully, he looked at length at the figure of John. At last, as though with sadness, he looked away from the painting, lowered the sheet, and went home, tired but happy.

Vronsky, Anna, and Golenishchev were particularly animated and gay on their way home. They spoke about Mikhailov and his paintings. The word "talent" they understood as an innate, almost physical ability, which did not depend on the heart or the mind, and with it they tried to define everything a painter experienced. This word occurred in their conversation with particular frequency because they needed it to name what they did not understand at all but liked to discuss. They said that it could not be denied that he had talent, but that his talent could not develop for lack of education—the general misfortune of our Russian painters. But the painting of the boys had left an impression on them, and again and again they returned to it.

"What a wonderful thing! How skillfully and yet how simply it was done! He himself doesn't know how beautiful it is. Yes, we absolutely must buy it," said Vronsky.

13

MIKHAILOV SOLD HIS painting to Vronsky and agreed to paint a portrait of Anna. On the appointed day he came and began to work.

After the fifth sitting the portrait impressed everyone, particularly Vronsky, not only by its likeness but by its unusual beauty. It was strange that Mikhailov could represent that special beauty of hers. One would have to know her and love her as I do to discover this in her, this most endearing expression of her soul, thought Vronsky, though only through this portrait had he discovered that most endearing expression of her soul. But the expression was so true that he and others thought that they had long known it.

"No matter how hard I tried, I never succeeded," he said of his own portrait of her, "and he just looked at her and did it. That's what I call technique."

"It'll come," said Golenishchev, trying to encourage him. He believed that Vronsky possessed both talent and, more important, the education that elevates one's understanding of art. Golenishchev's belief in Vronsky's talent found additional support in his own need of Vronsky's encouragement and praise of his articles and ideas, and he felt that this praise and encouragement should be mutual.

In a strange home, and particularly in Vronsky's *palazzo*, Mikhailov was completely different than in his studio. He was courteous but not friendly, as though afraid to become intimate with people he did not respect. He called Vronsky "Your Excellency" and, in spite of Anna's and Vronsky's invitations, never stayed for dinner and came only for the sittings. Anna treated him with particular kindness, and was grateful to him for the portrait. Vronsky was more than courteous to him, and evidently was interested in the painter's opinion of his painting. Golenishchev never missed a chance to expound to Mikhailov the true meaning of art. But Mikhailov remained equally cold to all of them. By the expression of his eyes Anna was aware that he enjoyed looking at her, but he avoided conversing with her. He remained stubbornly silent when Vronsky spoke of his work, as stubbornly silent when they showed him Vronsky's painting, and he evidently felt oppressed by Golenishchev's discourses and did not contradict him.

In general, as they got to know him better, they disliked him deeply for his restrained, unsympathetic, almost hostile attitude toward them. They were glad when the sittings came to an end, for they were in possession of a beautiful portrait and he stopped coming.

Golenishchev was the first to express the thought all of them shared, namely, that Mikhailov simply envied Vronsky.

"Perhaps he isn't envious, because he has 'talent.' But he is annoyed because a man of great means, a courtier, and, in addition, a count (they hate all this) does, without any particular effort, the same thing he does, who has devoted all his life to it, and does it as well if not better. What counts most is education, which he lacks."

Vronsky defended Mikhailov, but deep within his heart he believed it, because according to him a person of a different, lower world would have to be envious.

Since both he and Mikhailov had painted from the same model, the portrait of Anna should have shown Vronsky the difference which existed between him and Mikhailov. But he did not see it. He merely discontinued painting his own portrait of Anna, for he decided that it was unnecessary now that Mikhailov had done it. But he continued to work on his picture of medieval life. He himself, Golenishchev, and particularly Anna, found the painting to be excellent, for it far exceeded Mikhailov's painting in its resemblance to the masterpieces.

As for Mikhailov, although he had been intensely interested in doing Anna's portrait, he now was still happier than they, for with the sittings over he would no longer have to put up with Golenishchev's discourses on art and could forget about Vronsky's painting. He knew that Vronsky could not be prevented from amusing himself with painting; he knew that Vronsky and all the other dilettantes had a perfect right to paint as they pleased; but it annoyed him. There is no way to keep a man from making a large wax doll for himself and from kissing it. But if this man brings his doll, seats himself in front of a lover, and begins to caress it as the lover caresses his beloved, the lover will not like it. Mikhailov experienced the same unpleasant feeling when he looked at Vronsky's painting. He found it amusing, annoying, pathetic, and offensive.

Vronsky's infatuation with painting and the Middle Ages did not last long. He had enough artistic sense to realize that he should not finish his picture. His canvas remained unfinished. He felt vaguely that its defects, little noticed in the beginning, would become conspicuous if he proceeded. The same thing occurred to him as to Golenishchev, who felt that he had nothing to say and constantly deceived himself by the illusion that his idea had not yet developed, that he was nurturing it and preparing facts for it. But whereas Golenishchev was angered and distressed by this, Vronsky could not deceive or torment himself nor, particularly, could he grow angry. With his usual resoluteness and without any explanation or excuse, he gave up painting.

But without this occupation life for him and for Anna, who was surprised by his disenchantment, became so tedious in this Italian city, the *palazzo* suddenly appeared so old and dirty, so tiring had it become to look at the stains on the drapes, the cracks in the floors, the chipped plaster on the cornices, and so bored had they become with the same Golenishchev over and over again, with the Italian professor and the German traveler, that they had to make a change in their lives. They decided to go to Russia, to the country. In Petersburg, Vronsky intended that he and his brother would divide their property between them, and Anna planned to see her son. They intended to spend the summer at Vronsky's large ancestral estate.

14

LEVIN HAD BEEN married for over two months. He was happy, but not quite as he had expected. At every step he met with disillusion in his former dreams and with enchantments that were new and unexpected. Levin was happy, but on entering family life he saw at every step that it was not at all what he had imagined. At every step he felt like a man who had seated himself in a little boat after having watched with admiration how smoothly and gracefully it glided over the lake. He saw that it was not enough just to sit erect without rocking; he realized that at every moment he had to be mindful of his course, that he had to remember that under his feet there was water, that he had to row, though it put a strain on arms unaccustomed to this, and he saw that to observe had been easy but to do was very difficult, though a great joy.

When, as a bachelor, he happened to observe the life of a married couple, their petty cares, quarrels and jealousies, he just smiled within himself contemptuously. Not only did he believe that nothing like this could happen in his future married life but even outwardly, it seemed to him, his life would differ completely from that of others. Instead, in spite of his expectations, not only did his life with his wife fail to develop into anything unusual but on the contrary, it was comprised of the same insignificant trivialities that he had formerly despised but now, against his will, acquired unusual and uncontrovertible significance. And Levin saw that taking care of all those trifling details was not at all so easy as he had formerly thought. Though he believed that he had the most exact understanding of family life, Levin, like all men, unconsciously imagined that family life was nothing but enjoyment of the love, which shouldn't be hampered in any way, and from which one should not be diverted by petty cares. According to his understanding, he had to do his work and then rest in the happiness of his love. As for her, she merely had to be loved. But, like all men, he forgot that she, too, had to work. And he was surprised that not only during the first weeks but during the first days of their married life, she, poetical, charming Kitty, could be concerned with and could fuss over tablecloths, furniture, mattresses for the guests, a tray, the cook, dinner, and so on. While still a bridegroom, he was surprised at the resoluteness with which she refused to go abroad and decided to go to the country, as though she knew what had to be done and could concern herself with things other than love. He had been annoyed by it at that time, and now on several occasions he was annoyed by her petty cares and worries. But he saw that she needed this. And loving her, he could not but admire her cares, though he did not understand their purpose and found them amusing. He was amused by the way she arranged the furniture they had brought from Moscow, rearranged her own and his room, hung the drapes, designated future quarters for visitors and for Dolly, furnished the room for her new maid, gave orders for dinner to the old cook, and argued with Agafia Mikhailovna so as to ease her out of her housekeeping duties. He saw that the old cook smiled, admiring her and listening to her instructions, which were impractical and impossible. He saw that Agafia Mikhailovna shook her head thoughtfully and kindly as she listened to the orders of the young mistress concerning the pantry. He found Kitty unusually charming when, both crying and laughing, she came to him to complain that Masha, the maid, had been accustomed to regard her as a young girl, and so nobody obeyed her. All this seemed to him charming but strange, and he thought that things would go along better without all this.

He did not understand the feeling of change she was experiencing. At home she had sometimes wanted to have cabbage and kvas, or candy but had not been allowed any of them, whereas now she could order whatever she wished, could buy heaps of candy, could spend as much money as she wanted and order any pastry she liked.

She now dreamt happily of a visit by Dolly and her children, particularly because she would order for each child his favorite pastry, and because Dolly would appreciate her new home. She had become completely engrossed in her household tasks without knowing why. Instinctively feeling the approach of spring and knowing that bad weather also lay ahead, she was building her nest as well as she could and she hurried simultaneously both to build it and to learn how to do it.

Kitty's preoccupation with petty details, in such contrast with Levin's ideal of sublime happiness of their early period, was one of the causes of his disenchantment. And the charm of this preoccupation, the meaning of which he did not understand but could not help loving, was one of his new enchantments.

Another cause of both disillusionment and enchantment was their quarrels. Levin could never imagine that the relationship between his wife and himself would be other than tender, respectful, and affectionate, yet suddenly in their very early days they had a quarrel which resulted in her telling him that he did not love her but loved only himself, and she burst into tears and threw her hands into the air.

They quarreled for the first time when Levin went to a new farmstead and was delayed for half an hour because he tried a short cut and lost his way. On his return home he was thinking only of her, of her love, of his happiness, and the nearer he came to his house the greater grew his tenderness for her. As he burst into the room, he experienced the same emotion he had when he had come to the Shcherbatskys' to propose, or perhaps stronger. But he was struck by her gloomy expression, one he had never seen on her face. He wanted to kiss her, but she pushed him aside.

"What is it?"

"You're cheerful enough," she began, trying to appear calm and sarcastic.

But as soon as she began to speak, she burst into a torrent of reproaches, displaying the unreasonable jealousy which had tormented her as she sat motionless for the previous half hour on the windowsill. Now for the first time he understood clearly what he had not understood when he led her out of the church after their wedding. He understood that not only was she close to him, but that now he no longer knew where she ended and he began. He knew this from the distressing feeling of division which he was experiencing at that moment. At first he was offended, but he quickly realized that she could not offend him, that she was he himself. At that first moment he felt like a man who is suddenly struck on the back, turns around angrily looking for an assailant upon whom to be revenged, but sees that he was hurt through his own fault, that no one was to blame for it, that he must endure and assuage his pain.

Never again did he feel so deeply about it, but this first time he was long in recovering. His natural reaction was to protest, to prove that she was wrong. But this would only upset her further and intensify the disagreement that was causing them so much suffering. One natural feeling moved him to try to clear himself and to place the blame on her; another, a stronger feeling, drove him to settle their differences as quickly as possible without letting them grow stronger. It was disturbing to remain so unjustly accused, but to cause her pain by clearing himself would be still worse. He was like a man who, half-asleep and suffering pain, wants to tear out and rid himself of the source of his pain, but when he comes to his senses, realizes that the source of his pain is himself. All he could do was to help himself endure his pain and he tried to do so.

They made peace. Realizing but not admitting that she was wrong, she became more tender toward him, and they tasted the new, redoubled happiness of their love. But this did not prevent their disagreements from being repeated quite frequently, and for the least expected and most insignificant reasons. These clashes frequently occurred both because neither knew yet what was important to the other and because all during this early period both of them were often out of humor. When one of them was in good spirits and the other not, peace remained unbroken, but when both happened to be out of humor, they clashed for reasons of such insignificance that later they were at a loss to remember what they were. True, when both of them were in good spirits, their happiness doubled. Nevertheless, this early period was a trying one for both of them.

Throughout this early period they felt most acutely that the bond that united them was taut, as though being drawn either to one side or the other side. In general, the honeymoon, which is the month after the wedding, and of which, following tradition, Levin himself expected so much, not only was not a honeymoon but remained for both of them the most trying and most humiliating period of their lives. In later years both of them tried to erase from their memories all the ugly and shameful events of this unhappy period, during which both of them were seldom in a normal mood, seldom quite themselves.

Only after two months of married life, after their return from Moscow, where they had stayed for a month, did their lives begin to run more smoothly.

15

THEY HAD JUST arrived from Moscow and were glad to be alone. He was writing at the desk in his study. Wearing the dark lilac dress that she had worn in the early days of their marriage, had put on again that day, and that was particularly memorable and dear to him, she was seated with her *broderie anglaise* on the same antique leather divan that had always been in the study in his grandfather's and father's times. Thinking and writing, he was constantly and happily conscious of her presence. He had not stopped working on the farm and on his book, in which he intended to expound new agricultural principles. But while earlier his work and ideas had seemed to him mean and insignificant in the darkness enveloping his whole life, they seemed just as insignificant and mean now in the bright light of the happiness that illuminated his present life. He continued his work, but now he felt that

the focus of his attention had shifted, and that as a consequence his view of his work was much clearer and entirely
different. In the past his work had provided an escape from
reality; he had felt that without this work his life would be
too gloomy. Now he needed this occupation lest his life become too monotonously bright. Having brought out his papers
and reread what he had written, he was glad to see that the
work was worth resuming. It was new and useful. Many of his
former ideas seemed superfluous and extreme, many of the
gaps stood out clearly as he refreshed his mind on the whole
subject. He was now engaged in writing a new chapter on
the causes of the poor state of agriculture in Russia. He was
proving that the poverty of Russia had resulted not only from
the unequal distribution of land and from poor management,
but lately had been fostered by a foreign civilization, which
had been implanted unnaturally in Russia; especially by the
means of communication, the railroads, which had brought
about concentration in the cities; by emphasis on luxury. This
led—at the expense of agriculture—to the development of
industry, credit, and its satellite, stock-exchange speculation.
It seemed to him that when the wealth of a state developed
normally, all these phenomena took place only after much
labor had already been spent on agriculture, when it had been
put in a proper, or at least well-defined, condition. He believed that the wealth of the country should grow gradually,
and, particularly, in such a way that other facets of the national economy might not outstrip agriculture. He believed
that means of communication should correspond to the state
of agriculture, and that with our improper use of land, the
railways, built not for economic but for political reasons, were
premature. Instead of helping agriculture, as was expected,
they had outstripped it, and by creating industry and credit,
they impeded its development. Therefore he believed that
just as the premature and one-sided development of a single
organ of a living organism would impede its general development, so would credit, means of communication, and the
growth of manufacturing, all of which were undoubtedly
needed in Europe, where they were timely, only harm the
general development of wealth in Russia by shunting to one
side the most important task on hand, the development of
agriculture.

While he was putting his ideas on paper, she recalled how
excessively attentive her husband had been to the young

Prince Charsky, who had flirted with her quite tactlessly on the eve of their departure. To think that he is jealous, she thought. Heavens, how dear and foolish he is! Jealous of me! If he could only know that all of them mean no more to me than Piotr the cook, she thought, looking at the back of his head and his ruddy neck with a new feeling of possession. It's a pity to interrupt his work (though he'll have enough time for it!) but I must see his face. Will he feel that I'm looking at him? I wish he'd turn around—I wish it! and she opened her eyes wider in an effort to increase the intensity of her look.

"Yes, they drain off all the sap for themselves and shine with a false luster," he mumbled. He stopped writing, and sensing her glance and her smile, he turned around.

"What is it?" he asked, rising with a smile.

He turned around, she thought.

"It's nothing. I wanted you to turn around," she said, looking at him and trying to guess whether he was displeased or not at her interruption.

"Well, how good it is that we are alone! It's good for me, I mean," he said as he came over to her, beaming and smiling with happiness.

"It's wonderful for me! I'll not go anywhere, particularly to Moscow."

"And what were you thinking about?"

"I? I was thinking. . . . But no, go back to your writing, don't waste your time," she said, pursing her lips. "I have to cut these small holes. These."

She took the scissors and began.

"No, tell me," he said, sitting down next to her and watching the circular movement of the small scissors.

"What I was thinking? I was thinking about Moscow, about the back of your head."

"What right do I have to such happiness? It's not natural. It's too good," he said, kissing her hand.

"To me, on the other hand, the better it is the more natural it seems."

"Ah, you have a little curl," he said, carefully turning her head. "A little curl. Look, here it is. But we are busy."

The work did not proceed, and they broke apart guiltily when Kuzma came in to announce that tea was served.

"Have they arrived from the city?" Levin asked Kuzma.

"They have just arrived; they are unpacking."

"Don't be long," she said to him as she left the study, "or I'll read the letters without you. And let's play the piano, four hands."

When he remained alone, he put his notebooks in a new briefcase that she had bought for him and washed his hands in a new washstand with handsome accessories, which also had appeared with her arrival. Levin smiled at his thoughts and shook his head, disapproving of them. A feeling akin to guilt troubled him. There was in his present life something shameful, effeminate, Capuan, as he called it. It's wrong to live like this, he thought. It will soon be three months and I've done almost nothing. Today for the first time I began to work seriously, and the result? I dropped it as soon as I started. I've given up even my usual occupation. I've even neglected all the work on the farm. Either I'm sorry to leave her or I see that she's lonely. And I thought that life before marriage just drags on and doesn't count, and that real life begins after marriage. But soon three months will have passed and I have never lived such a useless, idle life. No, this can't go on; I must make a new start. Of course it's not her fault. She's not to blame for anything. I myself must be firmer, must uphold my masculine independence. Otherwise I may get used to this kind of life and make her like it too. . . . Of course, it's not her fault, he repeated to himself.

But it is difficult for one who is dissatisfied to refrain from blaming someone for his dissatisfaction, usually the very person who is closest to him. And it occurred vaguely to Levin that though it was not her fault (for she could never be at fault), it was the fault of her education, too shallow and frivolous (that fool Charsky—I know that she wanted to stop him but didn't know how). Yes, besides her domestic interests (she has them), her care for her toilette and *broderie anglaise,* she has no serious interests. She's not interested in my work, in the farm, in the moujiks, in music, though she is quite proficient in it, nor in reading. She doesn't do anything and is completely contented.

In his heart Levin blamed her, and did not understand that she was preparing herself for future activities, which were due to come, when she would be at one and the same time a wife to her husband and a housewife, and would bear, nurse, and rear children. It did not occur to him that she knew it instinctively and, preparing herself for this tremendous task, she did not reproach herself for the moments of lightheartedness and happiness in her love, which she enjoyed now as she gaily built her future nest.

16

WHEN LEVIN CAME upstairs, his wife was sitting at the new silver samovar with the new tea service. She had seated old Agafia Mikhailovna at the small table with her cup of tea, and was reading a letter from Dolly, with whom she had maintained a frequent correspondence.

"Look, your lady has seated me, ordering me to stay with her," said Agafia Mikhailovna, smiling amiably at Kitty.

Levin read in these words of Agafia Mikhailovna the outcome of the drama in which Kitty and Agafia Mikhailovna had lately taken part. He saw that in spite of all the worry the new lady had caused Agafia Mikhailovna by depriving her of the prerogatives of a housekeeper, Kitty had succeeded and had made Agafia Mikhailovna love her.

"Here's a letter to you which I have read," said Kitty, handing him a badly written letter. "It's from that woman. I think your brother . . ." she said. "I haven't finished it. And this is from my parents and Dolly. Just imagine, Dolly took Grisha and Tania to Sarmatsky's for a children's ball. Tania went as a marquise."

But Levin did not listen to her. His face flushed, he took the letter from Maria Nikolayevna, his brother Nikolai's former mistress, and began to read it. This was the second letter from Maria Nikolayevna. In the first she had written that his brother had driven her away for no fault of her own and with touching naïveté she added that though she again lived in poverty she was not asking anything for herself and did not want anything but was deeply aggrieved by the thought that without her Nikolai Dmitrievich would perish on account of the poor state of his health, and she asked his brother to look after him. Now she wrote something else. She had found Nikolai Dmitrievich in Moscow, they had again come together, and she had gone with him to a city in the province where he had obtained a position. But he had quarreled with his superior, and they had left for Moscow. On the way there he fell so sick that he probably would not re-cover, she wrote:

"He always speaks of you, and there is no money left."

"Read what Dolly writes about you," Kitty started with a smile, but she stopped suddenly when she noticed the changed expression on her husband's face.

"What is it? What's the matter?"

"She writes that Nikolai is dying. I must go to him."

Kitty's expression changed suddenly. All thoughts of Tania as a marquise and of Dolly vanished.

"When will you go?" she asked.

"Tomorrow."

"I'll go with you, may I?" she asked.

"Kitty! Why should you?" he asked reproachfully.

"Why shouldn't I?" she asked. She was hurt by the apparent reluctance and annoyance with which he received her offer. "Why shouldn't I go? I'll not be in your way. I—"

"I'm going because my brother is dying," said Levin. "Why should you go?"

"Why? For the same reason as you."

Even in such a grave moment she is concerned only about becoming lonesome if left by herself, thought Levin. And the pretext that she used in such a serious matter angered him.

"It's impossible," he said sternly.

Agafia Mikhailovna, seeing that they were about to quarrel, quietly put down the cup and left the room. Kitty did not even notice. The tone of her husband's last words offended her, particularly because he evidently did not believe what she had said.

"And I say that if you go I'll go with you; I definitely will," she said hastily and angrily. "Why is it impossible? Why do you say that it's impossible?"

"Because I have to go God knows where, over bad roads, stop at inns. You'll be in my way," answered Levin, trying to control himself.

"Not at all. I'll not need anything. If it suits you, it will suit me. . . ."

"Well, there's the mere fact that that woman is there, one with whom you mustn't associate."

"I don't know who is there and I don't care. I know that my husband's brother is dying and my husband is going to him, and I'm going with my husband to—"

"Kitty! Don't get angry. But think how grave this matter is

and how much it pains me to see that you are involving your
own weakness, your reluctance to remain alone. Well, if you'll
be lonely, go to Moscow."

"You see, you *always* suspect me of these wicked, mean
thoughts," she said, tears of hurt and anger in her eyes. "It's
not that, it's not weakness. I know that my duty is to be with
my husband when he's in trouble, but you deliberately try to
hurt me, deliberately refuse to understand . . ."

"No, this is terrible! Am I some sort of slave?" exclaimed
Levin, rising, no longer able to restrain his annoyance. But at
the same moment he felt that he was punishing himself.

"Then why did you marry? You could have remained free.
Why did you, if you regret it?" she said, and she jumped to
her feet and ran into the drawing room.

When he came to her, he found her racked with sobs.

He began to speak, no longer seeking words to make her
change her mind but only to calm her. But she did not listen
to him and did not agree to anything. He bent down, and
though she resisted, took her hand. He kissed it, kissed her
hair, and again kissed her hand, but she kept silent. But when
he took her face with both his hands and said, "Kitty," she
suddenly collected herself, cried a little, and they made peace.

They decided to go together the next day. Levin told his
wife that he believed that she wanted to go only to be helpful
and agreed with her that the presence of Maria Nikolayevna
at his brother's bedside would not present any impropriety.
But deep within his heart he was displeased with her and with
himself. He was displeased with her because she could not
bring herself to let him go when he had to (and how strange
it seemed to him that he, who only so recently had not dared
to dream of the happiness of her love for him, now was unhappy because she loved him too much!) and displeased with
himself because he had not shown enough strength of character. Still less did he believe, deep in his heart, that it did not
matter that the woman was with his brother, and he was
terrified at the thought of all the conflicts that might await
them. And the mere thought that his wife Kitty, his own
Kitty, would be in the same room with that wench made
him shudder with aversion and horror.

AT THE PROVINCIAL capital, the hotel where Nikolai Levin
lay was one of those provincial hotels that are built according
to the newest and highest standards and are intended to be
kept in the highest state of cleanliness, comfort, and even
elegance. But thanks to the type of guests who patronize them,
they turn with surprising speed into dirty inns with preten-
sions to modern improvements, and through this very preten-
tiousness they become worse than the old, avowedly dirty
hotels. This hotel had already come to that state. The veteran
in a dirty uniform, who smoked a cigarette at the entrance
and was supposed to play the part of doorman; the dismal and
depressing cast-iron staircase; the insolent waiter in his dirty
swallow-tailed coat; the dining room with dusty bouquets of
artificial flowers adorning the table; the dirt, dust and filth
everywhere; and with this, the hotel's smug air of bustling
activity, like that of a modern railroad station—all this, contrasting with their own new life, oppressed the Levins most
heavily, particularly because the impression of falseness the
hotel made did not correspond at all with what awaited them.

As always, after they had been asked what price they
wanted to pay for the room, it turned out that no good room
was vacant. One good room was occupied by a railroad in-
spector, another by a Moscow lawyer, a third by Prince
Astafyev from the country. There remained one dirty room,
but they were promised that the room adjoining it would be
vacant toward evening. Annoyed with his wife because it had
turned out as he had expected, namely, that at the moment
of their arrival, when his heart was deeply troubled at the
thought of his brother, he had to take care of her instead of
hastening directly to his brother, Levin took her into the room
assigned to them.

"Go on, go!" she said, giving him a timid and guilty look.

Without a word he went out the door and here came face
to face with Maria Nikolayevna, who had found out about his
arrival but had not dared to come into the room. She was
exactly the same as when he had seen her in Moscow: the
same collarless and cuffless woolen dress, the same good-natured, dull, pockmarked face, somewhat plumper than before.

"Well, how is he?"

"Very bad. He stays in bed. He's been waiting and waiting for you. He. . . . You . . . and your wife."

At first Levin could not understand why she was embarrassed, but she quickly explained.

"I'll get out of the way; I'll stay in the kitchen," she said. "He'll be very happy. He's heard that she's here. He knows her and remembers that he saw her abroad."

Levin understood that she was referring to his wife and did not know what to say.

"Let's go, let's go!" he said.

But as soon as he started, the door of his room opened, and Kitty looked out. Levin blushed, ashamed and irked by his wife for having put herself in this difficult situation, but Maria Nikolayevna blushed still more deeply. She shrank, and, embarrassed to tears, she seized the corners of her kerchief with both her hands and rolled them up with her red fingers, not knowing what to do or what to say.

For a moment Levin saw the expression of eager curiosity with which Kitty looked at this awful woman, who was completely beyond her comprehension. But it lasted only a moment.

"Well, how is he?" she asked, turning to her husband and then to her.

"But we can't talk in the hall," said Levin, glancing with annoyance at a gentleman who at that moment passed along the hall with a springy step, presumably on his own business.

"Come in then," said Kitty, addressing Maria Nikolayevna, who had regained control of herself. But noticing her husband's frightened face, she added, "Both of you go and let me know when to come," and she went back into the room. Levin went to his brother.

He had never expected to see and feel what he did in his brother's room. He had expected to find unchanged the state of self-deception, which he had heard was typical of consumptives, that had impressed him so deeply during his brother's visit the previous fall. He expected to find the physical signs of approaching death more pronounced, his weakness increased, his body more wasted, yet with all this his condition remaining almost the same as before. He expected that he himself would feel the same pity at the approaching loss of his beloved brother and the same fear of death he had felt then, but to a greater degree. And he was prepared for this, but found something quite different.

In a small, dirty room, the painted panels of its walls befouled by spittle, its foul air choking, a thin partition separating it from another room from which a conversation could be heard, on a bed removed from the wall, lay a body covered by a blanket. One arm rested on top of the blanket; its hand, enormous as a rake, in some incomprehensible way attached to a sort of long spindle, thin and straight from its beginning to its middle. A head lay sideways on the pillow. Levin could see the thin hair at the temples, wet with perspiration, and the tightly drawn forehead, almost transparent.

No, this awful body cannot be my brother Nikolai, thought Levin. But as he approached and looked at the face, there could no longer be any doubt. Though his face had changed terribly, Levin had only to glance at those vivid eyes, lifted toward him as he entered the room, to notice the slight movement of the mouth under the matted mustache, in order to recognize the frightening truth that this corpse was his living brother.

As he entered the room his brother's shining eyes looked at him sternly and reproachfully. And immediately with this look there was established a living relationship between living people. Levin at once became conscious of the reproach in the look fixed on him, and he felt a twinge of remorse for his happiness.

When Konstantin took his hand, Nikolai smiled. It was a faint, scarcely noticeable smile, but in spite of it the stern expression of his eyes did not change.

"You didn't expect to find me like this," he said with difficulty.

"Yes . . . no," said Levin, faltering. "Why didn't you let me know earlier, at the time of my wedding? I inquired about you everywhere." He had to speak in order not to keep silent, but he did not know what to say, the more so because his brother did not say anything but just kept his eyes fixed on him, evidently trying to grasp the meaning of every word. Levin told his brother that his wife had arrived with him. Nikolai expressed his pleasure, but said that he feared he might frighten her by his condition. A silence ensued. Suddenly Nikolai stirred and was about to say something. Judging by the expression of his face, Levin expected to hear something particularly meaningful and important, but Nikolai spoke of his state of health. He blamed his doctor, regretted that the renowned Moscow doctor was not there, and Levin understood that he still had hope.

Availing himself of the first moment of silence, Levin rose, anxious to rid himself at least for a moment of his torment, and said that he would go fetch his wife.

"All right, and I'll have them clean up here. I know, it's dirty and smelly here. Masha, straighten up the room," the patient said with difficulty. "After you've finished, you leave," he added, looking at his brother inquiringly.

Levin made no reply. He went into the hall and stopped. He had promised to bring his wife, but now, realizing what he felt, he decided that he would do the opposite and would try to convince her not to go to the sick man. Why should she suffer as I do? he thought.

"Well, how is he?" Kitty asked, fearfully.

"It's terrible, terrible! Why did you come?" asked Levin.

Kitty kept silent for a few seconds, looking at her husband, pitifully and timidly. Then she went over to him and took his arm in both her hands.

"Kostia, take me to him. It will be easier for us when we are together. You just take me to him, please, and then leave," she said. "You must understand that it's much harder on me to stay here without seeing him. There I may perhaps be useful both to you and to him. Please allow me!" she begged her husband, as if her future happiness depended on this request.

Levin had to give in, and having calmed down and completely forgotten about Maria Nikolayevna, he went back to his brother, accompanied by Kitty.

Walking with a light step and casting frequent glances at her husband with an expression of courage and sympathy, she entered the sick room, and without hurrying, she turned and closed the door noiselessly. With a soft step she quickly crossed over to the sick man's bed, approaching him so that he did not have to turn his head, at once pressed his large bony hand into her cool young one and with that subdued vivacity, inoffensive and sympathetic, which is peculiar to women, she began to talk to him.

"We used to see each other in Soden, but we never met," she said. "You didn't imagine that I would be your sister-in-law."

"You would not have recognized me," he said with the smile that had lit his face when she entered.

"Yes, I would. I am so glad you let us hear from you. Not a day passed without Kostia's mentioning you and worrying about you."

But the sick man's animation did not last long.

She had scarcely finished speaking when his face again assumed the stern, reproachful expression of a dying man's envy for the living.

"I'm afraid that you're not quite comfortable here," she said, turning away from his searching look and looking over the room. "We'll have to ask the landlord for another room," she said to her husband, "so we can be nearer."

18

LEVIN COULD not look at his brother without agitation and could not be natural and calm in his presence. When he entered his brother's room, his eyes and attention automatically blurred and he did not see or distinguish the details of his brother's condition. He smelled the horrible odor, saw the filth and disorder, knew how his brother was suffering, heard him moan, and felt that nothing could be done. It never occurred to him to look into all the details of the sick man's state, to find out how that body lay there under the blanket, and what were the positions of the cramped, emaciated calves, loins and back, to see whether they could not be eased, or to do something that though not making the patient comfortable, would at least reduce his discomfort. A chill ran down his spine when he began to think of all these details. He was fully convinced that nothing could be done either to prolong his life or to relieve his suffering. But the sick man was conscious of his brother's conviction that he could not be helped in any way, and this irritated him. This depressed Levin still more. It was a torment to remain in his brother's room, but it was still worse to stay away. And frequently, under various pretexts, he left the room and came back, not having the strength to remain alone.

But Kitty thought, felt, and acted quite differently. At the sight of the sick man she felt pity. And in her woman's heart this pity did not at all create the feeling of horror and aversion which it had created in her husband but aroused a need for action, a need to learn all the difficulties of his condition and

to try to alleviate them. And since she had not the slightest
doubt that it was her duty to help him, she did not doubt that
it could be done; and she began immediately to do it. Those
details the mere thought of which terrified her husband, at
once drew her attention. She sent for a doctor, sent to the
pharmacy, had her own maid, who had come with her, work
with Maria Nikolayevna, sweeping, dusting, and washing,
washed and rinsed something herself, and placed something
under the blanket. Under her direction things had been
brought into and taken out of the sick room. She herself went
to her own room several times, paying no attention to the men
who passed her in the corridor, obtained and brought sheets,
pillowcases, towels, and shirts.

A waiter, who was serving a group of engineers in the public
dining room, several times responded to her call with an angry
expression on his face, but he could not help complying with
her orders because she gave them with such amiable persistence that he could not ignore her. Levin did not approve of
all this. He did not believe that it could help the sick man in
any way. Most of all he feared it might offend the sick man.
But though the sick man seemed not to be pleased with all
this, he was not angry but merely embarrassed, and, in general, he appeared to show some interest in what she was doing
for him. When he returned from the doctor's, where Kitty had
sent him, Levin opened the door and came in at the moment
when, at Kitty's orders, they were changing the sick man's
underwear. The long white frame of his back, with its huge
projecting shoulder blades, protruding ribs and vertebrae, was
bare, and Maria Nikolayevna and the waiter were entangled
in the sleeve of the shirt and could not insert his long dangling
arm into it. Kitty, who quickly closed the door behind Levin,
was not looking in the sick man's direction, but when she
heard him moan she hurried over to him.

"Hurry," she said.

"Don't come here," the sick man said angrily. "I myself. . . ."

"What did you say?" asked Maria Nikolayevna.

But Kitty heard him and understood that he was embarrassed and uncomfortable to be undressed in her presence.

"I'm not looking, I'm not looking!" she said, adjusting his
arm. "Maria Nikolayevna, you go to the other side and
straighten it out."

"Please go to our room. There's a vial in my little bag," she
said to her husband. "You know, in the side pocket. Please

bring it, meanwhile they'll straighten up everything here."

When Levin returned with the vial, he found the sick man lying in bed and everything around him completely changed. The air, foul before, now smelled of perfumed vinegar, which Kitty sprayed through a tube, extending her lips and puffing out her rosy cheeks. There was not a speck of dust anywhere, and there was a rug beside the bed. The vials, the pitcher, the linens, and Kitty's *broderie anglaise* were neatly arranged on the table. The sick man's medicine, his powders and a candle were arranged on another table next to him. The patient himself, washed and combed, lay between clean sheets, propped up on high pillows, wearing a clean shirt with its white collar around his unnaturally thin neck, his face expressing new hope and his eyes fixed on Kitty.

The doctor Levin had brought, whom he had found in the club, was not the same one who had been treating Nikolai Levin and whom he disliked. The new doctor reached for his stethoscope and examined the patient, shook his head, prescribed a medicine, and in particular detail first explained how to take the medicine and then what diet to keep. He advised giving the patient raw or soft-boiled eggs and seltzer water with fresh milk at a certain temperature. When the doctor left, the sick man said something to his brother. Levin heard only the last words, "Your Katia," but by the way he glanced at her, Levin understood that he was praising her. Then he called Katia (the name he used for her).

"I'm already much better," he said. "With you I would have recovered long ago. This is fine!" He took her hand and was about to put it to his lips, but as though fearing that she might not like it, he changed his mind, releasing it and only caressed it. Kitty took his hand in both of hers and pressed it.

"Now turn me on my left side and go to bed," he said.

No one but Kitty could make out what he had said. She understood because she was continuously watching for what he might need.

"On the other side," she said to her husband. "He always sleeps on that side. Turn him over, it's awkward to call the servants. I can't do it. Can you?" she addressed Maria Nikolayevna.

"I'm afraid," replied Maria Nikolayevna.

However horrified Levin was to take into his arms this awful body and to reach for those places under the blanket that he did not want to know about, he submitted to his wife's request with a resolute expression, so familiar to her, put his hands under the blanket, took hold of his brother, and in spite of his strength, was astonished by the unusual weight of the emaciated body. While he turned him and felt his brother's immense, wasted arm around his neck, Kitty turned over the pillow quickly and noiselessly, puffed it up, adjusted his head and straightened his thin hair, which again clung to his temple.

The sick man did not release his brother's hand. Levin felt that he wanted to do something with his hand and that he was pulling at it. Levin gave in with a sinking heart. Yes, he pulled it toward his lips and kissed it. Levin broke into sobs and, unable to utter a word, left the room.

19

"Thou hast hid these things from the wise and the prudent and hast revealed them unto the babes." So thought Levin about his wife, while talking to her that evening.

Levin recalled the saying from the Gospel not because he considered himself so wise. Without considering himself wise, he could not help knowing that he was more intelligent than his wife and Agafia Mikhailovna, and he could not help knowing that when he thought of death, he thought with all the powers of his mind. He also knew that many men of high intellect, whose ideas on this subject he had read, had thought about it but did not know a hundredth part of what his wife and Agafia Mikhailovna knew. However great was the difference between these two women, Agafia and Katia, as his brother Nikolai called her and as Levin particularly liked to call her now, in this matter they were entirely alike. Both of them knew beyond any doubt what life was and what death was, and though they absolutely could not answer or even understand the questions which occupied Levin, both of them had no doubts concerning the meaning of these phenomena. Their views on this subject were identical, and moreover these views were shared by millions of others. That they really knew what death was was proved by the fact that without a moment's hesitation they knew how to deal with the dying and were not afraid of them. But Levin and others, though they could discuss death at length, evidently did not comprehend it, because they were afraid of it and were absolutely ignorant of what to do when a person was dying. If Levin were now alone with his brother Nikolai he would look at him in horror, would wait with still greater horror, and would be able to do nothing else.

Moreover, he did not know what to say, how to look, how to walk. To speak of extraneous matters seemed to him offensive and therefore forbidden; nor should he talk of depressing subjects or death. And to remain silent was also wrong. If I look at him, Levin thought, he might think that I'm studying him and am afraid of him. If I don't look, he might believe that I'm thinking of something else. If I walk on tiptoe, he might dislike it; if flatfooted, I'll feel guilty." But Kitty did not think of herself and had no time for it. She thought of him because she knew something, and everything was turning out well. She talked about herself and about her wedding, she smiled and pitied him, caressed him and spoke of cases of recovery, and everything sounded well; obviously she knew what to do. The proof that her actions and Agafia Mikhailovna's were not instinctive, animal, and irrational was that both Agafia Mikhailovna and Kitty demanded that in addition to physical care, to help in alleviating his suffering, a dying man be given something that was more important than physical care and had no connection with the physical world. Speaking of an old man who had died, Agafia Mikhailovna had said, "Well, thank God, he received communion and extreme unction. May God grant everyone such a death." Likewise Katia, in addition to taking care of the sick man's linen, his bedsores, and medicines, on the first day succeeded in persuading him that he must receive communion and extreme unction.

When they returned for the night to their two rooms, Levin sat down with his head bowed, not knowing what to do. Not only did he fail to order supper, prepare for the night and think over what they were going to do, he could not even speak to his wife: he felt guilty. Kitty, on the contrary, was more active than usual. She was even more vivacious than usual. She ordered supper brought up, she herself unpacked, herself helped to make the beds, and she did not forget to sprinkle them with bedbug powder. She was excited and alert, as men are before a battle or a fight, in dangerous and fateful moments of life, those moments when a man once and forever shows his worth and proves that all his past has not been in vain but has prepared him for this moment.

She worked with such efficiency that before twelve o'clock all the things in the room had been arranged with such neat-ness and precision and in such a particular manner that the hotel room resembled her room at home. The beds were made, the brushes, combs, and hand mirrors laid out, and the napkins spread.

Levin considered that it was now unforgivable to eat, to sleep, even to talk, and felt that every movement he made was improper. But she arranged the little brushes, doing it, however, in such a way that there was nothing offensive in it.

They could not, however, bring themselves to eat and were long in falling asleep, even after a much-postponed bedtime.

"I'm so glad I persuaded him to receive extreme unction tomorrow," she said, sitting in her dressing jacket before her traveling mirror and combing her soft, fragrant hair with a fine-toothed comb. "I've never seen it, but, as mother told me, during it they say prayers for recovery."

"Can you really believe that he might recover?" asked Levin, watching the narrow part of her hair on her shapely little head steadily disappearing behind the comb as she brought it forward.

"I asked the doctor. He says that he won't last more than three days. But do they really know? But I'm glad I persuaded him," she said, peering at her husband through her hair. "Anything can happen," she added, with the odd, somewhat arch expression that always appeared on her face when she spoke of religion.

After the discussion of religion they had had before they were married, neither he nor she had mentioned it again, but she dutifully attended church services and said her prayers, always with the same calm conviction that this was the way things should be done. In spite of his assurances to the contrary, she was firmly convinced that he was as good a Christian as she, or even better, and that everything he said on the subject reflected one of his ridiculous male peculiarities, just as with the *broderie anglaise*, of which he said that while good people mend holes, she created them deliberately, and so on.

"Well, this woman Maria Nikolayevna could not have accomplished all of this," said Levin. "And . . . I must admit, I'm very, very glad that you came. You are so pure that. . . ." He took her hand, but did not kiss it (to kiss her hand while so near the presence of death seemed to him improper) and only squeezed it while he looked into her serene eyes with a feeling of guilt.

"You would have suffered too much if you were alone," she said, and raising her arms so that they hid the blush of pleasure on her cheeks, she coiled her braids and pinned them on the back of her head. "No," she continued, "she didn't know how. . . . Fortunately, I learned much at Soden."

"Were there such sick people there, too?"

"Worse."

"It frightens me that I can't help seeing him as he was in his youth. . . . You'd scarcely believe that he was such a fine young man, but I didn't understand him then."

"I do believe it. I feel that we *could have been* good friends," she said, and frightened by her own words, she looked at her husband and tears came to her eyes.

"Yes, you *could have been*," he said sadly. "He's truly one of those men of whom it is said that they are not of this world."

"We still have, however, many hard days left, and now it's time to go to bed," said Kitty, looking at her miniature watch.

20

THE NEXT DAY the sick man received communion and extreme unction. During the ceremony Nikolai Levin prayed ardently. His large eyes, fixed upon an icon that had been placed on a card table covered with a colored napkin, expressed such ardent entreaty and hope that Levin was afraid to look at him. Levin knew that this ardent prayer and hope would make it still more difficult for him to part with life, which he loved so much. Levin knew his brother and the course of his thoughts. He knew that he had become an unbeliever not because he found it easier to live without faith, but because the modern scientific explanation of natural phenomena gradually supplanted his religious beliefs. Levin therefore understood that his brother's present return to religion was not genuine, had not been brought about by the same logical process, but was only transient and covetous, prompted by a frantic hope for recovery. Levin also knew that Kitty had enhanced this hope by her stories of miraculous recoveries of which she had heard. All this Levin knew and with torment and anguish he watched his beseeching look full of hope, his emaciated hand, which he raised with difficulty to his tightly drawn forehead to cross himself, his sharp shoulders, and his hollow, rattling chest, which could no longer contain that life for which the sick man prayed.

During the ritual Levin also prayed and did what he, an unbeliever, had done a thousand times. He said, addressing God, "If you exist, bring to pass that this man recovers (you have done this many times in the past), and you will save him and myself."

After the anointment the sick man suddenly felt much better. He did not cough at all for a whole hour, smiled, kissed Kitty's hand, tearfully thanked her, and said that he was well, had no pain at all, had an appetite and felt strong. He even sat up by himself when they brought him soup, and asked for a second cutlet. No matter how hopeless his condition was, no matter how obvious it was by looking at him that he could not recover, during this hour Levin and Kitty were both in a state of happy excitement, fearful, however, lest they be mistaken.

"Is he better?"

"Yes, much better!"

"Remarkable."

"There's nothing remarkable about it."

"But he is better."

Thus they spoke in whispers, smiling at each other.

The illusion did not last long. The patient fell asleep peacefully, but in half an hour a cough awakened him. At once all his hopes and the hopes of everyone around him vanished. The reality of suffering destroyed completely all traces of the former hopes of Levin, Kitty, and the sick man himself.

Without even recalling what he had believed half an hour earlier, as though ashamed to think of it, he asked for the iodine, which he inhaled from a jar covered with perforated paper. Levin handed him the jar and at once the same look of frantic hope with which he received the extreme unction was now fixed on his brother, as though asking him to confirm the doctor's words that the inhalation of iodine performed miracles.

"Where's Katia?" he whispered hoarsely, looking around, after Levin had reluctantly confirmed the doctor's words. "She's not here, so I may say it. . . . It was for her that I played the comedy. She is so dear, but you and I can no longer deceive ourselves. This is what I believe in," he said, and squeezing the jar with his bony hand, he began to inhale the iodine.

Around eight in the evening, when Levin and his wife were having tea in their room, Maria Nikolayevna ran in, panting. She was pale and her lips trembled.

"He is dying!" she whispered. "I'm afraid that he'll die any moment."

They ran to his room. He was sitting up in bed, leaning on his arm, his long back bent and his head lowered.

"How do you feel?" Levin asked him in a whisper after a silence.

"I feel that I am going," answered Nikolai with difficulty but with unusual clarity, slowly forcing out the words. He did not raise his head, but just directed his eyes upward, missing his brother's face. "Katia, go away!" he added.

Levin straightened quickly and with a commanding whisper made her leave the room.

"I am going," he said again.

"What's makes you think so?" said Levin just to say something.

"Because I am going," he repeated, as though pleased with this expression. "It's the end."

Maria Nikolayevna came over to him.

"Lie down, you'll feel better," she said.

"I'll soon lie quietly, dead," he said derisively and angrily. "All right, help me to lie down, if that's what you want."

Levin laid his brother on his back, sat down near him, and, scarcely breathing, stared at his face. The dying man lay with his eyes closed, but the muscles of his forehead stirred now and again, as in a man absorbed in deep and intense thought. Levin was unconsciously wondering what was going on within his brother's soul, but in spite of all his efforts to follow him, he saw by the expression of his calm, stern face and by the play of the muscle above his eyebrow that what to Levin still remained as dark as before was becoming clear to the dying man.

"Yes, yes, that's so!" said the dying man, slowly pacing his words. "Wait." He again fell silent. "That's it!" he said suddenly, drawing out his words and calming down, as though everything had been resolved for him. "Oh, God!" he said and sighed heavily.

Maria Nikolayevna felt his feet.

"He's getting cold," she whispered.

The patient lay motionless for a long time, very long, as it seemed to Levin. But he was still alive, and sighed occasionally. Levin was already worn out by the mental strain. He felt that in spite of all his efforts he could not understand what "that's it" meant. He felt that he had not been able to keep up with the dying man for a long while now. He could no longer think of the problem of death itself, but in spite of himself thoughts came of what he would have to do now, right away: closing the dead man's eyes; dressing his body; ordering a coffin. And, strange as it seemed, he felt entirely unconcerned, felt no sorrow, had no feeling of impending loss and, still less, any pity for his brother. If he had any feeling for his brother now, it was rather one of envy for the knowledge which the dying man had but which he could not possess. He continued thus to watch over him for a long while, always awaiting the end. But the end did not come. The door opened and Kitty appeared. Levin rose to stop her. But as he was rising, he heard the dying man stir.

"Don't go," said Nikolai and he extended his hand. Levin gave him his and angrily motioned to his wife to leave.

With the dying man's hand in his, he sat for half an hour, an hour, and yet another hour. He no longer thought of death. He thought of what Kitty was doing, of what kind of people lived in the next room, and wondered whether the doctor owned the house in which he lived. He was hungry and sleepy. He carefully freed his hand and felt his brother's legs. The legs were cold, but the sick man still breathed. Levin was again about to leave on tiptoe, but the sick man stirred again and said, "Don't go."

It was daybreak. The sick man's condition remained the same. Levin slowly withdrew his hand and, without looking at his brother, went to his room and fell asleep. When he woke up, instead of being informed that his brother had died, as he had expected, he was told that he had returned to his former state. He again began to sit up, to cough, to eat, to talk, again stopped talking about death, again began expressing his hope for recovery, and became even more irritable and gloomy than before. No one, not his brother nor Kitty, could calm him. He was angry at everyone, his words were disagreeable, he reproached everyone for his suffering, and he demanded that the renowned doctor be summoned from Moscow to examine him. To all inquiries about his condition he gave the same answer, expressing it with anger and reproach.

"I'm suffering terribly, unbearably!"

His suffering increased, particularly from the bedsores, which no longer responded to treatment, and he grew increasingly surly at those around him, reproaching them for everything and particularly for their refusal to bring the doctor from Moscow. Kitty did her best to help him, to calm him, but it was all in vain, and Levin saw that she herself was worn out in body and in spirit, though she would not admit it. The sense of death, which he had aroused in everyone the previous night when he bade farewell to life and called for his brother, was gone. Everyone knew that his death was unavoidable and imminent, that he was already half in the arms of death. Everyone wished for the same thing—that he die as soon as possible; but everyone, concealing this desire, handed him medicines, looked for new medicines and doctors, and deceived him, themselves, and each other. All of this was deceit, mean, offensive, blasphemous deceit. And this deceit affected Levin most painfully both because of his nature and because he loved his brother more than anyone else.

Levin, who had always been preoccupied with the thought of reconciling his two brothers before Nikolai's death, wrote to Sergei Ivanovich and on receipt of his answer he read the letter to the sick man. Sergei Ivanovich wrote that he could not come, but he asked his brother's forgiveness in deeply moving words.

The sick man said nothing.

"What shall I write to him?" asked Levin. "I hope that you're not angry with him."

"No, not at all!" replied Nikolai, annoyed by the question. "Tell him to send me the doctor."

Three more tormenting days passed. The patient remained in the same state. Everyone who saw him now felt that they wanted him to die: the waiter, the landlord, the guests, the doctor, Maria Nikolayevna, Levin, and Kitty. Only the sick man did not share this feeling; he, on the contrary, was angry that they had not summoned the doctor, continued to take the medicines, and spoke of life. Only in those rare instances when the opiate brought him a moment of relief from his suffering did he say, half-asleep, what he felt more deeply than anyone else, "Ah, if only the end would come!" or, "When will it end?"

His suffering, gradually increasing, had its effect in preparing him for death. There was no position in which he did not suffer, there was not a moment when he could forget himself, there was no spot on his body, no limb that did not give him pain, did not torment him. Even memories, impressions, and thoughts of his body now raised in him the same aversion as the body itself. The sight of other people, their words, his own memories—all this caused him only suffering. All those

around him felt it and unconsciously did not permit themselves, while in his presence, any unrestrained movement,
conversation, or expression of their wishes. All his life now
fused into one sensation of suffering and the desire to rid
himself of it.

Evidently a radical change was taking place within him,
one that would make him look at death as the fulfillment of
his desires, as his good fortune. Formerly, every specific desire
produced by suffering or privation, such as hunger, fatigue,
or thirst, was fulfilled by the functioning of the body, bringing
satisfaction. But now privations and suffering received no
relief, and any attempt to allay them brought new suffering.
Therefore all his desires fused into one—a desire to free himself of all his suffering and of its source, his body. But he had
no words to express this desire of his to be set free, and therefore he did not speak of it but followed his habit and demanded the satisfaction of desires which could no longer be
fulfilled. "Turn me on the other side," he would say, and at
once demanded to be turned back to his former position.
"Give me some bouillon. Take away the bouillon. Tell me
something. Why are you silent?" And as soon as they began to
talk, he closed his eyes and showed fatigue, indifference, and
aversion.

On the tenth day after their arrival in the city, Kitty fell
ill. She developed a headache, vomited and could not get out
of bed the entire morning.

The doctor explained that the illness was the result of
fatigue and excitement, and advised her to avoid emotional
strain.

After dinner, however, Kitty got up and as usual took her
work and went to the sick man's room. When she entered, he
glanced at her sternly and, when she told him that she was
not well, he smiled contemptuously. That day he continuously
blew his nose and moaned pitifully.

"How do you feel?" she asked him.

"Worse," he said with difficulty. "I am in pain."

"Where do you feel pain?"

"All over."

"He will die today, you'll see," said Maria Nikolayevna, and
though she whispered, the patient, very sensitive, as Levin
noted, could have heard her. Levin hushed her and glanced
at the sick man. Nikolai had heard. But these words made no

impression whatever on him. His look was as reproachful and intent as before.

"What makes you think so?" Levin asked her, when she followed him into the hall.

"Because he's begun to pull at his nightshirt," said Maria Nikolayevna.

"What do you mean?"

"This is what he's doing," she said, tugging at the folds of her woolen dress. Indeed, he had noticed all day that the patient clutched at his clothing as if trying to pull something off.

Maria Nikolayevna's prediction proved to be true. Toward nightfall the sick man no longer had the strength to raise his hands, and stared straight ahead without changing his expression of deep concentration. Even when his brother or Kitty bent over him so that he might see them, his look did not change. Kitty sent for the priest to read the prayer for the dying.

While the priest read the prayer, the dying man showed no sign of life; his eyes were closed. Levin, Kitty, and Maria Nikolayevna stood at his bedside. The priest had not yet finished the prayer when the dying man stretched, sighed, and opened his eyes. After he had finished the prayer, the priest touched the dying man's cold forehead with the cross. Then he slowly wrapped the cross in the stole, and, after standing silently for about two minutes, he felt the large bloodless hand that was growing cold.

"He has passed away," said the priest, and he was about to leave. But suddenly the matted mustache of the dying man twitched, and from the depth of his chest came a sound, distinct and harsh in the silence.

"Not quite. . . . Soon."

And within a minute his face brightened, a smile appeared under the mustache, and the women in the group busied themselves gravely with dressing the dead man.

The sight of his brother and the proximity to death re-awakened in Levin the feeling of dread aroused by the inscrutability and, at the same time, the nearness and inevitability of death, the same feeling that had taken possession of him that evening in the fall when his brother had come to visit him. This feeling was even stronger now than before; even less than before did he feel capable of understanding the meaning of death, and its inevitability seemed to him

even more terrifying. But now, thanks to the presence of his
wife, the feeling did not lead him to despair. In spite of death,
he felt the need to live and love. He felt that love was saving
him from despair and that this love was becoming still
stronger and purer under the threat of despair.

No sooner had the mystery of death, still uncomprehended,
come to pass before their eyes, when another one, as incomprehensible, arose, calling for love and life.

The doctor confirmed what he had suspected regarding
Kitty. Her indisposition was due to pregnancy.

21

EVER SINCE Aleksei Aleksandrovich gathered from his conversations with Betsy and Stepan Arkadievich that all that was
demanded of him was that he leave his wife alone and not
annoy her with his presence, and that his wife herself wanted
this, he felt so utterly lost that he could make no decisions of
his own, did not know himself what he now wanted, and
putting himself into the hands of those who were glad to busy
themselves with his affairs, he agreed to everything demanded
of him. Only when Anna had left his home and the English
governess sent to inquire whether she should have dinner with
him or separately did he, for the first time, understand his
situation clearly; and it frightened him.

The most painful part of this situation was his complete
inability to connect and reconcile his past with what was now
taking place. He was not troubled by that past in which he
had lived happily with his wife. He had already gone through
the suffering caused by the transition from that period to the
discovery of his wife's infidelity; that situation had been painful but understandable. If his wife, having revealed to him
her infidelity, had left him at that time, he would have been
distressed, unhappy, but not in the hopeless and incomprehensible situation in which he now found himself. He simply
could not reconcile his recent forgiveness, his tenderness, his
love for his sick wife and a stranger's child, with what was
now taking place, when as a reward for all of this, he remained
alone, disgraced, ridiculed, not needed by anyone and despised
by all.

For the first two days after his wife's departure Aleksei

Aleksandrovich received petitioners, his office manager, attended the sessions of the committee and had his dinner in the dining room as usual. Without realizing why he was doing it, during these two days he used all his energies to appear calm and even indifferent. When he answered questions about the disposition of Anna Arkadievna's rooms and belongings, he did his utmost to appear as a man to whom the event that had happened was not unforeseen and who did not see in it anything that by its nature would set it apart from ordinary events. He succeeded in these efforts, and nobody could detect any signs of despair in him. But on the second day after her departure, when Kornei handed him a bill from the milliner's that Anna had forgotten to pay and reported that the store clerk was waiting, Aleksei Aleksandrovich called for the clerk.

"I beg Your Excellency's forgiveness for daring to disturb you. But if you command me to apply to Her Excellency, would you be kind enough to give me her address?"

Aleksei Aleksandrovich was lost in thought, as it seemed to the clerk, but suddenly he turned around and sat down at the table. He rested his head on his hands and remained in this position for a long time. Several times he tried to say something, but he could not.

Kornei understood how his master felt and he asked the clerk to come another time. Alone again, Aleksei Aleksandrovich realized that he could no longer maintain a mask of calmness and firmness. He ordered that his waiting coach be dismissed and that no visitors be admitted, and he did not appear for dinner.

He felt that he could not endure the weight of universal scorn and malevolence, which he read clearly on the faces of the clerk, of Kornei, and of everyone, without exception, whom he had met during those two days. He felt that he could not avert this general hatred of him, for the hatred was not due to his being wicked (in that case he could have tried to improve) but to his being shamefully and repulsively unhappy. He knew that because of this, because his heart was tormented, people would have no mercy on him. He felt that people would destroy him as dogs destroy a badly injured dog that is whimpering with pain. He knew that he could only protect himself from people by hiding his wounds from them, and he had been unconsciously trying to do so for two days, but now he felt that he no longer had the strength to continue the unequal struggle.

His despondency was intensified by his awareness of being utterly alone in his affliction. It was not only in Petersburg that he lacked even a single person to whom he could express his feelings, one who would sympathize with him not as a high official, not as a member of the upper class, but simply as a man who was suffering—nowhere could he find such a person.

Aleksei Aleksandrovich had been an orphan. He had one brother. They did not remember their father, and their mother died when Aleksei Aleksandrovich was ten years old. Their fortune was small. Their uncle Karenin, an important official and previously the late Emperor's favorite, had brought them up.

After graduating from the gymnasium and university with honors, Aleksei Aleksandrovich at once began a promising career with his uncle's help and from that time devoted all his energy to advancing himself in service. Aleksei Aleksandrovich had not made friends at the gymnasium, university, or later in the service. Closest to his heart was his brother, but he served in the diplomatic corps and lived mostly abroad, where he died soon after Aleksei Aleksandrovich's marriage.

While he was serving as governor, Anna's aunt, a rich provincial lady, brought him and her niece together. No longer a young man, but young for a governor, he was placed by Anna's aunt in such a situation that he either had to declare his intentions or leave the city. Aleksei Aleksandrovich hesitated for a long while. There were as many reasons for the step as against it, and there was no decisive reason for making him violate his rule to refrain from action when in doubt. But through a friend, Anna's aunt persuaded him that he had already compromised the young lady and that as an honorable man it was his duty to propose. He proposed and gave his bride and wife all the affection of which he was capable.

The attachment he felt toward Anna had removed from his heart the last trace of any yearning for intimacy with other people. And now among all his acquaintances he had not even one close friend. There were many so-called connections, but no bonds of friendship. There were many people whom Aleksei Aleksandrovich could invite to dinner, could ask for assistance in a case in which he was interested, or for help for some petitioner, or with whom he could discuss without restraint the actions of others and of the government. But his relationship with these people was confined to one area, clearly defined by tradition and habit, from which it was impossible to depart. There was one former university classmate with whom he had later become intimate and to whom he could speak about his misfortune; but this friend was serving as the head of a remote school district. And of those who lived in Petersburg the only ones to whom he was close enough to confide in were his office manager and his doctor.

Mikhail Vasilievich Sliudin, his office manager, was a straightforward, clever, good-natured and upright man, who, Aleksei Aleksandrovich felt, was personally well disposed toward him. But five years of an official relationship had erected between them a barrier against heart-to-heart conversations.

Aleksei Aleksandrovich, after signing some papers, kept silent for a long while, glancing at Mikhail Vasilievich; several times he tried to say something, without success. He had already prepared the sentence: "Have you heard of my misfortune?" But he ended by saying, as usual, "Well, please take care of this," and with that he dismissed him.

The other person was his doctor, who also was well disposed toward him. But they had already long agreed, without saying so, that both were overburdened with work and could not be distracted.

As for his friends among the ladies, the foremost among them Lydia Ivanovna, Aleksei Aleksandrovich gave them no thought. All women, just because they were women, were frightening and repugnant to him.

22

ALEKSEI ALEKSANDROVICH had forgotten Countess Lydia Ivanovna, but she had not forgotten him. At this most difficult moment, when he was lonely and despondent, she came to see him, and without having been announced, entered his study. She found him in the same position in which he had been sitting, his head in his hands.

"*J'ai forcé la consigne*," she said, walking in briskly and breathing heavily, as a result of her agitation and rapid pace.

"I know everything, Aleksei Aleksandrovich! My good friend!" she continued, firmly shaking his hand with both of hers and looking with her lovely pensive eyes into his.

Aleksei Aleksandrovich rose with a frown, disengaged his hand and offered her a chair.

"Be seated, Countess! I'm not receiving anyone because I'm not well, Countess," he said, his lips trembling.

"My good friend!" repeated Countess Lydia Ivanovna, her eyes fixed on him. Suddenly the inner corners of her eyebrows rose, forming a triangle on her forehead, and her homely yellow face became still homelier. But Aleksei Aleksandrovich felt that she pitied him and was on the verge of tears. He was moved deeply; he seized her plump hand and covered it with kisses.

"My dear friend!" she said in a voice choked with emotion. "Don't let your misfortune overwhelm you. Your misfortune is great, but you must find consolation."

"I am crushed; I am broken; I am no longer a man," said Aleksei Aleksandrovich, releasing her hand but still looking into her tear-filled eyes. "My situation is terrible because nowhere, even within myself, can I find the strength I need."

"You will find that strength. Don't look for it in me, though I want to assure you of my devotion," she said with a sigh. "Your strength you will find in love, the love which He has bequeathed to us. His burden is light," she said with that enraptured look which Aleksei Aleksandrovich knew so well. "He will support and aid you."

Though these words expressed her admiration for her own exalted feelings and represented a new mood of mystic rapture that had recently become fashionable in Petersburg and that seemed to Aleksei Aleksandrovich entirely unnecessary, now he was pleased to hear them.

"I am weak; I am broken. I foresaw none of this, and now it's beyond me."

"My dear friend!" repeated Lydia Ivanovna.

"It's not the loss of what no longer exists; it's not that," continued Aleksei Aleksandrovich. "I have no regrets. But I cannot but feel ashamed before the world for the situation in which I find myself. It's wrong, but I can't help it."

"It was not you who performed that high act of forgiveness, for which I and everyone else admire you, but He who dwells in your heart," said Lydia Ivanovna, raising her enraptured eyes. "You, therefore, cannot be ashamed of your deed."

Aleksei Aleksandrovich frowned, laced his fingers, and began to crack his knuckles.

"You'd have to know all the details," he said in a thin voice. "A man's strength has its limits, Countess, and I've reached the limits of my strength. All day long today I've had to take care of the household, as a result" (he emphasized the words "as a result") "of my new, lonely situation. The servants, the governess, bills. . . . This petty fire has consumed me and I can't endure it any longer. At dinner . . . yesterday I nearly left the table. I couldn't bear the way my son looked at me. He didn't ask me the meaning of all of this, but he wanted to, and I couldn't endure his look. He was afraid to look at me, and that's not all. . . ."

Aleksei Aleksandrovich was about to mention the bill that had been presented to him, but his voice trembled and he stopped. He could not think of this bill, written on blue paper, for a hat and some ribbon, without pitying himself.

"I understand, my friend," said Countess Lydia Ivanovna. "I understand completely. You will not find aid and consolation in me, though I came just to help you if I could. If I could only relieve you of these petty, humiliating cares. I know that a woman's presence is needed here, a woman's supervision. Will you permit me?"

Aleksei Aleksandrovich pressed her hand gratefully in silence.

"We will take care of Seryozha together. I'm not very good at practical matters. But I'll do my best; I'll be your housekeeper. Don't thank me. It's not I who am doing this. . . ."

"I can't help thanking you."

"But, my friend, do not yield to the feeling of which you spoke, of being ashamed of that which is the highest achievement of a Christian: 'he that humbleth himself shall be exalted.' And you must not thank me. We must thank Him and ask Him for help. In Him only will we find peace, consolation, salvation, and love," she said, and raising her eyes to heaven, she began to pray, so Aleksei Aleksandrovich thought, judging by her silence.

As Aleksei Aleksandrovich listened to her words now, the expressions that had formerly sounded, if not offensive, at least excessive, now appeared natural and comforting. Aleksei Aleksandrovich did not like this new ecstatic spirit. He was a believer, but he was interested in religion mainly from the political point of view. The new trend, which permitted giving religion a new interpretation, offended him as a matter of principle, just because it opened the door to controversy and analysis. Formerly his attitude toward these new teachings had been cold and even hostile, and he had never argued with Countess Lydia Ivanovna, who was ardently interested in them; by keeping silent he had studiously avoided being drawn into arguments. But now for the first time he listened to her words with pleasure, and within his heart did not oppose her.

"I am very, very grateful to you, both for your deeds and for your words," he said when she had finished praying.

Countess Lydia Ivanovna once again pressed her friend's hands.

"Now I'll begin to act," she said after a silence, smiling and wiping the remaining tears from her face. "I'm going to see Seryozha. Only in case of urgent need will I apply to you." And she rose and left the room.

Countess Lydia Ivanovna went into Seryozha's room and, covering the cheeks of the frightened boy with her tears, she told him that his father was a saint, and that his mother had died.

Countess Lydia Ivanovna kept her promise. She actually took upon herself the management of Aleksei Aleksandrovich's household. But she had not exaggerated when she said that she was not experienced in practical matters. All her orders had to be changed because they could not be fulfilled, and the changes were made by Kornei, Aleksei Aleksandrovich's valet, who now inconspicuously managed the entire Karenin household, and when he helped his master to dress, calmly and cautiously informed him of all that had to be done. But Lydia Ivanovna's help was none the less of the greatest importance: she had brought Aleksei Aleksandrovich moral support by making him aware of her love and esteem, and particularly, as she felt it comforting to think, by nearly succeeding in converting him to Christianity, in other words, changing him from an indifferent and inactive believer into an ardent and confirmed follower of the new interpretation of Christian teachings that had recently spread in Petersburg. It was not hard for Aleksei Aleksandrovich to accept these new teachings. Like Lydia Ivanovna and others who shared these views, he was completely devoid of a penetrating power of imagination, a spiritual faculty through which concepts

created by the imagination become so vivid that they demand
to be harmonized with other concepts and reality. He found
nothing impossible or improbable in the concept that death,
while it existed for the unbeliever, did not exist for him, that
since he had implicit faith—he being the only judge of its
extent—his soul was already free from any sin, and that he
was already experiencing full salvation here on earth.

True, Aleksei Aleksandrovich felt vaguely that this concept
of his faith was shallow and erroneous. He knew that when
he had not in the least considered his act of forgiveness a
manifestation of some higher power but had abandoned himself directly to this feeling, he had felt much happier than
now, when he at every moment remembered that Christ dwelt
in his soul, and that even when signing papers he was fulfilling
His will. But Aleksei Aleksandrovich had to think this way; in
his humiliation he had an urge to feel more exalted than
others, even if in his imagination only, so that he, despised by
everyone, might despise others, and this urge was so strong
that he held on to this imaginary salvation as though it were
true.

23

COUNTESS LYDIA IVANOVNA, when a very young, enthusiastic
girl, had been married off to a rich, aristocratic, most kindly
and dissolute hedonist. During the second month of their
marriage her husband left her, replying to her rapturous assurances of her tender feelings for him mockingly and even
malevolently, something that those who knew the count's good
heart and who saw no faults whatever in the enthusiastic
Lydia were at a complete loss to understand. Since then they
had lived apart, though they had not been divorced, and when
husband met wife, he never failed to treat her with a
venomous derision, the cause of which was impossible to
understand.

Countess Lydia Ivanovna had long since lost her love for
her husband, but since then she had never ceased to be in
love with someone. She was simultaneously in love with
several persons, both men and women. She was in love with
almost every person who was outstanding in some respect.
She was in love with all the new princes and princesses who
through marriage became related to the Czar's family. She

had been in love with a metropolitan, a coadjutor, and a priest. She had been in love with a journalist, three Slavs, with Komisarov, with a cabinet minister, a doctor, an English missionary, and Karenin. All these loves, now waning, now waxing, did not prevent her from maintaining the widest and most complicated court and social connections. But after the misfortune that had befallen Karenin, since she had taken him under her special protection, since she had busied herself in the Karenin household, concerning herself with his welfare, she felt that her other loves had not been real and that now she was really in love with Karenin alone. The feeling she now had for him seemed to her stronger than all her former ones. After analyzing this feeling and comparing it with earlier ones, she saw clearly that she would not have been in love with Komisarov had he not saved the Czar's life, would not have been in love with Ristich-Kujitsky if no Slav problem had existed, but that she was in love with Karenin for his own sake, for his noble, misunderstood soul, for his thin voice, dear to her, with its drawling intonations, for his weary look, for his character, and for his soft white hands with their bulging veins. She was not only happy to see him but she sought in his face signs of the impression which she made upon him. She wished him to like her not only for her speeches but for her entire person. For him she now dressed with greater care than ever before. She caught herself dreaming of what might have happened if she were not married and he were free. She blushed in agitation when he entered the room; she could not restrain her happy smile when he said something nice to her.

For the past few days Countess Lydia Ivanovna had been in a state of great excitement. She had learned that Anna and Vronsky were in Petersburg. She had to spare Aleksei Aleksandrovich the pain of meeting her, spare him the torment of even knowing that this terrible woman was in the same city as he and that at any moment he might meet her.

Through her acquaintances Lydia Ivanovna was kept informed of the plans of those "awful people," as she called Anna and Vronsky, and during all that time she endeavored to direct the movements of her friend in such a way that he might not meet them. A young adjutant, a friend of Vronsky's, who supplied her with this information and who hoped to obtain a government grant with her help, told her that they had wound up their affairs and were to depart the following day.

Lydia Ivanovna had begun to feel reassured, when on the following morning she received a letter written in a hand that she recognized with alarm. It was Anna Karenina's handwriting. The envelope was as thick as though made of bast, and the exquisitely fragrant, rather long, yellow notepaper bore a huge monogram.

"Who brought it?"

"A hotel messenger."

For a long while the countess could not bring herself to sit down to read the letter. She often suffered from attacks of short breath, and the excitement had brought one on now. When she had calmed down, she read the following letter in French.

MADAME LA CONTESSE,

The Christian sentiments which fill your heart provide to me the temerity, which I realize is unforgivable, to write to you. I am distressed by my separation from my son. I beseech you to permit me to see him once before I leave. Forgive me for reminding you of myself. I am applying to you and not to Aleksei Aleksandrovich only because I do not wish to cause any suffering to that magnanimous man by reminding him of my existence. Knowing your friendship with him, I am sure that you will understand. Will you send Seryozha to me, or shall I come to the house at an appointed hour, or will you let me know where I can see him outside the house? I do not believe that I will be refused, knowing the magnanimity of him on whom the decision depends. You cannot imagine how great is my longing to see my son, and therefore you cannot imagine how deep will be my gratitude to you for your help.

ANNA.

Everything in this letter irritated Countess Lydia Ivanovna: its contents, the reference to Aleksei Aleksandrovich's magnanimity, and particularly its—as it seemed to her—free and easy tone.

"Tell the messenger that there will be no answer," said Countess Lydia Ivanovna. Quickly opening the writing pad, she wrote to Aleksei Aleksandrovich that she hoped to see him shortly after noon at the court reception.

"I must talk to you on a serious and melancholy matter. We

*can make arrangements there. It would be best in my house,
where I can serve you your tea. It is urgent. He gives us a
cross to bear, but He also gives us the strength for it,"* she
added, to prepare him in some measure.

Countess Lydia Ivanovna usually wrote Aleksei Aleksandrovich two or three notes a day. She liked this way of communicating with him; it had an element of elegance and
mystery that her oral communications lacked.

24

THE RECEPTION was drawing to its end. Those who were departing met each other, chatted about the latest news, the
newly granted rewards and the new assignments of key
officials.

"It would be nice if Countess Maria Borisovna were war
minister and Princess Vatkovsky chief of staff," said a little
gray-haired old man in a gold-embroidered uniform, addressing a tall, beautiful lady-in-waiting who had inquired of him
about the new assignments.

"And I their adjutant," replied the lady-in-waiting with a
smile.

"You already have your appointment. Yours is in the department of religion. With Karenin as your assistant."

"How are you, Prince?" said the little old man, shaking
hands with a man who approached him.

"What were you saying about Karenin?" asked the prince.

"He and Putyatov have received the order of Aleksandr
Nevsky."

"I thought that he already had it."

"No, Look at him," said the little old man, pointing with
his embroidered hat at Karenin, who was dressed in a court
uniform with a new red sash over his shoulder and had stopped
in the doorway with one of the influential members of the
State Council. "Happy and contented, like a copper kopeck,"
he added, stopping to shake hands with a handsome, athletic-
looking Gentleman of the Bedchamber.

"No, he's grown old," said the Gentleman of the Bedchamber.

"He worries. Lately he's been continuously submitting
projects. And now he won't release his unfortunate listener
until he's explained every single detail to him."

"What do you mean grown old? *Il fait des passions.* I think that Countess Lydia Ivanovna is jealous of his wife now."

"Hold on! Please don't say anything bad about Lydia Ivanovna."

"Is there anything wrong with her being in love with Karenin?"

"Is it true that Karenina is here?"

"Not here in the palace, of course, but in Petersburg. Yesterday I met her with Aleksei Vronsky, *bras dessus bras dessous,* on Morskaya street."

"*C'est un homme qui n'a pas . . .*" the Gentleman of the Bedchamber was about to say, but he stopped to make way for a member of the Czar's family, bowing as he did.

Thus they spoke ceaselessly about Aleksei Aleksandrovich, judging and ridiculing him, while he blocked the way of the member of the State Council whom he had trapped, not interrupting his exposition for a moment lest he lose his listener, and he expounded on his financial project to him in detail.

Almost at the same time as his wife left him, Aleksei Aleksandrovich had reached a stage most disheartening to any government official: advancement in his career had come to an end, and everyone saw it clearly but Aleksei Aleksandrovich, who did not yet realize it. Whether it was his encounter with Stremov, the misfortune brought upon him by his wife, or simply the fact that Aleksei Aleksandrovich had reached his predestined limits, that year it had become clear to everyone that his career had come to an end. He still occupied an important position and still was a member of numerous commissions and committees, but he was now a person whose abilities had been spent and of whom nothing more could be expected. Whatever he said, whatever he proposed, was received in a manner that seemed to show that these propositions had long been known and were just what was not needed.

But Aleksei Aleksandrovich was not aware of this and, just the opposite, when prevented from participating directly in government affairs he saw more clearly than ever the failures and errors of others, and he considered it his duty to point out measures for correcting them. Soon after his separation from his wife he began to write a report on the new court, the first of an endless series of reports he was to write on all branches of government, reports of value to no one.

Aleksei Aleksandrovich not only failed to see the hopelessness of his situation as a government official and not only failed to worry about it, but he was more satisfied with his own work than ever before.

"He that is unmarried careth for things that belong to the Lord, how he may please the Lord: but he that is married careth for the things that are of the world, how he may please his wife," said the apostle Paul, and Aleksei Aleksandrovich, who in all his actions now followed the Gospel, often recalled this verse. It seemed to him that ever since his wife had left him, by these very projects he served God better than before.

The obvious impatience of the council member, who was anxious to leave him, did not trouble Aleksei Aleksandrovich. He broke off his discourse only when his listener, availing himself of an opportunity when a member of the Czar's family passed by, had slipped away.

Left alone, Aleksei Aleksandrovich bent his head, collected his thoughts, then absently looked around and walked over to the doorway, hoping to find Lydia Ivanovna.

And how strong and hearty they all are, thought Aleksei Aleksandrovich, looking at the powerfully built Gentleman of the Bedchamber, with his well-groomed, perfumed side-whiskers, and at the ruddy neck of a prince in a tight uniform, as he passed them. It is truly said that everything in this world is evil, he thought, once again casting sidelong glances at the calves of the Gentleman of the Bedchamber.

Moving unhurriedly, Aleksei Aleksandrovich bowed with his usual air of weariness and dignity to the gentlemen who were gossiping about him, and looking in the direction of the door, searched for Countess Lydia Ivanovna.

"Ah, Aleksei Aleksandrovich!" said the little old man, with a malicious twinkle in his eyes, when Karenin came up next to him and coolly greeted him. "I have not yet congratulated you," he said, pointing to the newly awarded sash.

"Thank you," replied Aleksei Aleksandrovich. "What a *beautiful* day," he added, emphasizing, as was his custom, the word *beautiful*.

He knew that they were laughing at him, but he expected of them nothing but malice. He had become accustomed to it.

When he caught sight of Countess Lydia Ivanovna as she came through the doorway, her yellow shoulders rising above her décolletage, and her beautiful, pensive eyes looking at him invitingly, Aleksei Aleksandrovich smiled, revealing his unimpaired white teeth, and walked over to her.

Lydia Ivanovna had spent much effort on her toilette, as she had done of late with all her toilettes. She dressed now for a completely different purpose than she had thirty years earlier. In those days she wanted to adorn herself somehow, and the more the better. Now, on the contrary, her adornments were invariably so ill-suited to her age and her looks that her sole concern was that the contrast between her attire and her looks not be too shocking. With Aleksei Aleksandrovich she had reached this goal, and she seemed to him attractive. In the sea of ill will and derision that surrounded him, she was the only isle on which he had found not only good will but even love.

Passing through all those derisive looks, he was as naturally drawn toward her enamored look as a plant is drawn toward light.

"Congratulations!" she said, her eyes indicating the sash.

Restraining a smile of satisfaction, he shrugged his shoulders with his eyes closed, as though saying that this could bring him no pleasure. But Countess Lydia Ivanovna knew well that this was one of his great joys, though he would never admit it.

"How is our angel?" asked Countess Lydia Ivanovna, referring to Seryozha.

"I can't say that I'm completely pleased with him," said Aleksei Aleksandrovich, raising his brows and opening his eyes. "Nor is Sitnikov pleased with him." (Sitnikov was the tutor who had been entrusted with Seryozha's secular education.) "As I've told you, there is about him some indifference to those most important problems that should touch the heart of every man and every child," said Aleksei Aleksandrovich, beginning to expound his views on the only subject that interested him other than his official duties—the subject of his son's education.

When Aleksei Aleksandrovich, with Lydia Ivanovna's help, had again returned to active life, he felt that it was his duty to busy himself with the education of his son, now in his care. He had never concerned himself before with problems of education and he now devoted some time to the study of the theory of education. After reading a few books on anthropology, pedagogy, and didactics, Aleksei Aleksandrovich formed a plan for his son's education, and after inviting one of the best Petersburg pedagogues to provide guidance, he undertook the task. He was now constantly preoccupied with this matter.

"Yes, but his heart? I find he has his father's heart, and with such a heart a child cannot be naughty," said Lydia Ivanovna enthusiastically.

"Yes, perhaps. . . . As for me, I perform my duty. That's all I can do."

"Please come to see me," Lydia Ivanovna said after a silence. "I have to talk to you on a melancholy matter. I would give much to spare you certain memories, but others don't think the same way. I've received a letter from *her. She* is here, in Petersburg."

Aleksei Aleksandrovich shuddered at the mention of his wife, but at once his face assumed a deathlike immobility that expressed his complete helplessness in this matter.

"I expected it," he said.

Countess Lydia Ivanovna looked at him in rapture, and the greatness of his soul moved her to tears of ecstatic admiration.

25

WHEN ALEKSEI ALEKSANDROVICH entered Lydia Ivanovna's small, cozy sitting room, filled with old china and hung with portraits, the lady of the house was not yet there. She was changing her clothes.

On a round table, covered by a cloth, there was a Chinese service and a silver teapot heated by an alcohol lamp. Aleksei Aleksandrovich absently scanned the numberless familiar portraits that adorned the room and, sitting down at a table, he opened the Bible that lay there. The rustle of the countess' silk dress distracted him.

"Well, here we can sit comfortably," said Countess Lydia Ivanovna with a nervous smile, hurriedly making her way between the table and the divan, "and we will talk while we have our tea!"

After a few preliminary remarks, Lydia Ivanovna, breathing heavily and blushing, handed Aleksei Aleksandrovich the letter which she had received.

After reading it he remained silent for a long while.

"I don't believe that I have the right to refuse her request," he said, timidly raising his eyes.

"My dear friend! You can't see evil in anyone."

"On the contrary, I see that everything is evil. But is that right? . . ."

On his face was the expression of hesitation and longing for advice, help, and guidance in a matter that was beyond his comprehension.

"No," interrupted Countess Lydia Ivanovna. "There is a limit to everything. I understand immorality," she said, not quite sincerely, for she never could understand what made women immoral, "but I can't understand cruelty, and to whom? to you! How can she remain in the same city as you? Well, you live and learn. The world is full of surprises. And I am learning to understand how virtuous you are and how base she is."

"And who should cast the first stone?" asked Aleksei Aleksandrovich, evidently pleased with his role. "I've forgiven completely and therefore cannot deny her the love—which she needs—the love for her son."

"But is it love, my dear friend? Is it sincere? I admit you have forgiven her, still forgive . . . but have we the right to trouble the heart of this angel? He believes that she is dead. He prays for her and prays to God to forgive her sins. . . . It's better this way. Otherwise what will he think?"

"I never thought of that," said Aleksei Aleksandrovich, evidently agreeing with her.

Countess Lydia Ivanovna covered her face with her hands and was silent. She prayed.

"If you were to ask me," she said, finishing her prayer and looking at him, "I would advise you not to do it. Don't I see how you suffer, how this has opened old wounds? But suppose you were to be selfless, as always. What would it lead to? To new suffering for you and anguish for the child. If she had a trace of human feeling left in her, she herself would not wish to do this. No, without any hesitation, I advise you not to do it, and if you'll permit me to, I'll write to her."

Aleksei Aleksandrovich agreed, and Countess Lydia Ivanovna wrote the following letter in French.

DEAR MADAM,

To remind your son of you may make him ask questions to which no answer could be given without arousing in him a spirit of condemnation of what should be sacred to him. I therefore ask you to accept your husband's refusal in the spirit of Christian charity. I pray that the Almighty will be merciful to you.

COUNTESS LYDIA.

This letter accomplished the secret purpose Lydia Ivanovna had been concealing from herself. It insulted Anna most painfully.

Aleksei Aleksandrovich, for his part, on returning home from Lydia Ivanovna's, could not that day busy himself with his usual activities nor find the peace of mind that he had had before and that is given to a man who believes and has been saved.

The memory of his wife, who had wronged him so grievously, and toward whom he acted like a saint, as Countess Lydia Ivanovna so justly put it, should not have troubled him. But he could not remain calm, he could not follow the book he was reading, he could not rid himself of the tormenting memories of his relationship to her, of the errors that, as it seemed to him now, he had committed in his behavior toward her. He bitterly repented the manner in which, on their return from the races, he had received her revelation of her unfaithfulness to him (particularly that he only demanded that she observe propriety but had not challenged her lover to a duel), and the memory of this distressed him. He was also distressed when he recalled the letter he had written to her, and especially his forgiveness, which nobody had wanted, his caring for the child of a stranger, and this memory filled him with burning shame and remorse.

With the same feeling of shame and repentant regret he reviewed in his mind his entire life with her and remembered the awkward words in which, after long hesitation, he had proposed to her.

But where did I do wrong? he asked himself. And this question invariably led to another—whether the others, the Vronskys, Oblonskys . . . those Gentlemen of the Bedchamber with their thick calves, whether they felt differently, loved differently, married differently. And this brought to his mind a whole host of sound, strong, self-assured men whom he always unwittingly watched with attention and curiosity. He tried to rid himself of these thoughts, tried to convince himself that he did not live for this temporary life but for the eternal one, and that there was peace and love within his heart. But the fact, as it seemed to him, that he had committed some insignificant errors in this transient, insignificant life, distressed him as though the eternal salvation in which he believed did not even exist. But these doubts did not last long, and soon Aleksei Aleksandrovich's soul again regained its state of peace and detachment, helping him to forget what he did not wish to remember.

26

"WELL, KAPITONYCH?" asked Seryozha, rosy and cheerful as he returned from a walk on the eve of his birthday. He handed his Russian-style coat, gathered at the waist, to the tall old doorman, who smiled down at the little boy from his great height. "Well, did the clerk come, the one who's always bundled up? Did Papa see him?"

"He did. As soon as the office manager left, I announced him," the doorman said, winking gaily. "Sit down, please. I'll take them off."

"Seryozha," said his tutor, a Southern Slav, who had stopped at the doorway to the inner rooms. "Take them off yourself."

But though Seryozha heard his tutor's weak voice, he did not pay any attention to him. He stood there, holding on to the doorman's belt and looking into his face.

"Well, did Papa do for him what he asked?"

The doorman nodded.

Both Seryozha and the doorman were interested in the clerk, who, always bundled up in his clothing, had already come seven times to petition Aleksei Aleksandrovich. Once Seryozha met him in the entrance hall and heard him beg the doorman pitifully to announce him to Aleksei Aleksandrovich lest he and his children perish.

Since then, having once again met the clerk in the entrance hall, he had been interested in him.

"Well, was he very happy?" he asked.

"Of course! As he left, he almost jumped for joy!"

"Well, did they bring anything?" asked Seryozha after a silence.

"Yes sir," said the doorman in a whisper, nodding. "Something arrived from the countess."

Seryozha knew that the doorman meant that a birthday present had arrived from Countess Lydia Ivanovna.

"You don't say? Where?"

"Kornei took it to your father. I think it's really something."

"How big? Like this?"

"Smaller, but very good."

"A book?"

"No, something really good. You'd better go; Vasili Lukich is calling you," said the doorman. On hearing the approaching steps of the tutor, he carefully removed the boy's hand, its glove half off, from his belt, and with a wink he indicated Lukich with his head.

"Just a minute, Vasili Lukich!" called Seryozha, with the gay and kind smile that always appeased his stern tutor.

Seryozha was too gay, he felt too happy, not to share with his friend the doorman the joy of yet another family event, about which he had learned from Countess Lydia Ivanovna's niece during his walk in the Summer Garden. This joy seemed to him particularly significant because it coincided with the clerk's joy and his own when he learned that toys had arrived. It seemed to Seryozha that this was a day in which everyone should be joyful and gay.

"Do you know that Papa received the Aleksandr Nevsky?"

"Of course I know. Visitors have already come to congratulate him."

"Well, is he happy?"

"Who wouldn't be happy to receive the Czar's favor? It means that he earned it," the doorman said in a stern and serious tone.

Seryozha became thoughtful and looked into the doorman's face, which he knew in minute detail, particularly his chin, which protruded between his gray side whiskers. This chin nobody but Seryozha knew, for he always looked at it from below.

"And how long has it been since your daughter visited you?" The doorman's daughter was a ballet dancer.

"How can she come on weekdays? They also have their studies. And you have to study, sir. You'd better go."

When he came into his room, instead of attending to his lessons, Seryozha told his tutor that he believed that what they had brought was probably a locomotive. "What do you think?" he asked.

But Vasili Lukich thought only of the grammar lesson

Seryozha had to prepare for the teacher who was expected at two o'clock.

"One minute, Vasili Lukich, just tell me," he said quickly, already seated at his desk with a book in his hand. "What is higher than the Aleksandr Nevsky?"

Vasili Lukich replied that the Vladimir was higher than the Aleksandr Nevsky.

"And then?"

"The highest is the St. Andrew."

"And higher than the St. Andrew?"

"I don't know."

"Even you don't know?" and Seryozha leaned on his hands and became engrossed in thought.

His reflections were most complex and various. He imagined that his father would suddenly get both the Vladimir and the St. Andrew, and that as a result, he would be much kinder during the lesson that day, and that he himself, when he grew up, would get all the orders, including the one they would create above the St. Andrew. As soon as they would create it, he would get it. And if they created higher ones, he would get them, too.

The time passed in such reflections, and when the teacher arrived, the assignment on adverbs of time, place, and manner had not yet been prepared, and this not only displeased the teacher but upset him. Seryozha was affected by the teacher's feelings. He did not feel guilty about his failure to prepare his assignment. No matter how eagerly he had tried to do it, he had failed completely. While the teacher explained it to him he believed that he understood it, but as soon as he remained alone, he absolutely could not remember or understand that such a short and simple word as *suddenly* was an "adverb of manner of action." Nevertheless, he felt sorry that he had upset his teacher and he wanted to comfort him.

He chose the moment when the teacher looked at the book in silence.

"Mikhail Ivanovich, when is your saint's day?" he suddenly asked.

"You had better think of your work. For an intelligent person the saint's day is of no importance. It's the same kind of day as any other, a day of work."

Seryozha looked attentively at his teacher, at his sparse beard, his glasses, which had slid down his nose, and became so profoundly absorbed in reflection that he no longer heard anything the teacher was explaining. He knew that the teacher did not believe what he was saying and he felt this in the tone of his voice. Why have they all decided to speak in the same way and say only the most useless and boring things? Why doesn't he want me near him, why doesn't he love me? he asked himself sadly, and he could find no answer.

27

AFTER THE LESSON with his teacher came the lesson with his father. While waiting for his father, Seryozha sat down at the table, toyed with a penknife and sank into reverie. One of Seryozha's favorite occupations was looking for his mother during his walks. He did not believe in death in general and particularly in her death, though Lydia Ivanovna had told him about it and his father had confirmed it. Therefore, even after he had been told that she had died, he looked for her during his walks. Every full-figured, graceful lady with dark hair was his mother. At the sight of such a woman a feeling of tenderness stirred in his heart, making him gasp and bringing tears to his eyes. And he expected that at any moment she would come over to him and lift her veil. He would see her entire face, she would smile, she would embrace him, he would smell her fragrance, would feel the touch of her gentle hand, and would cry with happiness, as on that evening when he had lain at her feet, she had tickled him, and he had laughed loudly, biting her white hand with its rings. Then, when he accidentally heard from his nurse that his mother had not died, but that his father and Lydia Ivanovna had told him that for him she was dead because she was not good (which he absolutely could not believe because he loved her), he continued to search and wait for her. That morning such a lady with a lilac veil was in the Summer Garden, and with a sinking heart he hoped that it was she and he watched her as she came along the walk in their direction. But this lady did not come over to them and disappeared somewhere. That day, more than ever, Seryozha overflowed with love for her, and now, without noticing it, while waiting for his father, he cut the whole edge of the table with his penknife, thinking of her and looking straight ahead with his shining eyes.

"Papa is coming," said Vasili Lukich, interrupting his thoughts.

Seryozha jumped to his feet, walked over to his father, kissed his hand and looked at him intently for signs of joy at having received the Aleksandr Nevsky.

"Did you have a nice walk?" asked Aleksei Aleksandrovich, seating himself in his armchair. He reached for the Old Testament and opened it. Though Aleksei Aleksandrovich had told Seryozha many times that every Christian should know the Bible well, he very often had to consult the Old Testament, and Seryozha noticed it.

"Yes, I had a very nice time, Papa," said Seryozha, seating himself sideways on the chair and rocking it, something that was forbidden. "I saw Nadenka." (Nadenka was the niece and ward of Lydia Ivanovna.) "She told me that you received a new order. Are you glad, Papa?"

"First of all, please stop rocking," said Aleksei Aleksandrovich, "and secondly, it is not the award that counts but the work. And I would like you to understand this. You see, if you work, if you study only to receive a reward, the work will seem difficult. But when you work," said Aleksei Aleksandrovich, recalling how that morning, in the knowledge that he was carrying out his duty, he had performed the tedious task of signing one hundred and eighteen papers, "and love your work, you will find your reward in it."

The tender and happy look disappeared from Seryozha's eyes, which he lowered under the weight of his father's look. His father's tone was the same old familiar one he always used with him, to which Seryozha had already learned to accommodate himself. His father always spoke to him—so Seryozha thought—as though he were addressing some boy whom he had created in his imagination, one of those boys who are found in books, but who was totally unlike Seryozha. And when he was with his father, Seryozha always tried to play the part of that same boy from the books.

"You understand, I hope," said his father.

"Yes, Papa," replied Seryozha, pretending to be that imaginary boy.

The lesson consisted of memorizing some verses from the New Testament and of repeating the beginning of the Old Testament. Seryozha knew the verses from the New Testament fairly well, but as he recited them, his attention was drawn so closely to the bone structure of his father's forehead, which made a very sharp angle at the temple, that he grew confused and ran together verses that ended and began with the same word. It was clear to Aleksei Aleksandrovich that he did not understand what he was saying, and this vexed him.

He frowned and began to explain what Seryozha had already heard many times but could never remember, although he understood it perfectly, as he could not remember that *suddenly* was an adverb of manner of action. Seryozha looked at his father fearfully and had only one thought: would his father make him repeat what he had said, as he often did, or wouldn't he. And this thought alarmed him so profoundly that he no longer understood anything. But his father did not make him repeat it and moved on to the lesson in the Old Testament. Seryozha recited correctly the course of events, but when he had to answer questions on the prophetic meaning of some of the events, he showed complete ignorance even though he had already been punished in connection with this assignment. And when it came to the ancient patriarchs, he could not answer at all, looked lost, cut the table and rocked the chair. He knew none of them except Enoch, who had ascended to heaven while still alive. He used to remember their names, but now he forgot all of them, especially because Enoch was his favorite figure in the Old Testament, and in his mind Enoch's ascendance to heaven while alive was the source of a long procession of thought which he followed now with his eyes fixed on his father's watch chain and on the partly fastened button on his vest.

Seryozha did not at all believe in death, about which he had been so often told. He did not believe that people whom he loved might die, and particularly that he too might die. To him it was utterly impossible and incomprehensible. But he was told that everyone dies. He even asked those whom he trusted about this, and they confirmed it. The nurse said the same thing, though reluctantly. But Enoch did not die and therefore not everyone dies. And why couldn't everyone deserve well of God and be taken to heaven? thought Seryozha. The wicked, in other words, those whom Seryozha did not like, could die, but all the good people should be like Enoch.

"Well, name the patriarchs."

"Enoch, Enos."

"Yes, you have already said those. That's bad, Seryozha, very bad. If you don't try to learn what is most important for a Christian," said his father, rising, "what could interest you? I am displeased with you, and Piotr Ignatich" (who was the chief teacher) "is displeased with you. . . . I must punish you."

His father and his teacher were both displeased with Seryozha, and he really was not doing well in his studies. But it could not be said that he was not bright. On the contrary, he was much more capable than the boys the teacher cited to Seryozha as examples. According to his father, he did not want to learn what he was taught. But actually he could not learn it. He could not do it because his soul confronted him with demands more urgent than those posed by his father and his teacher. These two sets of demands contradicted each other, and he actually struggled against his teachers.

He was nine years old, still a child. But he knew his soul, it was dear to him, he guarded it as the eyelid guards the eye and admitted to it no one without the key of love. His teachers complained that he did not like to study, but his soul overflowed with the thirst for knowledge. And he learned from Kapitonych, from his nurse, from Nadenka, from Vasili Lukich, but not from his teachers. The water that his father and teachers expected would fall on their mill wheels had long since seeped away and was doing its work elsewhere.

His father punished Seryozha by forbidding him to visit Nadenka, Lydia Ivanovna's niece, but this punishment turned out to Seryozha's advantage. Vasili Lukich was in good spirits and showed him how to make windmills. The entire evening was spent in this work and in dreams of making a windmill on which they could ride; they would hold on to the wings with their hands or they would tie themselves on and ride. That entire evening Seryozha did not think about his mother, but when in bed, he suddenly remembered her and prayed in his own words that the next day, on his birthday, his mother would stop hiding and would come to see him.

"Vasili Lukich, do you know what I prayed for that was extra?"

"To become a better student?"

"No."

"Toys?"

"No. You won't guess. A very good thing, but a secret. When it comes true, I'll tell you. You haven't guessed?"

"No, I can't guess. You tell me," said Vasili Lukich, smiling one of his rare smiles. "Well, lie down and I'll put out the candle."

"What I prayed for I can see better without the candle. Oh, I almost told you my secret," said Seryozha, laughing gaily.

After the candle had been taken away, Seryozha felt and heard the presence of his mother. She stood over him and caressed him with a loving look. But then the windmills appeared, and the penknife. Everything grew confused and he fell asleep.

28

WHEN THEY ARRIVED in Petersburg, Vronsky and Anna stayed in one of the best hotels. Vronsky had separate quarters on the lower floor, and Anna, the baby, wet nurse, and the maid were upstairs in a suite of four rooms.

On the very first day of his arrival Vronsky went to see his brother. There he met his mother, who had arrived from Moscow to attend to some personal matters. His mother and sister-in-law met him as usual. They inquired about his trip abroad, spoke of mutual friends, but said not a word about his affair with Anna. But when his brother came to see Vronsky the next morning, he himself inquired about her, and Aleksei Vronsky declared to him firmly that he looked upon his relationship with Karenina as upon a marriage, that he hoped that she would obtain a divorce, that he would marry her, that until then he considered her as much a wife to him as any married woman is to her husband, and he asked him to tell this to their mother and to his wife.

"I don't care if society doesn't approve," said Vronsky, "but if my relatives want to maintain a family relationship with me, they must maintain that same relationship with my wife."

The older brother, who always respected the opinions of the younger, could not be quite sure whether he was right or wrong until society decided this question. But he, for his part, had nothing against it and went along with Aleksei to see Anna.

In the presence of his brother, as in the presence of others, Vronsky addressed Anna as "you" and treated her as a close friend, but it was assumed that his brother understood their relationship and they spoke about Anna's intention to go to Vronsky's estate.

In spite of all his experience with high society, Vronsky, as a result of his new situation, harbored a strange illusion. One could have expected him to understand that society was closed to him and Anna. Yet he conceived some vague idea that this was true only in the old times, but that now, with the rapid progress that was being made (without noticing it he had become a partisan of every kind of progress), the opinions of society had now changed and the question of whether they would be received by society had not yet been settled. Of course, he thought, the court circles will not receive her, but those who have been close to me can and must see it in its proper perspective.

One can endure several hours of sitting cross-legged without changing his position if he knows that nothing prevents him from changing it. But if he knows that he must sit cross-legged, he will be seized with cramps, his legs will begin to twitch, and they will tend to move in the direction he would like to stretch them. The same was true of Vronsky's feelings toward society. Though deep within his heart he knew that society was closed to them, he tried to find out whether it had not changed, and whether they would be received. But very soon he found that though society remained open for him personally, it was closed to Anna. As in the game of cat and mouse, the arms raised for him were immediately lowered for Anna.

The first lady of Petersburg high society whom Vronsky saw was his cousin Betsy.

"At last," she cheerfully greeted him. "And Anna? I am so glad to see you! Where are you staying? I imagine how horrible Petersburg looks to you after your wonderful trip. I can visualize your honeymoon in Rome. What about the divorce? Is it all settled?"

Vronsky noticed that Betsy's enthusiasm subsided when she learned that the divorce had not yet been granted.

"They will cast stones at me, I know," she said, "but I'll go to see Anna. Yes, I'll go without fail. How long will you stay here?"

And indeed she came to see Anna that same day, but her tone was not at all the same as it used to be. Evidently, she was proud of her courage and hoped that Anna would appreciate her faithfulness. She spent no more than ten minutes there, told her the social news, and when leaving, she said:

"You didn't tell me when you expect to get the divorce. Of course, I myself am free from prejudice, but the bigots will freeze you with their looks until you're married. And it can be done so easily nowadays. *Ça se fait.* So you're leaving Friday? What a pity that we won't see each other again."

By Betsy's tone Vronsky should have surmised what he might expect from society. But he made one additional attempt, with his family. He pinned no hopes on his mother. He knew that his mother, who had so ardently admired Anna at the beginning of their acquaintance, was unmerciful toward her now for being the cause of her son's failure in his career. But he placed great hopes on Varia, his brother's wife. He believed that she would not cast stones and would simply and unreservedly visit Anna and receive her.

The day after he arrived, Vronsky went to see her, and finding her alone, frankly expressed his wish to her.

"You know, Aleksei," she said after listening to him, "how I love you and how ready I am to do anything for you. But I've kept silent because I know that I can be of no help to you or Anna Arkadievna." She was careful in pronouncing the name Anna Arkadievna. "But please don't think that I condemn her. I couldn't. Perhaps in her place I would have done the same. I will not and cannot go into detail," she said, looking shyly at his somber face. "But one must call a spade a spade. You want me to visit her, receive her, and thus restore her to society. You have to understand that I *cannot* do it. My daughters are growing up, and I must live with society for my husband's sake. Suppose I visit Anna Arkadievna. She will understand that I can't invite her to my house, or that I would have to arrange it so that she might not encounter those whose views are different, and this would offend her. I can't help her up. . . ."

"But I don't consider that she has fallen any lower than many of the women whom you do receive!" Vronsky interrupted with a still gloomier look. He rose in silence, for he understood that his sister-in-law's decision was final.

"Aleksei! Don't be angry with me. Please understand that it's not my fault," Varia said, looking at him with a shy smile.

"I'm not angry with you," he said, with the same gloomy expression, "but I'm doubly hurt. I'm also hurt because this destroys our friendship. And if it doesn't destroy it completely, it weakens it. You must understand that there's no other way for me either."

And with this he left.

Vronsky understood that further attempts were useless, and

that to spare himself annoyance and insults, so painful to him, he would have to spend the few days in Petersburg as in a strange city, avoiding all his former contacts with society. One of the most annoying aspects of their situation in Petersburg was that it seemed that Aleksei Aleksandrovich and his name were everywhere. No conversation could be started which would not turn to the subject of Aleksei Aleksandrovich. It was impossible to go anywhere without meeting him, or so it seemed to Vronsky, as it seems to a man with a sore finger who, as though deliberately, bumps this same sore finger against everything.

His stay in Petersburg seemed to Vronsky all the more difficult because all that time he observed in Anna a new mood, which he could not comprehend. Now she appeared to be in love with him, and now cold, irritable, strange. Something was distressing her, she was concealing something from him, and it seemed that she did not notice the insults that poisoned his life and that, in view of her sensitive nature, should have been even more painful.

29

ONE OF ANNA's purposes in going back to Russia was to see her son. From the day she left Italy the idea of seeing him never ceased to agitate her. And the closer she came to Petersburg, the greater seemed to her the joy and significance of the forthcoming meeting. She did not even ask herself how she would arrange this meeting. It seemed to her that it would be natural and simple to see her son if she were in the same city as he. But when she arrived in Petersburg, she quickly perceived her new situation in society, and she realized that it would be difficult to arrange the meeting.

By now she had been in Petersburg for two days. She had not stopped thinking of her son for a moment, but she had not seen him yet. She felt that she had no right to go to his house, where she might meet Aleksei Aleksandrovich. She might not be admitted and might be subjected to insults. And it was painful even to think of writing to her husband or to have anything to do with him. She could enjoy peace of mind only when she did not think of her husband. She would not be satisfied by merely seeing her son during his walks after finding out where and when he took them; she had been so long preparing herself for this meeting, she had so much to tell him, she longed so to embrace him and to kiss him. Seryozha's old nurse could help and advise her. But she no longer lived in Aleksei Aleksandrovich's home. Two days passed in these doubts and in attempts to find the nurse.

After learning of the close friendship between Aleksei Aleksandrovich and Countess Lydia Ivanovna, Anna, on the third day after her arrival, decided to write her a letter, something that cost her much effort. In it she deliberately stated that permission to see her son depended on the generosity of her husband. She knew that if her husband saw this letter, he would continue to play the role of a magnanimous man and would not refuse her request.

The messenger who delivered the letter brought back the cruelest and most unexpected answer—that there would be no answer. She had never felt so humiliated as at the moment when, after calling in the messenger, she heard from him a detailed report of how he had waited and later had been told, "There will be no answer." Anna felt humiliated and insulted, but realized that from her point of view Countess Lydia Ivanovna was right. Her distress was all the more painful because she had no one with whom to share it. She could not and would not reveal it to Vronsky. She knew that though he was the main cause of her misfortune, the problem of her meeting her son would seem to him of very little importance. She knew that he would never be able to fathom the true depth of her suffering. She knew that she would hate him were he to respond coldly when told of it. And she feared this more than anything else in the world, so she hid from him everything that concerned her son.

She spent the entire day at the hotel, trying to think through a way of meeting her son, and decided to write to her husband. She was composing the letter when they brought her the letter from Lydia Ivanovna. The countess' silence had subdued and humbled her, but this letter, and everything she read between its lines, provoked her so deeply, so offensive did this malice seem to her when compared with her proper, passionate tenderness toward her son, that she became aroused against others and ceased blaming herself.

This coldness, this false feeling, she said to herself. All they want is to insult me and torment the child, but shall I give in to them? Certainly not. She's worse than I. At least I don't lie. And then and there she decided that the very next day, which was Seryozha's birthday, she would go directly to her husband's house, would bribe the servants, would resort to deceit, but would see her son without fail. She would bring down the wall of shameful deceit with which they had surrounded her unfortunate child.

She rode to a toy shop, bought a number of toys, and thought out a plan of action. She would arrive early in the morning, at eight o'clock, when Aleksei Aleksandrovich probably was not yet up. She would have money on hand to bribe the doorman and the servant to admit her, and without lifting her veil, she would tell them that she had come from Seryozha's godfather to congratulate him and that she had been told to put the toys next to the boy's bed. She prepared everything but the words she would say to her son. No matter how hard she thought, she could find none.

The next morning at eight o'clock Anna stepped out alone from a hired coach and rang the bell at the large entrance to her former home.

"Go and see what it's about. There's a lady there," said Kapitonych, not yet dressed but wearing a coat and galoshes, as he looked through the window and saw a lady wearing a veil and standing right at the door.

As soon as the doorman's assistant, a young man whom Anna did not know, opened the door, she went in, and taking a three-ruble note from her muff, she hurriedly thrust it into his hand.

"Seryozha . . . Sergei Alekseich," she said and was about to walk ahead. After he examined the bill, the assistant doorman stopped her at the other glass door.

"Whom do you wish to see?" he asked.

She did not hear his words and did not answer.

Noticing the stranger's confusion, Kapitonych himself came out to her, stopped her at the doorway and asked what he could do for her.

"From Prince Skorodumov to Sergei Alekseich," she said.

"He is not up yet," said the doorman, looking at her intently.

Anna had not expected the sight of the completely unchanged entrance hall of the house in which she had spent nine years to affect her so deeply. Memories, one after another, both joyous and painful, crowded into her mind and for a moment she forgot why she was there.

"Would you care to wait?" asked Kapitonych, helping her with her fur coat.

After helping her, Kapitonych glanced at her face, recognized her, and in silence bowed deeply.

"Come in, Your Excellency," he said to her.

She wanted to say something, but her voice failed her. She looked at the old man with guilty entreaty, and then ascended the staircase with a quick, light step. Leaning far forward and clumsily running in his galoshes up the stairs after her, he tried to overtake her.

"The tutor is there. Perhaps he is still undressed. I'll announce you."

Anna kept ascending the familiar staircase without understanding the old man's words.

"Here, to the left, if you please. Pardon me, it is not so clean here. The master now occupies the former parlor," said the doorman, panting. "Please wait for a second, Your Excellency. I'll look in," he added, and going past her he opened the door cautiously and disappeared behind it. Anna stopped and waited. "He has just awakened," said the doorman as he came out from behind the door.

And at the moment when the doorman said this, Anna heard the sound of a child's yawn. Just from the sound of this yawn she recognized her son and saw him as though he were standing in front of her.

"Let me in, I say. Let me in!" she cried, and went in through the high doorway. A bed was to the right of the door, and on it was a boy, sitting upright, his shirt unbuttoned. He bent backward and stretched, completing his yawn. At the moment his lips met they folded into a blissful drowsy smile, and with this smile he fell back slowly and pleasurably.

"Seryozha," she whispered, coming over to him with a noiseless step.

During her separation from him and during the state of overflowing love for him she had been in constantly of late, she had visualized him as a four-year-old child, as she liked best to remember him. Now he was not even the same as when she had left him; he resembled still less the four-year-old and had grown taller and was thinner. What had happened? How thin his face was! How short his hair! How long his arms! How he had changed since she had left him! But it was he, with his head, his lips, his tender little neck and his broad little shoulders.

"Seryozha!" she repeated right up against the boy's ear.

He got up again on his elbow, turned his tousled head around, as though looking for something, and opened his eyes. For a few moments he gazed quietly and questioningly at his mother, who stood in front of him without moving, then suddenly smiled a blissful smile, closed his sleepy eyes again and fell, not backward, but toward her, toward her arms.

"Seryozha! My darling boy!" she said, catching her breath and embracing his chubby body.

"Mama!" he repeated, wriggling under her hands so that various parts of his body could touch them.

Smiling sleepily, his eyes still closed, he brought his arms from the back of the bed, clasped her shoulders with his plump little hands, and clung to her with the sweet sleepy aroma and warmth that only children possess, rubbing his face against her neck and shoulders.

"I knew," he said, opening his eyes. "Today is my birthday. I knew you would come. I'll get up right away."

And while he said this, he was falling asleep.

Anna gazed at him hungrily. She saw how he had grown and changed during her absence. She both recognized and did not recognize his bare legs, grown so long, sticking out from under the blanket, recognized his cheeks, now grown thin, and the close-cropped curls on the back of his head, which she had kissed so often. She touched each of these and could say nothing. Tears choked her.

"Why are you crying, Mama?" he asked, now fully awake. "Mama, why are you crying?" he exclaimed in a tearful voice.

"I? I won't cry any more. . . . I am crying for joy. I haven't seen you for such a long time. I won't, I won't," she said, swallowing her tears and turning aside. "Well, now it's time for you to dress," she added, as she calmed down. She fell silent, and holding his hand, she sat at the bedside on a chair on which his clothes had been laid out.

"How do you dress without me? How . . ." she was about to say with genuine cheer, but she could not and again turned aside.

"I don't wash with cold water. Papa forbade it. And you haven't seen Vasili Lukich, have you? He'll come. But you're sitting on my clothes." And Seryozha burst into loud laughter.

She looked at him and smiled.

"Mama, darling, sweetheart!" he cried, again throwing himself into her arms and hugging her. It seemed that only now, seeing her smile, did he clearly understand what had happened. "You don't need this," he said, taking off her hat. And as though seeing her anew without her hat, he again began to kiss her.

"Well, what did you think happened to me? You didn't think that I'd died?"

"I never believed it."

"You didn't, my dear one?"

"I knew, I knew," he said, repeating his favorite words, and seizing the hand with which she was stroking his hair, he pressed her palm to his lips and covered it with kisses.

30

IN THE MEANTIME Vasili Lukich, who at first did not know who the lady was and then, learning from the conversation that she was none other than the mother who had deserted her husband, whom he never had met because he had become a member of the household after she had left, was in doubt whether to enter the room or not, or whether to inform Aleksei Aleksandrovich. Deciding at last that it was his duty to waken Seryozha at a certain hour, that it was not his concern to find out who was sitting there, the boy's mother or someone else, but that he had to perform his duty, he dressed, went up to the door, and opened it.

But the caresses of the mother and son, the sound of their voices, and the words they said—all this made him change his mind. He shook his head, sighed, and closed the door. I'll wait ten minutes more, he said to himself, clearing his throat and drying his tears.

At the same time the servants were in a state of great excitement. Everyone had learned that the mistress had arrived, that Kapitonych had admitted her, and that she was in the nursery. Everyone knew that the master always went there between eight and nine in the morning and everyone understood that the meeting of husband and wife was inconceivable and should be forestalled. The valet Kornei went down to the doormans' room to find out how she had gained admittance, and hearing that it was Kapitonych who had admitted and escorted her, he chided the old man. The doorkeeper remained stubbornly silent, but when Kornei told him that for this he should be discharged, Kapitonych whirled toward him and, waving his arms in front of Kornei's face, cried:

"Yes, you wouldn't have let her in. I served her for ten years and she showed me nothing but kindness, but you would have gone up and said to her, 'Please, go away!' You're the sly one! Yes! Let's not forget how you rob the master and steal his raccoon-fur coats."

"Hey! You stupid soldier!" said Kornei contemptuously, and he turned toward the nurse who was coming in. "You be the judge, Maria Efimovna. He admitted her without saying a word to anyone," said Kornei, addressing her. "Aleksei Aleksandrovich will emerge any moment now and will go to the nursery."

"Trouble, trouble!" said the nurse. "You, Kornei Vasilievich, somehow delay the master, and I'll run there and try to make her leave. Oh, what trouble!"

When the nurse entered the nursery, Seryozha was telling his mother how he and Nadenka had fallen, how they had slid downhill, turning head over heels three times. She listened to the sounds of his voice, saw his face and its changing expressions, felt his hand, but did not understand what he was saying. She had to go, she had to leave him—that was the only thing she felt and knew. She heard Vasili Lukich, as he came over to the door, clearing his throat, and she heard the nurse approach, but she sat as if frozen, lacking the strength to utter a word or to rise.

"Mistress, dear!" said the nurse, coming over to Anna and kissing her hands and shoulders. "What great joy God has sent to the boy on his birthday. You haven't changed at all."

"Ah, my dear nurse, I didn't know that you were staying here," said Anna, coming to herself for a moment.

"I don't live here, I live with my daughter. I came only to congratulate the boy, Anna Arkadievna, my dove!"

Suddenly the nurse burst into tears and again fell to kissing her hand.

Seryozha, his eyes and smile sparkling, tapped on the rug with his chubby bare feet, holding on to his mother with one hand and to the nurse with the other. The tender love of his beloved nurse for his mother delighted him.

"Mama! She often comes to see me, and when she comes . . ." he started, but stopped, seeing that the nurse was whispering something to his mother, and that the mother's face expressed fear and something like shame, which was so unbecoming to her.

She turned back to him.

"My darling," she said.

She could not say goodbye—but her face expressed it, and he understood. "My dear, dear Kootik," she said, using the name she had used when he was little. "You won't forget me? You . . ." but she could not continue.

How many words came to her mind later, words she could have said! But then she neither knew what to say nor how. But Seryozha understood everything she wanted to say. He understood that she was unhappy and that she loved him. He even understood what the nurse had whispered to her. He heard the words "always between eight and nine," and he understood that she was referring to his father, and that his father and mother must not meet. All this he understood, but one thing was beyond him: why had her face shown shame and fear? . . . She was not guilty, but she was afraid and ashamed of something. He wanted to ask a question that would dispel all his doubts, but he dared not; he saw that she was suffering and felt sorry for her. In silence he pressed close to her and then whispered:

"Don't go yet! He won't come so soon!"

His mother held him away from her to see whether he meant what he said, and in the frightened expression on his face she read that not only was he referring to his father, but he seemed to be asking what he should think of his father.

"Seryozha, my dear child," she said, "love him. He is better and kinder than I. I have wronged him. When you grow up, you will understand."

"No one is better than you!" he shouted in despair, on the verge of tears, and clasping her shoulders, he drew her toward himself with all his strength, his arms trembling under the strain.

"My darling, my little one," said Anna, crying in the same weak, childlike way as he.

At that moment the door opened and Vasili Lukich came in. There was a sound of steps at the other door, and the nurse, frightened, whispered, "He is coming," and handed Anna her hat.

Seryozha fell on the bed and burst into sobs, burying his face in his hands. Anna removed his hands, kissed his wet face once more, and went out the door with a quick step.

Aleksei Aleksandrovich was coming in her direction. Seeing her, he stopped and bowed his head.

Though she had just said that he was better and kinder than she, after a quick glance in his direction that took in his entire person in detail, she was seized with a feeling of aversion and ill will toward him and envy for having her son. With a quick movement she lowered her veil and, her pace quickening, she almost ran from the room.

She had not had the time to give him the toys that she had selected in the shop the previous day with such love and sadness, and she brought them home with her.

31

No MATTER HOW much Anna had longed to see her son, how long she had been thinking of it and preparing herself for it, she had never expected the meeting to affect her so profoundly. When she returned to her lonely suite in the hotel, it took her some time to realize why she was there. Yes, all that's over and I'm again alone, she said to herself, and without removing her hat she sat in the armchair at the fireplace. She fixed her eyes upon the bronze clock that stood on a table between the windows and became lost in thought.

The French maid, whom she had brought from abroad, came to help her dress. She gave her a surprised look and said:

"Later."

The servant offered her coffee.

"Later," she replied.

The Italian nurse, having dressed the baby girl, came in and brought her over to Anna. The chubby, well-fed baby caught sight of her mother and, as always, turned her bare little arms palms down, her wrists looking as though a thread had been tied around them. Smiling with her tiny, toothless mouth, she began to wave her hands as a fish waves its fins, rustling the starched folds of her little embroidered skirt. One could not help smiling nor refrain from kissing this little girl. One could not help giving her a finger, which she would grasp, shrieking happily and bouncing her entire body. One could not help giving her one's lips which, as though kissing, she would draw into her little mouth. Anna did all of this, took her in her arms, dandled her, kissed her fresh cheeks

and bare little elbows. But at the sight of this child, she saw
still more clearly that the feeling she had for her was not even
a feeling of love when compared with what she felt for
Seryozha. Everything about this little girl was lovely, but
somehow she didn't move her heart. On the first child, though
born of an unloved man, she had lavished all her love, which
before had found no satisfaction. The girl was born under
the most trying circumstances, and not even a hundredth part
of the attention was bestowed upon her in comparison with
the first child. Moreover, everything in regard to the girl lay
in the future, whereas Seryozha was almost a man, and a
man whom she loved. Thoughts and feelings already contended within him; he understood, loved, and judged her, she
thought, as she recalled what he had said and how he had
looked at her. And she was separated from him forever, not
only physically but also spiritually, and this could not be
remedied.

She gave the child back to the nurse, dismissed her and
opened the locket that contained a portrait of Seryozha when
he was almost the same age as the girl was now. She rose,
took off her hat and reached for the album which lay on the
little table and which contained pictures of Seryozha at various ages. She wanted to compare the different pictures and
began to take them out of the album. She removed all of
them but one, the best. He was sitting astride a chair, dressed
in a white shirt, his eyes frowning and his lips smiling. This
was his best and most characteristic expression. With her
small, nimble hands, their slender white fingers moving that
day with unusual tenseness, she repeatedly grasped the corner
of the picture, but it kept slipping and she could not get it
out. The paper knife was not at hand so she took a small
picture which lay nearby (it was a picture of Vronsky taken
in Rome, one in which he wore a round hat and had long
hair), and with it she pried loose her son's picture. "Yes,
there he is!" she said, glancing at the picture of Vronsky and
suddenly recalling who was the cause of her present misfortune. She had not thought of him even once that morning.
But now, suddenly seeing this manly, noble face, so familiar
and dear, she felt a sudden surge of love for him.

"But where is he? How could he leave me alone with my
suffering?" she suddenly thought reproachfully, forgetting
that she herself had been concealing from him everything
about her son. She sent for him, asking him to come at once.

She waited with a sinking heart, thinking of the words in which she would tell him everything and of the expressions of love with which he would console her. The servant returned with a reply that he had a guest, but that he would come at once, and that he inquired whether she could receive both him and Prince Yashvin, who had arrived in Petersburg. "He's not coming alone, though he hasn't seen me since dinner yesterday," she thought, "and I'll not be able to tell him everything, since he's coming with Yashvin." And suddenly a strange thought occurred to her: perhaps he did not love her any longer.

Reviewing the events of the last few days, it seemed to her that in everything she could find confirmation of this frightening assumption: in the fact that he did not dine at home yesterday, that he insisted that they stay in separate apartments in Petersburg, and that even now he was not coming alone to see her, as though avoiding a tête-à-tête with her.

But he must tell me so. I must know it. If I know it then I'll know what to do, she said to herself, lacking the fortitude to visualize her situation were she to convince herself of his indifference. She thought that he no longer loved her, she felt close to despair, so she was especially excited. She rang for the maid and went into the dressing room. She dressed with greater care than she had recently, as though if he did not love her any longer, he might fall in love with her again on account of a dress or coiffure that was most becoming to her.

She was still not ready when she heard the bell ring.

When she entered the drawing room, it was not he but Yashvin who met her look. Vronsky was examining the pictures of her son, which she had left on the table, and he was in no hurry to look up at her.

"We have met," she said, putting her small hand into Yashvin's huge one. He felt self-conscious (in sharp contrast with his enormous size and coarse features). "We met last year, at the races. I'll take them," she said, snatching the pictures of her son from Vronsky, who had been examining them, and looking at him significantly with her sparkling eyes. "How were the races this year? I watched them at the Corso in Rome instead. But you don't like life abroad," she said with a kind smile. "I know about you and your tastes, though we have seldom met."

"That makes me very unhappy, because my tastes are mostly bad," said Yashvin, biting his left mustache.

Noticing after a short conversation that Vronsky was glancing at the clock, Yashvin asked her how long she would stay in Petersburg, and straightening his huge frame, he reached for his cap.

"Not long, I believe," she replied, casting an embarrassed look at Vronsky.

"Then we won't see each other?" asked Yashvin, rising and turning to Vronsky. "Where are you dining?"

"Have dinner with us," said Anna resolutely, as though angry at herself for her embarrassment, but she blushed as she always did when she revealed her situation to someone new. "The dinners are not good here, but at least you two will be together. Of all his comrades in the regiment, Aleksei loves no one so much as you."

"I'll be glad to," said Yashvin, with a smile which showed Vronsky that he was much taken with Anna.

Yashvin bowed and left. Vronsky remained.

"Are you leaving too?" she asked.

"I'm already late," he said. "Go ahead! I'll be with you in a moment," he cried to Yashvin.

She took his hand, and with her eyes fixed upon him she searched her mind for words that would make him stay.

"Wait, I have to ask you something," she said, and taking his short-fingered hand, she pressed it against her neck. "Is it all right that I invited him to dinner?"

"It's fine!" he said with a calm smile which showed his even teeth, and he kissed her hand.

"Aleksei, your feelings toward me haven't changed?" she asked, pressing his hand with both of hers. "Aleksei, I'm miserable here. When will we leave?"

"Soon, soon. You'd scarcely believe how hard our life here is for me, too," he said, withdrawing his hand.

"All right, go, go!" she said, her feelings hurt, and she walked away quickly.

32

WHEN VRONSKY RETURNED, Anna was not yet home. He was told that soon after he had left, a lady had come to visit her, and that they had left together. She had left without saying where she was going, she had not returned yet, and that morning she had also gone somewhere without telling him—

all this, together with the strangely excited expression on her face that morning and the recollection of the resentment with which, in the presence of Yashvin, she had almost torn the pictures of her son from his hand, made him thoughtful. He felt that he had to talk to her. He waited for her in the drawing room. But when Anna returned she was not alone; she brought along her aunt, an old maid, Princess Oblonsky. This was the same lady who had come in the morning and with whom Anna had gone shopping. Anna apparently did not notice the worried and questioning expression on Vronsky's face, and cheerfully described to him what she had bought that morning. He saw that something unusual was going on within her: there was intense concentration in her sparkling eyes when, in passing, she rested them on him, and she spoke and moved with that nervous speed and grace that had enchanted him so delightfully during the early period of their intimacy but troubled and frightened him now.

Dinner was served for four. Everybody was ready to leave for the small dining room when Tushkevich arrived with a message for Anna from Princess Betsy. Princess Betsy apologized for not coming to say goodbye. She was not well but asked Anna to come to see her between half past six and nine. Vronsky glanced at Anna when he heard this stipulation of a time for her visit, for it showed that measures had been taken so that she might not meet anyone. But Anna seemed not to have noticed it.

"I'm very sorry, but just between half past six and nine I can't go," she said with a faint smile.

"The princess will regret it deeply."

"And so do I."

"You're probably going to hear Patti?" asked Tushkevich.

"Patti? You have given me an idea. I'd go if we could get a box."

"I can get one," volunteered Tushkevich.

"I would be very, very grateful to you," said Anna. "Would you like to stay for dinner?"

Vronsky shrugged his shoulders almost unnoticeably. He was at a complete loss to understand what Anna was doing. Why had she brought this old princess, why had she invited Tushkevich to dinner, and, most surprising, why was she going to reserve a box? Was it possible in her situation to think of going to Patti's subscription concert, where the entire society she knew would be present? He cast a thoughtful glance at her, but she replied with that same challenging look, both gay and despondent, the meaning of which he could not understand. At dinner Anna was unnaturally gay; she seemed to flirt with both Tushkevich and Yashvin. When they rose from dinner and Tushkevich went after the tickets, Yashvin went out to smoke and Vronsky took him to his apartment downstairs. After a short while he ran back up. Anna was already dressed in a light silk and velvet décolleté gown, which she had ordered in Paris. The costly white lace on her head framed her face, displaying her radiant beauty to the greatest advantage.

"Are you really going to the theater?" he asked, trying not to look at her.

"Why do you say that with such alarm?" she asked, again hurt because he did not look at her. "Why shouldn't I go?"

She seemed to have failed to understand the meaning of his words.

"Of course there is no reason why you shouldn't," he said, frowning.

"That's exactly what I say," she responded, deliberately ignoring his ironic tone and quietly pulling on her long, perfumed glove.

"Anna, for God's sake! What's the matter with you?" he said, trying to reason with her exactly as her husband once did.

"I don't understand your question."

"You know that you mustn't go."

"Why? I'm not going alone. Princess Varvara went to dress; she's going with me."

He shrugged his shoulders with an air of bewilderment and despair.

"But don't you know . . ." he began.

"But I don't want to know!" she almost shouted. "I don't want to. Do I regret what I've done? No, no, no! And if I were to start again, I would do just the same. There's one thing which is important to us, to you and to me, and that is whether we love each other. Nothing else matters. Why do we live here separately and not see each other? Why can't I go? I love you, and the rest doesn't concern me," she said in Russian, with a sparkle in her eyes, singular and incomprehensible to him, "providing you haven't changed. Why don't you look at me?"

He looked at her. He saw all the beauty of her face and

her dress, which was always so becoming to her. But now it was exactly this beauty and elegance that vexed him.

"You know that my feeling can't change, but I ask you, I beg you not to go," he said, again in French, his voice beseeching tenderly but his eyes cold.

She did not hear his words, but she saw the coldness of his look and replied with annoyance:

"And I would like you to explain why I mustn't go."

"Because it may cause you . . ." and he halted.

"I don't follow you. Yashvin *n'est pas compromettant,* and Princess Varvara is no worse than the others. . . . Here she is."

33

IT WAS THE first time that Vronsky felt annoyed, almost angry with Anna for her deliberate refusal to understand her situation. This feeling was the more intense because he could not reveal to her the cause of his annoyance. If he had told her directly what he thought, he would have said, "For you to appear in the theater in this attire, in the company of a princess so well known to everyone, means not only to acknowledge your situation as a lost woman but to challenge society, in other words to renounce it forever."

He could not say this to her. But how can she fail to understand this, and what can she be thinking? he asked himself. He felt that simultaneously his respect for her was decreasing and his awareness of her beauty was increasing.

Frowning, he returned to his room and sat down next to Yashvin, who had stretched his long legs on a chair and was drinking cognac and seltzer water. He ordered the same.

"You were talking about Lankovsky's Moguchi. It's a fine horse and I advise you to buy it," said Yashvin, glancing at his comrade's gloomy face. "Its hindquarters droop some, but you couldn't ask for better legs or head."

"I think I'll buy it," said Vronsky.

The conversation about horses interested him, but he could not forget Anna for a moment, unconsciously listening to the sounds of steps in the hall and now and then glancing at the clock on the mantlepiece.

"Anna Arkadievna ordered me to tell that she has left for the theater," a servant announced. Yashvin poured another glassful of cognac in the effervescing water, drank it and rose, buttoning his coat.

"Well, let's go," he said with a faint smile under his mustache, showing by this smile that he understood the cause of Vronsky's gloomy mood but considered it of no importance.

"I'm not going," Vronsky said gloomily.

"But I must, I promised. Well, goodbye. Why don't you take a seat in the orchestra? Take Krasinsky's seat," he added as he was leaving.

"No, I'm busy."

A woman who is your wife spells trouble; a woman who is not your wife spells calamity, thought Yashvin, as he emerged from the hotel.

Left alone, Vronsky rose from his chair and began to pace the room.

What day is it? The fourth subscription. . . . Egor, his wife and mother will probably be there. In other words—all of Petersburg. She has arrived by now, has taken off her coat and has appeared before the public. Tushkevich, Yashvin, Princess Varvara . . . he thought, visualizing them. But what's the matter with me? Am I afraid, or have I put her under Tushkevich's protection? No matter how you look at it, this is stupid, stupid. . . . And why has she put me in such a situation? he asked, waving his hands.

As he did this, his hand brushed against the little table with the seltzer water and decanter of cognac and knocked it over. He tried to catch it, missed, and in annoyance kicked it and rang the bell.

"If you want to stay with me," he said to his valet, who came in, "you must know your duties. See that it doesn't happen again. Clean it up."

The valet, knowing that it was not his fault, was about to protest, but as he glanced at his master, he understood from the expression on his face that it was best to keep silent. Moving quickly, he got down on the rug and began to pick up both the whole and broken glasses and the bottles.

"This is not your work. Send the servant to clean it up and get out my swallow-tailed coat."

Vronsky entered the theater at half-past eight. The performance was in full swing. The little old attendant helped Vronsky with his coat, recognized him, addressed him as "Your Excellency," and told him he needed no ticket but should simply call Fyodor. There was no one in the bright hallway but an attendant and two servants with fur coats over their arms, listening at the door. From behind the closed door could be heard the delicate staccato accompaniment of the orchestra and a solo female voice singing an aria with unusual clarity. The door opened, letting out an attendant who hurriedly slipped through. The aria, which was drawing to an end, came through clearly to Vronsky's ears. But the door closed at once and Vronsky did not hear the end of the aria or the cadenza, but by the thunder of the applause from behind the door he understood that the cadenza was over. When he entered the hall, brightly lit with chandeliers and bronze gas brackets, the noise continued. On the stage, the singer, her bare shoulders and diamonds aglitter, bent over and smiled, and with the help of the tenor who held her hand, gathered the bouquets which sailed clumsily over the footlights. She moved over toward a gentleman, his hair glistening with pomade and parted in the middle, who offered her something, holding out his long arms over the footlights, while those in the orchestra and in the boxes, all astir, strained forward, shouted and applauded. The conductor on the podium helped to deliver the gifts and straightened his white tie. Vronsky walked into the middle of the parterre, stopped and looked about. That day he paid less attention than usual to the familiar surroundings, the stage, the noise, to this so well known, so uninteresting, motley herd of spectators in the fully packed theater.

As always, there were ladies in the boxes, and officers in the rear of the boxes; the same—God only knew who—ladies in gay dresses, the same uniforms and dress coats; the same dirty crowds in the gallery, and among all this multitude, in the boxes and the first few rows, there were about forty *genuine* men and women. And Vronsky quickly directed his attention to these oases and at once established contact with them.

The act had ended when he entered and so, without going into his brother's box, he went over to the first row and stopped at the footlights with Serpukhovskoy, who had bent his leg and was tapping the wall with his heel. He had seen him from afar and had beckoned to him with his smile.

Vronsky had not yet seen Anna and deliberately refrained from looking in her direction. But by the direction of people's stares he knew where she was. He looked around slowly but did not look in her direction. Expecting the worst, he searched for Aleksei Aleksandrovich. To his good fortune, Aleksei Aleksandrovich was not in the theater that day.

"How little of the military is left in you," Serpukhovskoy said to him. "A diplomat, an artist, something like that."

"Yes, as soon as I returned home, I put on my swallow-tailed coat," replied Vronsky, smiling and slowly reaching for his binoculars.

"In this respect, I confess, I envy you. When I return from abroad and put on this," he said, touching the *fourragère*, "I miss my freedom."

Serpukhovskoy had long since given up all hope for Vronsky's government service, but he loved him as before and was now particularly considerate of him.

"It's a pity that you missed the first act."

Scarcely listening to him, Vronsky moved his binoculars from the dress circle to the lower tier and scanned the boxes. Next to a lady wearing a turban and a little old bald man who blinked angrily in the lens of the moving binoculars, Vronsky suddenly caught the sight of Anna's face, proud, strikingly beautiful and smiling in its frame of lace. She was in the fifth box, twenty paces from him. She was sitting up front and, turning slightly, was saying something to Yashvin. The way she held her head on her beautiful shoulders and the restrained yet animated radiance in her eyes and in her entire face made her look exactly as he remembered her at the ball in Moscow. But now her beauty affected him in a completely different way. There was nothing mysterious in his feeling for her, therefore, though her beauty attracted him even more profoundly than before, it also offended him. She did not look in his direction, but Vronsky felt that she had already seen him.

When Vronsky again directed the binoculars toward her, he noticed that Princess Varvara's face was unusually flushed, that she smiled unnaturally and kept glancing at the adjoining box. But Anna, tapping on the red plush with her folded fan and looking intently somewhere else, did not see and evidently did not wish to see what was going on in the adjoining box. The expression on Yashvin's face was the one he displayed when he was losing in a card game. Frowning, he pushed his left mustache deeper and deeper into his mouth and cast sidelong glances at the adjoining box.

This box, to their left, was occupied by the Kartasovs. Vronsky knew them and he knew that Anna had met them.

Madame Kartasov, a thin little woman, was standing in her box and, turning her back on Anna, was putting on her cape, which her husband held for her. Her face was pale and angry and she was saying something excitedly. Kartasov, a fat, bald gentleman, glanced continuously at Anna and tried to calm his wife. When his wife left, he tarried for a long while, trying to catch Anna's eye and evidently wishing to bow to her. But Anna seemed to ignore him deliberately, and with her back toward him was saying something to Yashvin, who inclined his cropped head toward her. Kartasov left without bowing and the box remained empty.

Vronsky did not understand what had actually happened between the Kartasovs and Anna, but he understood that it was something humiliating for Anna. He understood it by what he had witnessed and most of all by the expression on Anna's face. She, he knew, had summoned all her strength to be able to play the role she had undertaken. And she had fully succeeded in playing the role of appearing outwardly calm. Those who did not know her and her circle, who had not heard all the expressions of sympathy, indignation or astonishment on the part of the women, who were aroused by her daring to appear so conspicuously in her lace headdress and in all her beauty, admired the serenity and beauty of this woman without suspecting that here were the emotions of one exposed to public shame.

Knowing that something had happened but not knowing what it was exactly, Vronsky was in a state of distress and alarm, and in the hope of finding out what had happened he went over to his brother's box. He purposely chose an aisle on the opposite side from Anna's box and at the exit ran into his former regimental commander, who was conversing with two friends. Vronsky heard them mention the name of the Karenins and noticed how hurriedly the regimental commander called to Vronsky, at the same time giving a meaningful look to his friends.

"Ah, Vronsky! When will we see you at the regiment? We can't let you go without a party. You're our old wheel horse," said the regimental commander.

"I'm sorry, but I have no time for it. Some other time," said Vronsky, and he ran upstairs to his brother's box.

The old countess, Vronsky's mother, with her steel-gray curls, was in his brother's box. In the hallway Vronsky ran into Varia and Princess Sorokin.

After she had taken Princess Sorokin to Countess Vronsky, Varia extended her hand to her brother-in-law and at once began talking on the subject which concerned him. She was upset to a degree he had seldom witnessed.

"In my opinion it was base and vile, and Madame Kartasov had no right to do it. Madame Karenina . . ." she began.

"But what happened? I don't know."

"Why, haven't you heard?"

"It seems that I'm the last to hear."

"Is there a more wicked creature than this Madame Kartasov?"

"But what did she do?"

"My husband told me. . . . She insulted Karenina. Her husband began to talk to her from his box, and Madame Kartasov made a scene. They say she said something insulting in a loud voice and then left."

"Count, your mother wants you," said Princess Sorokin, looking out of the door of the box.

"I've been waiting and waiting for you," his mother said with a mocking smile. "We never see you any more."

Her son saw that she could not restrain an exultant smile.

"How are you, *Maman?* I was coming to see you," he said coldly.

"But why aren't you going *faire la cour à Madame* Karenine?" she added when Princess Sorokin stepped away. "*Elle fait sensation. On oublie la Patti pour elle.*"

"*Maman*, I asked you not to speak to me on this subject," he said with a frown.

"I say what everybody says."

Vronsky made no answer, and after exchanging a few words with Princess Sorokin, he left. In the doorway he met his brother.

"Oh, Aleksei!" said his brother. "How vile! What a stupid thing. . . . I was just going over to see her. Let's go together."

Vronsky paid no attention to him. He walked downstairs with a quick step; he felt that he must do something, but he did not know what. He was disturbed both by annoyance with her for having placed herself and him in such an embarrassing situation and by pity for her in her distress. He went down into the parterre and proceeded directly to Anna's box. Stremov was standing at the box, talking to her.

"There are no tenors nowadays. *Le moule en est brisé.*"

Vronsky stopped, bowed to her and greeted Stremov.

"I think you came too late and missed the best aria," Anna said to Vronsky with what seemed to be a mocking look.

"But I'm not much of a connoisseur," he said, looking at her sternly.

"Just like Prince Yashvin," she answered with a smile. "He finds that Patti sings too loud."

"Thank you," she said, taking with her little hand in its long glove the program Vronsky had picked up, and at this moment her beautiful face suddenly quivered. She rose and went to the rear of the box.

During the next act, when Vronsky noticed that her box was empty, he rose, and hushed by the audience which was listening in silence to the cavatina, he left the theater and drove home.

Anna was already at home. When Vronsky came in she was in the same attire as at the theater. She sat in the first armchair against the wall and looked straight ahead. She glanced at him and at once resumed her former position.

"Anna," he said.

"It's all your fault, only yours!" she cried, rising with tears of despair and anger in her voice.

"I asked you, I begged you not to go. I knew that it would be unpleasant."

"Unpleasant!" she cried. "It was terrible! As long as I live I shall not forget it. She said that it was a disgrace to sit near me."

"The words of a stupid woman," he said. "But why run the risk, why provoke. . . ."

"I hate your composure. You shouldn't have brought me to this. If you really loved me. . . ."

"Anna! What has my love to do with this . . . ?"

"Yes, if you really loved as I do, if you suffered as I do . . ." she said, looking at him with an expression of fear.

He pitied her, yet he was annoyed. He assured her of his love, for he saw that only this could calm her now, and he uttered no reproachful words, but in his heart he reproached her.

And these assurances of his love, which seemed to him so trite that he felt compunction in uttering them, she drank in, gradually calming down. The following day, completely reconciled, they left for the country.

PART SIX

1

DARIA ALEKSANDROVNA and her children were spending the summer at Pokrovskoe with her sister Kitty Levin. The house on her own estate had fallen apart completely, and Levin and his wife had induced her to spend the summer with them. Stepan Arkadievich approved of this arrangement whole-heartedly. He said that he regretted that his work deprived him of what would be his greatest happiness—spending the summer with his family in the country—and, remaining in Moscow, he occasionally spent a day or two in the country. Besides the Oblonskys, their children and the governess the Levins also had as their guest that summer the old princess, who considered it her duty to watch over her inexperienced daughter who was *in that condition*. In addition, Varenka, Kitty's friend from abroad, had kept her promise to visit her when Kitty would marry, and she was now her friend's guest. All these people were relatives and friends of Levin's wife. And though he loved them all, he somewhat missed the Levin peace and order, now smothered by the influx of the "Shcher-batsky element," as Levin termed it to himself. Of his relatives only Sergei Ivanovich visited them that summer, but even he was not of the Levin bent but of the Koznyshev, so that the Levin spirit was vanishing completely.

In the Levin house, which had been so long empty, there were so many people now that almost every room was occu-pied and almost every day as they sat down at the table the old princess had to count those present and to remove the thirteenth grandchild to a separate small table. And Kitty, who had thrown herself into the running of the household, found herself completely involved in the procurement of chickens, turkeys, and ducks, of which a great supply was needed to satisfy the summer appetites of the guests and children.

The whole family was sitting at the dinner table. Dolly's children, their governess and Varenka were planning where they should go to gather mushrooms. Sergei Ivanovich, whose intellect and erudition commanded general respect bordering on adulation, surprised everyone by entering into the discussion of mushrooming.

"Take me, too. I am very fond of gathering mushrooms," he said, looking at Varenka, "I regard it as a very good pastime."

"We'll be happy to," said Varenka, blushing. Kitty and Dolly exchanged meaningful glances. The offer of the learned and intelligent Sergei Ivanovich to go mushrooming with Varenka confirmed some of the conjectures on which Kitty had been speculating lately. She hurriedly began to talk to her mother so that her look might not be noticed. After dinner, Sergei Ivanovich sat down with his cup of coffee at the window in the drawing room, resuming a conversation with his brother and glancing at the door from which the children would emerge to go to gather mushrooms. Levin sat on the window sill next to his brother.

Kitty stood next to her husband, obviously waiting for the conversation, which did not interest her, to end so that she might tell him something.

"You have changed much since your marriage, and for the better," said Sergei Ivanovich to his brother, smiling at Kitty and also evidently little interested in the conversation, "but you have remained faithful to your zeal for defending the most paradoxical propositions."

"Katia, it's not good for you to be standing," said her husband, offering her a chair and giving her a significant look.

"Well, we have no time for this now," added Sergei Ivanovich, as the children came rushing out.

At the head of the group, in her tight stockings, was Tania, who galloped sideways, waved her basket and Sergei Ivanovich's hat, and ran straight toward him.

She boldly ran up to Sergei Ivanovich, her sparkling eyes so much like her father's handsome ones, and handed him his hat. She indicated that she wanted to put it on him, tempering her boldness with a shy and gentle smile.

"Varenka is waiting," she said, carefully putting the hat

on him when she saw by Sergei Ivanovich's smile that she might do so.

Varenka stood in the doorway, having changed into a yellow cotton dress, her head covered with a white kerchief.

"I'm coming, I'm coming, Varvara Andreyevna," said Sergei Ivanovich, finishing his coffee and placing a handkerchief and the cigarette case in his pockets.

"How charming my Varenka is! Isn't she?" Kitty asked her husband as soon as Sergei Ivanovich rose. She said it loud enough so that Sergei Ivanovich might hear, which evidently was her purpose. "And how beautiful she is! What noble beauty! Varenka!" cried Kitty, "will you be in the woods near the mill? We'll join you."

"You completely forget your condition, Kitty," said the old princess, hurriedly emerging from the doorway. "You mustn't shout that way."

Varenka, hearing Kitty's voice and her mother's reprimand, came over to Kitty with a quick, light step. Her movements, the blush that covered her animated face—all this showed that something unusual was going on within her. Kitty knew what it was that was so unusual and watched her attentively. She called Varenka now only to give her her silent blessing for the important event that, according to Kitty, should take place that afternoon in the woods.

"Varenka, I'll be happy if one thing happens," she whispered, kissing her.

"Aren't you going with us?" Varenka asked Levin in embarrassment, pretending that she did not hear what had been said.

"I'll go, but only as far as the threshing barn and I'll remain there."

"Why do you want to go there?" asked Kitty.

"I have to look over the new wagons," replied Levin. "And where will you be?"

"On the terrace."

2

THE ENTIRE COMPANY of women congregated on the terrace. They always liked to sit there after dinner, but that day they also had business to attend to. Besides sewing chemises for the baby and knitting swaddles, which kept all of them busy, that day they were occupied with making preserves without adding water, a method new to Agafia Mikhailovna. Kitty was introducing this new method, which had been used in her mother's house. Agafia Mikhailovna, who had earlier been entrusted with this matter, believed that whatever had been practiced in the Levin house could not be wrong and added water to the strawberries, asserting that it could not be done otherwise. She had been discovered doing so, and now the raspberry preserves were being prepared publicly, and Agafia Mikhailovna had to be convinced that good preserves could be prepared without adding water.

Agafia Mikhailovna, her face flushed and worried, her hair matted, her thin arms bare to the elbows, shook the pan in a circle over the brazier and looked gloomily at the raspberries, with all her heart yearning for them to congeal and remain uncooked. The princess, feeling that Agafia Mikhailovna's resentment was probably directed toward her as the principal adviser in preparing the raspberry preserves, pretended that she was busy with something else and was not interested in the raspberry preserves, and she spoke on extraneous matters, all the while casting sidelong glances at the brazier.

"I myself buy some cheap material for the maid's dresses," said the princess, continuing the conversation which they had started. "Isn't it time to skim, my dear?" she added, turning to Agafia Mikhailovna. "You certainly mustn't do it, it's too hot," she said, stopping Kitty.

"I'll do it," said Dolly, and she rose, began to move the spoon carefully over the foaming syrup, and in order to free the spoon from the scum that adhered to it, rapped it occasionally on a plate which was already covered with multicolored, yellowish-pink blotches of scum, the blood-colored syrup oozing from it. How they will relish it with their tea! she said to herself, thinking of her children and remembering how she herself, as a child, had marveled that adults did not eat the tastiest part—the scum.

"Stiva says that it's better to give them the money," said Dolly, resuming the interesting conversation on how to make presents to the servants, "but. . . ."

"How can you give them money," chorused the princess and Kitty. "They appreciate presents."

"Last year, for instance, I bought for our Matriona Semionovna not poplin but something like it," said the princess.

"I remember that she wore it on your saint's day."

"A lovely design, simple and refined. I would have made such a dress for myself if she hadn't had it. It resembles Varenka's. So nice and inexpensive."

"I believe that it's ready now," said Dolly, letting the syrup drip from the spoon.

"When it stops dripping, then it's ready. Cook it a little longer, Agafia Mikhailovna."

"These flies!" Agafia Mikhailovna said crossly. "It won't make any difference," she added.

"Ah, how sweet it looks! Don't frighten it," Kitty said suddenly, watching a sparrow which was sitting on the railing and had begun to peck at a raspberry, bending its tiny stem.

"Yes, but keep away from the brazier," said her mother.

"À propos de Varenka," said Kitty in French, as they had been doing all this time so that Agafia Mikhailovna might not understand them. "You know, Maman, for some reason I expect the decision today. You know what I mean. How wonderful it would be!"

"Look at the cunning matchmaker!" said Dolly. "How cautiously and skillfully she has brought them together!"

"But tell me, Maman, what do you think?"

"What should I think? He" (the word he meant Sergei Ivanovich) "could at any time make the best match in Russia. He's no longer so young, but I still think that even now there are many who would want him. . . . She's very sweet, but he could. . . ."

"No, you must understand, Mother, why nothing could be better either for him or for her. First of all, she's charming," said Kitty, bending one finger.

"One can see that he likes her very much," confirmed Dolly.

"And then, his social standing is so high that neither his future wife's wealth nor her social position would mean anything whatsoever to him. He needs only a good, charming, quiet wife."

"Yes, with her one could certainly enjoy a quiet life," confirmed Dolly.

"Third, she must love him. And it is. . . . I mean it would be so wonderful! . . . I'm waiting for them to come out from the woods, when everything will be settled. I'll see it at once in their eyes. It would make me so happy! What do you think, Dolly?"

"But don't get so excited. You simply mustn't get excited," said her mother.

"I'm not excited, Mother. It seems to me that today he will propose."

"What a strange thing happens when a man proposes. . . . The barrier that existed suddenly collapses," said Dolly with a pensive smile, remembering her past with Stepan Arkadievich.

"Mama, how did Papa propose to you?" suddenly asked Kitty.

"There was nothing extraordinary about it, very straightforward," replied the princess, but at this question her face suddenly brightened.

"But how did it happen? You probably loved him even before you were allowed to speak to each other."

Kitty was particularly delighted that she could now discuss as an equal with her mother the most important events in the life of a woman.

"Of course I loved him. He used to visit us in the country."

"But how did it come about, Mama?"

"You probably think that you've invented something new. It came about the same way; it was decided through our eyes and smiles. . . ."

"How well you put that, Mama! It really was through our eyes and smiles," confirmed Dolly.

"But what words did he say?"

"What words did Kostia use?"

"He wrote with a piece of chalk. It was wonderful. . . . How long ago it seems!" she said.

And the three women were absorbed in the same thoughts. Kitty was the first to break the silence. She remembered the winter which had preceded her marriage, and her infatuation with Vronsky.

"Only one thing—Varenka's former love," she said, remembering this as a natural consequence of her own thought. "I wanted somehow to tell Sergei Ivanovich about it, to prepare him. Men, all of them," she added, "are terribly jealous of our pasts."

"Not all," said Dolly. "You are judging by your husband. He is still distressed at the memory of Vronsky. He is, isn't he?"

"It's true," replied Kitty with a pensive smile in her eyes.

"But what I don't understand," said the princess, in defense of the maternal care she had given her daughter, "is what there is about your past that disturbs him. That Vronsky courted you? That happens to every girl."

"No, we aren't talking about that," said Kitty, blushing.

"But just a moment," continued her mother. "After all, it was you yourself who didn't allow me to speak to Vronsky. Don't you remember?"

"Oh, Mama!" Kitty said with a pained expression.

"Nowadays there's no way to hold you girls back. Your relationship with him could not have gone beyond what was proper. Otherwise I would have spoken to him myself. But, my dear, you mustn't get excited. Please, remember that and calm down."

"I'm quite calm, *Maman*."

"How fortunate it was for Kitty that Anna arrived just then," said Dolly, "and how unfortunate for her. How things change!" she added, struck by her own thought. "Anna was so happy then, and Kitty fancied herself unhappy. How completely things change! I often think of her."

"She's not worth thinking about. A vile, horrible, heartless woman!" said the princess, who could not forget that Kitty had married Levin and not Vronsky.

"What pleasure does it give you to talk about this?" said Kitty with annoyance. "I don't think about it and I don't want to. . . . I don't want to think about it," she repeated, listening to the familiar sound of her husband coming up the terrace steps.

"What is it that you don't want to think about?" asked Levin, entering the terrace.

But nobody answered, and he did not repeat the question.

"I'm sorry to have invaded this female domain," he said, looking at everyone with displeasure and feeling that they had been discussing something which they would not have done in his presence.

For a moment he felt that he shared the feelings of Agafia Mikhailovna, her resentment against preparing preserves without water and against the alien Shcherbatsky atmosphere in general. But he smiled and walked over to Kitty.

"Well?" he asked, looking at her with the same expression everyone now had when addressing her.

"I'm fine," said Kitty with a smile. "And what about you?"

"Those wagons can carry three times as much as a cart. Well, shall I go for the children? I've ordered the horse harnessed."

"Why, you don't intend to take Kitty in the wagonette, do you?" asked her mother reproachfully.

"But we'll drive at a walking pace, Princess."

Levin never addressed the princess as *Maman*, as one would expect, and the princess did not like this. But though Levin was very fond of the princess and respected her, he could not call her *Maman* without violating the memory of his dead mother.

"Let's go together, *Maman*," said Kitty.

"I don't want to be a witness to such recklessness."

"Then I'll walk. Walking is good for me," said Kitty. She rose, went over to her husband and took his arm.

"It's good when in moderation," said the princess.

"Well, Agafia Mikhailovna, are the preserves ready?" asked Levin, smiling at Agafia Mikhailovna and eager to cheer her up. "Is the new way all right?"

"It's probably all right. But to our way of thinking it's overcooked."

"All the better, Agafia Mikhailovna, then it won't turn sour. Our ice has melted and there's no place to keep it," said Kitty. She immediately understood her husband's intention and addressed the old woman with the same feeling. "But your pickles are such, mother says, as she's never tasted before," she added, smiling and straightening the old woman's kerchief.

Agafia Mikhailovna looked at Kitty angrily.

"Don't try to comfort me, ma'am. I can just look at you and him and cheer up," she said, and this rude reference to her husband as "him" rather than as "his honor" moved Kitty.

"Come with us to gather mushrooms. You'll show us where to look for them." Agafia Mikhailovna smiled and shook her head, as though to say, Even if I wanted to get angry with you, I couldn't.

"Follow my advice, please," said the old princess. "Place some paper soaked in rum over the preserves, and they'll never mildew, even without ice."

3

KITTY WAS particularly happy to be alone with her husband
because she had noticed that when he came onto the terrace
and asked but was not told what they had been discussing,
a shadow of worry had passed over his face, which always
reflected vividly all his emotions.

When they had walked ahead of the others and moved out
of sight of the house onto the smooth, dusty road strewn with
grains and ears of rye, she leaned more heavily on his arm
and drew it toward her. He had already forgotten the momentary unpleasantness. The thought of her pregnancy had
not left him for a moment, and now, alone with her, this
closeness to the woman whom he loved filled him with a delight, still new to him, joyous and completely free of sen-
suality. They had nothing particular to say to each other,
but he wanted to hear the sound of her voice, which like her
look, had changed with pregnancy. There was an air of mild-
ness and gravity in her voice as well as in her look, such as
is usually found in people constantly preoccupied with something they love.

"Won't you get tired? Lean harder on me," he said.

"No. I'm so glad to have a chance to be alone with you, and
I must confess that good as it is to be with them, I miss our
winter evenings together."

"That was good, but this is still better. Both are better,"
he said, pressing her arm.

"Do you know what we were discussing when you entered?"

"Preserves?"

"Yes, preserves, and then the way people propose."

"Ah!" said Levin, listening more to the sound of her voice
than to her words, all the time watching the road, which now
led through the woods, and avoiding those places where she
might stumble.

"And about Sergei Ivanovich and Verenka. Have you noticed? . . . I do hope it happens," she continued. "What's
your opinion?" and she looked into his face.

"I don't know what to say," Levin replied, smiling. "In
this respect Sergei seems very strange to me. I've told
you. . . ."

"Yes, that he was in love with the girl who died. . . ."

"That happened when I was still a child. I know it from hearsay. I remember him as he was then. He was unusually charming. And since then I've watched his way with women: he's courteous, he likes some of them, but you have the impression that to him they're not women but just people."

"Yes, but now with Varenka. . . . It seems that there's something. . . ."

"Perhaps there is. . . . But you have to know him . . . he's an unusual, remarkable person. He lives only a spiritual life. He's a man whose soul is too pure and sublime."

"What do you mean? Would this debase him?"

"No, but he's so accustomed to living a purely spiritual life that he can't adjust himself to reality, and Varenka is, after all, reality."

Levin was used to expressing his thoughts freely now, without taking pains to present them in exact terms. He knew that in such intimate moments as these his wife would understand just by a hint what he meant to say, and she did understand.

"Yes, but she doesn't have the same matter-of-factness that I do. I know that he would never fall in love with me. But she's a completely spiritual person. . . ."

"On the contrary, he's so fond of you, and it always gives me such pleasure to see how my people love you. . . ."

"Yes, he's kind to me, but. . . ."

"But not as with our late Nikolenka. . . . You fell in love with each other," Levin said, completing her thought. "Why shouldn't I talk about him?" he added. "Sometimes I reproach myself: we'll end by forgetting him. What a terrible, yet charming man he was! . . . Yes—what were we talking about?" said Levin after a silence.

"You think that he's not capable of falling in love," said Kitty, expressing his thought in her words.

"It's not that he's not capable of falling in love," said Levin, smiling, "but he lacks the weakness that's necessary. . . . I've always envied him, and even now when I'm so happy, I still envy him."

"Do you envy him for not being capable of falling in love?"

"I envy him because he is better than I," said Levin with a smile. "He doesn't live for himself. All his life is dedicated to duty. Therefore he can be calm and contented."

"And you?" Kitty asked with a mocking but loving smile.

She would have been absolutely unable to account for the line of thought that had resulted in this smile; but her conclusion was that her husband, who admired his brother and humbled himself before him, was not sincere. Kitty knew that this insincerity resulted from his love for his brother, from his feeling of guilt for being too happy, and particularly from his unflagging eagerness to become a better man. She loved this feeling in him and therefore smiled.

"And you? Why aren't you contented?" she asked with that smile.

He was delighted by her disbelief in his dissatisfaction with himself and unconsciously provoked her to explain the reason for her disbelief.

"I'm happy, but I'm not satisfied with myself . . ." he said.

"But how can you be dissatisfied if you're happy?"

"How can I explain it to you? . . . Within my heart I wish for nothing else but that you may not trip. Ah, but you mustn't jump so!" he said, interrupting the conversation with a reproach when she stepped too quickly over a tree branch that was lying in their way. "But when I think of myself and compare myself with others, particularly with my brother, I feel that I'm not good."

"But in what respect?" Kitty continued with that same smile. "Don't you also do things for others? And what about your small farmsteads, your work on the estate, your book? . . ."

"No. I know, particularly now, that it's your fault," he said, squeezing her arm. "It's not the same thing. I'm doing everything perfunctorily. If I loved my work as I love you . . . but lately I've been doing it as though I'd been ordered to."

"And what do you think about Papa?" asked Kitty. "Is he also bad because he hasn't done anything for the common good?"

"He? No. But one would have to possess the simplicity, the purity, and goodness of your father, and what do I have? I do nothing and it torments me. You're the cause of it. When you weren't here and *this* hadn't come yet," he said, pointing to her midriff with a look that she understood, "I devoted all my energy to work. But now I can't do it, and I feel guilty. I do it as though I've been ordered to, I pretend. . . ."

"Well, would you like to change places now with Sergei Ivanovich?" asked Kitty. "Would you like to work for the common good and to love only this assigned task as he does?"

"Of course not," said Levin. "But then I'm so happy that

I understand nothing. . . . So you think he'll propose today?" he added after a short silence.

"I do and then I don't. But I do so wish that it would happen. Wait." She bent down and picked a camomile flower from the edge of the road. "Well, Count: will he or won't he propose," she said, handing him the flower.

"He will, he won't," Levin kept repeating, tearing off the narrow white petals, the road's dust on them.

"No, no!" Kitty cried, seizing his hand and stopping him as she anxiously watched his fingers. "You tore off two just then."

"Well then, this small one won't count," said Levin, tearing off a short, half-grown petal. "And now the wagonette has caught up with us."

"Aren't you tired, Kitty?" exclaimed the princess.

"Not at all."

"Perhaps you'll sit in here, providing the horses are gentle and continue at a walking pace."

But it did not pay to do so. It was not far, and they all went on foot.

4

SURROUNDED BY the children, with whom she kept busy good-naturedly and cheerfully, and evidently excited by the thought that the man she liked might propose, Varenka looked very attractive, with her white kerchief over her black hair. Sergei Ivanovich walked at her side, feasting his eyes on her. As he looked at her he recalled all the charming words he had heard her say, all the good he knew about her, and realized more and more clearly that his feeling toward her was that special feeling that he had experienced many years earlier and only once in his lifetime, in the days of his early youth. The feeling of joy awakened by his nearness to her continued to grow stronger, reaching such a stage that when he had found and placed in her basket a huge birch mushroom, curling at the edges and held on a slender stem, and looked into her eyes and noticed the blush of joyous and fearful agitation that spread over her face, he himself became confused, remained silent, and gave her a smile which said too much.

If this is so, he said to himself, I must think it over and come to a decision, and not abandon myself to a passing fancy like a boy.

"Now I'll go and gather mushrooms by myself, or else no one will notice my contribution," he said, leaving the edge of the woods, where they had been walking on low, silky grass amidst scattered birch trees, for the middle of the woods, where the white trunks of the birch trees were interspersed with gray aspens and dark hazelbushes. After he had gone about forty paces and had come behind a spindle bush in full flower, its catkins rose-red, Sergei Ivanovich stopped, knowing that he could not be seen. Complete silence surrounded him. Only overhead, in the birch trees under which he was standing, flies hummed incessantly like a swarm of bees, and from time to time he could hear the sound of children's voices. Suddenly, not far from the edge of the woods, there sounded the contralto voice of Varenka calling Grisha, and a joyous smile appeared on Sergei Ivanovich's face. Conscious of this smile, he shook his head in disapproval of his state of mind, reached for a cigar, and was going to light it. It took a long time before he succeeded in lighting a match on the trunk of a birch tree. At each attempt the tender membrane of the white bark clung to the tip of the match and smothered the flame. At last one of the matches caught, and the aromatic smoke of the cigar spread like a wide, billowing tablecloth and rose forward, above the bush under the drooping branches of the birch. Watching the band of smoke, Sergei Ivanovich proceeded slowly, pondering his present state.

But why not? he thought. If this were only a passing, passionate impulse; if I merely felt this attraction, this mutual attraction (and I may call it mutual), and suspected that it might go contrary to the whole pattern of my life; if I felt that by yielding to this attraction I might betray my calling and my duty . . . but such is not the case. The only thing I can have against it is that after I lost Marie, I promised myself to remain faithful to her memory. This is the only thing I have against my present feeling. . . . It's important, Sergei Ivanovich said to himself, conscious at the same time that this consideration could be of no importance to him personally and could only possibly impair other people's opinion of his role as a romantic. And aside from this, no matter how much I may search, I'll find nothing to be said against my feeling. Even by using reason alone, I couldn't have come to a better decision.

However many women and girls of his acquaintance he recalled, he could not think of a single one who so completely possessed all the qualities, literally all of them, that he, after calm reasoning, wanted in a wife. She had all the charm and freshness of youth, but she was not a child, and if she loved him, she loved sensibly, as a woman should. This was one of her virtues. Then, far from being a woman of society, she apparently even had an aversion toward it, yet at the same time she was familiar with the ways of society and had all the manners of a well-bred lady, without which Sergei Ivanovich could not visualize anyone as his life's companion. And last, she was religious, not as a child is, unconsciously religious and good, as, for instance, Kitty was, but her whole life was based on religious convictions. Even in other details Sergei Ivanovich found in her all that he wanted to find in a wife: she was poor and lonely and would not bring with her a host of relatives and their atmosphere into her husband's house, as he saw Kitty doing, but would feel obligated to her husband for everything, and this, too, he had always expected in his future family life. And this girl who possessed all these qualities loved him. He was modest but could not help seeing it. And he loved her. There was one objection—his age. But he came from long-lived stock, he did not yet have a single gray hair, no one would credit him with his forty years, and he remembered Varenka saying that only in Russia did people of fifty consider themselves old, but in France a man of fifty looked upon himself as *dans la force de l'âge,* and a man of forty—*un jeune homme.* But does age mean anything when one feels that he is as young at heart as he was twenty years earlier? Wasn't it a young feeling that he now experienced when, emerging again toward the edge of the woods, but from the opposite side, he saw in the bright light of the slanting rays of the sun the graceful figure of Varenka in her yellow dress, a basket in her hand, as she walked with her light step past the trunk of an old birch? Wasn't it a young feeling that made the impression of Varenka fuse with the impression of the view which had struck him with its beauty—the view of the yellowing oat field bathed in the slanting sunbeams, and beyond the field, of the far-off old forest, dappled with yellow and vanishing in the azure distance? His heart contracted with joy. A feeling of tenderness possessed him. He felt that he had come to a decision. Varenka, who had just bent down to pick

up a mushroom, rose with a supple movement and looked
around. Tossing aside his cigar, Sergei Ivanovich headed
toward her with a resolute step.

5

VARVARA ANDREYEVNA, when I was still young, I created my
ideal of a woman, the one with whom I would fall in love and
whom I would be happy to call my wife, I have lived a long
life and now for the first time I have found in you everything
for which I have been searching. I love you and I ask for your
hand.

Sergei Ivanovich was saying this to himself as he came within ten steps of Varenka. She was on her knees, using her hands
to protect a mushroom from Grisha and calling little Masha.

"Here, here! Little ones! There are lots of them here!" she
cried in her pleasant, low-pitched voice.

She saw Sergei Ivanovich approach but did not rise nor
change her position; but everything told him that she knew
he was approaching and that it made her happy.

"Well, did you find anything?" she asked, turning her
lovely face and smiling gently from under the white handkerchief.

"Not a single one," said Sergei Ivanovich. "And you?"

She did not answer, busy as she was with the children who
surrounded her.

"And that one, near the twig," she said, pointing out to
little Masha a small mushroom whose pink, resilient crown was
being cut into by a dry blade of grass from which it was
trying to free itself. She rose after Masha had picked up both
halves of the mushroom she had broken. "It reminds me of my
childhood," she added, walking away from the children with
Sergei Ivanovich.

They took a few steps in silence. Varenka felt that he
wanted to say something; she guessed what it was, and her
heart sank with joyous excitement and fear. They were now
so far that no one could hear them, but he still did not begin.
It would have been better if Varenka had remained silent. It
would have been easier to say what they had intended to say
after a silence than directly after their remarks about mushrooms. But against her will, as though inadvertently, Varenka

said, "So you didn't find any? Well, there are always fewer inside the woods."

Sergei Ivanovich sighed and said nothing. He was annoyed that she had begun to talk about mushrooms. He wanted her to return to the words she had used in mentioning her childhood, but as though against his will, after a short silence he remarked in reply to her last words:

"I've only heard that white mushrooms grow mainly at the edge of the woods, but I can't tell which are the white ones."

A few more minutes passed; they walked away still further from the children and were completely alone. Varenka's heart pounded so that she heard it beat and felt that she was blushing, paling, and blushing again.

To be the wife of such a man as Koznyshev, after her position with Madame Stahl, seemed to her the height of happiness. In addition, she was almost sure that she was in love with him. And now it was about to be decided. She was frightened. She was frightened by what he would say and by what he would not say.

It would have to be decided now or never. Sergei Ivanovich felt the same. Everything in Varenka's look, in her blush, in her downcast eyes, betrayed painful expectation. Sergei Ivanovich saw it and felt sorry for her. He even felt that it would be insulting to say nothing. In his mind he quickly went over all the reasons in favor of his decision. He repeated to himself the words in which he had intended to propose. But instead of these words, moved by some unexpected thought, he suddenly said:

"What then is the difference between a white and a birch mushroom?"

Varenka's lips trembled with agitation as she answered, "There is almost no difference in their crowns, only in their stems."

And as soon as she pronounced these words, both he and she knew that all was ended, that what had to be said would remain unsaid, and their agitation, which had reached its highest point, began to subside.

"The stem of a birch mushroom reminds me of a two-day old stubble on the chin of a dark-haired man," said Sergei Ivanovich, now calm.

"Yes, that is so," Varenka replied with a smile, and unconsciously they changed the direction of their walk. They were approaching the children. Varenka was pained and ashamed, but at the same time she had a feeling of relief.

When he returned home, Sergei Ivanovich went over all his reasoning and decided that he had been mistaken. He could not betray the memory of Marie.

"Quiet, children, quiet!" Levin shouted somewhat crossly at the children, placing himself before his wife to protect her from the crowd of children who rushed toward them with shrieks of joy.

After the children, Sergei Ivanovich and Varenka also emerged from the woods. There was no need for Kitty to ask Varenka. By their calm and somewhat shamefaced expressions she knew that her plans had not matured.

"Well?" her husband asked as they were returning home.

"It didn't take," said Kitty, her smile and manner of speaking much like her father's, something Levin often noted with pleasure.

"What do you mean, it didn't take?"

"This is what I mean," she said, taking her husband's hand, lifting it, and touching it with her closed lips. "The way one kisses a bishop's hand."

"On whom didn't it take?"

"On either one. But it should have been done this way. . . ."

"Moujiks are riding by. . . ."

"They didn't notice."

6

During the children's tea the adults were seated on the balcony, conversing as if nothing had happened, though everyone, and particularly Sergei Ivanovich and Varenka, knew very well that a very important though negative event had occurred. Each of them felt like a pupil who, having failed in his test, had to repeat the grade or be expelled from school. All those present, also aware that something had happened, spoke with animation of unrelated matters. That evening Levin and Kitty felt particularly happy and in love with each other. And they felt guilty at being so happy in their love, for it intimated unpleasantly that others wanted to feel likewise but could not.

"Remember my words: Alexandre won't come," said the old princess.

That evening they were expecting Stepan Arkadievich to arrive by train and the old prince had written that he also might come.

"And I know why," continued the princess. "He says that the young couple should be left alone at this time."

"But Papa has already left us alone. We haven't seen him," said Kitty. "And what kind of a young couple are we? We are already so old."

"But if he doesn't come, I too will leave you, my children," said the princess with a sad sigh.

"Why, Mama?" cried both daughters.

"Just think how hard it is for him! Now. . . ."

And quite unexpectedly the old princess' voice trembled. Her daughters fell silent and exchanged looks. "*Maman* always manages to find something sad," their looks said. They did not know that no matter how much the princess enjoyed her stay with her daughter, or how certain she was that she was needed here, she had been feeling profoundly sorry for herself and her husband since their beloved youngest daughter had married, leaving their family nest empty.

"What is it, Agafia Mikhailovna?" Kitty suddenly asked the old nurse, who had stopped near her with a mysterious and meaningful expression on her face.

"About supper."

"Very well," said Dolly, "you go and attend to it and I'll go over the lesson with Grisha. He hasn't really done anything today."

"It's my turn, Dolly, I'll do it," Levin said, springing to his feet.

Grisha, who had already entered the gymnasium, had to redo his lessons during the summer. Daria Aleksandrovna, who had been studying his Latin with him while in Moscow, had set a rule when she arrived at the Levins': to go over the most difficult assignments in arithmetic and Latin with him at least once a day. Levin volunteered to take her place. But once she had listened to Levin conduct the lesson and had noticed that he did not do it as the teacher had been doing in Moscow, and though she was embarrassed and tried to spare his feelings, she told him resolutely that one must follow the textbook as the teacher did, and that she would prefer to do it herself again. Levin was annoyed at the lack of interest on the part of Stepan Arkadievich, who, instead of taking personal charge of his son's instruction, entrusted it to his wife, who was completely incompetent to do it. He was also annoyed by the teachers for teaching the children so badly. But he promised his sister-in-law that he would coach the boy the way she wanted. And he continued coaching Grisha, not in his own way, but following the book and, as a result, did it reluctantly, often forgetting the time for study. And that is what had happened that day.

"No, Dolly, I'll go. You stay here," he said. "We'll do everything as it should be done—following the book. But when Stiva comes, we'll go hunting and then I'll be excused."

And Levin went to Grisha.

Varenka told Kitty something along the same line. Even in the happy, well-managed Levin household Varenka found ways to be useful.

"I'll attend to supper, and you remain here," she said, and she went to see Agafia Mikhailovna.

"All right, but they probably didn't get any pullets. Then take ours. . . ." said Kitty.

"Agafia Mikhailovna and I will take care of it." And Varenka disappeared behind the door.

"What a dear girl!" said the princess.

"Not a dear, *Maman*, but a gem that is not often found."

"So you are expecting Stepan Arkadievich today?" said Sergei Ivanovich, evidently unwilling to continue the conversation about Varenka. "It's hard to find two brothers-in-law who resemble each other less," he said with a subtle smile. "One always active, happiest in the company of people as a fish in water, the other, our Kostia, lively, quick, considerate, but when among people, he either shrivels up or struggles senselessly as a fish on land."

"Yes, he's very thoughtless," said the princess, addressing Sergei Ivanovich. "I did want to ask you to talk to him about the fact that she" (she indicated Kitty) "must not remain here and must by all means go to Moscow. He said that he would invite a doctor. . . ."

"*Maman*, he'll do everything, he agrees to everything," said Kitty, annoyed that her mother was appealing to Sergei Ivanovich to interfere in this matter.

In the middle of the conversation they heard the sounds of snorting horses and of wheels rolling on the gravel of the alley.

Before Dolly had the chance to rise to meet her husband, Levin jumped down through the window of the room below, in which Grisha was having his lesson, and then helped Grisha down.

"It's Stiva!" shouted Levin from under the balcony. "We've finished, Dolly, don't worry!" he added and, like a boy, ran toward the carriage.

"*Is, ea, id, ejus, ejus ejus,*" shouted Grisha, bounding along the alley.

"And there's someone else. Probably Papa," shouted Levin, stopping at the entrance to the alley. "Kitty, don't walk down the steep staircase, but go around."

But Levin was mistaken in believing that the other man in the carriage was the old prince. When he came closer he saw that it was not the prince sitting next to Stepan Arkadievich but a handsome portly young man in a Scotch cap with its long ribbons hanging down in back. It was Vasenka Veslovsky, the Shcherbatskys' second cousin, a dashing Petersburg-Moscow young man, "a very nice fellow and ardent hunter," as Stepan Arkadievich introduced him.

Not in the least embarrassed by the disappointment he caused everyone by having appeared in place of the old prince, Veslovsky greeted Levin cheerfully, reminding him that they had met, and taking hold of Grisha, he lifted him into the carriage over the pointer that Stepan Arkadievich had brought along.

Levin did not take a seat in the carriage, but walked behind. He was somewhat annoyed that the old prince, whom he loved more the better he knew him, had not arrived, but instead here was this Vasenka Veslovsky, a totally alien and unwanted person. He seemed still more alien and unwanted to Levin when, on coming up to the porch where the whole animated crowd of adults and children had asembled, he saw that Vasenka Veslovsky was kissing Kitty's hand with particular tenderness and gallantry.

"Your wife and I are cousins and old friends," said Vasenka Veslovsky, again shaking Levin's hand vigorously.

"Well, is there any game?" Stepan Arkadievich asked Levin, barely managing to address his greetings to everyone. "He and I have the most savage intentions. . . . Why, *maman*, they haven't been in Moscow since then. . . . Well, Tania, I've something for you. You'll find it in the back of the carriage," he said, turning in every direction. "How lovely you look, Dollenka," he said to his wife, kissing her hand once more, holding it in his own, and patting it with his other hand.

Levin, who a moment earlier was in the happiest frame of mind, now looked gloomily at everyone and nothing pleased him.

Whom did he kiss yesterday with those same lips? he thought, watching how affectionate Stepan Arkadievich was with his wife. He glanced at Dolly and felt a dislike for her, too.

She has no faith in his love. Why then does she look so happy? It's disgusting! thought Levin.

He glanced at the princess, who had seemed so dear a moment ago, and did not care for the manner in which she was welcoming this Vasenka with his ribbons, as though to her own home.

Even Sergei Ivanovich, who also came out on the porch, seemed to him distasteful for the sham friendliness with which he met Stepan Arkadievich, for Levin knew that his brother did not like and did not respect Oblonsky.

And Varenka also seemed to him offensive, as, with the air of a *sainte nitouche* she met this gentleman, whereas all she thought about was how to get married.

But most offensive of all was Kitty, with her way of entering into the general spirit of gaiety with which this gentleman was celebrating his arrival in the country, as though it were a holiday for himself and everyone else, and Levin particularly disliked the peculiar smile with which she replied to his.

Speaking in loud voices, they all entered the house, but as soon as everyone was seated, Levin turned around and left.

Kitty noticed that something was bothering her husband. She tried to find a moment to talk with him privately, but he hastily left her, saying that he had to go to the office. It had been a long time since he considered his business affairs as urgent as he did that day. It's a holiday for all of them in there, he thought, but affairs here know no holiday, they brook no delay, and without them life cannot go on.

7

LEVIN returned home only after his wife had sent word that supper was ready. Kitty and Agafia Mikhailovna were on the stairs, conferring about the wines for supper.

"Why are you making such a fuss about it? Serve the usual."

"No, Stiva won't drink it. . . . Kostia, wait, what's the matter?" asked Kitty, hurrying after him. But without waiting for her, he strode grimly toward the dining room and there at once entered into the lively general conversation led by Vasenka Veslovsky and Stepan Arkadievich.

"Well, are we going hunting tomorrow?" asked Stepan Arkadievich.

"Please, let's go," said Veslovsky, seating himself sideways on another chair and folding his plump leg underneath him.

"I'd be very glad to. Have you already hunted this year?" Levin asked Veslovsky, staring at his foot, but speaking with feigned courtesy, a trait of his that was so familiar to Kitty and so unbecoming to him. "As for double snipe, I doubt whether we'll find many, but there will be plenty of woodcocks. But we'll have to leave early. Won't you be tired? Are you tired, Stiva?"

"I, tired? I've never yet been tired. Let's stay up all night. We'll take a walk."

"Good enough, let's not sleep tonight. Excellent!" interjected Veslovsky.

"Oh, we know very well that you can stay awake and disturb the sleep of others," Dolly said to her husband with a scarcely noticeable touch of irony, which she now almost always used when she addressed her husband. "But in my opinion it's time to retire . . . I'll go without supper."

"No, stay for a while, Dollenka," said Stepan Arkadievich, going over to her around the large table at which they were having their supper. "I still have so much to tell you!"

"I wonder."

"You know, Veslovsky has been to see Anna. And he is going again. They're only seventy versts from you. And I, also, will go to see her, without fail. Veslovsky, come here!"

Vasenka came over to the ladies and sat next to Kitty.

603

"Oh, please tell us, have you seen her? How is she?" asked Daria Aleksandrovna, turning to him.

Levin remained at the other end of the table, and without interrupting his conversation with the princess and Varenka, he noticed that Stepan Arkadievich, Dolly, Kitty and Veslovsky were engaged in an animated and mysterious conversation. And not only did he see that this was a mysterious conversation but he also noticed on his wife's face the serious expression with which she looked fixedly on the handsome face of Vasenka as he related something with great animation.

"Theirs is a very pleasant home," Vasenka related about Vronsky and Anna. "Of course I'm not the one to judge, but there's a true family spirit in their home."

"And what do they intend to do?"

"It seems that they plan to spend the winter in Moscow."

"How nice it would be to meet in their home! When are you going?" Stepan Arkadievich asked Vasenka.

"I'll spend the month of July with them."

"And will you go?" Stepan Arkadievich asked his wife.

"I've wanted to go for a long time and I'll go without fail," answered Dolly. "I feel sorry for her and I know her. She's a fine woman. I'll go alone, after you leave, and I'll be in no one's way. It'll be even better without you."

"Very well," said Stepan Arkadievich. "And you, Kitty?"

"I? Why should I go?" said Kitty, flaring up. And she glanced at her husband.

"Have you met Anna Arkadievna?" Veslovsky asked her. "She is a charming woman."

"Yes," she replied to Veslovsky's question, blushing still more. She rose and went over to her husband.

"So you are going hunting tomorrow?" she said.

During these few moments Levin's jealousy had grown very intense particularly because of the blush which covered her cheeks when she spoke to Veslovsky. Now, listening to her words, he understood them in his own way. However strange it seemed to him later when he thought of it, it was obvious to him now that when she asked him whether he would go hunting, she did it only because she wanted to know whether he would afford this pleasure to Vasenka Veslovsky with whom, in his opinion, she was already in love.

"Yes, I am," he replied in an unnatural voice, offensive to himself.

"No, it would be better for you to stay here tomorrow, for

Dolly hasn't seen her husband for such a long time. Go the day after tomorrow," said Kitty.

The meaning of these words Levin interpreted thus: "Don't separate me from *him*. I don't care if you go, but let me enjoy the company of this charming young man."

"Well, if you want us to, we'll stay at home tomorrow," Levin replied with strained courtesy.

In the meantime Vasenka, completely unaware of the suffering his presence had been creating, rose from the table after Kitty, and watching her with a smiling and affectionate look, went over to join her.

Levin saw that look. He paled and could not catch his breath for a moment. How dare he look at my wife that way? he thought, seething with fury.

"Then tomorrow? Do let's go!" said Vasenka, sitting on a chair and again, as was his habit, doubling his leg underneath him.

Levin's jealousy grew still more intense. He already visualized himself as a betrayed husband, whom his wife and her lover needed only as a means to enjoy the comforts and pleasures of life. . . . Yet, in spite of this, he kindly and courteously inquired of Vasenka about his hunting, his gun and boots, and agreed to go hunting the next day.

To Levin's good fortune, the old princess put an end to his suffering by rising and advising Kitty to go to sleep. But even here Levin was not spared new suffering. Taking leave of his hostess, Vasenka again wanted to kiss her hand, but Kitty, blushing, withdrew it and said to him with a naïve rudeness for which her mother reprimanded her later:

"This is not our custom."

In Levin's opinion, she was guilty of having encouraged such a relationship, and more so for showing so awkwardly that she enjoyed it.

"But who wants to sleep?" asked Stepan Arkadievich who, after the several glasses of wine he had consumed at dinner, was now in his most charming poetic mood.

"Look, Kitty," he said, pointing to the moon which was rising from behind the linden trees. "How beautiful! Veslovsky, this is the time for a serenade. You know, he has a good voice, and we were singing some songs on the way over. He brought some beautiful music, two new songs. We should sing them with Varvara Andreyevna."

After the group broke up, Stepan Arkadievich and Veslovsky continued to walk along the alley, practicing a new song.

Seated in a chair in his wife's bedroom, Levin listened gloomily to their voices and kept stubbornly silent as she repeatedly inquired what was the matter with him. But when at last she herself asked with a shy smile, "Perhaps there was something about Veslovsky that you didn't like?" he broke down and told her everything. What he was saying offended her and so vexed him all the more.

He stood in front of her with a frightening gleam in his eyes under his frowning brows and pressed his strong hands against his chest, as though trying to exert all his efforts to control himself. The expression on his face would have seemed grim and even cruel if it had not revealed his suffering at the same time, and this moved her. His jaw trembled and his voice faltered.

"I want you to understand that I'm not jealous. Jealousy is an abominable word. I can't be jealous and believe that. . . . I can't tell you what I feel, but it's horrible. . . I'm not jealous, but I'm offended; I'm humiliated when someone dares to think, dares to look at you in such a way. . . ."

"But in what way?" asked Kitty, trying to recollect as conscientiously as possible all the words and gestures of that evening and all their nuances.

Deep within her heart she felt that there had been something just at the moment when he came over to her at the other end of the table, but she did not dare to confess it even to herself, and still less to tell it to him and thus cause him still more suffering.

"But what could be attractive about me as I am now? . . ."

"Ah!" he shouted, clutching at his head. "You shouldn't have said that. It means, if you were attractive. . . ."

"No, Kostia, wait, listen to me!" she said, looking at him with an expression of suffering and sympathy. "What can you be thinking? When no other men exist for me, not one! . . . Would you like me to see no one?"

At first she was offended by his jealousy. She was annoyed that she was not permitted to enjoy the smallest diversion, the most innocent one. But now she would sacrifice not only such trifles but everything to bring him peace of mind and to spare him the agony he was suffering.

"Please understand how horrible and ridiculous my situation is," he continued, whispering despondently. "He's here in my house; he has actually committed no impropriety, except to act with undue familiarity and to double his leg under him. He considers this to be excellent manners so I must be courteous to him."

"But, Kostia, you are exaggerating," said Kitty, deep in her heart rejoicing in the intensity of his love for her, expressed now in this fit of jealousy.

"Most terrible of all is that you, who are now so sacred to me, as you always have been, that we are so happy, so unusually happy, and suddenly such trash. . . . Not trash, why should I abuse him? I've nothing to do with him. But why should my happiness, and yours . . . ?"

"You know, I understand how it happened," Kitty began.

"How? How?"

"I noticed how you looked when we were talking at the table."

"Well?" Levin said fearfully.

She told him what they had talked about. And while telling it, she breathed heavily with excitement. Levin kept silent; then he looked intently at her pale, frightened face and suddenly clutched at his head.

"Katia, I'm torturing you! My darling, forgive me! It's insanity! Katia, it's insanity. Katia, it's all my fault. Does such a trifle justify this suffering?"

"No, but I feel sorry for you."

"For me? For me? Who am I? A madman! . . . But why should you suffer? It's terrible to think that any stranger may upset our happiness."

"Of course, this is what's so painful. . . ."

"Very well then, I'll ask him to spend the whole summer here, and I'll treat him with the utmost courtesy," said Levin, kissing her hands. "You'll see. Tomorrow. . . . Of course, we are going tomorrow."

8

THE NEXT MORNING the ladies had not yet arisen when the hunter's vehicles, a wagonette and a small cart, were already standing at the entrance. Laska, who ever since early morning had known that they were going hunting, had yelped and leaped to her heart's desire. She was now seated on the wagonette next to the coachman, and excited and displeased with the hunter's tardiness, she stared at the door through which they had not yet emerged. Vasenka Veslovsky came out first, in new, large boots, which reached to the middle of his thick thighs, a green blouse tied with a new cartridge belt smelling of leather and wearing his cap with its ribbons and carrying a brand-new, English hammerless gun without a sling. Laska bounded toward him, greeted him, and after a few leaps, asked him in her own way whether the others would emerge soon. Getting no reply, she returned to her observation post and again sat motionless, turning her head sideways and pricking one ear. At last the door opened with a crash, and out came Krak, Stepan Arkadievich's yellow spotted pointer, flying, turning and leaping in the air, followed by Stepan Arkadievich himself with a gun in his hand and a cigar in his mouth. "Quiet, Krak, quiet!" he called gently to the dog, which threw its paws up on his chest and stomach and entangled itself in the game bag. Stepan Arkadievich was dressed in torn pants and a short coat, his feet in coarse wrappings with low boots over them. On his head he wore a dilapidated hat, but his gun was a jewel of the latest model, and his game bag and cartridge belt, though worn, were of the best make.

Vasenka Veslovsky was not yet familiar with this mark of true hunter foppery—to be dressed in rags but have hunting gear of the best quality. He understood it now, looking at Stepan Arkadievich, whose elegant, well-fed, cheerful figure of a gentleman sparkled in these rags, and he decided that without fail he would be dressed in the same style at the next hunt.

"Well, what about our host?" he asked.

"A young wife, you know," said Stepan Arkadievich with a smile.

"Yes, and such a charming one."

"He's already dressed. He probably ran up to see her once more."

Stepan Arkadievich had guessed right. Levin had run back to his wife to ask her once more whether she had forgiven him for the foolish way he had acted the day before, and also to ask her to be more careful for the sake of Christ. Most important, she should avoid the children, for there is always a danger that they might push her. Then she had to assure him once more that she was not angry with him for leaving her for two days, and he begged her not to fail to send him a note the next morning by mounted messenger, even if she were to write no more than two words, so that he might know that everything went well with her.

As always, Kitty was sorry to part with her husband for two days, but noticing how animated he looked now, how unusually large and strong he appeared in his hunting boots and white shirt, and observing the hunter's peculiar sparkle of excitement, incomprehensible to her, she forgot her worries because of his pleasure and parted with him cheerfully.

"I'm sorry, gentlemen!" he said, running out on the porch. "Did you pack breakfast? Why is the sorrel on the right? Well, it doesn't matter. Here, Laska, sit!"

"Put them with the heifers," he said, addressing the cowherd who was waiting for him at the porch to ask what to do about the bullocks. "I'm sorry, here's another rascal coming."

Levin jumped off the wagonette, on which he had already seated himself, and went toward the carpenter, who was coming up to the porch with a yardstick.

"You didn't come to the office yesterday, but now you are delaying me. Well, what is it?"

"Allow me to add another flight. Just three steps. We'll fit it exactly. It'll be much more convenient."

"You should have listened to me," Levin replied with annoyance. "I told you that first you should make the stringboards and then the steps. You can't correct it now. Do as I tell you; build a new one."

What happened was that in the wing the carpenter was building he had made a mistake in the construction of the staircase by building it separately without first measuring the angle of ascent. The result was that all the steps slanted when the staircase was put in place. And now the carpenter wanted to add three steps to the staircase.

"It would be much better."

"But where will it reach with your three steps?"

"If you please," the carpenter said with a contemptuous smile, "it'll come up just to the right point. You see, it'll start at the bottom," he said with a convincing gesture, "and will go up, and up, and come to the right place."

"But three steps will make it longer. . . . Where will it reach then?"

"You see, it'll start at the bottom and will get there," the carpenter continued, obstinately and persuasively.

"It'll reach the wall at the ceiling."

"If you please, it'll start at the bottom and will go up and reach its place."

Levin reached for the ramrod and began to draw the design of the staircase on the ground.

"Well, do you see now?"

"As you say," said the carpenter, his eyes suddenly brightening. Evidently he at last understood what had to be done. "It seems that I will have to build a new one."

"Well, do as you're told!" cried Levin, taking his seat in the wagonette. "Let's go! Filipp, hold the dogs!"

With his family and farm cares behind him, Levin experienced such a deep feeling of joy and anticipation that he had no desire to talk. In addition, he was seized with a feeling of intense agitation, which every hunter experiences as he approaches the scene of action. All that interested him now was whether they would find any game in the Kolpensky marsh, whether Laska would compare well with Krak, and whether he would be a good shot that day. Would he disgrace himself in the presence of the stranger? Would Oblonsky outshoot him? Such were his thoughts.

Oblonsky felt the same, and he too was not given to talk. Only Vasenka Veslovsky chattered happily without stopping. Listening to him, now, Levin felt guilty for having been so unjust to him the night before. Vasenka was indeed a nice fellow, simple, good-natured, and cheerful. If Levin had met him when he was single they would have become friends. Levin somewhat disliked his festive attitude toward life and the air of undue familiarity in his elegance. He seemed to ascribe to himself without any hesitation some special importance because of his long nails, his cap, and the like; but one could forgive him this on account of his good nature and his decency. Levin liked him because he was well brought up, because his French and English were excellent, and because he was a man of his own group.

Vasenka greatly admired the Don steppe horse attached to the left. He kept praising it.

"How nice it would be to gallop over the steppe on this horse. Don't you think so?" he asked.

There was something savage and poetic in his vision of riding this horse of the steppe, and though it made little sense, his naïveté, particularly when combined with his handsome appearance, kind smile, and graceful movements, was very appealing. Whether it was because his nature pleased Levin, or because Levin, eager to atone for the injustice of the day before, was trying to find in him only good, he enjoyed his company.

After they had covered about three versts, Veslovsky suddenly discovered that he was missing his cigars and wallet and did not know whether he had lost them or left them behind on the table. There were three hundred and seventy rubles in the wallet, so the matter had to be attended to.

"If it's all right with you, I'll gallop home on this Don trace horse. I'll enjoy it! All right?" he said, ready to mount the horse.

"No, why should you?" replied Levin, calculating that Vasenka weighed at least two hundred and fifteen pounds. "I'll send the coachman."

The coachman left on the trace horse, and Levin himself now drove the remaining pair.

9

"WELL, WHAT'S OUR ITINERARY? Tell us in detail," said Stepan Arkadievich.

"Our plan is as follows. We are going as far as Gvozdev. On this side of Gvozdev there's a double-snipe marsh, and beyond Gvozdev there are some excellent snipe marshes where double snipe also may be found. It's hot now, and toward evening (it's about twenty versts) we'll arrive. We'll do some hunting in the evening, stay overnight, and in the morning we'll move to the large marshes."

"And isn't there anything along the way?"

"There is, but it'll delay us, and it's hot. There are two fine places, but there's not much there."

Levin himself would have liked to stop at these places, but they were close to his house, he could go there at any time, and, moreover, they were not large enough for three hunters. That is why he hid the truth by saying that there wasn't much there. When they came alongside the small marsh, Levin wanted to pass it by, but the experienced hunting eye of Stepan Arkadievich immediately noticed the grassy marsh which was visible from the road.

"Shall we go in?" he asked, pointing at the marsh.

"Please, Levin! An excellent idea!" Vasenka Veslovsky began, and Levin could not decline.

Even before they had a chance to stop, the dogs, over-taking one another, dashed toward the marsh.

"Krak! Laska! . . ."

The dogs returned.

"It'll be too crowded for three. I'll remain here," said Levin, hoping that they would find nothing but lapwings which, frightened by the dogs, were swaying in their flight, wailing pitifully above the marsh.

"No, come with us, Levin! Let's go together!" said Veslov-sky.

"There's really not enough room. Laska, back! Laska! You don't need another dog, do you?"

Levin remained at the wagonette and watched the hunters with envy. The hunters covered all of the small marsh. Be-sides a little hen and some lapwings, of which Veslovsky bagged one, there was no other game.

"You see, I didn't begrudge you the marsh," said Levin, "but it was just a waste of time."

"But we enjoyed it. Did you watch us?" said Vasenka Veslovsky, awkwardly climbing into the wagonette with his gun and lapwing in his hand. "How neatly I got it! Don't you agree? Well, when are we coming to the real thing?"

Suddenly the horses dashed forward. Levin's head struck against the barrel of a gun and a shot sounded. Actually the shot had sounded earlier, but this was how it seemed to Levin. It turned out that Vasenka Veslovsky, when pulling the triggers, had pulled one only, leaving the other still cocked. The shot went into the ground without harming any-one. Stepan Arkadievich shook his head and laughed re-proachfully at Veslovsky. But Levin could not bring him-self to chide him. First of all, any reproach would seem to have been provoked by the danger they had escaped and by the lump that had appeared on his forehead; second, Veslovsky, at first sincerely upset, now laughed at the general alarm so good-naturedly and so infectiously that no one could have restrained his own laughter.

When they arrived at the second marsh, which was quite large and would take up much of their time, Levin urged them to pass it by. But Veslovsky again had his way. And again, since the marsh was too narrow, Levin, as the generous host, remained with the carriages.

As soon as they reached the place, Krak made straight for the hummocks. Vesenka Veslovsky was the first to run after the dog. And before Stepan Arkadievich had a chance to come up, a double snipe rose into the air. Veslovsky missed, and the bird alighted in an unmown meadow. This bird was assigned to Veslovsky. Krak again found it, pointed, and Veslovsky shot it and returned to the carriages.

"Now you go, and I'll remain with the horses," he said.

Hunter's envy began to stir in Levin. He handed the reins to Veslovsky and went into the marsh.

Laska, who had long whined pitifully and complained of the injustice, made straight for the familiar, reliable hummocks where Krak had not gone.

"Why don't you stop her?" cried Stepan Arkadievich.

"She won't frighten them," replied Levin proudly, as he hurried after the dog.

The nearer Laska came to the familiar hummocks, the more she concentrated on her search. A small marsh bird distracted her attention just for a moment. She made a full circle before the hummocks, started to make another one, then suddenly trembled and froze.

"Go, Stiva, go!" cried Levin, feeling that his heart had begun to pound and that suddenly all sounds, irrespective of their origin, were assailing him sharply but in disorder, as though some bolt had been slid, freeing his strained sense of hearing. He heard the sound of Stepan Arkadievich's steps and mistook them for the distant tread of horses. As he stepped on the corner of a hummock, he heard the brittle sound it made as it broke off, pulling the grass out by the roots, and he mistook the sound for a flight of double snipe. He also heard not far behind the sound of water splashing, something for which he could not account.

He took each step with care and approached his dog.

"Fetch!"

It was not a double snipe but a woodcock that flew up from underneath the dog. Levin aimed, but while he was doing so, the same sound of water splashing grew louder, came nearer, now combined with Veslovsky's voice shouting something in a strange manner. Levin saw that he was aiming behind the woodcock, but he fired nevertheless.

Convinced that he had missed, Levin looked around and

noticed that the horses and the wagonette were no longer on the road, but in the marsh.

Veslovsky, eager to watch the shooting, had driven into the marsh, and there the horses had stalled.

Where the devil is he going? Levin said to himself, returning to the mired carriage. "Why did you drive in here?" he asked him coldly, and with the help of the coachman began to free the horses.

Levin was annoyed because he had interfered with his shooting, because his horses had stalled in the mud, and mostly because neither Stepan Arkadievich nor Veslovsky had helped him or the coachman to unharness and free the horses, for neither of them had the slightest idea of how to do it. Without a word in response to Vasenka's assurances that it was completely dry there, Levin and the coachman worked in silence in their efforts to free the horses. But when in the heat of the work he noticed how Veslovsky pulled the wagonette by its splashboard with such concentrated effort that he broke it off, Levin reproached himself for being so cold to Veslovsky under the influence of his feeling of the previous day, and he tried to make up for his coldness with particular friendliness. When everything had been set right and the carriages had been brought out to the road, Levin called for lunch.

"'Bon appetit—bonne conscience! Ce poulet va tomber jusqu'au fond de mes bottes,'" said Vasenka, quoting a French proverb, and his cheer restored, he finished off a second pullet. "Well, our troubles are over. Now everything will go well. But to atone for my crime, I should sit on the box. Shouldn't I? Eh? No, no, I'll be Automedon. You'll see how I'll get you there!" he replied, refusing to yield the reins when Levin asked him to let the coachman take his seat. "No, I must atone for my crime, and I'm very comfortable on the box," he replied, and he drove on.

Levin was somewhat worried lest he tire the horses, particularly the sorrel on the left, which he could not control; but he unconsciously surrendered to his cheerfulness, listened to the songs that Veslovsky kept singing all the way as he sat on the box, to his stories, watched his demonstration of how to drive a four-in-hand in the English style, and in this general happy frame of mind they arrived at the Grozdev marsh after lunch.

10

VASENKA DROVE the horses so fast that they arrived at the marsh too early, and it was still hot.

As they approached the main marsh, their primary destination, Levin was unconsciously thinking of how to rid himself of Vasenka and do his hunting without anyone's interference. Stepan Arkadievich evidently wished the same, and on his face Levin saw an expression of the preoccupation in which every true hunter is always absorbed before the beginning of the hunt, and of the good-natured cunning that was peculiar to him.

"How shall we proceed? It's an excellent marsh, I see. Look at the hawks," said Stepan Arkadievich, pointing to two large birds that hovered over the sedge. "Where there are hawks, there surely is game."

"Well, look, gentlemen," said Levin, with a somewhat gloomy expression on his face, as he pulled up his boots and inspected the caps on his gun. "Do you see that sedge over there?" He pointed to a somber islet of dark verdure amid an immense, half-mowed, wet meadow, which stretched along the right bank of the river. "The marsh begins right here in front of us where, as you see, it is greener. From here it goes over to the right, where the horses are walking; there you find the hummocks and double snipe. And it runs around the sedge up to that alder grove, coming right up to the mill. It's there, where you see that inlet. That's the best spot. Once I bagged seventeen snipe there. We'll separate, each party taking one of the dogs, and we'll meet at the mill."

"Well, who is going to the right and who to the left?" asked Stepan Arkadievich. "There's more space to the right. You two go there, and I'll go to the left," he said with feigned casualness.

"Excellent! We'll outshoot him. Well, let's go, let's go!" interjected Vasenka.

Levin could not do anything but agree, and they parted.

As soon as they entered the marsh, both dogs began searching together in the direction of the rust-colored pool. Levin was familiar with Laska's way of searching, careful and hesitant. He knew the place and expected to find a flock of snipe there.

"Veslovsky, walk alongside me," he said in an anxious voice to his companion, who splashed behind him in the water. After the accidental shot on the Koepensky marsh, Levin unconsciously felt uneasy about the direction in which Vasenka pointed his gun.

"No, I won't be in your way. Don't worry about me."

But Levin could not help thinking about him and recalled Kitty's words as he left her. "Be careful not to kill one another." The dogs came closer and closer, passed each other, each following its own scent. The wait for the snipe was so intense that the smack of his heel as he pulled it out of the rusty mud sounded to Levin like the cry of a snipe and he clutched at the gun and pressed its butt.

"Bang! Bang!" a shot sounded at his ear. It was Vasenka's shot at a flock of ducks that hovered over the marsh and at that moment flew toward the hunters in an unusually large group. Levin scarcely had time to turn around when he heard the cry of a snipe, then of another, and a third, and about eight more rose into the air, one after the other.

Stepan Arkadievich shot one at the very moment when it was about to begin its zigzag, and the snipe plumped into the swamp. Unhurriedly, Oblonsky aimed at another one, which was still flying low over the sedge, and at the sound of the shot this snipe also dropped, and it could be seen struggling in the mowed sedge, flapping its uninjured wing, showing its white underside.

Levin was not so lucky. He aimed at the first snipe too soon and missed it. When he aimed again, as the bird began to rise, another snipe flew out from under his feet, distracted him, and he missed again.

While they were reloading their guns, another snipe rose in the air, and Veslovsky, who had already managed to reload, emptied two charges of small shot over the water. Stepan Arkadievich picked up his snipe and glanced at Levin with his sparkling eyes.

"Well, now we'll separate," said Stepan Arkadievich, limping slightly on his left leg, and, keeping his gun ready, he whistled to his dog and headed off to one side. Levin and Veslovsky went to the other.

It had always been the case with Levin that after missing the first shots, he would grow excited and upset, and then his shots would be bad for the entire day. That is what happened that day. There were a great many snipe. They constantly flew out from underneath the dog and the hunters' feet. Levin could have improved his score, but the more he fired, the deeper was his disgrace before Veslovsky, who kept shooting whether he needed to or not, not in the least embarrassed at not having scored at all. Levin fidgeted, hurried and fretted increasingly, and reached such a state that he almost gave up all hope of hitting anything. It seemed that Laska also felt this. She scented with less zeal and seemed to be casting puzzled and reproachful glances at the hunters. Shots followed one another. Gun smoke hung over the hunters, but the large, spacious net of the game bag contained only three small snipe. And of them, one was shot by Veslovsky and another belonged to both. In the meantime, from the other part of the marsh could be heard the sound of infrequent but, as it seemed to Levin, effective shots by Stepan Arkadievich, and after almost every shot the cry, "Krak, Krak, fetch!"

This disturbed Levin still more. The snipe ceaselessly circled in the air over the sedge. Their cries on the ground and caws in the air could be heard continuously from all sides. The snipe that had been disturbed earlier and had risen into the air first, now alighted in front of the hunters. Instead of two hawks, now dozens of them hovered, screeching, over the marsh.

After they had covered more than half the marsh, Levin and Veslovsky came to a place where the moujiks' meadows, which reached to the sedge, were divided into long strips, marked here by a path of trampled grass and there by a narrow line of cut grass. Half the strips were already mowed.

Though there was little hope of finding as many snipe in the unmowed grass as on the mowed, Levin had promised to meet Stepan Arkadievich, and walked along the mowed and unmowed strips with his companion.

"Hey, hunters!" cried one of the moujiks, who was seated at a cart with no horse. "Come here and have a drink and a bite!"

Levin looked around.

"Come on!" cried the cheerful, ruddy, bearded moujik, grinning and showing his white teeth as he lifted the greenish jug, which sparkled in the sun.

"*Qu'est-ce qu'ils disent?*" asked Veslovsky.

"They're inviting us to have some vodka. They've probably been dividing the meadows. A drink would be good," Levin said, not without cunning, hoping that Veslovsky would be tempted by the vodka and would go over to them.

"Why do they want to treat us?"

"Well, they're just having a good time. Go over to them. You'll find it interesting."

"*Allons, c'est curieux.*"

"Go yourself. You'll find the way to the mill," cried Levin, and turning around, he was pleased to see that Veslovsky, bent, his tired feet stumbling, with his gun in his outstretched hand, was making his way from the marsh toward the moujiks.

"What about you?" the moujik cried to Levin. "Don't be afraid. You'll taste our pie."

Levin would have very much liked to have a drink of vodka and a piece of bread. He was exhausted, and it was an effort to drag his stumbling feet through the swamp, and for a moment he hesitated. But the dog pointed. At once his fatigue left him, and he easily walked on through the swamp toward the dog. A snipe flew out from under his feet. He fired and killed it, but the dog still pointed. "Fetch!" Another rose from under the dog. Levin fired. But it was his unlucky day: he missed, and when he looked for the one he had shot, he could not find it either. He searched all through the sedge, but Laska did not believe that he had killed it, and when sent to look for it, she only pretended to do so and actually did not.

But even without Vasenka, whom he blamed for his failure, matters did not improve. There were a great many snipe here, but Levin missed one after the other.

It was still hot in the slanting rays of the sun. His clothes, thoroughly drenched with perspiration, clung to his body; his left boot, full of water, was heavy and made a smacking sound; drops of perspiration rolled down his face, smeared with gunpowder; he had a bitter taste in his mouth, a smell of gunpowder and rust in his nose; his ears were constantly filled with the cry of the snipe; he could not touch the barrels of his gun, they were so hot; his heartbeat was rapid and short; his hands trembled with excitement; his tired feet tripped and stumbled on the hummocks and in the mire; but he kept walking and shooting. At last, after a shameful miss, he flung down his gun and his hat.

I must get hold of myself! he said to himself. He picked up his hat and his gun, called Laska, and left the marsh. When he came to a dry place he sat down on a hummock, removed his boots, emptied the water from them, went to the marsh, had a drink of water that tasted of rust, wetted the heated barrels of the gun, and washed his face and hands. Refreshed and firmly resolved to control himself, he moved to the place where the snipe had alighted.

He tried to be calm, but the same thing happened again. His finger pulled the trigger before he took aim at the bird. Things were going from bad to worse.

He had only five birds in his bag when he came up from the marsh to the alder grove where he was to meet Stepan Arkadievich.

Before seeing Stepan Arkadievich he caught sight of his dog Krak, who jumped out from behind an upturned alder stump. Black with the stinking marsh slime and bearing the air of a victor, he sniffed at Laska. Following Krak, the impressive figure of Stepan Arkadievich appeared in the shade of the alder trees. He was coming toward him, still with a slight limp, his face flushed and perspiring, his collar unbuttoned.

"Well? You've done a lot of shooting," he said with a gay smile.

"And you?" asked Levin. But there was no need to ask, for he saw that his game bag was full.

"Can't complain."

He had fourteen birds.

"A beautiful marsh! Veslovsky was probably in your way. It's awkward for two to share one dog," said Stepan Arkadievich, tempering his triumph.

11

WHEN LEVIN and Stepan Arkadievich came into the moujik's house where Levin usually stopped, Veslovsky was already there. He was sitting in the middle of the room on a bench, holding on to it with both hands, while a soldier, the hostess' brother, was pulling off his slime-covered boots, and he was laughing his infectious, gay laugh.

"I've just arrived. *Ils ont été charmants.* Just imagine, they've dined and wined me. What wonderful bread! *Délicieux!* And the vodka! I've never drunk anything tastier! And they absolutely refused to accept money. And they kept saying something like, 'no offence meant.'"

"Why should they take money? It means they were treating you. Their vodka was not for sale," said the soldier, as he finally pulled off the wet boot together with a blackened sock.

Though the house was filthy, befouled by the hunter's boots and by the dirty dogs who were licking themselves; though the air became permeated with the smell of the marsh and of gunpowder; though there were no knives or forks, the hunters drank their tea and ate their supper with an appetite one has only at a hunt. Washed and clean, they went to the hay barn, where the floor had been swept and where the coachmen had prepared their masters' bedding.

Though it was getting dark, none of the hunters felt sleepy.

After alternating between reminiscences and stories about shooting, dogs, and former hunts, the conversation settled on a subject that held everyone's interest. After listening to Vasenka's repeatedly expressed admiration for these charming overnight lodgings, for the scent of the hay, for the broken cart (which he had taken for broken because it had been detached from its forward section), for the good nature of the moujiks who had treated him with their vodka, for the dogs which lay each at its master's feet, Oblonsky described to them the delights of the previous summer's hunt at Maltus' estate. Maltus was a well-known railroad magnate. Stepan Arkadievich described the marshes Maltus had bought up in Tver province, the care given to their preservation, the carriages and dogcarts which conveyed the guests, and the breakfast tent which was pitched near the marsh.

"I can't understand you," said Levin, sitting up in the hay. "Aren't you disgusted with these people? I know that a bottle of Lafitte goes well at lunch, but doesn't this very luxury disgust you? All these people, like the tax farmers we used to have, arouse universal contempt by the way they make their money. But they disregard this attitude toward them, and then with their ill-got wealth they buy themselves out of the contempt in which they had been held."

"Quite true!" interjected Vasenka Veslovsky. "Quite true!

Of course, Oblonsky is doing it out of *bonhomie*, and then others say, 'But Oblonsky goes there.'"

"Not at all," said Oblonsky, and Levin detected a touch of humor in his voice. "I just don't consider him more dishonest than any other rich merchant or nobleman. All of them earned their money in the same way, by their work and their wits."

"But what work? Do you call it work when they obtain a concession and then sell it?"

"Of course it's work. It's work in the sense that if it weren't for him or others like him, we'd have no railroads."

"But it's not like the work of a moujik or a scientist."

"I agree, but it's labor in the sense that the activity achieves results—a railroad. However, you believe that railroads are useless."

"No, that's another matter. I'm ready to admit they're useful. But any gain that's out of proportion to the labor spent on it is dishonest."

"But who's going to establish the proportion?"

"Gain by dishonesty, by cunning," said Levin, feeling that he could not clearly draw the line between what is honest and dishonest, "such as gain made by the banks," he continued, "is evil. This acquisition of enormous fortunes without labor is the same evil that was practiced by the tax farmers, but in a different form. *Le roi est mort, vive le roi!* No sooner was tax farming abolished than railroads and banks appeared. This is also gain without labor."

"All this is possibly true and ingenious. . . . Down, Krak!" Stepan Arkadievich shouted at the dog, which scratched itself, turning up the hay. He was evidently convinced that his views were correct, and therefore spoke with calm deliberation. "But you didn't draw the line between honest and dishonest work. Is it dishonest to receive, as I do, more salary than my chief clerk, though he's more competent than I?"

"I don't know."

"Then let me tell you: when you gain for your labor on your farm, let us say, over five thousand rubles, whereas our host the moujik can't make more than fifty rubles, however hard he may work, it's as dishonest as when I get more than my chief clerk, and when Maltus makes more than a railroad mechanic. Nevertheless, I discern some completely unreasonable hostility in the attitude of society toward these people, an envy, it seems to me—"

"No, that's not true," said Veslovsky. "It isn't really envy, but there's something unclean about such affairs."

"No, wait," continued Levin. "You say its unjust for me to make five thousand rubles while the moujik makes only fifty. That's true. It's unjust, and I feel it, but—"

"It is indeed. Why do we eat, drink, hunt, do nothing, while he toils without respite?" said Vasenka Veslovsky, evidently for the first time in his life seeing the problem clearly and therefore facing it with complete sincerity.

"Yes, you feel it, but you don't hand your estate over to him," said Stepan Arkadievich, as though deliberately provoking Levin.

It seemed that a hidden hostility had developed between the two brothers-in-law lately, as though since the time they had married two sisters, they had become rivals in their attempt to prove who could mold a better life; and this hostility expressed itself now in the conversation, which was verging on the personal.

"I don't hand it over because nobody demands it of me, and even if I wanted to, I couldn't give it away," replied Levin. "To whom could I give it?"

"Give it to this moujik. He won't refuse."

"But how should I give it to him? Should I take him to a law office to sign over a deed?"

"I don't know, but if you're convinced that you don't have the right—"

"I'm not at all convinced. On the contrary, I feel that I have no right to give away my property, that I have my duties toward my land and my family."

"Wait a moment! If you believe that this inequality is unjust then why don't you do something to—"

"I do do something, but negatively. In other words, I won't try to increase the inequality that exists between his state and mine."

"Well it's a paradox, if I may say so."

"Yes, a kind of sophistry," Vasenka Veslovsky agreed. "Ah! Our host," he said to the moujik who was entering the barn through the creaky gate. "Why aren't you asleep yet?"

"What do you mean asleep? I thought that you gentlemen were asleep, but I heard you talking. I'm looking for a hook. She won't bite, will she?" he added, stepping warily in his bare feet.

"And where will you sleep?"

"Outside, while the horses graze tonight."

"Ah, what a night!" said Veslovsky, looking at the corner of the house and at the unharnessed wagonette, visible in the dim light of the afterglow within the frame of the large barn gate, now wide open. "Listen, I hear women singing, and truly, not at all badly. Who's that singing, my host?"

"Those are maidservants, from nearby."

"Let's take a walk! We won't sleep anyway. Oblonsky, let's go!"

"I'd like both to lie here and to go," answered Oblonsky, stretching. "It's such a pleasure to lie here."

"Then I'll go alone," said Veslovsky, jumping up and putting on his boots. "Good night, gentlemen! If it's fun, I'll call you. You treated me to game, and I'll not forget you."

"A fine fellow, isn't he?" said Oblonsky, after Veslovsky had left and the moujik had closed the gate after him.

"Yes, a fine fellow," replied Levin, continuing to think of the subject of the conversation just concluded. It seemed to him that, to the best of his ability, he had expressed his thoughts and feelings clearly. Nevertheless, both of them, both sincere and quite intelligent, said in one voice that he comforted himself with sophistries. This troubled him.

"And that's the way it is, my friend. One must choose one of two things: either he must admit that the present social system is just, and then defend his rights; or he must confess that his are unjust privileges, as I do, and enjoy them."

"No, if they were unjust, you wouldn't be able to enjoy these privileges; at least I wouldn't. To me the most important thing is to know that I'm committing no wrong."

"Well, on the other hand, why shouldn't I go?" said Stepan Arkadievich, evidently tired by the strain of thinking. "We're not sleeping anyway. Let's go!"

Levin made no answer. He was preoccupied with the remark which he had made that he acted justly in a negative sense. Is this negative approach the only possible way to act justly? he asked himself.

"What a strong smell fresh hay has!" said Stepan Arkadievich, rising. "I'm sure I wouldn't be able to sleep. Vasenka is up to something there. Do you hear the laughter—hear his voice? What do you say? Let's go!"

"No, I won't," replied Levin.

"Can this also be a matter of principle?" asked Stepan

Arkadievich with a smile, searching for his cap in the darkness.

"Not of principle, but why should I go?"

"You know that you'll cause yourself trouble," said Stepan Arkadievich, as he rose and picked up his cap.

"Why?"

"Don't I see the position you've put yourself in with your wife? I noticed that the question of whether you would or would not go for a two-day hunt seemed to you of paramount importance. All this is a pleasant idyl, but it can't last a lifetime. A man must be independent; he has his own male interests. A man must be masculine," said Oblonsky, opening the gate.

"What do you mean? That I should go and dally with the maidservants?" asked Levin.

"Why not, if it gives you pleasure. *Ça ne tire pas à conséquence.* It won't harm my wife, but it will give me pleasure. The most important thing is to guard the sanctity of the home. At home don't permit yourself any liberties. But don't tie your hands."

"Perhaps you're right," Levin said drily, and he turned on his side. "We start early in the morning. I'll wake no one and leave at dawn."

"*Messieurs, venez vite!*" cried Veslovsky, who had returned. "*Charmante!* I've discovered her. *Charmante,* a true Gretchen. We've already become friends. Very pretty, indeed!" he related, with a look of approval that seemed to indicate she had been created so attractive for his sake alone and that he was pleased with the opportunity presented to him.

Levin pretended to be asleep, and Oblonsky, having put on his slippers and lit a cigar, left the barn, and soon their voices faded.

Levin could not fall asleep for a long while. He heard his horses munch their hay, then the host and older son getting ready to go to the field for the night. After that he heard the soldier settle for the night on the other side of the barn with his nephew, the host's little son. In his thin voice the boy related to his uncle his impression of the dogs, which seemed to him frightening and huge, and he asked what these dogs were going to catch. The soldier replied in his husky and sleepy voice that tomorrow the hunters would go into the marsh and fire their guns, and to put an end to the boy's questions, he said, "Sleep, Vaska, sleep, or watch out!" and he soon began to snore. A stillness descended, and all that could be heard was the munching of the horses and the cries of snipe. Must it be negative only? he asked himself again. Well, what of it? It's not my fault. And he began to think of the morrow.

I'll leave early in the morning, and promise myself not to get excited. The snipe are plentiful. And there are double snipe as well. And when I return, there'll be a note from Kitty. Yes, perhaps Stiva is right. I don't act manfully with her; I've become womanish myself. . . . But what shall I do? Again the negative!

In his sleep he heard the laughter and gay chatter of Veslovsky and Stepan Arkadievich. For a moment he opened his eyes; in the bright light of the rising moon he saw them standing at the open gate and talking. Stepan Arkadievich said something about the freshness of the girl, comparing her with a little fresh nut, just shelled. Veslovsky, laughing infectiously, repeated the words that evidently a peasant had said to him, "You'd better go after your own!" Half asleep, Levin said:

"Gentlemen, tomorrow at daybreak," and fell into a deep sleep.

12

LEVIN AWOKE at daybreak and tried to awaken his companions. Vasenka, lying face down, one of his stockinged legs outstretched, slept so soundly that no reply could be elicited from him. Oblonsky, still half asleep, refused to leave so early. Even Laska, who slept curled up at the edge of the hay, rose reluctantly and lazily, stretching and straightening her hind legs one after the other. Levin put on his boots, took his gun, carefully opened the squeaking door of the barn, and went outside. The coachmen were asleep at the carriages; the horses dozed. Only one of them lazily munched its oats, scattering them all over the trough by its snorting. The sky was still gray.

"What made you get up so early, my dear?" asked his hostess, who had emerged from the house and addressed him as an old friend.

"Going hunting, auntie. Do I get to the marsh this way?"

"Go straight over the back yards, along our threshing

barns, my dear, and through the hemp fields. There's a path there."

Walking carefully in her bare, sun-tanned feet, the old woman showed Levin the way, and at the threshing barn moved back the fence to let him pass.

"Go straight and you'll come right to the marsh. Our lads took the horses there yesterday evening."

Laska ran happily ahead along the path. Levin followed her with a brisk, light step, frequently glancing at the sky. He did not want the sun to rise before he reached the marsh. But the sun did not tarry. The moon, which had still been shining when he started, now only gleamed like quicksilver; the early morning glow one could not help noticing in the sky was now almost gone; the patches on the remote field, which had been indistinct earlier, now stood out clearly. They were shocks of rye. Invisible without the sunlight, the dew on the tall, aromatic hemp, which had already scattered its pollen, wetted Levin's legs and his shirt above his waist. In the transparent stillness of the morning, the softest sounds could be heard. Whistling like a bullet, a bee flew past Levin's ear. He looked around and saw another, and then a third. All of them came from behind the apiary fence, and rising over the hemp, they disappeared in the direction of the marsh. The path led straight to the marsh which could be recognized by the mist rising from it, in some places dense, in others light, so that the sedge and willow bushes seemed like islets swaying in the mist. On the edge of the marsh at the road the boys and moujiks who had watched the horses during the night lay, covered by their coats, all of them sleeping until the sun would rise. Not far away were three hobbled horses. One of them clanked its fetters. Laska ran alongside her master, looking around and asking to be allowed to go ahead. After he passed the sleeping moujiks and came to the first bog, Levin inspected his caps and released the dog. One of the horses, a sleek three-year-old chestnut, seeing the dog, shied, raised its tail, and snorted. The other horses were startled too and, splashing the water with their hobbled legs and pulling their hoofs out of the sticky ground with a plopping sound, they leaped out of the marsh. Laska stopped, looked at the horses with disdain and at Levin questioningly. Levin stroked Laska and whistled, signifying that she was allowed to start.

Laska ran over the quivering swamp, happy and intent. As she ran into the marsh, Laska immediately detected, amidst the familiar scents of the roots, marsh grasses, slime, and the alien smell of horse dung, the pervading scent of the bird, that fragrant bird that agitated her most of all. In some places on the moss and swamp dock this scent was very strong, but it was impossible to determine in which direction the scent grew stronger and in which it grew weaker. To do this she had to move ahead and face the wind. Mindless of the movements of her legs, Laska moved ahead in a tense trot so she could stop at any moment if she had to. She dashed to the right, away from the predawn breeze from the east, and turned into the wind. Inhaling through distended nostrils, she felt at once that this was not only their scent, but that *they* themselves were there, in front of her, and not one but many. Laska reduced her speed. They were there, but exactly where she could not yet tell. To find the exact spot she began to circle, when suddenly her master's voice distracted her. "Laska, here!" he said, pointing to the other side. She stopped, asking him whether it would not be better to continue what she had started. But he angrily repeated his order, pointing to a tussocky hummock, flooded with water, where, she knew, nothing could be found. She obeyed, pretending to search in order to please him, and, after she looked all over the hummock, she returned to her former place and immediately picked up the scent again. Now, with no interference on his part, she knew what to do. She did not look down at her feet and was annoyed if she tripped over a tall tussock or fell into the water, but with her strong, supple legs she overcame these difficulties and began to make a circle that would reveal everything to her. *Their* scent affected her more and more strongly and with more and more clarity, and suddenly it became completely clear to her that one of them was there, behind that hummock, within five paces of her, and she stopped, her entire body rigid. On account of her short legs she could not see anything in front of her, but by the smell she knew that it was sitting no further than five paces from her. She stood there, sensing it with increasing distinctness, and the expectation delighted her. Her tail was drawn tight and shuddered at its tip only. Her mouth was slightly open, her ears pricked. One ear had got folded over itself while she was running. She breathed heavily but cautiously, and still more cautiously she turned to her master, with her eyes rather than with her head. She saw his familiar face with those same frightening eyes as he walked, stumbling over the hummocks, unusually slowly, it seemed to her. Though he appeared to be walking slowly, he was actually running.

Observing the peculiar manner of Laska's search, as, her mouth slightly open, she kept close to the ground, pushing her rear legs out in great strides, Levin understood that she had caught the scent of double snipe. Praying to God within his heart to grant him success, particularly with the first bird, he ran up to Laska. When he came right up to her, he looked straight ahead from his full height and saw with his eyes what she had smelled with her nose. Through a small opening between two hummocks he sighted a double snipe on one. It turned its head and listened. Then, slightly opening and then folding its wings, it twitched its tail awkwardly and disappeared behind a hummock.

"Go! Go!" Levin shouted, pushing Laska from behind.

But I mustn't go, thought Laska. Where should I go? I smell them from here, but if I move ahead I'll get confused and won't know who they are or where they are. But he pushed her with his knee and said in an excited whisper, "Go, Lasochka, go!"

Well, if he wants me to go, I'll do it, but I won't be responsible, she thought, and with all her might she darted between the hummocks. She no longer smelled anything and only saw and heard without understanding.

Within ten paces of where she had been a double snipe rose with a throaty cry and with the hollow sound of its wings, typical of snipe. And after the shot its white breast thudded against the water of the swamp. Another one did not wait for the dog and rose into the air behind Levin.

When Levin turned toward it, it was already far off, but his shot reached it. After flying about twenty paces, the second snipe climbed sharply, turned over and over, like a ball thrown into the air, and fell heavily onto a dry spot.

Well, that's more like it, thought Levin, putting the warm fat snipe into his game bag. "Well, Lasochka, isn't this more like it?"

When Levin moved on after loading his gun, the sun had already risen, though it could not yet be seen behind the clouds. The moon had lost all its luster and remained in the sky like a small white cloud; the stars were no longer visible.

The marsh grass, which earlier, while wet with dew, had gleamed with a silvery sheen, now glittered like gold. The rusty patches were now amber. The bluish grass changed into yellowish green. Near the river the marsh birds stirred in the small bushes, which sparkled with dew and cast long shadows. A hawk awoke, and sitting on a haycock, turned its head from one side to the other, viewing the marsh with displeasure. Jackdaws flew over the field and a barefoot boy was already driving the horses toward an old man, who rose from under his coat, scratching himself. Gun smoke, white as milk, hung over the green grass.

One of the boys ran up to Levin.

"Uncle, there were ducks here yesterday!" he cried, and then followed him at a distance.

And the approval expressed by the boy doubled Levin's pleasure in bagging here, in sight of the boy, three more snipe, one after the other.

13

THE HUNTER'S BELIEF that if you do not miss the first beast or bird the hunt will be successful, proved true.

It was after nine o'clock in the morning when Levin returned to the lodgings, tired, hungry and happy, after having covered about twenty miles, with nineteen fine snipe and one duck, which he had tied to his belt, for there was no room for it in the game bag. His friends had long since awakened and had managed to work up an appetite and have breakfast.

"Wait, wait, I know there're nineteen," said Levin, counting for the second time the snipe and double snipe, which now no longer presented as impressive a sight as earlier, when they had risen into the air; they were twisted, dried, and caked with blood, their little heads hanging to one side.

The count was correct, and Levin was pleased with Stepan Arkadievich's envy. He was also glad that on his return to the lodgings a messenger was waiting with a note from Kitty.

I am well and cheerful. Don't worry about me. You have even more reason to be calm than before. I have a new guardian, Maria Vlasievna." (She was the midwife, a new and important person in Levin's family life.) *"She has come to see me. She found me very healthy, and we asked her to stay until you return. Everyone is cheerful, healthy, and, as for you, please don't hurry, but if the hunt is good, stay another day.*

These two joyful happenings—the successful hunt and the note from his wife—were so great that Levin took lightly the two small unpleasantnesses which happened later. One of them was that the chestnut trace horse, which evidently had been overworked the previous day, now refused to take food and looked dispirited. The coachman said it had been pushed too hard.

"It was overdriven yesterday, Konstantin Dmitrievich," he said. "And no wonder. They drove it badly for ten versts."

The other trouble, which at first upset his good humor but which he later laughed at heartily, was that nothing remained of the food that Kitty had furnished them in such abundance that it seemed it would last for a week. When he returned from the hunt, tired and hungry, Levin dreamed so fondly of the patties that, while still approaching the lodgings, he scented their fragrance and tasted their flavor as Laska scented game, and he immediately ordered Filipp to get him some. As it turned out, not only the patties but the pullets as well were gone.

"Some appetite!" said Stepan Arkadievich, laughing and pointing to Vasenka Veslovsky. "I myself don't suffer from a lack of appetite, but his is unbelievable. . . ."

"Well, what can we do?" said Levin, looking at Veslovsky despairingly. "Then give me some beef, Filipp."

"They ate up the beef too, and the bone I gave to the dogs," replied Filipp.

Levin was deeply offended and said with annoyance, "They could at least have left me something," and he felt like crying.

"Then prepare some game," he said to Filipp in a trembling voice, trying not to look at Vasenka, "and stuff it with nettles. And at least get me some milk."

Later, after he had drunk his milk, he felt ashamed for having displayed his annoyance to a stranger and began to laugh at this hunger-induced temper.

In the evening they covered another field, where Veslovsky bagged a few birds, and at night they returned home.

They were as gay on their return home as they had been on the way to the hunt. Veslovsky sang and recalled with pleasure his adventures with the moujiks who had treated him with vodka, saying to him, "No offence meant." He told his companions of his gay nocturnal adventures, of the servant girl and of the moujik, who had asked him whether he was married and when told that he was not said to him, "Don't run after the wives of others, but do your best to get your own." These words particularly amused Veslovsky.

"All in all, I'm enjoying this outing immensely. And you, Levin?"

"Very much," Levin replied sincerely. He was particularly happy to know that not only was he now free from that feeling of animosity toward Vasenka Veslovsky he had at home, but that, on the contrary, he had the friendliest feelings toward him.

14

THE NEXT DAY, at ten o'clock, after he had attended to his affairs, Levin knocked at the door of the room where Vasenka had spent the night.

"*Entrez*," Veslovsky cried. "Please excuse me, I've just finished washing," he said with a smile, standing before him in his underwear.

"Please don't be embarrassed," said Levin, taking a seat at the window. "Did you sleep well?"

"Like a log. And how would today be for a hunt?"

"What will you have, coffee or tea?"

"Neither. I'll have breakfast. I really feel guilty. The ladies, I presume, are already up. It would be nice to take a walk. Please show me your horses."

After they had walked in the garden, stopped at the stable, and even performed some exercises on the parallel bars, Levin and his guest returned and entered the drawing room.

"It was a splendid hunt and a most interesting experience," said Veslovsky, coming over to Kitty, who was seated at the samovar. "What a pity that ladies are deprived of these pleasures!"

After all, he has to say something to the lady of the house, thought Levin. He again saw something in his smile, in the victorious air with which his guest addressed Kitty.

The princess, who was seated at the other end of the table next to Maria Vlasievna and Stepan Arkadievich, called Levin to her side and began to discuss plans for moving to

Moscow for Kitty's confinement and for renting an apartment. Just as all the preparations for their wedding had seemed to Levin unpleasant and offensive by their insignificance when compared with the majesty of the event, so these preparations for the coming childbirth, the time of which they somehow counted on their fingers, also seemed offensive, and even more so. All this time he had tried to ignore these conversations about methods of swaddling the baby; he tried to turn his eyes away from the endless mysterious knitted bands, the small linen triangles, which Dolly ascribed particular importance to, and so on. The coming birth of his son (he was sure it would be a son) had been promised to him, but he still could not believe it, so extraordinary did it seem to him. On the one hand, it appeared to be a boundless and therefore impossible happiness—and on the other, it was such a mysterious event that an imagined understanding of what was going to happen, and the consequent preparations for it as though it were an ordinary event brought about by human beings, seemed to him revolting and humiliating.

But the princess misunderstood his feelings, and his reluctance to think and speak on this subject she mistook for thoughtlessness and indifference, so she harassed him. She had been asking Stepan Arkadievich to look for an apartment and now she called Levin to her side.

"I don't know anything, Princess. Do as you please," he said.

"We must decide when to move."

"I really don't know. All I know is that millions of babies are born outside Moscow and without doctors in attendance. . . . Why then—"

"Well, in that case—"

"No, we'll do as Kitty desires."

"This mustn't be discussed with Kitty. Do you want me to frighten her? Only last spring Natalie Golitzyn died through improper care."

"I'll do as you say," he replied gloomily.

The princess began to say something, but he did not listen. Though his conversation with the princess had upset him, his sullen mood was not because of that but because of what he saw taking place at the samovar.

No, it's impossible, he thought, looking from time to time at Vasenka, who was bending toward Kitty, telling her something with his beautiful smile, and at her, flushed and animated.

There was something unclean in Vasenka's pose, in his look, and in his smile. Levin even saw something unclean in Kitty's pose and look. And again darkness engulfed him. Again, as the other day, he felt that he had been abruptly cast down from the heights of happiness, composure, and dignity into the abyss of despair, ill will, and humiliation. Again he felt an aversion to everyone and everything.

"Then do as you please, Princess," he said, and he looked around again.

"Heavy is the crown of Monomach," Stepan Arkadievich said to him jokingly, apparently referring not only to the conversation with the princess but also to the cause of Levin's concern, which he had noticed. "How late you are today, Dolly!"

All rose to greet Daria Aleksandrovna. Vasenka rose for a second, and with the lack of courtesy toward the ladies typical of the new generation, he bowed almost imperceptibly and resumed his conversation with a laugh.

"Masha has worn me out. She didn't sleep well and is terribly cranky today," said Dolly.

The conversation Vasenka had started with Kitty again centered on the topic of the previous day, on Anna and on the question of whether love may disregard social conventions. Kitty did not enjoy this conversation; it disturbed her by its substance, by the tone in which it was conducted, and particularly by the unfavorable impression she knew it would make on her husband. But she was too simple and too naïve to know how to stop the conversation or even how to conceal the shallow pleasure she derived from the obvious attentions of this young man. She wanted to stop the conversation but did not know how. Anything she did, she knew, her husband would notice and would misinterpret. And in fact, when she inquired of Dolly about Masha, and Vasenka, while waiting for the sisters' dull conversation to end, looked at Dolly without interest, this question seemed to Levin to be an artificial, repulsive device.

"Well, are we going mushrooming today?" asked Dolly.

"Please, let's go. I'll go too," said Kitty with a blush. Out of politeness, she wanted to ask Vasenka whether he would also go, but she did not. "Where are you going, Kostia?" she asked her husband apologetically as he passed her with a resolute step. This apologetic expression confirmed his suspicions.

"The machinist arrived while I was away, and I haven't had the chance to see him yet," he said, without looking at her.

He went downstairs, but before he could leave his study he heard his wife's familiar step; she was walking faster than she should have.

"What is it?" he asked her drily. "We're busy."

"Will you excuse me," she said, turning to the German machinist. "I have something to tell my husband."

The German was about to leave, but Levin said to him, "Don't disturb yourself."

"Does the train leave at three?" asked the German. "I may be late."

Levin did not reply and walked out with his wife.

"Well, what do you want to tell me?" he asked her in French.

He did not look at her; he did not want to see how, in her present condition, her whole face trembled, and how pitiful and crushed she looked.

"I . . . I want to say that it's impossible to live like this . . . that this is torture. . . ." she said.

"There are servants here in the pantry," he said angrily. "Don't make a scene."

"Then let's go here."

They were standing in the hallway. Kitty wanted to enter the next room, but there the English governess was giving Tania her lessons.

"Well, let's go into the garden."

In the garden they came upon a moujik who was sweeping the path. Without even considering that the moujik might see their faces, hers tear-stained and his excited, without even considering that they looked like people who were fleeing from some misfortune, they walked rapidly, feeling that they had to have a heart-to-heart talk and to undeceive each other, to be alone together, to free themselves of the torment which both of them had been suffering.

"We can't live like this! It's torture! I'm suffering and so are you. What for?" she said when at last they came to a secluded bench in the corner of the linden tree alley.

"But just tell me: wasn't there something improper, unclean, humiliating, and horrible in his tone?" he said, resuming the same pose in which he had stood facing her that previous night, his fists against his chest.

"There was," she said in a tremulous voice. "But, Kostia, don't you really see that it's not my fault? All morning I've wanted to change it, but these people. . . . Why did he come? How happy we were!" she said, sobs choking her and shaking her whole body, which by now had grown heavier.

The gardener was surprised that though nothing had pursued them, though they had nothing from which to flee, and though they could have found nothing particularly joyous on the bench, when they went back past him their faces were calm and radiant.

15

AFTER CONDUCTING his wife upstairs, Levin went to Dolly's part of the house. Daria Aleksandrovna had also been deeply upset that day. She paced the room and spoke angrily to her little daughter, who stood in the corner wailing.

"You will stand there in the corner the whole day; you will eat dinner by yourself; you will see none of your dolls; and I will not make you a new dress," she said, running out of punishments.

"She's a nasty girl!" she said, turning to Levin. "Where did she acquire such a horrible disposition?"

"But what has she done?" Levin asked, quite indifferently. He wanted to consult Dolly on a matter of his own and was disappointed to have come at the wrong time.

"She and Grisha went to the raspberry patch and there . . . I'm ashamed to tell you what she did. How badly I miss Elliot! This one pays no attention at all, a real machine. . . . *Figurez-vous que la petite. . . .*"

And Daria Aleksandrovna told him of Masha's crime.

"That doesn't prove anything. It's not at all a sign of a nasty disposition, just a childish prank," Levin said, trying to calm her.

"But why are you upset? Why have you come?" asked Dolly. "What's going on in there?"

And by the tone of the question Levin knew that it would be easy for him to tell her what he had intended to.

"I haven't been in there, but Kitty and I were alone in the

garden. We quarreled for the second time since . . . Stiva arrived."

Dolly looked at him with her wise, understanding eyes.

"Well, tell me please, in all sincerity, wasn't . . . not Kitty's but that gentleman's tone one that a husband might find unpleasant? No, not just unpleasant, but horrible and offensive?"

"Well, what can I say? . . . Stay there in the corner!" she said, addressing Masha, who noticed a faint smile on her mother's face and was about to turn around. "According to social standards, he behaves like any other young man. *Il fait la cour à une jeune et jolie femme,* and the husband, if he's a man of the world, should only be flattered."

"Yes, yes," Levin said gloomily, "but you noticed it?"

"Not only I but Stiva, too. After tea he told me openly, '*Je crois que* Veslovsky *fait un petit brin de cour à* Kitty.'"

"Splendid! Now I know. I'll drive him out of the house."

"What do you mean? Have you gone mad?" Dolly cried in alarm. "Come to your senses, Kostia!" she added, and she began to laugh. "Now you may go to Fanny," she said to Masha. "Well, if you want to, I'll tell Stiva. He'll take him away. We can tell him that you are expecting visitors. In general, he doesn't fit in with us."

"No, no, I'll do it myself."

"But you'll quarrel."

"Not at all. I'll enjoy it," said Levin, and his eyes actually shone with pleasure. "Well, forgive her, Dolly! She won't do it any more," he said, referring to the little culprit, who had not gone to Fanny, but, glancing from under her brows, stood hesitatingly in front of her mother, awaiting and seeking her look.

Her mother glanced at her. The little girl burst into sobs, burying her face in her mother's lap, and Dolly laid her thin, gentle hand on the child's head.

What do we have in common with him? thought Levin, and he went to find Veslovsky.

As he passed through the entrance hall, he ordered the carriage to be readied immediately for a trip to the railroad station.

"A spring broke yesterday," replied the servant.

"Then the tarantas, but hurry up. Where's the guest?"

"He went to his room."

When Levin came in, Vasenka was adjusting his leggings for

a ride on horseback, after having removed his belongings from his suitcase and laying out his music.

Either because of some unusual expression on Levin's face, or because Vasenka himself felt that *ce petit brin de cour* he had begun did not fit in with this family, he was somewhat (as much as a man of the world can be) embarrassed by Levin's visit.

"Do you ride in your leggings?"

"Yes, it's so much cleaner this way," said Vasenka, putting his fat leg on the chair, fastening a lower hook, and smiling cheerfully and good-naturedly.

Most likely he was a nice fellow, and Levin felt sorry for him and ashamed of himself as a host when he noticed the shyness on Vasenka's face.

On the table there lay a piece of the stick that they had broken that morning, during their gymnastics, when they tried to straighten the warped parallel bars. Levin took it in his hand and began to break off the splinters at its broken end, unable to find a way to start the conversation.

"I wanted. . . ." He was ready to stop, but suddenly, remembering Kitty and everything that had happened, he looked resolutely into his eyes and said, "I've ordered the carriage for you."

"What do you mean?" asked Veslovsky in surprise. "Where are we going?"

"It's for you, to the railroad station," Levin said gloomily, picking at the point of the stick.

"Are you leaving, or has anything happened?"

"As it happens, I'm expecting guests," said Levin, his strong fingers picking at the stick more and more rapidly. "I'm really not expecting any guests, and nothing has happened, but I'm asking you to leave. You may interpret my rudeness any way you like."

Vasenka straightened.

"I would ask *you* to explain to me . . ." he said with dignity, when at last he understood.

"I can't explain it to you," Levin said softly and slowly, trying to mask the trembling of his jaw. "And it would be better for you not to ask."

And since all the splinters had already been picked clean, Levin grasped the thick end of the stick with his fingers, split it in two and carefully caught a piece which fell.

Probably the sight of his straining arms, of those same

muscles that he had felt that morning during their gymnastics, and of his shining eyes, his soft voice, and his trembling jaw, impressed Vasenka more than his words. He shrugged his shoulders, smiled contemptuously, and bowed.

"May I see Oblonsky?"

His shrug and smile did not anger Levin. What else can he do? he thought.

"I'll send him to you at once."

"What kind of nonsense is this?" said Stepan Arkadievich, after he had learned from his friend that he was being driven out of the house. He found Levin in the garden, where he was walking while waiting for his guest to depart. "*Mais c'est ridicule!* What stung you? *Mais c'est du dernier ridicule!* What did you imagine, when a young man. . . ."

But the spot where Levin had been stung was evidently still quite painful, for he paled again and hastily interrupted Stepan Arkadievich when he tried to explain to him why all this had happened.

"Please don't explain. I can't act otherwise. I feel very much ashamed before you and him. But to him, I believe, it'll be no great misfortune to leave, whereas to me and my wife his presence has been disagreeable."

"But he has been insulted. *Et puis, c'est ridicule.*"

"And I have been both insulted and tormented. It's not my fault, and there's no reason for me to suffer!"

"Well, I didn't expect this of you! *On peut être jaloux, mais à ce point, c'est du dernier ridicule!*"

Levin quickly turned away, went to the far corner of the alley and continued his solitary pacing up and down. He soon heard the rattle of the tarantas and through the trees he saw Vasenka riding along the alley, seated on the hay (unfortunately there was no seat in the tarantas), wearing his Scotch cap and bouncing with every jolt.

What now? thought Levin, when a servant ran out from the house and stopped the tarantas. It was the machinist, about whom Levin had completely forgotten. Bowing, the machinist explained something to Veslovsky. Then he climbed into the tarantas, and they left together.

Stepan Arkadievich and the princess were incensed by Levin's behavior. And he himself felt not only *ridicule* in the extreme but unforgivably guilty and disgraced. But he remembered how much he and his wife had suffered, and when he asked himself how he would act again in similar circumstances, he replied that he would do the same.

In spite of all of this, toward the end of the day everyone but the princess, who had not forgiven Levin his behavior, became unusually animated and cheerful, like children after punishment or grownups after a wearisome official reception, so that in the evening, in the princess' absence, the expulsion of Vasenka was mentioned as an event of the distant past. And Dolly, who had inherited from her father the gift of telling amusing stories, made Varenka convulse with laughter when she related for the third or fourth time, each time with new humorous additions, how she had been about to put on her new little bows in the guest's honor and to enter the drawing room, when she heard the rattle of the venerable contrivance. And who was in that contrivance? Vasenka himself, seated on the hay with his Scotch cap, his music, and his leggings.

"You should have at least ordered the coach for him. But you didn't. . . . And I hear the shout, 'Stop!' Well, I think, he's forgiven. And then I see that they have seated the fat German next to him, and they drive them both off. . . . And so my little bows are wasted. . . ."

16

DARIA ALEKSANDROVNA carried out her intention to visit Anna. She was very sorry about upsetting her sister and displeasing her brother-in-law. She understood how right the Levins were in refusing to have anything to do with Vronsky. But she considered it her duty to visit Anna, and to show that her feelings had in no way changed in spite of the change in Anna's situation.

In order not to depend on the Levins for this trip, Daria Aleksandrovna sent to the village for some horses. But when Levin found out about it, he came to chide her.

"Why do you believe that I'm against your going? Even if it were so, I would find it still more unpleasant if you didn't take my horses," he said. "You never told me that you had decided to go. As for hiring horses in the village, first, it would reflect unfavorably upon me, and, most important, they'll undertake it but will never get you there. I have horses. And if you don't want to upset me, take mine."

Daria Aleksandrovna had to give in, and on the appointed day Levin readied a team of four horses for his sister-in-law and also arranged for a relay. The teams, made up of draft and saddle horses, looked very unattractive, but they could be relied upon to take Daria Aleksandrovna to her destination in one day. Now, when the horses were also needed for the princess and for the midwife, who were both leaving, it was hard for Levin to spare them, but the duties of a host did not permit him to let Daria Aleksandrovna, his guest, hire horses and in addition, he knew that Daria Aleksandrovna needed the twenty rubles they asked for the journey. Her financial affairs, which were in a very bad state, concerned Levin as much as his own.

On Levin's advice, Daria Aleksandrovna left at daybreak. The road was good, the carriage comfortable, the horses ran briskly, and on the box, beside the coachman, sat the office clerk, who acted as a footman and was sent by Levin for Daria Aleksandrovna's safety.

Daria Aleksandrovna dozed, waking only when they approached the inn where they were to change horses.

After having tea at the same well-to-do moujik's where Levin had stopped on his way to see Sviazhsky, and a chat with the women about their children and with the old man about Count Vronsky, whom he praised highly, Daria Aleksandrovna resumed her journey at ten o'clock. At home, busy with her children, she never had time for meditation. But during this four-hour trip, all the thoughts held in check until now suddenly crowded into her head, and she reviewed her whole life in a way she had never done before, in a most thorough manner. Her thoughts seemed strange, even to herself. First she thought of her children, and although the princess and, more important, Kitty (she relied more on her) had promised to look after them, she nevertheless felt uneasy. I hope that Masha won't be mischievous again, that the horse won't kick Grisha, and that Lily's upset stomach won't get worse, she thought. Then the problems of the moment began to give way to the problems of the near future. She began to think that for the coming winter they would have to rent a new apartment in Moscow, change the furniture in the drawing room, and have a fur coat made for their oldest daughter. Then her attention was drawn to the problem of the more remote future: how would she bring up the children? It's not so hard with the girls, she thought, but what about the boys?

True, I'm coaching Grisha now, but it's only because I'm free and don't have to take care of a baby. Of course, I can't rely on Stiva. And I'll bring them up with the aid of good people. But what if there's another child? . . . And the thought occurred to her—how wrong the statement is that woman has been cursed with the pains of childbearing. Giving birth is easy; carrying the child is torture, she thought, remembering her last pregnancy and the death of her last child. And she recalled her conversation with the young peasant woman at the inn. When asked whether she had any children, the pretty young woman replied cheerfully:

"I had a little girl, but the Lord released me and I buried her during Lent."

"Well, are you very sorry?" asked Daria Aleksandrovna.

"Why should I be? As it is, the old man has enough grandchildren. It would be nothing but trouble. I couldn't work or do anything. I'd be tied down."

Daria Aleksandrovna was shocked at this answer, in spite of the good nature of the lovely young woman. But now she unconsciously remembered these words. There was some truth in this cynical remark.

And in general, thought Daria Aleksandrovna, reviewing all the fifteen years of her married life, it's been pregnancy, nausea, dullness, apathy, and mainly ugliness. Kitty, young, pretty Kitty, she too has lost all her good looks, and when I'm pregnant, I look ugly, I know it. Childbirth, suffering, ugly suffering, and that last minute . . . then nursing, sleepless nights, the awful pain. . . .

Daria Aleksandrovna shuddered just at the memory of the pain her cracked nipples had caused her with almost every child. Then the children's illnesses, the unceasing worry; and bringing them up, their nasty dispositions (she remembered little Masha's misbehavior in the raspberry patch), lessons, Latin—everything is so confusing and difficult. And above all —the death of a child. And again her imagination brought back that implacable memory, always oppressing her mother's heart, the memory of her youngest baby boy, who died of quinsy. She recalled his burial, the general indifference toward the little rose coffin, and her lonely heart that was rent with pain as she looked at the pale little forehead, with its curls at the temples and the little mouth open in wonderment, visible within the coffin just as they were about to put on the rosy lid with its embroidered cross.

And what is the purpose of all this? What will come of all this? Only that I, without a minute's rest, either pregnant or nursing, always angry, querulous, worn out and wearing others out, disliked by my husband, will pass through my life, and some unhappy, badly brought up, pauper children will grow up. Even now, if it weren't for Levin I don't know how we'd have spent the summer. Of course, Kostia and Kitty are so considerate that we feel completely at ease; but this can't go on. They'll have their own children and won't be able to help us; even now they're pressed for money. Well, can I expect help from Papa, who has almost nothing left for himself? So—I can't bring up my children myself, but only with the humiliation of being helped by others. Well, let's suppose that I'll be most fortunate, that all the children will survive, and that somehow I'll raise them. At best they will not be scoundrels. That's all I can hope for. And for this alone, so much suffering, so much toil. . . . My whole life has been wasted! She again remembered what the young peasant woman told her, and she was again repelled at the thought. But she could not deny that there was some shocking truth in her words.

"Well, Mikhaila, is it still far?" Daria Aleksandrovna asked the office clerk, to rid herself of her fearful thoughts.

"It's seven versts from this village, they say."

The carriage drove down the village street to a small bridge. A crowd of cheerful women, with coiled sheaf binders hanging over their shoulders, walked along the bridge, chattering loudly and gaily. The women stopped on the bridge, viewing the carriage with curiosity. All the faces turned to her seemed to Daria Aleksandrovna to be healthy, gay, and teasing her with their enjoyment of life. Everyone lives and enjoys life, Daria Aleksandrovna kept thinking after she had passed the women. The horses trotted up the hill and again she bounced pleasantly on the soft springs of the old carriage. But I am released from a jail-like life, where worries are killing me, to gain just one moment's respite. They are all so alive, these peasant women, my sister Natalie, Varenka, and Anna, whom I am going to visit, but not I.

And they assail Anna. Why? Am I any better? I, at least, have a husband whom I love. Not as I would like to love, but I do love him, whereas Anna did not love her husband. Was it her fault? She wants to live. God has planted this desire in our souls. It's very possible that I'd have done the same. And

"They're coming here! There they are!" cried the moujik. "See how fast they are coming!" he said, pointing to the road where four horsemen and a charabanc with two passengers were riding toward them.

It was Vronsky, his jockey, Veslovsky and Anna on horseback, and Princess Varvara and Sviazhsky in the charabanc. They had gone for a ride and to inspect the newly arrived harvesting machines.

When the carriage stopped, the horsemen proceeded at a walking pace. Anna and Veslovsky led the way. Anna, mounted on a short, stocky colt with a cut mane and a short tail, rode at an even pace. Dolly was struck by her beautiful head, the black hair showing from underneath her tall hat, her full shoulders, her slender waist in her black riding habit, and her whole calm, graceful bearing.

At first she thought that it was improper for Anna to ride horseback. In her imagination Daria Aleksandrovna related horseback riding to frivolous, youthful coquetry, which, in her opinion, was not becoming to Anna in her situation; but when she looked at her closely, she quickly became reconciled to her riding. In spite of Anna's elegance, everything was so simple, calm and dignified in her bearing, attire, and movements that nothing could seem more natural.

Alongside Anna, Vasenka Veslovsky, in his Scotch cap with its waving ribbons, rode a gray, nervous cavalry horse. He stretched his thick legs forward, and clearly admired himself, and Daria Aleksandrovna could not restrain a happy smile as she recognized him. Behind him rode Vronsky. He was on a thoroughbred bay, which evidently was excited by the gallop. He pulled at the bridle, trying to restrain the horse.

He was followed by a short man in a jockey's uniform. Sviazhsky and the princess, in a brand-new charabanc, drawn by a large black trotter, tried to catch up with the horsemen.

The moment Anna recognized Dolly as the little figure pressed against the corner of the old carriage, her face quickly lit up with a happy smile. She cried out, started in the saddle, and touched her horse to a gallop. When she rode up to the carriage, she jumped down without assistance, and holding her skirt, ran toward Dolly.

"I thought it was you, but I didn't dare believe it. What a pleasure! You can't imagine how happy I am to see you!" she said, now pressing her face against Dolly and kissing her, and now moving away and looking at her with a smile.

"How wonderful, Aleksei!" she said, turning to Vronsky, who had dismounted and was coming toward them.

Vronsky took off his tall gray hat and came over to Dolly. "You can't imagine how glad we are that you've come," he said, giving his words a particular meaning and, with his smile, displaying his strong white teeth.

Vasenka Veslovsky, without dismounting, took off his cap and greeted the guest, cheerfully waving the ribbons over his head.

"It's Princess Varvara," said Anna in reply to Dolly's inquiring look when the charabanc rolled up.

"Oh!" said Daria Aleksandrovna, and unconsciously her face showed displeasure.

Princess Varvara was her husband's aunt. Dolly had known her a long time but had little respect for her. She knew that Princess Varvara had spent her whole life as a toady to her rich relatives. But that she, her husband's relation, now stayed with Vronsky, who was a stranger to her, offended Dolly. Anna noticed the expression on Dolly's face and, blushing with embarrassment, dropped the edge of her skirt and tripped on it.

When the charabanc stopped, Daria Aleksandrovna went over to it and greeted Princess Varvara coldly. She knew Sviazhsky, too. He inquired about his eccentric friend and his young wife, and after a quick glance at the ill-matched horses and the patched splashboards of the carriage, he offered the ladies the charabanc.

"And I'll ride in this vehicle," he said. "The horse is tame, and the princess is an expert driver."

"No, you stay where you are," said Anna as she came up, "and we'll drive in the carriage," and taking Dolly's arm, she led her away.

Daria Aleksandrovna was dazzled by the elegant charabanc, a kind she never had seen; by the beautiful horses, and by the elegant, brilliant people around her. But most of all she was struck by the change that had taken place in her beloved old friend Anna. Another woman in her place, less observant, who had not known Anna before, and particularly one who had not been occupied with thoughts like those that had occupied Daria Aleksandrovna during her journey, would have noticed nothing unusual in Anna. But now Dolly was struck by that temporary kind of beauty that a woman possesses only in moments of love, which she now saw in Anna's face. Everything in her face: her deeply dimpled cheeks and chin, the curve of her lips, the smile that seemed to flit over her face, the sparkle in her eyes, her graceful and brisk movements, her sonorous voice, even the air of both kindness and anger with which she replied to Veslovsky when he asked her permission to mount her cob in order to train it to start to gallop with the right leg—all this was unusually attractive; and it seemed that she herself knew it and rejoiced in it.

When the two women took their seats in the carriage, both suddenly felt embarrassed. Anna's embarrassment was caused by the attentive and questioning way Dolly looked at her, Dolly's by Sviazhsky's remark about the "vehicle," which made her ashamed of the dirty old carriage in which Anna took a seat next to her. Filipp the coachman and the clerk felt the same. To hide his embarrassment, the clerk bustled about, helping the ladies into the carriage, but Filipp grew sullen, preparing himself in advance to resist this outward show of superiority. He smiled ironically as he sized up the raven trotter, and had already made up his mind that the raven horse pulling the charabanc was fit only for a "promenade," and on a hot day would never make forty versts in one stretch.

All the moujiks at the cart rose, exchanged remarks, and watched with gay curiosity how the guest was being received.

"How happy they are! They probably haven't seen each other for a long time," said the curly haired old man with the bast band in his hair.

"Well, Uncle Gerasim, if we had the raven stallion to draw the sheaves, we'd have done it in no time."

"Look, is that a woman in those pants?" asked one of them, indicating Vasenka Veslovsky, who was taking his seat on the lady's saddle.

"No, it's a man. See how easily he did it."

"Well, lads, we'll have no time for a nap, I believe."

"What nap?" said the old man, squinting at the sun. "Look it's past noon. Get your hooks and let's go!"

18

ANNA LOOKED at Dolly's thin, careworn face, its wrinkles filled with dust, and wanted to tell her what she was thinking, namely, that Dolly had grown thin. But remembering that her own appearance had improved and that Dolly's look confirmed this, she sighed and began to talk about herself.

"You look at me," she said, "and wonder whether I can be happy in my situation. Well, you'd be surprised. I'm ashamed to confess it, but I am . . . unforgivably happy. I'm under a magic spell, as in a dream, one where you're frightened and anxious, and then suddenly wake up and find that all these fears are gone. I've woken up. I knew anxiety and fright, but now I've been so happy for such a long time, particularly since we arrived here . . . !" she said, looking at Dolly with a shy and inquiring smile.

"How glad I am!" said Dolly with a smile. Unconsciously she smiled more coldly than she wanted to. "I'm very glad for you. Why didn't you write to me?"

"Why? . . . Because I didn't dare . . . you forget my situation. . . ."

"To me? You didn't dare? If you knew how I . . . I think. . . ."

Daria Aleksandrovna wanted to tell her of her thoughts of that morning, but somehow she felt now it would be out of place to do so.

"Well, more about that later. What are all these buildings?" she said, to change the subject, and she pointed at the red and green roofs that could be seen behind the green hedges of acacias and lilacs. "Like a little town."

But Anna made no reply.

"Wait, how do you look at my situation? What do you think of it?" she asked.

"I believe . . ." Daria Aleksandrovna began, but at this moment Vasenka Veslovsky, having started the cob from the right leg, galloped past them in his short jacket, thudding heavily against the suede of the lady's saddle.

"Success, Anna Arkadievna!" he cried.

Anna did not even glance at him. And again it seemed to Daria Aleksandrovna that it was inconvenient to start such a long conversation in the carriage, so she expressed herself briefly.

"I have no opinion," she said. "I've always loved you, and if you love, you love the whole person, as he is, not as you would want him to be."

Anna turned her look away from her friend, half-closed her eyes (this was a new habit, one Dolly had not noticed in her before), and sank into thought, trying to grasp the full meaning of these words. After she evidently had understood them the way she wanted to, she again looked at Dolly.

"If you had any sins," she said, "they would all be forgiven for your arrival and for your words."

And Dolly saw that tears appeared in her eyes. She pressed Anna's hand in silence.

"What are those buildings then? How many there are!" she said, repeating her question after a short silence.

"These are the employees' homes, the stud, and the stables," replied Anna. "And the park starts here. All this had been neglected, but Aleksei restored everything. He's very fond of this estate, and something I least expected, he's completely given himself up to it. And then, he's such a gifted man! Whatever he starts, he does perfectly. He's not only not bored, but he works with enthusiasm. And I see that he's turned into a careful, efficient landlord, and in the management of the estate he's even become miserly. But only there. When it's a question of tens of thousands, he doesn't think of money," she said, with that joyful, roguish smile with which women, when speaking of the men they love, often discuss their secret traits, known to them alone. "Do you see that large building? It's the new hospital. I think it'll cost him more than a hundred thousand rubles. It's his *dada* now. And do you know how it started? The moujiks, it seems, asked him to reduce the rents on the meadows, but he refused, and I accused him of being a miser. Not just because of this of course, but because of a combination of things, he began building a hospital to prove, as you see, that he was no miser. If you prefer, *c'est une petitesse*, but I love him the more for it. And now you'll see the house. It was built by his grandfather, its exterior hasn't been changed at all."

"How lovely!" said Dolly, looking with wonder at the beautiful, colonnaded house that stood out against the various shades of green of the old garden trees.

"It's beautiful, isn't it? And the view from the house, from its upper storey, is magnificent."

They drove into a courtyard covered with gravel and decorated with flowers, where two laborers were placing rough-edged, porous stones around the loosened soil of a flower bed; and they stopped at the covered entrance.

"Ah, they've already arrived," said Anna, noticing the horses that were being led away from the porch. "Isn't that a beautiful horse? He's a cob. My favorite. Bring him here and get me some sugar. Where is the count?" she asked the two uniformed footmen who rushed forward. "Ah, there he is!" she said, catching sight of Vronsky and Veslovsky, who were coming toward her.

"Where will you put the princess?" Vronsky asked Anna in French, and without waiting for an answer, again greeted Daria Aleksandrovna, now kissing her hand. "I suggest the large balcony room."

"Oh, no, it's too far! The corner room would be better—then we'll see more of each other. Let's go!" said Anna, giving her favorite horse some of the sugar that had been brought by the servant.

"*Et vous oubliez votre devoir,*" she said to Veslovsky, who had also come onto the porch.

"*Pardon, j'en ai tout plein les poches,*" he replied, smiling and reaching into his vest pocket.

"*Mais vous venez trop tard,*" she said, using her handkerchief to wipe her hand, which had been moistened by the horse when it took the sugar. Then she turned to Dolly. "I hope you've come to stay a while. For one day only? But that's impossible!"

"I promised, and the children . . ." said Dolly, embarrassed both because she had to reach for her traveling bag in the carriage and because she thought her face was probably covered with dust.

"No, Dolly, darling. . . . Well, we'll see. Come!" And Anna took Dolly to her room.

This room was not the main guest room suggested by Vronsky, but one for which Anna apologized to Dolly. And though offered apologetically, it was furnished at a level of luxury that Dolly had never lived in and that reminded her of the best hotels abroad.

"My darling, how happy I am!" said Anna, still in her riding habit, and she sat down for a moment next to Dolly. "Tell me about your family. I saw Stiva for a moment only. But he doesn't know what to say about the children. How's my favorite, Tania? She must be a big girl now."

"Yes, quite big," Daria Aleksandrovna replied abruptly, surprised at herself for talking so coldly about her children. "We're enjoying our stay with the Levins," she added.

"If I could only be sure," said Anna, "that you don't condemn me. . . . All of you should have come. After all, Stiva is an old and close friend of Aleksei," she added and suddenly blushed.

"Yes, but we are so comfortable . . ." said Dolly in embarrassment.

"Well, I'm talking such foolishness only because I'm happy. But I'm so glad to have you, darling, and that's the only thing that matters," said Anna, again kissing her. "You haven't told me yet what you think of me. I want to know everything. But I'm glad that you'll see me as I am. Most of all, I wouldn't like people to think that I'm trying to prove something. I'm not trying to prove anything; I only want to live and to wrong no one but myself. It's my right, isn't it? This, however, could become a long conversation, and we'll talk about it at length later. And now I'll go change my dress and send you a maid."

19

WHEN DARIA ALEKSANDROVNA remained alone, she surveyed the room with the eyes of a housewife. Everything that she had seen when she was approaching the house and was going through it, and what she saw now in her room, impressed her with its abundance and smartness and with that air of the new European luxury, which she had only read about in English novels and had never seen in Russia, particularly in the country. Everything was new, from the new French wallpaper to the carpet that covered the entire floor. The bed, with its springs and mattress, had a peculiar kind of bolster and small pillows in silk cases. The marble washstand, the dressing table, the couch, the tables, the bronze clock on the mantel, the curtains and the drapes—everything was new and expensive.

The smartly attired maid who came in to offer her services was combed and dressed more fashionably than Dolly, and looked as new and expensive as the rest of the room. Daria Aleksandrovna was pleased with her politeness, cleanliness, and complaisance, but she did not feel at ease with her. She was embarrassed by her patched blouse, which, to her bad luck, had been packed with her things by mistake. She felt awkward about the patched and darned spots, which she was so proud of at home. At home everyone realized that for six blouses one needed more than eighteen yards of nainsook at sixty-five kopecks, which amounted to more than fifteen rubles not counting trimming and labor, and that thus these fifteen rubles had been saved. But the maid made her feel not really ashamed but uncomfortable.

Daria Aleksandrovna was greatly relieved when her old friend Annushka came into the room. The mistress needed the smart-looking maid, and Annushka remained with Daria Aleksandrovna.

Evidently Annushka was very glad that Daria Aleksandrovna had come, and she talked ceaselessly. Dolly noticed that she wanted to express her opinion about her mistress' situation, particularly about the count's love for Anna Arkadievna and his devotion to her, but Dolly insisted on stopping her whenever she began to talk about this.

"I grew up with Anna Arkadievna; she is dearer to me than anyone else in this world. Well, it's not for us to judge. But such a love, I believe—"

"Then, please, have it washed, if possible," interrupted Daria Aleksandrovna.

"Very well. We have two laundresses for the small things, but the linen is washed by machine. The count himself attends to everything. Such a husband. . . ."

Dolly was glad when Anna came in and put an end to Annushka's chatter.

Anna had changed into a simple, white batiste dress. Dolly looked keenly at this simple dress. She knew what that simplicity meant and at what expense it had been purchased.

"My old friend," said Anna, referring to Annushka.

Anna was no longer embarrassed. She felt completely calm and collected. Dolly saw that by now she had freed herself completely of the initial impression her arrival had made and had assumed a superficial, indifferent tone, as though she had locked the door to her feelings and innermost thoughts.

"And how is your little girl, Anna?" asked Dolly.

"Annie?" (This was how she referred to her daughter, Anna.) "She's fine. She has improved a great deal. Would you like to see her? Come, I'll show her to you. We've had a great deal of trouble with the nurses," she began. "We have an Italian wet nurse, She's good, but so stupid! We wanted to send her away, but the girl has become so accustomed to her that we still keep her."

"And what have you decided . . ." Dolly began, intending to ask her what the child's name would be. But noticing that

Anna suddenly frowned, she changed her question. "What have you decided to do? Have you already weaned her?"

But Anna understood.

"That's not really what you meant to ask, is it? You were going to ask about her name—am I right? It worries Aleksei. She has no name, or rather her name is Karenin," said Anna, half-closing her eyes so that the eyelashes joined and only they were visible. "But," she said, her face suddenly brightening, "we'll talk about it later. Come, I'll show her to you. *Elle est très gentille.* She has already begun to crawl."

The splendor of the nursery impressed Daria Aleksandrovna even more than that of the rest of the house. Here there were small carriages ordered from England, implements for training the child to walk, a special divan built like a billiard table for the child to crawl on, rocking chairs, and special bathing basins of a new style. All this was English, strong and well built, and obviously very expensive. The room was large, very high and bright.

When they entered, the little girl, dressed only in a shirt, was seated in her tiny chair at a table, eating her bouillon, which dripped onto her chest. A Russian girl who assisted in the nursery was feeding the child and evidently helping herself as well. Neither the nurse nor the wet nurse was there. They were in the next room, and from there could be heard their conversation in a peculiar French that was their only means of communicating with each other.

On hearing Anna's voice, a tall, smart English nurse, with an unpleasant and insincere expression on her face, appeared in the doorway, rapidly shook her fair ringlets and at once began to apologize, although Anna was not blaming her for anything. To every word of Anna's she continued to reply hastily, "Yes, my lady."

The dark-browed, dark-haired, rosy-faced little girl, with her sturdy, ruddy body covered with goose flesh, delighted Daria Aleksandrovna, in spite of the stern look she gave the stranger; she even envied her her healthy appearance. She also was charmed by the way the baby crawled. None of her children had crawled that way. This child looked unusually sweet when they placed her on the rug and tucked her dress up in back. Like a little animal, looking now and then at the grownups with her large, sparkling black eyes, and evidently enjoying the general admiration, she smiled and held her legs sideways, leaned firmly on her arms, quickly raised her entire back, and again pushed her arms forward.

But the general atmosphere of the nursery, and particularly the English nurse, did not appeal at all to Daria Aleksandrovna. Only after realizing that a good woman would be unwilling to serve in such an unconventional family as Anna's did Daria Aleksandrovna understand how Anna, with her knowledge of people, could engage such an uncongenial and unrespectable person as that English nurse. Moreover, from a few words, Daria Aleksandrovna at once understood that Anna, the wet nurse, the nurse, and the baby were not entirely accustomed to each other, and that the mother's visit to the nursery was an unusual occurrence. Anna wanted to give the baby her toy, but could not find it.

But most surprising of all, when asked how many teeth the baby had, Anna made a mistake and was completely unaware of the two latest teeth.

"Sometimes I feel downhearted, as though I'm not wanted there," said Anna as she left the nursery, lifting her train so that she might not upset the toys that were standing at the door. "It was not like this with the first one!"

"I thought the opposite," said Daria Aleksandrovna shyly.

"Oh, no! You probably know that I saw Seryozha," said Anna, half-closing her eyes, as though gazing at something in the distance. "But we'll talk about it later. You'd scarcely believe it, but I feel like a hungry person who has been suddenly given a full dinner and doesn't know where to begin. That full dinner is you and the conversations we'll have, which I couldn't have with anyone else. But I don't know which conversation I should start first. *Mais je ne vous ferai grâce de rien.* I must unburden myself completely. But now I must give you a brief account of the company which you'll meet here," she said. "I'll begin with the ladies. Princess Varvara. You know her, and I know your and Stiva's opinion of her. Stiva says that her only purpose in life is to prove her superiority over Aunt Katerina Pavlovna. It's true, but she is kindhearted and I'm very grateful to her. There was a time in Petersburg when I needed *un chaperon*. She turned up then. But, truly, she's very kind. She eased my situation considerably. I see that you don't understand the full burden of my situation . . . as it was there, in Petersburg," she added. "Here I'm completely tranquil and happy. But about this we'll talk later. I must continue down my list. Then there's

Sviazhsky. He's the local marshal of nobility and a very decent person, but he seeks some favor of Aleksei. You see, since we've settled in the country, Aleksei, with his wealth, can exert great influence. Then there's Tushkevich—you've seen him. He used to be with Betsy, but they let him go and he came over to us. He, as Aleksei says, is one of those men who are very pleasant when they are taken for what they try to appear to be, *et puis, il est comme il faut,* as Princess Varvara says. Then there's this Veslovsky . . . you know that one. A very nice boy," she said, and a roguish smile curved her lips. "What's that unbelievable story we heard about Levin? Veslovsky told Aleksei about it, but we can't believe it. *Il est très gentil et naïf,*" she said with the same smile. "Men need diversion and Aleksei needs company; therefore I value these people. It must be lively and gay with us so that Aleksei may not wish for anything new. Then you'll see the manager. A German, a very good man, who knows his business. Aleksei regards him highly. Then there's the doctor, a young man, not quite a nihilist, but, you know, he eats with his knife, yet a good doctor. And the architect. . . . *Une petite cour.*"

20

"Well, here's Dolly, Princess. You were so eager to see her," said Anna, coming out together with Daria Aleksandrovna onto the spacious stone terrace, where Princess Varvara was seated in the shade at an embroidering frame, working on a cover for Count Aleksei Kirillovich's armchair. "She says she won't have anything until dinner, but will you order lunch to be served, please? And I'll go call Aleksei and all the rest."

Princess Varvara received Dolly kindly and somewhat patronizingly, and at once began to explain to her that she had made her home with Anna because she had always loved her more than did her sister Katerina Pavlovna, the one who had brought up Anna, and that now, when everyone had forsaken Anna, she considered it her duty to help her in this transient, most difficult period.

"Her husband will grant her a divorce and then I'll return to my secluded life, but right now I can be useful to her and, unlike the others, I'll fulfill my duty, however hard it is on me. And how nice of you to come! They live exactly like the happiest of married couples. God will be their judge, not we. And didn't Biriuzovsky and Avenieva. . . . And Nikandrov himself, and Vasiliev and Madame Mamonov, and Liza Neptunov. . . . No one said anything against them. And in the end they were received everywhere. And then *c'est un intérieur si joli, si comme il faut. Tout-à-fait à l'anglaise. On se réunit le matin au* breakfast *et puis on se sépare.* Until dinner everyone does as he pleases. Dinner is at seven. It was very kind of Stiva to send you here. He should stick to them. You know, Vronsky can accomplish anything through his mother or his brother. And they are very generous. Did he tell you about his hospital? *Ce sera admirable.* Everything is brought from Paris."

Their conversation was interrupted by Anna, who had found the men in the billiard room and was coming onto the terrace in their company. There was still some time before dinner, the weather was beautiful, so several suggestions were made for passing the remaining two hours. There were many ways of passing the time at Vozdvizhenskoe, and none of them were like those at Pokrovskoe.

"*Une partie de lawn tennis,*" Veslovsky suggested with his handsome smile, "We'll be partners again, Anna Arkadievna."

"No, it's hot. I'd rather walk in the garden and then go for a boat ride to show the river banks to Daria Aleksandrovna," proposed Vronsky.

"Whatever you decide," said Sviazhsky.

"I believe that Dolly would enjoy a walk most of all. And then a boat ride," said Anna.

That is what they decided. Veslovsky and Tushkevich left for the boathouse to get the boat ready and to wait for the others.

They walked along the path in pairs, Anna with Sviazhsky, and Dolly with Vronsky. Dolly felt somewhat embarrassed and worried in the completely unfamiliar surroundings she found herself in. In theory, abstractly, she not only justified but even approved of Anna's step. As frequently happens with irreproachably moral women who tire of the monotony of their moral lives, from a distance she not only did not blame Anna for this sinful love but even envied her. Moreover, she loved Anna with all her heart. But when she actually saw her amidst these strangers, with their elegant ways, new to Daria

Aleksandrovna, she felt uncomfortable. Most unpleasant to her was Princess Varvara, who had forgiven them everything for the comforts she was enjoying.

In general, Dolly approved of Anna's action in theory, but she did not enjoy seeing the man for whom it had been done. Moreover, she had never liked Vronsky. She believed him to be too proud, although she could not find anything in him that he should be proud of other than his wealth. But against her will, here in his own home, he appeared to her more imposing than before, and she did not feel at ease with him. In his presence she felt as she had with the maid because of her patched blouse. Just as the patches had made her feel not exactly ashamed but uncomfortable with the maid, so with him she was always not exactly ashamed but uncomfortable on account of herself.

Dolly felt embarrassed and tried to find a topic of conversation. Though she considered that such a haughty person would not like to hear his house and garden praised, she was unable to find another subject and told him how much she liked his house.

"Yes, it is a beautiful building, and in the fine old style," he said.

"I very much liked the courtyard that faced the porch. Was it always like this?"

"Oh, no!" he answered, and his face beamed with pleasure. "If you could have seen that courtyard last spring!"

And then, first cautiously, and then with increasing enthusiasm he began to point out to her in detail the various attractive features of the house and the garden. One could see that, having devoted so much effort to the improvement and embellishment of his estate, Vronsky felt the urge to boast about it to a visitor and was wholeheartedly glad to hear Daria Aleksandrovna's praise.

"Perhaps you would like to see the hospital, if you're not tired? It's not far. Let's go!" he said, looking into her face to make sure that she really was not bored.

"Will you go, Anna?" he asked.

"We'll go along—all right?" she said, addressing Sviazhsky. "*Mais il ne faut pas laisser le pauvre* Veslovsky *et* Tushkevich *se morfondre là dans le bateau.* We must send them word. Yes, it'll be his monument," said Anna, turning to Dolly with the same roguish, knowing smile with which she had spoken about the hospital earlier.

"Oh, what a grand undertaking!" said Sviazhsky. But in order to show the independence of his opinions, he at once added a slightly disapproving remark. "I am, however, surprised, Count," he said, "that you, who are doing so much for the health of the peasants, aren't interested in schools for them."

"*C'est devenu tellement commun les écoles*," said Vronsky. "You know, that isn't the reason. I was just carried away," he said. "This is the way to the hospital," he said, addressing Daria Aleksandrovna, and he pointed to a side exit from the alley.

The ladies opened their parasols and turned onto the side path. After a few turns they passed through a gate, and Daria Aleksandrovna saw, facing her on a rise of ground, a large red, almost-completed building of elaborate design. The iron roof, still unpainted, glared blindingly in the bright sunlight. Next to this building another was rising, enclosed in scaffolding on which workmen in aprons were busy laying brick, pouring mortar from wooden pails and checking the courses with their levels.

"How rapidly your work is progressing!" said Sviazhsky. "The last time I was here the roof wasn't up yet."

"Everything will be ready by fall. Inside, everything's nearly finished," said Anna.

"And what's the new building going to be?"

"The doctor's apartment and the pharmacy," replied Vronsky, and noticing the architect in his short coat coming toward him, he apologized to the ladies and went over to meet him.

He walked around the lime pit, from which the workers were taking the slaked lime, then stopped and began a heated discussion with the architect.

"The pediment is still too low," he said when Anna asked what was wrong.

"I told you that the foundation should have been higher," said Anna.

"Of course it would be better, Anna Arkadievna," said the architect, "but it's too late now."

"Yes, I'm very much interested in it," replied Anna to Sviazhsky, who expressed his surprise at her knowledge of architecture. "The new building must match the hospital. But it was thought up later and started without a plan."

After he finished his conversation with the architect,

Vronsky joined the ladies and led them inside the hospital.

Though outside they were still working on the cornices, and the lower floor was still being painted, the upper floor was almost completely finished. They ascended a wide cast-iron staircase to a landing and entered the first large room. The walls were made of imitation marble, the immense plate glass windows were already installed, and only the parquet floor remained to be finished. The carpenters, who were planing a square of the floor, stopped their work to take off the bands they had tied their hair with and to greet the visitors.

"This is the waiting room," said Vronsky. "There'll be a desk here, a table, a closet, and nothing else."

"Come this way. Don't go near the window," said Anna, feeling the paint to see whether it was dry. "Aleksei, the paint is already dry," she added.

From the waiting room they went into the hallway. Here Vronsky pointed out ventilators of the latest design. Then he showed them marble bathtubs, beds with unusual springs, then the wards, one after another, the store room, the linen room, new-style stoves, carts that could be pushed noiselessly along the hallway with needed supplies, and many other things. Sviazhsky expressed his appreciation of everything, as one who was familiar with all the latest improvements. Dolly simply looked with wonder at all of these things that she had never seen before, and in her desire to understand them she asked detailed questions, to Vronsky's apparent pleasure.

"Yes, I believe that it'll be the only perfectly equipped hospital in Russia," said Sviazhsky.

"And will you have a maternity ward?" asked Dolly. "It's so urgently needed in the country. I often—"

In spite of his usual courtesy, Vronsky interrupted her.

"This is not a lying-in home, but a hospital for the treatment of all diseases, except the contagious. And look at this. . . ." and he rolled up a wheelchair for convalescents, recently ordered. "Look at it!" He sat and began to wheel it. "The patient cannot walk yet, he's still weak or his legs are affected, but he needs air, and he can move around in this chair. . . ."

Everything interested Daria Aleksandrovna; she liked everything, but most of all she was taken by Vronsky and his sincere, naïve enthusiasm. Yes, he's a very kind, fine man, she thought, not listening but looking at him, trying to fathom his expression, and in her imagination putting herself in Anna's place. She liked him so much in his present animated state that she understood how Anna could have fallen in love with him.

21

"No, I THINK that the princess is tired, and that horses don't interest her," Vronsky said to Anna who had proposed walking to the stud farm where Sviazhsky was eager to see a new stallion. "You go there. I'll take the princess home and we'll have a chat," he said. "If you don't object," he added, turning to her.

"I don't know anything about horses, and I'll be happy to," said Daria Aleksandrovna, somewhat surprised.

She saw on Vronsky's face that he had something to ask her. She was not mistaken. As soon as they returned through the gate into the garden, he looked in the direction in which Anna had gone and, convinced that she could neither hear nor see them, he began:

"You've probably guessed that I want to talk to you," he said, looking at her with laughing eyes. "I know that you are Anna's friend." He took off his hat and, reaching for his handkerchief, wiped his balding head.

Daria Aleksandrovna made no reply and only looked fearfully at him. When they were alone, she suddenly became frightened; she feared his laughing eyes and stern expression.

The most diverse conjectures of what he intended to tell her flashed through her mind. He may ask me to move in, bringing my children, and stay as their guest, and I'll have to refuse; or that I should create a circle of friends for Anna in Moscow. . . . Or is it about Vasenka Veslovsky and his relationship with Anna? Or perhaps about Kitty and about his feeling of guilt? She foresaw only what would disturb her but could not guess what it was he wanted to tell her.

"You have such an influence over Anna, and she's so fond of you," he said. "Please help me."

Daria Aleksandrovna looked inquiringly and shyly at his forceful face, which emerged, now completely and now partly, from the shade of the linden trees into the sunshine, and then darkened once again in the shade. She waited for him to go on, but he walked beside her in silence, his cane catching in the gravel.

"Since, of all Anna's former friends, you're the only woman who's come to see us—I'm not counting Princess Varvara—I understand that you did it not because you regard our situation as normal, but because, knowing all the difficulty of this situation, you still love her as before and want to help her. Am I right?" he asked, glancing at her.

"Oh, yes!" said Daria Aleksandrovna, folding her parasol. "And—"

"But," he interrupted, and unconsciously, without realizing that he was making his companion uncomfortable, he stopped, causing her to stop as well, "no one feels all the hardship of Anna's situation more deeply and more strongly than I. And it's quite understandable, if you would do me the honor of regarding me as a man with a heart. I am the cause of this situation, and therefore it weighs on me."

"I understand," said Daria Aleksandrovna, unconsciously admiring the sincere and unhesitant way in which he spoke. "But precisely because you feel that you're the cause of this situation, I'm afraid that you also exaggerate it," she said. "I realize that her position in society is difficult."

"It's hell!" Vronsky interjected, frowning gloomily. "It's hard to imagine any worse mental torment than what she endured during the two weeks in Petersburg . . . and I'd like you to believe that."

"But here, until either Anna . . . or you begin to miss society. . . ."

"Society?" he said contemptuously. "What do I need of society?"

"Until then—and it may be forever—you're happy and contented. I see how happy Anna is, completely happy—she has already managed to tell me about it," said Daria Aleksandrovna with a smile. But unconsciously, while saying this, she developed some doubts about Anna's being really happy.

But Vronsky, it seemed, had no such doubts.

"Yes," he said, "I know she's become herself again after all her suffering. She is happy. She's happy in her present situation. But I? . . . I dread what awaits us. . . . I'm sorry, perhaps you would prefer to walk?"

"It doesn't matter."

"Then let's sit here."

Daria Aleksandrovna sat down on a garden bench in a corner of the alley. He stopped in front of her.

"I see that she's happy," he repeated, and Daria Aleksandrovna felt still more uncertain of Anna's happiness. "But can it go on like this? Whether we acted right or wrong is another question. But the die is cast," he said, changing from Russian to French, "and we are bound for life. We are joined by bonds of love, most sacred to us. We have a child, we may have more. But the law and our present situation create numberless complications, which she, enjoying her present peace of mind after all her trials and suffering, neither sees nor wants to see. And it's quite understandable. But I can't help seeing the truth. According to law, my daughter is not mine, but Karenin's. I refuse to accept this deceit!" he said with an energetic gesture of rejection, looking at Daria Alkesandrovna with a half-gloomy and half-questioning expression.

She said nothing but just kept looking at him. He continued:

"And when a son is born to me, he, my own son, will legally be a Karenin and will be the heir neither to my name nor to my fortune, and no matter how happy we may be in our family life, no matter how many children we may have, there will be no legal bond between me and them. They will remain Karenins. Please understand the hardship and the horror of this situation. I've tried to talk to Anna about it. It irritates her. She doesn't understand, and I have no way of telling *her* everything. Now look at it from another side. I'm happy in her love, but I must keep occupied. I've found my occupation. I'm proud of it; I consider it more honorable than the occupation of my former comrades at the court and in the service. And, without a doubt, I wouldn't change it for theirs. I work here without leaving the place, I'm happy and contented, and we need nothing else for our happiness. I love what I'm doing here. *Cela n'est pas un pis-aller;* on the contrary. . . ."

Daria Aleksandrovna noticed that during this part of his confession he grew confused, and she could not completely understand the reason for his stumbling. But she felt that once he had begun to reveal his intimate thoughts, which he could not speak of to Anna, he was now revealing all, and that the problem of his activities in the country belonged to the same group of intimate thoughts as the problem of his relationship with Anna.

"Now, I'll continue," he said, regaining control of himself. "It's most important and urgent that, while working, I should be sure that my work will not die with me, that I leave heirs. I've no such assurance. Just imagine the state of a man who knows beforehand that the children born to him and his beloved wife will belong not to him, but to another person, who will hate them and will not want to know them. That's horrible!"

He fell silent, apparently deeply moved.

"Yes, of course. I understand. But what can Anna do?" asked Daria Aleksandrovna.

"Well, this brings me to the purpose of our conversation," he said, making an effort to calm himself. "Anna can help; it depends on her. . . . Even to petition the Czar for the adoption of our child, she must first get a divorce. And this depends on Anna. Her husband agreed to grant a divorce—your husband almost succeeded in arranging it. Even now, I know, he couldn't refuse. All she has to do is to write to him. At that time he plainly said that if she expressed her desire he would not refuse it. Of course," he said gloomily, "it's just another of the cruel hypocrisies that only heartless men like that are capable of. He knows how painful it is for her to even think of him, and, knowing this, he demands a letter from her. I know it would be torture for her. But the reasons are so vital that one has *passer pardessus toutes ces finesses de sentiment. Il y va du bonheur et de l'existence d'Anne et de ses enfants.* I'm not speaking of myself, though it's very hard on me, very hard," he said, with a threatening expression for whoever made it so difficult for him. "And so, Princess, I shamelessly hold on to you, as to my anchor of salvation. Help me make her write to him and ask for a divorce."

"Yes, of course," said Daria Aleksandrovna thoughtfully, remembering vividly her last meeting with Aleksei Aleksandrovich. "Yes, of course," repeated Daria Aleksandrovna resolutely, thinking of Anna.

"Make use of your influence on her, make her write to him. I don't want to . . . and I don't believe I can talk to her about it."

"Very well, I'll talk to her. But why doesn't she think of it herself?" asked Daria Aleksandrovna, for some reason suddenly recalling Anna's strange new habit of half-closing her eyes. And she recalled that Anna did it just when her innermost thoughts dwelt upon the problems of her life. As though she wants to close her eyes on her life so that she may not see everything, thought Dolly. "I'll talk to her without fail both for her sake and my own," replied Daria Aleksandrovna to his words of thanks.

They rose and went toward the house.

22

WHEN SHE saw Dolly, who had returned before her, Anna looked intently into her eyes as though inquiring about the conversation she had had with Vronsky, but she did not ask about it in words.

"It seems to be time for dinner," she said, "and we've scarcely seen each other. I'm counting on the evening. Now I must go to dress. You too, I suppose. All of us are dusty after our visit to the building."

Dolly went into her room and was amused. She had nothing else to put on. She had already put on her best dress. But to go through the motions of getting ready for dinner, she asked the maid to clean her dress, changed the cuffs and the bow, and covered her head with lace.

"This is all I could do," she said, smiling at Anna who came out in a new dress, the third, and again an exceedingly simple one.

"Yes, we are very formal here," she said, as though apologizing for her smart appearance. "Aleksei has seldom enjoyed anything so much as your visit. He's positively in love with you," she added. "I hope you aren't tired."

They had no time to talk before dinner. When they entered the drawing room, Princess Varvara and the gentlemen, in their black frock coats, were already there. The architect was dressed in a swallow-tailed coat. Vronsky introduced the doctor and the manager to the guest. The architect had been introduced earlier, at the hospital.

The portly butler, shining with his round, clean-shaven face and starched white tie, announced that dinner was ready, and the ladies rose. Vronsky asked Sviazhsky to escort Anna Arkadievna, while he escorted Dolly. Veslovsky was quicker than Tushkevich in offering his arm to Princess Varvara, so that Tushkevich, the manager, and the doctor walked alone.

The dinner, the dining room, the dinner service, the servants, the wine, and the food not only conformed to the general style of latest luxury of the home but seemed even to exceed everything else by their splendor and newness. Daria Aleksandrovna took in this unaccustomed luxury. She could not hope to make use in her household of anything she observed here—so much did this life exceed her own in luxury. But, as a housewife, she unconsciously tried to learn all the details of what she saw, asking herself by whom and how all this had been done. Vasenka Veslovsky, her husband, even Sviazhsky, and many others whom she knew, never thought about it and unquestioningly believed what every gracious host wished his guests to believe, namely, that all this good order in his home had not been achieved at the expense of any effort on his part but had come about by itself. But Daria Aleksandrovna knew that even porridge for the children's breakfast never came about by itself, and that therefore someone's careful attention was being given to maintain this complex and excellent order. And by Aleksei Kirillovich's look, by the way he surveyed the table, motioned to the butler, and offered Daria Aleksandrovna a choice of hot or cold soup, she understood that all of this was being done and maintained through the attention of the master himself. Anna's part in it was probably no greater than Veslovsky's. She, Sviazhsky, the princess, and Veslovsky all were guests, enjoying everything which had been prepared for them.

Anna was the hostess only insofar as she guided the conversation. It was very difficult for her to do it at this small dinner party on account of the presence of the manager and the architect, people of a completely different world, who tried not to be overawed by the unfamiliar luxury and who could not sustain a long general conversation. Nevertheless, Anna guided this difficult conversation with her usual tact and ease, even enjoying it, as Daria Aleksandrovna noticed.

The conversation touched on Tushkevich and Veslovsky's boatride, which they had taken by themselves, and Tushkevich began to tell about the latest races at the Petersburg Yacht Club. But Anna, availing herself of a break in the conversation, at once turned to the architect to draw him out of his silence.

"Nikolai Ivanovich," she said, referring to Sviazhsky, "was amazed to see how quickly the building had gone up since he was here last. . . . Even I wonder at the rapid progress of the work as I visit and watch the building every day."

"It's a pleasure to work with His Excellency," said the architect (he was a respectful and quiet man, conscious of his own dignity). "It's quite different from dealing with the provincial authorities. Whereas there you get entangled in red tape, here I explain the matter to the count, and after a short discussion, we come to a decision."

"American methods," said Sviazhsky with a smile.

"Yes, there they build efficiently. . . ."

The conversation changed to the abuse of power by the United States government, but Anna at once directed it to another subject so as to draw the manager out of his silence.

"Have you ever seen a harvesting machine?" she asked Daria Aleksandrovna. "We were returning from inspecting some when we met you. It was the first time I had seen them."

"And how do they work?" asked Dolly.

"Exactly like scissors. They have a board with many small scissors. Like this."

With her beautiful white hands, covered with rings, Anna took a knife and fork and began to demonstrate. She apparently knew that nobody would understand what she was trying to explain, but knowing that her voice was pleasant and her hands attractive, she continued the explanation.

"They are rather like penknives," said Veslovsky flirtatiously, his eyes fixed on Anna.

Anna smiled faintly but made no reply.

"Karl Fiodorovich, they work like scissors, don't they?" she said, turning to the manager.

"*O ja*," replied the German. "*Es ist ein ganz einfaches Ding*," and he went into an explanation of the mechanism.

"It's a pity that it doesn't bind. At the Vienna exposition I saw a machine that binds with wire," said Sviazhsky. "Such a machine is more economical."

"*Es kommt drauf an . . . Der Preis vom Draht muss ausgerechnet werden*." And the German, drawn out of his silence, addressed Vrosnky. "*Das lässt sich ausrechnen, Erlaucht*." The German was about to reach into his pocket for his pencil and notebook in which he made all his calculations, but remembering that he was at dinner and noticing Vronsky's cold look, he restrained himself. "*Zu kompliziert, macht zu viel Klopot*."

"*Wunscht man Dochots, so hat man auch Klopots*," said

Vasenka Veslovsky, teasing the German. *"J'adore l'allemand,"* he said, turning to Anna with the same smile.

"Cessez," she said to him with mock sternness.

"We expected to find you on the field, Vasili Semyonovich," she said, turning to the doctor, a sickly looking man. "Weren't you there?"

"I was there, but I vanished into the air," replied the doctor, joking in his gloomy way.

"Then you must have had quite a bit of exercise."

"It was excellent."

"Well, how is the old woman? It's not typhus, I hope."

"Not typhus, but she's pretty low."

"What a pity!" Anna said, and having accorded her share of courtesy to the members of the household, she turned to her own group.

"And yet, Anna Arkadievna, it would be hard to build a machine from your explanation," said Sviazhsky jokingly.

"But why?" Anna asked with a smile which showed that she knew that there was something charming in her description of the way the machine worked, and that Sviazhsky had noticed it. This new trait of youthful coquetry made a disagreeable impression on Dolly.

"But Anna Arkadievna's knowledge of architecture is amazing," said Tushkevich.

"Why, only yesterday I heard Anna Arkadievna discussing architraves and plinths," said Veslovsky. "Am I saying it right?"

"It's not surprising at all, when you see it and hear it discussed so often," said Anna. "And you probably don't even know what houses are made of."

Daria Aleksandrovna saw that Anna did not enjoy the flirtatious tone that was being used between herself and Veslovsky but yielded to it unconsciously.

In this respect Vronsky did not act at all like Levin. He apparently attached no importance to Veslovsky's chatter, and on the contrary, even encouraged this kind of banter.

"Well, Veslovsky, tell us. How are building stones held together?"

"By cement, of course."

"Bravo! And what is cement?"

"Well, it's something you spread. . . . well, putty," said Veslovsky, causing loud, general laughter.

The conversation among the guests, with the exception of

the doctor, the architect, and the manager, all of whom maintained a gloomy silence, was uninterrupted and either flowed smoothly, or caught on something, or cut someone to the quick. At one point Daria Aleksandrovna felt hurt and became so excited that her face grew flushed, and only later did she think that perhaps she had said something uncalled for and unpleasant. Sviazhsky mentioned Levin, relating his strange view that machines can bring only harm to Russian farming.

"I haven't the privilege of knowing this gentleman, Mr. Levin," said Vronsky with a smile, "but most likely he never saw the machines he condemns. And if he saw one and tried it out, he did it carelessly, and it must not have been an imported one but some Russian model. What kind of views could he have then?"

"Nothing but Turkish views," said Veslovsky with a smile, turning to Anna.

"I can't defend his point of view," said Daria Aleksandrovna, suddenly angered, "but I can say that he is a very learned man, and if he were here, he would know how to answer you, although I don't."

"I'm very fond of him, and we are very good friends," said Sviazhsky with a good-natured smile. *"Mais pardon, il est un petit peu toqué.* For instance, he maintains that neither the zemstvo nor the courts of arbitration are needed, and he refuses to take part in any public activities."

"It's our Russian apathy," said Vronsky, pouring some ice water from a decanter into a thin-stemmed glass, "our failure to meet the duties our privileges impose upon us and the consequent rejection of these duties."

"I know of no one who's more faithful in the performance of his duties," said Daria Aleksandrovna, vexed by Vronsky's condescending tone.

"I, on the contrary," continued Vronsky, whose feelings, for some reason, were obviously hurt by this conversation, "I, on the contrary as you see me, am very grateful for the honor they have done me in electing me honorary justice of the peace, thanks to Nikolai Ivanych." (He indicated Sviazhsky.) "I believe that my duty to travel to the sessions, to try a case concerning a moujik's horse, is as important as anything else that I'm able to do. And I'd be honored if they were to elect me to the county council. Only in this manner can I make up for the advantages which I enjoy as a landowner. Unfortunately, people don't understand the important part that the big landowners should play in the government."

It seemed strange to Daria Aleksandrovna to hear the self-assurance with which he expressed his views at his own table. She recalled that Levin, who held opposite views, was as resolute in his judgments at his table. But she loved Levin, and therefore took his part.

"Then we may rely upon you, Count, to come to the next sessions?" said Sviazhsky. "But you must leave earlier to be there by the eighth. Would you do me the honor of coming to me?"

"And I partly agree with your *beau-frère*," said Anna, "but in a different way," she added with a smile. "I'm afraid that lately we have become too much involved in these civic affairs. Just as in former times we had so many officials that each case had to have its own official, so it is now with participants in public affairs. Aleksei has been here only six months, and I believe he is already a member of five or six different public institutions—a public guardian, judge, member of the county council, juryman, and a member of some equestrian commission. *Du train que cela va* all his time will be taken up in these affairs. And I'm afraid that attending to so many duties becomes little more than formality. Of how many institutions are you a member, Nikolai Ivanych?" she asked, turning to Sviazhsky. "More than twenty, I believe?"

Anna was jesting, but her tone betrayed irritation. Daria Aleksandrovna, who had been attentively watching Anna and Vronsky, noticed it at once. She also noticed that during this conversation Vronsky's face immediately assumed a serious and stubborn expression. Princess Varvara, eager to change the subject, began hurriedly to speak about their Petersburg acquaintances. Observing this and recalling how Vronsky had spoken to her in the garden, unexpectedly bringing up his public activities, Dolly understood that these public activities were the cause of a secret disagreement between Anna and Vronsky.

The dinner, the wine, the service—all were excellent, but they were of a kind that Daria Aleksandrovna had seen at formal dinner parties or balls, to which she was no longer accustomed to. There was the same impersonal and strained atmosphere; and since the day was an ordinary one and the group of guests small, all this made a disagreeable impression on her.

After dinner they sat for a while on the terrace. Then they

started a game of lawn tennis. The players, divided into two groups, took their positions on carefully leveled, hardened croquet grounds, on both sides of a net stretched between two gilded posts. Daria Aleksandrovna tried to take part in the game, but for a long while she could not understand it, and when she did, she was so worn out that she sat down beside Princess Varvara and simply watched the players. Her partner, Tushkevich, also gave up, but the rest continued to play for a long while. Both Sviazhsky and Vronsky played well and with concentration. They carefully watched the approaching ball, deftly ran up to meet it, neither hurrying nor delaying, and bounding into the air at the right moment, they struck the ball with the racket adroitly and accurately, tossing it over the net. Veslovsky was the least skillful. He fussed too much, but his gayety inspired the players. He laughed and shouted ceaselessly. With the ladies' permission, he, like the other gentlemen, took off his frock coat, and his large, handsome figure, with the white sleeves of his shirt, his flushed perspiring face, and his quick movements, were a memorable sight.

When Daria Aleksandrovna went to bed that night, every time she closed her eyes she saw Vasenka Veslovsky flying about the croquet grounds.

But while the game was going on, Daria Aleksandrovna was unhappy. She did not like the flirtation between Anna and Vasenka Veslovsky, which they continued during the game, and the unnatural way grownups generally behave when, without children, they play a children's game. But not to upset the other players and to pass the time in some manner, she again joined them after a rest, and pretended that she was enjoying herself. All that day it seemed to her that she was performing on stage in the company of actors who were superior to her, and that her poor acting was causing the entire performance to fail.

She had come with the intention of spending as long as two days if she enjoyed herself. But that same evening, during the game, she decided to leave the next day. The tiresome cares that beset a mother, so hateful on her way here, now, after a day spent without them, seemed to her quite different and drew her back.

After evening tea and a night boat ride, when Daria Aleksandrovna entered her room alone, took off her dress, and sat down to arrange her thinning hair for the night, she felt greatly relieved.

She did not even enjoy the thought that Anna would soon come to see her. She wanted to be alone with her thoughts.

23

DOLLY WAS ABOUT TO go to bed when Anna entered, dressed in a robe.

Several times during the day Anna had begun to speak to her on subjects close to her heart, but each time, after a few words, she stopped. "We'll talk about this later, when we're alone. I have so much to tell you," she would say.

Now they were alone, and Anna did not know what to say. She was seated at the window, looking at Dolly. She reviewed in her mind what had seemed to her an inexhaustible store of topics for intimate conversation, but she could find none. It seemed to her at that moment that everything already had been said.

"Well, how is Kitty?" she asked with a heavy sigh and a guilty glance at Dolly. "Tell me the truth, Dolly, is she angry at me?"

"Angry? No," said Daria Aleksandrovna with a smile.

"She doesn't hate or despise me?"

"Oh, no! But you know, such things are never forgiven."

"Yes, of course!" said Anna, turning away and looking through the open window. "But I wasn't at fault. And who is at fault? What do we mean by being at fault? Could it possibly have been otherwise? Well, what do you think? Could it have happened that you might not be Stiva's wife?"

"Truly, I don't know. But tell me. . . ."

"Wait, we haven't finished about Kitty. Is she happy? They say he's a fine man."

"More than just a fine man. I don't know a better."

"Ah, I'm so glad to hear that! More than just a fine man," she repeated.

Dolly smiled.

"But tell me about yourself. We must have a long talk. And I spoke to . . ." Dolly did not know how to refer to him. It seemed awkward to her to call him either "the count" or "Aleksei Kirillovich."

"To Aleksei," said Anna. "I know that you had a talk. But I wanted to ask you frankly: what do you think about me, about my life?"

"How can I give you a quick answer? To tell you the truth, I don't know."

"But just the same, tell me. . . . You see how I live. But don't forget, you came in the summer and you see us when we are not alone. . . . We came here in the early spring, lived all alone and will live all alone, and I want that more than anything else. But just imagine me living alone, without him, and this will come to pass. . . . All indications are that this will happen often, that half of his time he'll spend outside his home," she said, rising and moving closer to Dolly.

"Of course," she interrupted as Dolly was about to object, "of course, I won't hold him by force. I'm not holding him even now. This is the racing season, his horses are running, and he goes there. I'm happy for him. But think about me, just imagine my situation. . . . But why talk about it?" She smiled. "Well, what did you two talk about?"

"He talked about the same things that I want to talk to you about, so it's easy for me to take his part. It's about whether it's possible, whether something can be done . . ." Daria Aleksandrovna faltered, "to correct, to improve your situation. . . . You know my views. . . . Nevertheless, if it's possible, you should get married. . . ."

"In other words, a divorce?" said Anna. "You know that the only woman who came to visit me in Petersburg was Betsy Tverskoy. You know her, of course. *Au fond c'est la femme la plus depravée qui existe.* She had had an affair with Tush-kevich, betraying her husband in the vilest way. And she told me that she didn't want to know me as long as my situation remained so unconventional. Don't imagine that I'm making comparisons. . . . I know you, my darling. But unwillingly I recalled it. . . . Well, what did he tell you?" she repeated.

"He said that he suffers both for you and for himself. Perhaps you'll call it egoism, but what a rightful and noble egoism! First of all, he wants to legitimize his daughter, to be your husband, to have his rightful claim on you."

"What wife, what slave can be as enslaved as I am in my situation?" she interrupted gloomily.

"But his main wish is . . . that you should not suffer."

"That's impossible! Go on."

"Well, his most proper wish is that your children bear his name."

"What children?" asked Anna, without looking at Dolly and half-closing her eyes.

"Annie and those that will come. . . ."

"He shouldn't worry on this account, for I'll have no other children."

"How can you be so sure that you won't have any more?"

"I won't because I don't want any."

Though deeply agitated, Anna smiled, noticing the naïve expression of curiosity, surprise and horror on Dolly's face.

"The doctor told me after my illness. . . ."

. . . .

"Impossible!" said Dolly, opening her eyes wide. To her it was one of those discoveries the results and effects of which are so tremendous that for a moment one feels that he cannot comprehend all of it but must give it a great deal of thought.

This discovery, which had suddenly made clear to her what she formerly could not understand about families that had only one or two children, stirred in her so many thoughts, considerations and contradictory feelings that she could not say anything and only stared wide-eyed in surprise at Anna. It was the same thing she had dreamt about only that day on the way there, but now that she had learned that it was possible she was horrified. She felt that such a solution was too simple for such a complex problem.

After a silence, all she could say was, *"N'est-ce pas immoral?"*

"Why? Think a moment. I had to choose between two things—either to be pregnant, in other words, ill, or to be a friend and companion to my husband, to one who is the same as my husband," said Anna with a deliberate air of levity and lightheartedness.

"Of course, of course," repeated Daria Aleksandrovna, listening to the same arguments that she herself had employed but not finding them so persuasive as before.

"You and others," said Anna, as though guessing her thoughts, "still may hesitate, but I. . . . You must understand that I am not his wife; he loves me while he still loves me. How can I keep his love? By this?"

She placed her white hands in front of her stomach.

As usually happens in moments of great agitation, thoughts and memories crowded in on Daria Aleksandrovna's mind with uncommon speed. I've failed to hold Stiva, she thought. He's left me for others, and the first one he betrayed me for failed to hold him, though she was always gay and beautiful. He left her and took another. Is it possible that in this way Anna will succeed in attracting and keeping Count Vronsky? If he seeks, he will find elsewhere still more attractive and gay toilettes and manners. And however white and beautiful her bare arms are, however beautiful her full figure and her flushed face under her black hair, he will find some still more beautiful, just as they are sought for and found by my disgusting, pitiful, dear husband.

Dolly made no reply and just sighed. Anna heard that sigh, which expressed Dolly's disagreement, and continued. She had in store some other arguments, so potent that they were irrefutable.

"You say that it's wrong. But we must consider everything," she continued. "You forget my situation. How can I wish to have children? I'm not talking about the suffering; I'm not afraid of it. But think who my children would be. Unfortunate children who would bear a stranger's name. Their very birth would make them ashamed of their mother, their father, their birth."

"That's exactly why you must get a divorce."

But Anna did not listen to her. She was anxious to air the rest of her arguments, which she had so many times employed to convince herself.

"Why am I endowed with reason if I don't use it to keep from bringing forth ill-fated children?"

She looked at Dolly, and without waiting for an answer, continued:

"I would always feel that I'd wronged these unfortunate children," she said. "If they don't exist, at least they aren't unfortunate; but if they were unfortunate, I alone would be to blame."

These were the same arguments Daria Aleksandrovna herself had employed; but now she listened to them and could not understand them. How can you wrong a being who doesn't exist? she thought. And suddenly the thought occurred to her: would it be better in any respect for her darling Grisha never to have existed? And this appeared to her so preposterous and so strange that she shook her head to rid herself of this whirling confusion of insane thoughts.

"I don't know, but it's wrong," was all she said, with an expression of disgust on her face.

"But don't forget who you are and who I am. . . . Moreover," added Anna, who in spite of the power of her arguments and the weakness of Dolly's, still seemed to admit that what she said was wrong, "don't forget the most important thing—that now I'm not in the same situation as you. Your problem is whether to decide to have no more children, and mine whether I want any. It's a great difference. You must understand that in my situation I cannot want them."

Daria Aleksandrovna did not object. She suddenly felt that a great distance now separated her from Anna, and that there existed questions on which they would never agree and which it would be better not to discuss.

24

"THEN IT'S ALL the more necessary for you to rearrange your situation, if possible," said Dolly.

"Yes, if possible," said Anna, her voice suddenly sounding quite different, soft and sad.

"Is a divorce impossible? I was told that your husband had agreed to it."

"Dolly, I don't like to talk about it."

"Then we won't," Daria Aleksandrovna said quickly, noticing an expression of suffering on Anna's face. "I just want to say that you view things too darkly."

"I? Not at all. I'm gay and content. You saw, *je fais des passion*, Veslovsky. . . ."

"To tell you the truth, I didn't like Veslovsky's manner," said Daria Aleksandrovna, anxious to change the subject.

"Oh, come now! It only flatters Aleksei, and nothing else. But he's a boy, and like putty in my hands. You see, I manipulate him as I wish. He's like your Grisha. . . . Dolly," she suddenly said, changing the subject, "you say that I view things darkly. You couldn't understand. It's too terrible. I try not to see at all."

"But you must, I believe. You must do everything you can."

"But what can I do? Nothing. You say that I should marry Aleksei and that I'm not thinking of it. Not thinking of it!" she repeated, her face flushed. She rose, straightened, sighed deeply and began to pace the room with her light step, stopping occasionally. "I'm not thinking? There isn't an hour of the day when I don't think of it and don't reproach myself for thinking . . . because such thoughts may drive one mad. They may drive one mad . . ." she repeated. "When I think of it I can't fall asleep without morphine. Well, let's discuss it calmly. They tell me—divorce. First of all, *he* won't grant it. *He* is now under the influence of Countess Lydia Ivanovna."

Daria Aleksandrovna sat erect in her chair, showing compassion and suffering on her face, and she turned her head to follow Anna as she paced the room.

"You have to try," she said softly.

"Suppose I try. What would it mean?" she said, expressing a thought that had evidently occured to her a thousand times, that she knew by heart. "It would mean that I, who hate him and at the same time admit that I have wronged him—I consider him a magnanimous person—that I would have to humble myself and write to him. . . . Suppose I force myself to do it. Then I will either receive an abusive reply or his consent. Suppose I receive his consent . . ." at that moment Anna was on the other side of the room and stopped to straighten the window curtain. "I'll receive his consent, but what about . . . my son? I know that they won't let me have him. And, holding me in contempt, he'll be raised by his father, whom I left. You must understand that I love these two beings equally, Seryozha and Aleksei, and more than myself."

She came to the middle of the room and stopped in front of Dolly, pressing her hands against her heart. In her white peignoir her figure seemed particularly large and broad. She bowed her head, and as she looked up with her moist, sparkling eyes at tiny, slender, pathetic Dolly, in her patched dressing jacket and night cap, her whole body trembled with emotion.

"These are the only two beings that I love, and one excludes the other. I cannot bring them together, but that's the only thing I want. And without that nothing else matters. Nothing matters. It will end somehow, and this is the reason why I cannot and do not like to speak of it. Therefore don't reproach me, don't blame me for anything. You are so pure that you can't understand all these things that cause me suffering."

She came over to Dolly, sat beside her, and, looking into her face with a guilty expression, took her hand.

"What are you thinking? What do you think of me? Don't despise me. I don't deserve to be despised. I am only unhappy. If anyone is unhappy, it is I," she said, and turning away, she began to cry.

When she remained alone, Dolly said her prayers and went to bed. While talking to Anna, she pitied her with her whole heart; but now she could not force herself to think of her. The memories of her home and children, awakened by her imagination, were now endowed with an unusual, unfamiliar charm and shone with a new brilliance. Her world now seemed to her so attractive and so dear that nothing would induce her to spend another day outside it, and she decided that she would leave the next day without fail.

In the meantime, Anna returned to her sitting room, took a little glass and poured in a few drops of medicine, the main ingredient of which was morphine, drank it, and after sitting motionless for a short while, calmed down. In a happy frame of mind she went into the bedroom.

When she entered the bedroom, Vronsky glanced at her intently. He looked for the effects of the conversation that he knew she must have had with Dolly, since she had spent such a long time in her room. But in her expression, which showed that she was restraining her animation and concealing something from him, he could find nothing but her beauty, still enchanting though now familiar, her awareness of her beauty, and her desire that it captivate him. He did not want to ask her about their conversation, hoping that she would tell him herself. But she only said:

"I'm glad that you like Dolly. You do, don't you?"

"Yes, but I've known her for a long time. She's very kind-hearted, I believe, *mais excessivement terre-à-terre*. Still, I'm very glad that she's come."

He took Anna's hand and looked inquiringly into her eyes. She understood the look differently and smiled at him.

The next morning, in spite of her host's entreaties, Daria Aleksandrovna prepared to leave. Levin's coachman, in his not-so-new coat and would-be coachman hat, sullenly and resolutely drove the horses, ill-matched in color, and the carriage, with its patched splashboards, toward the canopied, sand-strewn entrance.

Daria Aleksandrovna did not enjoy the procedure of parting with Princess Varvara and the gentlemen. After spending a day with them, both she and her hosts felt that they did not suit each other, and that it was better for them not to come closer. Only Anna felt sad. She knew that now, with Dolly's departure, no one would ever stir up in her heart the feelings that had been awakened by this visit. It was painful to her to awaken them, yet she knew that they were the best part of her soul, and that this part was being rapidly submerged in the kind of life she was leading.

When they got out to the field, Daria Aleksandrovna experienced a pleasant feeling of relief, and was about to ask her men how they liked their stay at the Vronskys' when suddenly the coachman Filipp himself said:

"They may be rich, but they gave the horses only three measures of oats. They ate it before the roosters crowed. What are three measures? Just a taste. Yet now you can get oats at the inns at forty-five kopecks a measure. But when visitors come to us, we give their horses as much as they can eat."

"A stingy master," echoed the clerk.

"Well, did you like their horses?" asked Dolly.

"Their horses are first rate. And the food was good. But I found it rather tiresome there. Didn't you, Daria Aleksandrovna?" he said, turning his handsome, kind face to her.

"I did, too. Well, will we reach home by evening?"

"We should."

When she returned home and found everyone in excellent health and more dear than ever, Daria Aleksandrovna related with great animation all the details of her visit, of the hospitality with which she had been received, of the luxury and good taste of the Vronskys, of their amusements, and did not allow anything to be said against them.

"You have to know Anna and Vronsky—and I've come to know him better—to understand how touchingly kind they can be," she said now with complete sincerity, forgetting the vague feeling of dissatisfaction and awkwardness she had experienced there.

Vronsky and Anna had spent the summer and part of the fall in the country in the same circumstances, still taking no steps to obtain the divorce. They had decided that they would not go anywhere; but both of them felt, as they continued to live alone, particularly in the fall and without visitors, that they could not endure such a life and would have to change it.

Their life seemed to leave nothing to desire; they were wealthy, enjoyed good health, they had a child, and both were busy. Even without guests Anna paid the same attention to her appearance, and read a great deal, novels as well as serious books, which were in vogue then. She ordered all the books that were favorably reviewed in the foreign newspapers and magazines she subscribed to, and read them with the close attention with which one reads only in solitude. In addition, she studied books and technical magazines on all those matters Vronsky was engaged in, so that he often turned directly to her with his problems on agronomy, architecture, and even horsebreeding and sports. He marveled at her knowledge and memory, but at first, through lack of confidence, he sought confirmation of his views; she would find the answers to his inquiries in books and show them to him.

The furnishing of the hospital also interested her. She not only assisted him in his work, she thought up and arranged a a great deal on her own. But still, the object of her greatest care was herself—she herself, in so far as she remained dear to Vronsky and could make up for all that he had left behind. Vronsky appreciated this desire of hers, which had become the only purpose of her life, the desire not only to please him but also to serve him, and yet at the same time he was weighed down by the thought of the amorous net she was trying to ensnare him in. As time passed, the more often he found himself ensnared in this net the more anxious he was not exactly to free himself of it but to test it, to see whether it impaired his freedom. Except for this ever-growing desire to be free, not to have scenes every time he had to go to the city for meetings or the races, Vronsky would have been entirely contented with his life. The part he had taken upon himself —the part of a rich landowner, one of those who should comprise the center of Russian aristocracy—not only completely suited his taste but after living like this for half a year now afforded him ever-increasing pleasure. And his work, which absorbed him and interested him with growing intensity, was progressing well. In spite of the enormous cost of the hospital, machines, cows ordered from Switzerland and many other things, he was convinced that he was not wasting but increasing his wealth. In the matter of his income, such as the sale of timber, grain, and wool, or the lease of his lands, Vronsky could be hard as flint and hold to his price. In the management of this large estate and of his others, he adhered to the simplest methods, which involved no risks. He was exceedingly thrifty and economized even on petty expenses. In spite of all the cunning and shrewdness of the German, who kept trying to tempt Vronsky into purchases by presenting his estimates in a way that made it seem, at first, that a large sum was needed, and that after consideration the thing could be done more cheaply and give an immediate profit, Vronsky did not give in. He listened to the manager, asked questions, and agreed with him only when what was going to be ordered or installed was the latest model, still unknown in Russia and bound to arouse general awe. Moreover, he allowed himself to assume a large expenditure only when he had spare money; and before going into the expense, he acquainted himself with all the necessary details and insisted on getting the best for his money. Therefore it was clear from the way he was conducting his affairs that he was not wasting but increasing his fortune.

In October there were elections of the nobility in Kashin Province, which included the estates of Vronsky, Sviazhsky, Koznyshev, Oblonsky, and a small part of Levin's.

These elections attracted public attention for several reasons, among them the kind of people who were taking part in them. They were much discussed and long awaited. Some people who had never taken part in local elections came for these from Moscow, Petersburg, and abroad.

Vronsky had promised Sviazhsky long ago that he would attend them.

Before the elections, Sviazhsky, who had often visited Vozdvizhenskoe, came to fetch Vronsky.

On the eve of that day, Vronsky and Anna almost quarreled on account of the intended trip. It was fall, the most tedious, oppressive season in the country, so Vronsky, anticipating her objections, declared his intention to make the trip in a stern and cold tone, one he had never used before with Anna. But to his surprise, Anna received this news very calmly, and only asked when he would return. He looked at her intently, wondering at her composure. She smiled at his look. He knew this ability of hers to withdraw into herself, and knew that she used it only when she had made some decision by herself, without revealing her plans to him. He feared it, but he was so anxious to avoid a scene that he pretended to—and with some sincerity did—believe in what he wished to believe in: her reasonableness.

"I hope you won't be lonesome."

"I hope not," said Anna. "I received a box of books from Gautier yesterday. No, I won't be lonesome."

If she wishes to assume this attitude, it's all for the best, he thought. Otherwise it would be the same thing over and over again.

And so he left for the elections without challenging her to reveal her thoughts. It was the first time in their life together that they had parted with something left unsaid between them. On the one hand it disturbed him, and on the other he believed that it was better this way. At first it'll be as it is now, somewhat vague and obscure, but later she'll get used to it. At any rate, I can give her anything but my male independence, he thought.

26

IN SEPTEMBER LEVIN moved to Moscow for Kitty's confinement. He had already spent a month in Moscow without doing anything, when he was invited by his brother Sergei Ivanovich to accompany him to Kashin Province. Sergei Ivanovich had an estate there, and being deeply involved in the forthcoming elections, was making ready to leave for them. Levin had a vote in Seleznev County in the province. In addition he had some urgent business to attend to in Kashin concerning a trusteeship and the receipt of money for his sister, who lived abroad.

Levin still hesitated, but Kitty, who saw how bored he was in Moscow and advised him to go, had ordered for him, without his knowledge, a nobleman's uniform costing eighty rubles. And the eighty rubles that had been spent on the uniform were Levin's main reason for going; he left for Kashin.

The first five days in Kashin Levin spent visiting the assembly daily and attending to his sister's affairs, in which he met with little success. All the marshals of nobility were busy with the elections, and it was hard to expedite the simplest matter connected with the trusteeship. In the other matter—the receipt of the money—he also encountered difficulties. After much effort he obtained the release of the money. It was ready to be paid out, but the notary, a most obliging person, could not write out the order because the chairman had to sign it, and the chairman, without having delegated his authority, was attending the sessions. All these efforts, visits to one office after another, conversations with fine, kindhearted people who wholeheartedly sympathized with the petitioner's difficulties but could not help him, all this exertion that had led to nought, created in Levin a painful feeling like the feeling of annoyance and helplessness one has in a dream when he attempts to use physical force. He often had this feeling when he spoke to his agent, a most genial person. It was obvious that the agent was doing everything within his means and exercising all his mental faculties attempting to relieve Levin of his difficulties. "Try this," he would often say. "Go to this or that office," and the agent would work out a complete plan to avoid a fateful initial stumbling block in the affair. But at once he would add, "They'll still delay it, but try anyway." And Levin went everywhere, trying his best. Everyone was kind and courteous, but it always turned out that what had been skirted reappeared at the end and again blocked the way. Levin was particularly annoyed because he was completely unable to understand against whom he was struggling and who profited from his case had not been settled. This, it seemed, nobody knew, including his agent. If Levin could understand this, as he understood that you cannot reach the railroad ticket office unless you take your place in the waiting line, he would not have felt so deeply offended and annoyed. But no one could explain why the difficulties he had encountered in his case existed.

But Levin had changed much since his marriage. He was patient, and if he did not understand why everything had been arranged this way, he said to himself that since he did not know everything he could not judge, that probably it was the way it had to be, and he tried not to resent it.

Now, attending the elections and taking part in them, he again tried to refrain from judging and arguing, but to understand as much as possible of this matter in which all these honorable and good men, whom he respected, were so deeply and wholeheartedly involved. Since Levin's marriage so many new and important facets of life were revealed to him that formerly, because of his lighthearted attitude toward them, he had considered worthless, that in these elections he also sought the profundities he presumed were there.

Sergei Ivanovich explained to him the meaning and significance of the upset which was expected in these elections. The marshal of the province was, by law, in charge of many important public functions—trusteeships (the same office that was now causing Levin so much trouble), the rich treasury of the noblemen, boys', girls', and military gymnasiums, general education as introduced by the new law, and, finally, the zemstvo. The marshal of the province, Snetkov, was a man of the old school of noblemen, one who had squandered an enormous fortune, a kindhearted man, honest in his own way but completely ignorant of the spirit of the new era. In all matters he always took the part of the nobility: he openly opposed the spread of popular education; he was trying to reduce the zemstvo, which should have been of such great importance, to the state of a class institution. It was necessary to replace him with a vigorous, modern, active, completely different man, and to continue the conduct of affairs in such a manner that the nobility, not as such, but as a participant in the zemstvo, could avail itself of all the advantages of self-government. In rich Kashin Province, which always, in every respect, had been in the van, there had grown up such a vigorous civic element that once the proper conduct of government was established here it could serve as a model for other provinces, even for all of Russia. That was why this matter was so important. To replace Snetkov as marshal of the nobility they expected to elect either Sviazhsky or, still better, Nevedovsky, a former professor, an unusually intelligent person and a close friend of Sergei Ivanovich.

The session was opened by the governor, who delivered a speech to the noblemen, exhorting them to elect officers without bias and consider only their merits and the good of the fatherland. He hoped, he said, that the highborn noblemen of

Kashin would perform their duty scrupulously and would prove worthy of that great confidence that the monarch had in them, as they had done in previous elections.

After finishing his speech, the governor left the hall, the noblemen following noisily and with animation, some even with sincere enthusiasm, and they stood around him while he put on his fur coat and talked amiably to the marshal of the province. Levin, eager to understand everything thoroughly and to miss nothing, was present in the crowd and heard the governor say, "Please tell Maria Ivanovna that my wife sends her regrets. She had to visit the orphanage." Then all the noblemen, in a gay mood, picked up their fur coats and left for the cathedral.

In the cathedral Levin, together with the others, raised his hand, and repeating the words of the priest, swore a most solemn vow that he would perform everything as the governor had asked. Church services always affected Levin, and when he pronounced the words, "I kiss the cross," and looked at the crowd of young and old men repeating the same words, he was moved.

On the second and third days the subjects of discussion were the nobility's finances and the girls' gymnasium. These subjects, as Sergei Ivanovich explained, were of no consequence, and Levin, busy with his own affairs, did not follow them. On the fourth day they were auditing the provincial finances at the desk of the marshal of the province. And here, for the first time, the new party clashed with the old. The commission that had been entrusted with auditing the funds reported to the assembly that everything was in order. The marshal of the province rose, thanked the noblemen for their confidence, and shed a tear. The noblemen loudly congratulated him and shook his hand. But at that moment one of the noblemen of Sergei Ivanovich's party declared that he had heard that the commission had not audited the funds, considering that this would be an insult to the marshal. One of the commission members inadvertently confirmed this. Then a short, young-looking but exceedingly venomous gentleman suggested that the marshal of nobility probably would have been pleased to render an account of the funds, and that the excessive thoughtfulness of the commission members had prevented him from enjoying this moral satisfaction. Then the members of the commission retracted their declaration, and Sergei Ivanovich began to prove logically that it must be admitted that either the funds had been audited or that they had not, and he discussed this dilemma in detail. A garrulous member of the other party attacked Sergei Ivanovich. Then Sviazhsky spoke, and he was followed by the venomous gentleman again. The debate went on for a while and led to nothing. Levin was surprised that they had argued so much on this subject, particularly because when he asked Sergei Ivanovich whether he believed that the funds had been misappropriated, Sergei Ivanovich answered:

"Oh, no! He's an honest man. But we had to attack this old-fashioned, paternalistic way of managing the nobility's affairs."

On the fifth day they elected county marshals. For some counties it was a turbulent day. Unanimously, without balloting, Sviazhsky was elected marshal of Selesnev County, and he gave a dinner party that day.

27

THE SIXTH DAY was set aside for the election of the marshal of the province. The large and the small halls were crowded with noblemen in various uniforms. Many had arrived for that day alone. Old acquaintances who had not seen each other for a long time, some from the Crimea, some from Petersburg, and others from abroad, met in the halls. A debate was in progress at the desk of the marshal of the province, under a portrait of the Czar.

In the large and small halls the noblemen separated into opposing groups, and by their hostile and mistrustful looks, by the sudden interruption of a conversation at the approach of a stranger, by the whispers in which some spoke even after they had retired to a remote hallway, one could see that each side kept its secrets from the other. In their appearance, the noblemen were sharply divided into two groups, the old and the new. Most of the old were dressed in their old, buttoned uniforms, with swords and hats, or in the uniforms of their respective services: navy, cavalry, or infantry. The uniforms of the old noblemen were old-fashioned, the shoulders slightly puffed; they seemed too small, short in the waist, and tight, as though their owners had outgrown them. But the younger ones were dressed in unbuttoned noblemen's uniforms, low at the waist and broad in the shoulder, with white vests, or in the black-collared uniforms of Ministry of Justice, embroidered with laurel leaves. And some of the younger men wore court uniforms, adding color to the crowd.

But the division into young and old did not coincide with party divisions. Some of the young noblemen, as Levin observed, belonged to the old party, and, on the other hand, some of the very old noblemen kept whispering to Sviazhsky and apparently were ardent supporters of the new party.

Levin stood in a small hall, where the noblemen smoked and were served refreshments, next to a group of members of his party, listening to what they were saying and vainly struggling to understand them. Sergei Ivanovich was at the center of the group. He was listening to Sviazhsky and Khliustov, the marshal of another county and a member of their party. Khliustov had refused to go with the members from his county to ask Snetkov to run for re-election, but Sviazhsky was persuading him to do so, and Sergei Ivanovich approved of this plan. Levin could not understand why the opposition party should ask the marshal to run for re-election when they wanted to defeat him.

Stepan Arkadievich, who had just had a smoke and a drink, came over to them in the uniform of a Gentleman of the Bedchamber, wiping his mouth with a perfumed, bordered, batiste handkerchief.

"We were taking our positions, Sergei Ivanovich!" he said, smoothing his whiskers.

And, after listening to the conversation, he agreed with Sviazhsky's plan.

"One county will do, and that Sviazhsky is in opposition is already quite apparent," he said, his words understood by everyone but Levin.

"Well, Kostia, it has caught your fancy, too," he added, turning to Levin and taking his arm. Levin would have been glad if that were true, but he could not comprehend what was going on, and when they had moved a few steps away from the group, he told Stepan Arkadievich that he could not understand why the marshal of the province should be asked to stand for re-election.

"Oh, *sancta simplicitas!*" said Stepan Arkadievich, and in brief and clear terms he explained to Levin what was going on.

If, as in former elections, all the counties asked the marshal to stand for re-election, he would have been elected without a ballot. This was to be avoided. But now eight counties had agreed to do it. If two refused to nominate him, Snetkov might decline to stand for re-election. Then the old party, its plans upset, might nominate another of its members. But if only one county, Sviazhsky's refused, Snetkov would run for office. And he would be nominated, with some of the opposition's votes deliberately cast in his favor. This would confuse his party so that when the opposition candidate was presented, even some of the other party might vote for him.

Levin understood, but not completely, and he was going to pose additional questions when suddenly everyone began talking and moving noisily into the large hall.

"What's the matter?" "What is it?" "Who?" "A warrant? For whom?" "What?" "They're ruling him out?" "It's not a warrant." "They won't admit Flerov." "What if he is to stand trial? They'll end by admitting no one." "It's an outrage!" "It's illegal!" Levin heard on all sides. Together with the others, who hurried about for fear of missing anything, Levin moved into the large hall, where the crowd of noblemen pushed him in the direction of the desk of the marshal of the province, where a heated dispute was in progress between the marshal, Sviazhsky, and other leaders.

28

LEVIN WAS STANDING some distance away. The heavy, hoarse breathing of a nobleman beside him and the squeak of another's thick-soled shoes prevented him from hearing clearly what was going on. He could hear from afar only the gentle voice of the marshal, the shrill voice of the venomous nobleman, and then Sviazhsky's voice. As far as he could tell, they were arguing about the meaning of the regulation and of the words "one who has to stand trial."

The crowd separated to make way for Sergei Ivanovich, who was coming up to the desk. Sergei Ivanovich, after waiting for the venomous nobleman to finish his speech, said that in his opinion the most proper method was to refer to the regulation, and he asked the secretary to find it. The regulation stipulated that in case of a disagreement the issue should be settled by a vote.

Sergei Ivanovich read the regulation and began to explain it, but he was interrupted by a tall, stout, stooped landowner with a dyed mustache, dressed in a tight uniform, its collar pressing the back of his neck. He came up to the desk, pounded on it with his ring and shouted:

"A ballot! No use arguing. A vote!"

Here several voices suddenly spoke at once, and the tall nobleman with the ring, becoming more and more incensed, shouted louder and louder. But it was impossible to make out what he was saying.

His proposal was the same as Sergei Ivanovich's. But he evidently hated him and all his party, and this feeling of hatred communicated itself to all the members of his party, arousing in their opponents the same hostile feeling, kept under better control, however. Shouts filled the air, and for a moment everything was in such confusion that the marshal of the province had to call for order.

"A vote! A vote! A nobleman understands. We have shed our blood. . . ." "The Czar has faith in us. . . ." "No checking on the marshal, he is not a clerk. . . ." "And this is different. . . ." "Let's vote!" "What an outrage!" were some of the wrathful, unrestrained shouts heard on all sides. And there was even more animosity and fury in their eyes and on their faces than in their words. They expressed implacable hatred. Levin was at a complete loss to understand what was going on and was amazed by the passion with which they were trying to decide whether to vote on Flerov's case or not. He forgot, as Sergei Ivanovich later explained to him, the syllogism according to which, for the sake of general welfare they had to remove the marshal of the province from his office; he could be removed only by the majority of votes; to have this majority of votes they had to allow Flerov to vote; to allow Flerov to vote they had to show how the regulation should be interpreted.

"And since one vote may decide the whole issue, we must be serious and consistent if we want to work for the public welfare," concluded Sergei Ivanovich.

But Levin had forgotten this, and he was depressed as he saw these fine people, whom he respected, in this state of disagreeable, fierce excitement. To rid himself of this oppressive feeling, he did not wait for the end of the debate but went into the hall, empty except for the waiters at the refreshment bar. As he watched them wipe dishes and arrange plates and glasses, and looked at their quiet though animated faces, Levin experienced a sudden feeling of relief, as though he had emerged from a foul-smelling room into the fresh air. He began to pace up and down the room, glancing at the waiters with pleasure. He was particularly taken with one waiter who wore gray side whiskers and displayed his contempt for the others, the youngers ones, who made fun of him, as he showed them how to fold napkins. Levin was about to enter into a conversation with the old waiter when the secretary of the noblemen's trusteeship office, a little old man whose gift was to know all the noblemen of the province by their names and patronymics, distracted him.

"Please come, Konstantin Dmitrievich," he said. "Your brother wants you. They are voting on the issue."

Levin entered the hall, received a small white ballot, and followed Sergei Ivanovich up to a desk at which Sviazhsky stood with an important and ironic expression, holding his beard in his fist and sniffing it. Sergei Ivanovich put his hand into the box, placed the ballot in it, and after giving Levin his place, remained nearby. Levin came up, but completely forgot what was going on, and in embarrassment turned to Sergei Ivanovich and asked, "Where shall I put it?" He asked this softly, hoping that in the conversation going on around them no one else would hear the question. But the conversation had died down, and his inappropriate question was overheard. Sergei Ivanovich frowned.

"That's a matter of one's convictions," he said sternly.

A few people smiled. Levin blushed, hurriedly shoved his hands under the cloth and put his ballot to the right because he held it in his right hand. After he had placed it there he remembered that he should have put in his left hand as well, and he did it, but it was too late now; becoming still more embarrassed, he hurriedly retreated to the back of the room.

"One hundred and twenty-six fo'! Ninety-eight against!" sounded the voice of the secretary, who could not pronounce his *r*'s. Laughter could be heard—they had found a button and and two nuts in the box. The nobleman was allowed to vote and the new party had gained a victory.

But the old party did not yet consider itself defeated. Levin heard that Snetkov had been asked to stand for re-election, and he saw a group of noblemen crowding around the marshal of the province, who was saying something to them. Levin came closer. Replying to the noblemen, Snetkov spoke of the confidence the noblemen placed in him, of their love for him, which he did not deserve, for all his merit consisted only of his devotion to the noblemen, whom he had served devotedly for twelve years. Several times he repeated the words, "I have served you to the best of my ability, faithfully and honorably. I appreciate the privilege, and thank you," and suddenly he stopped, choked with tears, and left the hall. Whatever was the cause of his tears—his awareness of the injustice being done to him, his love for the nobility, or the strain he had been laboring under, knowing that he was surrounded by enemies —his emotion communicated itself to others, most of the noblemen were moved, and Levin felt a tenderness toward him.

In the doorway the marshal of the province accidentally bumped into Levin.

"I'm very sorry," he said, addressing him as a stranger, but then he smiled shyly when he recognized Levin. It seemed to Levin that he wanted to say something but could not because of his agitation. The expression of his face, his entire bearing in his uniform with its medals and white, gallooned trousers, and his hurried step reminded Levin of a baited animal that sees its chances for escape are small. This expression on the marshal's face particularly moved Levin because only the day before, on his sister's business, he had visited him at home and had observed him in all his dignity as a kindhearted family man. It was a large house, with old, ancestral furniture; the old servants not smartly dressed and somewhat dirty, but respectful, evidently former serfs who had not changed masters. His wife, a stout, kindhearted lady in a lace bonnet and a Turkish shawl, patted a pretty grandchild, her daughter's daughter. His young son, in the sixth class of the gymnasium, had just come from school and greeted his father, kissing his large hand. And the kind words and the gestures of the master of the house were impressive. The previous day all this had unconsciously inspired Levin with respect and sympathy for him. But now Levin was moved by the sight of this old man; he felt pity for him and wanted to say something friendly to him.

"It looks as though you'll be our marshal again," he said.

"I doubt it," said the marshal, looking around fearfully. "I'm tired and old. There are those who are worthier and younger than I; let them serve."

And the marshal left through a side door.

The most solemn moment had arrived. They were going to

cast their ballots. The leaders of both parties counted the black and white ballots on their fingers.

By the debate on Flerov the new party had not only acquired an additional vote but also had gained some time to fetch three noblemen who, by a stratagem of the old party, had been prevented from taking part in the elections. Two of the noblemen, who had a weakness for the bottle, had been made drunk by Snetkov's agents, and the uniform of the third had been taken away from him.

When the members of the new party learned about this, they managed to send some of their men in a hired cab to provide one of the noblemen with a uniform and to bring one of the drunken ones.

"I brought one; I poured water on him," said the landowner who had been sent after him to Sviazhsky. "He'll be all right."

"He's not too drunk, I hope, and won't fall," said Sviazhsky, shaking his head.

"No, he's strong enough. So long as they don't give him any more to drink. I told the bartender not to give him a drink under any circumstances."

29

THE NARROW HALL where they smoked and had their refreshments was crowded with noblemen. The agitation grew more intense, and all faces showed anxiety. Most excited were the leaders, who knew all about the ballots and kept count of them. They made plans for the forthcoming contest. But the rest, like soldiers before a battle, though preparing themselves for the fight, were looking for diversions too. Some had their snacks, either standing or seated at the table; others walked up and down the long room, smoking and conversing with friends whom they had not seen for a long time.

Levin did not feel like eating, was not a smoker, and had no desire to join his group, namely, Sergei Ivanovich, Stepan Arkadievich, Sviazhsky and the others, because Vronsky, dressed in the uniform of a master of the horse, was with them and was engaged in a lively conversation. Levin had noticed him at the balloting of the previous day and had carefully avoided him. He went over to the window and sat down, watching the various groups of people and listening to the conversations around him. He felt sad, particularly because, as he noticed, everyone was animated, preoccupied, and busy, and only he and a little very old toothless man in a naval uniform, who sat down, mumbling, next to him, were indifferent to what was going on and had nothing to do.

"What a rascal! I told him, but he didn't bother to listen. And, of course, he couldn't collect it in three years," said a short, stooped landowner energetically. His pomaded hair fell upon the embroidered collar of his uniform; the heels of his new boots, evidently ordered for these elections, resounded on the floor. After casting a look of displeasure at Levin, the landowner turned away sharply.

"Yes, dirty business. No doubt about it," said a short landowner in a thin voice.

Following them, a large group of landowners, who crowded around a stout general, hastily moved in Levin's direction. Evidently they were looking for a place where they could talk to each other without being overheard.

"How dare he say that I ordered his trousers to be stolen! He probably bartered them for a drink. Damn his princehood! He has no right to talk this way. It's a damned outrage!"

"But wait! They cite the regulation," members of the other group argued, "which says that the wife must be registered as a noblewoman."

"The regulation be damned! I say what I feel. I'm an aristocrat. My word is enough."

"Let's go, Your Excellency, *fine champagne.*"

Another crowd followed a nobleman who was shouting; it was one of those who had been made drunk.

"I've always advised Maria Semionovna to lease it because she would make no profit," a gray-mustached landowner, dressed in the uniform of a colonel of the old general staff, said in a pleasant voice. He was the landowner Levin had met at Sviazhsky's. He immediately recognized him. The landowner also recognized Levin, and they greeted each other.

"I'm very glad to see you. Of course! I remember you very well. Last year at our Marshal Nikolai Ivanovich's place."

"Well, how's the farm going?" inquired Levin.

"The same way, always at a loss," said the landowner, coming up to Levin. He smiled gently, but his face expressed composure in the conviction that that was the way it had to be. "And how do you happen to be in our province? Have you come to take part in our *coup d'état?*" he asked, pronouncing the French words clearly but incorrectly. "All of Russia has come here—Gentlemen of the Bedchamber and all but ministers of state." He indicated the impressive figure of Stepan Arkadievich who, in white trousers and the uniform of a Gentleman of the Bedchamber, passed by in the company of a general.

"I must confess that I have a very poor understanding of the importance of these elections," said Levin.

The landowner looked at him.

"What's there to understand? They have no importance. It's an institution that has decayed but continues to move through inertia. Look at those uniforms—even they tell you, 'This is an assembly not of noblemen but of justices of the peace, of permanent members of commissions, and so on!' "

"Then why do you come?" asked Levin.

"First of all, it's a habit. And then you have to maintain your connections. Some kind of a moral obligation. And to tell you the truth, personal considerations. My son-in-law wants to stand for office as a permanent member. He's not rich and needs help to be elected. But why do these gentlemen come?" he said, indicating the venomous nobleman who had spoken at the marshal's desk.

"This is the new generation of noblemen."

"Perhaps new. But they are not noblemen. They happen to own land, whereas we are landowners. Though members of the nobility, they deliberately undermine its cause."

"But you yourself say that it is an outmoded institution."

"Perhaps it's outmoded, but it still should be treated more respectfully. Take Snetkov, for example. . . . Whether right or wrong, we have been developing for a thousand years. Suppose you decide to plant a garden in front of your home; you make a plan, but on that plot there is a hundred-year-old tree. . . . Though it may be old and crooked, you wouldn't cut down the old thing for the sake of the flower beds but would plan them so that the tree remains. It takes more than a year to grow one like that," he said cautiously, and then immediately changed the subject. "Well, how's your farm coming?"

"Not so good. About five per cent."

"Yes, but you don't take into account your own work. After all, you're also worth something. I'll tell you about myself. Before I began farming, my salary in government service was three thousand rubles. Now I work harder than then, and like you, my gain is only five per cent, and even of that I'm not sure. And for my own labor I get no pay."

"Then why do you do it, if it's only a loss?"

"Well, I do it. It can't be helped. It's a habit, and one knows that that's the way it has to be. I'll tell you another thing," the landowner said, carried away by the conversation. "My son has no taste for farming. Evidently he will become a scholar. Then there'll be nobody to carry on. But one still keeps doing it. Just this season I planted a garden."

"Yes," said Levin, "it's quite true. I always feel that there's no actual profit in my farm, but I keep doing it. . . . One feels impelled by some kind of duty toward the land."

"Now listen to this," continued the landowner. "A merchant from the neighborhood came to see me. We took a walk around the farm and in the garden. 'Well,' he said, 'Stepan Vasilich, everything in your place is well kept, but the garden is neglected.' Actually it's well kept. 'If it were up to me,' he said, 'I would cut down those linden trees. But you must do it when the sap rises. You surely have a thousand such trees and from each you could get two fine painting boards. These boards are in great demand now, and you would have timber, too.'"

"And for this money he would buy cattle and land for a trifle and lease it to the moujiks," Levin said with a smile, evidently having heard such schemes before. "And he'll make a fortune for himself, but you and I, we'll be lucky if we hold on to what we have and leave it to our children."

"You've married, I hear," said the landowner.

"Yes," said Levin, proud and pleased. "Yes, it's somewhat strange," he continued. "And so we live, without gaining any profit, appointed like the ancient vestals to keep a fire going."

A smile played under the landowner's white mustache.

"And there are some among us, such as our friend Nikolai Ivanovich, and now Count Vronsky, who would introduce progressive farming. But so far it's come to nothing but a waste of money."

"But why don't we do what the merchants do? Why don't we cut down the trees in the garden for painting boards?" asked Levin, returning to the thought that had impressed him.

"Because, as you said, we have to guard the flame. The other is not the nobleman's way. And our duties as noblemen we perform not here, at the elections, but there, in our corners. We have our class instinct, which tells us what's right and what's wrong. The same is true of the moujiks, as I've observed.

If he's a good moujik, he'll rent as much land as he can. Even if the land is bad, he plows it. And he works it without a profit, at a loss only."

"Just like us," said Levin. "It was very nice to see you again," he said, noticing that Sviazhsky was approaching him.

"This is the first time we've seen each other since we met in your house," said the landowner, "and we've had a long conversation."

"Well, didn't you carp at the new ways?"

"We couldn't do otherwise."

"We unburdened our souls."

30

SVIAZHSKY TOOK LEVIN'S ARM and brought him to his group.

Now he could no longer avoid Vronsky. He was standing next to Stepan Arkadievich and Sergei Ivanovich, looking directly at Levin as he approached.

"I'm very glad to see you. I believe I had the pleasure of meeting you at . . . Princess Shcherbatsky's," he said, extending his hand to Levin.

"Yes, I remember our meeting very well," said Levin and blushing crimson, he immediately turned away and began talking to his brother.

Vronsky smiled faintly and continued his talk with Sviazhsky, evidently having no desire to enter into a conversation with Levin. But Levin, while talking to his brother, glanced at Vronsky frequently, trying to decide how to begin a conversation with him in order to make up for his rudeness.

"What's delaying us now?" asked Levin, looking at Sviazhsky and Vronsky.

"It's Snetkov. He must either decline or accept," replied Sviazhsky.

"Well, has he accepted or not?"

"That's the trouble, he has done neither," said Vronsky.

"And if he declines, who will run?" asked Levin, looking at Vronsky.

"Whoever wants to," answered Sviazhsky.

"Will you?" asked Levin.

"Anyone but I," said Sviazhsky, taken aback and casting a

frightened glance at the venomous gentleman who was standing beside Sergei Ivanovich.

"Who else? Nevedovsky?" asked Levin, feeling that he had made a blunder.

But this made matters still worse. Nevedovsky and Sviazhsky were the two candidates.

"As for me, I wouldn't do it under any circumstances," replied the venomous gentleman.

This was Nevedovsky himself. Sviazhsky introduced Levin to him.

"Well, has it captured even your interest?" asked Stepan Arkadievich, winking at Vronsky. "It's like the horse races. You could stake bets on it."

"Yes, it has," said Vronsky. "And once you tackle a job, you want to see it through. We'll fight!" he said, frowning and clenching his strong jaws.

"How shrewd that Sviazhsky is! Everything is so clear to him."

"Oh, yes," said Vronsky absently.

A silence ensued, during which Vronsky, since he had to look at something, looked at Levin, his legs, his uniform, then at his face, and noticing the gloomy look directed at him, said, just to say something.

"And how is it that you, a permanent country dweller, aren't a justice of the peace? You're not wearing the uniform of a justice of the peace."

"Because I maintain that it's an absurd institution," was the sullen reply from Levin, who had been waiting all this time for a chance to talk to Vronsky and make up for his rudeness at their first meeting.

"For my part, I disagree," said Vronsky in mild surprise.

"It's like a child's game," Levin interrupted. "We don't need justices of the peace. For eight years I haven't been involved in a single case. And when I did have one, the decision was entirely wrong. The justice lives forty versts from me. In a two-ruble case I'd have to employ a lawyer at the cost of fifteen."

And he related the story of a moujik who had stolen some flour from the miller and when reproached by the latter, sued him for slander. What he was saying was entirely out of place and foolish, and Levin himself felt it while telling the story.

"Oh, what an odd one he is!" said Stepan Arkadievich, with

his most benign smile. "But let's go. They are voting, I think. . . ."

And they parted.

"I can't understand it," said Sergei Ivanovich, who had noticed his brother's blunder, "I can't understand how anyone can be so completely devoid of any political discretion. This is what we Russians lack. The marshal of the province is our opponent, and you are his *ami cochon* and ask him to stand for re-election. And as for Count Vronsky. . . . I don't intend to become his friend; he invited me to dinner, but I won't go. He is, however, one of us, so why turn him into an enemy? Then you ask Nevedovsky whether he will run for office. That's not the way things should be done."

"Ah! I'm completely confused! And it's all nonsense," Levin replied gloomily.

"You call it nonsense, but when you involve yourself, you make a mess of it."

Levin fell silent, and they entered the large hall together.

The marshal of the province had decided to run, though he smelled the plot against him and though he had not been nominated unanimously. Silence descended upon the hall, and the secretary loudly declared that Captain of the Horse Guards Mikhail Stepanovich Snetkov would now stand for election for the post of marshal of the province.

Carrying small plates on which the ballots had been placed, the county marshals began to move from their desks toward the desk of the marshal of the province, and the balloting began.

"Put it to the right," whispered Stepan Arkadievich to Levin, when he and his brother came over to the desk, following the marshal. But Levin now forgot what they had explained to him, and was afraid that perhaps Stepan Arkadievich had made a mistake when he said, "to the right." Wasn't Snetkov their opponent? When he came over to the box, he held the ballot in his right hand; then, believing that he had made a mistake, he placed it in his left hand when he was directly beside the box, and then evidently put it into the left side of the box. An expert on balloting, who was standing beside the box and could tell just by the movements of the voters' elbow where they were placing their ballots, wrinkled his face with displeasure. Here he had no opportunity to exercise his insight. There was silence in the hall, and then the sound of the counting of the ballots. After a while a lonely voice announced the number of ballots for and against.

The marshal received a large majority. Talking noisily, everyone rushed toward the door. Snetkov entered, and the noblemen surrounded him, extending their congratulations.

"Well, is it all over now?" Levin asked Sergei Ivanovich.

"It's just beginning," answered Sviazhsky with a smile, instead of Sergei Ivanovich. "Another candidate may receive more votes."

Levin had completely forgotten about this. Only now did he remember that some sort of artful design was being carried out here, but it bored him to recall what it was. He was dejected and wished he could escape from this crowd.

Since no one paid any attention to him and since no one seemed to need him, he quietly proceeded toward the small hall where they served refreshments, and he felt greatly relieved when he again saw the waiters. The little old waiter offered him something to eat and Levin accepted. After eating a cutlet and some beans and conversing with the waiter about his former masters, Levin, reluctant to return to the hall where everything seemed to him so unpleasant, went up to the gallery.

The gallery was full of smartly dressed ladies who bent over the railing, eager not to miss a single word spoken downstairs. Around the ladies were sitting or standing elegant lawyers, bespectacled gymnasium teachers, and army officers. Everywhere they spoke about the elections, about the marshal, who was so tired, and about the debates, which were so clever. In one group Levin heard his brother being praised. One lady was saying to a lawyer:

"How glad I am to have heard Koznyshev. It was worth going without lunch. Charming! How clearly I could hear everything! Nobody speaks like that in your court. Only Meidel, perhaps, and even he is far from being so eloquent."

Levin took an empty seat and bent over the railing, watching and listening.

All the noblemen were seated in areas partitioned off for their respective counties. Standing in the middle of the hall, a man in uniform announced in a thin loud voice:

"Junior Captain Evgeni Ivanovich Apukhtin is nominated for the office of marshal of the province."

Dead silence followed, and then a weak, senile voice announced:

"Declined!"

"Aulic Councilor Piotr Petrovich Bohl is nominated for the office," the voice began again.

"Declined!" resounded a young, high-pitched voice.

A third person was named, and again the answer, "Declined!" It went on this way for about an hour. Bending over the railing, Levin looked and listened. First he wondered and wanted to know what it all meant. Then, after he had become convinced that he would never understand it, he became bored. But recalling the agitation and enmity he had seen on everyone's face, he grew sad. He decided to leave, and went downstairs. As he passed through the entrance hall of the gallery, he saw a dejected schoolboy with puffed eyelids who was pacing up and down. On the stairs he met a couple—a lady who walked rapidly, her heels resounding, and a nimble assistant public prosecutor.

"I told you that you wouldn't be late," said the prosecutor at the same time as Levin stepped aside to let the lady pass.

Levin was on the stairs on his way out and was reaching into his vest pocket for his coatroom ticket when the secretary caught up with him. "Come, Konstantin Dmitrievich, they're voting."

Nevedovsky accepted the nomination, though he had been declining it so persistently. Levin went up to the door of the hall; it was locked. The secretary knocked, the door opened, and two landowners with flushed faces rushed past Levin.

"I can't stand it any longer!" said one of the excited landowners.

Following the landowners there appeared the face of the marshal of the province. It was terrible to see, exhausted and frightened as it was.

"I told you not to let anyone out!" he shouted at the doorman.

"I let them in, Your Excellency!"

"Oh, Lord!" said the marshal of the province with a heavy sigh, and shuffling along in his white trousers, his head bowed, he proceeded through the middle of the room toward the large desk.

As had been expected, Nevedovsky was elected marshal of the province by a large majority. Many were joyous, many content, many happy, many elated, and many discontented and unhappy. The former marshal of the province was despondent, and he could not hide it. As Nevedovsky was leav-

ing the room, the crowd surrounded him and followed him
with jubilation, just as it had followed the governor on the
day he opened the assembly and just as it had followed
Snetkov when he had been nominated.

31

THAT DAY THE newly elected marshal of the province and
many members of the victorious new party had dinner at
Vronsky's.

Vronsky had gone to the elections both because he was
bored in the country and because he had to show Anna that
he was entitled to his freedom, and also to give Sviazhsky his
support in these elections and thus repay him for all the help
he had given Vronsky in the zemstvo elections. But the main
reason was his desire to fulfill conscientiously all the duties
that went with the position he had chosen, that of nobleman
and landowner; he had not in the least expected that he would
become so engrossed in the elections, that they would become
so vitally important to him, and that he would perform his
part so well. He was a complete stranger in this circle of noblemen, but apparently he was becoming popular and he was not
mistaken in thinking that he had already been gaining influence among them. This influence was contributed to by: his
wealth and noble rank; the magnificent town house placed at
his disposal by his old friend Shirkov, a financier who had
founded a flourishing bank in Kashin; Vronsky's excellent
chef, whom he had brought from the country; his friendship
with the governor, his comrade, and one of those comrades
whom he had patronized; but most of all, his frank manner—
he treated everyone alike and this had, within a short time,
induced the noblemen to change their belief that he was a
haughty person. He himself felt that except for that peculiar
person married to Kitty Shcherbatsky, who had poured forth,
in violent anger, and à propos de bottes, a torrent of preposterous nonsense, every nobleman he met was on his side.
He saw clearly, and others admitted it too, that he had made
a significant contribution toward Nevedovsky's victory. And
now, at his table, he celebrated Nevedovsky's election, pleased
by the triumph of his candidate. And the elections themselves had absorbed him so deeply that if he were to be

married within the next three years, he would think of running for office himself, just as, after his jockey won a race for him, he wanted to do it himself.

And now they were celebrating a jockey's triumph. Vronsky was seated at the head of the table, while at his right sat the young governor, a general in the Emperor's suite. To everyone else he was the master of the province, who had solemnly opened the elections, delivered a speech, and commanded the respect and obsequiousness of many. But to Vronsky he was Maslov Katka—his nickname in the School of Pages—who was shy in his company, and whom Vronsky tried *mettre à son aise.* On his left sat Nevedovsky, with his youthful, steadfast, malicious face. With him Vronsky was simple and respectful.

Sviazhsky accepted his defeat in good spirit. It was not even a defeat for him, as he himself said, addressing Nevedovsky with a glass in his hand: they could have elected no better man to lead the nobility in these new times. Therefore, he said, all honorable men welcomed and celebrated the victory won that day.

Stepan Arkadievich also was glad, because he was having a pleasant time and because everyone was pleased. At dinner they recalled some episodes of the elections. Sviazhsky mimicked the tearful speech of the marshal and, addressing Nevedovsky, suggested that His Excellency would have to find, instead of tears, another more effective method of auditing the accounts. Another nobleman jestingly related that footmen dressed in stockings had been hired for the marshal's ball and that now they would have to be sent away if the new marshal of nobility were against stockinged footmen serving at his ball.

During dinner, when they spoke to Nevedovsky they kept repeating, "Our marshal of the province" or "your excellency."

They pronounced these words with the same pleasure with which one addresses a young woman with the word *madame,* followed by her husband's name. Nevedovsky pretended to regard these titles not only with indifference but even with contempt, but it was obvious that he was happy and trying to control himself in order not to reveal his elation, which did not suit the new liberal opinions of this gathering.

At dinner they sent a few telegrams to people who were interested in the outcome of the elections. And Stepan Arkadievich, who was enjoying himself wholeheartedly, sent a telegram to Daria Aleksandrovna that read, "Nevedovsky *elected by majority of twelve. Congratulations. Tell others.*" He read it aloud, remarking, "We must share the happy news." But Daria Aleksandrovna only sighed when she received the telegram, thinking of the ruble it cost, and understood that this had been done at the end of a dinner. She knew Stiva's weakness to *faire jouer le télégraphe* at the end of a dinner.

Everything, including the excellent dinner with its wines bought bottled abroad and not from Russian wine dealers, was refined, simple and cheerful. The group of twenty men had been chosen by Sviazhsky from among those who shared the same views, were liberal-minded, kept abreast of the times, and at the same time were witty and decent. They drank a toast, half-jokingly, to the new marshal, the governor, to the director of the bank, and to "our kind host."

Vronsky was gratified. He had never expected to find such a pleasant atmosphere in the provinces.

They grew still merrier toward the end of dinner. The governor invited Vronsky to a concert for the benefit of "our Serbian brothers." His wife, who had arranged it, wished to meet Vronsky.

"There'll be a ball afterward, and you'll meet the belle of the province. She's truly remarkable."

"Not in my line," replied Vronsky, who liked this English expression, but he smiled and promised to come.

Just before the guests left the table, when everyone had lit his cigar, Vronsky's valet came over to him with a letter on a tray.

"By special messenger from Vozdvizhenskoe," he said with a meaningful expression.

"It's remarkable how closely he resembles Assistant Prosecutor Sventitsky," said one of the guests in French, referring to the valet, while Vronsky, frowning, read the letter.

The letter was from Anna. Even before reading it, he knew its contents. Expecting the elections to last only five days, he had promised to return on Friday. It was Saturday, and he knew that the letter would consist of reproaches for his failure to return on time. The letter he had sent her the previous night probably had not yet arrived.

The contents of the letter were as he had expected, but its tone was unexpected and particularly disagreeable.

Annie is very sick, and the doctor says it may be an inflamma-

tion. I'm at my wits' end here alone. Princess Varvara is of no help and only in the way. I expected you the day before yesterday and yesterday, and now I am writing to find out where and how you are. I wanted to go myself, but I changed my mind, knowing that you would not like it. Write a few words so that I may know what to do.

The child was ill, yet she was willing to come herself. Their daughter was sick, and yet this hostile tone.

The carefree and gay atmosphere of the elections on the one hand, and the cheerless, oppressive love he had to return to, on the other, struck Vronsky by their contrast. But he had to go, and that night he left for home by the first available train.

32

BEFORE VRONSKY left for the elections, Anna had come to the conclusion that the scenes that had been occuring between them at each of his departures could only estrange him instead of drawing him closer to her. Therefore she decided to use all her efforts to bear his absence calmly. But the cold, stern look he gave her when he came to tell her of his intended trip offended her, and even before he left, her calm had been shattered.

When, in her solitude, she reflected upon that look, which was an expression of his right to freedom, her thought always brought her to the same point—to the awareness of her humiliation. He has the right to go where and when he pleases, she thought. Not only to go on his trips but to leave me. He has all the rights, and I have none. But, knowing this, he shouldn't have done what he did. But what did he do? . . . He looked at me with a cold, stern expression. Of course, this is intangible and indefinable, but it has never happened before, and that look had a profound meaning, she thought. That look showed that his love is beginning to cool.

And though she had become convinced that his love was cooling, she could not help it, she could not change her relationship with him in any respect. Just as before, she could hold him only by her love and beauty. And just as before, by being busy in the daytime and taking morphine at night, she could suppress the terrible thoughts of what would happen if he stopped loving her. True, there still remained another way, not a method of attracting him—this she wanted to be achieved through nothing but his love for her—but a way to become closer to him and to put herself in a position that would prevent him from staying away from her. This way was divorce and marriage. And she began to wish it and decided to agree to it as soon as he or Stiva would mention it.

With such thoughts she spent five days without him, the days of his intended absence.

Walks, conversations with Princess Varvara, visits to the hospital, and, mainly, reading one book after another filled her time. But on the sixth day, when the coachman arrived without him, she felt that she could no longer suppress her thoughts about him and of what he was doing there. At that very time her child became ill. Anna undertook to take care of her, but even this did not distract her, particularly because it was not a serious illness. No matter how much she tried, she could not bring herself to love this child, nor could she feign love for her. Toward the evening of that day, remaining alone, Anna was seized with such fear for him that she was on the verge of going to the city, but, on second thought, she decided to write that self-contradicting letter which Vronsky had received and, without reading it over, she had it delivered by special messenger. The next morning she received his letter and regretted that she had written. She was frightened at the thought that again he would give her the stern look he had given her on departing, particularly when he found out that the child was not seriously ill. Nevertheless, she was glad that she had written. Within her heart Anna already believed that she was a burden to him, and that he regretted giving up his freedom in order to return to her; nevertheless, she was glad that he was coming. Though she might be a burden to him, he would be near her, she would see him and know his every movement.

She was sitting in the drawing room under the lamp, reading a new book by Taine, listening to the wind outside and awaiting the arrival of the carriage at any moment. A few times it seemed to her that she heard the sound of wheels, but she was mistaken. At last she heard not only the sound of the wheels, but also the shouts of the coachman and a dull sound at the canopied entrance. Princess Varvara, who was playing solitaire, also heard it, and Anna, flushing, rose, but instead of going downstairs as she had done twice earlier, she stopped. She suddenly felt ashamed of her deception, but most of all feared the way he would receive her. The feeling of offense had already passed; she only dreaded that he might be displeased. She recalled that her daughter had been quite well since the previous day—she was even annoyed with her child for having recovered just at the time when the letter had been dispatched. Then she remembered him, recalled that he was here, all of him, with his hands, his eyes. She heard his voice. And forgetting everything, she ran happily to meet him.

"Well, how is Annie?" he asked hesitatingly from downstairs, as Anna ran down to him.

He was sitting on a chair while the servant pulled off his traveling boots.

"She is better."

"And you?" he asked, brushing himself off.

She took his hand in both of hers and drew it to herself, without lowering her gaze.

"Well, that's fine," he said, looking coldly at her, her coiffure, her dress, which, he knew, she had put on for him.

He liked all of this, but he had liked it so many times! And his face assumed the stern, stony expression she feared so much.

"Well, that's fine. And how are you?" he said, wiping his moist beard with his handkerchief and kissing her hand.

It doesn't matter, she thought, as long as he's here, and when he's here, he cannot, he dare not, cease to love me.

They spent a happy and gay evening with Princess Varvara, who complained that in his absence Anna had been taking morphine.

"What else could I do? I couldn't sleep. . . . Thinking kept me awake. When he's here, I never take it. Almost never."

He told them about the elections, and Anna knew how to lead him by her questions to the topic he enjoyed most—his success. She told him all the domestic news that might interest him. And all her information was most entertaining.

But late in the evening, when they were alone, Anna, seeing that he was completely in her power again, wanted to erase the painful impression of the look he had given her on account of the letter.

"Tell me the truth. You were annoyed by my letter and didn't believe me."

As soon as she said this, she knew that however affectionate he was with her now, he had not forgiven her for that letter.

"Yes," he said. "Such a strange letter. First, Annie is sick, and then you want to go yourself."

"All of that was true."

"I don't doubt it."

"No, you have some doubts. You're not pleased, I see."

"Not at all. And if I'm displeased, it's only because you, it seems, refuse to admit that I have my duties. . . ."

"Duties to go to concerts. . . ."

"Well, let's not talk about it," he said.

"Why shouldn't we?" she asked.

"I simply want to say that sometimes I may have urgent business. For instance, now I have to go to Moscow in connection with my house. . . . Oh, Anna, why are you so irritable? Don't you know that I can't live without you?"

"If this is so," Anna said in a suddenly changed voice, "this life is a burden to you. . . . Yes, you come home for a day, and leave as they do who—"

"Anna, you are being cruel. I'm ready to give my life—"

But she was not listening to him.

"If you're going to Moscow, I'm going too. I won't remain here. Either we must part or live together."

"You know that that's my only desire. But for this—"

"I must get a divorce? I'll write to him. I see that I can't live like this. . . . But I'll go with you to Moscow."

"You sound as though you're threatening me. But I have no greater desire than never to part with you," Vronsky said, smiling.

But as he spoke these gentle words, his eyes flashed a look that was not merely cold but the hostile look of a man being hounded and driven to exasperation.

She noticed this look and understood its meaning correctly.

If that's the case, it spells disaster! his look said. It was a fleeting impression, but she never forgot it.

Anna wrote a letter to her husband asking for a divorce, and at the end of November, after parting with Princess Varvara, who had to go to Petersburg, she and Vronsky moved to Moscow. Expecting a reply from Aleksei Aleksandrovich any day and then the divorce, they now settled down together as husband and wife.

PART SEVEN

1

THE LEVINS were now in their third month in Moscow. The time had long since passed when, according to the most exact calculations of those who were versed in such matters, Kitty should have given birth to the child. But she still carried it, and there was no sign that the time for its delivery was closer now than it had been two months ago. The doctor, the midwife, Dolly, her mother, and particularly Levin, who could not think without fright of what was coming, began to grow impatient and worried. Only Kitty was completely serene and happy.

She was now fully conscious of the new feeling of love engendered within her for her future child, who to her was to some extent actually existing already, and she delighted in giving herself up to this feeling. The child was no longer completely a part of her, and at times it lived its own life, independent of her. She often deeply regretted this, but at the same time she felt like laughing with a strange new joy.

Everyone she loved was near her, and everyone was so kind to her and took such good care of her, and she saw everything in such a pleasant light that but for her awareness and feeling that all this must soon end she couldn't wish for a better and more pleasant life. The only thing that marred her delight in this life was that her husband was not as she liked him to be and as he had been in the country.

She had loved his calm, gentle, and hospitable manner in the country. But in the city he always seemed to be uneasy and on guard, as though afraid that someone might offend him or, more important, her. There, in the country, evidently knowing that he was in his proper place, he never hurried and was never idle. Here in the city he was always in a hurry,

as though fearing that he might miss something, but he had
nothing to do. And she pitied him. To others, she knew, he
did not seem pitiful. On the contrary, when Kitty watched
him among people, as we sometimes watch a person we love,
she tried to look at him as at a stranger in order to visualize
the impression he made on others. She noticed, actually with
jealous fear, that he was not only not pitiful, but very attractive
with his somewhat old-fashioned respectability, his shy courtesy with the ladies, his strong figure, and his unique, as it
seemed to her, and expressive face. But she did not see him
from the outside; she saw what was going on within him. She
saw that here he was not himself; otherwise she could not
account for his present state. Sometimes, in her heart, she
reproached him for being unfit for life in the city, but at other
times she agreed that it would indeed be hard for him to
arrange his life here to his satisfaction.

And in fact, what could he do here? He did not like to
play cards. He did not go to the club. And by now she had
learned what it meant to be friends of gay men like Oblonsky
. . . it meant to drink, and after drinking to go to certain places.
She could not think without horror of the places men frequent
on such occasions. To pay social calls? But she knew that this
meant looking for pleasure in the company of young women,
something she did not desire. To stay at home with her mother
and sisters? But however friendly and cheerful they were,
their conversations were always the same girlish nonsense, as
the old prince called the sisters' chatter. She knew that it
could not interest him. What else remained for him to do?
To continue writing his book? He did try that in the beginning,
and he visited the library to make notes for his book. But, as
he told her, the more idle he became, the more he was pressed
for time. And in addition, he complained, here he was talking
too much about his book, and this had thrown his ideas into
confusion and caused him to lose interest in them.

The only advantage to their life in the city was that here
they never quarreled. Whether it was because the conditions
of their life in the city were different or because both of them
had become more cautious and reasonable, in Moscow they
had none of the jealous quarrels they had been so apprehensive about when they moved to the city.

There even occurred an event of great importance to both
of them in this respect, namely, Kitty's meeting with Vronsky.
The old Princess Maria Borisovna, Kitty's godmother, who

was very fond of her, insisted on seeing her. Kitty, who in her condition visited no one, went with her father to pay a visit to the venerable old lady and met Vronsky there.

The only thing Kitty reproached herself for was that at that meeting, for a single moment when she recognized his once so familiar figure, now in civilian clothes, she could not catch her breath, blood rushed to her heart, and a bright blush, she felt, covered her face. But it lasted only a few seconds. Even before her father, who deliberately was speaking to Vronsky in a loud voice, had finished talking, she was completely prepared to face Vronsky, to speak to him, if necessary, exactly as she spoke to Princess Maria Borisovna, and, above all, in such a manner that everything, including the minutest intonation of her voice and smile, would have been fully approved by her husband, whose invisible presence at her side she seemed to feel at that moment.

She said a few words to him, even smiled calmly at his joke about the elections, which he called "our parliament" (she had to smile to show that she understood the joke). But she immediately turned to Princess Maria Borisovna and did not look at him again until he rose to leave. Then she glanced at him, but evidently only because it would be impolite not to look at a man when he is taking his leave.

She was grateful to her father for saying nothing about this meeting with Vronsky, but after the visit, from his particular tenderness toward her during their customary walk, she could see that he was pleased with her. And she was pleased with herself. She had not expected in the least to be able to find the strength to suppress somewhere deep within her heart all the memories of her former feeling toward Vronsky and not only to appear but actually to feel completely indifferent to him.

Levin blushed much more than she when she told him that she had met Vronsky at Princess Maria Borisovna's. It was very hard for her to mention it, but it was still harder to go on and describe the details of the meeting, because he asked no questions and only looked at her with a frown.

"I'm very sorry that you weren't there," she said. "Not that you weren't there in the room . . . in your presence I would have been less natural . . . I'm blushing now much more, much more," she said, blushing and almost crying. "But I wish you could have watched through a peephole."

Her honest eyes told Levin that she was pleased with her-

self, and though she blushed, he soon calmed down and began
to ask her questions, and this was all she wanted. When he
had found out everything, even the fact that it was only for
the first moment that she could not help blushing, but that
later she felt as easy and unconcerned as with any other person, Levin became completely cheerful and said that he was
very glad that it had happened, happy, that he would no
longer behave so foolishly as he had at the elections, and that
at his next meeting with Vronsky he would try to be as
friendly with him as possible.

"It has been so painful for me to think that there exists a
man who is practically an enemy, someone with whom it is
hateful to associate," said Levin. "I'm very, very relieved."

2

"WELL THEN, please stop at the Bohls'," Kitty said to her husband when he came to see her at eleven o'clock, before leaving. "I know that you're dining at the club—Papa entered
your name. And what are you doing in the morning?"

"I'll stop at Katavasov's only," said Levin.

"Why so early?"

"He promised to introduce me to Metrov. I'd like to talk
to him about my book—he's a renowned Petersburg scholar,"
said Levin.

"Oh yes, wasn't it his article that you praised so highly?
And then?" asked Kitty.

"To the court perhaps, on my sister's business."

"And to the concert?" she asked.

"I'd hate to go alone."

"Please go. They are performing some new compositions.
. . . You were so interested in them. I wouldn't miss it."

"Well, at any rate, I'll stop back before dinner," he said,
looking at his watch.

"Put on your frock coat, so that you may go directly to
Countess Bohl's."

"Must I really go there?"

"You must! He was in our house. What can you lose? You'll
stop there, take a seat, talk about the weather for five minutes,
get up, and leave."

"Well, you'd scarcely believe it, but I've become so unaccustomed to these things that they make me feel guilty. It's

ridiculous! A stranger comes in, sits down, spends some time uselessly, annoys his hosts, upsets himself, and leaves."

Kitty laughed.

"But you used to pay visits when you were a bachelor," she said.

"I did, but I always felt ashamed, and now I'm so out of practice that I swear I'd rather go for two days without food than pay this visit. It's so embarrassing! It seems to me that they'll be annoyed and say, 'Why have you come, if you had no reason?'"

"They won't be annoyed. I can assure you of that," said Kitty, looking into his face, laughing. She took his hand. "Well, goodbye. . . . Go to see them, please."

He kissed her hand and was about to leave when she stopped him.

"Kostia, you know, I have only fifty rubles left."

"Well, I'll stop at the bank. How much?" he asked with a look of displeasure that she knew well.

"Wait," she said, taking his hand and holding it. "Let's talk it over; it troubles me. It seems to me that I'm very economical, but money melts away rapidly. There must be something wrong."

"Not at all," he said, clearing his throat and looking at her with a frown.

She knew that cough. It was a sign of his deep dissatisfaction, not with her but with himself. And in fact, he was vexed not because their expenses were great but because he was being reminded of something that he knew was not as it should be but wanted to forget.

"I told Sokolov to sell the wheat and to get an advance on the mill. In any case we'll have money."

"But I'm afraid that in general our expenses are too high. . . ."

"Not at all, not at all," he repeated. "Well, goodbye, my dear."

"Really, I sometimes regret that I listened to Mama. How good it was in the country! But here I wear you all out, and we spend so much money—"

"Not at all, not at all. Since our marriage, I've never had any reason to say that things would be better if they were different. . . ."

"Really?" she asked, looking into his eyes.

He had said it without thinking, only to comfort her. But

when he glanced at her and saw her sincere, gentle, and inquiring eyes fixed upon him, he repeated the same words with his whole heart. I'm definitely neglecting her, he thought. And he thought of the event that was to happen soon.

"Well, soon? What do you think?" he whispered, taking both her hands.

"I've thought of it so often that now I've given up and just don't think."

"Aren't you frightened?"

She smiled contemptuously.

"Not in the least."

"Well, if anything happens, I'll be at Katavasov's."

"Nothing will happen. Don't even think of it. I'll go with Papa to the boulevard for a walk. We'll stop at Dolly's. I'll expect you before dinner. Oh, yes, do you know that Dolly's situation is becoming impossible? She owes everyone and has no money. Yesterday Mama, Arseni (as she referred to her sister's husband, Lvov), and I talked it over and we decided that you and he should force the issue with Stiva. It's an absolutely impossible situation. We can't talk about it to Papa. . . . But you and he—"

"But what can we do?" asked Levin.

"When you see Arseni, talk it over with him. He'll tell you what we decided."

"Well, with Arseni I agree in advance to anything. I'll go to see him. By the way, if I do go to the concert, I'll go with Natalie. Well, goodbye."

On the porch the old servant Kuzma stopped him. He had been with him when Levin was still a bachelor, and now he was in charge of the household in town.

"We've reshod Krasavchik," (the left shaft horse, brought from the country) "but he's still lame," he said. "What should we do about it?"

In the early days of their stay in Moscow, Levin was interested in the horses he had brought from the country. He wanted to keep this part of his expenses as low and as advantageous as possible. But it turned out that his own horses cost him more than the hired ones and he still had to hire a cabman.

"Send for the veterinary. Perhaps it's a bruise."

"And for Katerina Aleksandrovna?" asked Kuzma.

Levin was no longer surprised now, as he had been in the early days of their life in Moscow, that in order to ride from

Vozdvizhenka to Sivtsev Vrazhek they had to harness two strong horses to a heavy coach, drive this coach for a quarter of a verst through slush, leave it there for four hours, and pay five rubles for this. It seemed natural to him by now.

"Tell the cabman to bring a pair of horses for our coach," he said.

"Very good, sir."

After having resolved this difficulty, which thanks to the conditions of city life he could accomplish so simply and so easily, but which in the country would require a great deal of personal labor and attention, Levin went out on the porch, hailed a cab, got in, and left for Nikitskaya. On the way he no longer thought of money, but reflected on his forthcoming meeting with the Petersburg scholar, a specialist in sociology, and on the conversation he would have with him about his book.

Only in the very beginning of his stay in Moscow was Levin astonished by the unproductive but unavoidable expenditures demanded of him on all sides, which had seemed so unusual to a man from the country. But now he was used to them. What had happened to him, they say, happens to drunkards: the first glass—a stake in the throat, the second—a swooping hawk, and after the third—tiny birds. When Levin changed the first hundred-ruble note to buy uniforms for his servant and doorman, he could not help thinking of this expense. These uniforms were of no use to anyone, yet they seemed indispensable, judging by the surprise which Kitty and the princess showed when he hinted that one could get along without such uniforms. And he calculated that with this money he could hire two summer laborers, in other words, he could pay for about three-hundred working days with it, from Easter week until the fall fast, each working day spent in heavy toil from early morning until late evening. This first hundred-ruble note was the stake in the throat. The second note was changed to buy food for a dinner for his relatives, which cost twenty-eight rubles. And though Levin remembered that these twenty-eight rubles were the price of nine measures of oats, the product of sweat, groans, and the toil of reaping, binding, threshing, winnowing, sifting, and sacking, nevertheless this note was spent with much more ease. But now the changing of notes had long since ceased to awaken such reflections, and the money flew by like tiny birds. And he had long since given up considering whether the labor spent on gaining the money corresponded to the pleasure afforded by what had been acquired for this money. The farmer's consideration that there was a certain price below which each kind of grain should not be sold had also been forgotten. For a long time he had clung to his price for his rye, but now he had sold it at fifty kopecks a measure less than he had been offered the previous month. Even the consideration that with such expenses they would not be able to go the year without incurring debts, even this consideration was now devoid of any importance. Only one thing was required—to have money in the bank, without any consideration for where it came from, so as to be sure of food for the next day. And this rule he had heretofore observed—he always had money in the bank. But he had run out of it now, and he did not quite know where to get more. This was what had disturbed him for a moment when Kitty asked him for money, but he had no time to think it over. He rode along, thinking of Katavasov and of his forthcoming meeting with Metrov.

3

DURING THIS STAY in Moscow, Levin renewed his close friendship with his college classmate, Professor Katavasov, whom he had not seen since his marriage. He liked Katavasov for the clarity and precision of his views on life. Levin thought that the clarity of Katavasov's views was the result of his limitations, and Katavasov believed that Levin's inconsistency was the result of his lack of mental discipline. But Levin liked Katavasov's clarity, Levin's manifold inconsistencies pleased Katavasov, and they enjoyed meeting and arguing.

Levin read to Katavasov some excerpts from his book, and Katavasov liked them. When he met Levin at a public lecture the previous day, Katavasov told him that the renowned Metrov, whose article Levin liked so much, was in Moscow and showed great interest in Levin's work, which Katavasov had told him about, and that Metrov would be at his home the next day at eleven o'clock and would be very glad to meet him.

"You show definite improvement, my good friend, I'm happy to see," said Katavasov to Levin, as he met him in his small drawing room. "I heard a bell ring and I thought: is he really on time? . . . Well, what do you say about the Montenegrins? Born warriors!"

"Why?" asked Levin.

In a few words Katavasov related to him the latest news, and when they entered the study he introduced him to a short, thickset man of very pleasant appearance. It was Metrov. For a short while the conversation centered on politics and on the views the highest Petersburg circles maintained on the latest happenings. Metrov cited the words the Czar and one of the ministers were supposed to have said on this occasion, which he had learned from a reliable source. Katavasov, however, had heard, also as an authentic report, that the Czar had said something quite different. Levin tried to think up a situation in which both these sets of words could have been said, and on this note the conversation came to an end.

"Here you have a man who has almost completed a book on the natural relationship between labor and the land," said Katavasov. "I am no specialist on the subject, but as a naturalist I was glad to see that he doesn't consider mankind as something exempt from the laws of biology but on the contrary, he accepts its dependence on environment, and in this dependence he seeks the laws of its development."

"That's very interesting," said Metrov.

"I actually began to write a book on agriculture, but in studying the main element of agriculture—labor—I unconsciously came upon totally unexpected results," said Levin, blushing.

And as though putting out a feeler, Levin cautiously began to expound his views. He knew that Metrov had written an article that contradicted the generally accepted tenets of political economy, but from the expression on his intelligent and calm face, Levin did not know and could not guess how much hope he could have for Metrov's sympathy with his novel views.

"But in what do you see the specific traits of the Russian laborer?" asked Metrov. "Is it, so to say, in his biological nature, or in the conditions in which he is placed?"

Levin saw that this question implied an idea he did not agree with. But he kept explaining his theory, which maintained that the Russian laborer's attitude toward the land was entirely different from that of other nations. And to prove this statement he hastily added that, in his opinion, this attitude had resulted from the Russian nation's awareness of its mission to populate the immense unoccupied stretches of land in the East.

"It's very easy to fall into error when you try to reach conclusions about the mission of an entire nation," said Metrov, interrupting Levin. "The state of the laborer will always depend on his relation to land and capital."

And without giving Levin a chance to complete his explanation, Metrov began to expound the particulars of his theory.

What these particulars were, Levin could not understand, for he did not even try. He saw that, in spite of the article in which he rejected the teachings of the economists, Metrov, like the others, still examined the condition of the Russian laborer by taking into consideration nothing but capital, wages, and rent value. He had to admit that in the eastern part of Russia, which was the largest, rent value was zero, that wages for nine-tenths of eighty million of the Russian people were only at the subsistence level, and that capital investment consisted only of the most primitive implements. Still he looked at the conditions of every laborer only in the light of these considerations, even though he did not agree with the economists on many points and had his own new theory of wages, which he began to explain to Levin.

Levin listened reluctantly and at first made some objections. He wanted to interrupt Metrov, to express his own idea, which, he believed, would make any further explanation unnecessary. But when he had convinced himself that their views were so far apart that they would never understand each other, he made no further objections and simply listened. Although at this point he had no interest whatsoever in what Metrov was saying, he listened to him with some pleasure. His self-esteem was flattered by the fact that such a learned man, so willingly, with such attention, and with such confidence in Levin's understanding of the subject, was expounding to him his theory, sometimes referring to a substantial part of it merely with a hint. He ascribed this to his own worth, ignorant of the fact that Metrov, after he had spoken on the subject to all around him, was particularly willing to talk about it to any new listener, and in general talked willingly to anyone on this subject, which occupied him but which he still did not see clearly in his own mind.

"I'm afraid we'll be late," said Katavasov, looking at his watch as soon as Metrov had finished his discourse.

"There's a meeting today of the Society for the Advancement of Knowledge, in honor of the fiftieth anniversary of Svintich," replied Katavasov to Levin's question. "Piotr Ivanovich and I are going. I promised to read a paper on his contribution to zoology. Come with us; it'll be very interesting."

"Indeed, it's time to go," said Metrov. "Come with us and from there, if you like, to my place. I'd like you to read your work to me."

"Oh, no! It's not really finished. But I'll gladly go to the meeting."

"Well, my friend, have you heard the latest? I submitted a dissenting opinion," said Katavasov from the other room, where he was putting on his swallow-tailed coat.

And they began to discuss events at the university.

That winter, events of major importance were taking place at Moscow University. In the council, three of the older professors had rejected the opinions of the younger ones, and the latter had submitted a dissenting opinion. In the judgment of some, this opinion was shocking, but according to others it was realistic and well-founded, and the professors were divided into two parties.

One group, among them Katavasov, saw in the opposing party foul treachery and deceit; their opponents, meanwhile, saw them as juveniles who lacked respect for authority. Though Levin was not a member of the university, during his stay in Moscow he had heard of this case on several occasions, had discussed it, and had formed his own opinion. He took part in the conversation, which they continued on the street, as all three walked toward a building of the old university.

The meeting had already begun. Katavasov and Metrov took their seats at a cloth-covered table where six other persons were sitting, one of them hunched over a manuscript, reading it aloud. Levin sat down in one of the vacant chairs around the table and in a whisper asked a student who was seated next to him what was being read. The student, with a glance of displeasure at Levin, replied:

"A biography."

Though Levin was not interested in the biography of the scientist, he could not help listening, and he acquired some new and interesting information about the life of the illustrious scientist.

When the reader had finished, the chairman thanked him,

read some verses written by the poet Ment for this occasion, then said a few words of thanks to the poet. Then Katavasov, in his loud, high-pitched voice, read his report on the scientific works of the man they were honoring.

When Katavasov had finished, Levin looked at his watch, saw that it was after one, and decided that he would not have time to read his work to Metrov before the concert. As a matter of fact, he no longer had the desire to do so. While listening to the report he had also been thinking of their conversation. It was clear to him now that though Metrov's ideas might have some validity, his own did too. These ideas could become clear and lead to results only if each of them followed his own chosen path, but nothing would be accomplished by keeping each other informed of these ideas. And having decided to decline Metrov's invitation, Levin came over to him at the end of the meeting. Metrov introduced Levin to the chairman, with whom he had been discussing political events. And continuing this discussion, Metrov related to the chairman the same story he had told Levin, and Levin made the same remarks he had already made that morning, but, to avoid sounding repetitious, he added a new idea of his own that came to him at that moment. Then the conversation shifted again to the problem at the university. Since Levin had already heard all this, he hastened to tell Metrov that he regretted that he was unable to accept his invitation, said goodbye, and left for the Lvovs'.

4

Lvov, who was married to Natalie, Kitty's sister, had spent all his life in the capitals and abroad, where he had been brought up and had served as a diplomat.

The previous year he had retired from the diplomatic service, not on account of any difficulties (he had never had any difficulties with anyone), and had taken a position in the Imperial Court Department in Moscow in order to provide his two boys with the best possible education.

Though their views and habits differed sharply, and though Lvov was older than Levin, that winter they became close friends and grew fond of each other.

Lvov was at home, and Levin entered without being announced.

Lvov, dressed in a belted lounging jacket and suede shoes, was sitting in an armchair, and carefully holding his cigar, half ash, in his graceful outstretched hand, was reading, through his blue pince-nez, a book held on a reading stand.

His face, fine, handsome and still youthful, its aristocratic look enhanced by his curly, shining, silvery hair, lit up with a smile at the sight of Levin.

"Splendid! And I was just about to send my man to you. Well, how's Kitty? Sit down here, you'll be more comfortable. . . ." He rose and pulled up a rocking chair. "Have you read the latest report in the *Journal de St. Pétersbourg*? I find it excellent," he said, with a slight French accent.

Levin related the latest rumors from Petersburg as told to him by Katavasov, and after a few remarks on politics, told him about his introduction to Metrov and about the meeting. Lvov was quite interested.

"I envy you for having access to that interesting world of science," he said. And, as usual, as he warmed up to the conversation, he quickly changed to French, in which he was more at home. "True, I'm pressed for time. My position and tutoring the children prevent me from doing the same; and then, I'm not ashamed to say my education is not quite adequate."

"I don't agree," said Levin with a smile, admiring, as always, his friend's humble opinion of himself, which was quite sincere and was not expressed only out of a desire to appear or even actually to be modest.

"No, it's true! I realize now how poorly educated I am. In order to teach my children I must do a great deal of reviewing or even studying. For it's not enough to have teachers for them; you must have a supervisor as well, just as on your farm you must have laborers and an overseer. Look at this book," he said, pointing to Buslayev's grammar, which lay on the reading stand. "They require it of Misha, yet it's so difficult. . . . Please explain something to me. They say here. . . ."

Levin tried to explain to him that it would not do to try to understand, that one simply had to learn it. But Lvov did not agree.

"I think you're making fun of me."

"On the contrary, you'd scarcely believe how much I learn,

by watching you, of what I'll have to do in the education of my children."

"Well, there's nothing to learn from me," said Lvov.

"I only know," said Levin, "that I've never seen children better brought up than yours, and I couldn't wish mine to be better than yours."

Lvov evidently tried to hold back any display of pleasure, but his face lit up with a smile.

"I only hope that they'll be better than I. That's all I want. You can't imagine how much work must be done," he said, "with boys like mine, whose education has been neglected through life abroad."

"You'll make up for it. They are such bright boys. The main thing is moral education. That's what I learn when I watch your children."

"You say moral education. It's hard to imagine how difficult it is! No sooner do you overcome one trait than others appear, and the struggle begins again. Without the support of religion —you remember, we spoke about it—no father could bring up his children by his own efforts."

This conversation, on a subject that always interested Levin, was interrupted by the beautiful Natalie Aleksandrovna, who entered the room, dressed to go out.

"I didn't know you were here," she said. Evidently she did not regret but was even glad that she had interrupted a topic which was too familiar to her, one she had grown tired of. "Well, how's Kitty? I'm having dinner with her today. Now, Arseni," she said, turning to her husband, "you'll take the coach. . . ."

And a discussion ensued between husband and wife on the manner in which they would spend the day. Since the husband had to go to meet someone on official business, and his wife had to attend a concert and then a public session of the Southeastern Slav Committee, they had much to discuss and decide. Levin, as a member of the family, had to take part in this discussion. It was decided that Levin and Natalie would go to the concert and the public session; from there they would send the coach to fetch Arseni at his office, and he would call for Natalie and take her to Kitty; or, if he were not through with his business, he would send the coach back and Levin would take her.

"He's turning my head," Lvov said to his wife. "He assures

me that we have such fine children, whereas I know how many faults they have."

"I always maintain that Arseni goes to extremes," said his wife. "If you seek perfection, you'll never be satisfied. Papa is right when he says that when they were bringing us up, there was one extreme—we were kept on the mezzanine and the parents lived on the ground floor, and now it's just the opposite—parents are kept in the store room and the children live on the ground floor. Parents don't count now; everything is for the children."

"What's wrong with that if it gives you more pleasure?" said Lvov with his handsome smile, as he touched her hand. "If one didn't know you, he might think that you're not their mother but their stepmother."

"No, no extreme is good," said Natalie calmly, replacing his paper knife in its proper position.

"Well, come here, my perfect children," she said to the handsome boys who came in, and after a bow to Levin, went over to their father, evidently desiring to ask him something.

Levin wanted to talk to them, to hear what they would tell their father, but Natalie said something and at that moment Lvov's colleague Makhotin, dressed in a court uniform came into the room. They had to go together to meet someone. An animated conversation followed about Herzegovina, Princess Korzinsky, the duma, and the sudden death of Madame Apraksin.

Levin had completely forgotten his mission. He recalled it only as he was going into the entrance hall.

"Oh, yes, Kitty asked me to talk to you about Oblonsky," he said when Lvov, seeing his wife and Levin off, stopped on the staircase.

"Yes, *Maman* wants us, *les beaux-frères*, to force the issue with Stiva," Lvov said, blushing and smiling. "But then, why should I?"

"Then I'll do it," said Madame Lvov, smiling, as she stood in her white, fur-lined cloak, waiting for the conversation to end. "Well, let's go."

5

AT THE MATINEE concert, two very interesting pieces were to be performed.

One was a fantasia, *King Lear on the Heath,* and the other a quartet dedicated to the memory of Bach. Both of them were new and written in the new style, and Levin was eager to form an opinion of them. After escorting his sister-in-law to her seat, he leaned against a pillar and decided to listen to the music with as much attention and concentration as possible. Trying to avoid distractions and to prevent spoiling the effect of the music, he did not watch the conductor who, in his white tie, waving his arms, always so disagreeably diverts the attention of the listener; he did not look at the ladies in their hats, who for the concert had painstakingly tied ribbons over their ears, or at all the faces around him, either vacant or displaying interest in the most diverse things other than the music. He tried to avoid the connoisseurs of music and the chatterers, and remained standing, his eyes downcast, listening.

But the more he listened to the fantasia of *King Lear,* the less he felt able to form any definite opinion of it. It seemed that the musical expression of an emotion started again and again, began to develop, then quickly fell apart into fragments of newly begun musical expressions or just into very complex sounds, held together by nothing more than the whim of the composer. But the very fragments of these musical expressions, some of them finely constructed, sounded disagreeable because they were completely unexpected and arrived without any preparation. Gaiety and sadness, and despair, and tenderness, and triumph, appeared without any reason, like the emotions of a madman. And, as with a madman, these emotions subsided unexpectedly.

During the entire performance, Levin felt like a deaf man watching dancers. He was utterly confused when the performance came to an end, and he felt extremely tired from the strain of maintaining a completely unrewarded attention. Tumultuous applause broke out on all sides. Everyone rose and began to move around and talk. Anxious to clarify his own puzzlement through the impressions received by others,

Levin began to walk about, looking for connoisseurs, and he was glad to see one of those famous experts talking to his acquaintance, Pestsov.

"Wonderful!" Pestsov said in his deep bass. "How are you, Konstantin Dmitrievich? How unusually vivid and clearly outlined, as though painted in rich colors, is the part where you feel that Cordelia is approaching, where Woman, *das ewig Weibliche*, challenges Fate. Isn't that so?"

"But what does Cordelia have to do with it?" Levin asked shyly, having completely forgotten that the fantasia portrayed King Lear on the heath.

"Cordelia appears . . . here!" said Pestsov, tapping his fingers on the glossy program which he held in his hand, and he handed it to him.

Only now did Levin recall the name of the fantasia and hurriedly read the Russian translation of Shakespeare's verses, printed on the back of the program.

"Without it you couldn't follow the music," said Pestsov, addressing Levin, since his companion had left him and he had no one else to talk with.

During the intermission, Levin and Pestsov became involved in an argument concerning the merits and faults of the Wagnerian trend in music. Levin maintained that Wagner and his followers erred in allowing music to invade the domain of another art, that poetry likewise errs when it tries to picture the features of a face, something that should be done by painting, and, as an example of such an error, he mentioned a sculptor who sought to chisel in marble the shades of poetic images rising around the figure of a poet on a pedestal. "In these sculptured shades there is so little of the nature of a shade that they even have to hold on for support," said Levin. He liked this sentence, but could not remember whether he had said it before, perhaps even to Pestsov, and after saying it he felt embarrassed.

But Pestsov argued that art is universal and that it can reach its loftiest heights only in the union of all its forms.

Levin had no opportunity to listen to the second selection. Pestsov, who stayed beside him, kept talking ceaselessly, criticizing this piece for its excessive, sentimental, artificial simplicity and comparing it with the simplicity of pre-Raphaelite painting. At the exit, Levin met many other acquaintances with whom he exchanged remarks on politics,

music, and mutual friends. Among them was Count Bohl; he
had completely forgotten that he was supposed to visit him.

"Then go right now," Madame Lvov said to him, when he
told her about it. "Perhaps they won't be at home, and then
you'll come to fetch me at the meeting. I'll still be there."

6

"PERHAPS THEY are not receiving visitors now?" asked Levin,
as he went into the entrance hall of Countess Bohl's home.

"They are, sir. Come in, please," responded the doorman,
helping him with his coat without hesitation.

What a pity, thought Levin. Sighing, he took off one glove
and straightened his hat. Why did I come here? What will I
talk about?

Passing through the first drawing room, Levin met Countess
Bohl in the doorway. With a worried and stern face, she was
giving orders to a servant. Seeing Levin, she smiled and
invited him to the next, smaller drawing room, from which
could be heard the sound of voices. In this drawing room were
the countess' two daughters, seated in armchairs, and a Moscow colonel, an acquaintance of Levin's. Levin went over to
them, greeted them and sat next to them on the divan, his
hat on his knee.

"How is your wife's health? Did you go to the concert? We
couldn't go. Mama had to attend a funeral service."

"Yes, so I heard. . . . Such an unexpected death," said
Levin.

The countess entered and sat on the divan. She, too, asked
him about his wife and about the concert.

Levin replied and repeated his words about the unexpected
nature of Madame Apraksin's death.

"But then, her health never was good."

"Were you at the opera yesterday?"

"Yes, I was."

"Lucca was excellent."

"Yes, she was," he said, and since he did not care what
they thought of him, he began to repeat what he had so many
times heard about the singer's unusual talent. Countess Bohl
pretended to listen. Then, after saying as much as was required, he fell silent, and the colonel, who had said nothing

and relatives and at once mentioned those who were close to him.

After going though the first hall, divided by screens, and the partitioned room on the right, where there was a fruit bar, Levin overtook an old man who was walking slowly and came into the noisy, crowded dining room.

He passed along the tables, almost all of them occupied, and scanned the guests. Here and there he saw the most diverse people, old and young, some of whom he scarcely knew and others who were his close friends. No one looked sullen or worried. It seemed that all of them had left their worries and troubles in the doorman's room together with their hats and were now ready to enjoy the material blessings of life at their leisure. Sviazhsky was here, and Shcherbatsky, and Nevedovsky, and the old prince, and Vronsky, and Sergei Ivanovich.

"Ah! Why are you late?" asked the prince, smiling and giving him his hand over his shoulder. "How's Kitty?" he added, adjusting his napkin, which he tucked above a button on his vest.

"She's all right. The three of them are having dinner at home."

"Ah! more girlish nonsense! I see there's no room for you here. Go over to the other table and take a seat quickly," said the prince, and he turned away and carefully took a plate of turbot soup.

"Levin, here!" a friendly voice called to him from some distance. It was Turovtzin. He was seated next to a young officer, and beside them there were two chairs, which had been tipped forward. Levin was glad to join them. He always liked the good-natured reveler Turovtzin—he associated him with his reconciliation with Kitty—but that day, after all the strain of the learned conversations, it was a particular pleasure to see the good-natured Turovtzin.

"These are reserved for you and Oblonsky. He'll be here soon."

The officer with the erect bearing and constantly smiling eyes was Gagin, from Petersburg. Turovtzin introduced them.

"Oblonsky is always late."

"Well, here he is."

"You've just arrived, haven't you?" asked Oblonsky, hurrying over. "How are you? You haven't had a drink, have you? Well, let's go!"

Levin rose and followed him to a large table, laden with vodka and a very large variety of *zakuskas*. It could be assumed that from about two dozen different *zakuskas* one could easily select something to suit his taste, but Stepan Arkadievich ordered something special, and one of the uniformed waiters standing by quickly brought it. They had a glass of vodka and returned to their table.

While they were still having their soup, the waiter brought champagne to Gagin, who ordered four glasses filled. Levin did not refuse the wine offered him and ordered another bottle. He was hungry, ate and drank with great pleasure, and with still greater pleasure took part in the gay and easy conversation of his companions. Gagin, in a lowered voice, told them a new Petersburg story, and though risqué and silly, it was so funny that Levin burst into loud laughter, causing his neighbors to stare at him.

"This reminds me of the story 'That's the very thing which I can't stand.' Do you know it?" asked Stepan Arkadievich. "A wonderful story! Bring us another bottle," he said to the waiter, and he began to tell the story.

"With the compliments of Piotr Ilich Vinovsky," interrupted the little old waiter, bringing two slender glasses of sparkling champagne and addressing Stepan Arkadievich and Levin. Stepan Arkadievich took his glass, turned toward a bald, red-mustached man at the other end of the table, smiled at him and nodded his head.

"Who is he?" asked Levin.

"You met him once at my house, remember? A fine fellow."

Levin did the same as Stepan Arkadievich and reached for his glass.

Stepan Arkadievich's story also was funny. Levin told them his story, and they liked it, too. Then the conversation touched on horses, on that day's races and on Vronsky's horse Atlasny, which had so spectacularly come in first. Levin did not notice how quickly the dinner came to an end.

"Ah! There they are!" said Stepan Arkadievich toward the end of the dinner, bending over the back of his chair and extending his hand to Vronsky, who came over to him with a tall colonel of the Guards. Vronsky's face, too, beamed with the cheer and kindness the club instilled in everyone. With a gay air he leaned on Stepan Arkadievich's shoulder, whispered something to him, and with the same cheerful smile extended his hand to Levin.

"I'm glad to see you," he said. "I was looking for you at the elections, but was told that you had left."

"Yes, I left the same day. I just heard about your horse. Congratulations!" said Levin. "That was a very fast race."

"You keep horses too, don't you?"

"No, my father did, but I remember them and still know them."

"Where were you sitting?" asked Stepan Arkadievich.

"At the second table, behind the columns."

"We celebrated his victory," said the tall colonel. "The Emperor's Cup, for the second time! Would that I were as lucky with cards as he is with horses. Well, there's no use in wasting precious time. I'm going to the 'infernal' room," said the colonel, and he walked away from the table.

"That's Yashvin," Vronsky replied to Turovtzin, taking the vacant seat next to him. After he had had the glass of wine they offered him, he ordered a bottle. Whether influenced by the atmosphere of the club or by the wine he had drunk, Levin engaged Vronsky in a conversation about the best breed of cattle and was happy to feel no enmity toward the man. He even told him in passing that he had heard from his wife that she had seen him at Princess Maria Borisovna's.

"Ah, Princess Maria Borisovna, what a charming lady!" said Stepan Arkadievich, and he related a story about her that amused them all. Vronsky burst into such exceptionally good-natured laughter that Levin felt completely reconciled with him.

"Well, have you finished?" asked Stepan Arkadievich, rising and smiling. "Let's go!"

8

WHEN HE LEFT the table, Levin, accompanied by Gagin, passed through the high-ceilinged rooms toward the billiard room, feeling that his arms swung with particular ease and precision as he walked. As they passed through the large hall, he came across his father-in-law.

"Well, how do you like our temple of idleness?" asked the prince, taking his arm. "Let's take a walk."

"That's just what I wanted to do, walk and look around. It's so interesting."

"Yes, it's interesting. But my interest in it now differs from yours. As you look at these little old men," he said, indicating a club member who was coming in their direction, stooped, his jaw drooping, shuffling his feet in their soft boots, "you'd think they were born *shliupiks*."

"What do you mean by *shliupiks?*"

"I see that you don't know the word. It's one of our club terms. You know, in the game of egg rolling, when you roll an egg too long, it becomes a *shliupik*. The same thing happens to people like us. We keep coming and coming to the club, and eventually we turn into *shliupiks*. Well, you're laughing, but every one of us wonders when the time will come for him to turn into a *shliupik*. Do you know Prince Chechensky?" he asked, and by the expression on his face Levin understood that he was about to tell him an amusing story.

"No, I don't."

"How can that be? Everyone knows Prince Chechensky. Well, never mind. He spends all his time playing billiards. Three years ago he was not yet a *shliupik* and made a brave showing. But he himself referred to others as *shliupiks*. One day he came here, and our hall porter Vasili . . . you know him, that fat one. A great wit. Lo and behold, Prince Chechensky asks him, 'Well, Vasili, who's here? Any *shliupiks?*' And he replies, 'You're the third.' Yes, my friend, that's how it is."

Talking and greeting acquaintances, Levin and the prince passed through all the rooms: the large one, where tables had already been set up and steady partners were playing their little games; the parlor, where they played chess and where Sergei Ivanovich was sitting, engaged in conversation; the billiard room, in which a gay group of men, among them Gagin, had congregated at the divan where the room made a turn and were drinking champagne; they also looked into the "infernal" room, where a crowd of bettors stood around a table at which Yashvin was sitting. Trying to make no noise, they went into the darkened reading room too, where, under the shaded lamps, were seated a young man with an angry face, reaching for one magazine after the other, and a bald general who was engrossed in reading. They also entered the room the prince called the intellectual room. Here three gentlemen were engaged in a heated discussion of the latest political news.

"Let's go, Prince, everything is ready," said one of his partners when he found him there, and the prince left. Levin sat for a while, listening. But remembering all the conversations of that morning, he suddenly found himself terribly bored. He rose hastily and went to look for the gay company of Oblonsky and Turovtzin.

Turovtzin was sitting on a tall divan in the billiard room, a glass in his hand, and Stepan Arkadievich and Vronsky were engaged in conversation at the door in a far corner of the room.

"I wouldn't say that she's depressed, but this uncertainty and vagueness of her situation," Levin overheard them say and was about to turn aside hurriedly, but Stepan Arkadievich called to him.

"Levin," said Stepan Arkadievich; and Levin noticed that, as was always true of Stepan Arkadievich after a drink, or when he was deeply moved, not tears but a mist covered his eyes. And that day both had happened. "Levin, don't go," he said, and he squeezed his elbow, evidently anxious to keep him there at all costs.

"This is my truest, I would say, my best friend," he said to Vronsky. "And you, too, are very dear and close to my heart. And because both of you are good men, I know that you can become close friends."

"Well, we just have to kiss," Vronsky said, jesting good-naturedly, and he extended his hand.

He quickly took the extended hand and grasped it firmly.

"I'm very, very glad," said Levin, pressing his hand.

"Waiter, a bottle of champagne," said Stepan Arkadievich.

"And I, too, am very glad," said Vronsky

But in spite of Stepan Arkadievich's and their own desire, they had nothing to say to each other, and both felt it.

"You know, he hasn't met Anna," Stepan Arkadievich said to Vronsky. "And I'm very anxious to take him to her. Let's go there, Levin!"

"Really?" said Vronsky. "She'll be very glad to meet you. I'd go home right away, but I'm worried about Yashvin," he added, "and I want to remain here until he finishes playing."

"Why, are things going badly?"

"He keeps losing, and I'm the only one who can restrain him."

"Very well, a game of pyramids? Levin, will you play? Fine," said Stepan Arkadievich. "Arrange the balls for the pyramid," he said, turning to the attendant.

"It's waiting for you," replied the attendant, who had already placed the balls in the rack and, for diversion, was rolling the red ball back and forth.

"Well, let's play."

After the game, Vronsky and Levin took a seat at Gagin's table and, following Stepan Arkadievich's advice, Levin bet on the aces. Vronsky either remained at the table, surrounded by his acquaintances who kept coming over to him, or looked into the "infernal" room to see Yashvin. Levin felt pleasantly relaxed after the mental strain of that morning. He was glad that the hostility between him and Vronsky had come to an end, and a feeling of calm, decorum, and pleasure remained with him.

When the game ended, Stepan Arkadievich took Levin's arm.

"Well, let's go see Anna. Would you like to go now? She's at home. I promised her a long time ago that I'd bring you. What did you plan to do this evening?"

"Nothing special. I promised Sviazhsky that I'd go to the meeting of the Agricultural Society. But I'd rather go with you," said Levin.

"Splendid! Let's go! Find out whether my coach has arrived," Stepan Arkadievich said to a waiter.

Levin came over to the table, paid the forty rubles he had lost on the aces, paid his club bill, which in some mysterious way was known to a little old servant who stood at the door, and swinging his arms in a peculiar way, he walked through all the halls toward the exit.

9

"THE OBLONSKY COACH," shouted the doorman in an angry bass. The coach rolled up, and both men took their seats. Only for the first moments, until the coach rolled through the gates of the club, did Levin still experience the feeling of calm, pleasure, and unquestionable decorum in everything around him as he had experienced it in the club. But as soon as the coach came out into the street and he felt it bumping on the uneven road; when he heard the angry shout of a cabman who came in their direction; when he saw in the dim light the red sign of a tavern and of a small shop, the impression was shattered and he began to reflect on his actions and ask himself whether it was right to go to see Anna. What would Kitty say? But Stepan Arkadievich did not let him concentrate on his doubts, and as though divining them, allayed them.

"I'm very happy," he said, "that you'll get to meet her. You know, Dolly has wanted it for a long time. And Lvov visited her and has been visiting her. Though she is my sister," continued Stepan Arkadievich, "I may say without any hesitation that she's a remarkable woman. You'll see for yourself. Her situation is very difficult, particularly now."

"Why particularly now?"

"We are negotiating with her husband for a divorce. He agrees to it. But there are complications about the son, and the case, which should have been settled long ago, has been dragging on for the last three months. As soon as she gets the divorce, she'll marry Vronsky. How foolish it is, this old custom of walking around in a circle to the sound of 'Isaiah, rejoice.' No one believes in it, it only interferes with people's happiness," added Stepan Arkadievich. "And then their situation will be as normal as yours and mine."

"What's the difficulty now?" asked Levin.

"Oh, it's a long and tedious story. Everything is so uncertain with us. And here's the point. While waiting for the divorce, for the past three months she's been here in Moscow, where everyone knows him and her. She goes nowhere, sees none of the ladies except Dolly, because, you see, she doesn't want them to visit her out of pity. Even that stupid Princess Varvara has left her, considering it improper to stay with her. Well, another woman in her position wouldn't have been able to find the inner strength to endure it. But you'll see how she has arranged her life, with what poise and dignity. To the left, into the lane, across the street from the church!" shouted Stepan Arkadievich, leaning out of the window of the coach. "Whew! How hot it is!" he said, throwing open his fur coat, already unfastened in spite of the twelve-degree frost.

"But she has a daughter. Isn't she kept busy with her?" asked Levin.

"You seem to consider every woman just a female animal, *une couveuse*," answered Stepan Arkadievich. "You think she should be occupied with nothing but her children. No, Anna seems to be providing her with an excellent bringing-up, but we don't hear much about her. First of all, she's busy with her writing. I can already see your ironical smile, but it's uncalled for. She's writing a children's book and doesn't discuss it with anyone, but she has read it to me, and I showed the manuscript to Vorkuyev . . . you know, he's the publisher . . . and also a writer, I believe. He's well versed in these matters and says that it's a remarkable work. But don't think that she's one of those lady authors. Not at all. Above all she's a woman with a heart, as you'll see for yourself. She now has in her house an English girl, and there's a whole family for her to take care of."

"Why, is it some kind of philanthropy?"

"You look for the worst in everything. It's not philanthropy, just kindness. They, or rather Vronsky, had an English horse trainer, very competent in his profession, but a drunkard. He took to drinking completely, suffered *delirium tremens,* and the family remained without any source of support. She found out about it, helped the family, became involved, and now she has the entire family on her hands. But her help is not simply perfunctory, just giving them money. She herself coaches the boys in Russian to prepare them for the gymnasium, and she has taken the girl into her home. But you'll see for yourself."

The coach drove into the courtyard, and Stepan Arkadievich rang loudly at the entrance, where a sleigh was standing.

And without asking the servant who opened the door whether the lady of the house was at home, Stepan Arkadievich went into the entrance hall. Levin followed, more and more doubtful of the propriety of his actions.

Glancing at the mirror, he noticed that his face was flushed, but he was sure that he was not drunk, and he ascended the carpeted staircase behind Stepan Arkadievich. Upstairs the servant greeted Stepan Arkadievich as a friend of the family, and to his inquiry of who was with Anna Arkadievna, he replied that it was M. Vorkuyev.

"Where are they?"

"In the study."

After going through a small dark-paneled dining room, Stepan Arkadievich and Levin walked over a thick carpet and entered the semidark study, lit by a single lamp with a large, dark shade. Another lamp, with a reflector, burned on the wall, illuminating a large, full-size portrait of a woman that attracted Levin's attention. It was the portrait of Anna that had been painted in Italy by Mikhailov. While Stepan Arkadievich was behind a latticework screen, and the man's voice, which he had heard before, fell silent, Levin looked at the portrait. Brightly illuminated, it stood out in its frame and he could not take his eyes off it. He even forgot where he was, and without listening to the conversation, kept his gaze fixed upon the wonderful portrait. It was not a painting, but a living, beautiful woman, with black, wavy hair, bare shoulders and arms, and a faint, pensive smile on her lips with their delicate down; she looked at him triumphantly and tenderly, and this look disturbed him. She was not alive only because she was more beautiful than a living woman could be.

"I am delighted," he suddenly heard a voice say beside him, evidently addressing him. It was the voice of the same woman he had been admiring in the portrait. Anna had come over to him from behind the screen, and in the semidarkness of the room, Levin saw the woman of the portrait, in a dark, multicolored, predominantly blue dress, not in the same pose, not with the same expression, but at the same pinnacle of beauty that the painter had captured in the portrait. She was less glamorous in real life, but then there was some new attractiveness about her, which the portrait lacked.

10

SHE HAD RISEN to meet him without trying to conceal her pleasure in seeing him. And in her poise, which she displayed as she extended her small, strong hand, introduced him to Vorkuyev, and indicated a pretty red-haired girl who was sitting there at work, referring to her as her ward, Levin recognized the familiar and pleasing manners of a lady of high society who always remains calm and unaffected.

"I am delighted," she repeated, and when said by her, these simple words seemed to Levin to have somehow acquired a special significance. "I've known you and been fond of you for a long time, both because of your friendship with Stiva and because of your wife. . . . I knew her for a very short time, but she left with me the impression of a delightful flower, a real flower. And to think that she will soon be a mother!"

She spoke easily and unhurriedly, looking from Levin to her brother. Levin saw that he had made a good impression and at once was possessed with a feeling of ease, freedom, and pleasure, as if he had known her from childhood.

"Ivan Petrovich and I have purposely taken our seats in Aleksei's study," she said, replying to Stepan Arkadievich's request for permission to smoke, "to be able to smoke." And, glancing at Levin, without asking him whether he smoked, she reached for a tortoise-shell cigarette case and took a cigarette.

"How's your health today?" her brother asked.

"Fairly good. Nerves, as usual."

"Remarkable, isn't it?" said Stepan Arkadievich, noticing that Levin frequently glanced at the portrait.

"I've never seen a better portrait."

"And it resembles her so closely, doesn't it?" asked Vorkuyev.

Levin looked from the portrait to the subject. Anna's face shone with unusual radiance when she felt his look. Levin blushed, and to hide his embarrassment, was about to ask her whether she had seen Daria Aleksandrovna recently. But at that moment Anna herself addressed him.

"Ivan Petrovich and I have just been discussing Vashchenkov's latest paintings. Have you seen them?"

"Yes, I have," answered Levin.

"I'm sorry I interrupted you. You were about to say something. . . ."

Levin asked her whether she had seen Dolly recently.

"She was here yesterday. She's very much annoyed with the gymnasium on account of Grisha. It seems that the Latin teacher is unfair to him."

"Yes, I saw the paintings. I didn't like them too much," replied Levin, reverting to the conversation she had started.

But Levin's way of talking now was far from his matter-of-fact manner of that morning. Every word of his conversation with her assumed a special significance. It was a pleasure to talk to her, but a still greater pleasure to listen to her.

Anna not only spoke naturally and intelligently, but intelligently and freely, as though ascribing no value to her own thoughts, but prizing highly the thoughts of her companion.

The conversation touched upon the new trend in art and on the new biblical illustrations by a French painter. Vorkuyev accused the painter of realism bordering on vulgarity. Levin remarked that the French had developed symbolism in art as no other nation had, and that therefore they regarded the return to realism as a particular achievement. "And just the fact that they have stopped lying seems like poetry to them."

Never before had Levin ever derived so much pleasure in the expression of a brilliant idea. Anna's face brightened suddenly as she grasped its meaning. She laughed.

"I'm laughing," she said, "the way you laugh when you see a portrait that closely resembles the subject. What you said is a true description of modern French art: painting and even literature—Zola, Daudet. But perhaps it always happens that way: you build your conceptions out of symbolic figures created by the imagination and then, when all the *combinaisons* have been formed, you get tired of the invented figures. You begin to create more natural and realistic ones."

"That's quite true!" said Vorkuyev.

"So you've been to the club?" she asked her brother.

Yes, this is a woman! thought Levin, forgetting himself and staring persistently at her beautiful, animated face, which had completely changed by now. Levin did not hear what she was saying as she bent toward her brother, but he was struck by the change in her expression. Her face, earlier so beautiful in its composure, suddenly displayed a strange curiosity, anger, and pride. But this only lasted for a moment. She half-closed her eyes, as though trying to remember something.

"But then, nobody is interested in it," she said, and she addressed the English girl.

"Please order tea in the drawing room."

The girl rose and left.

"Well, did she pass her test?" asked Stepan Arkadievich.

"Very well. She's a bright and sweet child."

"You may end up by loving her more than your own."

"Those are the words of a man. You can't love more or less —my love for my daughter is of one kind, for her, another."

"I keep telling Anna Arkadievna," said Vorkuyev, "that if she were to devote to the cause of general education of Russian children at least one hundredth of the energy which she devotes to this English girl, Anna Arkadievna would perform a great and valuable service."

"Say what you will, I couldn't do it. Count Aleksei Kirillovich particularly encouraged me to take an interest in the village school." (While pronouncing the words "Count Aleksei Kirillovich" she glanced at Levin shyly and entreatingly, and he responded unconsciously with a look of respect and approval.) "I went there a few times. The children were very charming, but I couldn't involve myself in the work. You mentioned energy. Energy is based on love. But if there is no love, you can't order it. In this case I fell in love with the girl, and I don't know why myself."

She glanced again at Levin. And her smile and look both told him that she was addressing herself to him alone, placing great store by his opinion, and at the same time knowing already that they understood each other.

"I understand completely," replied Levin. "You can't take schools and such institutions to your heart, and that, I believe, is the reason such philanthropic institutions always accomplish so little."

She was silent for a while, and then smiled.

"Yes," she agreed, "I never could. *Je n'ai pas le coeur assez large* to love a whole asylum of repulsive little girls. *Cela ne m'a jamais réussi.* There are so many women who made their *position sociale* that way. And now more than ever," she said with a sad, trusting expression, addressing her remarks to her brother but evidently meaning them only for Levin. "And now, when I'm in such need of an occupation, I can't find one." And frowning suddenly (Levin understood that she was displeased with herself for having spoken about herself), she changed the subject. "I've heard," she said to Levin, "that you are a delinquent citizen, and I defended you as well as I could."

"How did you defend me?"

"That depended on the charge. Well, but won't you have some tea?" She rose and reached for a morocco-bound book.

"Let me have it, Anna Arkadievna," said Vorkuyev, indicating the book. "It's well worth it."

"Oh, no. It needs so much polishing."

"I told him about it," said Stepan Arkadievich to his sister, indicating Levin.

"You shouldn't have. My writing reminds me of those little carved baskets made by the convicts Liza Mertsalov used to sell me. In her society she was in charge of jails," she said to Levin. "The patience of those unfortunate people was unbelievable."

And Levin discovered a new trait in this woman, of whom he had grown so inordinately fond. In addition to being intelligent, graceful and beautiful, she was also honest. She did not try to hide from him all the difficulties of her situation.

After saying that, she sighed, and her face suddenly assumed a stern, stony expression. With this expression she looked even more beautiful than before, but it was a new expression; it was outside that circle of expressions that sparkled with happiness and transmitted it to others, something that had been captured by the artist in the portrait. Levin glanced again at the portrait and at Anna, as she took her brother's arm and moved with him toward the tall doorway. To his surprise, he had a feeling of tenderness and pity for her.

She asked Levin and Vorkuyev to go into the drawing room and she herself remained to talk to her brother. Is it about the divorce, about Vronsky, about what he was doing in the club, or about me? thought Levin. And he was so troubled by the question of what she was talking about with Stepan Arkadievich that he scarcely listened to Vorkuyev's words about the merits of the children's book Anna Arkadievna had written.

At tea they continued the same pleasant interesting conversation. Not only were they able at all times to find a subject for conversation but each one felt that, even without having the opportunity to say what he had in mind, he was willing to refrain from talking and to listen to what the others had to say. And everything they said, not only she but also Vorkuyev and Stepan Arkadievich, seemed to acquire for Levin a particular significance, thanks to her interest and remarks.

All the time that he was following this interesting conversation, Levin admired her—her beauty, her intelligence, her knowledge, and also her simplicity and sincerity. He listened, talked, and continued to think of her, of her inner life, trying to divine her feelings. Following some strange line of reasoning, he who had formerly criticized her so severely now took her part and at the same time pitied her and feared that Vronsky did not completely understand her. It was after ten when Stepan Arkadievich rose to leave (Vorkuyev had left earlier), but it seemed to Levin that he had just arrived. Levin also rose, regretfully.

"Goodbye," she said, holding on to his hand and looking into his eyes in a way which drew him to her. "I'm very glad *que la glace est rompue.*"

She released his hand and half-closed her eyes.

"Tell your wife that I love her as much as always, and that if she can't forgive me my situation, it is my wish that she never forgive me. To forgive, one must experience what I have experienced, and may God spare her that."

"I won't fail to tell her . . ." said Levin, blushing.

11

WHAT A WONDERFUL, charming, and pathetic woman! he thought, as he came out into the frosty air with Stepan Arkadievich.

"Well? Didn't I tell you?" Stepan Arkadievich said, seeing that Levin had been completely vanquished.

"Yes," said Levin thoughtfully, "a wonderful woman! Not only intelligent, but unusually warmhearted. I pity her with all my heart."

"And now, with God's help, everything will soon straighten out. Now then, in the future don't pass judgment," said Stepan Arkadievich, opening the doors of his coach. "Goodbye. We aren't going the same way."

Engrossed in his thoughts about Anna, about the straightforward conversation they had had, recalling in detail the expression of her face, Levin tried increasingly to put himself in her position, and, his heart full of pity for her, he arrived home.

At home, Kuzma informed Levin that Katerina Aleksandrovna was well and that her sisters had left only a short while ago, and he handed him two letters. Levin did not want to be distracted later, and he read the letters there in the entrance hall. One was from his steward, Sokolov. He wrote that he could not sell the wheat, that they were offering only five and a half rubles, and that he had no other way to get money. The other letter was from his sister. She reproached him for not yet having settled her case.

Well, we'll sell at five and a half, if they don't offer more, thought Levin, solving at once and with unusual ease the first problem, which previously had seemed to him to be so difficult. It's hard to believe how time flies by here, he thought, mindful of the other letter. He felt guilty for not yet having attended to his sister's request. I've again neglected going to the court, but today I really had no time for it. And having decided to do it the next day without fail, he went to his wife. While walking toward her room, Levin quickly reviewed in his mind the entire day. The day had consisted of listening to and partaking in a series of conversations. All the conversations centered on topics that would never have occupied his attention if he were alone and in the country, but here they were very interesting. And all of them were pleasant conversations; only twice were they not completely pleasant. Once was when he had told the story of the pike, and then there was something about his tender pity for Anna that was *not* quite right.

Levin found his wife in a sad and lonely mood. The dinner for the three sisters had been very gay, but afterward they kept waiting for him, everyone became bored, the sisters left, and she had remained alone.

"Well, what have you been doing?" she asked, looking into his eyes, their sparkle somewhat unusually suspicious. But, to permit him to give a full account, she masked her suspicion, smiled approvingly, and listened as he told her how he had spent the evening.

"Well, I'm very glad that I met Vronsky. I felt quite at ease and natural with him. You see, now I'll try never to see him again, but our relations are no longer strained," he said, and he blushed as he recalled that though he had intended "never to see him again," he had gone directly to see Anna. "We claim that peasants drink. I don't know who drinks more, peasants or members of our class; they, at least, drink on holidays, but we. . . ."

But Kitty was not interested in the drinking habits of the peasants. She saw that he was blushing and she wanted to know why.

"Then where did you go?"

"Stiva insisted that I go to see Anna Arkadievna."

Having said this, Levin blushed even more deeply, and his doubt as to whether he had been right or wrong in having visited Anna was completely resolved. He now knew that he should not have gone.

Kitty's eyes opened especially wide and flashed on hearing Anna's name, but she forced herself to control her agitation, and he was misled.

"Ah!" was all she said.

"I'm sure that you won't be angry with me for having gone there. Stiva asked me, and Dolly wished it," continued Levin.

"Oh, no," she said, but in her eyes he saw the effort she was making, which did not bode well for him.

"She's very kind, very, very pathetic, and a fine woman," he said. He described Anna's occupations to Kitty and delivered her message.

"Yes, of course she's very pathetic," said Kitty when he finished. "And from whom were the letters?"

He told her, and reassured by her calm tone, he left to change his clothes.

When he returned, he found Kitty still sitting in the chair. When he came over to her, she glanced at him and burst into sobs.

"What is it?" he asked, but he knew beforehand what it was.

"You fell in love with that disgusting woman; she bewitched you. I saw it in your eyes. Yes. Yes. What will it lead to? You were drinking, gambling, and then went . . . to whom? No, let's leave . . . I'm leaving tomorrow."

For a long while Levin could not calm his wife. At last she calmed down, but only after he had confessed that the feeling of pity, combined with the wine he had consumed, had confused him and made him fall under Anna's cunning influence, and he promised that he would avoid her. One thing he confessed most sincerely—that having stayed so long in Moscow, with nothing to do but talk, eat, and drink, he had lost his head. They continued talking until three o'clock in the morning. Only at three did they become sufficiently reconciled so that they could fall asleep.

12

AFTER SEEING HER guests off, Anna did not sit down but began pacing up and down the room. During the entire evening she had been unconsciously doing her best to arouse in Levin a feeling of love for her (as she had been doing lately with all young men). She knew that she had succeeded, as much as she could succeed with an honest, married man and during a single evening. She liked him very much, and in spite of the sharp difference, from a man's point of view, between Vronsky and Levin, she, as a woman, saw what they had in common, what made Kitty fall in love both with Vronsky and Levin. In spite of all this, as soon as Levin left the room she ceased thinking of him.

One thought, in different forms, haunted her constantly. If I have such effect on others, as, for example, on this devoted family man, why is *he* so cold to me? . . . Not exactly cold, he loves me, I know that. But something new separates us now. Why is he away the entire evening? He let me know through Stiva that he couldn't leave Yashvin and had to watch over his gambling. What kind of child is Yashvin? Suppose that it's true. He never lies. But there's something else in this truth. He's glad to have the chance to show me that he has other obligations. I know this and I agree to it. But why must he prove it to me? He wants to prove to me that his love for me must not obstruct his freedom. But I need no proof, I need his love. He should understand how difficult my life is here in Moscow. Is it a life? I don't live, I'm waiting for the dénouement, which keeps being put off further and further. Again no answer! And Stiva says that he cannot go to Aleksei Aleksandrovich. And I can't write again. I can't do anything, can't start anything, can't change anything. I restrain myself, wait, invent diversions—the English family, writing, reading, but all this is a sham, all this is the same as morphine. He should have pity on me, she said, feeling tears of self-pity coming to her eyes.

She heard Vronsky's abrupt ring and hastily wiped away her tears, and to hide her distress more completely, she sat down under the lamp and opened a book, feigning composure. She had to prove to him that she was displeased at his coming home later than he had promised; she had to show him only her displeasure, but under no circumstances her distress nor, most important, her pitiful state. She could have pity for herself, but not he. She did not want a clash and she reproached him for seeking it, but unconsciously she placed herself in an antagonistic position.

"Were you lonesome?" he asked, coming over to her with a gay and lively air. "What a terrible passion gambling is!"

"No, I wasn't lonesome; I've long since learned not to be lonesome. Stiva and Levin were here."

"Yes, they wanted to see you. Well, how did you like Levin?" he asked, sitting down beside her.

"Very much. They left not long ago. Well, how is Yashvin?"

"He was winning seventeen thousand. I called him and he was ready to leave. But he turned back and now he's losing."

"Then why didn't you remain there?" she asked, suddenly raising her eyes to him. The expression on her face was cold and hostile. "You told Stiva that you remained to take Yashvin home. But you left him there."

The same expression of calm readiness for a clash appeared on his face as well.

"First of all, I didn't ask him to tell you anything, and secondly, I never tell a lie. And, most important, I wanted to remain, and remained," he said with a frown. "Anna, why? Why?" he added after a moment of silence. He bent over her, and opened his hand, hoping that she would put hers in it.

This appeal to her tenderness made her happy. But some evil force prevented her from yielding to it, as though their state of hostility did not permit her to give in.

"Of course, you wanted to remain there and you did. You do anything you want. But why are you telling me this? Why?" she asked, her agitation increasing. "Is anyone contesting your rights? But you wish to show that you're right— well, have your wish."

His hand closed, he straightened, and his face assumed a still more stubborn expression.

"With you it's just a matter of stubbornness," she said with an intent look, suddenly finding the precise name for the irritating expression on his face, "nothing but stubbornness. For you it's a question of whether you have the upper hand over me, but for me. . . ." She again felt sorry for herself and almost began to cry. "If you only knew what this means to me! When I feel that you, as now, are hostile, yes, hostile, toward me. . . . If you only knew what this means to me! If you knew how close I am to a dreadful disaster at such moments, how much I fear myself!" And she turned away, stifling her sobs.

"But what are we quarreling about?" he asked, frightened by her expression of despair, and again he bent toward her, took her hand and kissed it. "What is it about? Do I seek any diversions outside our home? Don't I avoid the company of women?"

"Of course!" she said.

"But tell me what must I do for your peace of mind? I'm ready to do anything for your happiness," he said, moved by her despair. "I would do anything to spare you anguish such as you are enduring now, Anna," he said.

"It's nothing, it's nothing!" she said. "I don't know myself; perhaps it's my solitary life, or nerves. . . . Well, let's not talk about it. How were the races? You haven't told me," she said trying to mask her joy in the victory which she had gained, in spite of everything.

He asked for supper and began to discuss the races in detail. But in his tone, in his glances, which grew colder and colder, she saw that he had not forgiven her her triumph, that the stubbornness she was struggling against was again taking hold of him. He was colder with her than before, as though he regretted that he had given in. And recalling the words she had gained her triumph by, namely, "I am close to a dreadful disaster and fear myself," she understood that this was a dangerous weapon and could not be used again. She felt that, along with the love which united them, they were possessed by an evil, contentious spirit, which she could not expel from his heart and still less from hers.

13

THERE ARE NO CONDITIONS to which one cannot become accustomed, particularly if he sees that everyone around him lives in the same way. Three months earlier, Levin would not have believed that he could fall asleep peacefully under the conditions of a life such as he was leading, a life that was aimless, senseless, and moreover above his means. He would not have believed that after a drinking spree (he could not refer to what had happened in the club in any other way), after a preposterous display of friendliness toward a man with whom his wife had formerly been in love, and after a still more preposterous visit to a woman who could not be called other than lost, and after having been swept off his feet by that woman and having upset his wife, that after all of this he would fall asleep peacefully. But under the influence of fatigue, a sleepless night, and the wine he had consumed, his sleep was deep and peaceful.

At five o'clock, the squeak of a door opening woke him. He started and looked around. Kitty was not in bed beside him. But a light was moving behind the partition and he heard her steps.

"What is it?" he asked, half asleep. "Kitty, what is it?"

"It's all right," she said, emerging from behind the partition with a candle in her hand. "I wasn't feeling well," she said, with a particularly gentle and meaningful smile.

"What? Has it begun?" he asked, frightened. "We must send for the midwife." And he began to dress hastily.

"No, no" she said, smiling, as she restrained him with her hand. "It's probably nothing. I just wasn't feeling well. But it has passed."

And she came over to the bed, blew out the candle, lay down and remained still. Though he was suspicious of her quiet breathing, which she seemed to be trying to control, and even more of the peculiar tenderness and animation she had displayed as she came out from behind the partition and said, "It's all right," he was so sleepy that he dropped off at once. Only later did he recall her quiet breathing and understand all that had been going on in her dear, gentle heart as she lay next to him motionless, awaiting the greatest event in a woman's life. At seven o'clock the touch of her hand on his shoulder and a soft whisper awakened him. She seemed to be torn between her desire to talk to him and her regret at having to awaken him.

"Kostia, don't be frightened. It's all right. But it seems to me. . . . We must send for Lizaveta Petrovna."

The candle had been relit. She was sitting on the bed, holding in her hand the knitting she had been working on for the past few days.

"Please don't be frightened. I'm not afraid at all," she said, seeing his frightened face, and she pressed his hand to her heart and then to her lips.

He jumped up, scarcely conscious of himself, and, his eyes fixed on her, he put on his robe and stopped. He had to go but could not take his eyes off her. How dearly he loved her face, how well he knew her expression, her look! But he had never seen her as she was now. And recalling the worry he had caused her the previous evening, how vile and horrible he seemed to himself next to her as she was now! Her flushed face, framed by the soft hair which peeped out from under the nightcap, radiated joy and resolution.

However little of the unnatural and conventional there generally was in Kitty's character, Levin was nevertheless struck by what was revealed to him when all the covering was suddenly removed from her soul and its very essence shone in her eyes. And in this simplicity and revelation, she, the one he loved, stood out still more clearly. She looked at him with a smile. But suddenly her brows twitched, she raised her head, and coming over to him rapidly, she took his hand and pressed her whole body against him, enveloping him with her hot breath. She was suffering and seemed to be complaining to him of her suffering. And as usual, at first he believed that he was at fault. But her gentle look told him that not only did she not reproach him but that she was grateful to him for her suffering. But whose fault is it, if not mine? he thought, unconsciously seeking the one who was the cause of this suffering in order to punish him; but there was no one he could blame. She suffered, complained, and exulted in her suffering, rejoiced in it and loved it. He saw that something beautiful was happening within her heart, but what it was he could not understand. It was beyond his comprehension.

"I sent for Mama. And you hurry and fetch Lizaveta Petrovna. . . . Kostia! . . . It's all right, it has passed."

She stepped aside and rang.

"Well, you go now. Pasha is coming. I'll be all right."

And Levin was surprised to see that she had reached for her work, which she had brought in during the night, and begun to knit again.

As Levin was leaving through one door, he heard the maid come in through the other. He stopped at the door and heard Kitty give the girl detailed instructions and move the bed with her help.

He dressed, and while they were harnessing the horses, because it was too early for a cab, he hurried again into the bedroom, not on tiptoe, it seemed to him, but on wings. Two maids with serious faces were making changes in the room. Kitty paced the room, showing the maids what to do while she knitted rapidly.

"I'm going to the doctor's. They've already left to fetch Lizaveta Petrovna, but I'll stop there anyway. Do you need anything? And how about Dolly?"

She looked at him, but evidently was not listening to what he was saying.

"Yes. Go, go," she said quickly, frowning and waving her hand at him.

As he entered the drawing room, a pitiful moan came from the bedroom, but it died down at once. He stopped and for a while could not understand what it was.

Yes, that's her, he said to himself, and clutching at his head, he rushed downstairs.

Lord, have mercy upon us; forgive and help us! he kept repeating, the words suddenly and unexpectedly coming to his lips. And he, an unbeliever, repeated these words not with his lips alone. Now, at this moment he felt that nothing, neither his doubts, nor his awareness that logic did not permit him to believe, would in any way prevent him from turning to God. All this vanished from his soul like dust. To whom could he turn if not to Him in whose hands he was, with his soul and love?

The horse was not quite ready, but responding to the physical stress he was under and, mindful of what he was expected to do, Levin did not wait for the horse so as not to waste a moment, but set off on foot after ordering Kuzma to catch up with him.

On the corner a night sleigh sped past him. In the small sleigh Lizaveta Petrovna was sitting, dressed in a velvet coat, her head wrapped in a kerchief. "Thank God, thank God!" he said happily, recognizing her fair little face, which now had a particularly serious, even stern expression. Telling the driver not to stop he ran alongside the sleigh.

"About two hours, you think? No longer?" she asked. "You'll find Piotr Dmitrievich at home, but don't rush him. And get some opium at the pharmacy."

"Then you think that everything will go well? Lord have mercy upon us and help us!" said Levin, seeing his horse emerge through the gate. He leaped onto the sleigh next to Kuzma and told him to go to the doctor's.

14

THE DOCTOR was not up yet, and his servant said that he had gone to bed late, left orders not to be awakened, and would get up soon. The servant was cleaning lamp chimneys and seemed to be engrossed in his work. The servant's concentration on his work and his indifference to what was going on within Levin at first astonished him, but, on second thought, he realized that no one knew and no one could be expected to know what he felt, so it was all the more necessary for him to act calmly, deliberately, and resolutely in order to break through this wall of indifference and achieve his objective. I mustn't hurry and must overlook nothing, Levin said to himself, conscious of the intensification of his physical strength and of his power of concentration over anything that he had to do.

After learning that the doctor was not up yet, Levin chose the following plan out of the ones he had considered: he would send Kuzma with a note to another doctor, and he would go to the pharmacy to get the opium himself. If when he returned the doctor was not up yet, he would bribe the servant to wake him, and if the servant refused he would force his way and insist that the doctor get up.

In the pharmacy the lank pharmacist, showing the same indifference to Levin the servant had shown as he cleaned the lamp chimneys, was busy sealing powder wafers for a coachman who was waiting for them, and he refused to give him the opium. Trying not to hurry and to keep calm, Levin mentioned the names of the doctor and of the midwife and, explaining why he needed the opium, tried to persuade him to give it to him. Speaking German, the pharmacist asked someone behind the partition for advice on whether he should dispense it, and after receiving approval, he reached for a vial and a funnel, slowly poured the liquid from the large bottle into the vial, attached the label, sealed the vial, in spite of Levin's entreaties not to do it, and was even going to wrap it. This Levin could not endure; he quickly seized the vial from his hands and rushed out through the large glass door. The doctor was not up yet, and the servant, now busy spreading a rug, refused to wake him. Unhurriedly Levin reached for a ten-ruble note and, speaking slowly, yet losing no time, he handed it to the servant and explained to him that Piotr Dmitrievich (how great and important did the formerly insignificant Piotr Dmitrievich now seem to Levin!) had promised to go at any time, that he would certainly not be angry, and that therefore he must be awakened immediately.

The servant agreed, went upstairs, and then invited Levin into the waiting room.

Levin heard the doctor cough behind the door, walk about, wash, and say something. About three minutes passed, but they seemed to Levin longer than an hour. He could wait no longer.

"Piotr Dmitrievich, Piotr Dmitrievich!" he called in a beseeching voice through the open door. "Please forgive me. Let me talk to you the way you are. It's over two hours."

"Just a minute, just a minute!" the doctor replied, and Levin was astonished to hear the cheer in his voice.

"For a minute only."

"Just a minute."

Two more minutes passed while the doctor pulled on his boots, and two more while he put on his suit and combed his hair.

"Piotr Dmitrievich!" Levin was about to begin again in his pitiful voice, but at this moment the doctor came out, dressed and combed. Heartless people! thought Levin. They comb their hair while we are dying!

"Good morning!" said the doctor, extending his hand and seeming to tease him with his calmness. "Don't hurry. Well?"

Trying to be as thorough as possible, Levin began to relate all the unnecessary details regarding his wife's condition, constantly interrupting his tale with entreaties that the doctor leave with him at once.

"But don't be in such a hurry. You can't be sure yet. I'm probably not needed there, but I promised to come and I suppose I will. But it isn't urgent. Sit down, please. Would you like some coffee?"

Levin looked at him as though wondering whether he could be laughing at him. But the doctor did not even think of laughing.

"I know, I know," said the doctor with a smile. "I myself am a family man. At such moments we husbands are most pitiful creatures. I have a patient whose husband at such moments hides in the stable."

"But what do you think, Piotr Dmitrievich? Do you think that everything will go well?"

"All indications are for a safe delivery."

"Then you'll come at once?" asked Levin, casting a malevolent look at the servant who was bringing the coffee.

"In about an hour."

"No, for God's sake!"

"Then at least let me have my coffee."

The doctor reached for his coffee, and they both fell silent.

"The Turks, I see, are being soundly beaten. Did you read last night's telegram?" asked the doctor, chewing on a piece of bread.

"No, I can take it no longer!" said Levin, jumping up. "So you'll be there in a quarter of an hour?"

"In half an hour."

"Your word of honor?"

When Levin reached home, the princess was arriving, and he accompanied her to the door of the bedroom. There were tears in the princess' eyes, and her hands trembled. Seeing Levin, she embraced him and broke into tears.

"Well, my dear Lizaveta Petrovna?" she said, grasping the hand of the midwife as she emerged from the bedroom with a bright and grave face.

"Everything is fine," she said. "Make her lie down. It'll be easier."

From the moment he awakened and realized what was going on, Levin, without thinking, without forseeing anything, having locked up all his thoughts and feelings, was ready to endure anything that was in store for him. He was ready to endure it stolidly, without alarming his wife; on the contrary, he would calm her and sustain her courage. Judging by the answers to his questions of how long it usually lasted, Levin without even allowing himself to think of what would happen and how it would end, imagined that he was ready to suffer and control his emotions for about five hours, and it seemed to him that he would be able to do this. But when he returned from the doctor's and saw again how she was suffering, he began to repeat more and more often, "Lord, have mercy upon us and help us!" sighing and turning his head toward heaven. And he was afraid that he would break down, burst into tears, or run away. He was suffering terribly. But only one hour had passed.

But after this another hour passed, two, three, then the five hours that he had set as the limit of his endurance, but the situation remained the same. And he still endured it because there was nothing else to do but endure, feeling at every moment that he had reached the limit of his endurance, and that his heart would at any moment break with compassion.

But more minutes passed, and hours, and still more hours, and his feeling of anguish and terror grew in its intensity.

All the ordinary conditions of life, so necessary for understanding anything, no longer existed for Levin. He lost awareness of time. Some minutes—when she called him to her side and he held her perspiring hand, which either squeezed his with unusual strength or pushed him away—seemed to him to be hours, and some hours seemed like minutes. He was surprised when Lizaveta Petrovna asked him to light a candle behind the screen and he learned that it was already five o'clock in the afternoon. If he had been told that it was only ten in the morning he would have been no more surprised. He knew as little about where he had been all that time as about what had happened and when. He saw her burning face, sometimes puzzled and suffering, and sometimes smiling and trying to calm him. And he saw the princess, flushed, intense, biting her lips, her gray curls drooping, forcing herself to swallow her tears; he saw Dolly and the doctor, who was smoking thick cigarettes, and Lizaveta Petrovna, with her stern, resolute, and reassuring face, and the old prince, who paced the drawing room, frowning. But how they came and left, where they were, he did not know. The princess was now with the doctor in the bedroom, now in the study, where a table covered with a tablecloth had mysteriously appeared. But it was not she, it was Dolly. Then Levin remembered that they had sent him somewhere. Once he was told to move the table and the divan. He did it eagerly, thinking that this was needed for her, and only later did he find out that what he had been doing was preparing a place for himself for the night. Then they sent him to the study to ask the doctor something. The doctor answered and then began to talk about the difficulties in the duma. Then he was sent to the princess' bedroom to get an icon, in a gilded silver frame, with the help of the princess' old chambermaid; he climbed up into a closet for it, and broke the little icon lamp, and the princess' chambermaid asked him not to worry about his wife and the icon lamp, and he took the icon and put it at the head of Kitty's bed, carefully tucking it behind the pillows. But where, when, and why all this had happened, he did not know. Nor could he understand why the princess took his hand, looked at him with sympathy and asked him to calm down, Dolly tried to get him to eat something and led him away from the room, and even the doctor looked at him with a serious and sympathetic air and offered him some drops.

He only knew and felt that what was happening was like what had happened a year ago in the hotel in the provincial city where his brother lay on his deathbed. But there it was sorrow, and here joy. Yet that sorrow and this joy were both outside the ordinary conditions of life; in that ordinary life they were like openings through which could be discerned something of the most sublime nature. And as then, what was happening now was accompanied by hardship and anguish, and incomprehensibly as then, the soul, beholding this sublimity, rose to such heights as it had never known before, where reason could not follow.

"Lord, have mercy upon us and help us!" he kept repeating, feeling that in spite of such a long estrangement, which he had thought to be final, he was turning to God again as honestly and trustfully as in his childhood and early youth.

During these hours he was subject to two distinct moods. One when he was not in her presence—when he was in the company of the doctor, who smoked one thick cigarette after another and put them out on the edge of a full ash tray; or when he was with Dolly, or with the prince, when they spoke about dinner, about politics or about Maria Petrovna's illness, when Levin suddenly would completely forget for the moment what was happening and would feel as if he had just awakened. He was in another mood in her presence, at her bedside, when his heart was ready to burst with compassion but did not, and when he constantly prayed to God. And every time a cry would reach him from the bedroom and would rouse him from his momentary oblivion, he would suffer from the same strange delusion as had struck him at first; every time he heard that cry he would start, run to apologize, and then, while running to her, would recall that he was not at fault, and he would want to protect her, to help. But at the sight of her, he again would realize that he could not help, would become frightened, and would pray, "Lord, have mercy upon us, help us!" With the passage of time, both moods became more pronounced: he became calmer when he was not in her presence, completely forgetting about her; and both her own suffering and his feeling of helplessness in the face of it became more tormenting. He would jump up, intending to run somewhere, but would run to her.

Sometimes, after she had called him again and again, he resented it. But after seeing her meek, smiling face and hearing her words, "I've worn you out," he blamed God, but at the thought of God he at once asked for mercy and forgiveness.

15

HE DID NOT KNOW whether it was early or late. All the candles had already burned low. Dolly had just been in the study and suggested that the doctor take a rest. Levin sat, listening to the doctor's story about a quack hypnotist and staring at the ash of his cigarette. It was time for a rest, and he forgot himself. He forgot completely about what was going on. He listened to the doctor's story and followed him. Suddenly there sounded a terrifying cry. It was so terrifying that Levin did not even jump up, but, holding his breath, stared at the doctor with a frightened and questioning look. The doctor inclined his head sideways, listened, and smiled approvingly. Everything was so unusual that nothing could astonish Levin any longer. Probably that's the way it must be, he thought, and he remained in his seat. Whose cry was it? He jumped up and on tiptoe ran into the bedroom, went around Lizaveta Petrovna and the princess, and stopped at his usual place, at the head of the bed. The cry subsided, but something was different now. What it was he did not see and did not understand, nor did he want to see or understand. But he saw it on the face of Lizaveta Petrovna; her face was stern and pale and still as resolute, though her jaw trembled slightly, and her eyes were firmly fixed on Kitty. Kitty's burning, exhausted, perspiring face, a strand of hair clinging to it, was turned to him and searched for his look. Her raised hands asked for his. Seizing his cold hands with her perspiring ones, she began to press them against her face.

"Don't leave me! Don't leave me! I'm not afraid, I'm not afraid," she said rapidly. "Mama, take my earrings. They are bothering me. You aren't afraid, are you? Soon, soon, Lizaveta Petrovna. . . ."

She spoke very rapidly and tried to smile. Suddenly her face became distorted and she pushed him away.

"Oh, how terrible! I'm going to die, I'm going to die! Go, go!" she cried, and again she uttered the same terrifying shriek.

Levin clutched at his head and ran out of the room.

"It's all right, it's all right, everything is fine!" Dolly called after him.

But no matter what they said, he knew that now all was lost. Leaning his head against the doorframe, he stood in the next room and heard someone scream, a shriek the like of which he had never heard before, and he knew that it had been uttered by what formerly had been Kitty. As for the child, he had long since lost any desire for it. He now hated that child. He even did not pray any longer for her life, he only wished that her terrible suffering would come to an end.

"Doctor! What is it? What is it? Oh, Lord!" he said, seizing the hand of the doctor who entered the room.

"It's coming to an end," said the doctor. And the doctor's

face was so serious when he said this that Levin understood "it's coming to an end" meant that she was dying.

Without knowing what he was doing, he rushed into the bedroom. The first thing he saw was Lizaveta Petrovna's face. Her frown had deepened, and her expression was still sterner. Kitty's face was no longer there. Where it had been before there was something that was terrifying in the strain it showed and in the sounds it emitted. He pressed his head against the wooden bar of the bedstead and felt that his heart was about to burst. The blood-curdling shrieks continued, their terror intensifying, and as though having reached the limits of their terror, they died down suddenly. Levin did not trust his ears, but there was no doubt about it: the shrieking had died down, and there ensued a soft bustle, a rustle, and rapid breathing, and her faltering, living, gentle, and happy voice softly pronouncing the words, "It's over."

He raised his head. Unusually beautiful and peaceful, her arms resting helplessly on the blanket, she looked at him in silence and tried to but could not smile.

And suddenly, from the mysterious, frightening, unearthly world he had been living in the last twenty-two hours Levin felt he had been transported instantaneously into the former, familiar world, now shining with such an unusual luster of happiness that he could not endure it. All the taut strings snapped. Sobs and joyful tears, which he had never foreseen, so forcefully surged within him, agitating his entire body, that for a long while he could not utter a word.

He fell on his knees at his wife's bedside, pressing her hand to his lips, and the hand responded to his kisses with a faint movement of the fingers. In the meantime, there at the foot of the bed, in the nimble hands of Lizaveta Petrovna, there flickered, like the tiny flame of a lamp, the life of a human being who had never existed before and who, with the same rights as others and with the same importance to himself, would live and bring forth beings like himself.

"It's alive! It's alive! It's a boy! No need to worry," Levin heard Lizaveta Petrovna say as she slapped the baby's back with her trembling hand.

"Is it true, Mama?" Kitty's voice asked.

The princess' sobs were her only reply.

And in the midst of the silence, like an incontrovertible answer to a mother's question, there arose another voice, completely different from the other, restrained voices that were heard in the room. It was a bold, challenging voice, one that refused to consider anything, the voice of a new human being who had appeared mysteriously from somewhere.

If Levin had been told earlier that Kitty had died, that he had died together with her, that their children were angels, and that God was there before them, he would not have been surprised. But now, after returning to the world of reality, he had to strain his mind to realize that she was alive and well, and that the creature screaming so frantically was his son. Kitty was alive, her suffering was over. And he was inexpressibly happy. This he understood and this made him completely happy. But a child? From where, what for, who was he? . . . He was at a loss to understand this, and he could not become accustomed to the idea of his existence. It seemed unnecessary and superfluous, and it would be quite a while before he could become accustomed to it.

16

IT WAS after nine o'clock. The old prince, Sergei Ivanovich, and Stepan Arkadievich were sitting with Levin, and after talking about the young mother, were now conversing on other subjects. Levin listened to their conversation, but he could not help recalling what had happened prior to that morning and thinking of what he had been like the previous day, before these events. It seemed that a hundred years had passed. He seemed to have risen to an unattainable height, from which he was trying to descend so that he might not offend his companions. He took part in the conversation but constantly thought of his wife, of the details of her present state, and of his son, trying to accustom himself to the fact of his existence. The entire world of women, which after his marriage had acquired a new meaning for him beyond his comprehension, now, in his opinion, rose to heights his imagination could not envisage. He listened to the conversation about yesterday's dinner in the club and thought, what is she doing now? Has she fallen asleep? How is she? What is she thinking about? Is my son Dmitri crying? And in the midst of the conversation, in the middle of a sentence, he leaped to his feet and left the room.

"Send me word whether I may see her," said the prince.

"All right, right away," replied Levin, and without stopping he went to her.

She was not asleep but was conversing quietly with her mother, making plans for the christening of the baby.

Lying on her back with her arms on top of the blanket, her hair combed, wearing fresh clothes and a smart nightcap trimmed in blue, she met his look with one which drew him to her. This look, bright as it was, grew even brighter as he approached her. Her face mirrored the same change from the earthly to the unearthly that may be seen on the face of one who is deceased; but there it bids farewell, and here it bid welcome. An emotion such as had moved him at the moment of the child's birth again surged in his heart. She took his hand and asked whether he had slept. He could not answer and turned aside, aware of his state.

"I had a nap, Kostia!" she said. "And I feel much better."

She looked at him but suddenly her expression changed.

"Let me have him," she said, hearing the child cry. "Let me have him, Lizaveta Petrovna, and he will be able to see him."

"Here, let Papa see him," said Lizaveta Petrovna, lifting something and bringing it over, red, strange, and tremulous. "But wait, let's first dress him up," and Lizaveta Petrovna placed this tremulous, red object on the bed, began to unwrap and rewrap the baby, lifting and turning him over with one finger, sprinkling powder over him.

Looking at this tiny, pathetic creature, Levin vainly struggled to discover in his heart some signs of a fatherly feeling toward him. But he felt nothing but aversion. Yet, when the baby was uncovered, and there darted out the tiny, saffron-colored arms and legs, with their fingers and toes, and even with their thumbs and big toes which differed from the other fingers and toes, and when he saw that Lizaveta Petrovna compressed these tiny struggling arms, like little soft springs, wrapping them in linen bands, he was moved by such pity for this creature and seized with such fear that she might injure him, that he restrained her hand.

Lizaveta Petrovna laughed.

"Don't be afraid! Don't be afraid!"

When the baby was wrapped and transformed into a stiff pupa, Lizaveta Petrovna rolled him over, as though proud of her work, and stepped aside so that Levin might see his son in all his beauty.

Kitty fixed a sidelong glance in the same direction.

"Let me have him, let me have him!" she said, and she was even about to rise.

"What are you doing, Katerina Aleksandrovna! You are not permitted such movements. Wait a second and I'll hand him to you. Let Papa see what a fine fellow he is."

And with one hand Lizaveta Petrovna lifted up to Levin the strange, ruddy, rocking creature, who tried to hide his face under the edge of the swaddling band (with the other hand, using her fingers only, she supported the back of his unsteady head). And this creature also had a nose, eyes which looked sideways, and lips, which smacked.

"A beautiful baby!" said Lizaveta Petrovna.

Levin sighed unhappily. This beautiful baby aroused in him only a feeling of revulsion and pity. It was not at all the feeling he had anticipated.

He turned aside while Lizaveta Petrovna settled the baby against the unfamiliar breast.

Suddenly a laugh made him raise his head. It was Kitty who was laughing. The baby had taken the breast.

"Well, enough, enough!" said Lizaveta Petrovna, but Kitty would not release the baby. He fell asleep in her arms.

"Look now," said Kitty, turning the baby so that he could see him. The baby's senile-looking little face wrinkled still more deeply and he sneezed.

Smiling and scarcely restraining his tears of tenderness, Levin kissed his wife and left the darkened room.

What he felt toward this tiny creature was not at all what he had expected. There was no cheer or joy in this feeling; on the contrary, it was a new feeling of tormenting fear. It was the awareness of a newly created vulnerable area. And this awareness at first caused him such deep anxiety, and his fear lest this helpless creature suffer was so distressing, that the strange feeling of irrational joy and even pride he had felt when the baby sneezed, passed unnoticed.

17

STEPAN ARKADIEVICH'S affairs were in a bad way.

The money for two-thirds of the timber had already been spent, and by allowing a ten per cent discount, he had received in advance from the merchant almost the whole of the remaining third. The merchant would not advance any more money, especially since that winter Daria Aleksandrovna had for the first time openly asserted her rights to her inheritance and had refused to sign a receipt for the last third of the money. All his salary was being spent for the upkeep of the family and for paying petty debts, of which they could never rid themselves. There was no money left at all.

This situation was unpleasant, embarrassing, and had to be brought to an end, in Stepan Arkadievich's opinion. The cause, as he understood it, was that his salary was too small. The position he held had apparently suited him well five years earlier, but was no longer appropriate. Petrov, the director of a bank, received a salary of twelve thousand rubles; Sven-titzky, a member of a corporation, seventeen thousand; Mitin, who had founded a bank, fifty thousand. Evidently I've fallen asleep, and they've forgotten me, thought Stepan Arkadievich about himself. And he began to listen and to look around, and toward the end of the winter he discovered a very lucrative position, on which he first directed his attack from Moscow through his aunts, uncles, and friends, and then, when his scheme reached its final stage, he himself left for Petersburg in the spring. It was one of those positions which paid from one thousand to fifty thousand a year and which at that time had become more numerous than the former nests of bribery. It was a position as member of the Commission of the Joint Agency of the Mutual Credit Balance of the Southern Railways and Banking Institutions. This position, like others of its kind, required such great competence and such enormous energy as could scarcely be possessed by a single person. And since a person of such qualities did not exist, the next best thing was to have rather an honest than a dishonest man fill that position. And Stepan Arkadievich was not only an honest man (without emphasis on the word), but he was an honest man (with the word emphasized) in the particular meaning the word then had in Moscow when they said: an honest public figure, an honest writer, an honest magazine, an honest institution, an honest trend, which meant that that man or that institution was not only not dishonest, but that was able, on the right occasion, to take a dig at the government. In Moscow, Stepan Arkadievich frequented those circles where this emphasized word had been coined, and having a reputation as an honest (the word emphasized) man, he, more than anyone else, was entitled to the position.

The position paid from seven to ten thousand rubles a year, and Oblonsky could fill it without relinquishing his present government post. The appointment depended on two ministries, one lady and two Jews; and though all these people had already been prepared, Stepan Arkadievich had to see them personally in Petersburg. In addition, Stepan Arkadievich had promised his sister Anna that he would get from Karenin his final decision regarding the divorce. And, having wheedled fifty rubles from Dolly, he left for Petersburg.

While seated in Karenin's study, listening to his discourse on the causes of the poor state of Russian finances, Stepan Arkadievich waited only for him to finish so that he might speak of his own case and of Anna.

"Yes, that's quite true," he said when Aleksei Aleksandrovich stopped and took off his pince-nez, without which he could no longer read, and glanced inquiringly at his former brother-in-law. "That's true, with regard to details, yet the principle of our age is liberty."

"Yes, but I'm proposing another principle, one that includes the principle of liberty," said Aleksei Aleksandrovich, accentuating the word *includes* and replacing the pince-nez in order to read aloud once again the part of his discourse that expressed this idea.

Aleksei Aleksandrovich turned the pages of the beautifully written manuscript, with its wide margins, and reread the conclusive passage.

"I reject protectionism, not for the benefit of private groups but for the sake of the general welfare, for the lower and higher classes alike," he said, peering at Oblonsky over his pince-nez. "But *they* cannot understand this, *they* are moved only by their own interests and are carried away by empty slogans."

Stepan Arkadievich knew that when Karenin began to talk of what *they* did and thought, those same people who refused to accept his projects and were the source of all the evils which beset Russia, he was nearing the end of his speech. He therefore willingly renounced the principle of liberty and agreed completely. Aleksei Aleksandrovich fell silent and, lost in thought, turned the pages of the manuscript.

"By the way," said Stepan Arkadievich, "I've been wanting to ask you something. If, by chance, you see Pomorsky, drop him a hint that I'm very anxious to obtain the vacant post on the Commission of the Joint Agency of the Mutual Credit

Balance of the Southern Railways." Stepan Arkadievich was now accustomed to the name of that position, which was so near to his heart, and he pronounced it rapidly and correctly.

Aleksei Aleksandrovich inquired what the functions of that commission were and grew thoughtful. He wondered whether there was not something about that commission which contradicted his projects. But since the functions of that commission were very complex, and his own projects covered a very large area, he could not decide at once, and taking off his pince-nez, he said:

"Of course I can tell him. But why are you really interested in this position?"

"The salary is good, up to nine thousand, and my means—"

"Nine thousand," repeated Aleksei Aleksandrovich, frowning. The high salary reminded him that the position which Stepan Arkadievich was seeking was in this respect contrary to the essence of his projects, which always tended toward economy.

"I maintain, and have submitted a report on the subject, that in our time these exorbitant salaries are symptoms of the false economic *assiette* of our system."

"But what do you expect?" asked Stepan Arkadievich. "A director of a bank, for example, gets ten thousand, and deserves it. And an engineer gets twenty thousand. They hold responsible positions, whatever you say!"

"I believe that salary is the price paid for a commodity, and that it should be regulated by the law of supply and demand. And if salaries are fixed in violation of this law, as for instance, when I see two engineers graduating from the same school, both equally competent and able, and one receives forty thousand, while the other is content with two thousand; or when they appoint jurists or former hussar officers as bank directors at enormous salaries, though they are completely unqualified, I come to the conclusion that salaries are fixed not by the law of supply and demand but simply by favoritism. And this is abuse of power, important in its own right and because of its harmful influence upon the government service. I believe—"

Stepan Arkadievich hastened to interrupt his brother-in-law.

"Yes, but you must agree that here they are organizing a new, undoubtedly useful enterprise. Its work is vital, whatever you say. And they are particularly eager to see that the work is done by *honest* men," Stepan Arkadievich added, accentuating the word.

But Aleksei Aleksandrovich did not know what the Moscow emphasis on the word "honest" meant.

"Honesty is nothing but a negative trait," he said.

"Nevertheless, you'll do me a great favor," said Stepan Arkadievich, "if you drop a hint to Pomorsky. Just in passing. . . ."

"But I believe it depends more on Bolgarinov," said Aleksei Aleksandrovich.

"Bolgarinov, for his part, is completely agreeable," said Stepan Arkadievich, blushing.

Stepan Arkadievich blushed at the mention of Bolgarinov's name because that very morning he had gone to see the Jew Bolgarinov, and the memory of that visit was unpleasant. Stepan Arkadievich knew very well that the enterprise to which he was offering his services was new, vital, and honest; but that morning, when Bolgarinov, evidently on purpose, had made him wait in his anteroom for two hours together with other petitioners, he suddenly felt uncomfortable.

Whatever the reason—either that he, a descendant of Rurik, Prince Oblonsky, had waited for two hours in the anteroom of a Jew, or that for the first time in his life he had disregarded his ancestors' tradition of serving the government and was embarking on a new career—he felt very uncomfortable. During these two hours of waiting at Bolgarinov's, Stepan Arkadievich walked briskly about the anteroom, smoothing his side whiskers, entered into conversations with other petitioners, tried to create a pun to describe this experience of waiting in a Jew's anteroom, and used all his efforts to hide from the others and even from himself the emotions he was being subjected to.

All that time he felt uncomfortable and annoyed without knowing why; perhaps because nothing came of his pun, "I had business with a *Hebrew,* and *he brewed* but mischief," or for some other reason. After Bolgarinov finally received him with extraordinary courtesy, evidently triumphing over his humiliation, and almost refused his request, Stepan Arkadievich tried to forget his experience as quickly as possible. And remembering it only now, he reddened.

18

"And now there's another matter; you know what it's about. About Anna," said Stepan Arkadievich, after remaining silent for a few moments in an effort to rid himself of the unpleasant memory.

As soon as Oblonsky mentioned Anna's name, Aleksei Aleksandrovich's expression changed completely: it was no longer animated, as it had been, but weary and deathlike.

"What do you really want of me?" he asked, turning in his chair and snapping his pince-nez shut.

"A decision, some kind of decision, Aleksei Aleksandrovich. I'm appealing to you now" (not as to a wronged husband, Stepan Arkadievich was about to say, but fearing lest this harm his case, he changed it) "not as to a high government official" (which sounded out of place) "but just as to a man, a kindhearted man and a Christian. You should have pity on her," he said.

"Just what do you mean by that?" Karenin asked softly.

"You should have pity on her. If you had seen her as I did —I spent the entire winter with her—you'd feel sorry for her. Her situation is terrible, terrible indeed."

"I thought," replied Aleksei Aleksandrovich in a thinner, almost piercing voice, "that Anna Arkadievna had got everything she really wanted."

"Oh, Aleksei Aleksandrovich, for God's sake let's refrain from recriminations. Let bygones be bygones. You know what she wants and is waiting for—a divorce."

"But I thought that Anna Arkadievna would not want a divorce if I insisted on having custody of our son. I gave my answer accordingly and thought that the case was closed. And I consider it closed," shouted Aleksei Aleksandrovich.

"Please, don't get excited," said Stepan Arkadievich, touching his brother-in-law's knee. "The case is not closed. If you allow me to recapitulate, here's what happened. When you parted, your generosity was magnificent; you offered her everything—freedom, even divorce. She was grateful. No, don't think otherwise. Truly grateful. And so deeply that at those first moments, knowing how she had wronged you, she did not and could not think the whole matter through. She declined everything. But reality and time have shown how distressing and unbearable her situation is."

"Anna Arkadievna's life can be of no interest to me," Aleksei Aleksandrovich interrupted, raising his brows.

"I can't believe that," replied Stepan Arkadievich gently. "Her situation is both distressing to her and of no advantage to anyone. She deserves it, you may say. She knows that and asks nothing of you. She says sincerely that she dares not ask for anything. But I, her kin, and all who love her, ask you, beseech you. Why should she suffer? Who benefits by it?"

"Wait, it seems that you are putting me in the position of the defendant," said Aleksei Aleksandrovich.

"No, not at all, but please try to understand me," Stepan Arkadievich said, now touching his hand, as though convinced that by this gesture he could assuage his brother-in-law. "I only want to say that her situation is distressing, and that you can relieve it without losing anything. I'll arrange everything in such a way that you won't even notice it. After all, you promised."

"The promise was given earlier. And I thought that the problem of our son had decided the matter. I also hoped that Anna Arkadievna would be generous enough to . . ." Aleksei Aleksandrovich spoke with difficulty, his face turning pale, his lips trembling.

"She leaves everything to your generosity. All she asks, begs for, is to be relieved of her present impossible situation. She no longer asks for her son. Aleksei Aleksandrovich, you're a kind man. Put yourself in her place for a moment. For her, in her situation, the divorce is a matter of life and death. If you hadn't promised earlier, she would have reconciled herself to her situation and would have remained in the country. But you promised, and so she wrote to you and came to Moscow. And in Moscow, where a meeting with anyone is like a knife in her heart, she has been living for six months, awaiting your decision from day to day. It's like the life of a condemned man who has had the noose around his neck for month after month, facing either death or, perhaps, a pardon. Have pity on her, and then I'll take it upon myself to arrange everything. . . . *Vos scrupules.* . . ."

"I'm not talking about that . . ." Aleksei Aleksandrovich interrupted with disgust. "But perhaps I promised something I had no right to promise."

"You're not going back on your promise?"

"I've never refused to do what is proper, but I want to have time to reflect on the propriety of what I have promised."

"No, Aleksei Aleksandrovich!" said Oblonsky, jumping to his feet, "I can't believe that. She's unhappy as no other woman could be, and you can't refuse—"

"As long as what I promised is proper. *Vous professez d'être un libre penseur.* But I, as a believer, cannot act in such an important matter contrary to the teachings of Christianity."

"But in Christian lands, and in our own, as far as I know, divorce is permissible," said Stepan Arkadievich. "Our own church accepts divorce. And we see—"

"It's permissible, but not in that sense."

"Aleksei Aleksandrovich, I don't know you," said Oblonsky after a silence. "Wasn't it you (and weren't we grateful for it?) who forgave everything, and moved by Christian charity, were ready to make every sacrifice? You yourself said, 'when they take away thy cloak, give them thy shirt,' and now—"

"I beg you," said Aleksei Aleksandrovich in a piercing voice, leaping to his feet, his face pale, and his jaw trembling, "I beg you to stop. Please drop the subject. . . ."

"Of course! Please forgive me for the pain I may have caused you," said Stepan Arkadievich, smiling sheepishly and extending his hand. "I've only been doing my duty as a messenger."

Aleksei Aleksandrovich gave him his hand and grew thoughtful.

"I have to think it over and look for advice. I'll give you my final answer the day after tomorrow," he said after some reflection.

19

STEPAN ARKADIEVICH was about to leave when Kornei came in and announced:

"Sergei Alekseich!"

"Who is Sergei Alekseich?" Stepan Arkadievich was about to ask, but suddenly he remembered.

"Ah, Seryozha!" he said. "Sergei Alekseich, I thought, would be the director of some department." Then he remembered, "Anna asked me to see him."

And he remembered the meek, pathetic expression on

Anna's face as she parted with him and said, "You'll probably see him. Find out the details of where he lives and with whom. And, Stiva . . . if it's possible! It is possible, isn't it?" Stepan Arkadievich knew what the words "if it's possible" meant—if it would be possible to arrange the divorce with the provision that he give her their son. . . . Stepan Arkadievich saw now that they could not even think of it, but nevertheless he was glad to see his nephew.

Aleksei Aleksandrovich reminded his brother-in-law that they never spoke to the boy about his mother and asked him not to say a word to remind him of her.

"He was very ill after that meeting with his mother, which we failed to prevent," said Aleksei Aleksandrovich. "We even feared for his life. But proper treatment and sea bathing in the summer have restored his health, and now, on the advice of the doctor, I've placed him in a school. And, indeed, the company of classmates has had a favorable influence on him, and he's completely well and a good student."

"What a fine young man he is! No longer Seryozha, but a real Sergei Alekseich," said Stepan Arkadievich with a smile, looking at the handsome, broad-shouldered boy in a blue jacket and long trousers who entered, walking briskly and easily. The boy looked well and happy. He greeted his uncle as a stranger, but on recognizing him he blushed, as though something had offended and angered him, and he hastily turned away from him. The boy went over to his father and handed him his report card.

"Well, this is fine," said his father. "You may go."

"He's thinner and has grown; he's no longer a child, but a boy. I like that," said Stepan Arkadievich. "Do you remember me?"

The boy looked quickly at his father.

"I do, *mon oncle*," he replied, glancing at his uncle, and he lowered his eyes.

The uncle called the boy to his side and took his hand.

"Well, how is everything?" he asked, trying to start a conversation without knowing what to say.

The boy, red-faced and silent, cautiously tried to draw his hand away from his uncle's. And as soon as Stepan Arkadievich released it, like a bird that has been set free, he walked rapidly out of the room after a questioning glance at his father.

A year had passed since Seryozha had last seen his mother. Since then he had heard nothing more of her. And that same year he was placed in a school where he made friends and grew fond of them. He was no longer occupied with the dreams and memories of his mother, which had made him ill after their meeting. When they recurred, he studiously suppressed them, ashamed of them and believing that they suited girls but not a boy and a friend of other boys. He knew that his father and mother had quarreled, that the quarrel had separated them, that he was destined to remain with his father, and he tried to adjust to this idea.

He was annoyed when he saw his uncle, for by his resemblance to his mother, he brought back those very memories of which he was ashamed. He disliked that meeting all the more because, from some of the words which he had overheard while waiting at the door of the study, and particularly from the expression on the faces of his uncle and father he surmised that they had probably been talking about his mother. And in order not to criticize his father, with whom he lived and on whom he depended, and mainly in order not to succumb to the sentiment that in his opinion was so humiliating, Seryozha tried not to look at his uncle, who had come to disturb his peace, and he tried not to dwell on the memories he had revived.

But when Stepan Arkadievich, who had left the room after him, saw him on the stairs, called him to his side, and asked him how he was spending his time in school between classes, Seryozha, in his father's absence, entered into a conversation with his uncle.

"We play at railroad now," he said in reply to his question. "It's like this. Two boys take their seats on the bench. They are the passengers. And another stands up on the same bench. Everyone gets harnessed. You can do it either with your arms or with belts, and then they race through all the rooms. The doors are opened in advance. Of course, the conductor's part is very difficult."

"Is he the one who is standing?" Stepan Arkadievich asked with a smile.

"Yes, he has to be brave and quick, particularly if the train suddenly stops or someone falls."

"Yes, it's no joke," said Stepan Arkadievich, looking sadly into the boy's animated eyes, which resembled his mother's and were no longer childish, no longer completely innocent. And though he had promised Aleksei Aleksandrovich that he would not speak to the boy about Anna, he could not restrain himself.

"And do you remember your mother?" he suddenly asked.

"No, I don't," Seryozha said quickly. His face turned crimson and he lowered his eyes. And his uncle could no longer elicit anything from him.

Half an hour later, his Slav tutor found his pupil on the stairs, and for a long while he could not make out whether he was angry or crying.

"Well, you probably hurt yourself when you fell," said the tutor. "I warned you that it was a dangerous game. I'll have to tell the headmaster."

"If I'd hurt myself nobody would know about it. Of this you may be sure."

"Then what happened?"

"Leave me alone! I remember, I don't remember. . . . What business is it of his? Why should I remember? Leave me alone!" he said, no longer addressing himself to his tutor, but to the whole world.

20

As usual, Stepan Arkadievich did not waste his time in Petersburg. While in Petersburg, besides attending to his business—his sister's divorce and the new position—he wanted, as always, to breathe some fresh air, as he said, after Moscow's stuffiness.

Moscow, in spite of its *cafés chantants* and omnibuses, still remained a stagnant marsh. Stepan Arkadievich had always felt this way. After staying in Moscow for some time, particularly after living in close contact with his family, he felt his spirits sink. After remaining in Moscow for a considerable time, he would reach such a stage that he would begin to worry about his wife's bad moods and her reproaches, about the health and education of the children, and about the petty troubles at the office; even the fact that he was in debt troubled him. But as soon as he arrived and remained in Petersburg and mingled with those who lived, actually lived, and not just existed, as they did in Moscow, these thoughts vanished, melting away like wax before a fire.

His wife? . . . That very day he had spoken to Prince

Chechensky. Prince Chechensky had a family, a wife and sons, young men in the School of Pages, and another family, an illegitimate one, where he also had children. Though his first family was a very fine one, Prince Chechensky felt happier with the second. He took his older son on visits to the second family and told Stepan Arkadievich that he considered this advantageous to his son and that it broadened his mind. What would they say about this in Moscow?

His children? In Petersburg, children were not in the way of their fathers. Children were brought up in schools, and the absurd notion that was gaining strength in Moscow, with the Lvovs, for instance, that children should be given all the advantages of life and the parents only toil and care, did not prevail here. Here they understood that one must live for himself, in a manner befitting an educated person.

His position? Here service did not consist of incessant, hopeless drudgery as in Moscow. Here service was interesting. An accidental meeting, a service rendered, an apt remark, a gift for amusing mimicry—and one could suddenly make his career, like Briantsev, whom Stepan Arkadievich had seen the previous day and who was now a high dignitary. This sort of service was interesting.

But the Petersburg view of financial matters had a particularly relaxing effect on Stepan Arkadievich. On the previous day, Bartniansky, who spent at least fifty thousand a year judging by the style he lived in, expressed to him his remarkable opinion on this subject.

During a conversation before dinner, Stepan Arkadievich said to Bartniansky:

"You're a close friend of Mordvinsky, I believe. You can do me a favor. Please drop him a hint about me. There's a position which I'd like to obtain. As a member of the Agency. . . ."

"Well, I won't remember anyway. . . . But why do you want to involve yourself in these Jew railroad affairs? . . . Say what you want, it's disgusting!"

Stepan Arkadievich did not tell him that it was an important enterprise. Bartniansky would not have understood it.

"I need the money; I've nothing to live on."

"And yet you live."

"I do, but I'm in debt."

"You don't say! Is it much?" Bartniansky asked sympathetically.

"Very much, about twenty thousand."

Bartniansky broke into a loud, happy laughter.

"Oh, what a happy man!" he said. "I owe one and a half million and own nothing, and, as you see, I'm still very much alive."

And not only words but facts proved to Stepan Arkadievich how true that remark was. Zhivakhov owed three hundred thousand without a kopeck to his name, yet he lived, and in what style! Long ago everyone had given up on Count Krivtzov, but he kept two mistresses. Petrovsky had squandered five million yet continued to live in the same manner as before, and he even held a post as director of finances at a salary of twenty thousand. In addition, Petersburg had a pleasant physical effect upon Stepan Arkadievich. It rejuvenated him. In Moscow he occasionally looked into the mirror at his gray hair, dozed after dinner, stretched, ascended the stairs puffing and with slow steps, was bored by young women, and did not dance at balls. But in Petersburg he always felt ten years younger.

In Petersburg he experienced the same feeling which the sexagenarian Prince Oblonsky, Piotr, who had just arrived from abroad, had talked to him about the previous day.

"Here we don't know how to live," said Piotr Oblonsky. "I spent the summer in Baden, and would you believe it, I actually felt like a young man. You see a young woman, and all kinds of thoughts. . . . You have your dinner, a light drink, and you feel vigorous and cheerful. But I returned to Russia, had to join my wife in the country to boot, and you'd scarcely believe it, but two weeks later I put on my robe and stopped dressing for dinner. Then who thinks of young women? I really became an old man. All that remained was to seek the salvation of my soul. But I went to Paris and again recovered."

Stepan Arkadievich felt the same change as Piotr Oblonsky. In Moscow he let himself sink so low that, indeed, if he stayed there too long, he might even end up seeking the salvation of his soul. But in Petersburg he again felt like a human being.

For a long time a very strange relationship had existed between Betsy Tverskoy and Stepan Arkadievich. Stepan Arkadievich always flirted with her and jestingly told her the most indecent things, knowing that that was what she liked most. The day after his conversation with Karenin, Stepan Arkadievich went to see her and felt so young that in this flirting and

chatting he inadvertently went too far and did not know how
to retreat because, to his misfortune, not only was she unattractive to him but he actually felt an aversion toward her.
But she liked him very much, and that was the cause of their
flirtatious relationship. He therefore was very glad when
Princess Miakhky arrived and broke up their tête-à-tête.

"Ah, you are here!" she said when she saw him. "Well,
how's your poor sister? Don't look at me that way," she added.
"While everyone criticizes her, including those who are a
thousand times worse than she, in my opinion she's done a
fine thing. I can't forgive Vronsky for having failed to let me
know when she was in Petersburg. I would have visited her
and would have gone everywhere with her. Please give her
my love. Well, tell me about her."

"She's in a very difficult situation, she . . ." began Stepan
Arkadievich, naïvely taking Princess Miakhky's words, "Tell
me about her," at face value. But, according to her habit,
Princess Miakhky quickly interrupted him and began to talk
herself.

"She did what everyone, except me, does but conceals; but
she didn't want to deceive, which was a wonderful deed on
her part. And the best thing she did was to leave your brother-
in-law, that half-wit. Forgive me. Everyone insisted that he
was clever, but only I said that he was stupid. Now, since he's
tied himself up with Lydia Ivanovna and Landau, everyone
says that he's a half-wit, and though I like to disagree with
everyone, I can't do it in this case."

"Will you please explain to me," said Stepan Arkadievich,
"what the following means. Yesterday I went to see him about
my sister and asked him for a final answer. He did not give it
to me and said that he would think it over. But this morning,
instead of an answer, I received an invitation to visit Countess
Lydia Ivanovna this evening."

"Just as I thought," Princess Miakhky exclaimed happily.
"They'll ask Landau about it."

"Landau? Why? What is Landau?"

"Why, don't you know Jules Landau, *le fameux* Jules
Landau, *le clairvoyant*? He, too, is a half-wit, but your sister's
fate depends on him. That's what life in the provinces does
to you; you don't know anything. You see, Landau was a
commis in a store in Paris. Once he went to a doctor, fell
asleep in the waiting room, and in his sleep began to advise
the patients. His advice was wonderful. Then the wife of

Yuri Meledinsky—you know, that sick man—heard of this Landau and brought him to her husband. He's treating her husband. In my opinion he hasn't helped him at all, because he's still as weak as ever, but they have faith in him and keep him with them. And they brought him to Russia. Here everyone took a fancy to him and he began to treat everyone. He cured Countess Bezzubov, and she grew so fond of him that she adopted him."

"Adopted him?"

"Yes, adopted. And he's no longer Landau, but Count Bezzubov. But this isn't important. What matters is that Lydia—I'm very fond of her, but her head is not screwed on right—of course happened to meet this Landau, and now no decision is taken either by her or by Aleksei Aleksandrovich without Landau, and therefore the fate of your sister is now in the hands of this Landau, otherwise known as Count Bezzubov."

21

AFTER A MAGNIFICENT dinner and a large quantity of cognac at Bartniansky's, Stepan Arkadievich arrived at Lydia Ivanovna's only a little after the appointed time.

"Who else is here? The Frenchman?" Stepan Arkadievich asked the doorman, looking at Aleksei Aleksandrovich's familiar coat and at a strange plain coat with fasteners.

"Aleksei Aleksandrovich Karenin and Count Bezzubov," replied the doorman sternly.

Princess Miakhky guessed right, thought Stepan Arkadievich as he ascended the staircase. Strange! Nevertheless, it would be good to gain her friendship. She has such great influence. If she were to say a word to Pomorsky, it would be final.

It was still quite light outside, but in Countess Lydia Ivanovna's small drawing room the shades were drawn and the lamps already lit.

At a round table under a lamp were seated the countess and Aleksei Aleksandrovich, conversing softly. A short, lean man, with the hips of a woman, knock-kneed, unusually pale, handsome, with beautiful shining eyes and long hair which fell onto the collar of his frock coat, stood at the other end of the room, gazing at the portraits on the wall. After greeting the lady of the house and Aleksei Aleksandrovich, Stepan Arkadievich involuntarily glanced once again at the man he had not yet met.

"*Monsieur Landau!*" called the countess, addressing him gently and cautiously, to Oblonsky's surprise. She introduced them.

Landau hurriedly turned around, came over, smiled, pressed his limp, perspiring hand into the hand Stepan Arkadievich extended to him, and immediately turned back to the portraits. The countess and Aleksei Aleksandrovich exchanged significant glances.

"I'm very glad to see you, particularly today," said Countess Lydia Ivanovna, indicating to Stepan Arkadievich a seat next to Karenin.

"I introduced him to you as Landau," she said in a soft voice, glancing at the Frenchman and then quickly at Aleksei Aleksandrovich, "but he is actually Count Bezzubov, as you probably know. But he doesn't like the title."

"Yes, so I've heard," replied Stepan Arkadievich. "They say that he has completely cured Countess Bezzubov."

"She came to see me today and looked so pathetic," the countess said, turning to Aleksei Aleksandrovich. "This parting distresses her so deeply. It's such a blow to her!"

"Is he definitely going?" asked Aleksei Aleksandrovich.

"Yes, he is going to Paris. He heard a voice yesterday," said Countess Lydia Ivanovna, looking at Stepan Arkadievich.

"Ah, a voice!" repeated Oblonsky, realizing that one must be as circumspect as possible in this company, in which something unusual was happening or was going to happen, something to which he still lacked the key.

A momentary silence ensued, after which Countess Lydia Ivanovna, as though coming to the main topic of conversation, said to Oblonsky with a subtle smile:

"I have known you for a long time and am happy to become more closely acquainted. *Les amis de nos amis sont nos amis.* But to be a friend, you must fathom a friend's innermost feelings, and I'm afraid that you've failed to do so in regard to Aleksei Aleksandrovich. You understand what I mean," she said, raising her beautiful, pensive eyes.

"Countess, I understand in general that Aleksei Aleksandrovich's situation—" began Oblonsky, not quite grasping what she meant and therefore trying to speak in generalities.

"It's not the outward change of his situation," said Countess

Lydia Ivanovna sternly, her enamored look at the same time following Aleksei Aleksandrovich, who rose and went over to Landau. "His heart has changed, he has been given a new heart, and I'm afraid that you haven't fathomed completely the change that has occurred in him."

"Yes, I can understand this change in a general way. We've always been friends, and now . . ." answered Stepan Arkadievich, looking gently at the countess in response to her look and trying to figure out which of the two ministers she was closer to, so that he might know for whose favor to ask.

"The change that has occurred in him cannot abate his feeling of love for his neighbor; on the contrary, the change that has taken place in him necessarily intensifies that love. But I'm afraid that you don't understand me. Won't you have some tea?" she asked, indicating with her eyes a servant who had brought a tray with tea.

"Not quite, Countess. Of course, his misfortune—"

"Yes, a misfortune that has become his greatest happiness now that his heart has become new and filled with Him," she said, looking with affection at Aleksei Aleksandrovich.

I think I could ask her to drop a hint to both of them, thought Stepan Arkadievich.

"Of course, Countess," he said, "but I believe that these changes are so personal that no one, not even a close friend, likes to talk about them."

"On the contrary! We must talk about them and help each other."

"Yes, of course, but sometimes there may be such a difference of opinion, and then . . ." Oblonsky said with a gentle smile.

"There can be no difference of opinion about the sacred truth."

"Oh, yes, of course, but . . ." Stepan Arkadievich replied and, embarrassed, he fell silent. He understood that she was talking about religion.

"I believe that he's falling asleep," said Aleksei Aleksandrovich in a solemn whisper, coming over to Lydia Ivanovna.

Stepan Arkadievich looked around. Landau was seated at the window, leaning on the back and the arm of the chair, his head hanging. Noticing that they were looking at him, he raised his head with a naïve, childlike smile.

"Pay no attention," said Lydia Ivanovna, and she effortlessly moved up a chair for Aleksei Aleksandrovich. "I've noticed . . ." she started to say, when a servant entered the room with a letter. Lydia Ivanovna ran through the note rapidly, and after apologizing to her guests, wrote an answer with unusual speed, handed it to the servant, and returned to the table. "I've noticed," she said, continuing the remark she had started, "that Muscovites, particularly the men, are most indifferent to religion."

"Oh, no, Countess, it seems to me that Muscovites have the reputation of being most religious," replied Stepan Arkadievich.

"But as I understand, you, unfortunately, belong to the indifferent ones," Aleksei Aleksandrovich said, turning to him with a weary smile.

"How can one possibly be indifferent?" said Lydia Ivanovna.

"In this respect I'm not exactly indifferent; I'm rather in a state of expectation," replied Stepan Arkadievich with his most engaging smile. "I don't believe that my time for such problems has arrived yet."

Aleksei Aleksandrovich and Lydia Ivanovna glanced at each other.

"No one can ever know whether his time has or has not arrived," Aleksei Aleksandrovich said severely. "We mustn't think of whether we are ready or not, for grace is not subject to man's expectations. Sometimes it doesn't descend on those who labor for it, but on those who are not prepared, as with Saul."

"No, not yet, I think," said Lydia Ivanovna, who had been watching the Frenchman's movements.

Landau rose and came over to them.

"May I join you?" he asked.

"Oh, yes. I didn't want to disturb you," said Lydia Ivanovna, looking at him tenderly. "Please sit down."

"All we have to do is to avoid shutting our eyes, lest we fail to see the light," continued Aleksei Aleksandrovich.

"And if you only knew the happiness which we experience when we feel that He is always present in our hearts," said Lydia Ivanovna with a blissful smile.

"But one may sometimes feel unable to rise to such heights," said Stepan Arkadievich, feeling that he was acting against his conscience by acknowledging the sublime nature of religion, thus lacking the courage to confess his skepticism to a person who by one word to Pomorsky could secure the position he was seeking.

"Do you mean to say that his sin may hinder him?" asked Lydia Ivanovna. "But that's a fallacy. There's no sin for him who believes; his sin already has been expiated. *Pardon,*" she added, glancing at the servant who came in with another note. She read it and gave her reply orally. "Tell him, tomorrow, at the grand duchess'." Then she resumed the conversation, "There's no sin for him who believes."

"Yes, but faith without deeds is dead," replied Stepan Arkadievich, recalling this sentence from the catechism and only by his smile defending his independence.

"Here it is, from the Epistle of St. James," said Aleksei Aleksandrovich, addressing Lydia Ivanovna with a mild reproachfulness, evidently speaking on a subject they had discussed more than once. "What enormous harm has been caused by the false interpretation of this passage. Nothing keeps one from believing so much as this interpretation. 'I have no deeds, and therefore can have no faith.' But actually this is not stated anywhere, and just the opposite is said."

"To work for the sake of God, to save one's soul by fasts and toil," said Countess Lydia Ivanovna with disgust and contempt, "these are the savage notions of our monks. . . . Nothing of this is actually stated anywhere. It is much easier and simpler," she added, looking at Oblonsky with the same encouraging smile with which, at the court, she encouraged young ladies-in-waiting when they were confused by their new surroundings.

"We are saved by Christ, who suffered for our sake; we are saved by our faith," confirmed Aleksei Aleksandrovich, looking at her encouragingly.

"Vous comprenez l'anglais?" asked Lydia Ivanovna, and having received an affirmative answer, she rose and began to look on the shelf for a book.

"I would like to read to you *Safe and Happy,* or should I read *Under the Wing?"* she asked, looking questioningly at Karenin. After finding the book, she sat down again and opened it. "It's very short. They describe here a way to find faith, and the happiness, greater than anything on earth, with which it fills our souls. He who believes cannot be unhappy, because he's not alone. But you'll see for yourself." She was about to begin to read when the servant came in again. "Madame Borozdin? Tell her, tomorrow at two. . . .

Yes," she said, and holding her finger between the pages, she sighed and looked straight ahead with her beautiful, pensive eyes. "Here's how true faith works. Do you know Marie Sanin? Have you heard of her misfortune? She lost her only child. She was despondent. And then she found this Friend, and she is now grateful to God for the loss of her child. This is the happiness which faith brings."

"Oh, yes, it's very . . ." said Stepan Arkadievich, pleased that they were going to read and would give him a chance to collect his thoughts. No, I see it's better not to ask her anything today, he thought. If only I can get out of here without committing any blunders!

"You'll be bored," said Countess Lydia Ivanovna, addressing Landau. "You don't know English, but it's short."

"Oh, I'll understand," replied Landau with the same smile, and he closed his eyes.

Aleksei Aleksandrovich and Lydia Ivanovna exchanged meaningful glances, and the reading began.

22

STEPAN ARKADIEVICH was utterly bewildered by the new, unfamiliar subjects he was hearing discussed. The complexity of Petersburg life in general stimulated him, releasing him from the stagnation of Moscow; but these complexities he admired and understood in circles that were close and familiar to him. But in this alien environment he was bewildered, stunned, and most of what he heard he did not understand. Listening to Countess Lydia Ivanovna and feeling that Landau's beautiful, naïve, or perhaps roguish—he was not sure himself which—eyes were directed at him, Stepan Arkadievich began to experience a peculiar heaviness in his head.

The most diverse thoughts churned about in his mind. Marie Sanin is glad that her child died. It would be good to have a smoke . . . To achieve salvation you have only to believe, and the monks don't know how to do it, but Countess Lydia Ivanovna does know. . . . And why is my head so heavy? It it the cognac or because all this is so strange? But I believe that so far I haven't done anything improper. And yet I certainly can't ask a favor of her. I've heard that they

make you pray. I hope they won't insist that I do it. It would
be too silly. And the nonsense she's reading! But her pronunciation is good. Landau is Bezzubov. Why is he Bezzubov?
Suddenly Stepan Arkadievich felt that an uncontrollable
yawn was forcing his mouth open. He smoothed his side-
whiskers to mask the yawn and pulled himself together. But
a moment later he felt that he was asleep and was going to
snore. He awoke at the moment when Countess Lydia
Ivanovna said, "He's asleep."

Stepan Arkadievich awoke with a start and a guilty feeling that he had been caught sleeping. But he was quickly
relieved when he saw that the words "he's asleep" referred
not to him but to Landau. The Frenchman had fallen
asleep just as Stepan Arkadievich had. But Stepan Arkadievich's sleep, he thought, would have offended them (and he
was not really sure even of this, so strange did everything
seem to him now), whereas Landau's sleep delighted them,
particularly Countess Lydia Ivanovna.

"*Mon ami,*" said Lydia Ivanovna, cautiously holding the
folds of her silk dress so as not to make any noise and in her
excitement addressing Karenin not as Aleksei Aleksandrovich but as "*mon ami,*" "*donnez lui la main. Vous voyez?* Sh—
sh," she hushed the servant who came in once more. "Admit
no one."

The Frenchman was asleep or pretended to be, resting his
head on the back of the armchair, and as though trying to
catch something, he made faint movements with his perspiring hand, which was resting on his knee.

Aleksei Aleksandrovich rose, and though he tried to be
careful, he bumped against a table as he walked over and
put his hand into the Frenchman's. Stepan Arkadievich also
rose and, opening his eyes wide in his effort to awaken, if he
were still asleep, stared first at one and then at the other.
But all this was not a dream. Stepan Arkadievich felt that his
mind was becoming more and more confused.

"*Que la personne qui est arrivée la dernière, celle qui de-
mande, qu'elle sorte!*" said the Frenchman, without opening
his eyes.

"*Vous m'excuserez, mais vous voyez. . . . Revenez vers dix
heures, encore mieux demain.*"

"*Qu'elle sorte!*" the Frenchman repeated impatiently.

"*C'est moi, n'est-ce pas?*"

And after receiving an affirmative answer, Stepan Arkadie-

vich, no longer remembering that he intended to ask Lydia
Ivanovna for a favor, or that he had wanted to settle his
sister's case, and having one desire only—to leave that place
as soon as possible—went out on tiptoe and fled into the
street as from a house of contagion. For a long while he
conversed and joked with the cabman, trying to come to his
senses as soon as possible.

In the French Theater, where he arrived for the last act,
and later at the Tartars', over champagne, Stepan Arkadievich refreshed himself somewhat in a familiar atmosphere.
Nevertheless, all that evening he felt quite upset.

When he returned to Piotr Oblonsky's, where he was staying while in Petersburg, Stepan Arkadievich found a note
from Betsy. She wrote that she was very anxious to complete
the conversation they had begun and asked him to come to see
her the next day. No sooner had he read the note and frowned
at it when he heard from downstairs the sound of the heavy
tread of men carrying something weighty.

Stepan Arkadievich went out to see what it was. It was the
rejuvenated Piotr Oblonsky. He was so drunk that he could
not climb the stairs, but ordered himself set on his feet as
soon as he saw Stepan Arkadievich. Holding on to him, he
made his way to his room and there began to tell him how
he had spent the evening, then he fell asleep at once.

Stepan Arkadievich was in low spirits, a rare event for him,
and he was long in falling asleep. Whatever he recollected
was repulsive, but most repulsive of all was the recollection
of the evening spent at Lydia Ivanovna's, as of something
shameful.

The next day he received from Aleksei Aleksandrovich his
definite refusal to grant a divorce to Anna, and he knew that
the decision had been based on what the Frenchman had
said the previous evening in his sleep, real or feigned.

23

In family life, in order for anything to be undertaken, there
must be either complete discord between husband and wife
or they must live in cordial harmony. But when the relationship between them is vague, and neither of these conditions
exists, no undertaking can be embarked on.

Year after year, many families remain in their old surroundings, which have become hateful to both husband and wife, only because they do not completely disagree nor can they agree.

Neither Vronsky nor Anna could any longer endure their life in the heat and dust of Moscow, where the sun no longer shone as in springtime but as it does in summer. All the trees on the boulevards had long been covered with foliage, and their leaves were already laden with dust. But though they had long since decided to move to Vozdvizhenskoe, they did not do so, and because no harmony had prevailed between them lately, they remained in Moscow, which had become hateful to both of them.

The mutual resentment that divided them had no outward cause, and all their attempts to come to an understanding not only did not check but exaggerated this resentment. It dwelt within them and had been caused, in her case, by the cooling of his love for her, and in his case by his regret that he had put himself, for her sake, in a difficult situation which she was making still more difficult instead of easing. Neither of them revealed the causes of their irritability but considered the other unjust and tried to prove it on every occasion.

To her, all of him, all his habits, ideas, desires, his entire physical and emotional nature, manifested but one thing—love of women—and this love, which she believed should have been centered on herself alone, had cooled. Consequently, she reasoned, he must have transferred part of his love to another woman or other women, and she was jealous. She was jealous not of a woman but because of the cooling of his love. Having so far no object for her jealousy, she looked for one. The slightest hint made her transfer her jealousy from one object to another. Sometimes she was jealous of those vulgar women with whom thanks to his bachelor connections, he could so easily renew his contacts. Sometimes she was jealous of the ladies of society whom he might meet. And sometimes she was jealous of an imaginary young woman, one whom he would marry after he had broken with her. And this last kind of jealousy tormented her most of all, particularly because he himself, in a candid moment, had incautiously confided in her that his mother understood him so little that she had even tried to persuade him to marry Princess Sorokin.

And because she was jealous, Anna bore ill will toward him and looked for reasons for her ill will. She accused him of everything that made her situation difficult. The tormenting state of suspense between heaven and earth in which she lived in Moscow, the vacillating and dilatory ways of Aleksei Aleksandrovich, her seclusion—all this was his fault. If he had loved her, he would have understood all the hardship of her situation and would have saved her from it. It was also his fault that she lived in Moscow and not in the country. He could not bury himself in the country, as she desired. He needed society and he had put her in this terrible situation and did not care to see how unbearable it was. And it was his fault, too, that she had been separated from her son forever.

Even their rare moments of tenderness brought her no peace; in his tenderness she now discerned a shade of composure, of self-assurance, which he had not shown before and which irritated her.

It was now twilight. Anna was alone, waiting for his return from a bachelor dinner which he was attending. She paced up and down his study (a room where the street noises were least noticeable), recalling minute details of their quarrel of the previous day. Going back from the insulting words of that quarrel, words which she remembered so clearly, to the cause of it, she at last came to the beginning of their conversation. For a long while she could not bring herself to believe that the disagreement had stemmed from an innocuous conversation on a topic which was close to the heart of neither of them. And yet that was what actually had happened. It began with his derisive remark about girls' schools, which he considered unnecessary, and she went to their defense. He made a disparaging remark about women's education in general and said there was no point whatever for Hannah, Anna's English protégée, to be taught physics.

This provoked Anna. She considered it a contemptuous remark about her occupations. And she had contrived and pronounced a sentence that should have repaid him for the pain he had caused her.

"I don't expect you to understand me and my feelings, as only a man who loves can, but I relied upon your tact," she said.

And, indeed, his face flushed with annoyance, in reply he said something disagreeable. She did not remember now what she had answered, but here he suddenly remarked, evidently with one purpose only—that of repaying her for the pain she had caused him:

"You're right; your tenderness for this girl doesn't interest me, because I see that it's an affectation."

This cruelty of his, with which he was destroying the world created by her at such a cost to enable her to endure the hardship of her life, the injustice of his accusation of sham and affectation on her part, incensed her.

"I regret that you understand and consider natural only what is coarse and material," she said, and she left the room.

When he came to see her in the evening, they did not mention their quarrel, but they both felt that it had been patched up but not settled.

That entire day he had not been at home, and she felt so lonely and depressed at being at odds with him that she wanted to forget and forgive everything and make peace with him, and she was ready to blame herself alone and absolve him.

It's my own fault. I'm irritable and unreasonably jealous. We'll make peace and leave for the country. I'll be calmer there, she said to herself.

"Affectation," she suddenly recalled what had hurt her most of all, which was not so much the word as his intention to hurt her.

I know what he meant. He meant: it's an affectation on my part to love a strange child without loving my own daughter. What does he know about love for children, about my love for Seryozha, whom I've given up for his sake? But that desire to cause me pain! No, he loves another woman. It can't be otherwise.

And seeing that in her desire to calm herself she had completed the circle again that she had already traveled so many times and had returned to her earlier state of resentment, she was frightened by her own thoughts. Is it really impossible— can't I admit that it's all my fault? she asked herself, and she began to think it through again. He's truthful, honest, he loves me. I love him, and one of these days I'll get the divorce. What else do I need? I must be calm, I must trust him, and I'll accept the blame. Yes, now when he comes I'll tell him that I was wrong, though I wasn't, and we'll leave.

And in order to think no longer of this and not to yield to

her ill humor, she rang and asked that the trunks be brought in and packed for their departure to the country.

At ten o'clock Vronsky arrived.

24

"WELL, DID YOU have a good time?" she asked, going out to meet him with a guilty and humble expression on her face.

"The usual," he replied, and with a glance he saw that she was in one of her good moods. He had already become used to these changes and that day he was particularly glad to see her changed mood, because he himself was in the happiest frame of mind.

"What do I see! That's just fine!" he said, pointing to the trunks in the entrance hall.

"Yes, we must leave. I went for a ride and it was so pleasant that I felt a desire to go to the country. I'm sure that nothing keeps you here."

"It's just what I want. I'll come right back and we'll talk it over after I change my clothes. Order some tea, please."

And he went to his study.

There was something offensive in the words, "That's just fine!" as though he were addressing a child who had stopped being naughty; and still more offensive was the contrast between her abject and his self-assured tone. For a moment she felt a combative urge swell within her, but she forced herself to suppress it and met Vronsky as cheerfully as she had before.

When he returned to her, she told him how she had spent the day, and of her plans for their departure, partly repeating the words that she had prepared.

"You know, I almost had an inspiration," she said. "Why should we wait here for the divorce? We might as well be in the country. I can wait no longer. I don't want to hope; I don't want to hear about the divorce. I've decided that it would no longer affect my life. Do you agree?"

"Oh, yes!" he said, anxiously looking at her agitated face.

"Well, what did you do there? Who was there?" she asked after a silence.

Vronsky named the guests.

"The dinner was excellent, as was the boat race, and everything was quite pleasant, but in Moscow they can't do anything without something *ridicule*. A lady appeared, the Swedish queen's swimming instructor, and she demonstrated her art."

"How? Did she swim?" asked Anna, frowning.

"In some sort of red *costume de natation*, an old, ugly woman. Well, when do we leave?"

"What a stupid idea! Well, was there anything particular about her swimming?" asked Anna, without replying to his question.

"Absolutely nothing. I tell you it was silly and disgusting. When do you want to leave?"

Anna tossed her head, as though trying to rid herself of an unpleasant thought.

"When? The earlier the better. We'll not make it for tomorrow. The day after."

"No . . . wait. The day after tomorrow is Sunday, and I must be at *Maman's*" said Vronsky, embarrassed, for as soon as he mentioned his mother he felt Anna's intent, suspicious look. His embarrassment confirmed her suspicion. She flared up and turned away from him. It was now no longer the Swedish queen's swimming instructor whom Anna saw in her imagination. It was Princess Sorokin, who was staying with Countess Vronsky in the countess' Moscow suburban estate.

"Can't you go tomorrow?" she asked.

"No, I can't. The power of attorney and the money required for the business I am going on won't be ready tomorrow." he replied.

"In that case we're not going at all."

"But why?"

"I won't go later. Monday or not at all."

"But why?" said Vronsky, as though surprised. "It makes no sense."

"It makes no sense to you because you don't care for me at all. You don't want to understand my existence here. My only interest here has been Hannah. You call it affectation. You yourself said yesterday that I don't love my daughter, but that I pretend to love the English girl, and that this is not normal. I would like to know what kind of normal life I could have here?"

For a moment she came to herself and was terrified at having violated her resolution. But though conscious that she was undoing herself, she could not control herself, could not refrain from proving that he was wrong, could not give in to him.

"I never said that. I said that I didn't sympathize with this sudden passion."

"Then why don't you, you who always boast of your frankness, tell me the truth?"

"I never boast and never tell a lie," he said quietly, restraining the anger which was rising within him. "It's a great pity that you don't respect—"

"Respect was invented to cover the empty place that should have been filled with love. And if you no longer love me, it would be better and more honorable to say so."

"No, it's becoming unbearable," shouted Vronsky, rising from his chair. And stopping in front of her, he said slowly, "Why are you trying my patience?" He spoke in a manner that suggested that he could have said much more but was restraining himself. "It's not limitless."

"What do you mean by that?" she shouted, horrified by the unconcealed expression of hatred in his entire face and particularly in his cruel, terrible eyes.

"I mean . . ." he was about to begin, but stopped. "I must ask you what you want of me."

"What could I want? All I want is that you don't abandon me as you intend to," she said, divining everything that he meant but did not say. "But this is not what I really wish; this is of little importance. What I want is love, but I don't have it. Therefore, all is lost."

She went toward the door.

"Wait, wait! . . ." said Vronsky, without relaxing the frown on his brow, but taking her hand to restrain her. "What happened? I said that we must postpone our departure for three days, and you replied that I was lying, that I am a dishonorable person."

"Yes, I repeat that a man who can reproach me because he has given up everything for my sake," she said, recalling a previous quarrel, "is worse than a dishonorable man. He is a man without a heart."

"No, there's a limit to one's patience," he cried and abruptly released her hand.

He hates me, that's clear, she thought, and in silence, without turning around, she walked out of the room with a hesitating step.

He loves another woman, that's even clearer, she said to

herself, as she entered her room. What I want is love, but I don't have it. Therefore all is lost, she said, repeating the words she had said before. It must come to an end.

But how? she asked herself, sitting down in a chair before the mirror.

Thoughts of where she would go now—to her aunt who had brought her up, to Dolly, or just abroad by herself—and of what *he* was doing alone in his study, of whether this was the final quarrel or whether a reconciliation was still possible, of what all her former Petersburg acquaintances would now say about her, of how Aleksei Aleksandrovich would view it, and many other thoughts of what would happen now after their break came to her mind, but they did not occupy her completely. There lingered in her mind a vague thought, which was the only one that interested her but which she could not discern clearly. Recalling Aleksei Aleksandrovich once again, she also recalled her illness after childbirth and the feeling which did not leave then. Why didn't I die? she thought, recalling her words and feelings of that time. And she suddenly understood what was going on within her heart. Yes, she was occupied by a thought that would solve everything. Yes, to die . . . !

And the shame and disgrace of Aleksei Aleksandrovich of Seryozha, my own horrible shame, all this will be atoned for by death. To die—and he will feel remorse, he will pity me, love me, and will suffer for me. With a lingering smile of self-pity, she remained seated in the chair, taking off and putting back on the rings of her left hand, visualizing vividly all that he would feel after her death.

Approaching steps, his steps, distracted her. As though busy with sorting her rings, she did not even turn toward him.

He came over to her and, taking her hand, said softly:

"Anna, if you wish, we will go the day after tomorrow. I agree to everything."

She remained silent.

"Well?" he asked.

"You know yourself," she said, and at the same moment, no longer able to control herself, she broke into sobs.

"Abandon me, why don't you?" she said between sobs. "I'll leave tomorrow. . . . And I'll do more than that. Who am I? A depraved woman. A millstone around your neck. I don't want to torment you; I don't. I'll set you free. You don't love me, you love another!"

Vronsky begged her to calm down and assured her that there was not even the slightest basis for her jealousy, that he had never ceased loving her and never would, that he loved her more than ever.

"Anna, why torture both of us like this?" he said, kissing her hands. His face now expressed tenderness, and it seemed to her that she detected the sound of tears in his voice and felt their moisture on her hands. Instantaneously, her frantic jealousy turned into boundless passionate tenderness; she embraced him and showered kisses on his head, neck, and hands.

25

FEELING THAT THE reconciliation was complete, Anna eagerly began the next morning to prepare for their departure. Though in the conciliatory mood in which they had been the previous evening it had not been decided whether they would leave on Monday or Tuesday, Anna was busy making preparations for the trip, now not concerned in the least whether they would leave a day earlier or later. She was standing in her room over an open trunk, sorting belongings, when he came in earlier than usual, already dressed.

"I'll drive over to *Maman*'s. She can send me the money with Egorov. And I'll be ready to leave tomorrow," he said.

However good her mood had been, she was annoyed when he reminded her of his going to his mother's house.

"No, I myself won't be ready," she said, and at once she thought, This proves that it could have been arranged the way I wanted. "No, do as you intended. Go to the dining room; I'll join you shortly. I just have to put aside the things I don't need," she said, adding still another to the heap of dresses with which Annushka was already weighed down.

Vronsky was eating his steak when she entered the dining room.

"You'd scarcely believe how tired I've become of these rooms," she said, sitting down next to him for her coffee. "There's nothing more horrible than these *chambres garnies*. They are devoid of any expression, they possess no soul. This clock, these drapes, and particularly the wallpaper—they are a nightmare. I dream of Vozdvizhenskoe as of the Promised Land. Aren't you going to send off the horses?"

"No, they'll come after us. And are you going anywhere?"

"I planned to go to Wilson's. I must take some dresses over to her. So it is definitely tomorrow?" she said in a cheerful voice. But suddenly her face changed.

Vronsky's valet came in to ask for the receipt for a telegram from Petersburg. There was nothing unusual in the fact that Vronsky had received a telegram, but he, as though with the intent of concealing something from her, said that the receipt was in his study and hurriedly turned toward her.

"I'll be ready tomorrow without fail."

"Who sent the telegram?" she asked, without hearing what he said.

"Stiva," he replied, reluctantly.

"Why didn't you show it to me? What secret can there be between Stiva and myself?"

Vronsky called his valet back and told him to bring the telegram.

"I didn't want to show it to you because Stiva has a weakness for telegraphing. What was the use of sending the telegram when nothing was decided?"

"About the divorce?"

"Yes, he wires that he was unable to accomplish anything yet. He promised a final answer within a few days. Here, read it."

Anna took the telegram with trembling hands and read just what Vronsky had told her. But at the end there was added, *"There is little hope, but I will do everything that is possible or impossible."*

"I said yesterday that it made no difference to me when I received the divorce or if I received it," she said, her face flushed. "There was no need to hide it from me." In the same manner he may conceal or does conceal correspondence with other women, she thought.

"Yashvin wanted to come this morning with Voitov," said Vronsky. "It seems that he won everything from Pestsov and even more than he can pay, about sixty thousand."

"No," she said irritably, because by this change of subject he obviously was indicating to her that she was becoming irritable. "Why do you think that such information concerns me so much that it had to be withheld from me? I told you that I don't want to think of it, and I wish that you were as little interested in it as I."

"I am interested in it only because I want the situation to be clarified," he said.

"It is clarified not by its form but by love," she said, her irritation growing not because of his words but because of the air of aloof composure he maintained while speaking. "Why do you want it?"

My God, again love, he thought, frowning.

"You know why: for your and the children's sake," he replied.

"There will be no children."

"It's a great pity."

"You want it for the children, but you don't think about me," she said, having completely forgotten or having failed to hear that he had said *"for your* and the children's sake."

The problem of having more children had long been a cause of their disagreement and her resentment. His desire to have children she interpreted as his lack of concern for her beauty.

"Ah, but I said, 'For your sake!' Most of all for your sake," he repeated, his face creasing as though in pain, "because I'm sure that your irritability is caused primarily by the uncertainties of this situation."

Yes, now he has ceased pretending, and I can see all his cold hatred for me, she thought, without listening to his words, and she stared with horror at the coldhearted and cruel judge who looked through his eyes and provoked her.

"That's not the cause," she replied, "and I can't even conceive how my being completely within your power can be the cause of my irritability, as you call it. In what respect then is my situation uncertain? It's just the opposite."

"I'm very sorry that you refuse to understand me," he interrupted, persistent in trying to express his thought. "The uncertainty stems from your assumption that I am free."

"On this point you may rest assured," she replied, and she turned away from him and began to drink her coffee.

She picked up her cup and brought it to her mouth, her little finger extended. After a few swallows, she glanced at him and by the expression of his face she understood clearly that her hand, gesture, and the sound made by her lips revolted him.

"The opinions of your mother and her plans for your marriage don't concern me at all," she said, putting down the cup with a trembling hand.

"But we aren't talking about that."

"Yes, precisely about that. And, believe me, a woman without a heart, whether she is old or not, your mother or a stranger, is of no concern to me, and I don't want to know her."

"Anna, I beg you not to talk disrespectfully of my mother."

"A woman whose heart had not told her where her son's happiness and honor lie has no heart."

"I beg you again not to talk disrespectfully of my mother, whom I respect," he said, raising his voice and looking at her sternly.

She made no reply. Staring at him, at his face, his hands, she recalled in detail the scene of their reconciliation of the previous evening and his passionate caresses. Such caresses, the very same, he has bestowed, will and longs to bestow on other women! she thought.

"You don't love your mother. It's all words, words, words!" she said, looking at him with hatred.

"If such is the case, we must—"

"We must decide, and I have made my decision," she said, and she was going to leave, but at that moment Yashvin entered. Anna greeted him and stopped.

Why, at this moment, when a storm raged in her heart and she felt that her life was at a turning point which might lead to horrible consequences, why, at this moment, she had to dissemble in the presence of a stranger, who sooner or later would learn everything, she did not know. But she instantaneously allayed the storm, sat down, and engaged her guest in conversation.

"Well, how are your affairs? Did you collect your debt?" she asked Yashvin.

"Everything is fine. But it seems that I won't receive everything, and on Wednesday I must leave. And you?" asked Yashvin, looking at Vronsky with his eyes screwed up and evidently surmising that they had quarreled.

"I think the day after tomorrow," said Vronsky.

"I believe you've intended to go for a long time."

"But now it's definite," said Anna, with a direct look into Vronsky's eyes which told him that he should not even think that a reconciliation was possible.

"Do you really have no pity on that unfortunate Pestsov?" she asked, continuing her conversation with Yashvin.

"I've never asked myself, Anna Arkadievna, whether or not I have pity. After all, my entire fortune is here," he said, patting his coat pocket. "At this moment I'm a rich man, but I'll go to the club tonight and perhaps will return penniless. Remember, whoever sits down with me wants to take away my shirt, and I his. Well, we struggle against each other, and that's our pleasure."

"But if you were married, how would your wife feel?" asked Anna.

Yashvin laughed.

"Probably that's why I haven't married and have never intended to."

"What about Helsingfors?" asked Vronsky, entering into the conversation and glancing at Anna, who was smiling.

As their looks met, Anna's face suddenly assumed a cold and stern expression, as though she were saying to him, I haven't forgotten. It's still the same.

"Were you really in love?" she asked Yashvin.

"Heavens, how many times! But you see, some take their seats at cards always ready to leave when the hour of rendezvous arrives. And I may have my love affairs, but I always remember to be on time in the evening for the game. I always manage things that way."

"No, I'm not asking about that, but about what actually happened." She wanted to say "Helsingfors," but did not want to repeat Vronsky's words.

Voitov, who was buying a stallion from Vronsky, arrived. Anna rose and left the room.

Before leaving, Vronsky came into her room. She was about to pretend that she was looking for something on the table, but, ashamed of her pretense, she looked directly at him with her cold eyes. "What do you want?" she asked in French.

"Gambetta's certificate. I sold him," he said in a tone that said more distinctly than words that he had no time for explanations, and anyway they would be of no use.

I haven't wronged her in any way, he thought, and if she likes to torment herself, *tant pis pour elle*. But as he was leaving, it seemed to him that she said something, and his heart contracted with pity for her.

"What is it, Anna?" he asked.

"Nothing," she replied, just as coldly and calmly.

Well, if nothing, then *tant pis*, he thought, his coldness returning, and he turned and left. On his way out he saw her face in the mirror; it was pale, her lips were trembling. He was about to stop and say something comforting, but his legs had carried him out of the room before he thought of what to say. All that day he was away, and when he returned late in the evening, the maid told him that Anna Arkadievna had a headache and had asked not to be disturbed.

26

NEVER BEFORE had they remained unreconciled for a complete day. This was the first time. And it was not a quarrel. It was an open admission of complete estrangement. How else could anyone glance at her as he did, when he entered the room for the horse's certificate? How could he look at her, see her heart break with despair, and pass by in silence with such an indifferent and unperturbed expression? He had not only cooled toward her, he hated her because he loved another woman. There was no doubt about it.

And recalling all the cruel words he had said, Anna imagined still other words which he apparently wanted to say to her or could have said, and this kept increasing her resentment.

"I'm not holding you," he might have said. "You may go wherever you wish. You didn't want to divorce your husband, probably because you intended to return to him. Return to him. If you need money I'll give it to you. How much do you need?"

All the harsh words that a rude man might have said, he said in her imagination, and just as if he had actually said them, she would not forgive him.

And wasn't it just yesterday that he swore that he loved me, he, that sincere and honest man? Haven't I already given up hope many times without sufficient reason? she asked herself right afterward.

Except for the trip to Wilson's which took up two hours, Anna spent all that day trying to decide whether everything was over or whether there still was hope for a reconciliation, and whether she had to leave at once or should see him once more. She waited for him all day, and in the evening, before retiring to her room, she left word that she had a headache, telling herself, If, in spite of this message, he comes to see me, it'll prove that he still loves me. If he doesn't, it will mean that everything is over, and then I'll decide what I have to do. . . .

In the evening she heard the sound of his carriage at the door, the bell, his step, the words he exchanged with the maid. He believed what he was told, did not care to inquire about anything else, and retired. This meant it was all over.

And death appeared to her vividly and clearly as the only means to revive within his heart his love for her, to punish him, and to triumph in the struggle waged against him by the evil spirit that had taken possession of her heart.

Nothing mattered now: whether to go or not to go to Vozdvizhenskoe, whether to get or not to get the divorce from her husband; all that was pointless. The only thing that mattered was to punish him.

When she poured herself her usual dose of opium, the thought that she had only to take the whole vial at once in order to die seemed to her so easy and simple that she again indulged in delightful thoughts of how he would suffer, feel regret, and cherish her memory when it would be too late. She lay in her bed, and in the light of a single, burned-down candle stared with open eyes at the sculptured corner of the ceiling and at the shadow from the screen which partly covered it. She imagined vividly what he would feel when she was gone and she lived in his memory only. "How could I have said those cruel words to her?" he would say. "How could I have left the room without saying anything to her? But she is no longer. She has left us forever. She's there. . . ." Suddenly the shadow of the screen quivered, spread over the entire ceiling, and other shadows rushed to meet it; for a moment the shadows retreated, then rushed forward with renewed force, trembled, fused, and darkness enveloped her. Death! she thought. And such a terror seized her that for a long while she could not understand where she was; it took her a long time to find a match with her trembling hands and to light another candle in place of the one which had burned down and gone out. No, anything, but only to live! I love him. And he loves me. It has happened before and it will pass, she said to herself, feeling that tears were rolling down her cheeks as a result of her joy at having returned to life. And to seek relief from her fright she hastily went to him in his study.

He was fast asleep. She came over to him, and lighting his

face from above, she stared at him for a long while. Now, when
he was asleep, her love for him was so great that as she looked
at him she could not restrain her tender tears. But she knew
that if he were to awaken, he would give her the same cold
look to show how completely sure he was that he was right,
and before telling him of her love for him, she would have to
prove to him how much he had wronged her. Without awakening him she returned to her room, and after taking a second
dose of opium, toward morning she fell into a heavy, fitful
sleep during which she never ceased being conscious of herself.

Toward morning a horrible nightmare, one that had occurred repeatedly in her dreams even before her life with Vronsky, awoke her. A little old man with a matted beard bent over
a piece of iron and did something, muttering some absurd
French words, and, as always in that nightmare (and this was
what terrified her), she felt that the little moujik paid no
attention to her, but was busy stirring up some dreadful evil
against her with that piece of iron. She awoke in a cold sweat.

When she got up, she had only a hazy recollection of the
events of the previous day.

We quarreled. What happened has already happened
several times. I said that I had a headache, and he didn't come
to see me. We are leaving tomorrow. I must see him and
prepare for the trip, she said to herself. And, learning that he
was in his study, she went to see him. As she went through
the drawing room, she heard the sound of a carriage stopping
at the entrance, and looking through the window, she saw a
coach from which leaned a young girl in a lilac hat, giving
instructions to the servant who rang the bell. After some
conversation in the entrance hall, someone walked upstairs
and she heard the sound of Vronsky's step outside the drawing
room. He walked downstairs rapidly. Anna again went over to
the window. She saw him come out hatless on the porch and
walk over to the coach. The young lady in the lilac hat handed
him a large envelope. Vronsky smiled and said something to
her. The coach drove off; he ran rapidly up the staircase.

The haze that had enveloped everything within her heart
suddenly cleared. The pain of the previous day stabbed her
aching heart with renewed force. She could not understand
now how she could have humbled herself and remained with
him in his house for a whole day. She went into his study to
tell him of her decision.

"That was Madame Sorokin and her daughter, who brought

me the money and the papers from *Maman*. I couldn't get it yesterday. How's your headache? Better, I hope," he said quietly, not wishing to see and comprehend the somber and solemn expression on her face.

She stood in the middle of the room and stared at him in silence. He glanced at her, frowned for a moment, and continued to read the letter. She turned around and slowly began to leave the room. He still could have stopped her, but she had already reached the door, while he continued to read in a silence that was disturbed only by the rustle of a turned page.

"By the way," he said when she already was in the doorway, "we're definitely leaving tomorrow, aren't we?"

"You, but not I," she said, turning toward him.

"Anna, it can't go on like this. . . ."

"You, but not I," she repeated.

"This is becoming unbearable!"

"You . . . will regret it," she said, and she left.

Frightened by the expression of despair with which she had uttered these words, he jumped to his feet and was about to run after her, but he collected himself and resumed his seat, clenching his teeth and frowning. He resented this vague threat which, he believed, was improper. I've tried everything, he thought. There remains only one thing—to pay no attention, and he began to prepare himself to go to the city and again to see his mother, who had to sign the power of attorney.

She heard the sound of his step in his study and in the dining room. He stopped at the drawing room. But he did not turn toward her room and only gave instructions to the servant about the stallion, which was to be delivered to Voitov in his absence. Then she heard the carriage roll up, the door open, and he left again. But he came back into the entrance hall, and someone ran upstairs. It was his valet, who came up for the gloves which his master had forgotten. She went over to the window and saw him reach for the gloves without looking, tap the coachman on the back and say something to him. Then, without a glance at the windows, he seated himself in the carriage in his usual pose, crossed his legs, and while pulling on a glove, disappeared around the corner.

HE'S LEFT! It's all over! Anna said to herself as she stood at the window, and as an echo of this exclamation, the memory of the darkness which had enveloped her after the candle had gone out, and of the frightful nightmare, both fusing into one filled her heart with chilling terror.

"No, this can't be!" she cried, and she crossed the room and forcefully rang the bell. She was now so frightened at the thought of remaining alone that, without waiting for the servant to come in, she went to meet him.

"Find out where the count went," she ordered.

The servant replied that the count had gone to the stables.

"He ordered me to tell you that the carriage would be back at once, in case you wished to go for a ride."

"Very well. Wait. I will write a note. Send it with Mikhail to the stables. Make haste."

She sat down and wrote:

"*I am wrong. Come back, we must come to an understanding. For God's sake, come back, I'm frightened.*"

She sealed the envelope and handed it to the servant.

She was now afraid to remain alone, and following the servant, she left the room and went into the nursery.

What's happened! It's not the same, this isn't he! Where are his blue eyes, his sweet, shy smile? was her first thought when, instead of Seryozha, whom in her bewildered state of mind she had expected to find in the nursery, she saw her chubby, rosy daughter with her black, wavy hair. The girl was beating a cork hard and repeatedly against the table at which she was seated, and she gazed at her mother with her vacant eyes, black as currants. After replying to the English nurse that she was all better and would leave for the country the following day, Anna sat down beside the girl and began to roll the cork stopper in front of her. But the child's loud and ringing laughter and way she raised her eyebrows reminded Anna of Vronsky so vividly that, restraining her sob, she rose hurriedly and left the room. Is it really all over? No, it can't be, she thought. He'll come back. But how will he explain to me why he smiled and why he was so animated as he talked to her? But even if he doesn't explain, I'll trust him. If I don't, there's only one thing left for me, and I don't want that.

She looked at the clock. Twelve minutes had passed. Now he has my note and is on his way back. It won't take long now, ten more minutes . . . But what if he doesn't come? No, that can't be. He mustn't find me in tears. I'll go and wash. My, did I do my hair or not? she asked herself. She could not remember. She touched her head with her hand. Yes, I did, but I don't remember at all when I did it. She did not even trust her hand, and went over to the large mirror to see whether she had really done her hair or not. She had, but she could not recollect when. Who's that? she thought, looking in the mirror at her burning face, its eyes shining strangely and staring at her fearfully. Yes, it's me, she suddenly realized, and looking at herself from top to toe, she suddenly felt his kisses, shuddered and moved her shoulders. Then she raised her hand to her lips and kissed it.

What has happened? I'm losing my mind she thought, and she went to the bedroom, which Annushka was busy tidying up.

"Annushka," she said, stopping before her and staring at her, without knowing what she would say.

"You wanted to visit Daria Aleksandrovna," the maid said, understandingly.

"Daria Aleksandrovna? Yes, I'll go to see her."

Fifteen minutes there and fifteen back. He's on his way now, and he'll be here shortly, she thought; she reached for her watch and looked at it. But how could he leave me, seeing the state I was in? How can he go on, without making up with me? She went over to the window and looked out into the street. It was time for him to return. But she might have been mistaken in her calculations, and she began to reconsider the time when he left and to count the minutes.

While she was going over to the clock to check her watch, someone drove up. Looking through the window, she saw his carriage. But no one ascended the staircase, and the sound of voices could be heard downstairs. It was the messenger who had returned in the carriage. She went down to see him.

"I missed the count. He had left for the Nizhegorodsky Station."

"What do you mean? . . ." she asked the ruddy, cheerful Mikhaila, who returned her note to her.

Well, he never received it, she realized.

"Take this same note to Countess Vronsky's in the country. You know where I mean. And bring an answer at once," she said to the messenger.

And I, what will I do? she thought. Yes, I'll go to see Dolly. I'll go or I'll lose my mind. But I can still send him a telegram. And she wrote out a telegram: "*I must talk to you. Come at once.*"

After sending off the telegram, she went to change her clothes. After changing and putting on a hat, she looked again into the eyes of the plump, placid Annushka. Sincere compassion could be read in her small, kind, gray eyes.

"Annushka, my dear, what shall I do?" asked Anna, sobbing and sinking into an armchair helplessly.

"Why worry so much, Anna Arkadievna? Such things happen. Go for a ride; you'll distract yourself," said the maid.

"Yes, I'll go," said Anna, collecting herself and getting up. "And if you receive a telegram while I'm away, send it to Daria Aleksandrovna's. . . . No, I'll be back myself."

"Yes, I mustn't think, I must do something, I must go— the main thing is to get out of this house," she said, listening in terror to the furious pounding of her heart. She left hastily and seated herself in the carriage.

"Where to, ma'am?" asked Piotr, before taking his seat on the box.

"To the Oblonskys', on Znamenka."

28

THE WEATHER was clear. A heavy drizzle had fallen the entire morning, and it had cleared up only a short while earlier. The iron roofs, the flagstones of the sidewalks, the cobblestones of the streets, the wheels, leather, brass, and tin of the carriages, everything sparkled brightly in the May sun. It was three o'clock, the streets' busiest hour.

Anna was seated in the corner of the comfortable carriage, which bounded softly on its resilient springs in time to the horses' rapid gait, the wheels of the carriage rumbling incessantly. In the open air her impressions changed rapidly; she recalled anew the events of the last few days, and her situation appeared quite different than it had at home. Now even the thought of death did not seem to her so terrifying and so distinct, and death itself no longer seemed inevitable. Now she reproached herself for having so humbled herself. I beg him to forgive me. I give in to him. I admit that I'm the one to blame. Why? Can't I really live without him? And without answering the question of how she would live without him, she began to read the signs. OFFICE AND WAREHOUSE. DENTIST. Yes, I'll tell Dolly everything. She doesn't like Vronsky. It'll cause me shame and pain, but I'll tell her everything. She loves me, and I'll follow her advice. I won't give in to him. I won't let him lead me. Filippov, Bread . . . I've heard that they send his dough to Petersburg. Moscow water tastes so good. And the wells of Mytischen, and the pancakes. . . . And she recalled that long, long ago, when she was seventeen years old, she had gone with her aunt to Troitza. Those days we went by horse-drawn carriage, she thought—Was it really I with those red hands? How much of what then seemed to me so beautiful and unattainable has become worthless, and how much of what was then has now became unattainable forever! Could I have imagined then that I would suffer such humiliation? How superior and contented he'll feel when he receives my note! But I'll prove to him. . . . How that paint smells! Why do they keep painting and building? DRESSES AND FINERY, she read. A man greeted her. It was Annushka's husband. "Our parasites," she recalled Vronsky saying. Ours? Why ours? What's terrible is that the past can't be uprooted completely. It can't, but the memories can be suppressed. And I'll suppress them. And now she recalled her past life with Aleksei Aleksandrovich and how she had blotted it from her memory. Dolly will think I'm leaving a second husband and that therefore it's probably my fault. But do I really care to be right? I can't help it! she said, and she was about to cry. But her attention was quickly drawn to two girls and she wondered why they smiled so happily. Love probably —they don't know how cheerless it is, how base. . . . Children on the boulevard. Three boys are running around, playing horses. Seryozha! And I'm going to lose everything and won't have him back. Yes, everything will be lost if he doesn't come back. Perhaps he missed the train and is already back. There you go, looking for more humiliation! she said to herself. No, I'll go to Dolly and I'll tell her plainly, "I'm unhappy, I deserve it, I'm wrong, but still I'm unhappy. Help me." These horses, this carriage—how I loathe myself in this carriage!—are his. But I won't see them any more.

Thinking through all the words she would use in telling Dolly everything, and deliberately searing her heart, Anna ascended the stairs.

"Are there any visitors?" she asked in the entrance hall.

"Katerina Aleksandrovna Levin," replied the servant.

Kitty! That same Kitty whom Vronsky was in love with, thought Anna, the one he thinks of with love. He's sorry he didn't marry her. But he thinks of me with hatred, and he's sorry he bound himself to me.

When Anna arrived, the sisters were conferring about the feeding of the baby. Only Dolly came out to meet the guest, who by her arrival had interrupted their conversation.

"Oh, you haven't left yet? I wanted to come to see you," she said. "I received a letter from Stiva today."

"We had a telegram, too," replied Anna, and she turned around, expecting to see Kitty.

"He writes that he can't make out what Aleksei Aleksandrovich really wants, but that he won't leave until he has an answer."

"I thought that you had a visitor. May I see the letter?"

"Yes, Kitty's here," said Dolly in embarrassment. "She's in the nursery. She's been very ill."

"So I heard. May I see the letter?"

"I'll bring it in a moment. But he didn't refuse. On the contrary, Stiva still has hopes," said Dolly, stopping in the doorway.

"I have no hope, and I don't even care," replied Anna.

What is it? Does Kitty consider it beneath her dignity to see me? thought Anna, as she remained alone. Perhaps she's right. But it's not for her, who was in love with Vronsky, to show it to me, though it may be true. I know that in my situation no honorable woman can receive me. I knew that from that first moment I gave up everything for him. And here's my reward! Oh, how I hate him! And why did I come here? I feel even worse; my heart is even heavier. She could hear the two sisters conversing in the next room. And what am I going to tell Dolly now? Shall I please Kitty by telling her that I'm unhappy, and submit to her patronizing me? No, even Dolly wouldn't understand. And I have nothing to say to her. But I'd like to see Kitty and show her what contempt I have for everything and everyone, how little I care for anything now.

Dolly came in with the letter. Anna read it and handed it back in silence.

"I knew all this," she said. "And it doesn't interest me in the least."

"But why? I, on the other hand, still have hope," said Dolly, looking at Anna intently. She had never seen her in such an unusually irritable state. "When are you leaving?" she asked.

Anna looked straight ahead with half-closed eyes and made no reply.

"Is Kitty hiding from me?" she asked, looking at the door, her face flushed.

"Don't be silly! She's nursing her child and is having difficulties. I was advising her to. . . . She'll be very glad to see you. She'll be here in a minute," Dolly said awkwardly, unaccustomed to lying. "Here she is."

When she heard that Anna had arrived, Kitty decided not to come out, but Dolly made her change her mind. Having gathered her courage, Kitty did come out, blushed, went over to Anna and gave her her hand.

"I'm very glad to see you," she said in a trembling voice.

Kitty was troubled by the struggle going on within her between her hostility toward this evil woman and her desire to be lenient with her. But as soon as she saw Anna's beautiful and appealing face, all her hostility vanished at once.

"I wouldn't have been surprised if you hadn't wanted to see me. I've become accustomed to anything. Have you been ill? Yes, you've changed," said Anna.

Kitty felt that Anna looked at her with enmity. She believed that this hostility stemmed from the awkward situation in which Anna, who had formerly patronized her, now found herself, and she felt sorry for her.

They spoke about her illness, about her child, about Stiva, but apparently nothing interested Anna.

"I've come to say goodbye," she said, rising.

"When are you leaving?"

But Anna, without replying to her, turned again to Kitty.

"I am very glad to have seen you," she said with a smile. "I have heard so much about you from everyone, even from your husband. He visited me, and I liked him very much," she added, with unmistakably evil intent. "Where is he?"

"He left for the country," said Kitty, blushing.

"Be sure to give him my regards."

"Certainly," Kitty answered naïvely, looking into her eyes sympathetically.

"Goodbye, Dolly!" And after kissing Dolly and shaking hands with Kitty, Anna left hurriedly.

"Still the same, and still as attractive. She's so beautiful!" said Kitty, when she remained alone with her sister. "But there's something pathetic about her. Terribly pathetic!"

"Yes, there's something odd about her today," said Dolly. "When I saw her to the entrance hall, it seemed to me that she was ready to cry."

29

WHEN SHE TOOK her seat in the carriage, Anna's frame of mind was worse than when she had left the house. To her former torments there was now added the feeling of insult and rejection that she had been so clearly aware of during her meeting with Kitty.

"Home, ma'am?" asked Piotr.

"Yes, home," she answered, no longer thinking of where she was going.

How they looked at me, as at something terrible, incomprehensible and strange! What could he be telling that other one so heatedly? she wondered, watching two pedestrians. Is it really possible to tell another person what you feel? I wanted to tell Dolly, and it's a good thing that I didn't. How she would rejoice in my misfortune! She would conceal it, but her main feeling would be the satisfaction of seeing me punished for the pleasures she's envied me. As for Kitty, she would be still happier. I can see right through her! She knows I was more than ordinarily friendly with her husband. She's jealous and hates me. And despises me, too. In her eyes I'm an immoral woman. If I really were an immoral woman, I could make her husband fall in love with me . . . if I wanted to. And I wanted to. That one is contented with himself, she thought, looking at a stout, ruddy gentleman who was riding from the opposite direction; mistaking her for an acquaintance, he raised his glossy hat over his bald, shiny head, then discovered that he had made a mistake. He thought he knew me. And he knows me just as little as anyone else in this world. That's true of myself as well. I know my own tastes,

as the French say. They like that filthy ice cream. They're
sure of that, she thought, as she watched two boys stop an
ice cream vendor, who took down the tub of ice cream from
his head and wiped his perspiring face with the corner of a
towel. We all like what's sweet and tasty. If there's no candy,
then there's this filthy ice cream. Just like Kitty: if not
Vronsky, then Levin. And she envies me. And hates me. And
we all hate each other. I hate Kitty, and she hates me. That's
the truth. TIUTKIN, COIFFEUR. *Je me fais coiffer par* Tiutkin.
I'll tell it to him when he comes, she thought, and she smiled.
But at the same moment she recalled that she no longer had
anyone she could tell a funny story to. Besides, there's nothing
that's funny or amusing. Everything is revolting. The bells are
ringing for vespers. How carefully that shopkeeper crosses
himself! As though he were afraid he might drop something.
What are all these churches for, these bells, and this deceit?
Only to conceal the hatred we feel for each other, like those
cabbies, who wrangle so viciously among themselves. Yashvin
says, "He wants to take my shirt, and I his." That's the way
it is.

She was so deeply engrossed in these thoughts that she had
even forgotten her predicament when the carriage drew up in
front of her house. Only when she saw the doorman, who
came out to meet her, did she recall that she had sent a note
and a telegram.

"Any answer?" she asked.

"I will see at once," replied the doorman, and glancing at
the desk, he reached for a thin, square envelope with a telegram in it and handed it to her. "*I cannot come before ten
o'clock. Vronsky,*" she read.

"Has the messenger returned?"

"No, he has not," replied the doorman.

"Well, if that's the case, I know what I must do," she said,
and feeling a vague anger and an urge for revenge stirring
within her, she ran upstairs. I'll go to him myself. Before going
away forever, I'll tell him everything. I've never hated anyone
as much as I hate that man, she thought. Noticing his hat on
the rack, she shuddered with revulsion. She did not realize
that his telegram was a reply to hers, and that he had not yet
received her note. She visualized him now, conversing calmly
with his mother and with Mlle. Sorokin, rejoicing in her suffering. Yes, I must leave quickly, she said to herself, without
yet knowing where she would go. She wanted to flee as soon

as possible from the emotions she had experienced in this horrible house. The servants, the walls, the furniture, everything in this house aroused in her loathing and hatred and oppressed her like a weight.

Yes, I must go to the railroad station, and if he isn't there, I must go to his mother's house and expose him. Anna looked at the timetable in the newspaper. There was an evening train at two minutes after eight. Yes, I'll make it. She ordered fresh horses to be harnessed and busied herself with packing the things she would need for a few days. She knew that she would never return. Of the several plans that had formed in her mind, she had tentatively chosen one: after what would take place on the station or at the countess' estate, she would take the Nizhegorodsky line to the first town and remain there.

Dinner was on the table; she went over to it, sniffed the bread and the cheese, and finding that the smell of food nauseated her, she called for the carriage and went outside. The shadow cast by the house already extended to the other side of the street, the evening was clear, and it was still warm in the sun. And Annushka, who accompanied her with the luggage, and Piotr, who placed it in the carriage, and the coachman, who was evidently displeased, all of them revolted and irritated her by their words and actions.

"I don't need you, Piotr."

"And how about the ticket?"

"Well, do as you wish. I don't care," she said with annoyance.

Piotr jumped up on the box, and his arms akimbo, ordered the coachman to drive to the railroad station.

30

THERE'S THAT GIRL again! Once again everything is clear, said Anna to herself as soon as the carriage started, bounded slightly, and rattled along over the small cobblestones of the pavement. Again new impressions began to follow one another.

Oh yes, what was that interesting thought I had last? she tried to recall. Tiutkin, *Coiffeur*? No, not that. Oh, it was what Yashvin says: the struggle for survival and hatred are the only things that bind people together. No, your journey is in vain, she said, mentally addressing a group in a coach-and-four, evidently going to the country for a gay outing. And that dog you're taking along won't help you. You can't escape from yourselves. Looking in the direction Piotr had turned to look, she saw a factory hand, almost dead drunk, his head bobbing, being led away by a policeman. For him it was easy, she thought. But Count Vronsky and I didn't find that happiness, although we expected so much from it. And now for the first time, Anna turned that bright light in which she was seeing everything upon her relationship with him, something she had heretofore avoided thinking about. What did he seek in me? Not so much love as appeasement of his vanity. She recalled the early days of their liaison, his words, and the expression of his face, which reminded her of a devoted setter. And everything confirmed it now. Yes, there was an air about him of vainglorious triumph. Of course, there was love, too, but mainly there was pride in his success. He boasted about me. It's over now. There's nothing to be proud of. No longer pride but shame. He took everything he could from me, and he no longer needs me. I'm a burden to him, but he tries not to be dishonest with me. He let the secret out yesterday— he's waiting for the divorce, to marry me and burn his bridges. He loves me, but how? The zest is gone. This one wants to surprise everybody and is very much pleased with himself, she thought, looking at a ruddy-cheeked clerk riding a hired horse. It's true, I no longer please him as before. If I leave him, deep within his heart he'll be glad.

This was no guess; she saw it clearly in the penetrating light that now revealed to her the meaning of life and of the relationship between people.

My love is growing more passionate and more selfish while his is dying, and that's why we're parting, she went on thinking. And it can't be helped. To me, he alone is everything, and I demand that he give me more and more of himself. But he wants to get farther and farther away from me. We moved toward each other with the sole purpose of uniting, and now we are uncontrollably drifting apart. And it can't be changed. He tells me that I'm unreasonably jealous, and I, too, have said to myself that I'm unreasonably jealous. But it's not true. I'm not jealous; I'm dissatisfied. But—she opened her mouth; agitated by a thought that suddenly occurred to her, she changed her seat in the carriage. If I could be anything other than his mistress, who passionately loves nothing but his caresses! But I can't and don't want to be anything else. And having this desire alone, I arouse revulsion in him and enmity within myself and it can't be otherwise. Don't I know that he'd never think of deceiving me, that he has no designs on Mlle. Sorokin, that he's not in love with Kitty, that he wouldn't be faithless to me? I know all this but it brings me no comfort. If he, without loving me, remains kind and tender toward me only out of *obligation* and I don't have what I really wish, it's a thousand times worse than hatred. It's hell! And that's what has actually happened. He hasn't loved me for a long time. And where love ceases, hatred begins. These streets are completely unfamiliar. Hills and houses, houses. . . . And people in all these houses. . . . How many of them! There's no end to them, and they all hate each other. Well, let me decide what I'd want in order to be happy. Suppose I get the divorce. Aleksei Aleksandrovich lets me have Seryozha, and I marry Vronsky. When she thought of Aleksei Aleksandrovich, she, with sudden and unusual vividness, visualized him with his mild, lifeless, lusterless eyes, blue veins on his white hands, his intonation, and his cracking knuckles, and, remembering the feeling they had had toward each other, which was also called love, she shuddered with disgust. Well, suppose I get the divorce and become Vronsky's wife. Would Kitty stop looking at me the way she did this morning? No. And would Seryozha stop asking and wondering about my two husbands? And what sort of new feeling could I create between Vronsky and myself? Is it possible, if not to be happy, at least not to suffer any longer? No, absolutely not! she replied to herself, now without the slightest hesitation. It's impossible! Life is driving us apart; I'm the cause of his unhappiness and he of mine, and neither he nor I can be changed. Everything has been tried; the thread of the screw is worn down. Yes, there's a beggarwoman with a baby. She thinks people feel sorry for her. Aren't we all flung into this world only to hate each other and so to torment ourselves and others? Here come the schoolboys, laughing. Seryozha? she remembered—I thought that I loved him and I was moved by my tenderness. But then I lived without him, I exchanged him for another love and I didn't complain about the exchange as long as that love pleased me. And she remembered with disgust what she had then called love. And the clarity with which she now saw her own life and the life of others gladdened her. So it is with me, with Piotr, with the coachman Fiodor, with that shopkeeper, and with all these people who live there along the Volga, where these advertisements invite us to go, everywhere, always, she thought as she approached the low building of the Nizhegorodsky railroad station. Porters ran out toward her.

"To Obiralovka, madam?" asked Piotr.

She had completely forgotten where she was going and why, and only with great difficulty could she understand his question.

"Yes," she said to him, handing him her purse, and with her small red bag on her arm, she left the carriage.

Making her way through the crowd toward the first-class waiting room, she gradually recalled all the details of her situation and the decisions between which she had been wavering. And again, now hope, now despair that touched the old painful spots, began to lacerate the wounds of her tormented, violently throbbing heart. She sat down on a star-shaped divan to wait for the train, looking with disgust at the people coming and going (they all revolted her). She thought how, when she would arrive at the station, she would send a note to him, and what she would write. Or she saw in her imagination how he (failing to understand her suffering) would complain to his mother of his situation, how she would enter the room and what she would tell him. Or she thought how happy life could still be, how agonizingly she loved and hated him, how dreadfully her heart was pounding.

31

THE BELL RANG. Several ugly, insolent, young men passed by hurriedly, yet at the same time heedful of the impression they were making. Piotr, too, passed through the hall in his uniform and half-boots, with his dull, animal face, and came over to help her to the car. Some boisterous men grew silent when she passed them on the platform, and one of them whispered something about her to his companion, some vile remark, of course. She ascended the high step, and alone in the compartment, sat down on a soiled, once white, spring divan. The bag shook on the springs and came to rest. At the window, Piotr, with his stupid smile, raised his gallooned hat to say goodbye to her. The arrogant conductor latched the door. An ugly lady in a bustle (in her imagination Anna undressed the woman and was horrified by her ugliness) and a little girl, smiling unnaturally, ran past the window.

"Katerina Andreyevna has it, she has everything, *ma tante!*" cried the girl.

A little girl, and she, too, is misshapen and full of pretense, thought Anna. To avoid everyone, she rose quickly and took a seat at the opposite window of the empty car. A dirty ugly moujik in a cap, his matted hair protruding from underneath it, walked past the window, bending over the wheels of the car. There's something familiar about that ugly moujik, thought Anna. And recalling her nightmare and shuddering with fear, she went over to the opposite door. The conductor was opening it to admit a man and his wife.

"Would you like to go out?"

Anna made no reply. The conductor and the couple who entered did not see the horror on her face, covered by her veil. She returned to her former place and sat down. The couple seated themselves on the opposite side, trying to hide their inquisitive glances at her dress. Both husband and wife looked repulsive to Anna. The husband asked her permission to smoke, evidently not because he wanted to smoke but to say something to her. Receiving her permission, he addressed his wife in French, saying something that he needed to say even less than he needed to smoke. They forced themselves to talk nonsense only to make her listen to them. Anna saw clearly that they were sick of each other and hated each other. And one could not but hate such wretched monstrosities.

The second bell sounded, followed by the shuffle of luggage, noise, shouts, and laughter. To Anna it was so clear that no one had any reason to rejoice about anything that this laughter jarred her painfully, and she wanted to stop up her ears so as not to hear it. At last the third bell rang, a whistle sounded, the locomotive shrieked, a chain clanked, and the husband crossed himself. It would be interesting to ask what he meant by that, thought Anna, casting a vicious glance at him. She looked past the lady and through the window, at the people on the platform who had come to see the passengers off and now seemed to move backward. Jolting uniformly at the rail crossings, the car in which Anna was sitting passed the platform, a stone wall, the station signal and other cars; with a soft rumble the wheels rolled along the rails more smoothly and evenly; the window was lit by the bright evening sun, the wind rustled the curtain. Anna forgot about her fellow travelers, rocked slightly to the rhythm of the car, inhaled the fresh air and began to think again.

Yes, where was I? I was thinking that I couldn't conceive of a situation where life would not be a torment, that we're all created to suffer, we all know it and keep contriving means to deceive ourselves. But what can you do when you see the truth?

"Man is endowed with reason to rid himself of what troubles him," the lady said in French, stammering, but evidently pleased with her statement.

These words seemed to be an answer to Anna's thoughts.

To rid himself of what troubles him, Anna repeated. And, glancing at the ruddy-cheeked husband and his thin wife, she saw that the sickly wife considered herself a misunderstood woman, that her husband was unfaithful to her, and that he encouraged her to maintain that opinion of herself. It seemed to Anna that by focusing her beam of light upon them, she understood their entire story and saw into all the recesses of their hearts. But she found nothing interesting there and turned back to her own thoughts.

Yes, it troubles me profoundly, and my reason is given to me to rid myself of my troubles. Therefore I must do it. Why then shouldn't I blow out the candle if there is no longer anything to look at, when everything is repulsive to the sight? But how? Why did the conductor run along the foot board? Why are those young people in the other car shouting? Why are they talking? Why are they laughing? Everything is false, deceitful, fraudulent, wicked . . . !

When the train stopped at the station, Anna went out with the crowd of passengers, shrinking from them as from lepers, and she stopped on the platform, trying to remember why she had come here and what she had intended to do. Everything that had seemed possible to her before was so hard to understand now, particularly in this noisy crowd of ugly people who would not leave her alone. First the porters ran over to her, offering their services; then some young men, striking their heels against the boards of the platform and talking in loud voices, cast their glances at her, and then those who moved in her direction stepped aside the wrong way. Recalling that she intended to ride further if there was no answer from him, she stopped one of the porters and asked whether Count Vronsky's coachman was there with a note.

"Count Vronsky's? Some of his men were here. They met Princess Sorokin and her daughter. What does the coachman look like?"

While she was talking to the porter, the coachman Mikhaila, ruddy-faced, cheerful, in a smart Russian-style coat and with a watch chain, evidently proud that he had so well acquitted himself of his charge, came over to her and handed her a note. She opened it, and her heart sank even before she read it.

"I'm sorry that I missed your note. I'll be back at ten o'clock," wrote Vronsky in a careless hand.

Well! Just as I expected, she said to herself with a wicked smile.

"Very well, you may go home," she said softly, addressing Mikhaila. She spoke softly because the rapid throbbing of her heart interfered with her breathing. No, I won't let you torment me, she thought, addressing her threat not to him, not to herself, but to the cause of her agony, and walked along the platform past the station.

Two servant girls who were strolling about the platform, turned their heads, looked at her, and said something aloud about her dress. "Genuine," they said, referring to the lace on her dress. The young men would not leave her alone. They passed by again, looked into her face, and with a laugh shouted something in affected voices. The stationmaster who passed by asked her if she was a passenger. A boy, the kvas vendor, kept his eyes fixed on her. Oh, Lord, where shall I go? she thought, walking further and further along the platform. She stopped at its end. Some ladies and children who had come to meet a gentleman in glasses interrupted their loud laughter and conversation to look at her as she passed alongside. She hastened her step and walked away from them to the edge of the platform. A freight train was approaching. The platform shook and it seemed to her that she was again riding.

Suddenly, recalling the man who had been crushed by a train on the day when she first met Vronsky, she understood what she had to do. Rapidly and lightly she descended the steps that led from the water tower to the rails and stopped close to the freight train which was going by. She stared at the undercarriages of the cars, at the bolts and chains and the tall iron wheels of the slowly moving first car, trying to estimate the midpoint between the front and back wheels and the moment when this would be in front of her.

There, she said to herself, looking into the shadow of the car on the sand mixed with coal between the rails. There, into the exact midpoint, and I'll punish him and escape from everyone and from myself.

She wanted to throw herself under the midpoint of the first car as it moved up in front of her. But the red bag, which she began to remove from her arm, delayed her, and she was too late. The midpoint passed by. She had to wait for the next car. She was seized by a feeling like that which she had experienced when she was about to enter the water when she had gone bathing, and she crossed herself. The familiar gesture of the sign of the cross brought to her mind a host of memories from childhood and girlhood, and suddenly the darkness that had veiled everything from her eyes was torn asunder and for a moment her former life revealed itself in all its serene joys. But she kept her eyes fixed on the wheels of the second car as it rolled nearer. And at exactly the moment when the midpoint between the wheels arrived she tossed away the red bag, and hunching her head into her shoulders, she threw herself under the car on her hands; with a light movement, as though ready to rise at once, she fell on her knees. At the same moment she was horrified by what she was doing. Where am I? What am I doing? Why? She wanted to rise and draw back, but something enormous and implacable struck her head and dragged her along. "Oh Lord, forgive me all my sins!" she said, feeling that resistance was futile. The little moujik, mumbling something, was busy over his piece of iron. And the candle by which she had been reading a book full of trouble, deceit, misfortune, and evil, flared up brighter than ever, illuminating for her everything that until then had been enveloped in darkness, sputtered, began to fade, and then died out forever.

PART EIGHT

1

NEARLY TWO months passed. It was the middle of a hot summer, and only now was Sergei Ivanovich getting ready to leave Moscow.

During this period, important events had been occurring in the life of Sergei Ivanovich. About a year earlier he had finished his book, the fruit of six years of labor, with the title, *A Tentative Survey of the Foundations and Forms of Statehood in Europe and Russia*. Several chapters of the book and the introduction had been published in periodicals, and other parts had been read by Sergei Ivanovich to members of his circle, so that the ideas propounded in this work could not have been completely unknown to the public. Nevertheless, Sergei Ivanovich had expected that the publication of his book would make a deep impression upon the public and that if it would not create a revolution in scholarship, it would profoundly stir the academic world.

After painstaking revision, the book had been published the previous year and distributed among the booksellers.

Although he did not ask anyone about the book, although he replied with reluctance and feigned indifference when asked by friends how the book was selling, and although he did not even ask the booksellers about it, Sergei Ivanovich looked keenly and with careful attention for the first impression the book would make upon the general public and the literary world.

But a week had passed, then a second, and a third, and the book had apparently made no impression at all upon the public; his friends, the specialists and scholars, touched upon the subject of the book occasionally, evidently out of a sense of courtesy. But his other acquaintances, who were not interested in a book of scholarly content, did not talk to him about it at all. And the public was completely indifferent, particularly because it was occupied now with other matters. And neither did the press even mention the book during the entire month.

Sergei Ivanovich had calculated exactly the time required for a review of the book to be written, but a month passed, a second, and the same silence prevailed.

Only in the *Northern Beetle,* in a humorous column about the singer Drabanti, who had lost his voice, was Koznyshev's book mentioned in passing, in a few contemptuous words that showed the book had long since been condemned by everyone and was being exposed to general ridicule.

At last, after two months had passed, a critical review appeared in a serious periodical. Sergei Ivanovich knew the author of the review. He had met him once at Golubtsov's.

The author of the article was a very young, sickly man, a journalist, very clever as a writer, but very poorly educated and shy in his personal relations.

In spite of his thorough contempt for the reviewer, Sergei Ivanovich began to read the article with complete respect for it. The article was dreadful.

Evidently the reviewer had misunderstood the book completely. But he had selected quotations with such skill that for those who had not read the book (and apparently almost no one had), it became quite clear that the whole book was nothing but a collection of words, high-sounding and, to make it worse, improperly used (as he indicated by question marks), and that the author of the book was a totally ignorant man. And all of this was written with such wit that Sergei Ivanovich himself would not have declined to be blessed with it. This was what made the situation intolerable.

In spite of the extreme conscientiousness with which Sergei Ivanovich examined the soundness of the reviewer's arguments, he did not dwell for a moment on the defects and errors which had been ridiculed—it was obvious that they had been culled deliberately—but immediately and in spite of himself began to recall the smallest details of his meeting and conversation with the author of the review.

Could I have offended him in some way? Sergei Ivanovich asked himself.

And remembering that at their meeting he had corrected the young man in the misuse of a word that betrayed his ignorance, Sergei Ivanovich now found the clue to the meaning of the article.

After the publication of that article there ensued a dead silence about the book both in the press and in oral discussions, and Sergei Ivanovich realized that his creation, on which he had labored with so much love for six years, had passed by without leaving any trace.

Sergei Ivanovich's situation was all the more difficult because, with the completion of his book, he was deprived of the scholarly occupation that had formerly taken up most of his time.

Sergei Ivanovich was intelligent, learned, healthy, and active, and he did not know how to employ his energies. Discussions in drawing rooms, conferences, meetings and committees, or at any other place where discussions could be held, occupied him to some extent. But as an old city dweller, he did not allow himself to devote all of himself to conversation as his inexperienced brother usually did when he came to Moscow; there still remained much leisure and a reserve of intellectual power.

To his good fortune, at that time, which was most trying to him because of the failure of his book, such topics as the dissenters, the American friends, famine in Samara, the expositions, and spiritism, were supplanted by the Slav problem, which had previously only smoldered in society, and Sergei Ivanovich, who was one of those who had always kept it alive, now devoted himself to it completely.

At that time, the circle of people to which Sergei Ivanovich belonged did not discuss or write about anything else but the Slav problem and the Serbian war. All the things the idle public usually does to kill time were now done for the benefit of the Slavs. Balls, concerts, dinners, speeches, ladies' attire, beer, taverns—everything attested to sympathy for the Slavs.

Sergei Ivanovich disagreed with many of the particulars which were being written and said on this subject. He saw that the Slav problem had become one of those fashionable fads that, one succeeding the other, always keep society busy. He also saw that there were many who occupied themselves with this matter for vain and mercenary reasons. He realized that the newspapers published much that was unnecessary and exaggerated for the sole purpose of drawing attention to themselves and of outshouting one another. He saw that in this state of general enthusiasm many of those who were failures or felt they had been wronged, advanced themselves and were the most vociferous: commanders without armies, ministers without ministries, journalists without journals, politicians without followers. He realized that there was much about it that was frivolous and ridiculous. But he saw and agreed that it was a state of enthusiasm that was genuine, that constantly grew in intensity, that closely united all classes of society, and with which one could not but sympathize. The massacre of the Slavs, co-religionists and brothers, evoked sympathy with the oppressed and indignation against the oppressors. And the heroism of the Serbs and Montenegrins, who were fighting for a great cause, aroused in the entire nation a will to help their brothers, no longer by words but by deeds.

And this brought forth another phenomenon, which delighted Sergei Ivanovich: a manifestation of public opinion. The public had definitely expressed its will. The soul of the nation had found a way to express itself, as Sergei Ivanovich said. And the more he busied himself with this cause, the clearer it became to him that it was one bound to reach great proportions, to create an epoch.

He dedicated all of himself to the service of this great cause and forgot about his book.

His time was completely occupied now, so that he had no chance to reply to all the letters and demands addressed to him.

He had worked the entire spring and part of the summer, and it was not until July that he could get ready to go to his brother's place in the country.

He was going to take a two-week rest in the holy of holies of the nation, in the remote countryside, to delight in witnessing the national enthusiasm, of whose existence he and all other dwellers of the capital and other cities were thoroughly convinced. Katavasov, who for a long time had wanted to keep his promise to Levin to visit him, accompanied Sergei Ivanovich.

2

SERGEI IVANOVICH and Katavasov had scarcely reached the Kursk railroad station, which that day was particularly crowded, alighted from their coach and stopped to wait for their servant, who was riding up with their luggage, when a group of volunteers drove up in four cabs. They were met by ladies with bouquets of flowers and, followed by a crowd which rushed after them, they entered the station.

One of the ladies who were meeting the volunteers came out from the station and turned to Sergei Ivanovich.

"Have you also come to see them off?" she asked in French.

"No, Princess, I myself am leaving. To take a rest at my brother's. And do you always see them off?" asked Sergei Ivanovich, with a faint smile.

"Of course!" replied the princess. "Is it true that we've already sent off eight hundred? Malvinsky wouldn't believe me."

"Over eight hundred. If you count those who didn't leave directly from Moscow, it makes more than a thousand," added Sergei Ivanovich.

"There you are! Just as I said!" the lady interjected happily. "And is it true that almost a million has already been donated?"

"More, Princess."

"What wonderful news today! The Turks suffered another defeat."

"Yes, I read about it," said Sergei Ivanovich. They were referring to the latest telegram, which confirmed that for three days the Turks had been suffering defeats on all fronts and were in flight, and that a decisive battle was expected the following day.

"Oh, by the way, a fine young man applied, but they're giving him trouble, I don't know why. I know him, and I'd like to ask you to write a note in his favor. He was sent by Countess Lydia Ivanovna."

Having gathered all the details about the young man that the princess had, Sergei Ivanovich went into the first-class hall, wrote a note to the person on whom the case depended, and handed it to the princess.

"You know, that . . . er, celebrated Count Vronsky is

816

leaving on this train," she said with a triumphant and meaningful smile to Sergei Ivanovich when he sought her out and
handed her the note.

"I'd heard he was leaving, but I didn't know when. On this
train?"

"I saw him. He's here. Only his mother is seeing him off.
He's doing the best thing."

"So it would seem."

While they were talking, the crowd rushed past them to
the dining table. They, too, moved up, and heard the loud
voice of a gentleman who, with a glass in his hand, was
delivering a speech to the volunteers. "In the service of our
faith, humanity, and our brothers," the gentleman was saying,
his voice growing louder and louder. "In this great cause
Mother Moscow gives you her blessing. *Zhivio!*" he concluded, in a loud and tearful voice.

Everyone shouted *Zhivio!* and a new crowd rushed into
the hall and almost knocked the princess down.

"Ah, Princess, wonderful!" said Stepan Arkadievich as he
suddenly appeared, beaming a happy smile, in the midst of
the crowd. "His words were so beautiful, so warm, weren't
they? Bravo! Sergei Ivanovich, why don't you say something too, you know, a few words of encouragement? You
speak so well!" he added with a gentle, respectful, and cautious smile, holding his arm and gently pushing him forward.

"No, I'm leaving shortly."

"Where to?"

"To my brother's in the country," replied Sergei Ivanovich.

"Then you'll see my wife. I wrote to her, but you'll see
her sooner. Please tell her that you saw me and that everything is all right. She'll understand. And, by the way, please
tell her that I've been appointed a member of the Commission of the Joint. . . . Well, she'll understand. You know,
les petites misères de la vie humaine," he said, addressing
the princess somewhat apologetically. "And Madame Miakhky,
not Liza but Bibiche, is sending a thousand rifles and twelve
nurses. Did I tell you?"

"Yes, I've heard," replied Koznyshev reluctantly.

"It's a pity you're leaving," said Stepan Arkadievich. "Tomorrow we're giving a dinner for two who are leaving for
the war—for Dimer-Bartniansky from Petersburg, and for
our own Veselovsky, Grisha. Both of them are going. Veselov-

sky married recently. What a fine fellow! Isn't he, Princess?"
he asked, turning to the lady.

Without replying, the princess glanced at Koznyshev. But
the fact that Sergei Ivanovich and the princess seemed to
wish to get rid of him did not embarrass Stepan Arkadievich
in the least. Smiling, he looked first at the feather on the
princess' hat, then at those around him, as though remembering something. Seeing a lady who was going around
collecting donations, he called her and put a five-ruble note
in her collection box.

"While I still have money, I can't look at these boxes
without being moved," he said. "What do you say about
today's report? What heroes, those Montenegrins!"

"You don't say!" he exclaimed, when told by the princess
that Vronsky was leaving on that train. For a moment Stepan
Arkadievich's face expressed sadness, but a moment later,
when, walking with a slightly springy step and smoothing
his side whiskers, he entered Vronsky's compartment, Stepan
Arkadievich completely forgot his heartbroken sobs over the
corpse of his sister and saw in Vronsky only a hero and an
old friend.

"In spite of all his faults, we must do him justice," said
the princess to Sergei Ivanovich as soon as Oblonsky left
them. "What a truly Russian, Slav nature! But I'm afraid
it might be painful for Vronsky to see him. Say what you like,
I'm moved by that man's fate. Talk to him during the trip,"
said the princess.

"Yes, if I have the chance."

"I never did like him, but this atones for a great deal. He's
not only going himself, but he's taking a whole squadron
at his own expense."

"Yes, so I've heard."

The bell rang. Everyone crowded at the doors.

"There he is," said the princess, indicating Vronsky, in a
long coat and wide-brimmed black hat, walking arm in arm
with his mother. Oblonsky was walking alongside, conversing
with animation.

Vronsky frowned and looked straight ahead, as though
not listening to Stepan Arkadievich.

Probably at Oblonsky's suggestion he glanced in the direction of Sergei Ivanovich and the princess and raised his hat
in silence. His face had aged and seemed frozen into an
expression of suffering.

After coming out onto the platform, Vronsky silently allowed his mother to proceed and disappeared into the car.

The platform resounded with the sounds of "God Save the Czar" and with shouts of *Hurrah!* and *Zhivio!* One of the volunteers, a tall, very young man with a hollow chest, bade farewell with particular fervor, waving his felt hat and a bouquet of flowers over his head. From behind him, also bidding their farewells, could be seen two officers and an elderly man with a long beard and a greasy cap.

3

AFTER SAYING GOODBYE to the princess, Sergei Ivanovich entered the crowded car with Katavasov, who had come over to him, and the train started.

At the Tsaritsyn station, the train was met by a well-trained chorus of young men who sang "Glory." Again the volunteers bowed and leaned out of the windows, but Sergei Ivanovich paid no attention to them. He had had such frequent dealings with the volunteers that he knew their general nature and it did not interest him. But Katavasov, who had been busy with his scientific pursuits and had had no occasion to observe the volunteers, was deeply interested in them and asked Sergei Ivanovich questions about them. Sergei Ivanovich advised him to go into a second-class car to talk to them himself. At the next station Katavasov followed his advice.

When the train stopped, he went into a second-class car and made his acquaintance with the volunteers. They were seated in a corner of the car, talking loudly, and were evidently enjoying the attention they attracted among their fellow passengers and from Katavasov who had just come in. The loudest of them was the tall youth with the hollow chest. He was unmistakably drunk, and was relating an event that had happened in his school. Seated opposite him was an officer, no longer young, dressed in the Austrian-style military singlet of the Guards uniform. He listened to the speaker with a smile and now and then interrupted him. A third, in the uniform of an artilleryman, was seated on a trunk alongside them. A fourth was asleep.

Katavasov entered into a conversation with the youth and

learned that he had been a wealthy Moscow merchant who had squandered a large fortune before the age of twenty-two. Katavasov disliked him because he was effeminate, pampered, and of delicate health. Evidently he was certain, particularly now after a drink, that he was performing a heroic deed, and he boasted of it in the most disagreeable manner.

The other one, a retired officer, also made an unpleasant impression on Katavasov. He was apparently a man who had tried his hand at everything. He had been a railroad employee, a manager, had built his own factories, and talked about everything, using scientific terms unnecessarily and improperly.

On the other hand, Katavasov was much taken by the artilleryman. He was a modest, soft-spoken man, who evidently admired the erudition of the retired Guards officer and the heroic self-sacrifice of the merchant but said nothing of himself. When Katavasov asked him what had made him decide to go to Serbia, he replied modestly:

"Well, everyone's going. The Serbs have to be helped, don't they? It's a pity."

"Yes, and there's a shortage of you artillerymen particularly," said Katavasov.

"But I didn't serve long in the artillery. They may assign me to the infantry or cavalry."

"Why to infantry, when they need artillerymen most of all?" asked Katavasov, assuming from the artilleryman's age that he must have reached an important rank.

"I didn't serve for long in the artillery. I retired as an officer candidate," he said, and he began to explain why he had not passed the test.

All this made an unfortunate impression on Katavasov, and when at the next station the volunteers went into the station restaurant for a drink, Katavasov wanted to verify his unfavorable impression in a conversation with someone. One passenger, a little old man in a military coat, had listened attentively throughout Katavasov's conversation with the volunteers. When they remained alone Katavasov turned to him.

"What a variety of circumstances they come from, those men going there," he remarked vaguely, wanting to express his own opinion and at the same time learn what the old man thought.

The old man had been a military man and had taken part

in two campaigns. He knew what a true soldier was, and by
the appearance and conversations of these gentlemen and by
the daredeviltry with which they had applied themselves to
the bottle during the trip, he believed them to be poor
soldiers. In addition, he lived in a small town and was anxious
to tell Katavasov about a discharged soldier who went to the
war from their town and was a drunkard and a thief whom
no one would hire any longer. But, knowing from experience
that in the prevailing general mood it was dangerous to
express an opinion that contradicted the accepted one, and
particularly to decry the volunteers, he, for his part, tried
to sound out Katavasov.

"Well, they need men there," he said, his eyes smiling.
And they touched on the latest war reports and each concealed from the other that he failed to understand who would
be the enemy to be fought in the battle expected for the
next day, since according to the latest reports, the Turks had
been beaten on all fronts. And so, without expressing their
opinions, they parted.

Katavasov returned to his car, and involuntarily dissembling
his feelings, told Sergei Ivanovich that from what he had
seen of the volunteers, they were excellent fellows.

When the train stopped at a large station in a city, the
volunteers were again met with songs and shouts, the collec-
tors of donations again appeared with their boxes and the city
ladies presented flowers and accompanied the volunteers to
the station restaurant, but all this was done with much less
enthusiasm and on a smaller scale than in Moscow.

4

DURING THE LAYOVER at the provincial capital, Sergei Ivanovich did not go into the station restaurant but began to walk
up and down the platform.

When he passed Vronsky's compartment for the first time,
he noticed that the shades were drawn. But when he passed
it again he saw the old countess in the window. She called
him to her side.

"I'm here, as you see. I'll accompany him to Kursk," she
said.

"Yes, so I've heard," said Sergei Ivanovich, stopping at

the window and looking inside. "How noble on his part!" he added, noticing that Vronsky was not in the car.

"What else could he do after his misfortune?"

"What a catastrophe!" said Sergei Ivanovich.

"Oh, what I went through! But come in. . . . Oh, what I went through!" she repeated when Sergei Ivanovich entered and sat on the divan alongside her. "It would be impossible to imagine! For six weeks he talked to no one and ate only when I pleaded with him. And he couldn't be left alone for a moment. We took away everything he could have used to kill himself with. We lived on the ground floor, but all precautions had to be taken. You know, he shot himself once on account of her," she said, and the old lady wrinkled her brow at the recollection. "Yes, her end was fitting for such a woman. Even the kind of death she chose was mean and base."

"It's not for us to judge, Countess," said Sergei Ivanovich with a sigh, "but I understand how distressing it must have been for you."

"Oh, don't even mention it! I was at my country place and he was with me. They brought him a note. He wrote an answer and had it delivered. We had no idea that she was there at the station. In the evening, as I was getting ready to retire, my maid Mary told me that at the station a lady had thrown herself under a train. My heart sank. I understood that it was she. The first thing I decided was not to tell him. But he'd already been told. His coachman was there and saw everything. When I ran into his room he was no longer himself—it was frightening to look at him. He didn't say a word and rushed over there. I don't know what happened there, but when he was brought home, he was like a dead man. I wouldn't have recognized him. *'Prostration complète,'* the doctor said. Afterward he was nearly seized by madness."

"Oh, why talk about it!" added the countess, waving her hands. "A terrible time! No, whatever you may say, she was a wicked woman. What ungovernable passions! And it's all a desire to prove something particular. Well, she did it: she ruined herself and two excellent men—her husband and my unfortunate son."

"And what about her husband?" asked Sergei Ivanovich.

"He took her daughter. In the beginning Alyosha agreed to everything. But now he suffers bitter remorse for having given away his daughter to a stranger. But he can't go back on his

word. Karenin attended the funeral. But we saw to it that he
and Alyosha did not meet. For him, her husband, it was
in some ways easier. She had set him free. But my unfortunate
son had given her all of himself. He forsook everything,
his career, myself, but she showed no pity on him and deliberately crushed him. No, say what you want, her very death
was the death of a wicked, irreligious woman. May God
forgive me, but when I see how she ruined my son I can't
help hating her memory."

"And how is he now?"

"This Serbian war is a godsend. I'm old and understand
nothing about it, but it's a godsend. Of course, I, as a mother,
am frightened, and, most important of all, they say that
ce n'est pas très bien vu à Petersbourg. But what's to be done?
This was the only thing that could arouse him. Yashvin, his
friend, had lost everything and was preparing to go to
Serbia. He came to see him and persuaded him to do the
same. He's now occupied with it. Please talk to him; I'd like
him to have some diversion. He's so sad. And to make it
worse he has a toothache. He'll be very glad to see you.
Please talk to him. There he is, walking on the other side."

Sergei Ivanovich said that he would be very glad to and
crossed over to the other side of the train.

5

IN THE OBLIQUE evening shadow cast by a heap of sacks that
had been piled on the platform, Vronsky, in his long coat and
with his hat pulled over his eyes, his hands in his pockets,
paced up and down like a caged animal, turning abruptly
every twenty steps. As Sergei Ivanovich approached him it
seemed to him that Vronsky saw him but pretended that he
had not. It did not matter to Sergei Ivanovich. In his relationship with Vronsky he was above petty considerations.

At that moment, Sergei Ivanovich saw in Vronsky an outstanding champion of a great cause, and he considered it his
duty to lend him encouragement and approval. He approached
him.

Vronsky stopped, stared, and, on recognizing him, took a
few steps toward him and clasped his hand firmly.

"Perhaps you don't particularly want to talk to me," said

Sergei Ivanovich, "but couldn't I be of some service to you?"

"There is no one whom I would see with less displeasure than you," said Vronsky. "Forgive me. Life is no longer pleasant for me."

"I understand and would like to offer you my services," said Sergei Ivanovich, gazing into Vronsky's palpably anguished face. "Perhaps you need a letter to Ristich or to Milan?"

"Oh, no!" replied Vronsky, as though following him with difficulty. "If you don't mind, let's walk. It's so stuffy in the car. A letter? No, thank you. To die one needs no letters of introduction. Perhaps to the Turks . . ." he said, smiling with his mouth only. His eyes retained their angry and anguished expression.

"But perhaps it would make it easier for you to establish connections, which you will surely need, with a person who has been prepared. On the other hand, do as you please. I was very glad to hear of your decision. The volunteers have been the subject of too much criticism, but with a man like you, their standing in public opinion will rise."

"As a man," said Vronsky, "I am valuable because I consider my life to be of no value to me. And as for physical strength, I have enough to lead an attack on an enemy phalanx, to destroy it, or to die in the attempt—this I know. I'm glad to have something to lay down my life for, a life that has become not only useless to me but hateful. But it may be useful to someone." And he moved his jaw impatiently, because of the ceaseless, gnawing toothache, which even prevented him from speaking with the expression he desired.

"You'll be reborn spiritually, this I predict," said Sergei Ivanovich, who was moved. "To liberate our brothers from the yoke of oppression is a cause worth dying for or living for. May God grant you success in your deeds and peace in your heart," he added, and he extended his hand.

Vronsky clasped Sergei Ivanovich's extended hand firmly.

"Yes, as a weapon of combat I'm still of some use, but as a man I am a wreck," he said slowly.

The gnawing pain in one of his large teeth caused his mouth to fill with saliva, interfering with his speech. He fell silent, staring at the wheels of a tender that rolled slowly and smoothly along the rails.

And suddenly another feeling, not pain but of general acute emotional discomfort, made him forget his toothache momentarily. At the sight of the tender and the rails, and under the influence of his conversation with an acquaintance he had not seen since the catastrophe, he suddenly recalled *her*, or rather what still remained of her when he rushed like a madman into the railroad station. There on a table lay the bloodstained body, shamelessly exposed to the view of strangers, and still bearing ample signs of recent life. The unharmed head was thrown back, its heavy braids and waving hair gathered around the temples. Frozen on her beautiful face, with its half-opened rosy mouth, was an expression, strange and pathetic around her lips, but terrifying in the immobile, open eyes, an expression that seemed to be saying those frightening words—that he would suffer remorse—she had said to him in their quarrel.

And he tried to recall her as she had been, when, also at a railroad station, he met her for the first time, mysterious, beautiful, loving, seeking and offering happiness, and not cruel and vengeful as he remembered her at the last moment. He tried to recall his happiest moments with her, but those moments had been poisoned forever. He remembered only the triumphant fulfillment of her threat of remorse, needed by no one, but indelible. He no longer felt the toothache, and sobs distorted his face.

After passing the heap of sacks twice and regaining control of himself, he calmly turned to Sergei Ivanovich:

"Have you had any new reports since yesterday? Yes, they were repulsed for the third time, but a decisive battle is expected for tomorrow."

And after exchanging a few more remarks about Milan's proclamation as King and about the important consequences this act might have, they left, after the second bell, each for his own car.

6

UNCERTAIN OF THE time when he would be departing from Moscow, Sergei Ivanovich did not wire his brother to send to meet him at the station. Levin was not at home when, at about midday, Katavasov and Sergei Ivanovich, dark as pitch from the dust, drove up to the porch of the Pokrovskoe house in a small taranta they had hired at the station. Kitty, who was sitting on the balcony with her father and sister, recognized her brother-in-law and ran down to meet him.

"Aren't you ashamed not to have let us know?" she said, extending her hand to Sergei Ivanovich and offering her forehead to be kissed.

"We had a very pleasant journey and didn't want to inconvenience you," replied Sergei Ivanovich. "I'm so dusty that I'm afraid to touch you. I was so busy, I didn't know when I'd be able to leave. And," he said with a smile, "you, as always, enjoy your serene happiness in your untroubled backwater, outside the currents. And here is our friend Fiodor Vasilich, who has come at last."

"No, I'm not a Negro. I'll wash, then I'll look like a man," said Katavasov with his usual jocularity, extending his hand, and his teeth shone with particular brightness in contrast with his black, smiling face.

"Kostia will be very glad. He went to the farmstead. He should be back soon."

"Always busy with his farm. Truly, an untroubled backwater," said Katavasov. "And we in the city are all wrapped up in the Serbian war. Well, how does my friend look at it? Probably not exactly as others do."

"No, as everyone else, I believe," said Kitty, looking at Sergei Ivanovich with slight embarrassment. "Well, I'll send for him. By the way, Papa is visiting us. He recently arrived from abroad."

And after leaving instructions to send for Levin, to permit the dust-covered guests to wash—one in the study and the other in Dolly's large room—and to prepare lunch for the guests, she ran up to the balcony, availing herself of her right to move rapidly, something she had been deprived of during her pregnancy.

"It's Sergei Ivanovich and Katavasov, a professor," she said.

"Oh, it's too hot for such types," said the prince.

"No, Papa, he's very nice, and Kostia is very fond of him," said Kitty with a smile, as though pleading with him, when she noticed the mocking expression on his face.

"Oh, it's all right with me."

"And you, darling, go to them," said Kitty to her sister, "and entertain them. They saw Stiva at the station; he's fine. And I'll run over to Mitia. It would happen that I haven't fed him since morning. He's awake by now and probably screaming." And feeling the flow of her milk, she quickly went to the nursery.

Actually it was not a guess (her bond with the baby had not been broken yet), but by the flow of the milk within her, she knew unerringly of his need for food.

She knew he was screaming even before she reached the nursery. And indeed, he was screaming. She heard his voice and quickened her step. But the more rapidly she walked, the louder he screamed. His voice was strong, healthy, but hungry and impatient.

"Has it been long, nurse?" Kitty asked immediately, sitting down on a chair and getting ready to nurse the child. "Give him to me quickly. Oh, how slow you are, nurse! You can tie the bonnet later."

The baby screamed for his food frantically.

"But it must be done, little mother," said Agafia Mikhailovna, who was almost always present in the nursery. "He must be dressed properly. Goo, goo," she sang over him, paying no attention to his mother.

The nurse took the child to his mother. Agafia Mikhailovna followed, her face suffused with tenderness.

"He knows me, he does. Believe me, Katerina Aleksandrovna, he recognized me!" said Agafia Mikhailovna, trying to outshout the child.

But Kitty did not listen to her. Her impatience grew as rapidly as the child's.

Due to their impatience, the affair proceeded slowly. The baby grasped at what it was not supposed to and fretted.

At last, after a desperate choking scream and some fruitless sucking, things worked out and both mother and child simultaneously calmed down and remained tranquil.

"But, poor thing, he's wet with perspiration," Kitty whispered, feeling the baby. "Well, why do you think that he recognizes you?" she added, looking sidelong at the child's eyes, which looked roguishly, it seemed to her, from underneath the bonnet, which had slid down, at the little cheeks, puffing evenly, and at the circular gestures of his little hand with its rosy palm.

"It can't be! If he recognized anyone, it would be me," said Kitty with a smile, in reply to Agafia Mikhailovna's assurances.

She smiled because, though she said that he could not recognize anyone, in her heart she knew that not only did he recognize Agafia Mikhailovna but that he knew and understood everything and also knew and understood much of what no one knew, and that she, his mother, had found out and had begun to understand only through him. To Agafia Mikhailovna, to the nurse, to his grandfather, and even to his father, Mitia was a living creature who required only physical care. But for his mother he had long been a spiritual creature with whom a complex spiritual relationship had already been established.

"Well, when he wakes up, with God's help, you'll see it for yourself. As I do this, he'll light up, the darling. He'll light up like a bright day," said Agafia Mikhailovna.

"All right, we'll see then," whispered Kitty. "Now go; he's falling asleep."

7

AGAFIA MIKHAILOVNA LEFT on tiptoe. The nurse pulled down the shades, chased away two flies from under the muslin canopy of the child's bed, and a hornet that was beating against the window pane, and then sat down, fanning mother and child with a withered birch branch.

"What a hot day! Would that the Lord gave us some rain," she said.

"Yes, sh-sh, sh-sh . . ." was Kitty's only reply as she rocked gently and tenderly pressed Mitia's plump little arm, which seemed to have a thread tied around its wrist, and which he kept waving faintly as he opened and closed his eyes. This little arm troubled Kitty: she wanted to kiss it, but was afraid to do so lest she awaken the child. The little arm at last stopped moving, and the eyes closed. Occasionally, to continue what he had been doing, the baby raised his long curved eyelashes and glanced at his mother, his eyes appearing black and moist in the semidarkness. The nurse stopped fanning and dozed. The rumble of the old prince's voice and Katavasov's loud laughter could be heard from upstairs.

They've probably become involved in a conversation in my absence, thought Kitty, but still it's a pity Kostia isn't here. He probably stopped again at the apiary. Though I'm lonely when he goes there frequently, I'm glad for him. It distracts him. He's more cheerful now than he was in the spring. He was so gloomy and suffered so much then that I began to worry about him. "And how funny he is!" she whispered with a smile.

She knew what was troubling her husband. It was his lack of faith. If she had been asked whether she thought that in the future life her husband would be condemned if he persisted in his unbelief, she would have had to admit that he would be condemned. Nevertheless, his unbelief did not make her unhappy. And she, who admitted that there could be no salvation for an unbeliever, and who loved her husband's soul more than anything in this world, smiled as she thought about his lack of faith and said to herself that he was funny.

Why does he keep reading those philosophy books all year long? she wondered. If it's all explained in those books, he could understand it. But if what they say isn't true, then why read them? He says himself that he'd like to believe. Then why doesn't he? Maybe it's because he thinks too much. And he thinks so much because he's alone all the time. Always alone, alone. He can't talk about all these things with us. I think he'll be glad to have these guests, especially Katavasov. He likes to argue with him, she thought, but immediately diverted her train of thought to the problem of where to place Katavasov comfortably for the night, whether in a separate room or together with Sergei Ivanovich. And here a thought suddenly occurred to her, one that made her start with agitation and even caused her to disturb Mitia, for which he gave her a stern look. I don't think the laundress has brought the linen yet, and there's no clean linen for the guests. If I don't attend to it, Agafia Mikhailovna may make Sergei Ivanovich's bed with linen that's already been used; and at the mere thought of it Kitty felt the blood rush to her face.

Yes, I'll take care of it, she decided, and returning to her former thoughts, she recalled that there was something important and close to her heart that had not yet been thought through. She tried to remember what it was. Oh yes, Kostia the unbeliever, she remembered, smiling again.

Some unbeliever! I'd rather have him be the way he is than be like Madame Stahl, or as I wanted to be when I was abroad. No, he'll never pretend.

And she vividly recalled a recent manifestation of his goodness. Two weeks earlier, Dolly had received a contrite letter from Stepan Arkadievich. He implored her to save his honor by selling her estate so that he might pay his debts. Dolly was despondent, hated her husband, felt contempt for him, pitied him, decided to divorce him, to refuse, but ended by agreeing to sell her part of the estate. Later Kitty could not but smile with admiration as she remembered how her husband had felt embarrassed, how he had repeatedly made awkward attempts to solve this matter, in which he took a great interest, and how, at last, as the only solution which would help Dolly without hurting her, he had suggested to Kitty that she give her her part of the estate, something of which she had not thought before.

He an unbeliever? she thought. With his heart, with his fear of hurting anyone, even a child! Everything for others, nothing for himself. Sergei Ivanovich candidly believes that it's Kostia's duty to take care of his affairs. His sister, too. And now Dolly and her children are under his care. And all those moujiks who come to him every day, as though it's his duty to serve them.

"Yes, may you be just like your father, just like him," she said, handing Mitia to the nurse and touching his little cheek with her lips.

8

FROM THE MOMENT when, at the sight of his beloved brother dying, Levin for the first time envisaged the problems of life and death in the light of his new, as he called them, convictions, which from the age of twenty until thirty-four, unnoticed by him, had supplanted the beliefs of his childhood and youth, from that moment he was frightened not so much by death as by the idea of living without the slightest knowledge of what life was, whence it came, and what its purpose was. The organism and its decay, the indestructibility of matter, the law of conservation of energy, evolution—these were the words that had supplanted his former faith. These words and the ideas related to them served well for intellectual purposes; but in actual life they were useless, and Levin suddenly felt like a man who had exchanged a warm fur coat for a muslin shirt. When exposed to frost for the first time, such a man becomes convinced beyond doubt, not by his reasoning but by his whole being, that he might as well be naked and that he will unavoidably suffer a cruel death.

From that moment on, though he did not realize it and continued his former way of life, Levin never stopped fearing his own ignorance.

In addition, he felt vaguely that what he called his convictions not only displayed his ignorance but were actually a state of mind in which attainment of the knowledge he needed was impossible.

At first, his marriage and the new joys and new duties completely stifled these thoughts. But lately, after the birth of the child, while he lived in Moscow in idleness, Levin had been confronted, with increasing frequency and intensified persistence, by a problem that demanded solution.

The problem, as he saw it, was the following: If I don't accept the answers offered by Christianity to the problems life presents to me, which answers do I accept? And in the entire store of his convictions he failed completely to find not only answers but anything resembling an answer.

He was like a man who looks for food in stores that deal in toys or guns.

Involuntarily, and without being aware of it, he now looked in every book, in every conversation, at every person, for a connection with these problems and for the solutions they might offer.

In this connection, he was most surprised and disturbed to see that most of those of his circle and his age who had changed their former beliefs for the same new ideas as he had did not see anything wrong in this and were completely contented and composed. Therefore, in addition to the main problem, Levin was beset by others: are those people sincere? could they be pretending? or perhaps they perceived in a different way and more clearly than he the answers science gives to the problems that preoccupied him? And he carefully studied both the opinions of these people and the books which contained these answers.

One thing he had learned since he had become absorbed in these problems was that he was mistaken in still believing, as he had believed in his youth as a university student, that religion had outlived its era and no longer really existed. Every one of the worthy men close to him had faith. The old prince, and Lvov, of whom he had grown so fond, and Sergei

Ivanovich, and all the women believed, and his wife believed as he had in his early childhood, and ninety-nine per cent of the Russian people, the people who inspired him with the greatest respect, had faith.

The other thing was that, after reading many books, he had become convinced that those who shared his views learned nothing from them, and without trying to solve the problems he sought answers to, they simply ignored them. He felt that he could not go on living without finding an answer to these problems, but they sought answers to completely different problems, problems that could not possibly interest him, such as the evolution of organisms, the mechanical interpretation of the soul, and so on.

In addition, during his wife's confinement something unusual happened to him. He, the unbeliever, began to pray, and at the moment when he was praying, he believed. But that moment passed and he had no place in his life for the feeling of that moment.

He could not admit that then he had known the truth and that now he erred because as soon as he began to think calmly about it, all his arguments fell apart. Nor could he admit that he had erred then, because he cherished that emotional state, and to consider it a state of weakness would mean to defile it. He was in a distressing state of disagreement with himself, and he exerted every effort to overcome it.

9

THESE THOUGHTS WEARIED and tormented him with varying intensity, but they never left him. He read and thought, and the more he read and thought the farther he felt he was from the goal he was seeking.

Lately, in Moscow and in the country, having convinced himself that he would find no answer from the materialists, he had been reading and rereading Plato, Spinoza, Kant, Schelling, Hegel, and Schopenhauer, philosophers whose interpretation of life was not derived from the materialistic point of view.

It seemed to him that his thinking brought results when he read or when he formulated, himself, refutations of other theories, particularly the materialistic; but when he read or formulated solutions to problems, this invariably led to one and the same result. Following a given definition of vague terms such as "spirit," "will," "freedom," and "substance," and deliberately letting himself be caught in the verbal trap set by the philosophers or by himself, he seemed to begin to understand something. But as soon as he lost the thread of this artificial thought process, and then, turning back from life itself, tried to regain what had given him satisfaction when he had been following that thread—then the entire artificial structure fell apart like a house of cards and it became clear that the structure had been erected just by reshuffling the same words, without heed to something that was more important in life than reason.

Once, while reading Schopenhauer, he substituted the term "love" for "will," and this new philosophy comforted him for the one or two days that he clung to it. But it, too, fell apart when he later looked at it from the viewpoint of real life; it appeared to be like the muslin shirt, unsuited for giving warmth.

His brother Sergei Ivanovich advised him to read the theological works of Khomiakov. Levin read the second volume of Khomiakov's works, and in spite of the author's polemical, refined, and witty style, which at first repelled him, he was deeply impressed by his theology. In the beginning, he was struck by the idea that the understanding of religious truth had not been granted to one man but only to a body of men joined in love—the church. He was glad to think how much easier it was to gain faith in a church—which existed and remained alive, which was the object of all men's beliefs, which was headed by God and therefore was holy and infallible; how much easier it was to receive faith from the church, faith in God, the Creation, the Fall, and Redemption, than to begin with God, the remote, mysterious God, with Creation, and so on. But after reading a history of the church by a Roman Catholic writer, and a history of the church by an Orthodox writer, and seeing that each church in its very essence infallible, rejected the other, he was disappointed in Khomiakov's theology as well, and this edifice crumbled into dust as the philosophical structures had.

All that spring he was not himself, and he lived through terrible moments.

I cannot live without knowing what I am and why I'm

here. But I cannot know it; therefore I cannot live, Levin said to himself.

In the infinity of time, in the infinity of matter, in the infinity of space, there appears an organism, a bubble, which will hold for a while and will burst, and that bubble is myself.

It was a distressing fallacy, but it was the sole, final product of ages of man's intellectual efforts in this direction.

It was the ultimate postulate, used as the foundation of almost every branch of man's intellectual pursuits. It was the dominating belief, and out of all the others Levin unconsciously adopted this interpretation as the most logical one, without himself knowing how and when he had done so.

But it was not only a fallacy, it was a brutal joke on the part of some evil force, a wicked and repulsive force, to which one ought not to submit.

One had to free himself from this force. And the way to free himself was within the reach of every man. One had to end this dependence on evil. And there was one means for doing it—death.

And, though he was a happy and healthy family man, Levin several times was so close to sucide that he hid away a length of rope so that he might not hang himself, and he became afraid to carry his gun lest he shoot himself.

But Levin did not shoot or hang himself, and continued to live.

10

WHEN LEVIN considered what he was and what he lived for, he could find no answer and was driven to despair. But when he stopped asking himself these questions, it was as though he knew what he was and what he lived for, because he acted and lived resolutely and purposefully, and lately he had lived even more resolutely and purposefully than before.

When he returned to the country in the beginning of June, he resumed his usual occupations. Farming, his dealings with the moujiks and neighbors, household duties, his sister's and brother's affairs, for which he was responsible, his relationship with his wife, his relatives, care of the child, his new hobby of beekeeping, in which he had been absorbed since last spring, occupied all his time.

He was interested in these occupations not because he justified them by some set of general principles, as he had previously done. On the contrary, now after on the one hand suffering disappointment from the failure of everything he had formerly undertaken for the general welfare, and on the other hand being so deeply absorbed in his thoughts and the very multitude of his occupations, which crowded in on him from all sides, he abandoned all considerations of the general welfare, and his occupations interested him only because he believed that it was his duty to do what he was doing, and that he could not act otherwise.

Formerly (this had begun practically in childhood and continued to his maturity), when he had tried to do something for the benefit of everyone, of mankind, of Russia, of the entire village, he noticed that thoughts of doing it were pleasant but work itself never progressed. He was not absolutely certain that the undertaking was really necessary, and the work itself, which had seemed so immense in the beginning, gradually decreased and finally stopped. But now, after his marriage, he began to devote his time increasingly to his own interests, and though no longer experiencing any joy whatsoever when he was thinking of his work, he felt certain that what he did was needed, and he saw that it was progressing much more than before and that it was gaining in magnitude.

As though against his will, he now cut more and more deeply into the earth, like a plow, so that he could no longer withdraw without leaving a furrow.

There could be no doubt that the family had to live the way the parents and grandparents had been accustomed to, that it had to be brought up as they had been, and that the children had to be reared according to the same standards. This was as urgent as it is to have dinner when one is hungry. And to be able to accomplish this, just as to be able to provide for a dinner, the farm in Pokrovskoe had to be conducted in such a way that it brought a profit. Just as it was his duty to pay a debt, so it was to preserve his ancestral estate with such care that when his son received it from him as his patrimony, he would be as grateful to him as Levin had been to his own father for everything he had built and planted. Therefore it was his duty not to lease his land, but to work it himself, to breed cattle, to fertilize the fields, to plant trees.

He could not help but take care of the affairs of Sergei Ivanovich, of his sister, of all the moujiks who came to him for advice, having become accustomed to doing so, as one cannot help but take care of a child who is under his protection. He had to attend to the comforts of his sister-in-law and her children, who had been invited to stay with them, and of his wife and his own child, and he had to spend with them at least a small part of each day.

And all this, together with hunting and his new interest in beekeeping, filled Levin's entire life, which when he thought about it had no meaning for him.

Moreover, Levin not only knew distinctly *what* he had to do, he knew as distinctly *how* it had to be done as well as the respective value of each task.

He knew that he had to hire laborers as cheaply as possible; but, though it would be very profitable, he was not to hold them in peonage by advancing them less money than they were entitled to get. It was right to sell straw to the moujiks when they were short of fodder, though he felt sorry for them; but the inn and the saloon, though they brought profit, had to be closed. For illegal tree felling he had to fine as heavily as possible, but no fine was to be exacted if the peasants inadvertently drove their cattle into his fields, and though this annoyed the watchmen and undermined their authority, it was only right to return stray cattle to their owners.

It was right to lend money to Piotr, who paid the usurer ten per cent a month, and to release him from his debt; but for the moujiks who were in default of their payment of rent, he ought not reduce it nor extend the time of payment. He was obliged not to forgive the steward for having left a meadow unmowed, letting the grass go to waste; on the other hand, the eighty dessiatines on which a young forest had been planted were not to be mowed. He was in no position to be lenient with the laborer who had left for home at the height of the working season because his father had died, and however sorry he felt for him he had to fine him for the precious time he had missed; on the other hand, it was impossible not to give monthly stipends to the old house servants who were no longer useful for anything.

Levin also knew that on returning home he first had to go to see his wife who was not well; but the moujiks who had been waiting for him for three hours could wait a little longer. He knew that in spite of all the pleasure hiving a swarm gave him, he had to forego this pleasure, leaving the old man to do it without him, and he himself had to talk to the moujiks who had sought him out in the apiary.

Whether he was acting well or badly he did not know, and not only did he now refrain from trying to prove either point but eschewed talking and thinking about it.

Reasoning led him to doubts and prevented him from seeing what should and should not be done. But when he did not think but acted, he constantly felt that an infallible judge was present in his heart, deciding which of two possible actions was the better and which the worse; and as soon as he did not act as he should have, he knew it immediately.

Thus he lived, without knowing and without seeing any possibility of knowing what he was and what he lived for in this world. He was troubled by this ignorance so deeply that he feared that he might commit suicide, and at the same time he steadfastly blazed his personal, well-defined trail through life.

11

SERGEI IVANOVICH arrived at Pokrovskoe on one of Levin's most troubled days.

It was the busiest time of the season, when all the peasants abandon themselves to their work in an unusually intense spirit of self-sacrifice, one that does not reveal itself under any other conditions of life and that would be highly prized if those who displayed this quality prized it themselves, if it were not repeated every year, and if the consequences of this intensity were not so ordinary.

To mow and to reap rye and oats, to cart it away, to finish mowing the meadows, to plow the fallow land twice, to thresh, to plant winter crops: all this seems simple and ordinary. But to accomplish all this in time, it is imperative that all villagers, young and old, work during these three or four weeks without a stop, three times as hard as usual, on a diet of kvas, onions and black bread, carting the sheaves, threshing at night, and sleeping no more than two or three hours a day. And this happens in Russia every year.

Levin, who had spent most of his life in the country in a close relationship with the peasants, always felt during the working season that this general excitement communicated itself to him.

Early in the morning he rode out to see the first rye being sown and the oats carted and stacked and returned home when his wife and sister-in-law were beginning their day. He had coffee with them and then walked to the farmstead, where they were going to start a recently installed threshing machine to prepare seed for planting.

All that day, while he talked to the steward and the moujiks, and at home to his wife, to Dolly, to the children, and to his father-in-law, Levin kept thinking of the one thing that occupied him in addition to the cares of the farm. In everything he sought a clue to his question, "Who am I really? where am I? and why am I here?"

Standing in the cool shade of the newly thatched barn with its wattled walls of hazel, its fragrant leaves still unshed, pressing against the joists of freshly stripped aspen under the thatch, Levin gazed out through the open door, which was filled with the dense, bitter, dry, pirouetting dust raised by the threshing, or at the grass around the threshing floor, lit by the hot sun, and at the fresh straw that had just been brought in from the barn. Or he watched the white-breasted swallows with their mottled heads, flapping their wings and chirping, lingering in the doorway in their flight toward the roof of the barn. Or he observed the people who bustled about in the dark, dusty threshing barn. And he was occupied with strange thoughts.

What purpose does all this serve? he thought. Why am I standing here, making them work? Why do they rush about, trying to show me their eagerness? Why does this old woman, Matriona, my acquaintance, wear herself out? (I treated her when a beam fell on her during a fire) he thought, looking at the gaunt woman who was raking grain, stepping with difficulty on the rough, hard barn floor in her bare, tanned feet. She recovered then, but perhaps one of these days or maybe ten years from now she'll be buried, and nothing will remain of her, or of that smartly dressed woman in the red skirt, who with such deft and gentle movements is beating the chaff from the ears. They'll bury her, too, as they'll soon bury that skewbald gelding, he thought, looking at the horse, which painfully strained his belly, breathing rapidly through extended nostrils while he trod a sloping wheel moving underneath him. And they'll bury him, too, as well as Fiodor, who loads the machine, his curly beard full of chaff and his shirt torn at his white shoulder. He unties the sheaves, gives orders, shouts at the women, and with quick movements adjusts the belt on the flywheel. And, what's more important, they'll bury not only them but me as well, and nothing will remain. What's the purpose?

He pondered this and at the same time looked at his watch to see how much threshing had been accomplished in one hour. He had to know this in order to be able to make the daily assignment.

Almost an hour has gone by, and we've just started the third shock, thought Levin, and he walked over to the loader. Trying to outshout the roar of the machine, he ordered him to load more slowly.

"You're loading too rapidly, Fiodor! You see, it chokes, and the work slows down. Space it out."

Fiodor, black with the dust that clung to his perspiring face, shouted something in reply but still did not do as Levin wanted.

Levin came over to the drum, pushed Fiodor aside, and himself began to load.

After working until the peasant's dinner, which was not long in coming, he went out of the threshing barn, followed by Fiodor. They started a conversation, stopping near a neat yellow stack of rye that lay on the floor waiting to be threshed.

Fiodor was from a remote village, the same one where Levin had formerly let his land on a cooperative basis. Now he let it to the innkeeper.

Levin entered into a conversation with Fiodor about that land and asked him whether Platon, a rich and honest moujik from that village, would like to rent that land next year.

"The price is high. Platon would gain nothing from it, Konstantin Dmitrievich," replied the moujik, removing some grain from his perspiring chest.

"But why does Kirillov make it pay?"

"Mitiukha" (the moujik's contemptuous name for the innkeeper) "will always make his profit. He'll squeeze a man dry, but he'll get what he wants. He has no pity on his fellow Christian. But would Uncle Fokanych" (as he referred to the old Platon) "ever think of fleecing anyone? He'll lend money and sometimes cancel the debt. Or he won't collect all of it. He acts like a man should."

"Why should he cancel a debt?"

"Well, you see, there are all kinds of people. One lives for his own needs only, like that Mitiukha, thinking only of his belly, but Fokanych is an upright man. He lives for his soul. He remembers that there is a God."

"What do you mean he remembers that there is a God? How does he live for his soul?" Levin almost shouted.

"You know, by truth, by God's law. There are all kinds of people. Take you, for instance; you wouldn't wrong a man, either . . ."

"Well, goodbye!" said Levin, choking with excitement. He turned, took his walking stick, and hastily left for home. At the moujik's words that Fokanych lived for his soul, by truth, by God's law, a host of vague but important thoughts seemed to have broken out from their confinement, and all of them rushed toward a single goal, whirled about in his mind, blinding him with their light.

12

LEVIN STRODE along the highway, his attention drawn not so much to his thoughts (he could not yet distinguish them clearly) as to his emotional state, one he had never experienced before.

The words the moujik had spoken affected his soul like a spark of electricity, suddenly transfiguring and joining into one a whole host of uncoordinated, ineffective, separate thoughts that never ceased to occupy him. Without noticing it, he had been occupied with these thoughts even while speaking about leasing the land.

He was conscious of something new within his heart, and he was delighted to feel it, though he did not yet know what it was.

To live not for one's own needs but for God. For what God? And what could be more senseless that what he said? He said that we must not live for our own needs, in other words, we must not live for what we understand, what interests us, what we like, but that we must live for something incomprehensible, for God, whom no one can understand nor define. What is it then? Have I failed to understand Fiodor's meaningless words? Or having understood them, have I doubted their validity? Have I decided that they were foolish, vague and inexact?

No, I understood, and exactly the way he does; I understood it completely and more clearly than I have understood anything else in my life, and never in my life did I or could I doubt it. And not I alone but everyone in the world understands completely just this, and on this alone everyone has no doubts and always agrees.

Fiodor says that Kirillov, the innkeeper, lives for his belly. This is understandable and reasonable. As rational beings, all of us cannot help but live for our bellies. And suddenly the same Fiodor says that it's bad to live for one's belly, that one must live for truth, for God, and with this much of a hint I understand him! And I, and millions of others who lived in former ages and who live now, the moujiks, the poor in spirit, and the wise men who have thought and written about this subject, who say in their vague words the same things, we all agree on this one thing: what we live for and what is right. I and all mankind know one thing only, we know it definitely, incontrovertibly and clearly, and that is something that can't be explained by reason because it's beyond reason, it has no cause and can't have any consequences.

If goodness results from a cause, it's no longer goodness; if it has a consequence, leads to a reward, it isn't goodness then either. It means that goodness is beyond the law of cause and effect.

And this is exactly what I know, and what we all know.

Yet I've been looking for miracles, I was disappointed that I couldn't witness a miracle that would have convinced me. But here's that miracle, the only possible one—it always exists, it surrounds me on all sides, but I didn't notice.

What miracle could be greater than this?

Is it possible that I've found the solution to everything? Is it possible that now my suffering has come to an end? thought Levin, striding along the dusty road, conscious neither of heat nor of fatigue and feeling that his long suffering had come to an end. It was such a joyous feeling that he could scarcely believe it. He was choked with emotion, and lacking the strength to go further, he left the highway for the wood and sat down on the unmowed grass in the shade of some aspen trees. He removed his hat from his perspiring head, and

resting on his elbow, he lay in the lush, full-grown fores
grass.

Yes, I must collect myself and think it over, he thought
looking intently at the untroddened grass before him and
watching the movement of a small green beetle, which wa
climbing up a blade of couch grass and whose way wa
blocked by the leaf of a goutwort. I must start from the be
ginning, he said to himself, pushing the leaf of the goutwor
out of the beetle's way and bending another blade so that the
beetle might cross over to it. What makes me so happy
What have I discovered?

Formerly I said that in my body, in this grass, or in the
body of that beetle (look, it refused to cross over to the
other blade, it spread its wings and flew away) an exchange
of matter takes place in accordance with the laws of physics
chemistry, and physiology. And in all of us, in the asper
trees, and the clouds and nebulae, a process of evolution goe
on. An evolution from what? And into what? An endless evolu
tion and struggle? . . . As though there could be any kind o
direction and struggle within infinity? And I wondered that
in spite of my most concentrated mental efforts in that direc
tion, the meaning of life, the meaning of my motives and
longings and my endeavors, hadn't been revealed to me. Bu
within me the meaning of my motives is so clear that I've
always been guided by it, and I was surprised and happy
when the moujik expressed it to me as "one must live for God
for his soul."

I haven't discovered anything new. I've only learned wha
I knew. I've come to understand the force that gave me life
not only in the past but now, too. I've freed myself from
deceit; I've found the Master.

And he briefly reviewed the whole course of his thought
for the past two years, starting with the clear, obvious though
of death at the sight of his beloved, hopelessly sick brother

When he had understood then, clearly and for the firs
time, that nothing awaited anyone, including himself, othe
than suffering, death, and eternal oblivion, he decided tha
one could not go on living that way, that one must either find
a meaning in life so that it would no longer appear as a
cruel mockery on the part of some devil, or he must shoo
himself.

But he had done neither but had continued to live, t
reason and to feel, and had even married during that time

and experienced much joy and happiness so long as he did not think of the meaning of his life.

What did it mean then? It meant that he acted correctly but reasoned incorrectly.

He lived (without being conscious of it) in accordance with the spiritual truths he had imbibed with his mother's milk, but in his thinking he not only refused to acknowledge them but carefully avoided them.

It was clear to him now that he could go on living only thanks to the beliefs with which he had been brought up.

What would I have been, how would I have lived my life if I hadn't had these beliefs, if I hadn't known that one must live for God and not for his own needs? I would have become a robber, a liar, a murderer. None of the things that are the main joys of my life would have existed for me. And, exercising his imagination to the utmost, he still could not visualize the beastly creature he would have been if he had not known what he lived for.

I've been looking for an answer to my question. But reason couldn't provide the answer—it's inadequate for the task. Life itself gave me the answer, in my awareness of what's right and what's wrong. And I didn't acquire this knowledge myself; it was given to me as to anyone else, *given*, because there was no source to take it from.

How did I learn it? Was it by reasoning that I found out I must love my neighbor and not strangle him? It was told to me in my childhood, and I was happy to believe it because what was told me had been in my heart. And how was it discovered? Not by reason. Reason discovered the struggle for survival and the law that demands that I strangle anyone who interferes with the satisfaction of my desires. That's what reason teaches. But that one must love his neighbor, reason couldn't reveal, because that is unreasonable.

Yes, pride! he said to himself, turning on his stomach and trying to tie a few grass stems into a knot without breaking them.

And not just the pride of the mind but the stupidity of the mind. And mainly its guile, indeed, the guile of the mind. Indeed, the fraudulence of the mind, he repeated.

13

AND LEVIN recalled a recent scene involving Dolly and her children. The children, left alone, had begun to roast raspberries over candles and to pour streams of milk into their mouths. When their mother caught them doing this, she tried, in Levin's presence, to explain to them how much work the adults had to perform to create what they were destroying, to remind them that the work was being performed for their sake, that if they broke the cups, they would have nothing to drink their tea from, and that if they spilled their milk they would have no nourishment and would die of hunger.

Levin was struck by the calm, dispirited mistrust with which the children listened to their mother's words. They were only disappointed that they had to give up a game they enjoyed, and they did not believe a single word their mother said. And they could not believe it because they were unable to imagine how great was the number of the things they used and so could not realize that what they were destroying was the same as what they lived by.

It comes by itself, they thought, and there's nothing interesting or important about it, because it's always been and always will be. And always the same. We don't have to think about it; it's always prepared for us. But we want to make up something new, our own invention. That's why we decided to put raspberries in a cup and roast them over a candle, and pour streams of milk into each other's mouths. It's fun, and new, and it's no worse than drinking from a cup.

Don't we do the same thing, he thought, continuing his meditation, haven't I done it, when we seek by means of our reason to discover the purpose of the forces of nature and the meaning of man's life?

And don't all philosophical theories do the same when, by intellectual means, which to man is an alien and unnatural means, they lead him to the knowledge of what he has long known and knows so unerringly that without it he couldn't live? Can't it be clearly seen in the process of the development of each philosopher's theory that he knows beforehand what the chief meaning of life is, and knows it with the same certainty as the moujik Fiodor and no more clearly than he? And doesn't he merely by doubtful intellectual means try to come back to what everyone knows?

Well, suppose we leave the children to their own resources, have them make their own dishes, milk the cows, and so on. Would they think of playing pranks? They would die of hunger. Well then, suppose we are left on our own, with our passions, our ideas, without knowledge of the one God and Creator! Or without understanding what is good, without knowing what is morally wrong.

Well, try to build anything without such understanding! We only destroy because we are spiritually satiated. Just like the children!

Where did it come from, this joyous understanding I share with the moujik, which alone gives me peace of mind? Where did I get it?

I, who was brought up as a believer in God, a Christian, who have filled my entire life with all the spiritual blessings Christianity has given me, who have been filled to the brim by these blessings and live by them, I, without understanding them, am destroying them, like the children. In other words, I want to destroy what I live by. But when an important moment in life arrives, I, like the children when they are cold and hungry, come to Him, and even less than the children, who are reprimanded by their mother for their pranks, do I believe that my childish attempts to be unreasonable, on account of the abundance of things given to me, will be held against me.

Yes, what I know, I don't know by reason but because it's been given to me, been revealed to me, and I know it with my heart, through my faith in the main teachings the church proclaims.

The church! the church! repeated Levin. He turned over, and leaning on his elbow, gazed into the distance at a herd of cattle coming down to the river on the opposite bank.

But can I believe in everything the church teaches? he thought, testing himself and trying to remember everything that might upset his present peace. He deliberately recalled those teachings of the church that had always seemed to him particularly strange and hard to accept. The Creation? And how did I explain existence? Was it just by the fact that it existed? Or have I left it unexplained? The devil and sin? And how do I explain the nature of evil? . . . The Redeemer? . . .

But I know and can know nothing, nothing at all, except what I, together with all others, have been told.

And it seemed to him now that there was not a single tenet of the church that disagreed with the main principle, that man's only goal is to believe in God, in goodness.

For each tenet of the church could be substituted the belief that one must serve truth and not his own needs. And each of these tenets not only did not violate that belief but was essential for the great miracle that always unfolds on this earth. Through this miracle every man, together with millions of the most diverse people, wise men and fools, children and old people, everyone—the moujik, Lvov, Kitty, beggars and kings—is enabled to understand distinctly one and the same thing and to create the spiritual life that alone is worth living for and that alone we value.

Lying on his back, he now looked up at the cloudless sky. Don't I know that this is infinite space and not a spherical vault? But no matter how much I squint and strain my eyes, I cannot see it except as spherical and finite, and though I know that space is infinite, I'm indisputably right when I see a solid blue vault, more right than when I strain to look beyond it.

Levin now stopped thinking, and it was as though he were listening to mysterious voices, which both joyously and seriously conversed with each other on some subject.

Can this be faith? he thought, afraid to believe his good fortune. I thank you, O Lord! he said, swallowing the sobs that rose within him and drying with both hands the tears that filled his eyes.

14

LEVIN LOOKED straight ahead, saw the herd and then his small cart, drawn by Voronoy, and his coachman, who rode up to the herd and exchanged a few words with the herdsman. Then he heard the sound of the wheels and of the snorting of the well-fed horse as the cart drove closer. But he was so deeply engrossed in his thoughts that he did not even wonder why the coachman had come.

He thought of it only when the coachman drove right up to him and called him.

"The mistress sent me. Your brother has arrived with another gentleman."

Levin sat down in the cart and took the reins.

As though awakened from a dream, Levin was long in coming to himself. He looked at the well-fed horse, lathered on its thighs and neck where the straps had rubbed against its skin, looked at the coachman Ivan, who was sitting next to him, and remembered that he had been expecting his brother, that his long absence was probably worrying his wife, and tried to guess who the guest was who had arrived with his brother. And his brother, his wife, and the unknown guest appeared to him differently than before. It seemed to him that his relationships with all people would be different now.

There will no longer be that aloofness that always existed between my brother and myself; there will be no more arguments; there will be no more quarrels with Kitty; I'll be kind and attentive to the guest, whoever he is; and with the peasants, with Ivan—everything will be different.

Pulling on the reins to control the eager horse, which snorted with impatience and begged to be given free rein, Levin looked around at Ivan, who sat alongside him and, not knowing what to do with his hands now that they were free from work, constantly smoothed his shirt. Levin looked for a pretext to enter into a conversation with him. He wanted to say that Ivan should not have pulled the saddle so high, but it would sound like a rebuke, and he was seeking a friendly chat. But no other subject came to mind.

"Would you please drive to the right; there's a stump there," said the coachman, pulling at the rein which Levin was holding.

"Please leave it alone and don't try to teach me!" said Levin, annoyed by the coachman's interference. The interference annoyed him just as it usually did, and he was immediately sorry to see how erroneous was his assumption that his new spiritual state could at once change him in his dealings with reality.

When still a few hundred yards from his house, Levin saw Grisha and Tania running to meet him.

"Uncle Kostia! Mama is coming, too, and Grandpa and Sergei Ivanovich, and someone else," they shouted, climbing into the cart.

"Who is it?"

"A terrible man! And he swings his arms like this," said Tania, rising in the cart and mimicking Katavasov.

"Is he young or old?" asked Levin with a laugh, for Tania's performance reminded him of someone.

Oh, just as long as he's not an unpleasant man, thought Levin.

Only after he turned the corner of the road and saw the people who were coming in his direction did Levin recognize Katavasov in his straw hat, walking along, swinging his arms just as Tania had demonstrated.

Katavasov loved to discuss philosophy, of which he had acquired some knowledge from naturalists who had never actually studied it. And recently in Moscow, Levin had had frequent arguments with him.

And the first thing Levin remembered on recognizing him was one of those discussions in which Katavasov had evidently felt that he had proved his point.

No, I will by no means ever again argue or express my ideas thoughtlessly, he said to himself.

After alighting from the cart and greeting his brother and Katavasov, Levin inquired about his wife.

"She took Mitia over to Kolok." (This was the wood near the house.) "She wants to keep him there while it's so hot in the house," said Dolly.

Levin always tried to dissuade his wife from taking the child to the wood, for he thought it was dangerous, and this information displeased him.

"She carries him from place to place," said the prince, with a smile. "I advised her to take him to the icehouse."

"She wanted to go to the apiary. She thought you were there. We're going there," said Dolly.

"Well, what have you been doing?" asked Sergei Ivanovich, falling behind the others and taking a place alongside his brother.

"Nothing special. As always, busy with my farm," replied Levin. "Well, I hope you'll be able to stay a while. We have waited so long to see you."

"About two weeks. I have too much work to do in Moscow."

At these words, the eyes of the brothers met, and in spite of his usual eagerness, particularly now, to be on friendly and, more important, frank terms with his brother, Levin felt embarrassment when he looked at him. He lowered his eyes and did not know what to say.

Reviewing the subjects Sergei Ivanovich might like to discuss and that might distract him from the Serbian war and the Slav problem, at which Sergei Ivanovich had hinted when he mentioned his pressing work in Moscow, Levin inquired about Sergei Ivanovich's book.

"Well, has your book been reviewed?" he asked.

Sergei Ivanovich smiled at the pointed question.

"Nobody cares for it, and I least of all," he said. "Look, Daria Aleksandrovna, it's going to rain," he added, pointing with his umbrella to some little white clouds which appeared over the crowns of the aspen trees.

And these words were sufficient to re-establish the relationship between the brothers that though not hostile, was nevertheless cold, and that Levin was so eager to change.

Levin went over to Katavasov.

"How good of you to have decided to come," he said to him.

"I've long intended to. Now we'll have the chance to talk. Have you finished Spencer?"

"Not yet," said Levin. "Anyway I no longer need him."

"How is that? That's interesting. Why?"

"Because I'm now positive that neither in him nor in those like him will I find the answers to the problems that occupy me. Now. . . ."

But he was suddenly struck by the relaxed and gay expression on Katavasov's face, and he so deeply regretted that by these words he was obviously impairing his present emotional state that, remembering his intention, he stopped short.

"But we'll talk about it later," he added. "This is the way to the apiary, along this path," he told everyone.

As they walked along the narrow path, they came upon a small, uncut meadow, one part of which was completely covered by bright cowwheat, interspersed with numerous tall, dark green, full-grown bushes of hellebore. Levin placed his guests in the dark, cool shade of young aspen trees, on a bench and stumps prepared especially for those visitors to the apiary who were afraid of the bees, and he himself went into the cottage to bring bread, cucumbers, and honey for the children and adults.

Trying to make as few rapid movements as possible and listening to the bees, which flew past him more and more frequently, he walked along the path toward the cottage.

At the very entrance to the cottage a bee buzzed noisily as it became entangled in his beard, but he carefully set it free. On entering the darkened entrance hall, he took down his net from the wall, where it hung on a peg, put it on, put his hands in his pockets, and went into the enclosure of the apiary. In an area where the grass had been mowed the old beehives stood in regular rows, tied to pegs with bast fiber; all of them were familiar to Levin, each having its own history. Along the fence were the newer beehives, put there that year. Dazzling the observer's eyes, whirling and jostling, but remaining in the same place, bees and drones played at the entrances to the hives, and from them, always on the same course—toward the flowering linden trees in the wood, and back toward the hives—flew the worker bees, to collect their prize or coming back with it.

His ears rang ceaselessly with diverse sounds: of a busy worker bee rapidly flying by, of a drone buzzing idly, and of sentinel bees, alarmed and ready to sting their enemies in the defense of their fortune. On the other side of the fence the old man was busy shaving a hoop and did not notice Levin. Without calling him, Levin stopped in the middle of the apiary.

He was glad of the opportunity to be alone and to recover from the effects of reality, which had already succeeded in debasing his spiritual state to such an extent.

He recalled that he had already managed to become angry with Ivan, to show his coolness toward his brother, and to talk thoughtlessly to Katavasov.

Could it possibly have been only a momentary mood, one that will pass without leaving any trace? he thought.

But at the same moment, reverting to that mood, he was happy to feel that something new and important had occurred within him. Reality had only temporarily veiled the spiritual peace he had found: within him it still remained unimpaired.

Just as the bees, which now whirled around him, threatened and distracted him and deprived him of complete physical calm, making him shrink to avoid them, so did the cares that had beset him from the moment when he sat down in his cart deprive him of spiritual peace; but this lasted only while he was in their midst. And as, in spite of the bees, his physical strength remained unimpaired, so did his newly acquired spiritual strength remain unimpaired.

15

"Kostia, do you know whom Sergei Ivanovich traveled with on the way here?" said Dolly, after distributing cucumbers and honey among the children. "With Vronsky! He's going to Serbia."

"And not alone, but he is taking a squadron with him at his own expense!" said Katavasov.

"It's like him," said Levin. "Do volunteers really still go there?" he asked, glancing at Sergei Ivanovich.

Sergei Ivanovich made no reply. Working with a spatula in his cup, where a piece of white honeycomb lay at an angle, he was carefully trying to set free a bee that was caught, still alive, in the running of honey.

"Of course! You should have seen what went on at the station yesterday!" said Katavasov, noisily crunching a cucumber.

"I don't understand! For God's sake, explain to me, Sergei Ivanovich, where are all these volunteers going and whom will they fight?" asked the old prince, evidently continuing a conversation which had begun before Levin's arrival.

"The Turks," replied Sergei Ivanovich with a calm smile. He set free the bee, which, black with honey, stirred its legs helplessly, and transferred it to a sturdy aspen leaf.

"But who's declared war on the Turks? Is it Ivan Ivanych Ragozov, with Countess Lydia Ivanovna and Madame Stahl?"

"No one has declared war, but people sympathize with the sufferings of their fellow men and wish to help them," said Sergei Ivanovich.

"But the prince is not talking about help," said Levin, taking the part of his father-in-law, "but about war. The prince says that private citizens should not participate in a war without the permission of the government."

"Kostia, watch out, that bee! I'm sure we'll all be stung," said Dolly waving away a wasp.

"But it isn't even a bee, it's a wasp," said Levin.

"Well, what's your theory?" Katavasov asked Levin with a smile, evidently challenging him to a debate. "Why shouldn't private citizens have such a right?"

"Here is my theory. On the one hand, war is such a beastly, cruel and horrible affair that no man—let alone a Christian—

851

can take upon himself the responsibility of starting it. Only the government can do it; it is established for this purpose, and it wages war inevitably. On the other hand, in accordance both with theory and common sense, in matters of state, and particularly in the matter of war, citizens surrender their personal will."

Sergei Ivanovich and Katavasov were ready with their objections and spoke out at the same time.

"That's just the point, my friend. There are times when the government doesn't obey the will of the people, and then the public persists in asserting it," said Katavasov.

But Sergei Ivanovich evidently did not approve of this remark. He frowned at Katavasov's words and made a different statement:

"You're not presenting the problem correctly. This is not a declaration of war but simply an expression of a humane Christian feeling. They are slaughtering our brothers, our kin, our co-religionists. But suppose they were not our brothers and co-religionists but simply children, women, old men. Our feelings are aroused, and the Russian people hasten to lend their assistance to stop these horrors. Just imagine that you were walking in the street and saw some drunken men assault a woman or a child. I believe that you wouldn't start inquiring whether war had or hadn't been declared on these men, but you'd attack them and defend those whom they were assaulting."

"But I wouldn't kill them," said Levin.

"Yes, you would."

"I don't know. If I saw such a thing, I'd yield to my first reaction, but I can't foresee that. And there's no such immediate reaction to the oppression of the Slavs, and there can't be."

"Perhaps you don't have that feeling. But others do," said Sergei Ivanovich, frowning with displeasure. "The nation remembers the stories of the orthodox believers who suffered under the yoke of 'the infidel sons of Hagar.' The Russian people have heard of the suffering of their brothers and have responded."

"Perhaps," Levin said evasively, "but I don't see it. I'm one of the Russian people, and I don't feel it."

"Nor do I," said the prince. "I've lived abroad and read the papers, and I must admit that even before the atrocities were inflicted upon the Bulgars, I was at a loss to understand why the Russian people had been suddenly smitten with such love for their Slav brothers, whereas I don't feel any love for them. I was deeply upset and thought that perhaps I was some kind of a monster, or that it was the way Karlsbad had affected me. But when I came here, I felt reassured. I see that, besides myself, there are others who are interested only in Russia and not in their Slav brothers. Konstantin, for example."

"Personal opinions don't count here at all," said Sergei Ivanovich, "and I'm not interested in personal opinions when all of Russia, the whole nation, has expressed its will."

"I beg your pardon. I don't see it. The people don't know anything about it," said the prince.

"No, Papa . . . is it really so? What about what happened in church last Sunday?" asked Dolly, who had been listening to the conversation. "Please give me a towel," she said to the old man who was watching the children and smiling. "It's really impossible that everyone. . . ."

"And what actually did happen in church last Sunday? The priest had been ordered to read something. He did. They didn't understand a word and kept sighing, as they do at every sermon," continued the prince. "Then they were told that a collection was going to be made in the church for some soul-saving cause, and each donated his kopeck. But what it was for, they themselves didn't know."

"The people cannot help knowing; they are always aware of their destiny, which, at moments like the present one, becomes manifest," asserted Sergei Ivanovich with a glance at the old beekeeper.

The handsome old man, with a graying black beard and thick silver hair, stood motionless, and holding a bowl of honey, gently and calmly looked down from his height at the gentry, obviously without understanding or having any desire to understand.

"That's it exactly," he said, meaningfully shaking his head in reply to Sergei Ivanovich's words.

"Well, ask him. He doesn't know anything about it nor does he think about it," said Levin. "Mikhailych, have you heard about the war?" he asked the old man. "You remember what they read in the church. What do you think? Should we fight for the Christians?"

"Why should we think about it? Aleksandr Nikolayevich, the Emperor, has thought for us and will do so in every matter. He knows best. Shall I bring some more bread? Shall I give some more to this lad?" he asked Daria Aleksandrovna, indicating Grisha, who was finishing off the crust.

"I don't have to ask," said Sergei Ivanovich. "We have seen and continue to see hundreds upon hundreds who give up everything to serve a just cause. They come from all corners of Russia and express their thoughts and their aims clearly and openly. They bring their pennies or they go themselves, openly explaining why. What does this mean?"

"In my opinion," said Levin, becoming excited, "it means that in a nation of eighty million there will always be found not hundreds, as now, but tens of thousands who have lost their social standing, reckless people, who are always ready to join Pugachev's band, to go to Khiva, to Serbia. . . ."

"But I tell you that they're not in the hundreds, and that they're not reckless people but the finest representatives of the nation!" said Sergei Ivanovich, as vexed as though he were defending his last possession. "And what about the contributions? Here, one must agree, the whole nation expresses its will clearly."

"The word 'nation' is so vague," answered Levin. "Volost clerks, teachers, and perhaps one out of a thousand moujiks know what is happening. The remaining eighty million, like Mikhailych, not only don't express their will but haven't the slightest notion of what it is they should express their will about. What right, then, have we to say that this is the will of the people?"

16

SERGEI IVANOVICH, versed in dialectics, did not retort but immediately redirected the conversation.

"Yes, if you intend to comprehend the spirit of the people by mathematical means, you'll find, of course, that it's very difficult to accomplish. Suffrage hasn't been introduced in our country and shouldn't be, because it doesn't express the nation's will; but there are other means for doing this. It's in the air; it can be felt in one's heart. I'm not talking about the undercurrents, which stir in the stagnant expanse of the nation, and which are obvious to any unprejudiced observer. Look at our society in the narrow meaning of the word. All the most diverse sections of the intelligentsia, previously so hostile to one another, are united now. Every disagreement is gone; through every means society expresses the same feeling; all are aware of the spontaneous force that has swept them in the same direction."

"Yes, it's the newspapers that sound alike," said the prince. "That's true. Very much alike, like frogs before a storm. And on account of them nothing else can be heard."

"Frogs or no frogs, I don't publish newspapers and I don't intend to defend them; but I'm speaking of the unanimity of the intelligentsia," said Sergei Ivanovich, addressing his brother.

Levin was about to answer, but the old prince interrupted.

"Well, something else can be said about this unanimity," said the prince. "I have a son-in-law, Stepan Arkadievich; you know him. He has been made a member of some commission's committee, or something like that, I don't remember. But they have nothing to do—well, Dolly, it's no secret!—yet it pays eight thousand a year. Ask him whether his service is useful, and he'll prove to you that it's most useful. He's an honorable man, and one surely cannot doubt the usefulness of eight thousand rubles."

"By the way, he asked me to tell Daria Aleksandrovna that he has obtained the post," said Sergei Ivanovich with displeasure, believing that what the prince was saying was irrelevant.

"The same is true of the unanimity among the newspapers. I've been told that as soon as a war breaks out their income doubles. Why then shouldn't they believe that the destiny of the nation and the Slavs . . . and all of that?"

"There are many papers that I don't like, but what you say is unjust," said Sergei Ivanovich.

"I would impose only one condition," continued the prince. "Alphonse Karr expressed it very well before the war with Prussia. 'You maintain that war is necessary. Fine. Whoever preaches war should be assigned to a special front line legion to lead all others in the assault and attack.'"

"I can just visualize our editors then," said Katavasov with a loud laugh, visualizing the editors, whom he knew, in this crack legion.

"Of course they would run," said Dolly, "and only be in the way."

"And if they ran away, they should be met by canister shot or Cossacks with whips," said the prince.

"But this is a joke, and a bad joke at that, if you'll forgive me, Prince," said Sergei Ivanovich.

"I don't believe it's a joke, it—" began Levin, but Sergei Ivanovich interrupted him.

"Every member of society is called upon to perform some kind of work in accordance with his abilities," he said. "The intellectuals do their work by expressing public opinion. And the complete and unanimous expression of public opinion is the service performed by the press, and it's a happy phenomenon. Twenty years ago we would have kept silent, but now we hear the voice of the Russian nation, ready to rise as one man and to sacrifice itself for its oppressed brothers. This is a great step forward and an indication of our strength."

"But not just to sacrifice itself but to kill Turks," Levin said shyly. "People sacrifice themselves and are prepared to do so for the sake of their souls and not for murder," he added, unconsciously connecting this discussion with the thoughts with which he had been so profoundly occupied.

"What do you mean, for their souls? This, you know, is a troublesome concept for a naturalist. What is a soul?" Katavasov asked with a smile.

"Oh, you know!"

"I swear that I haven't the slightest idea," said Katavasov, laughing aloud.

"'I came not to send peace but a sword,' said Christ," retorted Sergei Ivanovich, citing with ease a verse from the Gospels, as though it were easy to understand. It was the one that had always troubled Levin the most.

"That's it exactly," again repeated the old man, who was standing near them, in reply to an accidental glance at him.

"No, my friend, you are beaten, thoroughly beaten," cried Katavasov gaily.

Levin blushed in annoyance, not because he had been beaten but because he had not controlled himself and had begun an argument.

No, I mustn't argue with them, he thought. They are clad in impenetrable armor, and I am naked.

He realized that he could not change his brother's and Katavasov's opinions, and that still less could he agree with them. What they preached was the same pride of the mind that had all but destroyed him. He could not agree that a handful of people, among them his brother, had the right to assert that they, together with the newspapers, expressed the will and convictions of the nation, convictions that found their fulfillment in revenge and murder. And this right was based only on what they had heard from several hundred glibly prating volunteers arriving in the capital. He could not agree with this because he could not discover such convictions either in the people in the midst of whom he lived nor in himself (and he would not consider himself as anything but one of those who constituted the Russian people). But the main reason he did not agree to this was that he, together with the rest of the Russian people, did not and could not know what this general good comprised, yet he knew firmly that this general good could be attained only through strict adherence to that law of good and evil which has been revealed to every man. Therefore he could not accept war nor advocate it for any public purpose whatever. He was with Mikhailych and the rest of the Russian people, repeating the words of the invitation, according to legend, to the Varangians: "Come and govern us. We joyously proffer our complete submission. All the toil, all the humiliation, all the sacrifice we take upon ourselves. But we shall not judge nor decide." And now, according to Sergei Ivanovich and others like him, the people were renouncing this right, which had been gained at such great cost.

He also wanted to add that if public opinion were the infallible judge, then why wasn't a revolution, or the commune, as lawful as the movement for the defense of the Slavs? But all these were arguments that would prove nothing. One thing he could see clearly—that at this moment the discussion was irritating Sergei Ivanovich, so it was wrong to argue with him. Levin fell silent, and then called his guests' attention to the clouds that had gathered, and suggested that they go home to avoid the rain.

17

SERGEI IVANOVICH and the prince got into the cart and left; the rest of the group walked home at a quickened pace.

But the cloud, now growing brighter and now darker, was moving up so rapidly that they had to increase their speed still more to arrive home before the rain. The clouds that preceded the main one, low and black as smoke mixed with soot, rushed across the sky with unusual speed. The house was only about two hundred paces away, but a wind arose, and the downpour threatened to follow it at any moment.

The children ran ahead, shrieking with fear and joy. Daria Aleksandrovna, struggling with her skirts that entangled her legs, no longer walked but ran, her eyes fixed on the children. The men, holding their hats, strode along. They had just reached the porch when a large drop fell, splashing on the edge of the iron gutter. Chattering gaily, the children, followed by the adults, ran under the roof for protection.

"Where is Katerina Aleksandrovna?" Levin asked Agafia Mikhailovna, who met them in the entrance hall with kerchiefs and wraps.

"We thought she was with you," she answered.

"And Mitia?"

"In Kolok, probably. The nurse is with him."

Levin seized the wraps and ran to Kolok.

During this short interval, the center of the cloud had moved up, covering the sun so completely that it became as dark as during an eclipse. The wind, as though persisting in having its way, stubbornly resisted Levin. Ripping leaves and blossoms from the linden trees and reducing the white branches of the birch trees to strange and ugly nakedness, it bent everything in the same direction: the acacias, flowers, burdocks, grass and treetops. The girls who worked in the garden ran screaming under the roof of the servants' hall. A white sheet of heavy rain had already enveloped the entire distant forest and half the nearby field, rapidly moving toward Kolok. The air was filled with dampness caused by a rain falling in fine driblets.

Lowering his head and struggling against the wind, which was tearing at the wraps, Levin had already run up so close to Kolok that he could make out the white object behind an oak tree, when suddenly everything burst into flame, the entire earth caught fire, and the vault of the sky seemed to crash overhead. When he opened his blinded eyes and peered through the heavy sheet of rain that now separated him from Kolok, Levin was terrified when, before anything else, he noticed the strangely changed position of the green crown of the familiar oak in the middle of the forest. Could it have been struck? Levin scarcely had time to ask himself the question when the crown of the oak tree picked up speed and disappeared, and he heard the crash of the huge tree as it fell against other trees.

The flash of lightning, the roar of thunder and the sudden feeling of cold about his body fused into one terrifying impression.

"My God! My God! Not on them!" he said.

And although he thought at once how senseless was his prayer that they might not be killed by the oak tree that had already fallen, he repeated it, realizing that he could do nothing better than to utter this meaningless prayer.

He ran up to the place where they usually went but did not find them.

They were at the other end of the wood, under an old linden tree, and were calling to him. Two figures in dark dresses (which had been light-colored before the rain) were bending over something. They were Kitty and the nurse. The rain had stopped, and it was beginning to grow brighter when Levin ran up to them. The lower part of the nurse's dress was dry, but Kitty's was drenched and clung to her body. Though it was no longer raining, they remained standing in the same position they had assumed when the storm broke. They were bent over the baby carriage with its green hood.

"Are you all right? Safe? Thank God!" he said and, splashing through the puddles in shoes that were loose and full of water, he ran over to them.

Kitty turned her wet, rosy face toward him, smiling shyly from underneath her hat, which was now shapeless.

"Well, aren't you ashamed? I can't understand how anyone could be so careless!" he burst out with annoyance.

"I swear it's not my fault. We were just going to leave when he demanded attention. We had to change him. We were just going to . . ." Kitty began to apologize.

Mitia was safe, dry, and continued to sleep.

"Well, thanks be to God! I don't know what I'm saying!"

They gathered up the wet diapers. The nurse took the child from the carriage and carried him. Levin walked alongside Kitty, ashamed of his outburst, and hiding the gesture from the nurse, squeezed his wife's hand.

18

THAT ENTIRE DAY, during the most diverse conversations, in which he employed only what may be termed the outer edge of his mind, Levin was disappointed that the change he had expected had failed to take place in him, yet he continued to be happily aware of the fullness of his heart.

It was too damp to go walking after the rain; moreover, the thunderclouds had not left the horizon, and here and there crossed along the edge of the sky, rumbling and growing darker. The whole group spent the rest of the day indoors.

They did not start any more arguments; on the contrary, after dinner everyone was in the best frame of mind.

First, Katavasov amused the ladies with his unusual jokes which always delighted everyone on first meeting him, and then prompted by Sergei Ivanovich, he related his very interesting observations on the differences between the nature and even the physiognomy of male and female houseflies and on their lives. Sergei Ivanovich also was in a gay mood, and at tea, encouraged by his brother, he expounded his views on the outcome of the Near East problem and explained it so clearly and so well that everyone listened with interest.

Only Kitty could not stay to hear him through, for she was called away to bathe the baby.

A few minutes after Kitty left, Levin, too, was called to the nursery.

He left his tea and went to the nursery, regretting the interruption of the interesting conversation, and also worrying about the reason why they had called him, since that happened only when something important came up.

Sergei Ivanovich's theory, which Levin had not heard in its entirety, and according to which the world of forty million liberated Slavs, together with Russia, were bound to begin a new epoch in history, seemed to Levin completely new and therefore aroused his deep interest in spite of the fact that he was disturbed and anxious to know why he had been called. But as soon as he was alone, after leaving the drawing room, he recalled his thoughts of that morning. And all these reflections upon the importance of the Slav element in world history appeared to him so insignificant compared with what was going on in his heart that he quickly forgot all of it and transported himself to the same state of mind in which he had been that morning.

He did not recall now, as he had in former times, the entire course of his thoughts (he did not have to do so). He recaptured at once the feeling that had guided him, which was connected with those thoughts and which had become still stronger within his heart and more distinct than before. It was not the same now as it had been on previous occasions when, seeking peace of mind, he had to retrace the whole course of his thoughts to find that feeling. On the contrary, now the feeling of joy and calm was more vivid than before, but the thought lagged behind the feeling.

He walked across the terrace, observed two stars that stood out against the sky, now grown dark, and suddenly recalled, Yes, when I looked at the sky, I thought that the vault I could see was not false, and with this there was something which I didn't think through completely, something which I hid from myself. But whatever it was, it cannot be challenged. As soon as I think it through, everything will become clear.

Just as he was entering the nursery he recalled what it was that he had hidden from himself. And this is what it was: if the main proof of the existence of the Deity lies in His revelation of what is good, why is this revelation confined only to the Christian Church? What is the relationship between this revelation and the beliefs of Buddhists or Mohammedans, who also believe in and practice what is good?

It seemed to him that he had an answer to this question; but he entered the nursery before he had had time to express it to himself.

Kitty, her sleeves rolled up, was standing at the basin over the baby, who was splashing in it, and hearing the sound of her husband's steps, she turned to him and beckoned to him with a smile. With one hand she supported the head of the chubby baby as he swam on his back, spreading his little legs apart, and with the other hand she squeezed a sponge over him with a steady pressure.

"Look! Look!" she said, when her husband came over to her. "Agafia Mikhailovna is right. He recognizes us."

She was referring to the fact, apparent beyond any doubt, that beginning with that day, Mitia could recognize familiar faces.

As soon as Levin came over to the basin, he was permitted

to witness an experiment which proved completely successful.
The cook, called in purposely for the experiment, bent over
the baby. He frowned and shook his head with distaste. Then
Kitty bent over him, and his face lit up with a smile, he
pressed his hand against the sponge, and puckered his lips,
uttering such a contented and strange sound that not only
Kitty and the nurse but also Levin were suddenly moved to
rapture.

The baby was lifted from the basin with one hand, doused
with water, wrapped in a sheet, dried, and, after he had uttered
a piercing cry, was handed to his mother.

"Well, I'm glad you've begun to love him," said Kitty to
her husband, after she had seated herself comfortably, the
child at her breast, in her usual place. "It makes me very
happy, for I'd already begun to worry about it. You told me
that you had no feeling toward him."

"No, did I really say that I had no feeling toward him? I
only said I was disappointed."

"Why were you disappointed?"

"I wasn't really disappointed in him, but in my own feeling.
I expected more. I expected that, as a welcome surprise, a
new, pleasant feeling would develop within me. But instead
of that, a feeling of disgust, of pity. . . ."

She listened to him attentively, the baby between them,
putting back on her slender fingers the rings she had taken
off when she was bathing Mitia.

"And, most important, it was a feeling of fear and pity
rather than pleasure. Today, after that scare during the storm,
I understand how I love him."

Kitty's face lit up with a smile.

"Were you very frightened?" she asked. "I was, too, but
I'm more frightened now that it's over. I'll go over to see that
oak. And how charming Katavasov is! And in general it's been
such a pleasant day. And, when you want to, you can be good
to Sergei Ivanovich. . . . Well, go to them, because it always
gets hot and stuffy in here after the bath. . . ."

19

WHEN HE left the nursery and was alone, Levin quickly reverted to his thought, in which there remained something not quite clear.

Instead of going to the drawing room, from which the sound of voices could be heard, he stopped on the terrace, leaned on the balustrade and looked at the sky.

Darkness had already fallen, and to the south, where he looked, there were no clouds. They remained on the opposite side. There lightning flashed and distant thunder rumbled. Levin listened to the sound of the drops in the garden as they fell regularly from the linden trees, and looked at a familiar triangle of stars and at the Milky Way, with its branches passing through the middle of it. At each flash of lightning, not only the Milky Way but also the bright stars disappeared, but as soon as the lightning faded, they reappeared in their former places, as though projected by some accurate hand.

But what really troubles me? Levin asked himself, feeling beforehand that the answer to his doubts was now in his heart, though he did not know yet what it was.

Yes, one obvious, incontestable manifestation of the Deity lies in the law of good and evil, which has been revealed to the world, which I feel within myself, and by the acceptance of which I wouldn't say that I've joined, but rather have been joined, with or against my will, with others into one body of believers, which is called the church. But the Jews, the Mohammedans, the Confucians, the Buddhists, what about them? he thought, asking himself the question that seemed to him so dangerous. Is it possible that these hundreds of millions are deprived of the greatest blessing, without which life has no meaning? He pondered, but then quickly corrected himself. But what am I really asking? he asked himself. I'm inquiring about the relationship of all the diverse religions of all mankind to the Deity. I'm inquiring about the general manifestation of God to all this universe, including those nebulae. What am I actually doing? An understanding has been unmistakably revealed to me personally, to my heart, one that's not attainable through reason, and I persist in my desire to express this understanding through reason and in words.

Don't I know that the stars don't move? he asked himself, gazing at a bright planet, which had already changed its position in relation to the topmost branch of a birch tree. But, while looking at the movement of the stars, I can't imagine that the earth turns, and I'm right when I say that the stars move.

And would the astronomers be able to understand and to calculate anything if they took into consideration all the complex and diverse movements of the earth? All their wonderful findings about distances, weight, movements, and deviations of the celestial bodies are based only on the illusory movement of these bodies around an immovable earth. This movement, the one I'm observing now, has been the same to millions of people for ages; it has been and always will be unchanged, and can always be verified. And just as the findings of the astronomers would be useless and unreliable if they weren't founded on the observations of an illusory heaven in its relation to a single meridian and single horizon, so would my findings be useless and unreliable if they weren't founded on that understanding of what is good that's always been and always will be the same for everyone, that's been revealed to me through Christianity and can always be ascertained within my heart. As for the problem of other religions and their relationship with the Deity, I have neither the right not the ability to decide.

"Oh, haven't you left yet?" he heard Kitty say suddenly as she passed in the same direction toward the drawing room. "Is anything troubling you?" she asked, looking keenly into his face in the light of the stars.

But she would not have been able to see his face distinctly were it not for another streak of lightning, which hid the stars and lit up his face. In the flash of lightning she observed his entire face, and seeing that he was calm and happy, she smiled at him.

She understands, he thought, she knows my thoughts. Shall I tell her or not? Yes, I'll tell her. But at the moment when he was about to start, she spoke to him.

"Oh, Kostia! Do me a favor," she said. "Go to the corner room and see how they've arranged it for Sergei Ivanovich. I feel embarrassed to do it. Have they put the new washstand there?"

"All right, I'll be sure to do it," said Levin, rising and kissing her.

No, I mustn't tell, he thought, as she went ahead of him. It's a secret for me alone, important and inexpressible in words.

This new feeling hasn't changed me, he thought, hasn't brought me happiness, hasn't suddenly enlightened me as I had dreamt, just like my feeling toward my son. Like that, it didn't come by surprise. Whether it's faith or not—I don't know what it is—but this feeling has entered as unnoticeably into my heart through suffering, and has seated itself there firmly.

Just as before I'll get angry with Ivan the coachman, I'll argue, I'll express my thoughts inopportunely; Just as before a wall will separate the holy of holies of my soul from others, even from my wife; Just as before I'll reproach her for my fear and I'll suffer remorse; Just as before I'll fail to understand through my reason why I pray but I'll continue to pray. But now my life, all my life, regardless of anything that may happen to me, each minute of my life, is not only not purposeless as it used to be but has the unmistakable purpose of goodness that I have the power to provide to it.

Annotated Bibliography

Berlin, Isaiah. *The Hedgehog and the Fox*. New York: Mentor Books, 1957.

An essay on Tolstoy's view of history as set forth in *War and Peace*.

Ellis, Havelock. *The New Spirit*. Washington, D. C.: National Home Library, 1935.

The essay on Tolstoy, which was written during his lifetime, traces Tolstoy's spiritual metamorphosis from the crisis of his fifties to the simple life of his old age at Yasnaya Poliana.

Farrell, James T. *Literature and Morality*. New York: Vanguard, 1947.

Contains six critical essays on problems dealing with *Anna Karenina, War and Peace,* and Tolstoy's portrait of Napoleon.

Fausset, Hugh. *Tolstoy: The Inner Drama*. London: Cape, 1927.

An exploration of Tolstoy's personality in relation to his art and his life.

Lavrin, Janke. *Russian Writers: Their Lives and Literature*. New York: Van Nostrand, 1954.

A survey of the growth and character of Russian literature with special emphasis on the nineteenth century. A chapter on Tolstoy and Dostoevsky discusses them in terms of their historical and cultural backgrounds.

Leon, Derrick. *Tolstoy: His Life and Work*. London: Routledge, 1944.

An exhaustive biography which includes much interesting material on the genesis of *Anna Karenina,* models for some of its characters, and contemporary views of this novel, including those of Dostoevsky, Turgenev, and Chekhov.

Mann, Thomas. *Essays*. New York: Vintage, 1957.

Includes his long analysis, "Goethe and Tolstoy," written in 1922, and his 1939 essay on *Anna Karenina*, which he regarded as "Tolstoy's artistically finest work," and "the greatest society novel in all literature" although it was in fact "an anti-society novel." In paperback.

Maude, Aylmer. *The Life of Tolstoy*. 2 vols. New York and London: Oxford University Press, 1931.

A rewritten and revised edition of a two-volume biography first published in 1908–1910, of which Bernard Shaw wrote: "It will stand, I think, among the big biographies of our literature."

Mirsky, Dmitri. *A History of Russian Literature from Its Beginning to 1900*. New York: Vintage, 1958.

Includes two studies of Tolstoy, as artist and as moral philosopher.

Redpath, Theodore. *Tolstoy*. New York: Hillary House, 1960.

A brief survey of Tolstoy's thoughts and fiction intended primarily for the general reader rather than the Slavonic specialist.

Simmons, Ernest Joseph. *Leo Tolstoy*. 2 vols. New York: Vintage, 1961.

A detailed and comprehensive biography of Tolstoy by an outstanding authority on Russian literature. The four parts of this two-volume work correspond to the four major periods of Tolstoy's life. In paperback.

Slonim, Marc. *The Epic of Russian Literature*. New York: Oxford University Press, 1950.

This systematic survey of Russian literature from the eighteenth century to our day includes a discussion of Tolstoy and his posthumous influence on Soviet literature.

Spector, Ivar. *The Golden Age of Russian Literature*. Caldwell, Idaho: Caxton, 1952.

A product of courses in Russian literature given at the University of Washington, Seattle, between 1931–1952, the book includes a long section on Tolstoy with a biographical sketch, plots, excerpts, and a selective bibliography.

Tolstoy, Countess Alexandra. *Tolstoy: A Life Of My Father*. Translated by Elizabeth Reynolds Hapgood. New York: Harper, 1953.

A comprehensive account of his life and work by Tolstoy's devoted daughter and faithful aide, who was with him to the last moment of his life.

Yassukovitch, Antonina, ed. *Tolstoi in English: 1878–1929*. New York: New York Public Library Bulletin, Vol. 33, No. 7, July, 1929.

A list of works by and about Tolstoy in the New York Public Library compiled by Antonina Yassukovitch with an introduction by A. Yarmolinsky.

Zweig, Stefan. *Adepts in Self-Portraiture: Casanova, Stendhal, Tolstoy*. New York: Viking, 1929.

A study of Tolstoy as an example of the introverted, subjectively minded artist whose typical method of expression is autobiography.

Bibliographical Note

AUTOBIOGRAPHY:

Last Diaries. Edited and translated by Leon Stilman. New York: Putnam, 1960.

Private Diary. Edited by Aylmer Maude. Translated by Aylmer and Louise Maude. New York: Doubleday, 1927.

Tolstoy: New Light on His Life and Genius. Edited by Rene Fülöp-Miller. Translated by Paul England. New York: Dial, 1931.

REMINISCENCES:

GORKI, M. *Reminiscences of Leo Nikolaievich Tolstoy.* Translated by S. S. Koteliansky and Leonard Woolf. New York: Viking, 1920. *Reminiscences of Tolstoy, Chekhov and Andreev.* Viking, 1959.

KUZMINSKAYA, T. A. B. *Tolstoy As I Knew Him.* Translated by Nora Sigerist and others. Introduction by Ernest J. Simmons. New York: Macmillan, 1948.

MAUDE, A. (ed.). *Family Views of Tolstoy.* New York: Houghton, 1927.

——. *The Tragedy of Tolstoy.* Translated by Elena Varneck. New Haven: Yale, 1933.

TOLSTOY, L. L. *Truth About My Father.* New York: Appleton, 1924.

TOLSTOY, S. A. *The Autobiography of Countess Tolstoy.* Translated by S. S. Koteliansky and Leonard Woolf. New York: Viking, 1922.

——. *Countess Tolstoy's Later Diary.* Translated by Alexander Werth. New York: Brewer, 1930.

——. *Final Struggle.* Translated with an introduction by A. Maude. New York: Oxford, 1937.

BIOGRAPHICAL AND CRITICAL STUDIES:

BAUDOUIN, C. *Tolstoy: the Teacher.* Translated by Fred Rothwell. New York: Dutton, 1924.

LAVRIN, J. *Tolstoy: an Approach,* New York: Macmillan, 1946.

ROLLAND, ROMAIN. *Tolstoy.* Translated by M. Miall. New York: Dutton, 1911.

SLONIM, MARC. *Outline of Russian Literature.* New York: Mentor, 1959.

STEINER, GEORGE. *Tolstoy or Dostoevsky.* New York: Knopf, 1959, (paperback, Vintage).

Suggested Further Reading

Principal Literary Works *

Major Novels

War and Peace (1865–69)
Anna Karenina (1875–78)
Resurrection (1899)

Shorter Novels

Childhood, Boyhood, Youth (1852, 1854, 1857)
Two Hussars (1856)
Family Happiness (1859)
The Cossacks (1863)
Polikushka (1863)
The Death of Ivan Ilych (1886)
The Kreutzer Sonata (1889)
Master and Man (1893)
Father Sergius (1898)
Hadji Murad (posthumous, 1911)
The Devil (posthumous, 1911)

Short Stories

The Raid (1852)
The Wood-Felling (1855)
The Snowstorm (1856)
Lucerne (1857)
Albert (1858)
Three Deaths (1859)
God Sees the Truth, but Waits (1872)
What Men Live By (1881)
Where Love Is, God Is (1885)
Ivan the Fool (1885)
Evil Allures, but Good Endures (1885)
Strider: The Story of a Horse (1886)
Walk in the Light While There Is Light (1893)
Three Questions (1903)
Memoirs of a Madman (posthumous, 1911)

---

* First Russian publication dates

871

Plays

   The Power of Darkness (1886)
   The Fruits of Enlightenment (1889)
   The Light Shines in Darkness (posthumous, 1911)
   The Live Corpse (posthumous, 1911)

Principal Critical, Religious, Philosophical Works

   A Confession (1879)
   What I Believe (1884)
   The Kingdom of God Is Within You (1893)
   Christianity and Patriotism (1894)
   What Is Art? (1898)
   What Then Must We Do? (1902)